THE FAIR ISLE TRILOGY

COMPLETE SERIES COLLECTION

TESSONJA ODETTE

TESSONJA ODETTE

TRILOGY

COMPLETE SERIES COLLECTION

CONTENTS

TO CARVE A FAE HEART

TO WEAR A FAE CROWN

TO SPARK A FAE WAR

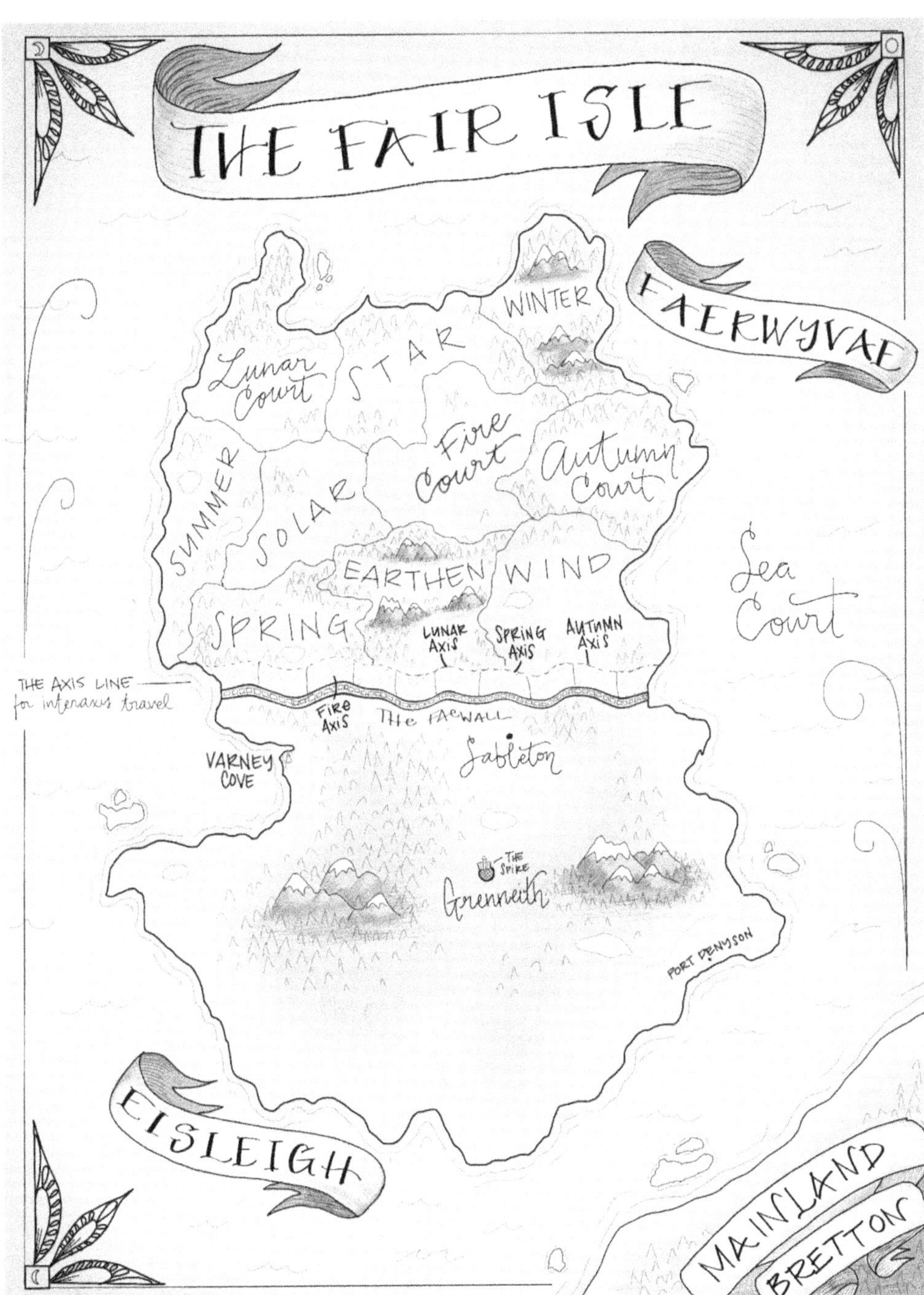

THE FAIR ISLE
FAERWYVAE
Lunar Court
STAR
WINTER
SUMMER
Fire Court
Autumn Court
SOLAR
Sea Court
EARTHEN
WIND
SPRING
LUNAR AXIS
SPRING AXIS
AUTUMN AXIS
THE AXIS LINE
for interaxis travel
FIRE AXIS
THE FAEWALL
Sableton
VARNEY COVE
THE SPIRE
Grenneith
PORT DENYSON
EISLEIGH
MAINLAND
BRETTON

TO CARVE A FAE HEART

BOOK ONE

1

———

Every young woman dreams of marrying a royal. A king, a prince, it doesn't matter, so long as he's richer than sin and handsome enough to fake a smile at. What else could a girl ask for?

Well, a working brain, for starters. And I do suggest all young women have one of those. That way, she'd know marrying a royal would be The. Worst. Thing.

You see, here in Eisleigh, all young women are eligible to be married off to a king. There's just one problem.

He'll probably eat you before you make it to your wedding bed.

And I'd rather not get torn to shreds by razor sharp fangs, thank you very much.

So you might be wondering why, after such a declaration, a sensible young woman like me would be traipsing through the woods toward the faewall in the middle of the night. I'll tell you why. To bribe my way to freedom.

Some might call it superstition to leave gifts for the fae. If fae weren't real, I'd agree. Unfortunately for the residents of Eisleigh, they are real. Dangerously, terrifyingly, blood curdlingly real. And I'm not about to offend them tonight.

I hear a rustling nearby. The snap of a twig to my left. The crinkling of falling leaves. I whirl to find nothing but the silhouette of an owl launching from a branch overhead to soar into the night sky. With a shaking breath, I pull my heavy wool cloak tighter around me and refocus on the path ahead. Even with the moonlight speckling the forest floor, I can barely make out the well-worn trail between the trees.

Yet I manage, trying my best not to trip on twining roots and rocks and all sorts of earthly assassins bent on making me regret coming here alone. It's usually Mother who comes to the faewall with me. Or Amelie, my sister. Tonight though, it's just me. I'm too old to need the protection of my mother, and Amelie—well, I'm usually the one protecting *her* even though she's two years older than I am. Besides, she has better things to do tonight.

You're welcome, Amelie. I hope you're enjoying your date. Hopefully my hard work can keep us both from certain doom! In all honesty, I can't blame her for not being with me tonight. For all she knows, this might be her last night of freedom.

Once the trees begin to thin, I catch a glimpse of the faewall up ahead. The wall is always an unsettling sight, no matter how many times I've seen it. It's composed of massive standing stones, twice my height and three times as wide, set a dozen or so feet apart. Between the stones, all you can see is dense mist towering high into the sky, showing nothing of the fae lands beyond. The wall spans from one end of the Fair Isle to the other, dividing it in half to separate the human lands of Eisleigh from the fae lands of Faerwyvae.

A shiver crawls up my spine as I approach the wall. There's no mistaking the danger radiating from between each pair of stones and the mist beckoning behind them. Each *between* is an entrance to Faerwyvae, the place humans never go on purpose and never return from when they do.

My heart quickens, and I pat the sheathed dagger that hangs from the belt around my waist, feeling the comfort of its weight against my hip. With slow, creeping steps, I make my way to one of the stones, then unshoulder my bag. From within, I remove a plate and saucer—both marked with my family surname and the name of my village on the bottom—and set them on the ground at the base of the stone. Then I take out a heel of fresh brown bread and a canteen of goat's milk, placing the bread on the plate and pouring the milk into the bowl.

My movements are routine and reverent, following the tradition Mother taught me every year to commemorate the anniversary of the Hundred Year Reaping. It's meant to curry favor with the fae in a way that will ensure my sister and I won't be chosen for the next Reaping. Since the Hundred Year Reaping comes at dawn tomorrow, I could use that favor now more than ever.

I stare at my offering, then look at similar ones farther down the wall. At the next stone over, I see a patterned scarf with a sparkling, moonlit brooch perched upon it. Farther down, I'm almost certain I see the silhouette of an entire deer corpse.

I return my attention to my offering of bread and milk. It's always been bread and milk, ever since I was a girl. Mother says anything fancier could draw the attention of the Reaping, while anything less could be seen as an insult fit for punishment. It seems the only way to guarantee my sister and I won't become the brides of monstrous fae is to remain respectfully unmemorable.

Why the fae give a lamb's ass about silly human offerings in the first place is beyond me. We couldn't possibly give them anything they don't already have in the fae lands. Besides, do fae even eat? Aside from human brains and the tears of young maidens?

I take one last glimpse at my offering, hoping it's enough to keep me and my sister safe, then turn around.

A new wall blocks my path.

A towering, brooding wall of shadow and teeth. I gasp and launch a step back. My vision clears and focuses, revealing the figure of a man, taller than me by two heads. He's dressed in dark, nondescript clothing beneath an equally dark cloak that makes it impossible to get an impression of anything but his face. That accounts for the shadows I saw at first glance. As for the teeth, I must have been mistaken, because there are none to be seen beneath his self-righteous smirk. My eyes trail from his mouth to his upturned nose and angled eyes.

A fae. Great.

It isn't unusual for fae to be seen on this side of the wall, but there are only two reasons one would be here at all. First, to cause trouble. This is most often performed by lesser fae—goblins, sprites, trolls. Second, to clean up said trouble. This is usually done by the fae ambassadors, sent by the high fae who like to pretend their kind mean us no harm. So which one is he? Trouble? Or charm?

It doesn't matter, I suppose. Even the most refined-seeming fae can tear out your heart before you see it coming.

I steady my breathing and put on a brave face, reminding myself to blink as I hold his gaze. If I forget to blink, he could maintain eye contact long enough to glamour me. Or, more accurately, he could maintain eye contact long enough to suppress the proper functioning of my amygdala.

This fae is just like any other creature, I remind myself. A dangerous creature, yes, but a creature bound by the laws of science. Science, I can understand. Science, I can confront.

Despite my mantra, I know I'm in the presence of danger. I'm vulnerable, small, wildly aware of my state of undress. My cloak suddenly seems too frail a thing to hide the fact that I'm wearing a thin cotton nightdress tucked into trousers. Why couldn't I have put on a proper top? Then again, I wasn't expecting to find anyone here, much less a fae. A towering, beautiful, horrible fae.

Luckily, his eyes don't stray to my clothing as he extends his hand toward the stones and the offerings at their bases. "Seeking favor, human? Hoping you'll be chosen to win the hand of King Aspen?" His voice is low and deep, dripping honey.

I suppress a laugh. Does he honestly believe any of us would *want* to be chosen as a bride of the fae? It's called the Reaping for a reason. Otherwise, we'd call it the Hundred Year Whimsy. Now, how do I answer that question without getting my face ripped off? "I ask only that my offering is received fairly and that my relationship with your kind maintains its good and distant standing."

His lips twitch, but I can't tell if he's on the verge of smiling or scowling. "Your gift comes too late. The Chosen have already been selected."

The blood leaves my face. The two Chosen have already been confirmed? But the announcement isn't made until dawn. "Is that why you're here? To finalize the names?"

"I just returned from doing so."

So he must be an ambassador after all. *But if he just came from finalizing the names...then that means...*

I can hardly finish the thought. No other village but my own is near this part of the faewall. I can only hope he came from farther south. With a deep breath, I say, "Might you tell me their names?"

He takes a step forward, a dangerous glint in his dark eyes. "For a price."

Of course. I should have known better than to step into that predictable trap. No peace of mind is worth making a bargain with a fae. "On second thought, I'll wait until dawn. I'll just be on my way then." I step to the side to skirt around him, but he's faster.

Again, his wall of a body is blocking me. "It will be an easy bargain. Give me your name and I'll give you theirs."

"Ha, I'm sure!" I regret the outburst as soon as it's made. Mother did say my mouth would be the death of me. But he's ridiculous if he thinks I'll fall for that! I know what he'd ask after I gave him my name. *Is that your true name you've given me?* Such an innocent question—if you're daft. But anyone who knows fae knows affirming he has my true name is all it takes to put me under his complete control. It would go beyond the power of a simple glamour, giving him the ability to make me do unspeakable things. A glamour, at least, ends by cutting eye contact. But giving one's name? Rumor has it only death can sever that level of control.

I gather my poise and put together a more polite reply. "Clever wording, but no, I will not give you my name."

He smiles wide. My eyes move to his mouth, looking for sharp teeth. In the dark, I barely get more than a flash of white between his full lips. "How about you *tell* me your name then. In return, I will tell you theirs."

My eyes flick back to his, and I turn his words over a few times in my head. I don't think he's left room for a trap. Breathe. Blink. Breathe. Blink. "Fine. I will tell you my name. It's Evelyn."

"Evelyn…"

I plaster a pleasant smile on my face. I'm sure it doesn't reach my eyes. "First names will do. Now it's your turn."

He glares, but his lips are curled with amusement. "You aren't afraid of me, are you?"

How could he ask me that? Surely, he can hear how loudly my heart is pounding in my chest. "Why would I be afraid?"

He lunges forward, lips peeling back with a snarl. Instead of lurching away, I stand my ground, dagger in hand as his fingers reach my neck. I raise my blade. He freezes, his nose an inch from the iron tip.

We hold our positions. His fingers are wrapped around my throat, the pressure uncomfortable, but not tight enough to constrict my breathing. My chest heaves. If he squeezes even the slightest bit more, I'll plunge my dagger into his eye socket. It wouldn't be easy. I've never killed a fae before, or anyone for that matter. But, as a more than capable surgeon's apprentice, I have a steady hand and am no stranger to cutting a blade into flesh. I know just how much pressure is needed to slice through every kind of tissue, know how deep and how hard I would need to thrust to reach vital organs.

His finger flinches at the base of my collarbone. I prepare to strike.

In the blink of an eye, he's taken a step back and his head is thrown back in bellowing laughter.

I keep my dagger raised, chest heaving with rage. "What's so funny?"

"I love being surprised. You're scared after all. Scared but unflinchingly prepared. You'd have killed me."

I swallow hard, resisting the urge to rub my neck as I glare back at him. "And you?"

He sobers from his laughter, but his smile remains wide. "I wasn't going to kill you. I simply wanted to see what you'd do. You're wise to carry iron around here."

"Thanks," I say through my teeth. "I'll be going now. Let me pass this time."

He turns to the side, extending a hand toward the forest in a perfect impersonation of a gentleman. I brush past him, the hilt of my blade still clenched in my fist.

"What about our bargain?" he calls after me. "Don't you want to know the names of the two Chosen?"

I pause, hesitating before I turn to face him. "Go on."

He doesn't move toward me, just holds my gaze for endless moments.

Breathe. Blink. Breathe. Blink.

Finally, he utters the words I'm waiting to hear. "Theresa and Maryanne Holstrom."

The Holstrom girls. From Sableton. *My* village. I should feel terror for them, anguish for their families. We grew up together, after all. But all I feel is relief. Sweet, overwhelming, glorious relief. I can't fight the smile that tugs at my lips, and I tip my head back and close my eyes. "Thank you," I whisper, although I don't know who I'm thanking. The fae? The stars? The Great Mother above?

I hear an amused laugh not too far away and remember the presence of the fae male. My eyes fly open and dart his way. But he's gone.

I whirl around, expecting him to be waiting menacingly behind me, but it seems the forest is empty. Good riddance. I return the way I came, no longer jumping at the sounds of snapping twigs or rustling leaves. Nothing can shake my joy right now. Nothing.

For the first time in my eighteen years of life, I can consider myself safe.

2

———————

My bed trembles beneath me as if the very earth is shaking. And yet, I can't be bothered by it. Not when there's such delicious sleep to be had.

"Evie. Evie! Get up!"

The voice startles me fully awake, and I open my eyes to find Amelie's face an inch from mine. I groan and roll away from her. The bed returns to shaking, in earnest this time. Amelie is on her feet, bouncing from one side of my mattress to the other.

"Evie, how can you sleep? You haven't heard the news yet!"

The news. She must mean the announcement of the Chosen. How long did I sleep? Finally, I roll onto my back and look up at my sister. Her copper hair is backlit by the morning sun coming in through my window. Her green eyes are bright beneath her long, feathery, black lashes. She's dressed in one of her finest daytime dresses, a cream, lowcut gown with a mauve floral pattern. Of course, she's outfitted in a fancy dress. That's how she celebrates.

Amelie plops down on the bed next to me and takes me by the shoulders. She's grinning so wide, I can see all her neat, perfect teeth. "It's the Holstrom girls! It isn't us!"

I realize I should act surprised. There's no reason to tell her about my encounter last night, which would be the only excuse I'd have for knowing the news she's bursting at the seams to share. I sit, trying to look eager. "Oh? The Holstroms?"

Amelie's smile turns into a frown as my blanket slides from my shoulders. I follow her gaze and realize I'm still wearing my cloak. She pulls back the rest of the blanket, revealing the dirty hem of my trousers and mud-splattered boots.

"Really, Evie? You didn't even bother to remove your shoes before bed?"

I stretch and shift my legs to hang over the side of the mattress, then begin working at the laces of my boots. "I was tired. You know, from securing our great victory?"

Amelie floats to my dressing table and stares at her reflection in the mirror that hangs above it, prodding at her brows and cheeks. "That explains why I didn't see you at the plaza. When Mother and I left to hear the announcement, your boots weren't by the front door. We figured you'd already left."

I kick off one of my boots and begin unlacing the next, still puzzling over how deeply I slept last night. I don't think I've ever slept so well in my life. Relief will do that to a girl, I suppose. "Did I miss anything? Aside from the announcement itself, I mean?"

Amelie whirls toward me, grinning. "You should have seen the look on Mrs. Holstrom's face when Theresa and Maryanne's names were called. She almost fainted!"

A pinch of guilt tugs my chest. Would our mother have fainted if she'd heard our names? But the sinking feeling evaporates before it can take hold. I'm still too grateful it wasn't us. "Fainted? That must have been a sight."

"*Almost* fainted. She did cry. A lot. The girls have already been taken beyond the wall. You should have seen the coach that came for them! Gold and pearl with dark, lustrous wood."

I stand and cross the cold floor to my window. "They've already been taken to Faerwyvae? What time is it?"

"It's almost noon." I meet Amelie's gaze and she frowns at my hair. She pats the chair at my dressing table. "Come. You look like a dead bird."

I should be offended, but I'm used to my sister finding fault in my appearance. She's always been the pretty one, the silly one, and the one most beloved by all the folk in our village. There's a reason she was out with a man last night while I was alone in the woods. She likes company and men and friends. I like practicality. And sleep.

I take a seat and Amelie stands behind me, immediately worrying at the knot in my hair that once was a braid. In the mirror, the contrast between us is stark. My sister is all copper hair, bright green eyes, pale peachy skin, and a smile that remains even when she's frowning—which she's doing now at my hair.

I, on the other hand, am a more subdued version of the girl behind me. My hair is a dark auburn that only looks remotely copper in direct sunlight, my eyes are a dull blue instead of green, my skin is far too bland to be considered peachy, and too dark to be considered fair. Then there's my smile. Let's just say the women in the village call it a *perpetual pout* when they're trying to be honest about my looks without being insulting. I do appreciate how sultry my perpetual pout makes me sound, but I know the truth of it. I look like I'm angry. All the time.

Once Amelie has finished undoing my braid, she sets to brushing out my tangles, a task that earns me a deeper frown from my sister. I smile. No matter how futile, she never gives up trying to make me presentable. "How was your date last night?"

I catch her eye-roll in the mirror. "It can hardly be called a date. It was nothing more than batting my lashes at Bertrand from across the parlor while stuck in awful chatter with his boring sisters for three hours straight." She pauses, then smiles. "We did kiss behind the stables before I left though. I thought we were going to be caught when his driver came looking for us. Thank the Great Mother Bertrand's fingers are like sausages, or he'd surely have had me out of my corset by then."

"Will you be seeing him again? Now that you know you're a free woman?"

"Why would I? I'm seeing Magnus tonight."

I furrow my brow. "Magnus?"

"Magnus Merriweather." She pauses her brushing, eyes going wide as she meets mine in the mirror. "I haven't told you, have I? That's the best part! After the announcement, Magnus invited me to dinner. Through his cousin, Annabel, of course. But I saw the way he looked at me from across the plaza. He and Theresa Holstrom were practically engaged. Now that she's...well, you know...he has to marry me!"

"Has to?"

"Well, Theresa was obviously his first choice, but I've always known I was a close second."

"And you're happy about that?"

Amelie's smile grows radiant as she returns to brushing my hair. "Magnus is the most handsome man in Sableton. Maybe all of Eisleigh, though I haven't traveled the Isle much, as you well know. But I can't imagine a man more dignified than he. And now he's stuck with me. I couldn't feel luckier, Evie."

I try my best to suppress my laugh. Despite Amelie being what I very much define as a *silly person*, I never go out of my way to make fun of her. She may be two years older, but she's more fragile than I am, like a tiny violet in a patch of weeds. That fragility was almost the death of her once. I'll never forget what it felt like to think I was going to lose her, and I've been fiercely protective of her ever since.

"We're both free women now," Amelie says, shaking me from my thoughts as she pins my fully brushed hair into a low chignon the way I like. She's given up trying to get me to wear my hair down like hers. "How are you going to celebrate?"

My eyes fall on the stack of books on my dressing table. All are either human anatomy or medical guides, to aid my studies as a surgeon's apprentice. Hidden beneath the stack of books is a letter. A letter I've read and reread a dozen times or more since receiving it last month. I've been waiting to respond to it until this very day—the day I can declare my absolute freedom.

I feel my cheeks flush before the words are out of my mouth. Not with shame. With excitement. "I'm going to mainland Bretton. To medical school. I'm going to become a *real* surgeon."

Amelie's eyes go wide as if I've just told her I plan on exchanging my head for a new one. "The mainland? You're leaving the isle?"

My heart drops at the hurt in her tone. It was always my plan to leave the Fair Isle after the Reaping. I would have left already if it would have been allowed. According to the treaty, all young women who would come of age during the Reaping are forbidden to marry or leave the isle three years prior. You can only imagine the influx of weddings and moves to the mainland that took place three years ago. I was livid Mother wouldn't comply with my wishes and leave with us immediately. Amelie was furious she was forbidden to marry at age seventeen. But mother was fixed on staying in Eisleigh, convinced our offerings would keep us safe. *I understand the fae,* she would say. *We will not be driven from our home or forced into rash behavior. We'll work with them. You'll be safe, I promise.*

Mother was right. We're free from the Reaping once and for all. Now I can do what I've always wanted to do. "I'll still visit you and Mother."

Amelie forces a smile, but I can tell she's hurt. "When will you go?"

"I've been invited to join the fall quarter at Bennings University of Medical Arts. It begins at the end of the month."

My sister sighs, pinning the last strand of hair in place. She steps back, admiring her work, then places a hand on my shoulder. "You'll see me get married at least, right?"

I feel my throat grow tight as I stand to face her. "Of course I will."

Amelie pulls me into a hug with her slender arms. My head barely reaches her shoulder. "It won't be the same without you."

I blink back tears. "Nothing will be the same without you."

She releases me but keeps her hands on my shoulders. "Have you told Mother?"

"Told me what?"

I whirl to find Mother standing in the doorway.

"Evie is leaving us for medical school on the mainland," Amelie says with a pout, then floats away from me, past Mother, to my door. "Meanwhile, I have a man to steal. Good day." With that, she disappears into the hall, leaving me to face Mother alone.

3

———————

"Is this true, Evelyn?" Mother asks, her voice soft. "You're moving to the mainland?"

I feel my shoulders collapse and have to turn away to avoid her tear-glazed eyes. "It shouldn't be a surprise." My voice comes out more defensive than I intend, but I'm not sure what to say. I wasn't ready for this conversation yet. *Thanks, Amelie.*

I grab a pile of clothes from my table and move behind my dressing screen. Again, I'm surprised to find my trousers so dirty and recall the night before. The wall. The offering. The fae male. I shake the memories from my mind and peel off the pants and nightdress and toss them to the floor. I don a fresh pair of wide-legged trousers, then retrieve my stiff corset from the floor. With a grimace, I wrap it around my waist. A moment later, I hear Mother's footsteps approach from behind, followed by the gentle pull of the laces. She knows better than to lace it as tight as Amelie's. Mother dislikes corsets almost as much as I do. However, she's convinced it's the burden we must bear for propriety's sake. At least until they fall out of fashion.

With my corset done, Mother returns to the other side of the screen, and I put on a cream satin blouse with round pearl-like buttons, followed by a short-waisted coat in a deep gray. I still can't meet Mother's eyes when I step out from behind my dressing screen, but I can feel her scrutiny at my trousers. I'm likely the only woman in my village who prefers trousers to dresses, and Mother hasn't decided her stance on them when it comes to propriety.

Not that propriety is Mother's only concern. She has her own curious ways, like her trailing scarves, colorful hair ornaments, and mismatched shawls. She's an odd mix of both me and Amelie, as if we were split from two sides of her personality, each taking an equal half. On one hand, Mother is whimsical, fair, and pretty like Amelie, with the same copper hair and green eyes. She knows how to fit into society and earn the acceptance of her peers. On the other hand, Mother has always been a bit of a secret rebel. She came to the Fair Isle from the mainland after she parted ways with my father. Yes, she *willingly* parted ways with a decent man, leaving the more traditional structure of the mainland for the less judgmental people of the isle. That's how she explains it, anyway. I've never known the residents of Sableton to be anything other than petty gossips with empty heads and rigid ways.

But the people here respect her, lone mother of two, witch of Sableton. Of course, she prefers the term healer. I prefer the term charlatan.

"When did you even apply to university?"

Finally, I meet her eyes. "I sent my application in the summer and received the reply a few weeks ago. They've invited me to join the next class. Ma, this is huge for me." I'm hoping the excitement in my tone will lift the corners of her mouth, but it doesn't.

"Why didn't you tell me?"

"Because I knew you'd be upset. Besides, I didn't want to say anything until we were safe from the Reaping."

"After all the work I've done to make sure I won't lose you, I'm going to lose you anyway."

I take a step toward her. "You did all that work to keep us *free*. That means giving me the freedom to choose."

Her eyes are pleading as she closes the distance between us and puts her hand on my cheek. "Couldn't you be happy here? Continue your path as a surgeon's apprentice for Mr. Meeks?"

With a groan, I skirt around her and head for my door. I hear Mother's footsteps fall behind me as I enter the hall and descend the stairs. "I don't want to be an apprentice forever. I want to be a full surgeon. Do you think Sableton has room for another one? No. Mr. Meeks will be surgeon here until he dies, and his son will be surgeon after him."

"Well, that's not a bad idea, Evelyn," Mother says as I reach the platform at the bottom of the stairs. "You could take the Meeks' example and do the same with me. You could learn my craft. You could help me run the apothecary."

Irritation courses through me. She's never stopped trying to convince me to *learn her craft*. I round on her. "Ma, we've had this discussion a million times. I don't want to brew silly potions and make up stories from tea leaves. I don't want to lay my hands on people until their made-up ailments dissolve from their imaginations."

Mother's face falls, and I know my words were too cutting. "Is that what you think I do all day? Fool around and take people's money for nothing? How do you explain the things I know? The miracles people experience after working with me?"

I release a sigh and continue down the hall, past the parlor and the door that leads to the public shop that is Mother's apothecary. "I didn't mean it like that. It's just...there's a rational explanation for everything. I'm sure what you do *helps* people. Just not in the way I want to help people."

"But you have so much potential. I can feel it in you."

I enter the kitchen, where I take a seat at the thick wooden table, reaching for what remains of this morning's loaf of bread. "Mr. Meeks says I have potential too. Real potential. He says I have a steady hand and the right disposition for surgery. When I graduate from university, I'll have the skills I need to make a difference in the world. I can do more than just make people feel better. I can *save lives*."

"Someday you'll realize you have the power to save lives already inside you."

A wave of anger sends heat to my cheeks. "You mean, like you?"

Tense silence grows between us, and a flash of guilt crosses Mother's face. "You'll never forgive me for what happened with your sister, will you? It kills me that your sister suffered for my mistake, but I promise you, I would have taken her to Mr. Meeks before things got too far."

Again, I know my words were too harsh, but it's the truth. Amelie nearly died four years ago, not because of some mistake, but because of Mother's entire belief system. Mother may help people in her own way, but she doesn't save lives. Pretending she can only hurts the people who actually need medical intervention.

I avert my gaze to avoid the hurt look on her face, instead taking in the jars of herbs lining the shelves spanning each wall, strands of drying plants hanging from the ceiling, tinctures and potions brewing on the countertops in glass jars. The sight makes my muscles tense. It's chaotic and messy and none of it is *me*. I crave the order and neatness of a sterile surgery room, not the messy kitchen behind an apothecary. I let out a heavy sigh. "Ma, you know I forgive you. Amelie forgives you. But the fact remains that Sableton isn't where I belong. Eisleigh isn't where I belong."

"You'll never be happy on the mainland. There's no magic there, no—"

"I don't believe in magic. You know this."

Mother's lips flicker into a sad smile, and her tone becomes wistful. "You used to believe in magic. You used to help me make draughts and potions. You used to sit at my side all day and read the tea leaves of the shop patrons. Don't you remember what it was like back then? Amelie would play the piano and sing while you and I would lay our hands on the sick and cleanse their energy. You were so powerful then."

I shake my head. "I was a child. A little girl who confused her imagination for magic and thought she gave offerings to the fae because they were friends with the humans. I know better now."

"If you don't believe in magic, how do you explain the fae?"

"The fae aren't magic. They're creatures like any other. Everything they do can be explained with science."

"Science doesn't explain everything," Mother says. "Sometimes you have to follow your heart."

With gritted teeth, I force a smile. "Lucky for me, both science and my heart are telling me to go to the mainland. That's my choice. You won't change my mind."

We hold each other's gaze, and I try my best to maintain my composure, even as Mother's eyes fill with tears. The bell rings from inside the shop. A male voice calls out, a patron entering the apothecary, but Mother makes no move to greet him. She looks like she wants to say more to me, to find the right words that will convince me to stay with her. *Nothing will convince me. Nothing.*

Finally, Mother averts her gaze and peeks out the window that looks into the shop. "Mr. Anderson is here for his tincture," she whispers.

I take the opportunity to shove a piece of bread in my mouth, but after the argument with my mother, its taste is bitter.

Mother leaves the table and heads to the doorway. She pauses beneath the arch, back facing me. Her voice comes out with more sorrow than I expect. "Don't lose all faith in magic, Evie. Keep at least a flicker of it alive in your heart and know no matter how far you go, you can always come back home."

She disappears into the shop, and I hear her cheerful voice greet Mr. Anderson. I should feel victorious after winning the argument with Mother. I should feel excited about medical school.

But all I feel is empty, the haunting tone of Mother's words still echoing through my head.

4

The tang of blood mixed with the sharp aroma of alcohol fills the air of the surgery room. I refuse to tremble as I hazard a glance at the mangled limb of the patient and what used to be a hand. All that remains are strands of tissue, muscle, and bone in unnatural angles dangling from the forearm. Hank Osterman groans on the operating table, writhing beneath my hands as I keep a firm grip on his shoulders.

"Chloroform, Miss Fairfield," Mr. Meeks says, his voice calm yet firm.

I rush to obey, soaking a cotton cloth in chloroform, then placing it inside the metal inhalation cone. "It's going to be all right, Mr. Osterman." I try to mimic Mr. Meeks' calming tone as I cover the patient's nose and mouth with the cone. After a few breaths, his groans subside and his body grows slack.

"Tourniquet," Mr. Meeks says.

I fix the strap above Mr. Osterman's elbow, then turn the screw that tightens the slack. The flow of blood begins to lessen.

"Bone saw."

I reach for the saw. My stomach dives as Mr. Meeks takes it from me. I'd hoped he would let me operate the bone saw this time. With hardly a blink, I swallow my disappointment and keep my eyes trained on Mr. Meeks' every move. His motions are smooth and deliberate. In no time, the lower arm is completely detached. I dispose of the mangled remains, then hand over clamps, needle, and thread, watching Mr. Meeks' deft fingers as he ties off arteries and stitches the skin together over the wound. Like always, I'm at a loss for words, awed with the power a surgeon like Mr. Meeks has. The power to save lives.

Sweat is dripping from my brow by the time the operation is over.

Mr. Meeks looks at me for the first time since the surgery began. His gray eyes crinkle at the corners as he smiles. "You did well, Miss Fairfield. I'm glad you were able to get here so quickly. It would have been quite the challenge without you, dear girl."

His praise lifts my shoulders, and I grin with pride. Never mind his tone erred on the side of patronizing. I like to tell myself he simply thinks of me too much like a daughter to forgo with the cosseting. "I'm glad I could be here too. Every chance I can learn the trade is a chance I'm eager to have."

"Yes, well, my son is on holiday on the mainland, as you know. Since he couldn't be here today, I'm pleased I was graced with the next best. Now, my dear, do clean up if you will. Mr. Osterman will be awake soon and I'd rather he didn't have to see this mess."

I deflate as Mr. Meeks shuffles out of the room. He didn't mean to insult me, I'm sure, but sometimes the old man can be quite daft, regardless of his genius status amongst the people of Sableton. I know he's fond of me as his apprentice, but he never hesitates to make it clear his son is his successor, not me. His special little fop of a son, who I'm sure hasn't spent half the time in the surgery room as I have. He clearly cares more about taking one holiday after the next than helping his dear old father.

Great Mother above, help the injured residents of Sableton once Mr. Meeks retires and leaves the village in the hands of his idiot son.

I shake out my wrists, realizing my nails have dug into my palms. *Never mind that. Never mind. It's not my concern anyway,* I remind myself as I grit my teeth and haul the tray of bloodied tools to the stove. *I'm going to medical school. I'm leaving Sableton behind for good.*

Once the tools have been cleaned, boiled, and dried, I untie my blood-stained apron, adding it to the basket of soiled laundry. I heft the basket and start toward the door when I hear a moan from behind me.

"Mr. Meeks!" I shout into the hall, then rush to the operating table where Mr. Osterman is beginning to stir. His eyelids flutter as he lets out another pained groan. Without so much as a tremble, I reach for the bottle of laudanum, extract a dropperful, then place the dropper between his lips. "This will help." He grimaces but doesn't fight me as I drop the liquid— thirty drops, with precision—into his mouth. I call for Mr. Meeks again. Even though I have everything under control, there's one thing I can't do alone, and that's help Mr. Osterman to the parlor. His towering weight would crush me, even if I could get him to walk mostly on his own.

The patient's groans subside, and his muscles begin to relax. "The fae did this," he mutters drowsily, one word rolling into the next. His lids are still fluttering over his eyes. "She tricked me. She made me put my hand...in a bear trap."

I freeze. A fae is responsible for this? Hank Osterman is one of the best hunters in Sableton. What kind of evil creature could trick him into doing such a thing? And why?

He lifts his head. It wobbles, giving him a glance at what remains of his arm before he rests it back on the table. He bares his teeth in an angry snarl. "I thought she was a woman. She *looked* like a woman."

His tone chills me, leaving me without a reply.

"Ah, Mr. Osterman, you're awake," Mr. Meeks says as he approaches the table, his surgeon's calm never faltering. "Come, let's get you to the parlor to wait for your wife."

"My wife," Mr. Osterman echoes.

"Yes, she's bringing the carriage. Come now." Mr. Meeks puts his hand behind the patient's head, helping ease him into a sitting position.

Mr. Osterman steadies himself with his good arm, and the amputated limb twitches, as if trying to copy the movement of the other. A wince of pain shoots across his face, and he closes his eyes.

I reach for the bottle next to me. "More laudanum."

Mr. Meeks shakes his head. "No, he's had enough for now. We'll send him home with a bottle for his wife to administer. Now, come Hank. On your feet."

Mr. Osterman doesn't obey. Instead, he opens his eyes and glances again at the severed arm. For endless moments he just stares at it. Then his shoulders heave, head falling into his remaining hand. Sobs tear out of him.

All I can do is stare with wide eyes as Hank Osterman—undoubtedly one of the strongest, burliest men in my village—is completely undone.

And the fae are to blame.

My heart sinks. I think about the Holstrom girls, gone nearly a week now. What's it been like living in Faerwyvae, in that horrible, monstrous place? Are they being tormented by the same heartless creatures that did this to Mr. Osterman? The thought ties my stomach in knots. Now that the giddy relief over Amelie's and my safety has worn off, it's much easier to feel bad for the Holstrom girls.

As the minutes tick by, Mr. Osterman's sobs don't seem to be letting up, no matter how much Mr. Meeks tries to console him. Finally, Mr. Meeks takes a step away and turns to me with a whisper. "Poor man. I wish we could have done more for him."

I keep my voice low. "He said a fae was responsible. Do you think he was glamoured?"

Mr. Meeks looks back at his sobbing patient, expression grave. "He may have been, although I'd be surprised if that were true. He was wearing rowan berries around the arm we removed. I think it may be a matter of simple fae trickery."

"Rowan berries?" I'm shocked. Not by Mr. Osterman wearing them, but by Mr. Meeks' belief in them. He's always sharing his scientific theories with me, explaining the fae through logic. I never took the wearing of rowan berries to be anything more than superstition. A false magic.

"Rowan berries have proven to be effective at preventing a glamour," he explains. "It hasn't been studied thoroughly, but those of us in the scientific community believe rowan berries release a chemical upon skin contact that somehow helps preserve the function of our amygdala in the presence of the fae. That way, one need not rely solely on severing eye contact to prevent a glamour."

Awe washes over me as my lips pull into a grin. Logic never ceases to have that effect. "That actually makes sense."

Mr. Meeks pats me on the head. "Such an apt pupil. Now, run along, Miss Fairfield. Mr. Osterman wouldn't want a young lady to witness him in such a state." He tilts his head back at the sobbing man.

My grin slips from my lips. I want to remind him I'm more than just some *young lady*. I'm a surgeon's apprentice and soon-to-be medical professional. However, Mr. Meeks has always been the one person I can't bring myself to argue with. His mentorship has been my ticket to freedom. If I spoke to him the way I speak to most people, I never would have gotten the apprenticeship, much less kept it for the last two years. Instead, I nod and wish him a good evening.

As I'm about to pass through the door, Mr. Meeks says, "Oh, and don't forget the laundry, dear."

I grit my teeth, finding the basket I'd dropped earlier when Mr. Osterman woke. With an irritated sigh, I take it to the laundry room.

The September air is mild when I leave Mr. Meeks' house, the sun beginning to set. At the end of the drive, a carriage comes my way. It must be Mrs. Osterman. I refuse to look inside as I pass it, not wanting to witness the woman's worry. She must be terrified for her poor husband.

I take my time back to Ettings Street, where most of the shops are located. Once there, I stop at the post. We already got our letters this morning, but I'm eager to see if anything has arrived for us since. It's silly of me to expect anything from the university so soon. It's only been four days since I sent my acceptance letter. But that doesn't stop me from checking twice a day. A girl can't be sensible in *all* things, you know.

I leave the post empty handed, then continue my walk. At the other end of Ettings is Mother's shop, Fairfield Apothecary, which is also our home. It's nestled between the baker and the dressmaker. You can imagine Amelie's delight to be so near a dressmaker. As for me...I prefer the bakery.

My stomach growls at the thought. Surgery always works up an appetite for me. After all the gruesome parts are well past done, of course.

I can think of nothing but warm soup and buttered bread as the bakery comes into view. Then something unusual snags my attention—a figure walking toward me with sure, calculated steps. It's then I realize how quiet Ettings Street is. The few villagers passing between shops seem frozen as they watch the figure make his way along the sidewalk.

He's fae.

My mind brings forth visions of the fae I met at the wall, and I try to find what I remember of his features in the male coming my way. But this fae is undoubtedly shorter, stouter. He wears thick-rimmed spectacles, which I didn't know fae wore, and a long, burgundy and bronze jacket that reaches his ankles. Beneath the jacket, he wears a pair of cream trousers, a russet waistcoat, and a bronze cravat in a floral pattern. The only similarity between him and the fae from the wall is the smug smile.

I don't meet his eyes as he passes by, but a shiver runs down my spine once he's behind me. I can guess where he's heading. He's clearly a fae ambassador and likely on his way to smooth things over with the Ostermans.

A fae drawing human blood could be seen as an act of war—*should* be seen as an act of war. Yet, I already know that's not how things will go. The ambassador has probably already spoken with the mayor, delivering sleek words and sorry excuses for the troublesome fae's unwitting behavior. Then he'll go to the Ostermans, offer to pay for the surgery we performed and make financial amends for loss of limb and income. The council will let it slide. Again. Just another accident. A misunderstanding.

I'm so angry, I could explode. It's then I notice the street has remained quiet. The villagers are still loitering outside the shops, staring at where the fae ambassador went. I whirl around, but he's out of sight. It makes me wonder if something else happened. Maybe the mayor *didn't* cave for once.

Whatever the case, the mood on Ettings Street has me rattled. I quicken my pace, forgetting the bakery as I make a straight line for home. That's when I realize the villagers aren't staring after the fae ambassador. They're watching *me*.

Nausea wrenches my gut as my mind begins to spin. There's a reasonable explanation for this. Maybe they're only staring because I had the nerve to walk past the fae while everyone else stood frozen in fear.

I want to be right. I have to be right.

As I reach the door to the apothecary, I'm surprised to find it in the process of opening. I'm more surprised when Harriet, the baker from next door, is revealed coming from behind it. Her face is pale, and when her eyes find me, her lips pull into a sympathetic frown. She reaches a hand and places it on my shoulder. "I brought you some bread, dearie."

"Bread," I echo, brows knitting together as I try to puzzle together her words with her expression. It isn't unusual for Harriet to bring us bread. We buy some from her almost daily. So why is she saying it like an apology?

Harriet nods. "I had plenty left over after I brought some to the Holstroms."

I stare at her, unable to make sense of her seemingly disconnected statements. "What's this all about?"

Her eyes widen and her mouth falls open, but she doesn't say anything.

Terror seizes my chest. "What's going on?"

She squeezes my shoulder. "You should talk to your mother."

I don't wait to see Harriet the rest of the way out the door before I rush into the shop. The front is empty, so I barrel into the kitchen, then to the parlor. That's where I find them.

Amelie is lying on the couch, her head in Mother's lap. Her cheeks are flushed and streaked with tears as she sobs uncontrollably into a white kerchief. Something sparkles from the finger of the hand she's dabbing her tears with. A ring.

I meet Mother's eyes and find her staring blankly ahead, face devoid of all color.

"Ma, what happened?"

She slowly turns to meet my gaze, but her expression remains empty. "The Holstrom girls are dead. You and Amelie are being sent to Faerwyvae in their place."

5

———————

Mother's words make no sense. They are neither rational nor reasonable. And they do nothing to stop my mind from spinning. There's no way she can mean what I think she means. My voice comes out shaky. "Ma, what are you talking about?"

She looks from me to Amelie, then strokes my sister's hair. Amelie lets out a louder sob.

"Let's speak in the kitchen." Mother gently scoots Amelie's head off her lap, leaving her to nestle deeper into the couch.

I follow her to the kitchen. "Please tell me what's happening. I feel like I'm losing my mind."

Her eyes are glazed as she takes two mugs and a jar of herbs, then sets them on the kitchen table. "The fae ambassador just left after coming here to tell me all of this. I've hardly had time to process it myself."

My eyes widen. The fae I saw a moment ago...he came from *here*? No wonder everyone was staring at me.

Mother spoons some herbs into the mugs, then places the kettle on the stove. She returns to face me. "He explained the Holstrom girls were... executed last night."

"Executed! Why?"

"All the ambassador would say is that the girls were found guilty of treason by King Aspen."

I put my hands on my hips. "We're supposed to believe sweet little

Theresa and Maryanne Holstrom committed treason against a fae king? That's insane. What exactly was their treasonous crime?"

She sighs. "You know how the fae are."

Cruel. Irrational. Evil. "You mean they offended him. Wore the wrong color on the wrong day of the week. Forgot to say some silly rhyme before eating fae food. Is that it?"

Mother doesn't answer. It's not like I expect her to know the truth anyway. The ambassadors never come with the truth. They come with excuses.

I grind my teeth. "Why are we being sent to Faerwyvae? They got their Chosen for the Reaping. It's not our fault the king executed them already."

She shakes her head. "The ambassador says the marriages hadn't taken place yet. The treaty states at least one marriage must take place between a Chosen and a fae every hundred years to secure the pact."

"What does the treaty say about the fae executing their fiancées? Drawing human blood is an act of war."

Her voice comes out soft. "So is treason." The emptiness in her tone is so resigned. So final. So hopeless.

I fight back tears, focusing instead on the flicker of indignation burning inside me. "You're just going to let this happen? You're going to let them take us?"

When she meets my eyes, her expression hardens, turning to anger. Not at me, I realize, but at the situation. "I don't know what else to do. I thought I did everything to keep the two of you safe. I thought you'd *always* be safe."

Anger is growing inside me too, and my words come out bitter. "You mean you never saw this in your cards? In your tea leaves? In all the times you took us to the wall with our offerings, promising us you *understood* the fae?"

"Evie, I—"

"Where is your precious magic now, Mother? Are your tinctures going to save us? Your potions and draughts? Do you have any mystical talismans to hang around our necks to ensure we don't lose our heads?" My words are laced with sarcasm, and I watch as she wilts beneath them.

As her expression falters, so does my heart. I shouldn't have said any of that; my anger isn't meant for her. Yet, I'm too full of fury to apologize. If I take it back now, the rage will rot inside me, eating me alive.

The kettle whistles from the stove, saving me from the tension growing between us.

"We were going to get married by the sea," says a wistful voice.

With a jump, I whirl around to find Amelie hovering in the doorway to the kitchen, eyes unfocused. I go to her, placing a hand on her arm.

She meets my eyes, then holds up a frail hand, the one bearing the ring. It's a ruby on a circlet of gold. "Magnus asked me to marry him this afternoon. Now I'll...I'll never..."

Mother pushes a mug of tea into Amelie's hands as a fresh sob escapes my sister's throat. "Drink."

Amelie does as told, then wanders back to the parlor. The sight of her uneven steps chills me to the bone.

Mother sighs, closing the lid to her jar of herbs with more force than necessary. "I should bring this to the Holstroms. It will help with their nerves. You may not believe in my craft, Evie, but I know Mrs. Holstrom will appreciate it."

I want to tell her laudanum would be far more effective than whatever herbal infusion she's created, but I hold my tongue. I've said enough already. And if I'm not ready to apologize...

I hold out my hand for the jar. "I'll take it to them."

Mother cocks her head, then seems to understand the olive branch I'm offering. "Very well. But don't stay long. The ambassador will be back at midnight..." Her words dry up, ending with a choked sound.

Midnight. Amelie and I will be taken to Faerwyvae at midnight.

The house suddenly seems too small for my swarm of thoughts, for the anger and confusion and shock swirling inside. I take the jar from Mother, then rush outside faster than I can blink.

I make my way to the Holstrom farm, which is on the northern edge of Sableton. The sky is almost dark by the time I arrive, but there's enough light to stop me when I reach their gate. For there in front of the farm lies a scene far more gruesome than anything I've witnessed during surgery.

The grounds in front of their stables and pens are littered with dismembered bodies. Animal bodies. Pigs, sheep, goats. Blood splatters the dirt, entrails stream between corpses. I take a step back, bile rising in my throat. This could be none other than the work of fae.

"Disgusting," says a voice at my side. I hadn't noticed Maddie Coleman arrive. She holds a basket full of coffee, chocolate, and other exotic food items. Her parents own the biggest merchant ships in Eisleigh, and her uncle is the mayor—which she thinks makes her Queen of Sableton. She wrinkles her nose at the scene before us but doesn't seem nearly as disturbed as I am. When she turns to me, her eyes fall on the jar of herbs in my hand. "What a quaint gift."

I watch as she sways side to side, as if trying to accentuate the oversized gift basket in her arms.

"Mother sent me," I say flatly.

"Mine sent me as well, although I doubt the Holstroms need it. Visitors have been coming all day." She returns to face the yard. "And yet, they still haven't managed to clean this unsightly mess. How are we supposed to make it to the front door without soiling our dresses?" Her eyes trail from the gore to my trousers, prompting a smirk. "Or should I say, dress?"

I glare at her. "They're probably too busy grieving their daughters to clean right now."

She turns her nose to the air, her blond curls at the sides of her head bobbing with the movement. "They deserve it. Their daughters committed treason, after all."

My mouth falls open, and I imagine punching Maddie Coleman in her perfect pink nose. "How can you say such a thing? You really think the Holstroms deserved the execution of their daughters? And for their entire farm to be destroyed?"

She rolls her eyes. "King Aspen gifted the Holstroms with enchanted farm animals, a blessing that would have led to riches for generations to come. And what does he get in return? Two treasonous girls."

"First off, the farm animals weren't enchanted, they were simply well-bred. Second, Theresa and Maryanne couldn't have done anything to deserve execution. You know that, right?"

She shrugs. "Perhaps the Holstroms wanted the war to return. Uncle says some residents of Eisleigh are in favor of another war to win the Fair Isle from the fae."

I'm surprised by this. Could some of our villagers actually want another war? Could the Holstroms be among those who do? I shake the idea from my head. There's no way the Holstroms would put their daughters' lives in danger in favor of war. Both the fae and the humans nearly perished during the last one a thousand years ago. The treaty was the only reason the bloodshed was able to end.

"I was supposed to be next in line, you know," Maddie says, eyes narrowed at me. "Marie and I were supposed to be chosen next if the Holstrom girls didn't work out. I was to marry King Aspen, and Marie was to marry Prince Cobalt. But *you* were chosen instead."

It takes me a moment to register what she's implying. "Wait...you *wanted* to be chosen for the Reaping? To be married off to a fae?"

"A fae *king*."

"A fae king with horns."

Maddie rolls her eyes. "He's called the *Stag King*. It's more likely he has antlers."

I flourish my free hand. "Wow, what a difference that makes."

"It does make a difference. And for someone who's always telling everyone how clever and sensible she is, you should get your facts straight before spouting off about them."

Heat rises to my cheeks. Since when does Maddie Coleman get the upper hand in an argument with *me*? "When did you become such a diehard fae lover? Last time I saw you in the presence of a fae, you ran screaming. You probably wet your knickers too."

"That was a goblin, not a king," she says. "Besides, I'd take horns, antlers, or fangs if it makes me a queen, not to mention the wealth and riches my family would be blessed with."

My eyes bulge with the restraint it takes to keep from laughing in her face. "Well, it turns out when the Great Mother was handing out working brains, she passed you over entirely. Regardless, I have the perfect solution for us both. If you want so badly to marry the Stag King, by all means, take my place."

Her mouth falls open, cheeks burning crimson as she processes my insult. Then with a scowl, she snaps her mouth shut and averts her gaze. "I can't."

"Why not? Your uncle is the mayor. He's in charge, isn't he?"

"My uncle is in charge of Sableton, but he has no control over the fae."

"What does that have to do with anything? The names have already been selected. If you were chosen as backup, then why are Amelie and I involved at all?"

Her lips press into a tight line, as if it pains her to say the next words. "You were chosen by the fae. It was a choice that overrode all previous selections."

My mind goes blank. "Why? Amelie and I have done nothing to attract the attention of the fae."

"You weren't selected as a pair, stupid," Maddie says. "*You* were selected. Personally. Your sister is only involved because of you."

I'm too shocked; I can't even bristle at her insult this time. "I was...selected?"

"The fae ambassador requested you by name. *First* name."

By name. My entire body goes cold.

6

I can do nothing but gape, words stripped from my lips as I make sense of Maddie's statement. I was chosen by name. Me. That can mean only one thing. I'm being punished.

I think back to my visit at the faewall and the cloaked fae ambassador. He's the only reason the fae would know me by first name and the only fae with motive to punish me. Images of my blade hovering in front of his face, ready to strike, flood my memory. But he attacked me first! Or was it my sharp tongue that sparked his ire?

It could have been anything, honestly. I frowned too much, spoke too much, spoke too little. Offended him with a misinterpreted gesture, said the wrong word in the wrong tone. Who knows what makes the fae react in anger? Why did they execute the Holstrom girls? Why did they slaughter their animals? Why did they trick Hank Osterman into sticking his hand in a bear trap?

There's no purpose trying to figure it out. The fae are unpredictable. Dangerous. And I'm about to be the bride of one.

The fight is leached from my bones. I can't even feel my rage anymore. Only hollowness remains.

I shove my mother's jar on top of Maddie's basket without a word, then turn away from the farm. Maddie calls after me, but I don't answer; I can't even make out what she's saying through the sound of blood rushing through my ears.

This is all my fault.

~

THE DARK OF NIGHT HAS FULLY SETTLED IN BY THE TIME I MAKE IT BACK TO
Ettings Street. My eyes are unfocused as I wander the sidewalk toward the
apothecary, only narrowing when I notice a hulking shape in front of the
shop. A carriage.

I stop, mind reeling as I process what time it might be. Surely it isn't
midnight yet! But the carriage parked in front of my home is undoubtedly
fae. I can't make out the color in the dark, but vines of gold twine up the
edges, glinting in the moonlight. The horses at the front of the carriage are
thin, dark, unearthly creatures.

With a shudder, I run to the door of the shop and dart inside. I find
Mother in the parlor. Her hands are on her hips as she scowls at a figure
standing in the middle of the room. He's stout and barely taller than Mother,
with neatly trimmed brown hair, pointed ears decorated with gold jewelry,
and brown slanted eyes behind horn-rimmed glasses. His jacket is pristine
lines of burgundy and bronze with elaborate golden clasps shaped like
leaves down the front. It's the fae I saw in the village earlier.

Mother whirls toward me with a sigh. She returns to face the fae, irritation tensing her posture. "I told you she'd be back," she snaps.

The ambassador shrugs. "You must understand my suspicion."

"No, I must not," Mother argues. "The girls aren't to be taken until
midnight. They still have three hours until then."

"I am simply here to assure they comply. Don't mind me. I won't be a
bother."

"No, you won't be," Mother says, "since you'll be waiting in your
carriage."

The ambassador looks shocked, his hand moving to his chest as if she
suggested he wait in a gutter. I'm equally surprised. Mother has never
spoken about the fae with anything but reverence and curiosity, or at the
worst of times, with amused frustration. It shows how hopeless our situation
really is.

When the ambassador makes no move to leave, she takes a step toward
him. "There's nothing in the treaty that states you are allowed in my house
while my children pack for their imprisonment. Now go. They'll be out the
door at midnight."

He sniffs, then turns on his heel.

I listen for the sound of the front door opening and shutting, then let out a heavy breath. "Three hours until midnight?"

Mother nods, her expression unreadable. She looks angry and hopeless all at once, but there's something else there I can't place. "I'll be in the kitchen," she whispers, then brushes past me out of the parlor.

I consider following her but don't. I'm not ready to face her after the hurtful things I said earlier. Especially since I know whatever I say to her next will be the last she'll hear from me again.

My throat feels tight as I make my way up the stairs toward my room. As I reach the top landing, I hear whimpering coming from the door straight ahead. Amelie's room. I tiptoe forward and peek through the crack between the door and the frame. Amelie is in the middle of her floor, surrounded by her favorite dresses. An overstuffed bag lies at her feet, more dresses spilling from it. I'm about to enter her room when I stop myself. How can I try to comfort her when I know I'm to blame? Does she already know? Does Mother know?

Tears spring to my eyes at the sight of my sister, but I force myself to leave, quietly crossing the hall to my bedroom. Once inside, I sit at the edge of my bed. Part of me wants to cry, to fall into a fit of sobs on my floor like Amelie. The other part of me won't let me cry, knowing I must be strong for the both of us.

My eyes rove my room, taking in everything I'm leaving behind. I expect to feel nostalgic, but I don't; I was already planning on leaving here anyway. My room isn't full of trinkets and luxuries like Amelie's is. My wardrobe isn't brimming with gowns and beaded slippers. The thing I treasure most of all lies on my dressing table—the invitation to university.

Longing tugs at my heart. My mind races to think of some way out of this. *Any* way out of this. I imagine sneaking out the back door, leaving before the ambassador returns to escort us to the carriage. How far could I get by midnight if I left now? I could take the money I've saved for university, use it to take me south where I can catch a ship to the mainland.

Excitement sparks within me, a smile nearly pulling at my lips. Then it all comes crashing down. I think of Amelie. What would happen to her if I ran away? Would they still take her? Punish her with a fate worse than being a fae's bride? No, I can't leave her, especially when I'm to blame for this mess. Could I convince her to come with me?

My sensible side takes over, and I know running away is neither logical nor possible. A marriage must take place for the treaty to be upheld. Our village has already lost two girls to the Reaping without securing the pact. What will happen if we break the treaty too? The council could select another set of Chosen. The fae could request another girl to be punished.

Or it could start a war. A war that brought near-annihilation a thousand years ago. A war I'd be responsible for.

I close my eyes, shutting the door to all my thoughts of escaping this. My dream of moving to the mainland is over. I won't be going to university nor will I become a great surgeon. I won't be anything but a bride. If the fae let me live that long.

Anger returns to me in a rush, making my hands clench into fists. I stand and stride over to my wardrobe, flinging the doors open with more force than necessary. From the bottom of the wardrobe, I extricate a bag. Beneath it lies a wooden case. I take that too and bring both to my bed. I open the case, revealing an array of tools—bone saw, tourniquet, scalpel, trephine, forceps, tenaculum, knives. My surgery kit, a gift from Mr. Meeks on my eighteenth birthday. A gift I never got to use.

Most significantly, the tools are carbon steel—an alloy I know contains iron. Whether an iron alloy has any effect on the fae, I don't know. But I'm willing to find out.

I close the box and place it at the bottom of the bag. Then I return to my wardrobe and pull out my cloak. From my dressing table, I retrieve my nightdress, an extra pair of trousers and a blouse, as well as my belt and dagger. I stuff the clothing in my bag and secure the belt around my waist. The dagger at my hip and the blades inside my bag have cooled some of my rage. I feel safe now. In control.

I may have to marry a monster. I may never get to leave Faerwyvae again. But I won't go down without a fight. The treaty may force me to marry, but as far as I know, it says nothing about letting a fae touch me or letting one come anywhere near me. In fact, I doubt it says anything about my husband needing to be alive for the treaty to remain valid.

I'll go to Faerwyvae. I'll do my part. I'll sacrifice myself for the safety of Eisleigh. But if any of the fae try to hurt me or my sister, I'll be ready. My future husband can try all he likes to touch me, but he'll find no luck with an iron blade between us.

I grin, but it's short lived as my thoughts return to Amelie. There will be times when my blade will only be able to protect one of us, times when we'll have to leave each other's sides. How will I keep her safe?

The door creaks open behind me, and I turn to find Mother in the doorway. We lock eyes, staring wordlessly, until she joins me at my bed. She places a stoppered jar on top of the clothing in my bag. "Tincture of iron, St. John's Wart, and daisy. Take half a dropperful daily."

She wants me to ingest...an iron supplement?

Everyone in Eisleigh knows iron is our greatest defense against the fae, something humans discovered during the war. Most people think it's magic that makes iron so harmful to the fae, but Mr. Meeks explains they have a severe allergy to the metal, preventing their blood from clotting and their wounds from healing. He says their olfactory system is highly attuned to it, allowing them to avoid it through scent. I think of the slaughtered animals at the Holstrom farm, of Hank Osterman's mangled arm. While I'm not sure having adequate levels of iron in my blood will keep me from getting killed by a fae, at least I'll less likely get eaten by one.

My mouth falls open, realizing Mother has never seemed more brilliant than she does now. Before I can thank her, she takes my hand and presses a pouch into my palm. "Salt all your food. Even a pinch will counteract any harmful magic. Turn your clothes inside out. And wear this at all times." She takes a long strand of odd-looking red beads and places them around my neck.

I run my fingers along the necklace. Dried rowan berries. I remember what Mr. Meeks said about them, how they help preserve proper brain function through skin contact. Mother has been selling them in her shop for years, something I'd always scoffed at before hearing Mr. Meeks' explanation today. For once, her craft has aligned with logic.

Yesterday's magic is today's science, Mr. Meeks likes to say.

Perhaps my mother deserves more credit. She may be giving people false hope with her silly magic, but only rarely do her treatments cause real harm. I'll never believe in her craft, but sometimes her treatments are rooted in science. She just doesn't know it.

More than that, she deserves credit for being my mother. For loving me with all my sharp words and harsh edges, hardly ever giving me more than a word of reproach when I cross the line. If she can love me with all my flaws, I can love her with all of hers. And I do. So much, I feel like my heart is being torn in two.

"Ma." The word comes out in a sob as I wrap my arms around her neck and breathe in her scent. Her arms go around me, and she rubs my back like I'm a child again. For a while, I let myself be a child, let Mother comfort me and stroke my hair. I take it all in—every word, every whisper, every angle of her face and shade of red in her hair—and lock it into my memory.

That's the only place I'll ever see her again.

7

———————

Three hours later, Amelie and I sit in the carriage across from the bespectacled fae ambassador, riding through the night toward the fae lands.

My eyes feel raw and red, my throat like sandpaper each time I swallow. At least my tears have dried. I refuse to show weakness in front of the fae male across from me.

Amelie, on the other hand, continues to whimper and cry. Her cheeks are red and coated in a sheen of fresh tears. We sit close, her arm entwined with mine, my wrist held in her vise-like grip. Her free hand tugs at the seam of her inside-out dress, then fiddles with the strand of rowan berries she wears. I can only imagine her distress at being forced to be dressed so unfashionably, regardless of circumstance.

Once Amelie falls asleep, head on my shoulder, the carriage goes silent. I force myself to stay awake as the hours pass, constantly checking on the presence of my dagger hidden beneath my cloak. The ambassador doesn't utter a word as he alternates between staring out the window of the carriage and leaning back for a nap.

It isn't until sunlight is beating my eyelids that I realize I've fallen asleep. I jerk upright, my hand flying to my dagger. Still there. The movement has woken Amelie, who lifts her head from my shoulder and sniffles. Her hand returns to squeezing my wrist.

Now that the sun has risen, warm light beams inside the carriage, drawing my curiosity. I lean forward just enough to see out the window. There I find sunlight diffused through a canopy of leaves in reds and golds and coppery brown, blinking like stars as they sway on the wind. The trees are birch and oak and others I can't identify. September may be beautiful in Sableton, but this is beyond any fall landscape I've ever seen. My breath catches in my throat, but I suppress my wonder, forcing my gaze away from the window as I settle back into my seat.

"We've entered Autumn, as you can tell," the ambassador says. He has a lazy, high-pitched way of speaking. It reminds me of the few nobles I've met, or snobs like Maddie Coleman.

His words puzzle me, and my intellectual needs override my desire to remain aloof. "When you say we've entered autumn, what exactly do you mean?"

"The Autumn Court, obviously," he says. "Your new home."

It never occurred to me to care to learn about King Aspen or the court he rules, but it does explain the unearthly beauty of our surroundings. Yet, his words, *your new home,* have left a sour taste in my mouth that no intellectual stimulus can erase.

His eyes move from me to Amelie. "There's no reason to be scared, you know. Honestly, it's silly the way you cower like that."

I shoot him a glare. "Silly? You think we're *silly*? Was it silly for the Holstrom girls to be executed?"

He lets out a trill of laughter. "Oh, that. Yes, I can see why that would frighten you. But you need not worry. That is, unless you're plotting treason. You don't seem the type though."

"Did Theresa and Maryanne seem the type?"

His brows furrow. "Now that I think about it, no, they didn't. Hmm." His smile returns as if we haven't been speaking about death and treason at all.

But I'm not done with the subject. "Why did they die?"

He shrugs. "We already told the human council. They performed an act of treason."

"Cut the lies," I say. "What's the real reason? What exactly did they do to earn a death sentence?"

"First off, fae can't lie. Second, that is a classified matter. If you'd like to ask the king when you meet him, perhaps he'll tell you. For now, just know their crime was grave indeed."

I roll my eyes. "Is that the same excuse you gave for poor Hank Osterman? I'm sure you were sent to tidy up that mess as well. Or did they send the ambassador in the black cloak instead?"

"Ambassador in a black cloak? Hank Osterman? I assure you, I know neither of these people. Care to enlighten me?"

I narrow my eyes at him. "I'm sure you know about Mr. Osterman. He lost his arm because of one of you. A fae tricked him into sticking his hand in a bear trap. What clever words were used to excuse that act?"

The ambassador pulls his head back in surprise. "You mean the Butcher of Stone Ninety-Four?"

"The what?"

"The Butcher of Stone Ninety-Four," the ambassador says, like it's supposed to be obvious. "That man is a menace. He comes hunting near the wall and enters Faerwyvae between stone ninety-four and stone ninety-five on the Spring axis. He enters only as far as he can get away with and leaves traps, hoping to catch the kind of fae he can sell for parts. Is that the man you speak of?"

"No, of course not! Hank Osterman would never—"

"He was injured just yesterday, right? Caught in his own bear trap? Fae trap, more like."

I hesitate. Mr. Osterman hadn't said if it was his own trap or not, but it's possible. "Yes, and one of your lesser fae—"

He hisses a sharp intake of breath. "Ah, we don't use that term. That's a human convention. Lesser fae and high fae are labels we in Faerwyvae take offense to. We prefer unseelie and seelie."

I glower. "One of your *whatever* fae tricked him into mangling his hand. He had to have his entire lower arm amputated."

The ambassador cackles. "Oh, Lorelei. What a scamp."

Heat rises to my cheeks. "A scamp. That's what you call a creature that tricks a man into losing his arm?"

"It's not like he didn't have it coming. She isn't the first fae the Butcher of Stone Ninety-Four has terrorized. He caught Lorelei's lover too. Probably sold her wings to a merchant and dumped her body in a ditch. Don't even get me started on the unicorns. I don't know how much longer I would have been able to cover for his treachery. Lorelei's little stunt likely saved us from war."

I'm at a loss for words. The ambassador must be mistaken. The fae may be adamant that they can't lie, but I'm sure it has more to do with cultural custom than physical ability. Besides, even if he were incapable of lying, it wouldn't mean he's telling the truth. He must not *know* the truth. Because the Hank Osterman I know would never hunt unicorns or kill fae. Would he?

"The lesson is, don't set traps and you'll be fine," the ambassador says.

"A simple matter then."

"Exactly!" he says with an approving nod.

I frown. Another stretch of silence falls over the carriage until a new question comes to mind. "Which are you? Seelie or unseelie?"

"Obviously, I'm seelie. I'm dressed in regal clothes and riding in a carriage, aren't I?"

"Is that all the difference amounts to?"

"Do you know nothing of Faerwyvae? Are you not taught our ways growing up, like we are taught about yours?"

We are, but I don't say so out loud. For the things we are taught about the fae are hardly flattering.

He huffs. "I'm an ambassador, not a nursery maid. Regardless, I'll educate you. All fae once were unseelie, which you so callously deem lesser fae. Back when the isle was ours alone and no human had set foot here, we were different. We were...creatures, you might say. Spirits. Animals. We were so alive back then." His voice sounds wistful. "Or so I'm told, at least. I'm hardly old enough to have been born that long ago. In any case, we didn't start to change until your kind came to the isle."

I find myself leaning forward, genuinely curious to hear what he has to say. I've been told about the war between the humans and fae, the repercussions, the treaty, but never anything about what the Fair Isle was like before.

He continues. "We were curious about these newcomers, and they were equally curious about us. There were mishaps and misunderstandings, of course, but for the most part, we were friendly with the humans. Then the humans started leaving us gifts, sharing their food. You taught us words, made us clothes. That's when we began to change."

"How did you change?"

"We began to feel like you, look like you, hurt like you. It was a curse. And a blessing. We experienced things we never had before. Love. Hate. Rage. Passion. Sorrow. Some of us welcomed these changes, exploring the vast array of new experiences. The others retreated from human settlements, vowing never to eat human food or wear human clothes again. That was the beginning of the divide between seelie and unseelie. The unseelie considered seelie fae unnatural, an abomination of what we were meant to be. They wanted the isle back, for the humans to be eradicated. The seelie, meanwhile, weren't willing to give their new identities away and wanted to protect their friends, the humans. And...well, you know the rest."

I'm not sure I do, but I can't find the words to admit it.

"Which one is my husband?" Amelie's voice startles me. It's the first time she's spoken since we left home. "Seelie or Unseelie?"

"Well, at present both King Aspen and Prince Cobalt are politically seelie," the ambassador says. "However, King Aspen tends to shift unseelie from time to time, both physically and politically. He has a temper, you know."

Amelie blanches, her hand clutching her rowan berries. "Which am I to marry?"

"That depends. Marriages from previous Reapings were made according to age. By the way, not all got to marry kings and princes, you know. You're lucky. The last Reaping from a hundred years ago paired the girls with minor cousins of the Summer Court Queen. Now, which of you is Evelyn Fairfield?"

"I am."

"Pleased to meet you, Miss Evelyn Fairfield," he says with a bow of his dark head. "My name is Foxglove. Forgive me for not introducing myself until now. I wanted to make sure the two of you had a good and proper sulk. Young human females seem fond of doing such. I take it you are the eldest?"

Amelie springs forward in her seat, an appalled look on her face. "Evie? Eldest! That's absurd."

I pat her knee and say to Foxglove, "Amelie is eldest."

Amelie leans back in her seat, arms crossed over her chest. "Why would you assume me to be the younger?"

Foxglove scratches the side of his head, then adjusts his spectacles. "I'm not sure. I do suppose you are taller, now that you are sitting upright and no longer have the tears of a small child in your eyes."

Amelie's mouth falls open. "Tears of a child? How rude! And another thing. Never mind how tall I am. Even if I wasn't taller, I'd still be older. Height is hardly an indication."

I suppress a grin. It's nice to see Amelie acting like herself again.

"I was certain height was an indication of human age, but I was obviously mistaken," Foxglove says.

"Does your kind keep growing forever, then?" I ask, imagining monstrous, mountainous fae strolling through the trees, heads above the treetops.

"Only for several hundred years. King Aspen has reached his full height by now, I'm sure, being the thousand years that he is."

Amelie lets out a gasp. "A thousand years? He's positively ancient!"

Foxglove nods. "He was born nearly the day the war ended. The tide turned upon his birth, and I say that with some irony, as his mother is

Queen of the Sea Court. She was unseelie through and through, as was her husband, King Herne of the Autumn Court. King Herne died during the war, however, leaving Melusine as regent. Somehow, against all odds, King Aspen was born in seelie form, taking his deceased father's place as heir to the Autumn Court. This, in turn, changed his mother's heart and brought the majority vote to side with the seelie. The Council of Eleven Courts forged peace with the humans through the treaty."

"You haven't answered my question," Amelie says with a pout. "Who are we each to marry?"

"As the eldest, you will marry King Aspen while Evelyn will marry his younger brother, Prince Cobalt."

Amelie's eyes go wide. "I have to marry the Stag King?"

"You do!" Foxglove says. "You're so lucky. The Stag King is quite yummy to look at. Plus, he has a huge...*kingdom*, as rumor would have it." He waggles his brows, his grin wide enough to show his slightly pointed teeth.

Fangs. I knew it—*wait*. Did he just make an innuendo? "Huge kingdom?"

He winks. "So I've heard. Prince Cobalt, on the other hand, has remained much more of a mystery. If he's taken many lovers, neither he nor they brag about it. Quite a shame. You'll have to let me know about his...kingdom yourself."

A blush of heat rises to my cheeks. I most certainly will not be reporting anything about Prince Cobalt's *kingdom*, for I plan on never laying eyes on it. I give a subtle pat to my dagger, taking comfort that it remains a presence at my side, then avert my gaze to the window, watching golden leaves fall.

8

———————

The journey through Autumn isn't easy, neither on my body nor my mind. Every muscle aches, both from sitting so long and from tensing due to nerves. Amelie and I were allowed two short breaks during our travels, and these were only to relieve our humanly urges, something I never care to relive again. Nothing could be more frightening than trying to squat behind a tree in the forest of the fae. I could swear every leaf, vine, and branch had eyes, watching me, mocking me. My only hope now is that our new home has a proper toilet.

Then again, whenever I think of our *new home*, my mind becomes frazzled, my muscles tense yet again, and I feel like my lungs will collapse in my chest. What awaits us at the end of this carriage ride?

Warm light of the setting sun blazes through the window of the carriage, bathing the inside in a red-orange glow. I lean forward, looking out the window. It seems the trees have cleared, and we are no longer in the dense forest. The sky is every shade of gold, pink, and orange, but the quality of color is unlike anything I've ever seen before. It glimmers and glows, enhanced by the red leaves of the trees covering the distant hillsides.

I lean back and Foxglove takes my place at the window. "Ah, we're almost to the palace," he says.

My heart begins to race. As much as I want the ride to be over, I'm not ready to enter the home of the king and my husband-to-be. The thought alone churns my stomach, making bile rise in my throat.

A moment later, the carriage begins to slow, and I feel the weight shift, as if we're making an ascent. Amelie grips my hand, chest heaving as she clutches her necklace. Her fingers tremble within mine. Or are mine the ones trembling? With a deep breath, I close my eyes, steadying my nerves and smothering my panic in a blanket of calm. The calm of a surgeon.

The carriage stops. "We're here," Foxglove says.

I force myself to open my eyes. *Breathe. Hold yourself together.*

Foxglove pushes open the carriage door and exits. Amelie's grip grows tighter, and neither of us makes any move to leave our seats. After a few moments, Foxglove peers back inside. "Come on. Did you not hear? You're home!"

Another deep breath. My free hand pats my dagger. As if moving through water, I slowly leave the seat and make my way to the door. Amelie trails behind me, her fingers laced in mine. Foxglove offers me his hand as I step from the carriage to the marble path beneath it. More light from the setting sun greets me outside, overwhelming my senses.

Foxglove extends his free hand, indicating the other side of the carriage. "Welcome to Bircharbor Palace."

I step away from the carriage and turn until massive golden spires come into view. My breath catches in my throat, and for one blessed moment, I forget my anxiety. The palace is more beautiful than any structure I've ever seen, with walls of red-orange carnelian, yellow citrine, and golden-brown tiger's eye. There's nothing behind the palace but blushing sky, no forest, tree, or shrub. It's as if the palace stands at the end of the world. A cool breeze brushes my face, slightly warmer than the autumn weather back home, and I catch the hint of salt on the air.

I'm nearly swept beneath the weight of my awe, but I dampen it, reminding myself this is not a beautiful palace but a prison. A place of death. I'm not standing before an architectural miracle but at the maw of a vicious beast.

I steal a glance at Amelie, who seems to be struck with the wonder I felt a moment ago. Her head tilts to the side as she studies the palace. The look on her face is the same she gets when considering a new gown.

"Come," Foxglove says and rounds the carriage.

We follow, but I freeze when we reach the horse-creatures that had been pulling the carriage. This is my first opportunity to see them up close and beneath proper light since our travels began. Last night, I had only the impression of something beastly and strange, but the sight before me is more chilling than I'd imagined.

The creatures have sleek, equine bodies covered in smooth black fur, and flowing manes of onyx hair. Their necks are longer and slimmer than a regular horse, curving sinuously, the legs more graceful and less jointed. Their teeth are bared, showing sharp razors of opalescent white. Their glowing yellow eyes seem to bore into us.

Foxglove rolls his eyes impatiently when he sees we've stopped following him. "Puca. Harmless, really, especially when you have them under control."

"And...you have them under control?" Amelie asks in her quavering voice.

Foxglove laughs. "They serve King Aspen. Puca are great for aiding transportation. Not nearly as fast as a kelpie, but let's not speak of them."

It's unnerving that he didn't answer the question, considering he supposedly can't lie.

"Impressed with the puca, are we?" A feminine voice draws my attention away from the creatures to the female fae approaching us. She's petite with brown skin and olive-green eyes, her face dusted with gold on her eyelids, lips, and over her cheekbones. Her hair is in wild, black curls, tangled with tiny sticks, leaves, and branches. She wears a gauzy gown in a deep bronze. It covers less skin than a nightdress and leaves little to the imagination, despite the fact that the thin fabric reaches past her ankles.

"Darling! It's so good to see you." Foxglove reaches out to her and they embrace, exchanging kisses on the cheek.

When she pulls away, she eyes Amelie and me, lifting an eyebrow as if uninspired by what she's found. "Are these the girls?"

"Yes, they are," Foxglove says. "Meet Amelie and Evelyn Fairfield."

She puts her hands on her hips. "Hey."

I hesitate, waiting for her to introduce herself. "And you are?"

"I'm to be your...what's it called?" She looks to Foxglove. "A slave? Servant?"

He laughs. "I think in the human world it's called a lady's maid, Lorelei."

"Yes. That." She doesn't look pleased.

Her name sparks recognition, and it takes me a moment to place it. "Wait, you're Lorelei? *The* Lorelei?"

She grins. "My reputation precedes me."

"For getting Hank Osterman's arm mutilated by a bear trap."

She lifts her chin with pride, as if I'd complimented her. "That was me."

A flush deepens in my cheeks, which Foxglove seems to notice. He steps toward me, hands fluttering in the air as if they can pull the tension from it. "Lorelei is serving you as punishment for her crime against the Butcher of

Stone Ninety-Four, or whatever human name you call him. See? Amends are made."

My eyes narrow at Lorelei, who seems to be relishing in my anger.

"Come now, Lorelei," Foxglove says. "You're supposed to make them feel welcome."

She plasters an exaggerated smile on her lips, then says in the most honey-sweet, high-pitched voice, "Oh, by all means. Welcome."

Foxglove claps his hands, then turns toward the palace. "That's better. Come along everyone."

I give Amelie's fingers a reassuring squeeze as we follow Foxglove and Lorelei toward the palace. We make our way down the marble path away from the carriage, then up massive, citrine steps. The enormous double doors are open wide, and two guards outfitted in bronze armor engraved with maple leaves stand on either side, golden spears in hand. I'm surprised to find one of the guards appears female, her features slightly more feminine than her counterpart, with a long brown braid of hair plaited down her back. I don't think I've ever seen a female guard in Eisleigh. Then again, I've hardly had the opportunity to meet any royal guards before this, considering Eisleigh's king resides on the mainland.

Inside the palace, I feel equally as overwhelmed as when I first saw the outside. Everything from the floor to the walls is constructed of stone in golds, reds, browns, and yellows. Golden arches and spiraling staircases steal my attention, then the smaller details like paintings, tapestries, and vases assault my senses.

Foxglove leads us through hall after hall, stair after stair. Orb-like lights hover above sconces along the walls, some strange sort of fae lighting. Oil, perhaps? They look nothing like the oil lamps back home. I make a mental note to investigate later before I remind myself I don't care about any of this. Returning my attention to our path ahead, I attempt to keep track of all the turns and twists. While it's impossible to gather my bearings completely, I get the sense we're winding deeper and higher into the palace.

By the time we come to a stop, I'm nearly out of breath. I try to keep my panting to a minimum while Foxglove approaches a set of double doors and pushes them open. He waves us forward, and Amelie and I step inside.

We enter a room in the same warm hues as the rest of the palace. An enormous bed lines the far wall, a wardrobe spans half the length of another wall, and a desk, dressing table, and dressing screen stand in a corner. In the middle of the room is a magnificent citrine tub. Wafts of steam curl up from the water inside.

"First things first," Foxglove says. "The two of you need to bathe before you meet your future husbands. You may either take turns or share the bath."

I didn't expect such a luxury to await me. In fact, I'm not sure what I expected, but it was supposed to be more terrifying than this.

"I will tell the king and prince you are here and arrange a meeting," Foxglove says. "Is there anything else you will require in the meantime? Lorelei can help you undress and wash—"

"No," I say. "We would like to bathe alone."

Lorelei shrugs. "Suit yourself."

"She'll be on the other side of the door if you need anything." Foxglove gives a bow of his head, then hurries to add, "Please don't plot murder or anything."

I frown at his back as he and Lorelei leave, closing the doors behind them.

Amelie finally lets go of my hand and looks around the room with mournful eyes. "This is really happening, isn't it?"

I sigh, wishing I'd wake up from this beautiful nightmare. But it isn't going anywhere, and it's only just begun. "Unfortunately, it really is."

9

The warmth of the bath soothes my muscles and calms my frazzled nerves. I know it's nothing more than a false sense of security, but the comfort lulls me into a feeling of safety. I wish I could stay in the bath all night.

Amelie sits across from me in the tub, playing with a sprig of rosemary. Other herbs and marigold blooms float on the water's surface, filling my senses with an intoxicating aroma. An aroma that reminds me of home. Of the apothecary kitchen. Of Mother.

"At least they've given us this room together," Amelie says, her frown flickering into a weak smile.

I don't want to crush her hope by telling her we'll likely be separated once our marriages take place, so I do nothing but nod.

"And this bath is nice," she says. "How do you think they keep the water warm?"

I don't have an answer to that and have been trying my best to tamp down any fascination with the palace or the fae. But I can't deny I am stimulated with all the questions brimming in the back of my mind. We must have been in the tub for an hour by now, and the water is still as warm as when we entered it. There's no drain, no visible plumbing, no heating element.

"It's magic, isn't it?" Amelie asks.

I shake my head. "You know I don't believe in magic."

"Even after all of this?" she says, waving her hand to indicate the room around us. "How else are those orbs of light staying lit? How else was a palace this big constructed?" She lifts her rowan berry necklace from her neck, the length of it trailing behind her to keep from soaking in the tub. "How else do magic talismans work against the fae?"

"It isn't magic. There's a perfectly logical—"

"—explanation for all of it," she finishes with me. "I know, but you don't have the slightest idea what that explanation could be, do you?"

"Actually, I know exactly how rowan works against the fae. You see—"

She splashes me, leaving me sputtering and blinking water from my eyes. When Amelie's face comes back into view, she's grinning mischievously.

I splash her back. "How dare you interrupt my scientific explications!"

She squeals, then launches more water at me. We fall into fits of laughter, and for a moment, it's like we're little girls again, sharing the tub while Mother scrubs our backs. The thought sobers me, and I'm again reminded of our situation.

Amelie seems to feel the same, her smile slipping back into a frown. Finally, she stands and reaches for one of the blanket-like towels on the floor. "I'm going to explore the wardrobe."

"Of course you are." Classic Amelie behavior. Solve all problems with clothes. The bath doesn't feel nearly as friendly now that I'm alone, so I follow suit. I step out of the tub and grab the towel, releasing a sigh as its warmth envelops me.

Amelie gasps, making me jump. My eyes locate my pile of discarded clothing. I'm ready to dive for my dagger buried beneath them when she gasps again, then turns toward me with a wide smile. She holds a shimmering pink dress up to herself, swishing the hem of the fabric back and forth. "Evie, can you even believe your eyes?"

I let out a sigh of relief and join her at the wardrobe to examine the gown. Its fabric is thin and gauzy, like Lorelei's, but the skirt is constructed of numerous layers, making it look like petals of a flower. Dresses may not be my favorite, but I must admit it's pretty.

She puts it back and pulls out another, this one in a seafoam green. Again, she holds it up to her body. "Each is more stunning than the last. Have you ever seen anything like this? What are you going to wear?"

I look back at my pile of clothes. "I'll probably wear my trousers."

Amelie's mouth falls open aghast. "No. How could you when you have all this at your disposal?"

A feeling of unease ties my stomach in knots. I feel oddly betrayed by

Amelie's excitement over the dresses. Aren't we supposed to be angry about all of this? Still, I can't bring myself to dampen her sudden joy.

She replaces the seafoam dress, then takes out another, purple this time. The skirt is made of shimmering silk decorated with tiny, amethyst jewels. The top is made from a similar silk in shades of purple, constructed of tiny, overlapping pieces of the cloth, making it look like scales. "Oh, I am definitely wearing this one."

"What if these are supposed to be formal dresses?"

She shrugs, letting the towel fall to the floor as she puts the dress over her head. "Who cares? If I'm going to get eaten by a fae king, at least I'll look good before I die."

I'm stuck between a gasp and a laugh, then that sense of unease returns. Again, I feel betrayed by how well Amelie seems to be adapting. How could she feel so lighthearted after spending the best part of our ride here sulking and crying? She's out of her wits. *I'm* being the sensible one. Aren't I?

A knock sounds on the other side of the door, and Amelie suppresses a shriek. She hurries to pull the dress the rest of the way down, succeeding just as Lorelei steps inside.

"Brought your things," the fae says, four bags in hand. Three are Amelie's, while one is mine. As she crosses the room, I realize for the first time that her gait is less than graceful. There's something crooked about the way she walks, her steps not dainty like Foxglove's.

She reaches the dressing table and hefts the bags on top of it. When she turns to face us, she catches us staring. Amelie tugs at her gown while I pull the towel tighter around me. "What?" she says, pulling her head back. "Did you not want your things?"

I lift my chin. "In the human world, a knock doesn't forewarn one entering. You usually await permission to enter first. Especially when one is known to be bathing."

A corner of her mouth lifts but her eyes narrow at me. "Well, aren't we fussy. I may be your lady's maid, but the first thing you need to get right is this: you aren't in the human world anymore. You're lucky you got a knock at all."

I glower. "I didn't ask you to be my lady's maid. In fact, tell the king we don't need one. Let him punish you elsewhere for your crimes."

Lorelei crosses her arms and strides up to me. I fight the urge to lean back as she holds my gaze with her furious olive eyes. "For one thing, I don't tell the king anything. He tells me. I am his subject as you are now too. For another, I shouldn't be punished at all. What I did to the Butcher was a favor to my people."

I remember what Foxglove said about the traps on the Faerwyvae side of the wall, about Mr. Osterman selling fae parts. "You see, that's where you're mistaken. Hank Osterman would never do what your kind are saying he did."

She bares her teeth. "Has it ever occurred to you that being human doesn't make you an authority on everyone of your kind? The man you call Hank killed my lover in front of my eyes. I watched him do it. How? My leg was stuck in one of his iron traps. I watched as he took Malan and cut the wings from her back with an iron blade, sliced out her emerald heart, then stuffed her body in a bag. I screamed the entire time. The only reason I'm alive is because I got lucky."

I blanch, taking an inadvertent step away from her. *No, she's wrong. This can't be true.*

She continues. "When he released me from the trap, I put myself under a glamour. It took all the strength I had not to give in to the pain from my wound. I could have let myself die, could have joined Malan in the otherlife, but I didn't. Instead, I thought of those I could help if I made the Butcher pay. So I glamoured myself as a beautiful human woman. I crawled away from him, and he saw it as a seduction, a tease. He followed me, reaching to touch me, to put his hands in all the forbidden places he craved. I finally pulled myself in front of another of his traps. He watched a beautiful woman open for him. And he did all the rest."

I feel like I'm going to be sick, her impossible words and my own logic battling for supremacy inside me. "It's still cruel," is all I can say. "You glamoured him—"

"No," she snaps. "I glamoured *me* alone."

I throw my hands in the air. "What's the difference?"

"Do you know nothing about our magic? Placing a glamour on a human controls them, lowers their inhibitions, allows us to suggest actions they readily accept."

This I know about, and there's a rational explanation to it. Mr. Meeks theorizes that the fae emit a certain hormone during prolonged eye contact —an automatic function for the fae. That hormone, unfortunately, is what suppresses our amygdala, compromising our response to danger, opening our minds to suggestion. That's why blinking is so effective at preventing a glamour. It keeps the fae from secreting whatever hormone is responsible for attacking our brains.

"Trust me, I know all about a fae glamour," I say, hazarding a glance at Amelie, who blanches. "I've seen it happen before."

"Then you'll know that's not what I did to the Butcher," Lorelei says.

"What exactly did you do to him, then?"

"Like I said, I glamoured *myself*, changing my appearance to look like a human instead. He saw a helpless woman before him. He could have done anything—ignored her to find the fae he'd captured, asked her what she was doing alone in the woods—but his vile urges were stronger."

I shake my head, unable to reconcile the man she's describing with the hunter from my village. He's lived in Sableton my entire life. He has a wife! Could it be I never knew him at all? That no one really knows him?

I remember what he said after he woke from surgery. *I thought she was a woman. She looked like a woman.*

Equally disturbing is Lorelei's assertion that she can glamour herself, change her appearance at will. I refuse to believe that's possible. Again, there must be a scientific explanation. Another undiscovered hormone the fae emit that wreaks havoc on our nervous systems, altering our perceptions, our interpretation of visual stimuli.

"Sorrow not," Lorelei says, a bitter edge in her voice as she lifts the hem of her dress. "He may have lost an arm, but iron through the leg is a lot to heal from for a fae."

I can't help but look at the flesh she's exposed. One of her legs is perfect, slim, and brown, while the other is scarred and misshapen, wrapped in thin vines like a makeshift cast.

She continues. "He, on the other hand, still has his wife while Malan will never again be amongst the living."

I shudder, my chest heaving. I want nothing more than to change the subject. For her to leave. To unsee the battered flesh of her leg.

"Can I wear this?" Amelie's voice comes out small. She strokes the skirt of the purple gown she's already wearing.

Lorelei swings her head toward my sister. Some of the fire seems to drain from her eyes, her shoulders slumping forward. "Yes. In fact, wear the nicest dress you can find in there."

I point to my bag on the dressing table. "I was going to wear—"

"Wear. A. Dress," Lorelei says, eyes locking back on me. "A fae dress. You are about to meet King Aspen and Prince Cobalt. This is not the time to argue about it or cling to your silly human ways."

Amelie squeals in delight and tosses the seafoam dress at me. I catch it with a resigned sigh.

"I take it neither of you need or want my help," Lorelei says, her tone still icy. "Meet me in the hall when you're dressed."

I feel empty after she leaves. Partially from guilt, but I'm used to my sharp tongue getting me into tight corners with others. What's more unsettling is the upside-down world I've been thrust into. One where fae find me ignorant and the people I've trusted my entire life are seen as monsters.

For the love of iron, is any of this real?

10

———

"Must I wear these?" Amelie asks.

I peer from behind the dressing screen to see my sister stroking the rowan berries around her neck. Her nose wrinkles, a frown tugging her lips as she stares into the full-length mirror next to the dressing table.

"Yes," I say, then pull back behind the screen. I'm wearing the seafoam dress after turning it inside out and back again several times. The fae dresses don't have visible seams and look appropriate worn either way. Not that I thought Mother's *wear your clothes inside out* suggestion would help anyway. I can think of no logic to such a superstition. But it was worth a try.

She lets out a heavy sigh. "But it doesn't match the dress."

"Neither does getting glamoured."

"That makes no sense, Evie. Besides, it's not like I'll do anything that will put me in a position to get glamoured. I know how to blink. I'm not stupid."

"I know you're not." She wasn't stupid when she fell under a glamour four years ago either, but I don't say so. Instead, I retrieve my dagger from the pile of clothes I've hidden it in, then strap the belt around my thigh. It's snug, but the gray leggings I found should keep it from chafing too badly. Luckily, the seafoam dress has several layers to the skirt, making the belt and dagger invisible to prying eyes. "Rowan works against the fae. We need to keep wearing the necklaces Mother made us. Make sure at least part of it is touching your skin at all times."

"Oh, *now* you believe in Mother's craft."

I roll my eyes, then check the fit of the dress. It feels fine. Unlike the dresses we wear at home, these ones are loose and flowing, easy to put on without much assistance. Best of all, no corsets.

I meet Amelie at the mirror, and she grins at my reflection. "You look beautiful, Evie!"

As much as I hate to admit it, the dress suits me, complementing the copper tones in my dark hair. I quickly look away, then approach the dressing table to rifle through my bag. "Did mother give you a pouch of salt and a tincture?"

Amelie drags her gaze away from the mirror with some difficulty, then stands at my side. "Yes, yes. Do we bring them both with us?"

"Bring the salt," I say, tying the pouch to my waist. Salt is another one of Mother's prescriptions I can believe in. While I don't believe it wards off magical enchantment—because, obviously, enchantment isn't real—I do believe it helps protect our digestive tracts from harm. Mr. Meeks once told me he theorized salt could counteract the harmful effects of fae food by neutralizing any acids and helping us digest unfamiliar components. "But take the tincture now. Half a dropperful like Mother said. Remember?"

She nods, then finds the pouch and bottle in one of her bags. Once she's finished tying her own pouch to her waist, we face each other.

"Ready?" I ask.

She blanches a little, then nods.

Lorelei waits for us outside our door. We find her leaning against the opposite wall with her arms crossed. "Finally," she mutters, then takes off down the hall.

As we follow, I try to memorize every turn we make, to familiarize myself with the halls and doors, but I keep finding myself drawn to Lorelei's now-unmistakable limp.

I avert my gaze back to our surroundings, to the staircase up ahead. We climb it, and I feel a cool breeze, again carrying the smell of salt. As we reach the top of the staircase, an enormous room comes into view. Open air greets us at the other side of the room from a wide expanse cut from the wall, lined with a white rail, and interspersed with citrine columns. The air is cool without being unpleasant, and the night is dark beyond it.

At the center of the room is a long table with two ornate chairs on each end. One chair is taller than the other, its legs and back in the shape of twining branches, or—more accurately—antlers. The chair on the other side is similar in design but with a shorter back. The table is laden with plates of food, thick yellow candles, and numerous cups and bottles. Along the length of the table are about a dozen much simpler chairs.

The room is empty, save for Foxglove, standing near the open expanse. Lorelei waves for us to follow as she crosses the room toward him.

He turns with a wide grin, adjusts his spectacles, then assesses Amelie and me. "Ah, much better. The king and prince will arrive shortly."

The smell of salt is stronger now, and I hear a rhythmic crashing. Curiosity draws me forward, and I look over the rail. Vertigo seizes me as the world seems to fall away, plummeting down into a black expanse below. I grab the rail, steadying myself, and blink a few times to clear my vision. Once stabilized, I see the palace is built at the edge of a sea cliff. The ocean sends waves lapping up and down the shore. As my eyes adjust to the moonlit dark, I notice something else about the shore. Dark holes pock the ground, like chasms. Some of the water reaches them, disappearing into their depths before the water recedes and gathers into another wave.

"King Herne built Bircharbor Palace at the edge of the sea," Foxglove explains, "to be near his mate, Queen Melusine."

"The Queen of the Sea Court," I say, remembering his story from earlier. "Didn't you say the king died in the war?"

"He did." His tone is mournful. "King Aspen could take up residence elsewhere in Autumn, especially considering Queen Melusine rarely visits land much these days. Yet he remains here. It is a lovely palace."

I lean over the rail again, watching the waves crash upon the shore. "What are those holes in the ground?"

"Ah, you'll have to look again when it's day. The beach gives way to coral and those are coral caves. Queen Melusine constructed them. Some think they lead to her underwater palace, but it's nothing more than a menace of a maze, if you ask me. Anyone who's ever tried to map the caves drowns by high tide. Even the sea fae who've tried never succeeded. Only Queen Melusine seems to know how to navigate them, and she prefers to keep her secrets to herself."

"The lesson being, don't go swimming," Lorelei says.

"Very true," Foxglove says with a grave nod. "Better avoided altogether. At low tide, you'll fall into a cave before you make it out to deep enough water for a swim. Even then, you'll find yourself trapped on the other side of the caves and get dashed into the coral. At high tide, you're lucky if the current doesn't suck you into the caves or worse."

"Or, again, dash you into the coral," Lorelei adds.

"Lesson understood," I mutter.

"I don't like swimming," Amelie says, wrinkling her nose at the sight of the dark ocean.

"Neither do I," Foxglove says. "The salt dries out my hair, and I can't get it looking right for days. I prefer to lie down for a seaside tan in the Summer Court, where the waves are less obnoxious."

A smile twitches at the corners of my lips. Despite my best efforts, Foxglove is growing on me.

"Are these our new guests?" A new voice rings out behind us, male, and dare I say...joyful?

The four of us whirl around to face the newcomer. Foxglove and Lorelei fall into easy bows while Amelie and I sink into clumsy curtsies half a minute too late. I wait until Foxglove and Lorelei rise before I do the same. Amelie's pinkie winds its way around my own.

Foxglove takes a step forward. "May I present to you Amelie and Evelyn Fairfield."

The fae male grins, taking confident steps toward us. His face is somehow both boyish and ancient at once, with dimpled cheeks, high cheekbones, and glittering blue eyes. His hair is straight and a deep shade of blue so dark it's almost black, loose strands falling over his forehead and brushing the tips of his pointed ears. He wears blue-black trousers and a jacket with an indigo waistcoat patterned with gold stitching and a blue cravat.

He bows, then looks from me to Amelie. "Pleased to make your acquaintance. I'm Prince Cobalt."

I can't take my eyes off him, much less speak. In all my terrified imaginings, I never thought a fae could look so regal, so kind, so...attractive. And he's—oh for the love of iron, he's Prince Cobalt. My husband-to-be. I can't tell if the thought terrifies me or excites me. Shame reigns supreme when I consider it could be the latter. I remind myself he's fae and recall everything I've heard about Faerwyvae. I can't afford to be flustered by a pair of blue eyes.

I open my mouth to relay a greeting, but Amelie beats me to it. "It's a pleasure." Her tone is formal, which I'm grateful for. By the look in her eyes, I can tell she's as enchanted as I am by his appearance. Still, she's keeping her composure, which means she has her head on her shoulders. Good.

A dark shadow looms behind the prince. Cobalt turns, bowing his head.

Again, Foxglove and Lorelei sink into bows. This time Amelie and I are quicker to catch on. When we rise from our curtsies, the Autumn King's eyes are on me.

I know he's the Autumn King, because never have I seen the season so perfectly embodied in a living being. Not only does he have an elaborate rack of dark brown antlers, but he wears bronze satin from head to toe. The jacket and trousers are a deeper shade of russet, but the waistcoat is closer to the red-bronze of fall treetops and is patterned in gold-stitched maple leaves. He has the same slim build as Cobalt but towers a head taller than the younger fae, not including the height of his antlers. Like his brother, the king has blue-black hair, but his is longer, curling at the nape of his neck. Aspen's eyes, however, are brown. Unlike Cobalt's, they don't glitter when he smiles, they narrow, and his smile is more smug than warm.

His gaze burns into me. "Evelyn," he says.

I hate how he says my name with such informality. Such scorn. I hate how the corner of his mouth turns up when he says it, like my name is a joke coming from his lips. Most of all, I hate the chill that runs down my spine when I hear it, sparking something familiar.

A dangerous echo.

I've heard that voice before. Seen that smirk.

In fact, I've told him my name.

11

I don't know how King Aspen could be the same fae I met at the wall, but I know it's him. Even with antlers and fashionable clothing, there's no mistaking his expression, his voice. He's the fae whose ire I've sparked. *He* brought me here.

Rage ignites within me, so hot it feels like it will boil over. I want to shout at him, to demand an explanation for why he sought fit to punish me. I almost do, when I remember I never confessed my guilt to my sister. She has no idea I even met a fae at the wall, much less drew enough attention to get us into this mess. I grit my teeth and meet his gaze with a glare.

"Pardon, Your Majesty, but *this* one is your bride-to-be, not she," Foxglove says, misreading the exchange between me and the king. He pushes my sister forward a step. "This is Amelie Fairfield, the eldest daughter of Maven Fairfield of Sableton Village."

King Aspen shifts his gaze to her, and Amelie forces an uncertain smile. His smirk disappears, and something crosses his face, but I can't read his expression. He almost seems taken aback. With a grunt of either acceptance or displeasure, he turns around. "Let's eat."

"You heard him," Foxglove whispers, waving for us to follow the king to the table.

As I move to obey, Prince Cobalt offers me a gentle smile and falls into step at my side. "That leaves you and me," he says. "To marry, I mean."

I don't say anything in reply.

As we reach the dining table, Cobalt steps in front of me and pulls out a chair. I hesitate before accepting the seat. He leans forward and pushes the chair in as I sit, bringing his face next to mine. He pauses with his lips by my ear and whispers, "I'm sorry for what happened to the girls before you, but I hope you can forgive me for saying...I like you better."

I'm surprised by this and turn toward him in time to see a blush creep up his cheeks. He catches my eyes and flashes me a smile, then makes his way to the seat at the end opposite his brother.

When I face forward, I meet Amelie's frown across the table. She turns her scowl to King Aspen, then loudly drags the chair away from the table. She sits, then pulls the chair forward in a few exaggerated scoots until she's nestled close to the table. The king pays her no heed, his eyes fixed firmly on his dinner plate.

"You can sit," he barks. I realize then that Foxglove and Lorelei had retreated to the edges of the room. "Both of you."

The two jump forward like timid pups eager to obey their master, then take seats at the table. Foxglove sits next to me, while Lorelei sits next to Amelie. I try not to meet Lorelei's eyes across the table.

Several figures enter the dining room—servants, from the look of their stoic expressions and reserved bearing. Most resemble the average, youthful human in stature and physical features, save the telltale ethereal beauty and pointed ears. Some, however, have additional attributes like upturned snout-like noses, whiskers, and even the odd tail. A few smaller fae are present with leathery skin and aged, wrinkled faces, limbs that appear more tree branch than arm or leg. Regardless of appearance, all are dressed in resplendent silks in russets, golds, reds, and browns.

One of the youthful fae, a male, approaches me and fills my goblet with a deep red liquid. Another, female as far as I can tell, with long, white whiskers framing a pink button nose, stands on my opposite side, heaping portions of food onto my plate from the many dishes on the table. The first servant moves on once my glass is full, but the second is still adding more food to my plate.

I manage to find my voice. "That's enough, thank you."

The fae steps away, and I look across the table at my sister. She wears an odd expression, somewhere between suspicion and longing, as she studies the items on her plate. With a lick of her lips, she reaches for a pastry.

I scoot forward and aim a kick at her shin. She scowls as my foot meets its mark, then meets my eyes with a questioning glare. I lift the bag of salt from my waist, widening my eyes in silent warning. *Salt your food.*

She gives me a nod of understanding, then retrieves her pouch. We each sprinkle our plates with a dusting of the pink crystals.

"What is this?" asks a dry, mocking voice. My eyes flash to the head of the table where King Aspen sits. His eyes rove from Amelie to me.

I'm at a loss for words as I seek an explanation that won't get me killed. Thankfully, Foxglove lifts his hand. "I believe it's a human folk remedy," he says. "They believe salt wards against evil."

"Salt." The king lets out a bark of cold laughter. His eyes lock on me. "You know we already use salt when cooking, right? And the salt sprays in from the ocean daily. If salt could do fae harm, we'd already be dead."

I'm still too furious to trust myself to speak. All I'd do is argue anyway. Besides, we don't salt our food to harm the fae, we do it to protect our digestive tracts. Instead of saying any of this, I deepen my glare, eyes still locked on the king, then dump another heaping pinch of salt on my plate.

He leans back in his chair with a dismissive snort.

"I think it's smart." Prince Cobalt's voice comes from the other side of the table, his gentle tone in contrast to his brother's. He smiles at Aspen, but his eyes are glowing with mischief beneath a raised brow. "They aren't the only ones with precautions in mind."

I look back at Aspen and realize a small tree-like fae is perched at his side, fork in mouth. The fae then reaches for Aspen's goblet and takes a sip. The king holds Cobalt's gaze for a few moments while the servant takes another bite of food from Aspen's plate.

Foxglove leans in close to me and whispers, "The king always has his food and drink tested before he eats."

The odd exchange makes much more sense now, but the tension between the two royals remains intact.

"You're right, brother," Aspen says in his cold, drawling voice. "One can't be too careful." The servant takes one more bite, then offers a bow. Aspen waves him away, then picks up his fork. "Eat."

Everyone except Amelie and I rush for their forks, but we follow suit shortly after. I push the food around my plate, trying to investigate what I've been served. It appears entirely recognizable, from the fillet of fish to the roasted potatoes and apple tart. The aromas are familiar as well, making my mouth water. I know I should eat. I *want* to eat. If only my stomach would agree. It's been in knots ever since I laid eyes on King Aspen, felt that anger rise inside me. How can I eat now?

I look at Amelie, who has already taken several bites from her plate. She meets my eyes, grinning while she chews. I force a grin, then with equal effort, bring a bite of food to my lips.

~

AFTER A MOSTLY SILENT DINNER, KING ASPEN AND PRINCE COBALT LEAVE THE dining room with curt farewells, and Foxglove and Lorelei guide us back to our room. Again, I try to memorize all the twists and turns, try to orient myself between the dining room and our bedroom. As far as I can tell, our bedroom is two floors down from where we ate.

Foxglove leaves us at our door, but Lorelei lingers in the doorway, leaning lazily against the frame. "Do you need me to stay?"

"That's not necessary," I say, trying to keep my voice neutral. I'm still not sure how to act around her after our argument.

She pushes off the door frame and lets out a yawn. "Fine. I'll be sleeping next door. Call if you need anything." With that, she closes the door and leaves me and Amelie alone.

Amelie rushes to the bed and flops belly down into the middle of it. It bounces, then sinks a little beneath her. "I'm so tired." Her face is pressed into a pillow, making her voice come out muffled.

I feel the same, in mind and body. Like Amelie, I want nothing more than to sink into the luxurious bed. But the pressure of the dagger belt around my thigh is too irritating to ignore. I grab my nightdress from my bag and take it behind the dressing screen. Once changed, I meet Amelie at the bed, slipping my sheathed dagger behind one of the pillows.

She lifts her face, blinking up at me. "Do you think the wardrobe has special nightdresses?"

I can't help but laugh. "I'm sure it does." Amelie scrambles out of bed and rushes to the wardrobe, while I turn down the covers and crawl beneath them.

After a time, Amelie twirls across the floor, a sheer, silky nightdress rustling around her ankles. She crawls into bed next to me. "This place has the best clothes."

"At least the fae realm has one thing going for it."

"It's really not as awful as I thought," she says. "I was certain I'd be fearing for my life by now. You know, monsters and goblins and harpies and such. But so far, no one has tried to so much as nibble me."

"That's because we haven't been left alone with our mates yet."

She's silent for a while, and I'm worried I've scared her. Then she scoots closer. "I don't like mine, Evie. He's so dour."

"No kidding."

"You clearly don't like him, either. I saw the way you glared at him. I was starting to think I'd missed something."

My muscles tense. Should I tell her? I'm not sure why I'm so afraid to confess my meeting with King Aspen at the wall. It's not like my good-natured sister would blame me forever. Besides, she's already adapting so well. But for some reason, I can't bring myself to talk about it. It feels... shameful. I don't even want to remember the way he said my name today, as if he has any right—

"Yours isn't so bad, though." Her voice shatters my thoughts. "He's a gentleman, at least. Perhaps you could come to like him."

"Perhaps I could wake up with horse hooves."

She giggles. "Do you think they throw balls in the palace?"

"Balls, human heads. Only time will tell."

"Really, Evie, you're so strange sometimes."

I don't reply. Instead, I close my eyes and try to breathe away the tension coursing through me. After a while, I hear Amelie's even breathing. Of course she falls asleep first. Of course she feels safe in this place of beautiful luxury. Of course I'm the only one aware of our fragile mortality in a place like this.

I toss and turn for what feels like hours, unable to relax, much less sleep. Finally, I give up. I grab a lightweight cloak from the wardrobe, wrap it around my shoulders, then slip out the bedroom door, leaving Amelie sleeping peacefully alone.

12

———————

I make my way back through the palace halls, trying to see if I can find my way to the dining room. Not for any particular desire to return there; it's more to lock down my sense of direction in the palace. If I can at least navigate between two places inside the palace, I'll feel like I'm in control of *something* again, no matter how small.

The halls are eerily quiet and eerily as dark, the orbs of light hovering above their sconces now diminished to a subtle glow. No one crosses my path, which I'm grateful for, despite getting lost numerous times. I eventually find myself in front of a familiar staircase and climb. When I reach the top, the dark, empty dining room opens before me.

My chest swells with pride. But now what? Do I just go back to my bedroom, see if I can reach it faster than I reached this place?

The sound of crashing waves calls to me, its rhythm softer than it had been earlier. And there's something else. Voices. Or music.

I tiptoe across the floor to the open expanse, placing my hands on the rail like I did before. The ocean is black beneath the moon, small waves gently rolling into the base of the cliff beneath the palace. Gone are the black chasms of the coral caves, as the tide has come in and hidden them beneath its watery depths. It chills me how much the shoreline can change in a matter of hours.

Music falls on my ears again, and I search the night for the source. There are large rocks near the cliff at the end of the shore, and I'm almost positive I see figures perched on top of them. Are they singing? There's a feminine trill in the air, both beautiful and terrifying.

Nearer movement draws my attention away from the rocks and back to the shore. There I see the forms of what appear to be women, skin white and glistening beneath the moon. Their bodies are naked, sinuous with their slow movements as they circle each other on the beach, laughing as the waves roll around their ankles. The way they move has me entranced, filling me with calm.

They're dancing.

"Selkies."

I whirl to find King Aspen behind me, expression hidden in shadow. My first instinct is to pat my dagger, until I remember tucking it behind my pillow. I clutch my rowan berry necklace and press myself as close to the rail as I can.

Aspen steps forward into the moonlight, then stands next to me at the rail. He's changed from his suit into a simple pair of dark trousers and a loose linen shirt. The shirt is open at the neck, revealing the golden skin of his upper chest. His expression is different than it was earlier, softer, eyes on the scene below us. "They come here to dance at night sometimes, leaving their sealskins on the rocks while they take the forms of human women."

As much as I don't want to speak to him, my curiosity again gets the better of me. "Are they the ones singing?"

"No, those would be the sirens upon the rocks."

I squint into the night, trying to make out more than vague silhouettes of the creatures.

Silence stretches between me and the king, and with it comes a growing tension. He's so close I can see the rise and fall of his chest from the corner of my eye. His hand rests on the rail, fingers glittering with red jewels, just inches from my own.

"How do you like it here?" His voice is irritatingly gentle.

That's all it takes to bring forth my anger. I round on him. "You mean, how do I like this prison you've brought me to?"

His brows furrow for the merest moment, then his eyes go steely, lips twitching into a smirk. "I take it you aren't impressed."

"Why are you punishing me?"

"Is that what I'm doing?"

"Answer my question," I say through my teeth.

"Ask a better one."

I cross my arms over my chest. "You're the fae from the wall, I know you are. What did I do to make you so angry that night? Why did you bring me here?"

He shrugs. "I'm sure you know what happened to the previous Chosen. Two girls needed to be brought in their place."

I let out a bitter laugh. "You think I don't know? Two other names had already been selected as backup by the council. You chose me by name."

He nods, unashamed. "Yes."

"Why? What did I do to deserve this? To be torn from my mother and my home? To drag my sister away from her fiancé?"

"You held an iron blade to me." He says it less like an accusation and more like an observation.

"You attacked me first! I was defending myself."

"Are we done?"

"No, we're not done. I want to know what happened to the girls before me. Why did you have the Holstrom sisters executed?"

Aspen's expression darkens. When he speaks, his tone is edged with razors. "You haven't once addressed me as Your Majesty since we began this conversation, nor did you bow."

I lift a shoulder in a shrug. "What are you going to do about it? Execute me, like you do everyone else who slights you? I'm sure you killed the Holstroms for far less, so what's the point of toeing the line?"

"You seem to have your opinion set about me and my involvement with the Holstroms. Why bother asking me at all?"

I open my mouth, but all I can think to say is, *this is just the way I am.* I must have truth. Order. Logic. My life is supposed to make sense. But what do the fae care about logic and order? This place is backwards, upside down, and dizzyingly frustrating. In this strange court, the fae are righteous and the villagers I've trusted my whole life are butchers, yet the ruler wears human clothes, serves human food, and expects to be treated according to human custom. It's enough to make my blood boil.

Instead of saying any of this, I turn to my only available weapon. My words. "I want to know what kind of monster I'm being forced to live with."

He shakes his head, a sneer curling his lip. "I thought you were smarter when I met you at the wall. I thought you had the sense to fear me."

I know I should back down now. I should bow. I should apologize. But I don't. "And I thought you'd have the sense to recall what else you learned about me. I'm prepared, remember? Just try and tear your fangs into me. We'll see if you like the taste of iron."

He holds my gaze, and I'm sure he's going to lash out at any moment. *I'm dead. I'm thoroughly dead.*

Then a wicked grin shatters his glower, and he throws his head back in laughter. When he returns his attention to me, his eyes are crinkled with amusement. It's not a comforting sight. "Fangs? What...do you think I want to *eat* you?"

He laughs again, and a blush creeps up my cheeks as I wait for him to sober. "Nothing I said was that funny."

"Fangs," he repeats. "Let me guess. You ingest iron of some sort? I can smell it on you."

The mention of him smelling anything about me makes my cheeks blaze. Still, I maintain my composure. "So what if I do?"

"I don't eat humans. I'm not that kind of fae." Despite his reassuring words, his tone is menacing.

"But there are types of fae who do eat humans?"

"Plenty."

I hope he can't see me blanch. "Regardless, I'm not harmless, you know."

"Yes, but I don't see that blade of yours. Even so, I could do worse at a distance."

My breath hitches as I imagine what kind of glamour he wants to force me under. "I'm prepared for that too."

He lifts his hand and I flinch away, but his fingers fall on the strand of rowan berries. The hair lifts on the back of my neck as he gives them a light tug. "Rowan," he says. "A lot of good that will do."

I lift my chin, breathing deeply to keep the trembling at bay. "It will keep you from glamouring me." For the love of iron, I hope it will. I blink several times for good measure.

"I don't need to glamour you to make you do what I want. If I wanted, I could make you fear me. Crave me. Love me."

His words are like a dangerous hiss, making my chest feel tight, like my lungs are shrinking into nothing. "I doubt that." I cringe at the uncertainty in my voice.

"All I'd have to do is glamour myself. I did it at the wall when we met. You never saw my antlers or anything other than my cloak and my face. You had no idea who I was."

My eyes flick to his antlers, taking in their size, their sharp tines. I swallow hard. "Yet I still charged you with a dagger."

He takes a step forward, closing the distance between us until I can feel the heat of his body. My eyes are locked on his chest as I press myself closer to the railing. There's no farther I can go without launching myself over the edge. "Look at me."

I don't know why I obey, but I do. Whether it's madness, stupidity, or something else, I want to look at him. I want to see what he can become. My eyes find his—a rich dark brown I can barely make out in the moonlight. A curl of blue-black hair falls into them, and I have a terrifying urge to sweep it away from his forehead. My breaths are growing ragged, shallow, the smell of his skin and clothes invading my senses, a spicy herbal aroma like rosemary and cinnamon as well as something earthy like fresh leaves. I try to hold my breath and avert my gaze, but that only shifts my attention to the curve of his lips.

He's beautiful, the most breathtaking creature I've ever seen. My mind reels to comprehend this, and I feel myself losing control, like my feet could fall out from under me at any moment.

A sound comes from somewhere nearby, and I blink a few times. Belatedly, I realized the sound was of someone clearing their throat.

Aspen's gaze lingers on me before he takes a step away and turns toward the figure standing on the other side of the room. It's Cobalt.

"I thought I heard voices," he says. "Wanted to make sure everything was well."

"All is well," Aspen says with a note of irritation in his voice. "I was showing our guest the selkies."

I lean to the side to widen the distance between me and the king. "And I was just leaving."

"Come," Cobalt says with a warm smile, "I'll walk you to your room."

I take a few steps away from the king; it's a miracle I can walk at all with the tremors of rage rushing through me. I pause. Without looking at Aspen, I whisper, "Don't do that to me ever again."

I can hear the grin in his voice. "Why? Did you like it too much?"

"I hated it. And if you ever so much as try a stunt like that again, I'll murder you in your sleep." I cross the room toward Cobalt, my lie ringing in my ears. I hate what he did. I hate that Lorelei was right, that the fae really can affect us by glamouring themselves. He may not have changed his appearance, but he altered my perception of him, made me see desire instead of danger. I hate that he has that kind of power over me. But during the glamour? I didn't hate it at all. I loved it. Loved staring at his lips, his eyes. Loved the pull between us, the smell of his skin, the heat of his body.

Rowan berries did nothing to prevent it. Blinking did nothing to stop it. Logic was nowhere to protect me.

That frightens me more than anything.

13

Cobalt and I walk side by side in tense silence. The farther we get from the dining room, the easier I breathe. I let the prince lead the way, not even bothering to pay attention to the journey this time. He slows his pace once we enter a familiar-looking hallway and stops outside a closed door. My room, I realize. I'm about to reach for the handle when Cobalt puts his hand on my arm. I flinch from his touch.

He draws his hand back, then faces me. "You shouldn't be alone with my brother."

I open my mouth, a spark of indignation heating my core. He may be my husband-to-be, but that doesn't mean he owns me or my actions.

He lowers his voice. "He's dangerous."

My anger cools, realizing he isn't chastising me. He's...scared for me. "Can you tell me what happened to the Holstrom girls?"

The prince looks at the floor, shuffling from foot to foot. "I shouldn't have said anything. He's my brother."

"Please tell me. I just want to know what's going on here."

Cobalt meets my eyes, lips pressed tight. "Honestly, I don't know what happened that night," he finally says. "All I know is that the Holstrom girls were alone with my brother when they..."

"When they what?"

"When they were killed."

The blood leaves my face. "You mean he murdered them? Then was their charge of treason a lie?"

"I don't know," he says in a rush. "Aspen claims they performed an act of treason in his presence, and he doled out justice immediately."

"Is there no formal justice system in Faerwyvae?"

"There is. Normally, criminals are imprisoned until they can stand trial before the Council of Eleven Courts. But if any ruler of the Eleven Courts sees fit to execute swift punishment, they may do so. It's rare though." He lowers his voice further. "And even though it was his right to do so, I think it was wrong. His actions nearly caused us to break the treaty. Luckily, the council was able to convince him to try another set of girls."

I hate the way he says that, *try another set of girls*, like we're nothing more than a pair of trousers for the king to wear or discard. "No one knows the supposed reason the Holstroms were charged with treason?"

Cobalt shakes his head. "There are rumors that the girls tried to kill him, but there's no proof, and Aspen won't share the entire story."

Probably because he can't lie. If the girls really did try to kill him, then it had to have been in self-defense. But even that is hard to believe. Theresa and Maryanne have always been the most timid, dutiful daughters in all of Sableton.

"Promise me you'll be careful," Cobalt says, brow furrowed.

His concern makes me uneasy, both the depth of it and the affability with which it's bestowed upon me. We've hardly spoken since we met, yet somehow he seeks to protect me. To care. Perhaps not all fae are as monstrous as I thought.

Still, his gaze makes me uncomfortable, his nearness reminding me too much of what it was like to be enraptured by his brother's glamour. "I'll be careful," I say, moving to my door.

He offers me a bow, and I return it with a curtsy. I watch him stroll down the hallway and out of sight before I slip into my room. As I close my door, I'm almost certain I see a dark figure looming at the other end of the hall.

MY SLEEP IS FITFUL, BUT I DO FINALLY MANAGE TO CATCH A FEW HOURS OF rest. When I wake, it's to the subtle sound of birdsong, an oddly harmonious blend of gull cries, raven caws, and songbird melodies coming from every direction around the palace. The lilting tunes are both familiar and strange, reminding me of the siren song last night.

That, of course, brings more unpleasant memories—the king, his close-ness, my loss of control, his brother's warning.

I can tell it's morning by how the sunlight blazes upon my eyelids, but I don't want to open them to confirm it. Perhaps if I keep them closed, the day will never proceed, and I won't have to leave this room. I smother my face in my pillow, then reach my hand beneath it until my fingertips touch my dagger. Safe. I'm safe. I'm in control.

I feel the weight of the bed shift next to me, followed by a peaceful sigh. "This is the most luxurious bed I've ever had the pleasure to lie in," comes Amelie's voice.

"How many beds besides your own have you lain in?" I tease, my words muffled in my pillow.

"Not nearly enough." Her tone is wistful. "I should have taken Magnus to bed, or at least behind the stables after he proposed. Can you believe Bertrand is the last man to have his hand down the front of my corset? What an unpleasant fact!"

I'm surprised she's able to speak of such matters so lightheartedly. It wasn't more than a day ago that she was sobbing uncontrollably over leaving home. Finally, I roll toward my sister and open my eyes. I flick her on her shoulder. "I thought you liked Bertrand!"

"Well, I did. But that was before Magnus."

"And now?" I ask. "Would you marry Bertrand if it meant we could go back to the way things were? Before we were sent here, I mean."

Her eyes unfocus, smile slipping from her lips, but she doesn't reply. She rolls onto her back, staring at the ceiling. I follow suit, noticing for the first time the canopy of red and gold leaves painted there in hyper-realistic detail.

Another sigh escapes Amelie's lips. "Do you think we could come to be happy here?"

I turn my head to face her, shocked at her words. "Happy? *Here*?"

She blushes, then rushes on to say, "I mean, I don't think I'll ever love the Stag King. He's too mean. But...do you think this arrangement could come to be worth it? This beautiful palace, these amazing luxuries. They're all ours!"

I hate to dampen her optimism, but I must be the voice of reason. She'll only get her heart broken if I don't. "Ami, we've been here less than a day. Just because they fed us, put us in a luxurious bedroom, and gave us an endless supply of gowns doesn't mean we're safe. The fae are dangerous."

"I know."

I sit up. "Do you, though? Do you have any idea what they're capable of, what they could do to us?"

She gives me a pointed look. "I know more than anyone what they're capable of, Evie. But what if all fae aren't...well, you know. Evil?"

"If you're thinking the fae here are worthy of your trust, you should reconsider. Have you forgotten what they did to the Holstrom sisters?"

She rolls her eyes. "No, of course I haven't."

I open my mouth to say more, to tell her what Cobalt hinted at last night, but I stop myself. I want her to be smart, not terrified. Instead, I say, "You need to be careful with King Aspen."

"Yet another thing I already know."

"*Really* careful."

She stands from the bed and faces me with her arms crossed. "Why must I be careful while you get to go on acting the same way you always do?"

"What's that supposed to mean?"

"I saw the way you looked at King Aspen. You could have melted iron with that scowl, and he noticed too. But did you lose your head? No."

"True, but King Aspen isn't my husband-to-be. He's yours."

"More of a reason for you to be careful, not me. Surely, he'd prefer his fiancée to remain alive."

"He didn't seem to mind murdering his last one."

"Murder!" She gasps, eyes growing wide. Finally, I've triggered her fear. "Do you really think..."

"I'm not trying to scare you. I just want you to be careful. In fact..." I say, then get up from the bed. Once I reach the dressing table, I begin to rifle through my bag. From the bottom, I retrieve my surgery kit. Amelie joins me, peering over my shoulder. I grab one of the smaller knives and face my sister. "I want you to keep this on you at all times."

She furrows her brow, looking at the knife as if it's some vile object. "I don't know how to use it."

"Take it anyway. I don't have a sheath for it, so wrap it in silk and tie it to your waist or around your thigh."

She presses her lips tight. I imagine she's considering how she can follow my instructions without them interfering with her clothing choices. Reluctantly, she takes the knife. "Are you going to carry one too?"

I go to the bed and pull my belt and dagger out from behind the pillow, then begin strapping it around my thigh. "I've been wearing this since we left home. Now, let's get dressed before Lorelei comes to wake us. We don't need her to see what we're hiding."

Amelie watches me as I finish strapping the belt. A mischievous grin plays on her lips. "Will you be wearing a dress then?"

I pause, realizing a dress will provide the only easy way to reach the dagger while hiding it from view. "I suppose."

She squeals, then runs to the wardrobe. "I'll pick one for you."

We finish dressing just before Lorelei knocks, once again barging through the doors before we can tell her to enter. This time, Foxglove follows in her wake.

"Good morning, good morning," he says. "And don't we look lovely."

Amelie and I are dressed in another set of fae gowns. My sister wears the shimmering pink one she was looking at yesterday, while I wear a pale blue dress with flowing, bell-like sleeves and two strands of pearls criss-crossing over the low-cut back. The skirt is loose with multi-layered ripples of floral-patterned fabric, hiding my dagger. My sister has her knife wrapped in pink silk and stashed in a tangle of gauzy sashes she wears around her waist.

"I was just about to do Evie's hair," Amelie says. Hers has already been brushed into long copper waves.

Foxglove nods. "Proceed. I can share what's on the agenda for today while you do so."

Lorelei steps forward, looking annoyed like always. "Need me for anything?"

Amelie hesitates before flashing her a smile. "Sure. You can hand me the hairpins."

"How nice," the fae mutters, then joins us at the mirror.

I pull up a chair and sit while Amelie attacks my hair with a brush.

Foxglove stands behind us. "King Aspen has finalized the date for your weddings. Normally, the hosting court of the Chosen is given one month to secure a wedding alliance to validate the treaty. But because of the mishap with the Holstrom sisters, our schedule got a bit thrown off. Worry not, we have it all sorted out. The human wedding ceremony will be exactly one month from now. The mate ceremony, however, will take place much sooner. It's scheduled ten days from now and will happen on the topmost balcony at sunset."

"The mate ceremony?" I echo.

"Yes. It's a fae celebration for paired couples. We don't call the resulting pair husband and wife; we call them mates. While it isn't nearly as binding as a human wedding, it is the closest thing we have here in Faerwyvae and is required by the treaty. It's usually reserved for noble pairings and alliances, situations where a bit of fanfare is needed. Afterward, you and your mates may perform...um...*the ritual.*"

I swallow hard, wondering if he's referring to consummation. "What exactly does *the ritual* mean?"

He hesitates before answering. "That's a private matter, one you will discuss with your mate. It's a very ancient and sacred ritual, one that is not discussed with such informality as we are speaking with now."

"Are you talking about sex?" Amelie doesn't so much as blush, just looks at Foxglove questioningly.

"Sex?" He puzzles over the word, then his eyes go wide with understanding. "Oh, you mean mating. Ha! No. Mating is not so sacred here in Faerwyvae. Honestly, your human ceremony puts much more emphasis on the sanctity of the mating act than we do. I mean, it is expected that you and your mate will...well, mate, but—for the love of oak and ivy, you're doing it all wrong. I can't stand by and watch this."

Foxglove steps forward, shoving Amelie out of the way and taking my hair in his hands. With deft moves, he undoes the few pins my sister already had arranged, then coils several strands of my hair at the base of my neck. He pins them in place, then pulls a few loose strands to frame my face.

"Now you," he says to Amelie, snapping his fingers for her to replace me in the chair.

I'm surprised when she rushes to obey. She never wears her hair up, preferring a longer style that showcases her natural color and texture. But when he finishes and steps aside, my sister is glowing, jaw hanging on its hinge. "I was offended at first, but my goodness, Foxglove! I've never done nearly such a beautiful job as that!"

"Obviously," he says, assessing his work with smug admiration. "I am a flower fae. I know a thing or two about beauty."

Even Lorelei looks impressed. "You're putting me out of a job. Perhaps you should be their lady's maid."

Foxglove scoffs. "I think not. Anyhow, let's not get off track. I haven't finished explaining the agenda."

I blush, remembering our mating conversation.

The ambassador continues. "With the mate ceremonies just ten days away, the king has decided you shouldn't be complete strangers by then. You will spend this time getting to know King Aspen and Prince Cobalt when they are free to entertain you. Which brings us to today's agenda. Amelie, the king will meet with you this afternoon in his study. Evelyn, during this time, Prince Cobalt will take you on a walk outside the palace."

My pulse quickens. Amelie and I are going to be separated. My sister will be alone with the Stag King. "Can't we get to know our fiancés within a group setting? The four of us? Perhaps you and Lorelei as well? I mean, it's hardly proper for us to be alone with..." I trail off at Foxglove's raised brow. Right. Human propriety doesn't mean much in Faerwyvae.

He laughs. "Oh, don't be frightened, my dear. Remember our chat yesterday? Don't set traps. Don't plot treason. Don't go swimming. Simple!"

I cross my arms, searching for the right argument.

Amelie sighs, then bounces the side of her hip lightly into mine. "I'll be fine, Evie."

I face her, hoping I can convey all the warning I can with my eyes. She tugs her rowan berry necklace, then brushes her fingers over the sashes at her waist. The sashes that hide the knife I gave her.

It isn't much, and it might not be enough. But in the end, it's all we can do.

14

——————

No hidden blade can comfort me as I find myself trekking through the woods a few hours later, marching up a steep incline behind Cobalt. All worry of Amelie has been swept from my mind, now that my main concern is trying to breathe properly.

Is he trying to kill me? He is. He must be.

Cobalt casts a glance behind him, winking when he meets my eyes. "Almost there, I promise."

I grind my teeth in reply, silently cursing Foxglove for describing my outing with Cobalt as a *walk outside the palace*. This isn't a walk. It's a hike. There's a distinct difference.

Cobalt, unwinded and unhindered by sweat and mortal lung capacities, leads the way higher and higher while I pant behind him, struggling to keep up with his long stride. He pauses and offers me his hand a few times, which I refuse. It only makes me want to hide my exertion better.

Thankfully, the incline begins to even out, the trees thinning until there's nothing but a vast field strewn with red leaves, like a blood-red sea. The field ends in a sharp edge that opens to nothing but blue sky. Cobalt sprints forward, then stops abruptly at the cliff's edge. When I make no move to run after him, he waves at me to hurry, face split into a wide grin. "Come on! You've got to see this."

I let out an irritated sigh, then slowly make my way forward. A delightful breeze brushes over my skin, drying the sweat from my brow. I pause several feet behind him, again that question nagging at me. *Is he trying to kill me? Did Cobalt bring me here just to push me off the edge of a cliff?*

My eyes shift from the prince's back to the view before us. All prior thoughts go still. A chill runs down my spine, but it isn't from fear. It's awe that has me in its grip. Below stretches red-orange hills rolling to the left and right, with endless ocean straight ahead. Bircharbor Palace is a tiny silhouette in the distance, perched at the edge of its cliff. Gulls soar high overhead in the clear blue sky, sunlight glinting off their feathers.

"Beautiful, isn't it?" Cobalt asks.

There's no point denying the truth. "It is."

"I've impressed you!" His smile is infectious, and I find myself averting my gaze to hide the tiny spark of joy fighting for dominance over my face. Cobalt doesn't seem to notice my struggle and turns away from the view to walk to the middle of the leaf-strewn field. There he plops down in the grass and begins unpacking the goods from the basket he brought.

I follow but hover a few steps away from where he sits.

He pats the grass next to him. "Come. I packed us a meal."

I stay where I am, eying the spread of cheese, nuts, and unfamiliar fruits he's laid out.

When he sees I haven't moved, he pauses and meets my eyes with another disarming grin. "I'm not going to hurt you, Evelyn. You're safe with me."

He can't lie, I remind myself. "Promise me."

"I promise I won't hurt you."

I let the vow hang between us for a few moments. While I don't believe a fae promise is a thing of magic like most people think it is, I know the fae put much stock into the word. A promise is a thing of deep reverence to them, like their inability to lie. It's something I can use like a shield.

With a deep breath, I take a seat opposite him, on the other side of the food-laden cloth. The earth is warm beneath me, the noonday sun beaming down upon us. My stomach rumbles at the sight of the meal, so I pick up a piece of cheese.

Cobalt takes a piece of fruit shaped like a pear, but with tiny red spikes all around it. He bites into it, spikes and all. "They aren't sharp," he says through the mouthful.

"Fae fruit, I'm guessing?"

He nods. "You have to try some. It's unlike anything you've ever had before."

I stare at the fruit with suspicion. "I'm not sure if that's a good thing."

"It is, trust me. Besides," he says, taking another bite, "you brought your salt, right? If you're worried, sprinkle some on every bite you take."

As much as I'd like to avoid all things fae and potentially dangerous, the fruit does look appetizing, especially the way the golden juice runs between Cobalt's fingers when he takes a bite. After the grueling hike, I could use something refreshing. I grab my pouch of salt, then choose a piece of fruit—one shaped like an apple but with an opalescent golden skin.

"Good choice. We call that an autumn equinox apple. You're going to love it."

He's right. Even with the salt, the flavor is overwhelmingly delicious. It's sweet and bright with a crisp, juicy texture. I close my eyes to enjoy the sensations.

"So...tell me about yourself," he says, popping a blood-red berry in his mouth. "What was life like for you before you came here?"

I salt my apple again and take another bite while I consider what to say. I'm hesitant to speak about anything personal, but I suppose it wouldn't hurt to share some. Right?

"Well, let's see. I grew up living in an apothecary run by my mother. For the past two years, I've been working as a surgeon's apprentice. And before I was forced to come here, I had plans to attend medical school on the mainland."

"Surgeon, wow. So, you cut up human bodies?" Cobalt asks as he grabs an apple like mine.

"I suppose you could say that, although it's more complicated. It's a healing practice. Surgery is often the difference between life and death for humans. Is there nothing like that here?"

He shrugs. "We aren't easy to kill. If there's ever a time we're wounded badly enough to require intervention, it usually means there's no coming back from it."

I take another bite of salted apple, pondering over what kind of wound would be bad enough to kill a fae. I've heard stories about the fae's impressive abilities to rapidly heal from injury, their supposed immortality. As far as I've been told, their main weaknesses are iron and ash. But can they heal from a wound inflicted by either material or is it always fatal? And what about a wound from an ordinary wood or metal? I know what kind of wounds can kill a man, but does the same apply to the fae?

"I'm sorry," he says quietly, shattering my morbid thoughts. "About you being forced to be here. I can tell you were passionate about your plans for school."

I nod but say nothing in reply. His words make me wonder if he knows why I was brought here—knows about my first meeting with his brother at the wall. If he does, he's doing a good job not bringing it up. Whatever the case, I'm done talking about myself. "Now it's your turn. Tell me about your adolescence."

He reclines on the bed of leaves, elbows supporting his weight. "Hmm. I am much older than you by several hundred years, so it'll take me a moment to think back that far."

"Several hundred years, you say? And to think you don't look a day over three-hundred and seventy-two."

"Ah, perfect. I was beginning to think my blues were showing. That's what humans get, right? Different colored hair with age?"

"Something like that." I take my last bite of apple and exchange the core for one of the pear-like fruits.

"Ha, thought so. Now, let's see. I was born the second son of Queen Melusine. She returned to the sea not long after I was born, which basically meant Aspen had to raise me, although he was barely more than an adolescent himself at the time."

"Your brother raised you? Does that mean the two of you are close?"

He ponders that for a moment. "I've lived with him my entire life, but I wouldn't say we've ever been close. I love him and I'm sure he loves me, but it isn't always smooth sailing between us. He frustrates me at times, and I know he resents me."

"Why would he resent you?"

His expression turns apologetic. "It's no secret many of the council would prefer to see me on the throne."

Part of me wonders if that wouldn't be a good idea. So far, Cobalt seems far more civilized than his brother. "How do you feel about that?"

"I just want what's best for Faerwyvae."

"Isn't that what every good king should want?"

He shifts, looking flustered.

My stomach drops, realizing my words are bordering on treason. There I go with that mouth of mine again. Time to change the subject. "Tell me more about your childhood. Who's your father? Foxglove said King Herne died before your brother was born, so I take it you don't share his paternity."

He shrugs. "I never met my father. He was one of Mother's many undersea consorts and never bothered coming to land to meet me. It's the unseelie way." There's a note of sorrow in his voice, and I can't help but feel a squeeze of sympathy for him.

"I don't remember my father," I say. "He parted ways with my mother when my sister and I were small. When Mother moved us to Eisleigh, he stayed behind. We've never heard from him since."

"I'm sorry. At least you had your mother, though. You must miss her terribly."

My throat tightens. I do miss her, and I can't fight my regret over the sharp words I said to her the night I left. She knows how much I love her, doesn't she?

"What's wrong?" Cobalt's brow is furrowed as he studies my face from his reclined position.

I don't want to tell him what's really on my mind. If I talk about my mother, I won't be able to trust myself not to cry. Instead, I voice another valid worry. "I just hope Amelie is faring well with your brother."

"You mean at her interrogation?"

I bristle at the word. "Why do you call it that?"

He frowns. "You know he's only spending time with her to make sure she doesn't plan on killing him, right?"

"Amelie? Kill King Aspen?" I may have given her a knife for protection, but if anyone were to kill the king, it would be me. Of course, I don't say so out loud.

"He thinks everyone is trying to kill him," Cobalt says, a note of irritation in his voice. "You've seen how paranoid he is, how he has his food tested before he eats it."

"Why is he like that? Does anyone have reason to kill him?" Aside from him being an insufferable prick, that is.

His eyes unfocus as he considers this. "He has many enemies—basically every fae on the Council of Eleven Courts. But I can't imagine they would target him with the kinds of underhanded assassination attempts my brother fears. If anything, they'd demand his removal from the throne."

"Why does the council hate him so much?"

"Well, to be honest, he's the most unstable ruler in Faerwyvae, always switching from seelie to unseelie and back again for no reason at all. I think he does it on purpose, just to stir chaos."

I remember what Foxglove told me during the carriage ride, about fae politics and the history of the original unseelie fae. "What do you mean he switches from seelie to unseelie? Do you mean politically or physically?"

"Politically. We all shift into our physical unseelie forms from time to time. But when it comes to politics, the rulers are supposed to take a firm stance on what each side represents. The unseelie ultimately want control over the isle. They were responsible for the war a thousand years ago and are the main supporters of going back to war and ridding the isle of humans. The seelie, on the other hand, are determined to keep war from ever reaching the isle again. They keep the unseelie in check and smooth things over with the humans when tensions arise."

"So, you're saying your brother constantly changes his mind about whether he supports war?"

"Yes, but it's more than that. I doubt he even cares about the politics at all, otherwise he wouldn't play the games he does. You see, in order to pass any new motions, the council needs a majority vote. Ever since the war ended, the council has remained mostly seelie. Occasionally, a ruler will change sides, especially when a court is inherited by a new ruler. But every time this happens, my brother switches sides too, to whatever opposes the newest change."

I furrow my brow. "Why would he do that?"

"To be difficult. There could be no other reason. If he was doing it to keep Faerwyvae from going to war, it would make sense. But he even shifts sides when an unseelie votes seelie."

"You think that's why the council dislikes him?"

"I know they do. The seelie hate him because his constant shifting keeps the council from getting anywhere near unanimously seelie, which in turn prevents them from bringing in new measures to further the seelie cause. If the council were to shift heavily seelie, they'd be able to make bigger and better changes. Changes that would do more than the treaty does now. Changes that could make human-fae relations even stronger."

"And the unseelie hate him for the same reason."

"Exactly. If the council were to shift heavily unseelie, the same would happen. Drastic changes but with an opposite result. However, the unseelie probably hate him more than the seelie do, on principle alone. It was his birth that ended the war. My mother turned seelie just as the council was ready to pass a motion that would rid the isle of humans."

I shudder at that. "Why did your mother turn seelie when Aspen was born?"

"I can't promise any of this is true," Cobalt says, "but the stories tell how Aspen was born in his seelie form and how my unseelie mother couldn't figure out how to care for him. She tried to nurse him with seawater, but he wouldn't take it. In a matter of hours, he was near death. Mother was so distraught about the possibility of losing the child that she became desperate. In a final attempt at saving her baby's life, she snuck past the war camps to the nearest human settlement and located a nursing mother, begging her to nurse Aspen. The woman agreed on one condition—that my mother make a bargain. End the war and the woman would nurse Aspen to full health. She'd even teach my mother how to care for the boy herself, if she'd agree to take on a seelie form."

"She made the bargain, I'm guessing?"

He nods. "She donned human clothing for the first time ever and learned to nurse her son. This changed her. Not only was she forced to make good on the bargain, but she found she wanted to rid the isle of war, to make the land safe for her newborn son. As Queen of the Sea Court and Regent of the Autumn Court, her vote on the council was substantial. When she turned seelie during that final council meeting, the war was over. The seelie vote won and they were able to forge the treaty we follow today."

"Considering the name of the fae council," I say, "Faerwyvae must have eleven courts. Aside from Autumn and Sea, what others are there?"

"There are three other seasonal courts in addition to Autumn," Cobalt says. "Spring, Summer, Winter. Then there are three elemental courts in addition to Sea; Wind, Fire, Earthen. The final three are celestial courts; Solar, Lunar, and Star. Sea, Winter, and Lunar have remained firmly unseelie the past few hundred years, with a couple others varying from time to time, based on the political climate. But no one has shifted sides as much as my brother."

I let his words sink in, awed over all the new information. Growing up, I only ever heard about the human side of the war, not the fae side. We were taught how the fae presented us with a treaty and that both our kind and theirs worked to finalize the terms. There are still a few things I never understood, however. "Do you know why the Hundred Year Reaping exists?"

"It's a demonstration of peace," he says. "When the war ended, the fae agreed to show our goodwill by exiling the King of the Fire Court. He was the first fae to engage the humans in organized violence and was determined to eradicate them. We bound him in iron and shipped him off to what you humans call mainland Bretton. Being so far from the Fair Isle and the magic here is certain death. And since we banished one of our kings to die, humans were required to make a similar sacrifice, especially considering they spilled the first blood that sparked the unrest to begin with."

More information I never knew. Was any of it true? Were the humans the ones to spill first blood? I always imagined it was the fae, creeping into human villages in the night, stealing children and slaughtering travelers.

More proof this world is upside down from everything I knew. "So, my people chose human girls to be their sacrifice?"

He nods. "Likely to atone for that first blood they spilled. It's said the Fire King took a human lover. Back then, human-fae pairings were forbidden. Humans were afraid any children born from such a union would become witches or demons. So when the Fire King's lover admitted to being pregnant with the child of a fae, they executed her. In retribution, he burned her village to the ground. That's what sparked the war. The Reaping is meant to repair that which was torn between the humans and fae, to maintain a balance of give and take between them. Two human girls are sent to a different court every hundred years, and at least one marriage alliance takes place. In exchange, the family is blessed with a gift from the court the girls are sent to."

"Is that why the two girls are almost always related? So the fae only have to gift one family?"

He shrugs. "Perhaps. Although I'd like to think it's so neither girl will be lonely."

This last part almost makes me laugh. I can't imagine the fae caring much about the emotions of their Chosen. I'm pondering everything else Cobalt said, eyes unfocused, when I remember the pear-like fruit in my hand. I've still yet to taste it. With a sprinkle of salt, I bite into it, finding the red spikes are soft and oddly flavorful after all, like ripe strawberries. But the flesh inside is even better, crisp, tart, and honey sweet. I take another bite and a wave of euphoric lightness floats to my head.

I only have a moment to realize something before my thoughts slip away into a chaotic jumble.

I never salted the second bite.

15

———————

I stare at the fruit, panic rising inside me. It only lasts a moment, however, before I find myself laughing, giddy over...something. Everything?

"Oh no." Cobalt sits upright, expression shifting between amusement and worry. "Did you take a bite of honey pyrus without salting it?"

The panic returns in a flash. "Yes. Is that bad?" My stomach churns, but not a moment later, my laughter is back. Cobalt is the one making me laugh. He's so funny. His face is funny. Everything is...*wow so pretty*. "Honey pyrus," I say slowly, my tongue feeling thick and heavy.

Cobalt's face is spinning as he inches closer to me. He's laughing now too, and it sounds like a thousand tiny bells. "Hey, I think it's best you lie down for a bit."

"Did you just say your words backwards?"

"Sure. Here, just lie back. The leaves will feel really nice. In fact, I'll join you. Honey pyrus no longer makes me feel as euphoric as you feel right now, but it does make me sleepy." He lays down next to me and pulls me down with him.

Or perhaps I fall down next to him. Either way, the ground is pulling me down and I'm sinking into an endless sea of vibrant red leaves. I could drown in it and I wouldn't mind. The sky is a swirling vortex of color over-head, clouds passing in shapes that make me laugh louder than I think I've ever laughed before. The panic continues to swell now and then, but I chase it away each time.

No, I'm not chasing panic.

I'm chasing a butterfly.

A ladybug.

No, a sprite.

A sprite with glowing yellow wings is leading me to more honey pyrus, which I'm desperate for. It's all I can think about. I just need more of that delicious fruit. Down the hill we go, and I'm laughing with every step, even when it leads me to tumble over roots and rocks. On and on we go, deeper into the woods. This is the most fun I think I've ever had. Why was I afraid earlier?

Afraid. Was I afraid? Should I be afraid?

The panic returns, and I come to a halt, looking wildly around me. I'm no longer on the leafy field next to Cobalt. I'm in the middle of a dense forest of oak and maple, and there's no one else in sight. Wasn't I chasing a sprite? I remember my craving for more honey pyrus, but it no longer has me in its grip. It's fear I feel now. And a pounding headache.

My legs feel suddenly weak beneath me, and I wince, my muscles screaming from exertion. Did I run all the way down the hill from the cliff? How long have I been out here alone? And...where exactly is *here*?

I look up at the canopy of orange leaves, finding daylight in the blue sky overhead. That's something, at least. I turn in a circle, trying to see if the ground hints at the beginning of an incline, but the forest is too dense. In fact, I don't remember going through a forest like this when Cobalt and I were on our way to the cliff. Our path from the palace took us through endless rows of slim white birches.

Panic rises further, sending my heart racing. *Calm down,* I tell myself. *Panic won't get you anywhere.* I take a step and nearly twist my ankle on a rock. In doing so, I catch sight of my tattered hem. It's torn in numerous places and pierced with twigs. I look at both arms, which are equally battered, tiny red scratches and blossoming bruises covering my flesh. What the blazing iron happened?

I remember the euphoric flavor of the honey pyrus, but the memory tastes sickly sweet, bringing bile to my throat. Before I know it, I'm doubled over and heaving out the contents of my stomach. Tears spring to my eyes, and I let out a moan of distress. I've hardly been more than tipsy from the occasional glass of wine, so this is a far cry from anything I've ever experienced before.

I curse myself for being so stupid as to try fae fruit in the first place, salt or no.

My hand flies to my side, finding my salt pouch gone. I likely left it at the picnic. Another thought crosses my mind, and I reach for my thigh, sighing with relief when I feel the hilt of my dagger.

I close my eyes, summoning a sense of calm. Control. With a deep breath, I lift my soiled hem and take one careful step and then another, avoiding ill-meaning rocks this time. I turn my head this way and that, seeking some sign of a worn path to no avail. Then I turn my eyes to the sky, trying to make out where the sun is. The sun set over the horizon behind the palace last night. If I can follow the trajectory of the sun, I might be able to find the palace. Maybe. It's the only logical step I can think of.

Here goes nothing.

HOURS PASS AND THERE'S STILL NO SIGN OF A TRAIL, MUCH LESS THE PALACE OR Cobalt or the cliff we picnicked on. I've yet to cross paths with any living being, save for birds and insects and the occasional rodent. This, at first, I was grateful for. Now I'm starting to wish I'd come across a fae. Surely, Cobalt will have sent someone to find me by now, right? Perhaps I should have stayed where I was.

"Help," I call out. "Can anyone hear me?"

Silence.

My heart feels like it will burst from anxiety and my feet are covered in blisters within the dirt-caked slippers I wear. I can't go much farther.

"Please." I try again, letting my voice carry throughout the quiet forest. "I'm lost and need help. I'm...fiancée of Prince Cobalt of the Autumn Court."

More silence.

This is the day I die after all. Not because of some vile fae, but because I'm an idiot who got tipsy on fae fruit and decided to run alone through the woods after what was probably an imaginary sprite. My throat feels tight and tears prick my eyes. I can't cry. I can't fall apart right now.

Control. Where is my control?

A sound comes from behind me. I whirl to find a dark shape in the distance. My breath catches, and I realize it's a black horse, similar to the ones I saw at the head of our carriage yesterday. What had Foxglove called them? Puca? It comes closer, slowly, and I fight the urge to flee.

"Did you come to help me?" I ask, trying to keep my voice steady.

"Come with me." The voice is somehow audible yet ethereal, as if carried not by vocal cords but the wind. The horse comes closer, and I see it's somewhat larger than the carriage-pulling puca. This one is more muscular too, with a long mane that blows in a wind I don't feel and eyes that gleam red instead of gold. It's beautiful.

I shudder. There's something sinister in this creature's beauty, reminding me of King Aspen's striking glamour. "Will you take me to the Autumn Court palace?"

"I will," says the ethereal voice. "I'll take you to Bircharbor Palace. Climb on my back."

I take an automatic step away as it approaches and lowers its head. Everything in me is screaming at me to run, but what other choice do I have? I'm lost with no guarantee I'll come across another fae before I get eaten alive by something worse. Besides, my mind is still too foggy from the honey pyrus to construct a tighter bargain. This one will have to do.

I grit my teeth and haul myself onto the creature's back. As soon as I'm righted upon it, it takes off. I reach for its mane, wrapping the thick strands of black around my hands to keep from falling off.

As the puca gallops through the forest, deftly avoiding branches and tree trunks as if by magic, I notice the forest begins to thin. It looks familiar as oaks and maples give way to stands of birch, and I'm almost positive it's the same way Cobalt and I came earlier. There's no sign of the prince or the cliff, but we can't be too far from the palace now.

My breathing begins to slow. Relief crawls over me bit by bit, and before long the ride becomes something close to enjoyable.

The sun is beginning its descent in the sky by the time the puca slows to a canter. The trees thin to a well-worn path, and a welcome sight comes into view—the palace. I sigh with relief, fully aware of the irony that I could feel so happy to return to what yesterday felt like a prison. Anything beats being alone in that eerie forest again.

"I brought you to the palace," says the puca. "Yes?"

"Yes, thank you."

As soon as the words are out of my mouth, the puca picks up pace again, charging forward. I feel like he's going to ram us both straight into the palace walls. I try to release his mane, hoping I can tumble from his back before we crash. To my horror, my hands are somehow stuck in place. It's not me holding the mane after all, but the mane holding onto me.

Before we slam into the palace wall, the creature veers sharply to the right. The golds of the palace speed past my vision and are replaced with the reds and pinks of the sunset behind it. The puca gallops ahead with no sign of slowing before we reach the end of the cliff.

I scream as the ocean comes into view below us, my stomach dropping as he leaps off the edge. We crash not too far down, the puca gaining purchase with little effort on a small outcropping of the cliff wall. It leaps and crashes again, jolting me with every landing. In a matter of seconds, we've descended the face of the cliff and are speeding along the narrow sliver of beach. Straight for the ocean.

I struggle to release the mane again, trying to reach my thigh, my dagger, but the strands of hair pull tighter and tighter. The tide is high, which means we plunge into the water before I can take a breath. There's no sign of the coral caves, no sign of anything but deep, dark water and the blinding sunset above.

The puca is equally as agile in the water as he was on land, and it isn't long before we clear the small inlet and move into the open ocean.

That's when the puca plunges beneath the waves.

I gasp for breath before the water closes over my head, but it isn't enough. My lungs are already screaming as the creature dives deeper and deeper into the ocean. I struggle, pulling at the puca's mane, but my hands have lost all feeling.

This is the end, I realize. I can hold my breath no longer.

Water floods my mouth as a wave of tiny bubbles crashes into me, obscuring my vision. The last thing I feel is a pair of hands encircling my waist.

16

When I wake, everything hurts. My eyes, my lungs, my throat. Every muscle feels like it's on fire. My eyelids flutter open, and I try to sit but can manage no more than lifting my head before a searing pain behind my eyes has me sinking back into the pillows beneath me.

"Evie!" The voice belongs to Amelie, though I don't dare open my eyes to find her. The pain in my head is too great.

"I'll help her sit," says another voice, which takes me a moment to recognize as belonging to Lorelei. An arm moves to my upper back, lifting me, and I feel a mountain of pillows fill the space behind me until I'm propped up slightly. "Drink this."

The rim of a cup touches my lips, and I don't bother to fight the warm liquid. I'd drink fae wine or the juice of a honey pyrus, if it meant quenching my razor-sharp thirst. The liquid tastes like a mild tea, like something Mother would have made me when I was sick. Its soothing effect is immediate, easing the pain in my throat and sending a wave of relaxation over me. Finally, I open my eyes.

Squinting into the semi-darkness of what appears to be my bedroom at the palace, I find Lorelei and Amelie hovering before me, concerned expressions on both their faces as they sit next to me on the bed.

"What happened?" My voice comes out like a croak, renewing the pain in my throat and lungs.

"Oh, thank the Great Mother above." Amelie brings a hand to her heart, shoulders drawing down with relief. "You are coherent."

My brow furrows at her words. She said it like she expected otherwise. "How long have I been asleep?"

Amelie and Lorelei exchange a glance. "What has it been? Three days?" Amelie asks.

Lorelei nods, then faces me. "You've been coming in and out of consciousness, but mostly sleeping."

"Three days?" I jolt forward, but the motion sends my head reeling again. Squeezing my eyes shut, I lie back until the pain recedes.

"Drink more," Lorelei prods.

I do as told, relishing the sweet, familiar herbs that remind me so much of home. When I open my eyes again, Amelie is grinning.

"Foxglove was sent to the village for a remedy," she says. "He brought you something from Mother's shop. Isn't that wonderful?"

I want to argue that he should have returned with antibiotics, but I can't help but admit how much comfort the tea is bringing me. "He...saw Mother? Did he say how she is?"

"I sent him with a letter, told her we're being treated well, aside from your unfortunate incident with the kelpie. She sent one back, expressing her love and wishes for you to return to full health. Would you like me to read it to you?"

"Yes—wait. The kelpie? Is that what the creature was?"

Amelie nods. "Cobalt told me all about it. You should have seen him! He looked quite the hero as he carried you in his arms through the castle, dripping water in his wake. His skin was blue too, it was so odd."

"He'd shifted into his unseelie form," Lorelei explains, "when he rescued you. He's a nix."

"He...rescued me?" I shudder, remembering the deadly ride on the puca —or kelpie, I should say—and how it drove us into the ocean and pulled me underwater. I remember the burning, searing pain as water entered my lungs, followed by the hands of someone pulling me by the waist. That's the last thing I remember. "Why did the kelpie try to kill me?"

"Apparently, dragging lost travelers to their deaths is their specialty, according to Prince Cobalt," Amelie says. "He had to sever the creature's mane with a shard of coral to release you from its grip."

"But how did Cobalt find me? We were separated during our picnic."

Amelie scoots closer, hands an animated flurry, as she explains. "He said he went looking for you when he realized you were missing. There was no sign of you, and he had no idea where you'd gone, but when he caught scent of the kelpie, he knew exactly what had happened. He followed the trail and dove in after you when he saw the kelpie drag you into the ocean." She puts her hand to her heart and sighs. "He's so romantic."

"Romantic? No. This entire situation—" I swallow my words as another wave of pain radiates through my skull. With a deep breath, I wait for the sharp ache to pass, and force my body to relax back into the pillows. I grind my teeth, hating how helpless I feel, how helpless I've been for three days. *Three days.* Anything could have happened in that time.

Amelie grabs my hand. "What's wrong? You look distressed."

I press my lips together, eyes flashing toward Lorelei.

As if the fae can sense my sudden tension, she stands from the bed. "I should go tell the king you've woken."

"Thank you, Lorelei," I say.

Once the door closes behind her, my eyes find Amelie again. I let out a deep sigh. "Tell me what's happened while I've been out."

She cocks her head. "What do you mean?"

"I mean, what have you been doing? Have you continued carrying your knife? And your rowan necklace?"

She rolls her eyes and pats the sash at her waist, then lifts the strand of rowan berries from beneath the bodice of her dress. "Yes, Evie, I've remained well protected. Not only that, but I managed to keep you protected as well. See? I trimmed my necklace in half to replace the one you lost. Yours didn't survive your little dunk in the ocean."

My hands fly to my throat, and I find the familiar feel of rowan berries. The new necklace is noticeably shorter than mine had been, and only now do I realize Amelie's is half as long as well. I must admit, I'm impressed by her consideration. I would have expected her to abandon the necklace altogether without me reminding her to wear it every day. "Thank you, Ami. Now, what else? Have you been alone with the king?"

"If you must know, I've seen the king for an hour each of the last three days."

I try to sit straighter at that, eager for everything she can tell me. "What have you done together? Did he...do anything to you?"

She stares at me with a pointed look and puts her hands on her hips.

"Ami, I need to know if you've been safe with him. If he tried to hurt you—"

"Then what? What would you do about it?"

I open my mouth, but no words come.

"Look, I know you care about me and you're afraid for the both of us. But you need to trust me to take care of myself sometimes. I'm not the same fragile girl I was four years ago."

I tense. Four years ago. When I almost lost her. It began with a fae glamour and nearly ended with my mother's folly. If it hadn't been for Mr. Meeks, Amelie would have died. I shudder, breathing the memories away. It's not something either of us like to talk about.

Still, she has a point. Amelie was never to blame for what happened to her back then. It could just as easily have happened to me. And this time, it did. This time, I'm the one who almost died. And if appearance is proof of circumstance, Amelie really does seem well. Her cheeks are rosy, her eyes are bright and alive. Perhaps I'm not giving my sister the credit she deserves.

I let out a heavy sigh. "I'm sorry, Ami. You're right. I've been treating you like you can't take care of yourself while I'm the one who keeps getting into these messes."

"These messes? Have there been multiple?"

I blush, again reminding myself she knows neither about me meeting Aspen at the faewall, nor about our tense conversation in the dining room the night we arrived. "So, at the risk of sounding like an overprotective little sister, what *can* you tell me about the past few days? No, better yet, what would you *like* to tell me? What wonderful things did I miss?"

Her smile returns, and she sits closer to me, folding her legs under her. "As you know, the king insists I spend time with him daily. He's not as bad as you think he is, Evie, although he's incredibly dull. Pleasant to look at, but no personality. He mostly sits at his desk in his study working while I talk and drink wine and eat the most decadent confections."

It's hard to reconcile my experience of the king with Amelie's. I can't imagine he and myself sitting alone in the same room without it ending with my knife at his throat. Never would I picture him as dull. Hostile, arrogant, and impossible maybe, but never dull. Then again, my sister is much more agreeable than I am. "What else?"

She lowers her voice. "Well, there's this handsome servant. I saw him yesterday when I asked Aspen to have some wine brought in for me during our daily chat. My goodness, Evie! I had no idea fae could be so beautiful."

I want to shake my head but know the movement will jar my skull. Instead, I settle for a smirk. "Leave it to you to find romance in captivity."

"It isn't hard. Have you even taken the time to look at the males here? I can hardly remember what Magnus looks like anymore."

"Wasn't it just three days ago you were lamenting over not having taken Magnus to bed?"

"I can still lament such a thing while making room in my new bed. Metaphorically speaking, of course. *You've* been taking all the room in my bed the last three nights."

I laugh, but sober quickly. Again, it's my turn to cut through Amelie's optimism with my brutal realism. I lower my voice. "You do know your bed is already spoken for, right?"

She shrugs.

"Ami, I'm serious."

"Oh really? I thought you were serious when you apologized for treating me like a helpless child."

I press my lips together. "You're right. I'm sorry. Again."

"My bed. My business."

I reach toward her and lay a feeble punch on her arm. "Not while I'm in it. Dirty harlot."

She giggles and punches me back. "Haggard prude." Before I can muster the energy to lay another blow, a knock sounds on the door. I expect it to be Lorelei returning, which means she'll barge in any moment. When the door remains closed, Amelie springs from the bed to see who's there.

"Your Highness," Amelie says. My heart races as Cobalt enters and approaches the bed. I find myself suddenly self-conscious, knowing I couldn't possibly be pleasant to look at after surviving a near-drowning and sleeping for three days. I do my best to summon an air of confidence and meet his smile with my own. "You'll forgive me for not standing to curtsy, I hope. I don't think my aching head would allow it."

"Only if you'll forgive me for not better protecting you on our picnic." There's remorse in his eyes, hesitation in his voice. He looks like he's worried I might be angry with him.

It gives me pause, and I choose my words with careful consideration as I navigate the best way to assuage his guilt. "Of course, I forgive you. Besides, if the rumors are to be believed, you did valiantly rescue me."

"Barely. If I had taken any longer...well, I don't even want to think about what could have happened."

I blush beneath his gaze and turn away, looking instead at Amelie. She, however, isn't looking at me at all. Instead she's swooning over Cobalt. When she finally meets my eyes, she arches a brow. I can almost hear her thoughts. *See? So romantic.*

Cobalt shakes his head as if to clear his thoughts. "Anyhow, I'd hoped you'd be well enough to join us for dinner, but you still seem out of sorts."

I cringe at the thought of leaving the bed. "I'll have to decline tonight, Your Highness. But I thank you for the invitation. And for your concern."

He turns to Amelie. "You'll join us, though, won't you? I'm sure my brother would appreciate your presence."

She beams at him. "Of course I will."

My eyes bore into Amelie, and I want to tell her she can't leave me. It takes all my willpower to remain quiet. *I have to trust her to protect herself. Especially when I'm in no position to leave my bed.*

"Very good," Cobalt says. "Dinner should be ready by now. I'll meet you and the others in the dining room. Would you be so kind to give me a minute more to speak with your sister?"

She looks from him to me, then back again, finally understanding his request for privacy. Again, it's a struggle not to tell her to stay. "Oh, yes! Yes. Of course." With a curtsy for him and a smile for me, she leaves the room.

As soon as Cobalt and I are alone, he sits at the edge of the bed. He seems suddenly shy, as if he's too embarrassed to meet my eyes, his gaze instead fixed on my hand. "I came to see you a few times."

His words spark a memory, his face looking down at me, my hand in his. Other similar memories flash through my mind, of the other faces who'd come to see me. Amelie, Foxglove, Lorelei, and—strangely—King Aspen. "I briefly remember, but I apologize if we exchanged any words. I remember nothing else."

He shakes his head. "We didn't speak. The most you produced was an incomprehensible mumble until now."

Heat rises to my cheeks. "How humiliating."

"Humiliated was how I felt when I woke up at our picnic and found you missing. I couldn't believe I'd fallen asleep." Finally, he meets my eyes and reaches a tentative hand toward mine until he covers my fingers in his.

I flinch at the touch but don't pull away. "Your hands are cold."

He grimaces. "Part of being a nix," he says. "That's a kind of sea fae. Do you dislike it? The cold, I mean. Or my touch?"

His vulnerability tugs at my lips, pulling them into a smile. "No, I don't dislike it."

He grins, keeping his hand in place. "I really am sorry for not protecting you better."

I want to argue that I don't need protecting, but the point would be moot. I've already proven the opposite to be true, as much as that fact irritates me to no end. "It's not your job to protect me. I should have protected myself better."

His brows knit together. "As your fiancé, it *is* my job. But it isn't just duty that makes me want to protect you." He averts his gaze, expression shy again.

I'm at a loss for words. Could Cobalt have actual feelings for me? I knew he was kind when I first met him. At the picnic, I realized he was easy to be around. But could our relationship mean more to him than a forced arrangement? Could he...*like* me?

Cobalt meets my eyes again, and I know no one has ever looked at me the way he's looking at me now. He's looking at me the way men usually look at Amelie. Like I'm worth looking at. Like I'm interesting. Fascinating. Pretty. "When I saw the kelpie take you underwater, I thought I was going to lose you forever."

My heart races beneath the weight of his stare. He inches forward, and I wonder if he's about to kiss me. My breath catches in my throat. Do I...want him to kiss me?

His eyes study my face, then stray down my neck, hovering over the skin exposed above my nightdress. There's a hunger in his eyes, something I'd be delighted to see in any other circumstance, but right now I'm painfully aware of how awful I must smell, how crazy my hair must be. Cobalt doesn't seem anything but pleased to be near me, but there's no way I'm going to experience my first kiss with my future husband from my almost deathbed. At least let me bathe first.

I pull my hand from beneath his and drag the blankets higher over my torso, wishing I could cover my face and the flush of heat I know is clear on my cheeks. "You should enjoy your dinner, Your Highness, and I should get some more rest."

He opens his mouth as if he wants to say something but resigns with a nod. "You're right. I shouldn't keep you up."

The disappointment in his voice makes my heart sink, and I have the overwhelming urge to see his smile return. "Will I see you tomorrow?"

I'm rewarded with his beautiful grin. "Of course."

When he departs, I'm left staring at the ceiling, puzzling over my thoughts and feelings. Cobalt was going to kiss me, I'm sure of it. And if I'd felt more confident, I would have let him.

I turn on my side and cover my head with my blankets. Amelie's question from just a few days ago rings through my head. *Do you think we could come to be happy here?*

I'm starting to wonder if that question wasn't so stupid after all.

17

———————

The next morning, I only feel half as terrible as I did the night before. Bright light streams through the windows, telling me I've slept late into the morning. Not only did I sleep late, but I slept deep too. The last thing I remember was my almost-kiss with Cobalt. I don't even remember Amelie coming to bed after dinner, or her getting up this morning.

Wait. Did she even come to bed?

My curiosity over her whereabouts is a welcome distraction from the other thoughts on the periphery of my mind—Cobalt's eyes as he drank me in, moments from closing the distance between us. And, of course, my subsequent reaction. It isn't long before those memories take over all other thought, making my heart race. At the time, pulling away from the potential kiss made sense. I was tired, dirty, weak—humiliatingly human. Now, after a full night's sleep, my reaction feels mortifying. He'd tried to kiss me. *Kiss* me. There was a strong part of me that wanted it. Yet, I rejected him.

Now I can only face the facts. I was scared. And not for the reasons I'm used to fearing about the fae. I was afraid because I'm not like Amelie, with her rotating list of endless suitors and lovers. The few courtships I had back home in Sableton were nothing to give up medical school for. Yet, none of those men had ever looked at me the way Cobalt did.

What would it have been like if I'd let him kiss me last night?

I let out something between a laugh and a frustrated moan as I smother my face in my pillow. A moment later, the sound of the door opening grabs my attention, sending me bolting upright. To my relief, there's no pain shooting through my skull at the motion.

"Good morning," Lorelei says in her bored tone. "Your sister said you might be up by now and would likely enjoy a bath."

"I would, thank you." I swing my legs over the side of the bed and place my feet on the cold marble floor. "Where is my sister, anyhow?"

She's taken aback for a moment, likely surprised I've accepted her help for once. "She was at breakfast. Now I believe she's walking the palace grounds."

I swallow the anxiety that bubbles up inside me. "Alone?"

"Well, Foxglove and I were at breakfast with her, but she didn't say if she was enjoying company on her walk or not."

I want to demand her reasoning for allowing Amelie to go anywhere alone but stop myself. Lorelei is our lady's maid, not our guard. And Amelie can take care of herself. At least, I promised I'd pretend to feel that way.

"King Aspen and Prince Cobalt will be at dinner tonight," Lorelei says. "They request the presence of both of you. That is, if you are feeling up to it."

"I am." Even if I hadn't been feeling better today, I'd still force myself to go. I've let Amelie out of my sight long enough.

"Very well. I'll put the order in for your bath."

After she leaves, I walk around the room, testing my legs after being dormant for so long. I move from the bed to the dressing table where I find my tattered gown—or what remains of it. To my relief, my dagger lays on the table next to it, belt intact. At least that wasn't lost during the struggle, although it didn't do me any good when I needed it. I set it behind the dressing screen so I can put it back on when I get dressed. When I return from behind the screen, wafts of steam draw my attention to the tub, which is suddenly full of swirling, fragrant water. I approach it, puzzling over how or when this happened. I've still yet to discover any source for the water to come through, not to mention the herbs and flowers floating on the surface.

Whatever the case, the bath is too tempting to linger outside it, and moments later I'm sinking into its comforting depths, forcing my questions and hypotheses to recede from my mind. I let out a heavy sigh, closing my eyes and feeling my muscles relax in response to the luxurious heat.

It's a struggle to pry my eyes open again when I hear the knock on the door. A moment later, Amelie bounds into the room and Lorelei follows closely behind. The two are laughing, as if sharing a joke, and I feel a squeeze in my chest. Since when did they become such fast friends?

"Lorelei, dear," Amelie says, "will you pick out a dress for my sister to wear today? She must look her best for dinner tonight. Oh, and see that Foxglove comes to do our hair."

"Of course," the fae says, then goes to the wardrobe.

Amelie comes to me and perches on the side of the tub. "You look much better today, Evie. How are you feeling?"

"I'm feeling well. How are you? Your cheeks are flushed."

She sighs, not meeting my eyes. "It's a beautiful day outside. I should have waited for you to wake before walking the grounds, but I just couldn't bear it. I'm sorry."

There's something about her tone and the way she averts her gaze that gives me pause. She's hiding something. "Who did you walk with in my stead?"

The pink in her cheeks deepens. "Oh, the palace is abundant with good company, if you know where to look. The residents and staff are most friendly, as you will soon learn once you're ready to move out and about again."

The residents and staff. Perhaps...a certain servant she mentioned last night? I catch a glimpse of Lorelei still digging through the wardrobe, back facing us. I lower my voice. "I didn't hear you come in last night."

"Ah, well I didn't want to wake you. I was quite discreet when I came to bed after dinner."

Her words weave double meanings in my mind, and I wonder if what I'm reading between the lines is truly there or simply my imagination. "How was last night's dinner, by the way?"

"Oh, very pleasant. I wish you would have been there. The food was divine, and the wine was even better." Her eyes take on a distant look, one that tells me more than her words can. I've seen this look before, many times. Amelie is in love.

The question is, with whom?

∿

I watch my sister like a hawk as we arrive at dinner later that night. We're dressed in flowing fae gowns—I in coral and Amelie in sky blue— with our hair expertly piled on the top of our heads, thanks to Foxglove. We meet the two royals in the dining room. Aspen and Cobalt sit at opposite ends of the long table, while Amelie and I sit across from each other. Like the first night, Foxglove and Lorelei sit with us, although this time they don't wait for Aspen to invite them. The mood feels much lighter than it had the first time we were here.

Well, I should say the mood of everyone *around me* seems lighter. I'm once again a ball of tightly wound nerves. It doesn't help that I can hear the rhythmic crashing of the ocean far below the palace, the sound coming through the open expanse at the other side of the room. A shudder crawls up my spine.

Amelie whispers something in Lorelei's ear, prompting a giggle from the fae. I feel that squeeze in my chest again. It's not that I dislike the friendship that seems to have bloomed between them. It's more that I hate feeling left out. My sister has always been my best friend. And I've always been her confidante.

Amelie catches my stare, then reaches across the table and puts her hand over mine. She turns her smile to Aspen. "Doesn't my sister look so much better, Your Majesty? She's like a rose come back to life after a winter frost, isn't she?"

Aspen doesn't so much as look up from his plate as servants pile it with one food item after the other. A second servant—the same wood-like fae from before—takes a dainty bite out of each piece that lands on the plate. "She looks the same as ever." His voice is flat, disinterested, with none of the seething danger I've heard when his words were meant only for me. Perhaps Amelie's perception of Aspen isn't too far off. Maybe for her, he really is as dull and harmless as she said.

Amelie laughs as if he's made some silly joke. She turns her smile to Cobalt next. "What do you think, Your Highness?"

With some trepidation, I lift my eyes to meet the prince's. It's the first time I've dared look at him since arriving to dinner. I've been too afraid to read what his expression might say. Too afraid I'll see none of the warmth I saw last night.

His lips pull into a shy smile and his eyes lock on mine before he answers. "She looks positively radiant. As much as I missed her presence at dinner last night, I'm glad she got some more rest." His eyes move from me to my sister. "It's just as you said. She's like a rose come back to life. I couldn't have put it any more eloquently myself."

My sister beams at him. "You're too kind, Your Highness. Now, how about some wine?"

I sit upright in my chair, eyes locking on the approaching servant. Is this the one Amelie was gushing over last night? The fae male steps forward and fills her glass. He's tall and slim with boyish good looks, pale golden eyes, and brown, tousled hair that brushes past his pointed ears to his shoulders. I watch the way Amelie smiles up at him, the way her gaze lingers on his when he bows to her. Is he the one? The one she's in love with?

"Evie, you must try this wine." My eyes flash to Amelie as she takes a sip. I didn't even catch if she salted it first. "I can't get enough these days."

The handsome servant lifts the decanter questioningly. I shake my head, but Amelie insists. The servant circles the table to fill my cup. I expect Amelie's gaze to follow his every move, but her eyes are on me, all innocence. Why is she being so difficult to read?

Once my cup is full, the servant returns to the far wall, and I lean toward my sister, lowering my voice. "Did you bring salt? I lost mine at the picnic."

She lifts her chin, a haughty grin on her face. She pushes a silk pouch across the table toward me. "Of course I did, silly."

I retrieve the bag of salt and sprinkle a dash in the wine, then over my plate. When I return it to my sister, she does the same. "Now try the wine already!"

Amelie watches eagerly as I take a sip. The flavor is sweet with just the right hint of bitterness, and the texture is as smooth as velvet. I can't help but close my eyes as I savor it.

"See?" Amelie winks. "Isn't it divine? It's one of the many pleasures I've enjoyed since coming here."

I narrow my eyes at her over the rim of my glass. "What other pleasures have you enjoyed, dear sister?"

"Oh, food, dresses, delightful conversation." Her eyes fall on each of us sitting at the table, ending with King Aspen, who has finally taken a bite from his fully tested plate. "And, of course, my time spent getting to know the king. He's been quite the gracious host, Evie."

Aspen looks up from his plate, as if only just remembering our presence. He grunts as he finishes chewing. "Now that you mention it," he says to my sister, "I'd like to request your presence tonight in my study after dinner."

Amelie smiles and bows her head. "Of course, Your Majesty. Will there be more wine? And chocolate?"

"Whatever you like," he says flatly.

She turns her grin to me, eyes sparkling. "See? Isn't he just a dear?"

I furrow my brow, trying to decipher my sister's tone. She's emphasizing her words, exaggerating her contentment. Is she trying to tell me...could Aspen be the one she's in love with?

I can't decide whether that's better or worse than her being in love with some random servant. On one hand, being in love with the man she's forced to marry is ideal. It means she has a chance at happiness, as opposed to risking her life while trying to hide an affair. On the other hand, I don't trust Aspen. He killed his last fiancée. And his brother's too.

"No, sweetie, he's a stag." Foxglove's words startle me from my thoughts.

Amelie lets out an easy laugh while I cock my head at him.

He rolls his eyes as if I'm daft. "She said, 'isn't he just a dear?' But he isn't a deer. He's a stag."

I blink, then realize the joke too late. My eyes meet Aspen's and find an amused smirk on his lips. When he looks at me, he wears the same smug expression I've seen before. The same irritating pride. The same stunning beauty. The kind only a blade can keep at bay. I pat the dagger strapped to my thigh. *Control. I'm in control.*

The king burns me with his stare a few moments longer, then returns his gaze to his food, bored again, as if I'd imagined the silent exchange. But I hadn't imagined it. He'd stared. Taunted me with his eyes.

Perhaps the Stag King isn't as dull as he's been pretending to be in front of my sister.

But why pretend at all?

What are you hiding, Aspen?

18

____

After dinner, Amelie and I walk arm in arm through the dark yet elegant halls toward Aspen's study. The king left dinner while the rest of us were still enjoying dessert. Now that every course has been served, it's time for Amelie to join her betrothed for their daily chat.

"You didn't have to come with me, you know," Amelie says. "Lorelei could have walked me here."

She's right, but there was no way I'd let her out of my sight until the last possible moment. Even though it meant I had to turn down Cobalt's company back to my room. "I know. It's just...after three days of unconsciousness, I missed you."

"How could you miss me if you weren't even awake?"

I shrug, then watch her out of the corner of my eye. A dainty smile pulls at my sister's lips while her free hand contentedly lifts and swishes the hem of her blue skirts, as if she's moments from spinning into a twirling dance. "Are you actually looking forward to spending time with Aspen?"

"He isn't as awful as you make him out to be, Evie." I'm surprised at the defensiveness in her tone. "You shouldn't be so quick to judge. You'd like him if you gave him a chance."

I slow our steps and gently turn Amelie to face me. "I didn't mean it like that, I swear. I'm merely curious how you feel. Do you like him then?"

She smiles. "He's boring, but he's not bad."

Not bad. That doesn't sound like something one would say about a lover.

Unless she's trying to hide that she's in love with him. But what would be the point? Surely, she'd know I'd be happy for her if I knew there was love involved. Wouldn't she? "Ami, tell me honestly. Are you in love with Aspen?"

The smile still plays at her lips, but she turns away from me and continues her slow steps down the hall. Again, she swishes the hem of her dress and spins in a circle. "Wouldn't it be for the best if we loved the men we were to marry? If we could find happiness in the best possible way?" Her voice is light, whimsical. Heavy with the adoration she's trying to suppress.

I catch up to her, tugging on the sleeve of her gown until she stops and faces me again. "Yes, I agree with you. And I know you're hiding your true feelings from me." She opens her mouth, but I continue before she can deny it. "I understand why. You feel like I've been judging you, underestimating you. Criticizing this place that you've already come to love. I need you to know that, while I may not trust Faerwyvae, or the king, or the creatures here, I trust you. Whatever brings you love and joy, I support it. You know that right?"

Tears well in my sister's eyes, and her face crumples. She reaches for me, pulling me into a tight embrace. "That means so much to me, Evie. You have no idea how much."

The longer we remain locked in the hug, the more ease I feel. The tension melts out of me, the warmth of my sister's arms like a blanket.

When we finally pull away, Amelie grins. "Everything is going to work out perfectly for both of us, I promise. You'll see." Her tone seems conspiratorial, but perhaps I'm imagining it. Before I can analyze further, she links her arm with mine and pulls me down the hall, a spring in her step. "Then when we're married, we'll have to compare notes. See whose *kingdom* really is bigger."

A burst of laughter escapes my lips, and we take turns hushing each other as we make our way down the quiet hall. We're still giggling when we reach a closed door flanked by guards. My heart sinks as Amelie pauses before it. This must be Aspen's study.

"Time for me to go," she says as she faces me. "I'm glad we talked."

I reach for her hand and squeeze it. "Me too."

As if he could sense our presence, the door sweeps open, revealing Aspen. He barely looks at us before he turns away and takes a seat behind a large, ornate desk, leaving the door open between us. "Come in," he says.

Amelie gives my hand a final squeeze, then enters the room. I watch as she takes a seat in a throne-like chair opposite his desk, next to a table laden with plates of chocolate and a decanter of wine. She squeals with delight as she pops a truffle into her mouth.

I'm about to remind her to salt the chocolates when Aspen's drawling voice startles me. "You may go. Unless you'd prefer to stay, of course."

I meet his eyes, finding that dangerous glint, that half-smirk. A blush creeps up my cheeks as I realize the absurdity of me hovering in his doorway, an uninvited onlooker on his private time with his betrothed. I tear my eyes away from his to light on my sister. She gives me a reassuring smile.

I barely turn away before I hear the door close behind me.

WHEN I RETURN TO MY ROOM, I CAN'T FIGURE OUT WHAT TO DO WITH MYSELF. I pace the length of the room, trying to occupy myself from thoughts of Amelie and Aspen. As much as I meant what I said to Amelie about supporting her, I can't shake my suspicion of the king. I can't fight the way my skin crawls when I think about the two of them as lovers. There's something so wrong about the pairing, although I can't say exactly what or why. Is it just because I know Aspen is dangerous? Or is it something else? Some fact I'm forgetting?

My door opens and I jump, startled from my thoughts. Lorelei enters and gives me a half-hearted curtsy. "I came to see if you needed help dressing for bed. I assume you don't, but—"

"Yes," I say, surprising myself. I'm eager not to be alone with my thoughts right now. Not to mention, I may be able to probe the fae for information.

Lorelei looks equally as surprised. "Very well. I'll find you a nightdress."

She goes to the wardrobe while I take my place behind the dressing screen. I quickly remove the belted dagger from my thigh and slip off my gown. I'm in the middle of hiding the dagger beneath the discarded dress when Lorelei approaches.

She pauses, studying me, then raises a brow at the heap of dress at my feet. "You don't need to hide it. Everyone knows you carry it. Same with your sister."

The blood leaves my face. "Oh?"

She hands me a nightdress in a blush-pink lace. "I mean, did you think we can't smell the iron on you? Besides, you weren't hiding much when Prince Cobalt carried you in from the ocean. The dagger around your thigh is no longer a secret, if it ever was before."

I pull the nightdress over my head to avoid meeting her gaze. "And you say everyone knows? That we carry blades among your kind?"

"Sure. Yet, the king doesn't seem to hold it against you. Which is surprising, considering his history."

"You mean his temper?"

"No, I mean the threats to his life."

I furrow my brow. "Do you really believe the last girls tried to kill him unprovoked?"

She shrugs, arms crossed. "I believe humans can be dangerous. I can say that from personal experience." The bite in her tone reminds me of the confrontation we had over Mr. Osterman. Lorelei may have become friendly with my sister, but there's still a chasm between us. The fae turns away. "Will that be all?"

She doesn't wait for me to answer before she begins to head toward the door, each step slightly uneven from her limp.

"Wait," I say as she reaches the door.

She pauses, then turns to face me.

I hesitate before rushing to ask, "Can I look at your leg?" She narrows her eyes at me, and I rush to add, "I'm a surgeon's apprentice. Well, I *was*, at least. I can't help but want to check on your leg and make sure it's healing well."

Lorelei doesn't move. "It's healing."

"I know, but...can I check on it? Please?"

Her expression softens, and she lets out a sigh. "Fine. What do I do?"

"Go ahead and lie on the bed." As she does so, I retrieve my surgery kit.

"What is that?" Lorelei sits upright, eyes on the kit as I make my way toward her.

"It's my surgery tools, although I doubt I'll need them. It just helps me feel more professional to have it by my side."

Her eyes go wide. "Don't you dare use them on me. I can smell the iron from here."

"I won't then." I push the kit away from me, and Lorelei settles back on the bed. A question I've had hovers in my mind, and I try to find a tactful way to ask it without making her suspicious. "My tools are carbon steel, an iron alloy. Is such a metal harmful to fae?"

"Normally only pure iron is lethal to us, especially if it maintains contact with our flesh for too long, but any iron injury weakens us until we fully heal, making even weaker human metals unbearable to touch." She lifts her head and eyes me with a scowl. "Don't get any ideas."

I kneel at the side of the bed next to her and adopt my most soothing bedside manner. "I won't hurt you."

Lorelei lets out a resigned grumble as she lifts the hem of her silky bronze dress to reveal the injured leg. My stomach churns to see her battered flesh again, to see the pink, puckered skin where iron teeth had torn it to shreds. I inspect every inch of the leg, looking for signs of infection. Although, I'm not entirely sure what to look for, aside from what I'm used to seeing in humans; I have no idea what to expect from fae infection.

Next, I gently prod the skin in places, asking Lorelei to tell me if anything feels tender. There are a few painful areas, but for the most part, her leg appears to be on the mend. Her bones seem to be set correctly. I'm almost certain I detect stitches in places, although they look nothing like the stitches I've seen. Hers are fine and delicate, weaving the skin together with little evidence of intervention.

"Who tended your wounds?" I ask.

She turns her head to face me. "I did some on my own. As a wood nymph, I was able to speak to the vines and roots to brace my leg and hold my torn flesh together so I could make it to Bircharbor. Gildmar did the rest."

"Who's Gildmar?"

"She's an Earthen fae employed by the Autumn Court for healing. She cleansed my wounds with herbs and stitched the deepest ones with spider silk."

"It looks like she did well. I'm going to check your range of motion now." I lift her leg, easing her to bend slightly at the knee. "Does it hurt when you walk or put weight on the leg?"

"A little." Her words are still laced with a bitter edge. "Other things hurt more. Things no one can ever heal."

My stomach sinks. I rotate her ankle slightly one way then the other. "What was she like?"

She furrows her brow. "Who? Gildmar?"

"No. Your lover. The one you lost."

Her eyes turn to the ceiling, a blank expression on her face. The weight of her leg seems to grow heavier, as if the question drained all the strength from her. I think she might ignore me, until she finally says, "Malan was beautiful. A pixie from the Spring Court with wings as pink and fine as cherry blossom petals. Her hair was the same color, a silvery-pink that always smelled of roses." She sighs. "Malan was the best part of me. She kept me kind. Made me laugh. I loved her."

My throat feels tight as tears prick my eyes.

Lorelei lifts her head to meet my gaze. "Are you finished?"

Her tone isn't unkind but snaps me out of my daze. I realize I'd released her leg, my hands frozen and resting lightly on her shin. With a shake of my head to clear it, I rise to my feet. "Yes. I feel confident you will heal well. I see no sign of infection and your range of motion is what I'd expect at this point of recovery."

Lorelei stands, shifting her weight from one foot to the other. "You know, it actually feels much better." She lifts her gown, examining her leg. "It looks better too. What is it a surgeon does, anyway?"

I'm torn between laughing and maintaining my professional manner. She must have thought my actions were more than simple inspection. How can I explain I didn't do a thing to help her? That whatever ease she feels is nothing more than a placebo? "A surgeon usually operates on tissues and organs with tools like the ones I have in my kit."

She takes a few steps, then flashes me a smile—something I've rarely seen from her. "Well, whatever you did, it worked. It hardly hurts."

"Perhaps the stretching and motion exercises helped," I say, not wanting to lose her gratitude by telling her the truth. "See if you can continue gentle stretches daily to improve your overall flexibility."

"Sure. Uh, thank you for this." She wrings her hands, as if suddenly uncertain around me, then bites her lip. "I suppose I should apologize, shouldn't I?"

I tilt my head. "For what?"

She sighs. "I'm not sorry for what I did to the Butcher—to your friend. But I know it must have hurt you to see him in pain. That I'm sorry for. And for saying you were a self-righteous harpy with a mouth bigger than her brain."

"You never said that."

She waves a dismissive hand. "Not to you, of course."

My lips tug into a smile. First Foxglove, now Lorelei is beginning to seem charming too. "I'm sorry as well. I misjudged you. It's just...I haven't had the best experiences with the fae."

"I doubt either of our kind have had many positive interactions since the war."

I nod. "You're right. It's funny, though. I grew up with a sort of terrified reverence for your kind, instilled by my mother. I was fascinated with what little I knew about Faerwyvae, with the idea of magic, but then...something happened. It changed everything I thought I knew."

My throat feels tight as the memory seizes me. Perhaps it's my worry over Amelie being alone with Aspen, but I can't shake the images that flood my mind—my sister's face, eyes alight with mischief as we ran through the woods toward the faewall. It was a perfect summer night, aside from the presence of Maddie Coleman. It was her dare that brought us to the faewall that night four years ago and sent the three of us circling one of the stones to prove we were brave enough to cross the wall. We'd maintained contact with the stone the entire time, holding our breath as we circled it to the fae side, then burst into fits of laughter when we returned safely to the human side seconds later. Our laughter died when we turned to run back home and saw the fae that stood before us.

Lorelei wrings her hands again, and her voice comes out soft. "You can tell me about it. If you want to, that is."

I consider shaking my head, telling her it's nothing, but I stop myself. After the vulnerability she shared with me tonight, perhaps I can return the honesty. I take a deep breath. "Four years ago Amelie and I met a goblin, tiny and horrid with sharp fangs and wrinkled, sagging skin. There was no mistaking it was there to cause mischief. We were frozen, terrified and fascinated at the unusual sight. It seemed it was equally fascinated with us. Amelie, in particular. Its beady eyes locked on hers, and she stared right back. After a while, she forgot to blink."

I remember my horror when Amelie's face went slack, recall the glint in the goblin's eyes when he realized he had her under his control. That's when Maddie Coleman ran screaming, leaving Amelie and me alone with the creature.

"The goblin ordered Amelie to come toward him, and she did. He ordered her to put her hand out, and she did. She paid me no heed as I tugged at her arms, pulled at the sleeve of her coat. All she could do was walk toward the creature, hand outstretched toward his vicious mouth, a placid smile on her face all the while. When he lunged forward to sink his teeth into her palm, I threw a rock, hitting him between the eyes. That's when Amelie was able to return to herself. We ran, but he chased us, nipping at our heels and shouting after us, saying if he didn't get a taste, he'd make our insides rot."

"You got free, though," Lorelei says.

"Yes. I don't remember when we could no longer hear him following, when his teeth and claws ceased to graze our heels. By the time we got home, the backs of our dresses were torn to shreds, our voices incoherent as we told Mother what had happened. She could hardly make sense of what we were saying. We just kept repeating that a fae had attacked and cursed us. All she could do was give comfort, tell us we were safe. Then later that night, Amelie collapsed, writhing in pain. She began vomiting, grasping her belly. She was certain the goblin's curse was coming to take her, insides rotting just like he said. Mother tried to break the curse using tinctures and counter-charms. We stayed up all night while she chanted over my sister, trying to purge the curse from her."

"Your mother is like you then?" Lorelei asks.

I shake my head. "No. My mother's craft is nothing like surgery, and surgery was what Amelie needed. It turns out, she wasn't plagued by a curse after all but a very serious medical condition. We only discovered this because I was stupid enough to try to return to the wall the next morning. I wanted to seek out the goblin, beg him to lift the curse from my sister. If that didn't work, I was prepared to offer myself in her stead. I couldn't bear to see my sister in pain and would rather die than lose her."

"What happened? Did you find the goblin?"

"No. Luckily, I was intercepted by Mr. Meeks, Sableton's surgeon. He saw me in distress heading toward the woods and made me tell him what was happening. Once I told him about Amelie, he insisted on seeing her. He raced home, got his surgery kit, then came to our house. That's when I learned the power of modern medicine and got to witness true healing. Amelie was never cursed. She was glamoured, yes, but what happened after was nothing more than a coincidence. My sister had developed appendicitis. If Mr. Meeks hadn't intervened, her appendix would have ruptured, and Amelie would have died."

Lorelei's eyes are wide. "I have no idea what an appendix is, but it sounds terrible."

Her statement shatters my somber mood, and I find myself laughing. She laughs with me, although it's clear from her expression that she isn't sure what we're laughing about. Once I begin to sober, I let out a heavy sigh. "Thank you for listening, Lorelei. That's not a story I like to tell, but oddly enough, it feels good to have told someone."

She smiles. "I think that's what a lady's maid is for, right?"

"Listening to me ramble on about my adolescence goes above and beyond the duties of a lady's maid." If I were ready to admit it, I'd say it falls into the realm of friendship.

"I never thought I'd hear that high praise from you," she says. "Is there anything else you need from me tonight?"

"No, go ahead and retire. I'll wait for Amelie to return."

"Very well." She offers a curtsy—one deeper than any she'd given me before—then leaves the room.

Once I'm alone, my eyes begin to grow heavy, muscles pulling with fatigue as if I really had performed a surgery. Or perhaps it's from the story I told. With slow steps, I retrieve my dagger from behind the dressing screen and stuff it beneath my pillow before crawling under the covers.

I'm determined to stay awake until Amelie returns. Then again, what if my suspicions are correct, and she's been sleeping elsewhere? Will she stay the night with Aspen?

The question makes my blood boil, but it quickly fades as sleep overtakes me.

In the night, I dream.

A dark figure looms over me, teeth sharp and glinting with moonlight as a snarl pulls at his lips. He lowers his face until it's hovering mere inches from mine. His chest heaves with anger.

It isn't a dream.

I reach for my dagger, hilt in hand and blade at the figure's throat. He pays me no heed as Aspen's voice growls, words rumbling with rage, "Where is your sister?"

19

____

His words echo through my mind. *Where is your sister?*

The question takes me by surprise, making my dagger hilt tremble in my fingers. Aspen's warm, wine-scented breath on my face brings me back to myself, reminding me of his proximity. As my eyes adjust to the moonlit dark, his shadowy features take shape in front of me. I press the blade to his throat, letting its edge break the skin. "Get. Off. Me."

He jolts back, wincing from the searing iron as I spring from the bed, keeping the dagger between us as I back up a few paces. It only deters Aspen a moment. He bounds toward me, and I retreat until I find my back pressed against a wall. Nothing but my dagger separates us as he closes the distance, the tip of my blade pressed to his sternum. With one thrust, I could have it buried in his chest.

Aspen doesn't seem to care. "Where is your sister?" he repeats.

I push his chest with my free hand, trying to force him back. It does nothing but shift the cloth of his shirt. "Why are you asking me? She was with you, you fool. Don't act like I didn't leave her in your study."

His chest heaves with rage. "She isn't there anymore. Where did she go?"

I narrow my eyes at him. "What, did she disappear into thin air?"

"No," he growls. "I left for only a few minutes. When I returned, she was gone."

"Gone? How is that—" My eyes widen, and I thrust the dagger tip forward. He winces and springs back a few inches. This time I'm the one closing the distance, forcing his retreat as anger heats my blood. My voice comes out with a snarl that could almost match his. "What did you do to her?"

"What did *I* do? Me?" His fingers lock around my wrist before I can prick him with my blade again. "I did nothing."

"Nothing?" I slam his chest again with my free hand. "Why else would she run away at the first chance? You did something to her. What did you do?"

"So, you admit she ran away."

My mouth hangs open. I struggle to free myself from his grip, but his fingers don't budge, suspending my wrist and dagger in midair. "Running away is the only logical conclusion based on what you've told me," I say through my teeth as I continue to struggle in vain.

"Where did she go?"

"I don't know."

"You're lying. You're in on it too. What are you planning? Aside from trying to kill me with this pathetic blade?" He turns my wrist, forcing my fingers to open. The dagger clatters to the floor, and he kicks it away.

I hold my ground, crossing my arms over my chest. "If I was trying to kill you, I would have slashed my blade through your throat when I had the chance. Besides, if one of us is lying, it's you."

He fixes me with a seething glare. "I can't lie."

"Then I suppose we're at an impasse, because I'm not lying either. What will you do next? Execute me for treason?"

Aspen holds me with a glower for what feels like an eternity. Finally, his breathing begins to steady, the heaving of his chest subsiding. He takes a step away but doesn't tear his eyes from mine. With a snap of his fingers, a warm light illuminates above the sconces in my room, bringing him into clear view. I try not to wonder at how the light could have responded to him like that, and instead take in his appearance. His hair is disheveled, and a thin, red line runs across his throat. It looks like dried blood, the superficial wound I gave him likely already healed beneath it. "You don't know where your sister is?"

"No. Like I said, last time I saw her, she was with you."

"She was there," he says, voice still much like a growl. "We spoke for a time until she requested more wine. I ordered some to be brought up, but the idiot servant brought honey pyrus wine. You, of all people, should know why that could have been disastrous. Still, she seemed as content as ever when I left to exchange it. When I returned, she was gone."

Wine. A servant. Could it be? What if I'd gotten our earlier conversation wrong? What if Amelie wasn't in love with Aspen after all? Would she do something so foolish as to run away with a handsome servant? Then again, perhaps it was a matter of Aspen catching a lingering glance between the two, igniting his jealousy. This entire confrontation could be a ruse to cover something far more devious. "Who brought the wine? Was it the same servant you used during your earlier visits with Amelie?"

"What does that have to do with anything?"

"Answer the question."

He runs his hands through the blue-black hair between his antlers. "I don't know. I have a lot of servants."

I squint at him, trying to decipher if there's deception beneath his words. I proceed with caution. "Did something else happen? When the servant brought wine? Did you...see something you didn't like?"

He tips his head back. "What is that supposed to mean?"

Footsteps sound in the hall outside my room. Aspen whirls around as several guards march in. One approaches Aspen. "Your Majesty," she says as she gives him a hurried bow, "someone was seen running toward the coral caves."

"When?" barks Aspen.

"Just now."

The caves. I'm too stunned to comprehend what this could mean. Was Amelie running away? *Truly* running away? She would have to be terrified out of her wits to do something as reckless as that. To leave me behind. My rage returns hotter than ever. "What did you do to her?"

Aspen ignores me. "Send guards after her."

The guard nods. "I've already dispatched some, Your Majesty, but the tide is already coming in. She won't make it long in there, nor will the guards."

He gives the fae a withering look, and his voice comes out cold. "Send guards to search every cave. I want the water up to their chins before a single one tries to return. And after that, I want guards stationed on the beach. If you don't find her alive, I want her body retrieved when it washes ashore."

The guard salutes and leaves my room, while I bristle at the carelessness of his words. "You're a monster."

He rounds on me. "I'm not the fool who ran into the caves. And if I find out you have anything to do with this, I'll throw you in the ocean after her." With that, he storms out of my room. I race after him, but before I reach my door, he shouts at the other guards who had remained in the hall. "Don't let her leave her room."

I halt as the fae guards bar my path. One reaches forward to slam my door shut. I'm left gaping, heart racing. What in the blazing iron is happening? All I can think of is my sister, running for the caves. Running from terror. From Aspen.

I channel my rage into beating my door with my fist, begging the guards to let me out. It doesn't matter that the action is fruitless. I must do something—*anything*—with my body to keep myself angry. Because if I'm not angry, I'll be anxious. Terrified. I'll lose my mind.

Hours pass, the light of dawn breaking through my windows, yet I continue to shout and throw my weight at the door. My voice is raw, shoulders and hands throbbing, by the time the handle begins to turn. I'm so shocked, I barely have time to move out of the way before the door swings open. Cobalt's eyes lock on mine, and before I realize what's happening, he pulls me into his arms. I hardly register the fact that I'm crying into his chest, my entire body racked with sobs.

He brushes a hand along my back, smoothing my hair. "Let's get you out of here," he whispers.

"Here's her cloak," says a voice behind me. Lorelei. She drapes the heavy fabric over my shoulders, and I pull it tight around me. That's when I remember I'm in nothing more than my nightdress. Cobalt rests his hand on my lower back and guides me out of the room. When we reach the hall, the guards are nowhere to be seen.

"I sent them on a false errand," he says. "I can't believe my brother locked you in your room when your sister is missing. That was cruel, and I'm sorry."

"He was only being cautious," Lorelei says from the other side of me, "but I agree. It wasn't the right thing to do in this situation."

I'm lost in a daze as we move through the halls of the palace. "Where are we going?"

"I don't know," Cobalt admits. "I just wanted to get you out of your room. I knew you'd be worried sick. I can take you to my room, if that makes you feel more comfortable."

Someone rounds a corner at the end of the hall, then begins racing toward us. As the figure closes the distance, I realize it's Foxglove. "They found someone," he says breathlessly.

The words make me alert, clearing the fog from my brain. "Where? Is it my sister? Is she all right?"

Foxglove wrings his hands. "They're bringing her from the caves now."

"Take me to the shore," I demand.

"My brother has the lower part of the palace heavily guarded," Cobalt says.

I face him. "I need to see her."

He holds my gaze. "You might not like what you see."

I don't want to consider what he means by that. Instead, I grit my teeth. "I don't care."

"The dining room," Lorelei says. She takes off down the hall, and I follow. Up the stairs we climb until we reach our destination. I rush to the other side of the dining room to the rail at the edge of the open expanse. There, beneath the dim light of the rising sun, I see the narrow sliver of beach, crawling with guards. The rest is hidden by the tide, revealing only the slightest hint of a cave as the crashing waves recede.

I hardly blink as I watch every movement of every guard, seeking any sign of my sister.

Foxglove gasps, then points toward the beach. "The cave. Look."

I watch as the rolling waves pull away from the shore, revealing movement at the mouth of the only visible cave. A guard pulls himself from the opening just as another wave crashes into him. He holds his ground until the water pulls away, then he reaches into the opening. His arms wrap around something that he hoists forward, a blur of white and blue. Another figure emerges from the entrance, pushing the bulk of their burden to the shore. Once the two guards are free from the cave, several more follow, all dripping seawater.

The first two guards reach for the bundle they'd pulled ashore. One lifts a set of pale arms. The other hoists up her legs. A third spreads a thin, blue fabric—what remains of a tattered dress—over her body like a shroud, covering even her face. What I can see of her hair looks nothing more than a mass of dark tangles, heavy with water and kelp. Still, I know it's her.

It's my sister.

She's dead.

My scream splits the air.

20

My feet fly beneath me as I tear across the dining room floor and down the stairs. I follow twists and turns, descending more stairs, taking any path that seems to lead me farther down in the palace. Shouts of caution follow me, but I ignore them. Ignore Cobalt as he takes hold of my arm and tries to make me stop.

I shake my arm from his grasp. "Let me go!"

He obeys but sticks close to my side as I take off running again. "My brother won't let you down there. As soon as he sees you, he'll lock you in your room again."

"I have to see her. I have to see my sister."

"There's nothing to see, Evelyn."

A fiery rage boils my veins, and I round on him. "Nothing to see? That was her body they pulled from the caves! How is that *nothing to see?*"

He opens and closes his mouth a few times. "It's just...why would you want to see that up close? You know she's...dead, right?"

His words drain the fight from me. The blood leaves my face, sending a wave of dizziness through my skull. I collapse to my knees, head hanging as tears obscure my vision. It's not that I didn't already know, but hearing him say it shatters all that remains of my feeble hope. "No. This can't be. She can't be gone."

Cobalt crouches next to me and places a hand on my shoulder. "I'm so sorry, Evelyn."

"Did he do it?" My voice comes out small. "Did Aspen have her killed when she was found? Or did she drown?"

He shakes his head. "I don't know. He's capable of anything, and if he finds you here, he'll have you sent back to your room. Or worse."

I wipe the tears from my cheeks and force myself to my feet, willing my mind to push emotion aside and find logic instead. I steady my expression beneath my surgeon's calm. "I still need to see her." At the horrified look on Cobalt's face, I add, "It's a human thing. We identify our dead."

"You know my brother won't let you see her right now. In fact, we need to get you higher in the palace before he—"

Footsteps sound down the hall, and before I can so much as think, Aspen rounds the corner, followed by a retinue of guards. He freezes when he sees me and Cobalt. "What is she doing here?"

With a deep breath, I square my shoulders and face him. "Where is she? My sister? What did you do with her body?"

A flash of surprise crosses his face. "You know about the body?"

"I saw her."

He takes a few steps toward me. "Did you, now?"

"I have a right to identify her body. Take me to her."

"You said you already saw her. Does that not qualify as identifying her?"

I stumble to find my reply. "It's—no, I—"

He turns to his guards, motions at a pair to his left. "Take her back to her room and make sure she stays inside this time. The Council of Eleven Courts will be here any moment."

The two guards surge forward, but I don't balk or argue or run. I simply burn Aspen with a hateful glare, then turn on my heel and begin walking in the opposite direction. I pay the guards no heed when they catch up.

"Don't touch her," Cobalt barks, when one tries to grab hold of me. "You may follow my brother's orders and accompany us, but I'll be walking her back to her room." Cobalt puts a hand on my lower back, his touch a steady guide as we make our way through the halls.

Only when I'm alone in my room do I let myself fall apart.

A DAY PASSES, THEN A NIGHT. I DON'T SLEEP AND I DON'T RECEIVE ANY visitors. I refuse the trays of food the guards push inside my door, letting the uneaten plates pile up on the floor. When morning breaks, my well of tears is fully dry and my sensible side tugs me back to reality.

My sister is gone. Dead. And there's nothing I can do to bring her back.

I'm tired.

I need to eat.

With shuffling feet, I cross the floor from the bed to the door, where the leftover food remains untouched. On my way, I find my dagger, lying useless on the floor where it landed after Aspen kicked it away. I retrieve it, then investigate the plates of food, finding a roll of bread as the only appetizing feature. I bite into it, not even caring that I haven't salted it. Luckily, the bread appears harmless, as it does nothing more than slightly quell the aching hunger in my stomach.

A knock sounds on my door, making me jump. Lorelei peeks inside, then enters, closing the door behind her. She meets my eyes with a look of apology. "Are you all right?"

I puzzle over the question before I answer. "I guess so," I lie. In truth, I'm not even close to all right. But she probably knows that.

"You are requested at breakfast," she says.

I set down the bread roll. "Just like that, my appetite is gone."

"I'm so sorry. I know the king is the last person you want to see right now, but his temper has calmed regarding you. By now he must realize you had nothing to do with your sister's disappearance."

"Yes, but how do I know *he* had nothing to do with it?" I mutter.

"He couldn't have wanted things to turn out the way they did," Lorelei says. "After every Reaping, the hosting court of the Chosen is put under deep scrutiny. The month leading up to the wedding that secures the treaty is a precarious time. Whatever happens between the hosting court and the Chosen is the difference between peace and war. You must see these mishaps have done nothing to benefit the king. They only make the council question his competence as a ruler. He could lose his throne if they find him unfit. Do you think he wants that?"

"Perhaps that's for the best."

Lorelei bites her lip before replying. "You know, he isn't so bad as you think he is."

I let out a bitter laugh. "Amelie said the same thing. And she's now dead."

"Fair enough," she says with a sigh. "I can't sway your opinion, especially when your loss is so raw. I, more than anyone, can understand that. But you must go to breakfast. Follow his summons. For now."

I meet her eyes. "What do you mean by that?"

She shrugs. "The council left at first light. That means they came to some conclusion about the treaty. For all you know, what happened with your sister could have broken it. Aspen could have been forced to step down. You might even be sent home."

Sent home. Relief washes over me, then terror. How can I return home without Amelie? How can I face my mother and tell her what happened? Something else tickles at my mind. "Wait. If the treaty is broken, wouldn't that mean war?"

She nods solemnly. "Yes."

I'm struck with a sudden resolve to know the truth. If there is to be war, I don't want to linger here any longer than necessary. Beyond that...I don't even want to think about it. "Fine, I'll go."

Once I'm bathed and dressed, Lorelei leads me to breakfast. I'm surprised to find it held in a smaller dining room, one I've never been to before. Whatever the reasoning for the change, I'm grateful for it. I don't think I could look at that open expanse in the formal dining room without remembering my sister's body. Not today.

Aspen hardly glances my way as I enter and take a seat at the small table, while Cobalt offers me a sad smile. The two brothers are already eating, and a plate of food has been laid out for me next to a bowl of salt. Once I salt my food, I push the items around the plate, but can't seem to bring any to my lips.

"I'm sorry about your sister."

I'm shocked to hear the words uttered from Aspen's end of the table. I look at him, but his eyes are on his food. My mouth feels too dry to respond.

"I shouldn't have locked you in your room either," he says. His words are strained, like it pains him greatly to admit his fault.

"No, you shouldn't have," I say. My voice comes out weak, but my anger is helping clear my mind from its daze. "Are you going to let me see her body?"

He takes his time chewing his food before answering. "No."

"Then your apology is wasted on me."

Silence falls over the table again, my scorn hanging over our heads like a shroud. I can feel Aspen's anger rolling in waves, but I try to pretend I don't notice.

Cobalt leans toward me, his voice low. "You should eat. The guards say you haven't touched the food that was brought to you."

I open my mouth to reply, but Aspen's voice halts my words. "Maybe she'd prefer wine," he says. With a snap of his fingers, a servant steps forward, decanter in hand.

My eyes jolt to the face of the servant, expecting to find the handsome male, but this one is unfamiliar to me.

"In fact," Aspen says, "all servants who have served me or any of my guests wine since the Fairfield girls arrived, please step forward."

The servants exchange hesitant glances. Then, one by one, several step forward from their places along the walls. I eye them all, then meet Aspen's penetrating gaze.

"Do any of these servants spark recognition?" he asks.

I'm about to say no, when I think I see the handsome one I remember from the other day. He shifts anxiously from foot to foot. "I don't understand," I say. "Why are you asking me this?"

Aspen narrows his eyes, fingertips steepled together as he leans back in his chair. "You seemed to suspect one of these servants after your sister went missing. Since you never explained yourself, I've come to suspect them too. Why did you ask me about a wine servant? About seeing something I didn't like?"

My mind goes blank as I seek an explanation. What can I say that won't condemn me or any innocent person? I have no idea if my suspicions are valid in the first place. Besides, it's *him* I'm more wary of.

I take a breath to calm myself, then meet his gaze. Two can play at this game. "You mistake me, Your Majesty. It wasn't your servants I suspected, but you."

A flicker of surprise crosses his face before he steels his expression. "Explain."

"Well, you see, I only brought it up because I thought perhaps you were a jealous male. There are many handsome fae here in the palace, but none could match the beauty of my sister. It made me wonder if you disliked the way they looked at her."

"You specified a wine servant. Why?"

I lift my shoulder in a casual shrug. "They seem to me more beautiful than the rest, that's all. If I were a jealous male, I might feel inadequate around them, king or no. And clearly," I wave my hand toward the servants around us, "they have you riled up indeed."

His knuckles go white as his fingers curl into fists. Perhaps I went too far. "Guards," he growls. Fae guards enter the room from the hall, bronze armor glistening in the light of the morning sun. "Take these servants to the dungeon. Execute them."

The guards surge forward to obey, and I leap to my feet. "What? Why?"

Cobalt stands as well. "This is absurd, brother. What did they do wrong?"

He says nothing as the servants are taken hold by the guards.

The horror on the servants' faces makes my stomach churn, heart racing as I watch their arms wrenched behind their backs as the guards shove them forward. I don't know why I should care. These fae are nothing to me. Yet, for some reason, I *do* care. The servants are likely innocent and are only being condemned because of something I said.

Before I have time to consider my actions, I'm rounding the table to approach the king. I place my hands on the tabletop as I lean toward him, lowering my voice to a furious whisper. "I'll admit, I suspected Amelie was in love with someone. I hoped it was you, but part of me wondered if she had feelings for someone else. Now that she's gone, we may never know. However, the truth remains that I was never worried one of these men would do her harm, but that *you* would. If you execute them all, it proves you have something to hide."

His lips return to their twisted smirk. "You want me to show them mercy, do you?"

"Yes," I say through my teeth.

He holds my gaze a moment longer. "Did you hear that?" His voice echoes through the room, stopping the guards in their tracks, freezing their attempts to funnel their prisoners into the hall. "Miss Fairfield requests mercy."

Silence answers. No one moves.

He returns his eyes to meet mine. "Fine. I'll heed your advice. I'll show them mercy. Considering you'll soon be their queen, I'll allow this choice to be yours."

His words send a wave of confusion through me. Their *queen*? Me?

He addresses the guards. "Take them to the dungeon for questioning only. At sunset tonight, release them and allow them to return to their stations."

Sighs of relief escape the prisoners, and the guards leave with them. The tension eases out of the room, yet I remain in place next to Aspen. Finally, I discover my words. "What did you mean about me becoming their queen?"

He smiles a devious grin, making my stomach drop. I know what he's going to say. "You're going to be my wife."

21

"No!" Cobalt and I shout at once.

Aspen seems unperturbed by our outbursts and returns to his meal, fork in hand. After taking a few bites, he says, "It's what the council thinks is best for the treaty to remain valid. A marriage must still take place."

"Then Evelyn can marry *me*," Cobalt says. "There's nothing in the treaty that says who the marriage should be made to, only that it is made to a fae of the hosting court."

Aspen fixes his brother with an indignant stare. "Yet, I am king, so I decide who she marries."

Cobalt's shoulders heave, and I expect him to shout. Instead, he lets out a growl of frustration and storms from the room.

"You get your way yet again." My voice is quiet, filled with iron. "Another potential bride. Another waiting victim. Another way to punish me."

He throws his fork down, letting it clatter on his plate. "If I wanted to punish you, I *wouldn't* marry you. Is that what you want? For the treaty to become invalidated? For war to rage over the isle? For every person you love to die?"

"You could allow me to marry Cobalt instead. The treaty would remain valid."

"I could," he says, face smug, "but I won't."

My fingers curl into fists, nails digging into my palms. "You have no claim to me just because you're king. I am not a thing to be owned."

He closes his eyes and rubs his temples with a groan, as if I'm the impossible one. His words come out strained through his clenched teeth. "I'm starting to believe war wouldn't be the worst idea. All I do is maintain the safety of the isle, yet I'm repaid with treason at every turn."

"Treason? You're out of your mind! No one is committing treason against you. If you had any sense at all, you'd see the real terror to the isle is you."

He rolls his eyes. "I don't care what you think of me. The choice is yours. Either you marry me, or the Fair Isle reverts to war. I'm getting tired of caring one way or another. What's it going to be?"

Fury roars through me, making my limbs tremble with rage. "I hate you."

His face twists into something between a glower and a menacing smile. "So much that you can't fathom marrying me for the sake of your people?"

I lean toward him. "So much that I will carve out your heart if you try to take me to your bed. I'll marry you. I'll sign the contract. But don't think for a moment we'll be anything more than cold allies."

His expression doesn't falter as he brings his face closer to mine. "So you accept my proposal?"

I hate the way my eyes are drawn to his mouth, the way he drags his tongue over his bottom lip, as if he's savoring the anger radiating off my skin. I want to shout at him, to slap the smug look off his face as his eyes rove over me, claiming me.

But I'll never be his.

With some effort, I push away from the table, away from him. Even when I turn away, I can still feel his eyes burning into me.

THE COOLNESS OF THE HALL OUTSIDE THE DINING ROOM IS A WELCOME comfort. I didn't realize until now how warm I'd become. Sweat drips down my neck and beads at my forehead. I quicken my pace, not quite knowing where I'm going. My only thought is to widen the distance between me and Aspen, to forget his words, to shake his face from my mind.

I don't even see the pair of arms that reach for me from the shadows of the hall. With a squeal, I leap back and draw my dagger, only to realize it's Cobalt.

"I didn't mean to startle you," he says, palms forward in surrender as his eyes dart from me to the dagger.

"It's all right," I say, releasing a heavy sigh and returning my blade to its sheath beneath my skirts. "What are you doing here, anyway?"

"I came out here to cool my rage, then decided to wait for you. We need to speak in private."

I nod, and he takes my hand. We move quickly down the hall until he pulls me into a room and closes the door. The room is small, curtains drawn shut, revealing mostly shadows and a few sparse furnishings.

"It's an unused parlor," Cobalt explains. "Used to be my mother's. Don't sit on anything. It hasn't been dusted in years."

I make no move to contradict his request, and we remain by the door. "What did you want to talk to me about?"

He takes my hands in his. When he meets my eyes, his expression falls. "I'm so sorry about all of this. I can't imagine how you must feel right now."

After my confrontation with Aspen, I only feel numb. "I don't think I've had enough time to process it all. I don't know how to feel or what to do."

"I still can't believe he'd do this. I know exactly why he's doing it too. He can't stand the idea of looking weak next to me, of the advantage it would give me if I were the one to secure the treaty with a marriage instead of him." He gives my hands a squeeze, expression pained. "He can't take you from me."

"Apparently, he can do whatever he wants." My voice is cold, bitter.

His hands move to my shoulders, bringing me closer to him. I can feel the coolness of his palms through the fabric of my dress. He lowers his voice. "Not if we act first."

"What do you mean? What could we possibly do?"

"We could leave together," he says, tone pitched with a blossoming excitement. "Perform the mate ceremony, then get married in secret. Our marriage would keep the treaty intact."

"But your brother," I argue. "He would never let us live after such a betrayal."

"We could fight him. We'd find no shortage of allies who would stand against him. I already told you how the council feels. They don't want him on the throne if he keeps acting this way."

For a moment, I let the fantasy take hold, let the idea weave images through my mind. I imagine me and Cobalt running away together, imagine us rising against Aspen, watching the council pull the throne out from beneath him. I think of a court ruled by Cobalt, gentle, kind, and fair. I think of the peace his steadfast nature would bring his people and mine. It's a beautiful fantasy, but I know it's just that. A fantasy. Cobalt may be able to gather allies, but is that enough to beat Aspen without getting himself killed in the process? And what about me? There's no fight left in my bones. Not after what happened to Amelie. Not after the hateful words spoken between me and Aspen.

"No," I say, my voice barely above a whisper. Slowly, I reach my hands to cover his, then pull them away from my shoulders. I give his hands a gentle squeeze, enjoying the coolness of his fingers, before I release them and take a step back. "I can't put you in danger."

"I don't care about the danger. I care about protecting you."

I offer him a sad smile, then pat the dagger at my thigh. "I'm not vulnerable."

"But I care about you."

My throat tightens. "If we care about each other at all, the best thing we can do is protect each other from Aspen's wrath. You may not care about the risk, but I do. I won't be able to live with myself if Aspen tries to hurt you. In fact," I take another step away from him until my back is against the door, "this is the last time we can meet like this. I won't do anything that rouses Aspen's suspicion against you. You saw what he nearly did to the servants."

He looks down at his feet, shoulders slumped. When he lifts his head, his expression sends shards of glass into my heart. "This is really what you want?"

I nod, then reach behind me for the handle.

"My feelings won't change." His voice breaks on the last word. "I'll do what I can to protect you, even if you become his wife."

"Thank you," I say, then open the door. I'm about to step into the hall when Cobalt stops me with a word.

"Wait."

Our eyes lock, and he closes the distance between us, hands framing my face. His lips find mine and press them into a firm kiss. It happens so fast, I can hardly comprehend it, much less enjoy it. I'm too stunned to move. If I were Amelie, I'd put my arms around his waist, pull him close to me, part my lips to allow the kiss to deepen.

But I'm not Amelie.

Thoughts of my sister drain me of all potential passion, making my shoulders go rigid. Cobalt must be able to tell, because he gently pulls away. "I'm sorry," he says. "I just had to do that once."

"I—I'm glad you did." *It might be the last kiss I'll ever have,* I think to myself.

"Also...there's something you should know. It's about the mate ceremony."

The worry in his eyes sends a chill down my spine. "What is it?"

"Aspen still plans to go through with the mate ceremony as previously scheduled, which will be in four days' time. Afterward, you'll be expected to participate in a fae ritual. You must refuse."

I remember what Foxglove had said about the mysterious ritual before we got sidetracked by talk of mating. It occurs to me I've yet to get a clear answer on what it involves. I furrow my brow. "Why?"

"Because it would mean giving my brother your true name."

My true name. *That's* what the fae sacred ritual is all about? My blood goes cold.

I've seen what a regular glamour nearly did to Amelie, but that's nothing compared to what a fae can do when he's been told he has your true name. Mr. Meeks says the hormone the fae release during prolonged eye contact is an unintentional function of their biology. Yet it's hypothesized that fae custom is the only thing preventing them from secreting the hormone purposefully and in greater quantity. The *true name* itself has no meaning. There's no secret name to utter, no chant to perform. It is but a statement that you are on a level of deepest intimacy, which to the fae, means they can do whatever they wish to you.

If Aspen had my true name, I'd be under his control with no free will of my own. My stomach churns at the thought.

"Promise me you won't do it."

"Trust me, I'll do whatever I can to avoid it." Even if it means my death, I don't add. Before he can say anything else to make me linger, I open the door and step into the hall. As I return to my room, all I can think about is Cobalt's crushed expression when I turned him down. I had no other choice. We'd never be able to survive Aspen's wrath.

I have to protect him. Protect Eisleigh.

I have to marry a monster.

22

———————

I count the days until the mate ceremony with numb awareness, stumbling in a daze, going through the motions. It feels like wading through mud, each day a struggle to get through. Most of the time, I try to turn off my emotions, following logic instead. Eat. Breathe. Do as I'm told.

Four.

I tolerate dress fittings with Lorelei, give half-hearted answers to Foxglove's questions about requested foods for the celebratory feast that follows the ceremony. He takes me through the steps of some strange dance I'm supposed to perform with the king. I learn it, memorize it, but I feel like I'm hardly there.

Three.

Foxglove says something about ribbons and masks. I nod, but the ribbons remind me too much of Amelie. She always loved pretty ribbons. I turn away from him to stare out the window for a while. That night I dream about seawater filling my lungs, of my sister calling my name as waves drag her into the coral caves.

Two.

When I wake, I force my pain to subside, put on my mask of calm. Try not to think of Amelie. More dress fittings. More masks and ribbons. Another round of practice for the dance.

One.

When the day arrives, I stand before my mirror, staring at the stranger in front of me. She wears my face, lips covered in a deep burgundy rouge, cheeks powdered a rosy blush. A russet-gold dusts my eyelids and lines my lower lashes, along with some rich browns and yellows. The makeup distracts from the dark circles I know lie beneath, and helps cover the ghostly pallor I've adopted as of late.

My eyes rove over my dress, a flowing gown of pale blue spider silk dotted with white pearls. The skirt is layered with a sheer fabric stitched with silk leaves in the same pale blue and flutters with every move I make. The colors on my face and dress bring to mind autumn leaves falling through a clear midday sky. To someone else, this would be a dream dress. To me, it's a nightmare.

It reminds me too much of a wedding gown.

Even though I know the mate ceremony isn't an actual wedding, it still makes my stomach churn. The way Foxglove explained it, the mate ceremony is a way for Aspen and me to present ourselves as a couple—*mates*. The first step in securing the alliance. The final step is our wedding ceremony. That will occur in just over two weeks.

I shudder.

"You look beautiful," Foxglove says, fixing a loose strand of auburn hair into place.

"He's right," Lorelei says. "There's no doubt you're the Queen of the Autumn Court."

Her words send a chill down my spine. Queen. I still haven't gotten used to the idea that I'm going to be a queen after we're married.

"Now for the final touches." Foxglove reaches for an elaborate mask from my dressing table and steps behind me to secure it over my eyes. It only covers the top portion of my face above my nose, but the embellishments adorning the top make the mask appear much larger than it is, creating a halo of robin feathers and golden leaves overhead. The mask itself is made of bronze, carved with elegant swirling patterns and decorated with pearls.

Next, Foxglove grabs a handful of long ribbons, motioning for me to raise my arms. He explained the ribbon part of the ceremony to me, but I'd only been half listening. Something about a ribbon representing each element, and how we'll have to untie them from each other. Foxglove ties the first—a red ribbon—around my hips, then a yellow one around my waist, a green one around my chest, and a blue one around my head and the mask. The bow of the final ribbon hangs slightly into my line of vision as it dangles from my brow.

"There," Foxglove says, admiring his work. He looks pleased, but I feel like a gaudy present as I look at my reflection.

"It's time," says a voice from the other side of my room. I find Cobalt hovering in my doorway. He wears a simple blue mask, lips pressed into a tight line. A pang of sadness tugs at my heart as I meet his gaze, but I quickly release it. I can't let myself consider regrets. No what-ifs. "Are you ready?" he asks.

"I suppose so," I say, trying to keep my voice neutral. I'm determined neither to fake joy nor reveal distress. I shall be calm. Composed.

Cobalt enters my room and meets me at the mirror. "I'll walk you," he says, extending his arm.

I hesitate, wondering if it's smart to walk with him. Then again, if Aspen didn't come to take me himself, perhaps he doesn't care. Without a second thought, I place my hand at his elbow and we leave my room. The halls are quiet and nearly empty, with most servants and guards congregating higher in the palace near the topmost balcony where the ceremony will take place.

Foxglove and Lorelei follow behind me and Cobalt as we make our way through the halls and up the stairs. We pass the landing that leads to the formal dining room, then climb another set of stairs even higher. Too soon, the sound of voices falls upon my ears. We come to the bottom of a final staircase that ends in bright sky overhead.

"I'll leave you here," Cobalt says, then leans in closer. With a shiver, I think he might steal a kiss, but his words whisper in my ear, "You remember what I told you? About the fae ritual?"

How could I forget? "Yes."

"You won't do it, right?"

I raise a brow. "Do I look crazy to you?"

"Well, you are about to become my brother's mate."

"Fair enough."

A shadow falls overhead, bringing my attention to the top of the stairs. I find a silhouette stark against the clear blue sky, a tall, lean frame with antlers. Even with Aspen's features obscured in shadow, I know he's glowering. But is it at me or his brother?

Cobalt all but leaps away from me, then proceeds up the stairs. As he reaches the top stair next to his brother, the two face each other. I can feel the tension between them until Cobalt turns ahead and continues out of sight.

Aspen faces me and extends his hand, like darkness itself beckoning me to join him.

"Go on," Foxglove says with a gentle touch on my shoulder.

With trembling steps, I make my way up the stairs, trying my best to keep my head held high. I'm momentarily blinded as I cross the threshold from the dim staircase to the open air of the balcony above. When my eyes adjust, I take in the wide platform opening before me. Its floor is of smooth citrine and the perimeter is lined with a golden rail. Two throne-like chairs perch on a raised dais at the far end, with a bronze silk rug leading to them from where I stand. On each side of this rug are nearly a dozen unfamiliar fae. Since the balcony is set at the pinnacle of one of the palace's highest towers, nothing but open sky surrounds us, giving way to views of distant hills colored in all shades of red, gold, and brown. The sound of crashing waves and crying gulls echo from far below.

It's the first time I've been here, and I must admit it's beautiful. For a moment, it's enough to make me forget the fae male before me.

All it takes is a breath for the moment to shatter. I can feel Aspen's eyes burning into me, hand still outstretched. My eyes flash toward him, taking in his elegant bronze suit beneath a red and gold cape lined with leaves and raven feathers. A crown of gold shaped like maple leaves and dotted with rubies sits between his twining antlers, slightly obscured behind the feathers of his mask. His mask matches mine, and the same four ribbons are tied around his body. Part of me wants to laugh at how comical the ribbons look in contrast to his regal bearing and elegant state of dress. But this is no time for laughter.

I swallow hard, then accept his hand, allowing him to steady me as I take the final stair to stand at his side. "You look beautiful." His words are so quiet, I have to question whether I heard him right.

"Meaningless flattery," I mutter through my teeth.

He lets out a low grumble and leads me forward. I try to remember what Foxglove told me during our preparations. *First, walk to the other end of the balcony, hand-in-hand with the king.*

We take a step, and the sound of harp begins to float in the air. Our next step prompts the beat of a low drum. I seek out the source of the music, finding a fae at the bottom of the dais, strumming an enormous harp. The fae has a feminine, human-like upper body and a long, fish-like tail. She must be a siren. Next to her sits a stout, heavyset fae with leathery skin and long, green hair who beats a wooden drum. The music picks up with every step we take, rumbling beneath my feet as we walk down the aisle between the fae.

My attention moves to these unfamiliar figures dressed in elaborate gowns and eccentric suits. These must be the ambassadors Foxglove told me about during our preparations. He said an ambassador from each court would be present for the ceremony today. Each fae wears a mask, although none are as embellished as mine and Aspen's. As we pass, they stare down at me with their piercing eyes. I do my best to keep my gaze trained straight ahead. My composure remains intact until we reach the other end of the balcony and I find a face I recognize. A *human* face. Sableton's vicar nods to me as we pass him, looking quite out of place in his somber black robes and unmasked face. I'm surprised by his presence, even though Foxglove did say a human would be here today to bring word of our actions back to Eisleigh's council. It just never occurred to me it would be someone I know.

Once we reach the base of the dais and the two thrones, we pause, then again face our audience. The music trails off into silence. My breaths grow shallow as I recall what's supposed to come next. Every pair of eyes is upon us, and I suddenly regret not paying more attention to the previous days' preparations. This ceremony may mean nothing to me, but that doesn't mean I want to look like an idiot in front of these strangers, not to mention Sableton's vicar. I blink a few times, clearing the fog from my mind. Aspen still clutches my hand, and I feel my palm growing sweaty in his.

"Are you ready?" he whispers.

"No."

I can see his smirk from the corner of my eye. Without another word, he lifts our hands, and the music begins again. The beat is deeper, heavier, the harp slow and sensuous. Dread fills me.

That's right. It's time for the stupid dance.

The fae shift to form a semi-circle around us. Aspen releases my hand and takes a step back. I mirror his steps, recalling all the times I practiced with Foxglove these last few days. We step in again, our hands touching, then break away once more. This time when we come back together, Aspen reaches for the red ribbon around my hips. It's a struggle not to flinch from his touch as he pulls one end of the bow. "The earth in you is the earth in me," he says, and the ribbon falls away from me.

We step away. Return. This time I must do the same with him. "The earth in you is the earth in me," I mutter, yanking on the ribbon until it comes from around his hips.

We step to the side, hands touching, then face each other again. He takes hold of the yellow ribbon at my waist. "The fire in you is the fire in me."

My turn again. The music pounds in rhythm with my heart, and somehow I manage to keep the beat with my motions. I take his yellow ribbon and echo his words.

We turn, backs facing each other. Step to the side. Face forward. Aspen takes the blue ribbon from my brow. "The air in you is the air in me."

Turn. Step. Turn. Echo. My breaths go heavy as we near the end of the dance. Step forward, step back. To the side, turn. Side. Turn.

We face each other, and Aspen pulls the green ribbon at my chest. "The water in you is the water in me."

Repeat. "The water in you is the water in me." My words come out breathless. From the exertion of the dance? From nerves? From the terror of what comes next?

He lifts his right arm out to the side, ribbons clutched in his fist. I do the same. With his other arm, he puts his hand at my lower back, pulling me close. My arm trembles as I mirror the motions. We circle and sway, circle and sway. Foxglove steps forward to take the ribbons from Aspen. Lorelei takes mine. Next, they move behind us and remove our masks. The freedom from the mask makes me feel surprisingly naked, and I wish I could shove it back on.

We pause. The music, however, continues. I feel the drumbeat in my bones, feel the harp rushing through my blood. It's dizzying, terrifying, invigorating. We release each other and press our palms together, bodies remaining close. Lorelei and Foxglove stand on each side of us, tying the ribbons around our joined hands. I lift my head and meet Aspen's eyes for the first time since we began the dance, meet his penetrating gaze with a glare. I know what happens next.

Before I can prepare myself, Aspen leans in and presses his lips to mine. A raging fire roars through my blood. I want to push him away, but with our hands bound, I can do nothing but squeeze my eyes shut and remind myself it will all be over soon. Besides, the ridiculous fae custom states we are to kiss until the ribbons are untied from our hands. It feels like an eternity that Aspen and I stand there, lips pressed limply together. I wonder how much longer it will be before Foxglove and Lorelei get on with it and free us already.

Aspen's lips flinch against mine, and for a moment I think he's going to pull away from the kiss early. But instead of pulling away, he moves closer, lips parting slightly to sink the kiss deeper. It ignites my rage, but I find myself leaning into the feel of his lips, the press of his torso against my breasts. The music seems to wrap around us, weaving our kiss into its song. Aspen's lips part again, and I find myself doing the same. His tongue brushes against mine. Something roars inside me, and I can't tell if my anger has reached new heights or burned into something else entirely.

Before I can ponder it further, the kiss ends and Aspen stands upright, a confused look in his eyes. Did he feel the rage coursing from my lips to his? Or is it that *something else* that has him so bemused?

It takes a few moments to realize our hands have been freed. I let go of him and take a step away, burning him with a glare. That kiss was far more than I signed up for. Not that I signed up for any of this.

He tears his eyes from mine and takes my hand again, raising our fists in the air.

Our audience erupts with cheers.

23

———————

With the ceremony over, we adjourn to the dining room for a celebratory feast. I'm about to take my usual seat at the middle of the table when Foxglove sidles up next to me. "Not anymore, sweet one," he whispers, then ushers me down to the end of the table, opposite of where Aspen sits. It's the secondary place of honor. Cobalt's usual seat.

"What about the prince?" I whisper.

"You're the king's mate now," he says, "and soon-to-be queen. Your place is here."

The king's mate. I grit my teeth, trying not to think about that infuriating kiss. As if he can sense my thoughts, Aspen lifts his eyes and meets mine from the other end of the table, a crooked smile quirking his lips. I avert my gaze and take my seat.

The guests quickly fill up the remainder of open chairs. Cobalt sits to the right of his brother at the other end, while Foxglove and Lorelei sit on either side of my end. I'm relieved to have them here, especially surrounded by so many strangers. The remaining guests are the fae ambassadors as well as Sableton's vicar. I'm surprised to see the latter take the seat opposite Cobalt, next to Aspen.

I look over the table, finding it laden with aromatic fruit, plates of oysters, bowls of violets, and towering tiered trays of chocolates. Several decanters of wine in every shade of red are set out. Everything is rich and decadent, evocative of sensuality. Even the room has been decorated to match the mood; deep red tapestries cover the walls, the floor is strewn with plush velvet pillows, and dark red lilies fill every vase.

My eyes rove to the fae ambassadors. They chat animatedly as they settle in, reaching for foods to fill their plates, holding their glasses for the servants to fill with wine. I can't see much of their faces, since only Aspen and I have taken off our masks, but they all appear quite civilized. I see a few whiskers, snouts and swishing tails, a few mouths with pointed teeth, but nothing I haven't already seen here at the palace.

I lean toward Foxglove. "Are all the fae ambassadors seelie?"

He nods approvingly. "You are correct in your observations. The ambassadors from every court, regardless of political affiliation, are seelie. This is because they must interact with humans on occasion, and we learned long ago that unseelie make terrible ambassadors to the human lands."

It makes me wonder what it would be like if I were in a room with unseelie fae instead. Are the unseelie kings and queens goblins and trolls? Vicious beasts like the kelpie? Whatever the case, the ambassadors are an interesting sight. Their gowns are bright and elaborate, like costumes in a play. The more masculine suits are composed of varied colors and fabrics, some with padded shoulders, others with trailing, glittering coattails.

A painful thought comes to mind. *Amelie would have loved to see this.* My throat tightens, lungs constricting as I try to keep the tears at bay.

To distract myself from my grief, I return my attention to the ambassadors and challenge myself to discern which fae belongs to which court. It takes a moment to recall all eleven courts Cobalt had named during our picnic, but I'm pretty sure I have them committed to memory.

I see a fae female with blue skin and a mask of seaweed and coral—an obvious Sea Court fae. A male with dark brown skin, a leafy-green suit, and moss for hair seems a candidate for Earthen. An androgynous fae next to him seems composed entirely of shimmering particles of glitter, making me think Star Court, while the next fae over must be Lunar, with her black dress speckled with glimmering opals and moon-white skin. Or did I get the two swapped? The pixie in a ruffled pink dress with wings the color of a robin's egg could be Spring. Or perhaps Wind? No, Wind must be the fae with the streaming hair that constantly moves as if in flight. And the two fae with golden skin and bright hair are equally convincing as both Fire and Solar.

I'm lost in my game of logic, certain the fae female in the revealing, paper thin gown in shades of green, orange, and blue is Summer Court, when the sound of my name startles me. Silence falls over the room. I find

Aspen's eyes at the other end of the table, lips pulled into his mocking grin as he raises a wine glass. All eyes lock on me, staring expectantly. Even the vicar watches from his seat next to Aspen. I feel my face flush with heat. What in the name of iron did I miss?

"He's raising a glass to you," Foxglove whispers under his breath, "as his mate."

With a trembling hand, I reach for my glass and lift it. "Thank you." My voice comes out flat and uncertain.

Most of the ambassadors smile with approval, while the rest squint at me, as if puzzling over a foreign object, but all reach for their glasses. Sound returns to the dining room, and before long, I'm once again forgotten in favor of the meal.

"Did he get the human gesture right?" Foxglove asks. "A *toast*, I think it's called? Silly name and quite deceptive."

"Yes, why? Was he trying to impress the vicar?"

"No," Foxglove says. "It was meant for you—"

"More wine?" A servant steps between us, decanter in hand.

I'm about to say no—I haven't had a single sip—when I recognize the server. I can't see him fully beneath the slim gold mask he wears, but I'm sure it's the handsome one I suspected Amelie might have been fond of. The thought sends another squeeze of pain to my chest. After a moment of hesitation, I say, "Please."

As he leans forward to fill my cup, he whispers, "Thank you. For asking the king to show us mercy."

"You're welcome. I'm glad he followed through with his promise to release you."

"Of course he did." He says it as if he's unable to comprehend my doubt.

Oh, to be fae and never have to question another's promise. I, on the other hand, never believed Aspen was going to release the servants after questioning, much less let them return to their previous posts. That's how much I trust *his* promises. Before I can say a word more, the fae flashes me a smile and moves down the table to serve the others.

"Are you going to eat anything?" Lorelei asks, raising a brow above her dainty green mask. I feel like it's all she's done the past few days—remind me to eat. She pushes a bowl of salt toward me.

With a sigh, I salt my food and wine, and pretend to enjoy my dinner.

❦

APPARENTLY, A CELEBRATORY FEAST IN FAERWYVAE CONSISTS OF SEVEN courses, four of which are wine. By the time we reach the end, the dining room is filled with laughter and chatter and all sorts of menacing sounds that make my head throb. All I want is quiet and to be alone.

I lean toward Foxglove. "Can I leave now?"

He's leaning back in his chair with his feet propped on the table, head thrown back in laughter at something Lorelei said. His spectacles rest on his forehead while his mask sits askew over his eyes. Lorelei sits on the table facing him and can barely finish her story, wine sloshing from the rim of her cup as her shoulders heave with snorts and giggles. Neither seems to have heard my question.

I rise to my feet, which gets their attention. "I'm leaving."

"No, my lovely," Foxglove says. "You must stay until the end."

I put my hands on my hips. "Why? Does it have anything to do with sealing the treaty? If not, I'm done here."

Lorelei's eyelids are heavy as she regards me. "It's important you stay until the end," she says, words slow and slurring together.

"But why?"

"For the treaty," Foxglove says, not nearly as intoxicated as Lorelei. "The ambassadors should see you retire with the king so they know you'll be mating."

I feel the blood leave my face. "But we aren't married yet. Humans don't mate until after marriage."

Foxglove throws his head back in bellowing laughter. "That's funny, dear."

"I'm serious."

"Honey, you are the king's mate now. That's all the permission you need to take him to bed. Besides, you'll be married in a couple weeks. There's no need to feel guilty about it."

It's not guilt I feel, but I don't say so. Propriety has never been my main concern in life, but I'd hoped the excuse would keep Aspen away for at least a while longer. My eyes flash to him at the other end of the table. The pixie in the pink dress leans over the table, lashes fluttering as she says something to him. His eyes lock on mine as he grunts his reply, his expression bored. She's clearly flirting with him, which is oddly irritating. Does she not realize she's at a mate ceremony? *His* mate ceremony? Then again, why do I care? She says something else, then pouts. He keeps his gaze on me as she flutters away.

Lorelei lifts my barely touched wine cup from the table, stealing my attention to her. "Come on, Evelyn, celebrate with us."

Anger roars through me. My words come out in a furious whisper. "This is not a time to celebrate. My sister is dead. Do you have no concept of grieving?"

The two fae seem to sober a little at my words. Lorelei sets down both cups of wine, while Foxglove's lips turn down in a frown.

Tears threaten to spill from my eyes, and I can feel the lump returning to my throat. Around me, the beautiful ambassadors laugh and chat and dance. A few have taken servants to the velvet pillows to kiss—perhaps more than kiss, if I dare look hard enough. The pixie is flitting in front of a guard, finger trailing over his bronze chest plate. The Sea Court ambassador has a servant—a female fae with a dainty pink bunny nose—giggling in her lap. It all seems garish against the landscape of my loss. Even if I wasn't wholeheartedly against this stupid ceremony to begin with, I wouldn't be able to celebrate. Not without Amelie.

I hold my breath, willing the pain to recede. I can't break down. Not now. Not in front of all these fae.

"May I have a word?" a quiet male voice asks.

I find the vicar at my side. His complexion has paled, likely from the excessive lust and frivolity around us. I can't imagine he feels anything close to comfortable here. With a deep breath, I don a shaky smile. "Of course."

He takes a few steps away from the table, and I follow. Once we're out of earshot of the others, he says, "I thank you for your greatest sacrifice for the good of Eisleigh. You have brought peace for another hundred years."

I'm not sure what to say, considering my sacrifice was forced upon me. "It is my duty."

"And how have you been treated since you've been here?"

I open my mouth, but no words come. What do I even say? *I was attacked by a kelpie, my sister is dead, and now I'm forced to marry a beastly fae. Oh, and did I mention, the monster I'm marrying may have murdered my sister?* I want to tell him this, but I don't, suddenly aware that everything I say could be taken back to the council and used as grounds to invalidate the treaty. "I've been treated...as expected," I finally say.

"Very good. I'll be sure to tell the council that you have taken the first step in securing the alliance. I'll be back to oversee your wedding." He pauses and looks around the room. "Where is your sister? I know her marriage alliance was forgone, which surprised the council, but at least yours will continue as planned. Still, I'm surprised she isn't here at all."

My mouth falls open. How does he not know? "My sister is—"

"There you are, my mate." Aspen steps between me and the vicar. "It's time for us to retire."

"But—"

He raises his voice over mine, addressing the room at large. "Thank you for attending our celebration and witnessing this first step in securing the treaty. You may stay or you may return to your courts, I don't care."

The ambassadors burst into laughter, although based on Aspen's disinterested tone, his words hadn't been made in jest.

He continues. "My mate and I will retire now." With that, he takes my arm and pulls me toward the hall. Before we reach it, I catch Cobalt's eyes flashing me a warning. I give him a subtle nod. *Don't worry, Cobalt. I know what happens next.*

In the hall, a pair of guards flank us, and I pull free from Aspen's grasp. "How does the vicar not know what happened to Amelie?"

He lets out an irritated grumble. "Come."

"No, not until you tell me."

His face transforms into a smile, but the effect is more devious than kind. "Our room is this way, mate," he says too loud, eyes flashing over my head.

I turn, finding a fae figure—the one from the Sea Court—hovering in the doorway of the dining room, her bunny-fae companion kissing her ear. Then another fae, the glittering one, peeks into the hall.

Now that I know we have an audience, I understand Aspen's forced smile. He extends his hand to me. I grit my teeth and take it.

I remain quiet as we continue down the halls, flanked by the two guards. The eerie feeling I'm being watched follows me. We ascend a staircase, and I wonder if he's taking me to the balcony where we had our ceremony. Instead, he stops before the final staircase that would lead there and turns to an ornate pair of doors protected by another set of guards who open them for us. Aspen all but pushes me inside before slamming the doors shut behind us.

"Do you want war?" he shouts, rounding on me.

"Excuse me?"

"Because that's what will happen if your people think your sister is dead."

My hands clench into fists. "Are you saying no one knows the truth? Not even our mother?"

"No one can know a thing until I am certain what happened."

My voice rises to a shout as I close the distance between us. "So you haven't taken her body to Mother to be buried? What are you doing with it then? Where is she?"

"Lower your voice," he hisses. "I am taking care of it."

My stomach churns. What does that mean? What does any of this mean?

He turns his back on me and storms over to a small table. There he pours wine from a decanter and swallows the glassful in a single gulp. As he stands there, eyes closed, I take in my surroundings.

We're inside an immense bedroom, lit by a fire roaring in a hearth as well as several of the orb-like lights above the sconces on the walls. The bed sits in the center of the room, the base consisting of elegant roots that seem to be growing straight from the floor, its posts of slender, white birch. Branches tangle overhead with red-orange leaves to form a canopy, and the blankets are bronze silk brocade.

I turn in a circle, taking in the rest of the room—furnishings of deep, dark wood, plush rugs, a turreted ceiling painted like an autumn sky. I've never seen such elegance, such autumn incarnate indoors. When I finish my circle, I'm again facing Aspen. I must have caught him off guard, because he watches me with the same curious look I saw on his face after our kiss.

I watch him right back, eyes narrowing to slits.

He sets down his glass. "We should perform the Bonding ritual."

The Bonding ritual. So that's what it's called. I cross my arms over my chest. "We most certainly will not."

His expression darkens. "Why did I expect anything else?" he mutters.

"Yes, why did you? We may have done a ridiculous dance and called it a ceremony, but I am not your mate. When we marry, it will be for alliance purposes only. Nothing more, and you know it. Do you really think I'm going to participate in a ritual where I give you my name?"

"You know."

I turn up my chin. "I should have been told sooner. Giving you my name—"

He takes a step toward me, and something like panic crosses his face. "Did it ever occur to you that I don't want to do this either? Especially when it means I have to give you my name in return?"

I'm surprised by this. He has to give me his name too? Cobalt only mentioned my part in the ritual. Still, what good will having his name do me? It's not like humans have access to whatever makes fae overpower us.

"I've been thwarted by your kind time and time again," he says. "Now I'm supposed to trust you with the one thing that could be my undoing."

"Well, it seems like forgoing the ritual will be mutually beneficial then."

He presses his fingers to his temples, grumbling something unintelligible. "Fine," he finally says. "We've both had a long day. We'll postpone the Bonding."

"We'll cancel it," I correct.

Aspen's jaw shifts back and forth. "We'll get some sleep and reassess in the morning."

"Then I'll be going." I spin on my heel toward the door.

Aspen strides toward me, blocking the door. "What do you think you're doing?"

"I already told you," I say with a sneer. "I will never allow you to bed me, not even for the sake of sleep. I'm returning to my room."

"How do you think that will look to the ambassadors? The vicar? I don't know who's a spy, who's plotting against me."

I let out a sharp laugh. "I know exactly who."

He tilts his head back, surprised. "Who?"

I cup my hand over the side of my mouth and motion him closer. My voice starts as a whisper and ends in a roar. "No one, you arrogant, self-obsessed, paranoid fool. No one is plotting against you. You're the one murdering humans and endangering the treaty, no one else!"

His chest heaves with rage, and I realize I've gone too far.

I try to keep my composure as I take a step away from him. "I should leave."

"No," he growls. "I will." With that, he storms to the doors and out of the room, leaving me in stunned silence.

24

———————

For minutes on end, I just stand there, unable to move. But can you blame me? Aspen left me in what is obviously his personal bedroom. I'm both too afraid to leave and too afraid he'll return at any moment.

When I finally get the nerve to further investigate my surroundings, I find my belongings have already been transferred here. One side of the wardrobe holds most of the fae dresses that used to be in my old room. The dressing table and screen have been brought over as well, taking up a corner of the room next to an enormous carnelian tub. My bag, my surgery kit, and all my stray items have been neatly arranged behind the dressing screen.

The only things missing are Amelie's. I blink back tears at the thought.

I find a nightdress in the wardrobe and change behind the screen, even though the room is empty. Then I take my dagger and wander the room again, investigating every crack, looking under every table and within every shadow. Once I've surmised no threat has been left for me, I make my way to the bed. My fingers tremble as I turn down the covers, peel back the spider silk sheets. This is Aspen's bed. *His bed.* The thought is equal parts disturbing and thrilling.

I allow the latter sensation to prevail, finding satisfaction in the fact that I've momentarily won. He forfeited his bedroom to *me*. And if he's going to be so difficult, I certainly won't suffer for it. Let him wander the halls or sleep in a closet, or whatever it is brooding fae do when their pride is wounded. Let me get a good night's sleep for once.

And I do.

I DON'T SEE ASPEN THE NEXT DAY. OR THE NEXT. I HARDLY SEE ANYONE AT ALL, for that matter, save for Foxglove and Lorelei. Since the king has yet to return to his bedroom since our argument, I begin to grow more and more comfortable, taking meals in there, snooping through Aspen's things. Yet I've found nothing to occupy me for long and spend most of my time alternating between grief and boredom.

By the third day, my curiosity is too strong. "Where are King Aspen and Prince Cobalt?" I ask Foxglove, meeting his eyes in the mirror as he twists a lock of my hair. "During the day, that is," I quickly add, in case I'm supposed to be keeping up the ruse that Aspen and I have been spending the night together.

"Hasn't your mate told you?" He places a jeweled pin in my hair. "The king has been inundated with correspondences regarding some issue with the humans."

"What kind of an issue?"

He shrugs. "It's not my place to know or say. I'm his ambassador, not his confidante. When I'm needed to go smooth things over, I'm sure he'll let me in on all the details."

I chew my bottom lip, wondering what this could be about. Is it about Amelie? Has Aspen finally decided to tell my people the truth? Or could he be trying to invalidate our alliance and break the treaty? The blood leaves my face at the thought.

"He must know you're restless with him so preoccupied," Foxglove continues. "Which is why he's brought a guest to visit."

"A guest? Who?"

His expression brightens. "I went out of my way to make it a quaint little human ritual. What do you call it...sitting for tea? I made up a room like a parlor and imported tea from your village. Isn't that too cute?"

"But who is my guest, Foxglove?"

He rolls his eyes. "It doesn't matter if I tell you. You don't know her. Not personally, at least, but once I'm finished with your hair...there!" He steps back and evaluates my auburn tresses. "Now I can take you to meet her."

I follow Foxglove out of Aspen's room and down the hall, eager to discover who my mysterious visitor will be. We stop at an open door, and I freeze when I see what's inside.

"You're impressed, right?"

I press my lips tight together, the strain of suppressing my laughter almost too much to bear. Inside the little room is a fine couch, a tea table, and an elegant chair. Surrounding these furnishings is an eyesore of human junk, from a grandfather clock to a coat stand dangling with numerous umbrellas, coats, and—oddly—a pair of boots. Everything is coated in doilies and frilly shawls, the floor sprawled with overlapping rugs of unfashionable design.

"Does it remind you of home?"

I'm not sure if I should be offended by that, considering he saw my home and should know this tacky room looks nothing like the parlor at the apothecary. "Yes," I manage to say. "Just with more...stuff."

"More character, you mean," he says. "I love human knickknacks. Some of these were left as offerings at the wall."

"Is this where our offerings end up?" I ask, lifting a corner of a yellowing doily. "In unused rooms at all the palaces?"

"Of course not." Foxglove says. "This just so happens to be my personal collection. When the king asked me to make you a private room to take guests, I figured I'd put these things to use. They didn't come cheap, you know. That rug itself cost me six garnets."

My eyes widen. "Are you saying our offerings are taken from the wall... and sold?"

"Only the most curious things. The rest is discarded. I'm sure hundreds of years ago, seelie fae were eager to get their hands on anything human. A new emotion to taste from a bite of pastry. A new human-like characteristic to learn from a pair of kid gloves. By now, Faerwyvae has enough human influence to keep the seelie quite satisfied."

"If our offerings are sold or discarded, how in the name of iron do the fae decide which girls to select for the Reaping?"

Foxglove shoots me an odd look. "The fae don't choose. Your human council does. The hosting court can override that decision with a choice of their own, of course, but that's a rare thing."

My head swims as I ponder the implications of everything he's saying. All those times Mother brought Amelie and me to the wall with our offering of bread and milk. All that time we thought the gesture would keep me and my sister safe from the Reaping. All that time we were wrong. It was my own people who were in charge all along.

"They're so precious, don't you think?" Foxglove says with a sigh, oblivious to my agitation. "Such silly, useless things. Yet, they have an irresistible charm."

"They sure do," I mutter.

Foxglove beams. "I'm glad you approve. Aspen will be pleased, and I'm sure your guest will be equally so."

"Where is my guest, anyhow?"

"She's waiting below. I wanted you to see your parlor before I brought her in. I can fetch her now if you're ready." He takes a step toward the door, then pauses, furrowing his brow. "You *do* like it right?"

I pull my lips into what I think is a warm smile. I'm sorely out of practice, but Foxglove deserves to see my gratitude. As gaudy as the room is, and as disappointed as I am to learn the futility of our offerings, I know his heart was in the right place. "Of course, Foxglove. I love it."

I take a seat on the couch as I wait for my guest. A few minutes later, Lorelei brings in a tray of tea, cookies, and salt. She freezes when she enters, looking around the room in terror. "What in all the rotting oak and ivy is this awful mess?"

I hush her. "Foxglove worked really hard on this."

"I can see that. The question is why?"

"He thinks it's what a human parlor looks like. Which is beyond me, considering he's the ambassador to the human lands."

She sets the tray on the table, nose wrinkled in disgust as she eyes her surroundings. "So you're saying every parlor doesn't look like this?"

"No, but don't tell Foxglove."

Noise sounds down the hall, and I rise to my feet. A moment later, Foxglove enters with a woman. A human woman. Her eyes widen as she enters the room, but other than that, her expression remains blank.

"Miss Fairfield, I'd like for you to meet Doris Mason," Foxglove says.

The woman curtsies, then takes a seat in the chair across from me. I return to my seat on the couch, pondering the familiar name. *Doris Mason.* Where have I heard that? Then it dawns on me. "You're the Chosen from the last Reaping."

"Yes," she says, her voice light and breathy.

"We'll give you some privacy," Foxglove says. Then he and Lorelei leave the room.

I'm left staring at Doris, a mingle of shock and confusion running through me. Doris was one of the Chosen from one hundred years ago. Yet she looks no older than Mother. Her eyes are distant and watery, their shade a dull gray, her hair is brittle wisps of dirty blonde, and she wears a thin green dress that barely reaches her calves.

"Is that tea?" she asks, eyes falling on the tray between us.

I shake my head to clear it. "Yes. So sorry. Where are my manners?" I pour two cups, then offer her a plate with a cookie.

As she sips her tea, a hint of clarity seems to focus in her eyes. "I haven't had tea in ages. Not like this, at least."

"It's a nice change from wine, isn't it?"

She nods.

I feel a flush of anxiety building as I search for what to say next. These situations have never been my forte, considering I'm not one for small talk. An intellectual debate with a magister would be more in my comfort zone. "Might I ask what village you were from?"

"Marchvale," she says. "I barely remember what it was like anymore. I'm sure it's changed since I last saw it."

"And you were sent to Faerwyvae with your cousin, right? To the Summer Court, if I remember correctly?"

"Yes, but Nadia passed away many years ago. It's been over sixty years that I've lived without her. It gets harder every day to remember her face."

Finally, a topic that piques my interest. I can think of no other way to pose my question but to be blunt. "How are you still alive when your cousin is not?"

She ponders my question, eyes wandering the cluttered walls. "You won't age the same way you used to," she says. "Being in Faerwyvae will change you a little. You'll be open to a very small amount of its magic. You can live longer than you would in Eisleigh, age less quickly. And so long as you live, your family and their descendants will be compensated back home. So, at least there's one motivation not to take your own life."

She says the last part so casually, it takes me a moment to realize she wasn't being sardonic. I make the firm decision not to laugh, then consider everything else she said. *Faerwyvae will change you. You'll be open to its magic.* I want to tell her I don't believe in magic, but the statement seems childish in this circumstance. Here sits a woman who wouldn't be alive, were she still in Eisleigh. Yet she hardly looks a day over forty. I know there's a scientific reason for this, but I haven't the slightest idea what it could be. "What about your cousin? Did she not age as slowly as you did?"

Doris shakes her head. "Nadia didn't fare so well. Probably because she had no children to live for, nor was she well-loved."

"Was her husband unkind to her?"

"I don't know if one could call a fae kind or unkind," she says. "They simply are what they are, despite the clothes they wear or the food they eat. Nadia and I were married to the Summer Queen's cousins, neither of whom wanted us. Neither kept us well, but I doubt either of our husbands thought they were doing anything but their utmost duties. Nadia's husband never visited her bed and chose to live with his favored lover instead. My husband visited my bed many times. But just as many times, he visited the beds of his numerous mates. I was breeding stock to him, a conduit to provide him heirs. And heirs I gave him. Many. I think that's the only thing the fae like about humans. We conceive well."

My stomach churns at that. "How are the children treated, being half-fae?"

"They are well," she says. "You'd hardly know they are half-fae at all, aside from their appearance. The magic here seems to favor them as if they were fully fae. My sons and daughters will far outlive me. Many of the children of the Chosen who preceded me are still alive today."

It had never occurred to me what became of any offspring between the fae and humans. If I'd given it any thought, I would have assumed the fae ate their half-human children. At least that assumption has been proven wrong. "Are any of the previous Chosen still alive in the other courts?"

She shakes her head. "I'm the last. No—I suppose there are two of us now. Three of us? Where is your sister?"

I can't bring myself to talk about Amelie, even though Doris might be the one person who could understand. "She isn't here," I say, then take a sip of my tea.

"I see." I'm not sure if I imagine it, but she seems to shoot me a knowing look. She then reaches across the table and gives my hand a squeeze. "Persevere, Miss Fairfield. If I can do it, so can you."

I look into her worn eyes, her empty expression, the lips that can barely form a smile. A morbid thought crosses my mind. *If this is what perseverance looks like...perhaps Amelie was the lucky one.*

25

———————

I can't shake my meeting with Doris, even long after she leaves. I'd always imagined the Chosen were unhappy with their predicaments —miserable, even—but seeing the evidence before me is more than I can handle. And hearing how she and her cousin were treated by their husbands...how did my people never hear of this?

My mood sours further when I open the bedroom door and find Aspen waiting inside, pouring a glass of wine from the bedside table.

"Come to steal your room back?"

He ignores me. "Did you enjoy your guest?"

I cross my arms over my chest. "You mean, did I enjoy that glimpse into my future? Did you arrange our meeting as some sort of threat?"

He sips his wine, not looking at me. "I thought you might be lonely for human company."

"So you sent me an abused old woman?"

He pinches the bridge of his nose and closes his eyes. "Ungrateful human."

"Have all the Chosen been treated so poorly? Used as breeding stock? Neglected until they died of loneliness?"

He sets down his glass and storms over to me. "I didn't wait here the past hour so you could return and gripe about Doris Mason. I came to tell you I'm leaving."

"Leaving?"

"I have to deal with a skirmish near the wall. Cobalt will be coming too, along with some of my guards and soldiers. That leaves you in charge of the palace. Try not to burn it down." He turns to leave.

I'm flummoxed as I process his words. "Wait," I call after him before he reaches the door. "What's the skirmish about? And how long will you be gone?"

He considers me a while before answering. His posture relaxes. "It's the Holstrom father. He wants my blood. I'll likely be gone no longer than three days."

I want to make a cutting retort, to tell him three days is far too short. But there's a fatigue in Aspen's bearing that I hadn't noticed until now, making me hold my tongue.

Aspen continues. "Mr. Holstrom won't leave the wall until I face him in person. His recklessness is putting both humans and fae alike in danger. So I'll go put an end to this stupidity."

"What are you going to do to him?"

He shrugs. "Give him what he wants."

I raise a brow. "What is that supposed to mean?"

"I'll offer him a bargain. Let him choose his weapon and draw blood from me in any way he likes without fear of reproach. Then we will call a truce and return to our lands."

"You're going to *let* him attack you?"

"Just once. If he continues to fight me after he draws blood, the truce is off."

It seems like an odd way to settle a dispute. Then again, it makes sense for the fae. Of course they would end conflict with a bargain. But will it be enough for Mr. Holstrom? Would the blood of an immortal king be enough to compensate for losing two daughters? *It will if it kills Aspen.*

He seems to read my mind, lips pulling into a smirk. "Perhaps you'll get your dearest wish and the Holstrom father will deal me a fatal blow."

"Perhaps."

He takes a step toward me, eyes locked on mine. "Maybe you should give me a kiss for luck. I am your mate, after all, about to go off to battle. You might never get the chance again."

I lift my chin, deepening my glare. "I'm counting on it."

With a laugh, Aspen turns and leaves the room.

∼

THE NEXT MORNING, I WATCH FROM MY WINDOW AS A RETINUE GATHERS ON THE palace grounds, preparing to leave. They look so small from this high up in the palace, but I'm certain I see Aspen riding at the head of the group on a black puca, his antlers clear even from this distance. Even if he had no antlers, I'd be able to recognize his haughty posture anywhere.

Cobalt must be down there too, and Foxglove. My heart sinks a little at the realization I'll no longer have Foxglove's company to entertain me for the next few days, just Lorelei.

The retinue files into a line, then departs the grounds. With a wide false smile, I pin Aspen's figure in my sight and give him a gracious wave. Never mind the fact he isn't looking. "Good riddance," I say in a singsong voice.

Relief washes over me when I see the last figure disappear into the trees of the forest at the edge of the palace grounds. Freedom. For three days I'll have no one to answer to but myself. I throw open the doors of my room, my joy fading as I see a pair of guards posted outside. Of course Aspen left guards. Or more likely *spies*.

No matter. I won't let it interfere with my plans. "Will one of you be a dear and have wine brought to me at once?" Then I close the door.

I dress quickly, not bothering to wait for Lorelei, then take a seat on the couch at the far end of the room, next to a round stump-like table.

When the knock comes, I sit upright. "Come in."

A servant enters bearing a tray. His slender legs end in dainty hooves, but disappointment flutters through me when I see his face. He's beautiful and youthful, like most of the fae living in the palace, but he's not the one I was hoping for. Still, I wave him forward, and he sets the tray on the table next to me.

"Will that be all?" he asks.

I look from him to the open door. The guards remain on each side, but their backs are to me. Not that it matters; for all I know, fae have superior hearing. I lower my voice anyway. "There is something else. First, tell me your name."

"My name is Ocher."

"Ocher, I hope you don't mind me asking...did you ever serve my sister?"

His brows knit together. "Yes," he says, hesitantly.

"Did you ever serve her while she was meeting privately with the king?"

"A time or two."

"Were you the one who served the wine the night she went missing?" I can't bring myself to say the truth. *The night she died.*

"No. That was Vane, I believe."

"Vane," I echo. My voice is still just above a whisper. "Do you think you could do something for me? Could you send him here?"

"I suppose so," he says, then blushes. "I mean, yes, of course."

"Very good." I smile, then raise my voice. "This is not the wine I wanted. I want the red wine that was served with breakfast yesterday morning. Why would I want this violet wine so early in the day?"

Ocher shifts from foot to foot. "Violet and red are merely different in flavor. Either can be consumed morning or—"

I turn my nose to the air, summoning the snobbery of Maddie Coleman, cringing at how uncomfortable it feels. "I can tell a difference. Now get on with it, or I'll tell the king you didn't listen to me."

He looks perplexed.

"And for your insolence, be sure you send another servant in your stead. I can't abide by this." I give him an exaggerated wink.

"Ah." He flashes me a knowing smile. "Understood. I'm so sorry. My mistake." He bows low, then backs out of the room, tray in hand.

I pace the room until my doors open once again. This time, I recognize the face of the fae. It's the handsome male, the one who thanked me for my mercy. As he approaches, I ask, "Are you Vane?"

"I am," he says in a whisper as he sets down the tray. "Ocher said you asked for me."

"I did, and I thank you for coming." One of the guards shifts outside my door but remains facing away from me. "I'll make this fast. Was anything amiss when you served my sister the night she disappeared?"

Color rises to his beautifully pale cheeks, and a flash of guilt crosses his face. "I brought honey pyrus wine. King Aspen was furious. But it was an accident, I swear—"

"Never mind that," I say. "What was she like when you saw her? Did she seem...troubled?"

He looks taken aback for a moment. "No, she looked serene. Smiling. Laughing. She seemed to think me bringing the wrong kind of wine was nothing more than a silly joke."

I chew my bottom lip. "Did anything else happen? You said Aspen was furious. What exactly did he do?"

"The king realized what kind of wine I'd brought almost as soon as I'd set it down. He stopped Amelie just before she went to pour herself a glass. Then he took the tray and said he'd get the wine himself. Made me take him to the kitchen and show him our wine stores, explain the mishap. He scolded me but nothing more. Then he left with a bottle of Bloodberry wine."

"Is that a…normal kind of wine?"

He shrugs, then points at the tray. "It's what I brought you here. It's served at most common meals. And it doesn't cause dangerous hallucinations in humans, if that's what you mean."

"What about when Aspen left you? Did he seem angry still? In any kind of rage?"

"No," Vane says. "I apologized so many times, he had to order me to stop. Once he left, he seemed perfectly forgiving, which is why I was so surprised when he ordered our execution the next day."

I press my lips tight together, wondering how much he knows about my responsibility for that predicament. "There's nothing else you can think of? Nothing that seemed strange?"

"After what you did to make the king find mercy, I wish there was something I could say to help you, but there isn't."

I sigh, all my hopes for potential answers dashed like waves upon jagged rocks. Then one more question comes to mind. "Were any of the servants overly friendly with Amelie? Was she *intimate* with any of them?" At another blush from Vane, I add, "That includes you."

"We all found her to be fair, for a human," he says, "but no one dared take her to bed or do more than look at her. No one would be so stupid to court the king's betrothed. In fact," he casts an anxious glance behind him at the guards outside the door, "I've likely overstayed my welcome."

I want to drill him with more questions, but he's probably right. Besides, I'm not sure what else to ask. All further questions I'd prepared hinged on him having something of value to tell me. "Very well. Thank you for speaking with me."

Once he's gone, I'm left alone to ponder the conversation. It leaves me just as frustrated as I was before. Speaking to Vane had been my one great idea, my one way to possibly gain some sense of control over the questions that continue to plague me. I should have known better than to get my hopes up. The longer I've been in Faerwyvae, the less control I seem to have. Nothing makes any more sense than it did when I arrived. There's no explanation for much of the fae's supposed magic, no clues to what happened the night Amelie died, and no evidence anything will ever make sense again.

There's only one thing left to do. I pour myself a glass of wine and sprinkle a pinch of salt into it. With a raise of my glass to no one, I mutter, "Might as well enjoy my freedom."

26

———————

Dread settles over me as the third day dawns since Aspen left, and I realize he'll be returning any time now. My days without him have been peaceful and uneventful. Then again, I suppose that's what they were like the few days leading up to his departure as well. Still, I can't help but think all that will eventually change. He'll hassle me to join his bed. Or try and get me to submit to the fae Bonding ritual. He'll stir my anger and I'll stir his, I just know it.

I freeze, noticing my inexplicable flush of excitement at the thought.

Well, I must be more bored than I thought.

The day comes and goes. Then another.

A new dread begins to emerge, one that has me pacing the open expanse in the dining room after breakfast while Lorelei watches with concern.

"What if something happened?" I mutter.

"The king will be fine, I'm sure of it," Lorelei says.

I roll my eyes. "Not to him. To the treaty or something."

"Give Foxglove some credit. He spins truces even better than he spins that pretty hair of yours. If they aren't back yet, it's likely only because they are negotiating the finer details."

"What if Mr. Holstrom refuses? I mean, *anything* could happen." In fact, I've spent the best part of two days analyzing every possible logical outcome. Most end in war. "Blazing iron, if my marriage to Aspen ends up being for nothing, I'll be livid. And if it turns out he's to blame for breaking the treaty, I'll kill him my—"

Shouts ring out somewhere inside the palace.

Lorelei rises to her feet. "What the bloody oak and ivy?"

I dart out of the dining room, then pause, listening for more sound. Another shout comes, then muffled, frantic voices.

Lorelei puts a hand on my arm to keep me from pursuing the source. "Don't. It might not be safe."

She's probably right, but I have to know what's going on. My eyes flash to the guards in the hall, the same two who guard my room. They've been following me at a distance everywhere I go since Aspen left, and I've given up trying to persuade them not to. Finally, they might be useful for once. "You," I point to one, a female with bright blue eyes and a distinctly feline face, "see what's going on and report back to me at once."

She stands at attention but doesn't move. Her expression is querulous as she ponders my request.

I square my shoulders, summoning the snobbery I feigned with the wine servant the other day. "As the king's mate and lady of Bircharbor Palace, I demand it."

The guard finally moves to obey, and Lorelei nudges her shoulder into mine. "Look at you, acting like a queen," she whispers.

We remain in the hall, waiting anxious minutes on end for the guard to return. When she does, she brings Foxglove as well. The ambassador's face is pale, expression troubled. Lorelei and I run to meet him.

"What's going on?" I ask.

"The king has been injured." Foxglove says. "Gravely so."

A surge of emotion rushes through me, but I can't identify what it is. Relief? Worry? Satisfaction? "What happened?"

Foxglove wrings his hands. "I finally convinced the Holstrom father to agree to a bargain. The king would be unarmored and allow Mr. Holstrom to draw blood using a weapon of his choice. The man chose a bow as his weapon and aimed for the king's heart."

At the look on Foxglove's face, Lorelei gasps, bringing her hands to cover her mouth. "Tell me he isn't dead."

"He isn't, but...the arrowhead was iron, of course. It got lodged between his ribs just below his heart. Prince Cobalt tried to free it, but the shaft was ash and burned his hands. He was only able to snap the shaft and potentially drove the arrowhead deeper."

Lorelei spins toward me and takes me by the shoulders. "You can help him."

My eyes go wide. "What?"

"You're a—whatever you call it—a surger."

"A surgeon," I correct, "and I, well, don't you have a fae healer? Gildmar?"

"Gildmar was summoned immediately," Foxglove says. "She met us on our way back to the palace and has already done what she can, but she can't get the arrowhead from between his ribs, especially with his blood becoming more and more poisoned with every minute the iron remains inside him. She can hardly go near the wound at this point, much less tend it."

A sense of purpose settles over me. This is exactly what I'm trained for. "I suppose I could help. Where is he?"

"He's in the east wing on the bottom floor."

"Let me get my things," I say. "Then take me there."

I CAN HEAR THE KING WELL BEFORE I SEE HIM. AS WE APPROACH THE EAST wing, moaning echoes from wall to wall, a guttural sound like a wounded animal. We reach the door at the end of the main hall and pause just inside. Aspen lies on a stone table and Cobalt paces the length of it, face twisted with worry. Next to the table stands a short fae with bark-like skin and branches of leafy hair, hand covering her mouth as if protecting herself from a foul smell.

I take a step inside, drawing Cobalt's attention. "Evelyn, what are you doing here?"

"I think I can help him."

Cobalt's brow furrows, either with concern or confusion. His voice comes out small. "You think you...can?"

I wonder if he meant to say *want to*. With a nod, I approach the table, Foxglove and Lorelei hovering just behind me. I note the smell of blood filling the air, something I am intimately familiar with. But another pungent odor assaults my senses as well. Tangy. Sharp. Dangerous.

"I can almost taste the iron in the air," Lorelei says with a cough. "Oak and ivy, that's strong."

Foxglove covers his mouth with his sleeve and takes a step back. With a deep breath, I look over the king. His face is covered in a sheen of sweat, teeth gritted, head lolling side to side as he moans in agony. His golden skin has faded so pale it's almost white, with an unhealthy blue tinge beneath it. His lips are chapped and peeling, and his eyes look sunken, a bruise-like purple surrounding them.

Cobalt faces the tiny fae. "Gildmar, show her the wound."

She eyes me for a moment, then reaches for the silk sheet covering Aspen's body and pulls it away from his neck. With a gasp, she springs away and drops the sheet as if it burned her.

"I'll do it." I take a cautious step forward, training my expression beneath my surgeon's calm despite my racing heart. With quick, deliberate movements, I set down my surgery kit and pull the sheet down, exposing Aspen's chest. The tang of blood and iron increase, and the fae step farther away. My hands tremble as I tuck the sheet around his waist and take in his damaged chest.

A poultice covers the wound, which is on his left side, not far from his heart. If he has a heart, that is. The skin around it is every shade of black, purple, and blue, with blue-black streaks spreading out in every direction across his torso. His breathing is shallow, labored. I don't need to know much about fae physiology to know Aspen is dying.

"What can I use as antiseptic?" I call out.

"Anti-what?" Gildmar asks, her voice like the creak of an old door.

I close my eyes, realizing—*of course*—they don't have antiseptic. Or know what it is. "Wine then. Someone get me wine. Now."

"I'll get some," I hear Cobalt say, followed by the sound of his feet tearing from the room.

I reach for the poultice, lifting a corner. "Has this helped at all?"

"It is slowing the iron poisoning his blood," Gildmar says, "but with the arrowhead stuck inside him, there's nothing I can use to stop it completely."

"I need clean cloth." Gildmar hands me strips of red spider silk. I've never used silk for dressing wounds, so I can only hope it will suffice. I set the cloth next to Aspen, then open my surgery kit.

Scalpel in hand, I return to Aspen.

His eyes fly open, a roar escaping his lips. "No!"

I look from his maniacal expression to the scalpel in my hand. Understanding dawns on me as I remember what Lorelei said about human metals —even weak ones—being unbearable to a fae with a current iron injury.

As Aspen's body begins to convulse, the scalpel slips from my shaking hands and clatters to the floor.

"Close it!" I hear Lorelei shout behind me. "Close that box!"

I sink to my knees, fumbling to replace the scalpel and shut the kit. Only when I secure the clasp does Aspen settle back down. I stand, finding the king once again listless. Fresh blood streaked with black oozes from his side beneath the poultice.

I'm frozen in place, at a loss for both words and actions.

"You can treat him," Gildmar says. "He's calm now."

"I can't use my tools," I whisper.

"No, but you can use mine." The little fae indicates a table strewn with herbs, poultices, shells, sticks, and sharp, white bones.

"I was trained to use tools. *These* tools." I point to my kit, lying useless on the floor.

"Your hands will work too."

I shake my head, backing toward the door. My breaths grow faster, shallower. "No. I can't do this."

Lorelei takes hold of my arm. "What's wrong?"

I meet her eyes, frantic. "I'm not trained for this. I have no idea what to do if I can't use my tools."

"You don't need your tools," she says. "Just do what you did for me."

I sigh. It's time to admit the truth. "I didn't do anything for you, Lorelei. I merely inspected your wound, helped you stretch. The fact that you felt better afterward was negligible. A placebo, if anything."

"Then how do you explain this?" She lifts the hem of her skirt, revealing her leg. Her smooth, unmarred leg with its perfect brown skin. I look to the other, thinking there must be some mistake, but both look exactly alike.

"It's a coincidence," I manage to say. "You were already on the mend."

She crosses her arms and lifts a brow. "Seriously? That's your best explanation."

I admit, I have no way to explain how she could have healed that much in a matter of days. "All I know is that it wasn't because of me."

Her eyes go steely, lips pressing into a tight line. "Don't you dare let my king die. Don't you dare give up right now, no matter how much you think his death might suit you."

Her words send a shock through me. The option of letting him die had yet to cross my mind, but now that I'm forced to consider it...would it be better if I simply did nothing? I look over at Aspen, watching the tendrils of black crawling over his torso. If I leave him be, the iron will poison his blood. He'll be dead before long.

I could let it happen. He did let my sister die, after all. And he may have been directly responsible for her death in the first place, not to mention the deaths of the Holstrom girls and who knows who else.

He deserves to die.

The thought makes my stomach churn. That's not how I was trained. Mr. Meeks taught me that a surgeon treats anyone, regardless of station or history. Some surgeons are even sent to treat convicted criminals sentenced to hang.

I may never become the medical professional I wanted to be, but that doesn't mean I'll stop being the apprentice I was trained to be.

My heart rate begins to slow, breaths growing deeper. I return to Aspen's side, meet Gildmar's eyes. "Hand me that shard of seashell, then fetch me strands of spider silk and a splinter-thin bone. And where in the blazing iron is that wine?"

27

———————

Cobalt brings the wine. I remove the poultice and pour the deep red liquid over the wound. Gildmar uses a dropper—much like the ones my mother uses for her tinctures—and drips honey pyrus extract into Aspen's lips, explaining it will help manage the pain. I wish we had laudanum, but the extract seems to work nearly as well. The king's body goes limp and his moaning ceases. Then, with deft fingers, I take the sharpest shard of seashell and make the incision, widening the opening on either side of the arrow shaft.

I ignore the blood that pours forth, ignore how much blacker it is than red. When I finally see the head of the arrow, I understand the problem. Its head is edged with four barbs. Removing it isn't simply a matter of turning the arrow to let it escape between two ribs. I'll need to twist it, angle it, pull it to the side. All without puncturing his internal organs.

For one moment, I freeze, unsure how to proceed. Gildmar has no forceps, no tweezers. I will have to use my hands through all of this. Without a second thought, I pour wine over my hands to clean them and reach inside the cut.

Time slows. I close my eyes, forgetting how far off protocol I've gotten, ignore the feeling of Aspen's blood and tissues on my skin. A calm certainty floods through me, and I follow it, find the tip of the arrow. I slide it to the side and Aspen groans.

"More honey pyrus," I say to Gildmar.

She moves to obey, and I shift the arrowhead again. One of the barbs is free. Then another. I rotate it slightly, turn it to the side.

Free.

The arrow comes away, and I toss it to the floor, knowing none of the fae can take it from me. I cleanse the wound again, check for internal damage. It's hard to tell considering everything is discolored with the tendrils of black, but he appears without further injury. I call for spider silk and bone, which Gildmar hands me. As quickly and as neatly as I can with the makeshift tools, I stitch him back together.

I tie the last stitch, then step back. Time seems to shift back to normal, and I release a heavy sigh. Only now do I realize the sweat on my brow and back of my neck. Only now does it dawn on me what I did.

I performed a surgery without normal tools. Unguided. And mostly with my hands.

I'm not sure whether I should be proud or horrified. More than anything, I'm exhausted. The surgery took mere minutes, but every part of me was in the task, focused like never before. Now I can feel the energy draining from me.

"You did it," Lorelei says, coming to my side.

Foxglove gives me an appreciative nod. "You saved the king."

"That you did," Gildmar says from the other side of the table. "Something not even I could do. If you hadn't been here...well, I suppose Cobalt would have had me executed for being the death of his brother."

"I wouldn't do that, Gildmar," Cobalt says.

"Well, you should," she says. "Luckily, you don't have to. Apparently, your brother won the golden lot when the Reaping brought this human girl to be his mate."

Cobalt's face falls, and my eyes snap away from him.

"I'm going to clean up," I say. "I'll return to check on the king after."

I make my way back to Aspen's room, wanting nothing more than to be rid of stairs. Why did he have to place his bedroom nearly at the top of the palace? By the time I reach it, I find a bath of steaming water waiting for me. I probably have Lorelei to thank for that, although I can't imagine how it was filled in the time it took me to get here. Without delay, I peel off my blood-stained dress and toss it in a heap in the corner of the room. If the fae don't have any powerful detergents to clean blood from silk, the dress is ruined. I hadn't considered asking for an apron before the surgery began.

A moan escapes my lips as I sink into the tub. I feel like I could fall asleep, but as soon as I try to relax, my mind wanders to dark thoughts, making my muscles tense yet again.

I saved the king when I could have killed him. Should I have let him die? My heart sinks at the thought.

No. I did what I was trained to do. What I've always wanted to do. I saved someone.

I just hope his life was worth saving.

Hours later I make my way back to the room where I performed the surgery, only to find Aspen's body being lifted by several guards. A wave of terror goes through me. Did something happen? Had my surgery failed to save him?

"What's going on?" I ask.

A hand falls on my shoulder, and I find Gildmar at my side. "Worry not," she says in her ancient voice. "He's recovering."

"Then where are they taking him?"

She looks at me, aghast. "To your rooms, of course. The king should recover in comfort and privacy, where his mate can tend to him with ease."

I hate the way she says *tend to him*, as if I'm Aspen's subservient woman, eager to fulfill his every need. But I understand the sentiment. I was responsible for healing him, after all. I can think of him more like my patient rather than my mate. Wouldn't I want my patient to heal in comfort?

"Of course," I say, trying to hide my irritation.

I follow the guards back to the bedroom, cursing the stairs twice over now that I've had to ascend them for the second time today, then watch as they lay Aspen on the bed. When they depart, Gildmar remains. "I brought you more extract of honey pyrus." She hands me a vial. "Give him more when he seems to be in pain."

"Thank you," I say, then set the vial on the bedside table.

"I'm still astonished you managed to save him when I could not." Gildmar's voice comes out small, heavy with remorse. Then her eyes meet mine. "I never knew humans had such powers. Where did you learn such healing?"

"My mo—" I stop short, realizing I was about to say *my mother* when I'd meant to say Mr. Meeks. The mistake unsettles me, unearthing a flood of memories from my childhood. Memories of me and Mother "treating" her patrons. She'd stand at their heads, burning herbs over them, administering tinctures, while I'd place my hands over their bodies. Mother would praise me for clearing their energy and aiding in healing, and I would swell with pride. It wasn't until Amelie nearly died that I understood my folly. That's when Mr. Meeks showed me what true medicine was. When I realized Mother wasn't a healer but a fraud at worst and an herbalist at best. When I stopped believing in magic.

I shake the memories from my mind. "Surgery is a miraculous thing," I say instead.

She gives me a wide smile, making the corner of her eyes crinkle on her brown, bark-like face. Then she takes her leave.

I'm left alone with Aspen dozing on the bed. With slow steps, I approach him and look him over. Outfitted in nothing but a clean, elegant robe of bronze silk, his chest rises and falls in an even rhythm, face slack, lips slightly parted. He looks nothing like the fierce, dangerous king I've come to know.

My eyes rove across his torso. His skin still looks pale, but a hint of gold has replaced the ghostly blue. At least the tendrils of black seem to have receded a bit, showing only a few thin veins peeking above the collar of his robe. I reach a hand toward the collar, slowly peeling it away to reveal the bandaged wound. The skin is still angry around it, red, black, and purple with plenty of black tendrils branching away, streaking in every direction.

I return the collar to cover his torso, but as I pull my fingers away, Aspen's hand covers mine, heavy and warm. My eyes flash to his face, but his eyes remain closed. His face contorts, head rolling slowly from one side to the other. He mutters something I can't understand.

I retract my hand from under his and rush to the bedside table. "You need more honey pyrus," I say, then pour a dropperful between his lips.

His face relaxes and his muttering fades.

I watch him for a few moments, wondering what exactly I've gotten myself into. How long will I have to play nursemaid to him?

"Evie." The word comes from Aspen's lips, slow and heavy.

I try to ignore the irritation that lights a fire in my chest at the sound of my nickname—the nickname only Amelie ever used for me. "Yes, it's me."

"Are you...going...to kill me?" Each word comes out with great effort, but a smile tugs at the corner of his lips, eyes remaining closed.

"No, I saved you. Only iron knows why."

He winces. "Don't say iron."

I say nothing, hoping the honey pyrus will return him to his slumber.

He lifts his hand, an action that seems to pain him, and motions me forward.

I take a hesitant step toward him, then another.

"Evie," he repeats.

"What?"

"I wanted it to be you."

My brows furrow. "You wanted it to be me for what? To save you? If you're telling me you got wounded on purpose just so I'd have to—"

"No. At the wall."

"The wall," I echo.

"When you told me your name. I wanted it to be you. To be my Chosen."

I clench my teeth, heat rising to my cheeks. "So, what? You killed the Holstrom girls so you could punish me instead?"

He shakes his head. "No. And I didn't want to punish you. I wanted you."

I roll my eyes. "You're clearly drunk on honey pyrus, Your Majesty."

"Don't call me that." His tone deepens, darkens, though his words still sound slurred and strained. "It's Aspen when we're alone."

"Fine, *Aspen*. I'll do you a favor and forget this conversation ever happened."

Aspen goes quiet for a few moments. "I didn't know you weren't eldest," he whispers, "until you arrived at the palace. I wanted to ask you if you'd be with me instead. Remember that night? The dining room?"

Heat rises to my cheeks, recalling the glamour he placed over himself. "How could I forget."

"I was going to ask you then. But you hated me so much."

A cold suspicion crawls up my spine. "Did you kill my sister? Did you kill her so you could have me instead?"

"No." I'm surprised at the certainty in his tone. "She was sweet. Kind. I would never have hurt her."

I shake my head. "Well, this is all coming a little too late. My sister is dead, perhaps because of you."

His expression flickers. With pain? Sorrow? "It wasn't her body."

Ice chills my blood. "What?"

"The body. On the shore. Not your sister." His face goes slack as he loses consciousness.

I move closer, putting my hands on each side of his face, lightly slapping his cheek. "What do you mean it wasn't her body? Wake up! Explain, damn you!"

He remains silent, motionless.

My mind spins with questions, anxiety building and building higher and higher until I think I will explode. Is what he said true? Or was he simply hallucinating and speaking nonsense? Was he playing with me, trying to get into my head?

All I know is I'll get those answers. I'll nurse this son-of-a-harpy back to health if it's the last thing I do. And if I find out he lied...well, that will be the last thing *he* will live to do.

28

———————

I continue to monitor Aspen, seeking any sign that he's returning to consciousness. The evening fades to night, and I alternate between dozing on the couch and checking Aspen for signs of life. I give him honey pyrus on occasion, but only partial doses. This means I have to administer it more often, but it also gives me the hope that I can catch him lucid.

So far, no luck. All he does is mutter and moan, face twisting in agony, each time he wakes. By morning, his skin is burning with fever.

I call for Gildmar and have her fetch me fresh spider silk cloth so I can change the dressing of his wound. She brings me more honey pyrus too, wine steeped with fae herbs, and an aromatic broth to try and feed Aspen. Each time I examine him, my stomach sinks. The tendrils of black have stopped receding. They aren't growing, but they no longer seem to be fading away. His skin grows hotter and hotter.

"Is there anything else we can do?" I ask Gildmar. A full day has passed since the surgery, and I'm beginning to lose hope he'll recover. "Are there any fae methods for reversing iron poisoning?"

She shakes her head. "A wound as bad as his could take months—years even—to fully recover from. It was too close to his heart, and the poisoning spread too fast."

"How long do you think he'll be like this? When will he wake?"

"Weeks, possibly."

My hands clench into fists. I can't wait weeks. Not after what he told me yesterday. I'll go out of my mind wondering if what he said about my sister is true.

"At least he has your care," she says. "I never thought much about human-fae pairings, aside from being a necessary function to maintain the treaty. But seeing you care for him like this...it makes me think I've been wrong about humans. Perhaps you aren't all greedy invaders. Perhaps this peace we have is worth keeping."

Guilt fills my stomach with lead. She has no idea I'm only caring for him in a purely professional manner. Has no idea my main motivation for bringing him back to health is to bleed answers from him. But if perpetuating the lie is what keeps humans and fae at peace...

"He's very important to me," I say with a pleasant smile.

She pats me on the shoulder. "I'm sure he feels the same about you. Now, I'll leave you to rest. I'm sure you haven't slept much."

I watch her shuffle out the doors, suddenly curious how old she is. She seems ancient compared to Aspen, and Aspen is a thousand years old. It's possible her age is unrelated to her appearance. Other Earthen fae might be like her, for all I know, considering the only other I've seen was the Earthen Court ambassador.

I return to Aspen's side, then press the back of my hand to his forehead. Still burning. I push his robe aside and check the black veins, trying to find evidence that they are fading. His torso is hot to the touch, even warmer than his forehead. I take a seat on the bed next to him, my fingers skating across his skin until they reach his wound. I lay my palm over the bandages.

"Come out of this, Aspen." My whisper sounds more like a hiss. "I'm not done with you yet. If you dare die on me, I will decimate your corpse and cut it into a thousand pieces, then feed you to a kelpie."

Heat radiates from his skin, warming my palm through the cloth dressing. I grit my teeth, anger seething toward the wound. Even after everything I did to accomplish a successful operation, it still wasn't enough. He's still suffering, fighting against a poison I don't understand. A poison no human antibiotic or fae remedy can help.

I hate feeling this helpless. Useless. Powerless.

I close my eyes, breathing away my anger. "Heal, damn you."

Aspen makes a noise and my eyes fly open. His face is contorted, twisted with pain, breaths labored. He tries to speak, but his open mouth pulls into a grimace.

I reach for the vial next to the bed and give him half a dropperful of honey pyrus. He doesn't immediately relax, but the furrows between his brow begin to lessen. After a few minutes, his breathing evens out. His expression still looks pained, but his jaw has unclenched.

My hand moves to his forehead, and I'm startled to find a sheen of sweat over the skin. The fever has broken. That is, if fae process illness like humans do.

He tries to speak again, and I realize he's asking for something to drink. I reach for the herbed wine. Despite my many protestations in favor of water, Gildmar insisted fae heal better with wine. I put the shallow bowl to his lips, help him incline his head to drink it. After a few swallows, he sighs, then lays back on the pillow.

"Aspen," I say, "can you hear me?" *Please be lucid. Please be lucid.*

"Yes." The word comes out like a croak.

"How do you feel?"

He grimaces. "Awful. Am I dead yet?"

"Not yet."

His eyelids flutter. "I can't...open my eyes. The light. It hurts."

I reach for a clean cloth and immerse it in a bowl of cool water. After I wring it out, I drape it over his eyes. "Better?"

"No. I need more honey pyrus. The pain. It's too much."

I return to my seat on the bed, leaning in close. "I'll give you more honey pyrus, but only after you answer my questions."

A corner of his lips twitches into a half smile. "Cruel human."

"Monstrous fae."

"What do you want to know?" His words are still thick and heavy, barely above a whisper, but at least they're coherent.

My pulse begins to race. "Yesterday you said the body you found on the shore wasn't my sister's. Was that true?"

He winces, but I can't tell if it's from pain or from the realization of what he said. "Yes," he finally confesses.

"What happened to Amelie?"

"I don't know. She was never found."

"Whose body was it, then? Who was the girl I saw being pulled from the caves?" The memory seizes me. Pale skin, face obscured by hair dark with water and tangled with kelp. There was no part of me that doubted it was my sister, but the truth is, I never saw the body close enough to know for certain.

"A selkie," Aspen whispers.

My eyes go wide. "A selkie? How did she die?"

"She must have lost her sealskin. Without it, a selkie can only live on land in seelie form until sunrise unless she dons human clothing."

"Was she the one your guards saw running into the caves?" I ask. "Or was that my sister?"

"Impossible to say."

My heart sinks. I thought I'd feel relief knowing there was a possibility Amelie was still alive, but now I'm just as disheartened as ever. If she really did run to the caves, then she could have been devoured by the sea or some fae monster, leaving no trace of her remains. Or she could be...anywhere. "You truly don't know where Amelie is? Why she disappeared?"

"I don't."

"Promise me."

His head moves, facing me, despite his vision obscured by the cloth. "I promise. I know nothing about her disappearance or her current whereabouts." After a moment, he adds, "Can you promise me the same? That you had nothing to do with it? That you have no part in any plot against the fae, my throne, or my life?"

"How can you ask me that? Of course I don't."

"The promise of a human means nothing when they can lie, but I want to hear you say it."

I swallow hard. "I promise. I had nothing to do with Amelie's disappearance, nor am I part of any plot against you, your throne, or faekind."

He sighs, face relaxing. "Is that all?"

I could leave him to rest, pour a dropper of honey pyrus between his lips now that he's answered my most pressing questions. But why waste the opportunity? "No. There's more I need from you. What really happened to the Holstrom girls? What treasonous act did they perform? I want you to tell me everything."

He lets out an irritated grumble. "At least give me more honey pyrus and wine first. If you're going to make me talk, I want to have a voice at the end of it. And sweet oblivion to slip into once it's over."

"Fine." I grab the vial. "I'll give you a few drops now, and a half-dropper after."

He parts his lips and I drop in the extract, followed by a few hearty sips of wine and broth.

Once he settles back down, I say, "Go on."

"Impatient human." His voice is gravelly, but somewhat stronger than before. "Very well. It was days before the mate ceremonies were to take place. The girls hadn't been here a week, even. They'd been cold, distant. Worse than you."

"I doubt that."

He continues. "Theresa came to me in the night. She'd barely said a word to me before this, but there she was, slipping into bed next to me, whispering, telling me she was eager to start living as mates now. I was perplexed but too intrigued to dismiss her. Not when she seemed to want it so badly."

My stomach churns, and an unexpected fury moves through me. "Spare me the details."

He smirks. "Are you judging me?"

"No."

"You are. I know humans hold mating as a sacred act, but most fae don't. However, it was that very realization that sparked my suspicion. I was on alert after that and grew even more concerned when she said she wanted her sister to join, that Maryanne couldn't bear the thought of becoming my brother's mate without having experienced a man before. The girl stepped out of the shadows and into the bed with us. Said I seemed like a lover who could provide the instruction she needed."

"I told you to spare me the details," I say through my teeth.

"You also said you wanted to know everything."

"Then get on with it."

I can tell he's amused by my discomfort. He continues. "After that, my suspicion only grew. I wasn't falling for their false passions, not even as Theresa climbed in my lap, trying to lull me with her words. Kissing me."

I hate the visions that swirl inside my imagination. Theresa and Maryanne Holstrom, Sableton's perfect little sweethearts, crawling all over Aspen, caressing him. Tasting him. My fingers dig into my palms as I try to quell my fury. Why do these visions infuriate me so?

"I knew they were up to something," Aspen says, "and I wanted to know what it was. I didn't close my eyes. Not when Maryanne turned my lips to hers. Not when Theresa lifted the iron blade, bared her teeth as she brought it down. My mind cleared at once, and I understood their true intentions. I blocked the thrust of the blade and turned it on her, then her sister. They were dead before their bodies struck the ground."

My fury extinguishes to horror. "You killed them. Without question. Without trial."

"They never had a chance." I'm surprised at the sorrow in his tone. "I was so enraged when I realized what was happening, I never stopped to think I could have overpowered them, could have kept them alive for questioning. Not even their bodies at my feet halted my anger. I was blinded by it. Swallowed by it. I shifted to my unseelie form and tore through Faerwyvae, past the wall, into your village. There I slaughtered every animal I'd gifted the Holstroms, my antlers tearing into flesh and bone, dooming the treaty, damning all of the Fair Isle to war."

Bile rises in my throat as my eyes flash to his twisting antlers. I shudder. "You really did it. You murdered the Holstrom girls and killed their animals."

"They were defenseless." His voice is a sorrowful whisper. "I can still smell the blood of the cows, the pigs, the sheep. Feel the resistance of their flesh as it met my antlers. I can still see the bodies of the girls, littering the floor. I've had that bedroom scoured and sealed off. Made a new one here."

I try to ignore how shaken he seems by relaying the tale. Try, instead, to see the monster he is. "You told my people it was treason."

"It was. They made an attempt on my life, and I delivered my cruel justice."

"And you expect me to believe you had nothing to do with my sister going missing?"

"I already promised you I don't," he says, his tone darkening. "I am not kind and I am not a hero, but I don't kill unprovoked. Your sister never did a thing to anger me. I may not have loved her, but I would never have wished her harm. And I never would have hurt the Holstrom girls if they hadn't come to kill me first."

I don't know what to think, what to believe. Could he be crazy? Could he have imagined the dagger in Theresa's hands? Misunderstood some unintentional gesture? Then again, their behavior in the first place is unimaginable. If they had the gall to seduce him in the night, days before their weddings, then it could be I never really knew them at all.

"Take me away, Evie," Aspen mutters. "Send me to oblivion. Let me forget."

With trembling fingers, I grab the extract and give him half a dropperful. He slips into unconsciousness before the vial returns to the table. I stare at him, pondering the duality between the vicious beast that kills defenseless girls, and the vulnerable king who mourns their deaths.

With every answer I get, my world shifts further upside-down.

Too shaken by the story to do anything else, I slide to the floor and cry into my hands.

29

———————

The next morning, I leave Aspen alone in his room so I can get some air. He managed to sleep through the night, and last time I checked his wound, the black tendrils were finally beginning to fade in earnest.

I find myself standing at the open expanse in the formal dining room, leaning against the rail as I breathe in fresh, salty air. It's so much better than the tension of the bedroom. The sea crashes at the shore then recedes, revealing entrances to the coral caves between each wave. I can't help but ponder what Aspen said.

Somewhere out there, Amelie could be alive.

"I hope you don't take offense, but you look terrible."

I turn to find Foxglove and flash him a smile. "I do take offense, but I think you must be right. Lorelei said the same thing earlier."

"Come," he says, "you should bathe. Dress. Let me brush out your hair."

I shake my head. "I don't want to disturb the king. He's been sleeping soundly all morning."

"We won't need to. Lorelei fetched some clothes from your room and brought them to your parlor. We've had a tub brought in as well."

I raise my brows. "Do I smell that awful?"

Foxglove does his best to hide his distaste, but it isn't working. "Humans do have rather...*odd* aromas that fae don't have. Besides, you could use the relaxation of a bath after everything you've done for His Majesty."

"Fine," I say with a sigh. "Take me to the bath."

He leads me to the garish parlor where I'd met with Doris Mason. Inside, I'm greeted by Lorelei and a steaming bathtub. Foxglove takes his leave and Lorelei helps me undress. She asks if I'd like privacy, but I make her stay with me. I've had enough alone time with my thoughts. Now I just need some company that isn't an unconscious Aspen.

She perches at the edge of one of the horrid chairs while I soak in the tub. We chat about mindless matters, sharing a few shallow laughs, but my worries aren't kept at bay for long. I need to tell someone about what I've learned. Perhaps I can trust Lorelei. Amelie seemed to.

"Aspen told me some things when he was awake," I say, trying to keep my tone nonchalant. I toy with my rowan berry necklace, keeping it from soaking too long in the water.

"Like what?"

I take a deep breath. "About Amelie."

She sits forward eagerly. "Does he know what happened to her?"

"No, but she might be alive." I watch her face for any indication that she already knows.

Her brows furrow. "Alive? But the body—"

"It wasn't Amelie's. It belonged to a selkie who lost her sealskin."

Lorelei is clearly perplexed. So she didn't know after all. "A selkie doesn't simply lose her skin. What happened to her? And what happened to Amelie?"

"He didn't have answers to either. I've been puzzling over it ever since. Why didn't he tell me? Why did he allow me and everyone else in the castle to believe Amelie died? Yet, he allowed the vicar to assume she's still alive and well."

Lorelei leaves the chair to crouch beside the tub, expression grave. She keeps her voice low. "Those questions are best saved for Aspen and asked in private. If he kept this information from us, it's for a reason. Don't tell anyone else."

"Why? What reason could he have for hiding it? He could be sending guards out looking for my sister. Instead, everyone thinks she's dead."

"I'm sure his most trusted guards know," Lorelei says. "There were many who witnessed the body they found. They will know the truth. He could have trackers seeking Amelie right now. If someone means him or her harm, it's best our efforts to find Amelie are made with discretion."

I nod. "Perhaps you're right. I just hate not knowing what's going on."

"I'm sure the king feels the same."

I chew my bottom lip. "He also told me about the Holstrom girls. He confessed to killing them, saying they came to assassinate him with a dagger. How do I know it's true?"

She lifts a shoulder in a shrug. "Guards found a blade in his room. It was of human design and was traced back to your village smith."

"But how do I know his account of things isn't skewed? I know he can't lie, but how do I trust his perspective is accurate?"

"You either trust him or you don't. I can't tell you how to feel. All I can say is I trust Aspen with my life."

A feeble smile tugs at my lips. "Even though he punished you by appointing you my lady's maid?"

"Meh," she says. "I've had worse company."

"Speaking of worse company." I jump at Foxglove's voice. He stands in the doorway looking flustered. He closes the door behind him, then lays out a sheer, spider silk dress in a deep plum color on top of the clothes Lorelei had brought. "We're going to need to speed up our plans. Forget just getting you clean. We need to make you look like a queen."

"What? Why?"

Foxglove gives me an apologetic smile and adjusts his spectacles. "It's time to meet your future mother-in-law."

I'm trembling by the time I'm dressed and ready to meet my guest, unsure what to expect. Foxglove has been cryptic at best, hushing every question with an admonition that I'll ruin my makeup if I keep talking. He painted my lips with rouge, powdered my cheeks with crystalline dust, and lined my eyes with black and gold kohl. My hair has been brushed out in long waves, something he insisted on doing instead of his usual updo. My dress is so sheer, I blushed when I first saw myself in the mirror.

Now, as I walk down the halls, I can feel each breeze as if I were naked. All the fae dresses have been light and gauzy, but this one is unlike any I've worn so far. The plum spider silk is tight around my torso, then flows outward at the waist, trailing past my ankles. Its plunging neckline reveals a generous portion of my curving breasts, and the silk barely covers the rest.

At least Foxglove let me keep my dagger strapped to my thigh, the only argument I won. I blanched when he muttered that I might end up needing it.

I tug at one of my long bronze earrings, fashioned into a strand of maple leaves. "Is all this really necessary?" I ask Foxglove.

He and Lorelei exchange a glance. "You'll see," he says.

I hold my breath as we enter the formal dining room. There at the other end, standing at the rail I left not long ago, is Queen Melusine. She's facing away from us, so all I see is a cascade of silky, indigo hair, pale blue arms, and a long, sinuous serpent's tail. As she turns, we sink into bows and curtsies. I'm grateful for the moment to compose myself before I face her, but the time to rise comes too soon, and I find myself straightening with Foxglove and Lorelei, pulse racing.

Now I can see Melusine fully, and my state of dress makes sense. The Queen of the Sea Court has a human-like upper body, both slim and seductively curving, breasts barely hidden beneath strands of her glossy, blue hair. Her face holds an unprecedented beauty with angled eyes the color of a stormy sea, high blushing cheekbones, a perfect nose, and full coral-red lips. Strands of pink coral hang from her ears and around her slim neck. The planes of her flat stomach disappear into scales that end in her shimmering blue-green tail.

I feel overdressed and hideous in her presence.

"Your Majesty," Foxglove says, taking a step forward. "Queen Melusine, I would like to introduce Miss Evelyn Fairfield."

Melusine smiles, showing rows of pointed teeth. *Fangs.* I resist the urge to back away from her. Fangs don't mean anything, I remind myself. Foxglove has fangs, and he's harmless. Pleasant, even. But the more I've gotten to know Foxglove, the more his pointed teeth seem dainty and fashionable. Melusine's, on the other hand, look anything but, with their sharp, serrated edges and elongated tips. Oddly, they do nothing to take from her beauty. Somehow, the danger they present makes her more breathtaking.

"Your Majesty." I curtsy again, doing my best to keep my composure.

She eyes me, nose turned up as if she's assessing an unusual speck of dirt. "Where is that son of mine?" Her voice is light, flowing. Like a melody. Every word carries the roar of the ocean, the song of the siren.

"Resting," Foxglove says. His voice sounds like shattering glass after the lilting tune of hers. "He's recovering from his injury."

Melusine looks displeased, though not surprised. She must already know what happened to Aspen. "And where is my other son? Where is dear Cobalt?"

"Here." Cobalt enters the room and bows before his mother, his moves flustered as if he'd rushed to make it here.

She wrinkles her nose at him as she eyes him from head to toe. "You dare greet me like that?"

He straightens, jaw shifting back and forth. "I take seelie form on land, Mother. You know this."

"I thought you'd have the decency to humor me, at least. Never mind, then. Take me to see Aspen."

"He's resting," Foxglove says again. "With his recovery so recently begun, we don't want to wake him."

Melusine throws her hands in the air. "Why did I come all this way if not to see my son?"

"Good question," Cobalt says. "Why did you come?"

She seems to ignore the ice in his tone. "This was my castle, once," she says. "I wanted to make sure it's in good hands."

"I'm more than capable of ruling in my brother's stead while he's incapacitated."

"You mistake me," she says. "I'm not curious about your hands, but hers." Her eyes slide to mine.

Cobalt follows her gaze, eyes going wide when they take in my appearance. He'd been so distracted by his mother, it's the first time he's looked at me since entering the room.

I resist the urge to cross my arms over my chest, and instead, put on my most convincing smile. "I am pleased to meet the mother of my mate," I say.

She slithers toward me on her serpent's tail while her upper body remains upright, bearing regal. Once she stops, I have to tilt my head to meet her eyes as she towers over me. "Are you?" she asks, tone mocking. "Are you truly pleased to meet me?"

"I am. I've heard so much about you."

She barks a musical laugh. "Not from Aspen, I'm sure. He barely considers me his mother anymore. He treats me as a fellow royal of the Council of Eleven Courts, nothing more."

"Still, I'm pleased to be in your presence just the same."

"Such human politeness," she says with disgust. "Fake."

"Mother," Cobalt says, a warning in his tone. "Aspen plans on making her his queen, which will make her nearly your equal."

She scoffs at that, eyes never leaving mine. "Nearly my equal. Ha! I see no crown on her head, nor have I gotten an invitation to her coronation. I've hardly heard more than whispers about this supposed upcoming wedding."

"There have yet to be any plans made for her coronation," Foxglove says, "all things considered. When Aspen recovers, I'm sure he'll—"

"Yes, I'm curious what he'll do with her." She slithers even closer, and I'm certain she sniffs at the air around me. "What are you to him?"

I swallow hard, hoping she can't hear my racing heart. "I'm his mate."

A corner of her lips pulls into a smile. "Are you though?"

"We performed the ceremony last week."

"Nothing more than a pretty show," she hisses. "Something tells me you have yet to become his true mate. You don't have the right...smell about you."

I want to argue that Foxglove and Lorelei had me bathed and cleansed until my skin was pink before I came to meet her, but I stop myself. First of all, my bathing habits are none of her business. And second, I have the feeling she isn't talking about *that* kind of smell. She's referring to something I don't understand. Something fae.

I realize another thing. Foxglove and Lorelei didn't have me dressed in silk and painted with rouge just to look pretty for the queen. They did it to give me an advantage. To place me as her equal. They wanted her to see me as someone to respect. And here I am cowering before her like a wounded dog.

I square my shoulders and stand at my full height. My voice takes on the same bored quality I've heard Aspen use so many times. Every word I'm about to say is a gamble, but I take it. "Well, this has been pleasant, hasn't it? Now, if we're done parsing words and smelling each other, I think I'll go check on my mate." I turn away from her, keeping my chin held high, then pause before I reach the hall. "I'll have someone fetch you when he wakes. If he wants to see you."

I enter the hall, and Foxglove and Lorelei follow. Only when I'm out of earshot, do I let out the breath I was holding. I don't dare look behind me, terrified I'll see a raging sea serpent charging after me, but we continue on, and my head remains attached to my shoulders.

Lorelei finally breaks the silence with a laugh. "Learning how to play the game, are we?"

"I'm playing it," I say. "Let's just hope I don't lose."

30

I'm still seething over my encounter with Melusine as I pace my room. Who does she think she is, coming here to look me over and try to make me feel inferior? How does she benefit from such actions, aside from potentially scaring me away? From what Cobalt told me, Melusine is politically unseelie, meaning she can't be too pleased her son's marriage is keeping the peace. Or perhaps she thinks I'm not good enough for her son, feeble human that I am.

"I'll show her who's feeble," I mutter as I pull the bronze earrings from my ears and toss them on the bedside table. I catch sight of Aspen and turn to face him, amazed at the color that has returned to his cheeks. With a sigh, I sit on the bed next to him to check his vitals. "No wonder you're so awful. I know where you get it now."

He says nothing, of course, sleeping peacefully while I touch his forehead. His temperature has gone down, and even the sheen of sweat has disappeared. I move my hand to his chest, intending to change the dressing over the wound.

Aspen's eyes fly open, and his hand circles my wrist. I lose my balance, toppling toward him. He catches my other wrist, then shifts his weight. Before I know it, I'm pinned to the bed, Aspen straddled over me. His lips peel back from his teeth, chest heaving as his eyes bore into me.

"You're clearly feeling better," I say with a sneer as I try to twist from his grasp.

"What are you doing here?"

"What do you think I'm doing? Tending your wounds, like I've done every nauseating hour since you were injured."

"Injured." He says the word as if it's foreign to him.

I freeze. "You don't remember?"

He searches my eyes, brows knitting together. "I was wounded."

"Yes. In your idiotic attempt to satiate Mr. Holstrom's bloodlust, you nearly got yourself killed."

"You...did something to me."

"It's called saving your pathetic life, and you're welcome."

He seems to relax and releases my wrists but doesn't move from over me. My body is still pinned between his legs and thighs.

I push at his chest, but he doesn't budge. "Will you get off me?"

His eyes widen as he looks at me as if seeing me for the first time. He takes in the sheer plum dress, eyes roving over the lowcut neckline. His lips twist into a mischievous smirk, making him look more like himself than he has in days. "Why, are you scared?"

I roll my eyes. "I'm scared you'll pull your stitches and all my hard work will be for nothing."

"No, you are scared of me," he says, voice low. "I can feel it."

I push at his chest again, tempted to punch him in his wound. It's then I realize the trails of black have all but disappeared from his torso. "I'm not scared. This is just highly inappropriate." But now that he mentions it, perhaps I should be afraid. He clearly isn't in his right mind, considering he woke up without memory of what happened. And even if he were in his right mind...my eyes involuntarily flash toward his antlers. If he wanted to, he could gut me here and now. I wouldn't have time to scream.

"You're thinking about what I did on the farm."

I shoot him a scowl. "So, you do remember."

A pained look crosses his face. "I won't hurt you, Evie."

I can't help but stare at his antlers again, imagining them covered in blood and gore.

Aspen seems amused. "Curious? You keep looking."

"Yes, I keep looking. There's a pair of razor-sharp antlers just inches from my face. I'm trying not to get stabbed in the eye." My words come out more breathless than I intend.

"I'm more than capable of handling my antlers. And how do you know they are razor sharp if you've never felt their cut?"

Part of me wants to push him away, make him stop his teasing, but another part of me is morbidly fascinated with his antlers, now that I know what they are capable of. There's something enticing about facing the danger of them. I want to touch them, admire them, the same way I want to admire a well-crafted blade or scalpel. Do they feel like bone? Rock?

He rolls his eyes as if he can hear my thoughts. "You can touch them. You're probably the first human in my presence who hasn't tried."

The first human who hasn't tried. This makes me think of my sister. Did *she* try to touch them? Were they ever close enough for her to do so? Or did she simply ask in her charmingly naive way? Without realizing it, my hand moves toward them, pulled by an invisible force.

Aspen leans closer, bracing himself on his forearms.

My fingers find the tip of one of the tines. It's sharp, but not enough to pierce skin without pressure. I'm surprised to find how smooth the surface is, covered in soft velvet. I run my fingertips down the length of the main beam, then trace one of the lower tines that branch off it. I'm mesmerized. Thrilled to be touching such a delicate yet powerful weapon.

Aspen shudders.

I pause, my sense of self-awareness returning. "What was that for?"

"My antlers are very sensitive," he says. His voice is quiet, breathy. "Every touch is both pleasure and pain."

I pull my hand away, heat flooding my cheeks. I had no idea antlers held sensation. "Why in the bloody name of iron didn't you tell me you could feel that?" I say through my teeth.

"Because I didn't want you to stop."

His words pull the breath from my lungs, and the intensity of his gaze holds me in place. This close, I can see his eyes like I never have before. They aren't brown like I originally thought, but every color of autumn. Golds, bronze, emerald, and ruby swirl in his irises. I can't stop myself from thinking it—*he's beautiful.* The most beautiful creature I've ever seen. And he's looking at me like I'm beautiful too. A luxurious feast for a starving man. His full lips are so close to mine, I can feel his breath, smell the rosemary on his skin. I can't help but remember our kiss during the mate ceremony, and that same strange fire roars in my chest.

As if he can feel it too, he closes the distance between us, lips crushing into mine. I don't think to stop him, to fight him. I give in to the kiss, let it deepen. My body hums with a hungry desire, eager to consume more of him.

With his knees, he pushes one of my legs aside, then the other. As a reflex, I wrap them around his waist, drawing him closer. My lips part for his tongue, and a soft moan escapes his mouth. I bring one hand to his lower back, and the other explores the firm muscles of his chest, careful not to skate too close to his wound.

One of his hands leaves the bed to do some exploring of its own. I feel his fingers caress my neck, then turn my head to the side so his lips can trail over the skin where his fingers just were. His kisses move down my neck and across my collar bone, then trace lower along the neckline of my dress.

When his lips return to mine, I claim them eagerly. His hand slides from my neck and over the curve of my breast. I gasp, feeling the trail of his fingers through the spider silk, sensations multiplied as if his fingers were flames. His thumb makes lazy circles over the crest of my breast, and a shock of pleasure runs through me, so intense I arch my back to meet it. A fire ignites at the apex of my thighs, and I think I will die if it isn't quelled.

His other hand finds my knee, traces up my thigh. I know where it's going and I don't care. I want it to go higher. Want him everywhere all at once. I have no control, no awareness but him. His fingers reach my dagger belt. He winces, then jolts upright. It's enough to shatter the moment, bringing clarity to my mind.

My breaths come out heavy as I recover from the spell of passion. The spell that had me powerless. Vulnerable. Completely unlike myself. I pull away from him, straightening my dress. "What in the name of iron was that?"

Aspen puts the tip of his thumb to his mouth, as if soothing a burn. He winces again, shaking out his hand. "Why are you wearing that damn thing?"

I ignore the question, scooting farther away from him. "You did it again, didn't you? You glamoured yourself to make me want you."

His expression darkens. "Is that the only way you can imagine kissing me? Under the pretense of a glamour? Am I really so disgusting to you?"

"Yes, you're disgusting." I slide from the bed and to my feet, eyes locked on him, ready for any sign that he'll pounce. "Only a disgusting creature would use a glamour to seduce a woman."

He shakes his head. "If that's what helps you sleep at night."

"Speaking of sleeping at night," I say, moving to the wardrobe. I grab a nightdress, a robe, and a heavy blue gown. "The bedroom is yours again. I'll sleep in my parlor."

"You liked your parlor, then?" He grins, eyes alight with mischief.

I don't rise to the bait. With my head held high, I stride to the doors, ignoring the attention of the guards waiting outside. "Oh, and by the way," I call out behind me, "your mother's here."

The last thing I see before I slam the doors is Aspen's look of utter horror.

31

The couch in my parlor isn't nearly as comfortable as Aspen's bed, nor the couch in his room that I'd been sleeping on while he'd been recovering. I don't know how much of that is due to a discrepancy in quality or from the weight of my humiliation.

Every time I close my eyes, I see Aspen's face, feel Aspen's lips, hear his breath in my ear. I see myself pulling him closer, hips writhing against his. The fire ignites all over again, and I hate it. I cover my eyes with my hands, as if that could banish the visions in my mind. As if it could make me forget the taste of his lips.

My humiliation turns to fury when I wake the next morning. I go over my list of reasons why I hate Aspen, King of the Autumn Court.

I hate that he glamoured himself.

I hate that he tried to seduce me.

I hate that he made me feel out of control.

I hate his lack of apology.

Hate the way he looked at me.

Hate the way he kissed.

The way he breathed.

The way his hands felt on my—

A knock sounds on the parlor door.

Snap out of it, Evie. I steady my ragged breathing just in time to greet Lorelei.

"You're requested on the balcony," she says, looking both flustered and pleased. "The king has fully recovered and will be holding audience with Queen Melusine."

I furrow my brow. "The balcony?"

"That's where you had the mate ceremony."

"Yes, but why are we going there?"

"Aspen holds court there. It's his throne room of sorts."

"I see." I twist my fingers together, anxiety building in my chest. "Must I go?"

"I think it's wise. You'll be sitting at the king's side where his queen would be. It's a bit of a power move, hosting his mother before his throne as opposed to over breakfast."

"I suppose that does sound important." My heart sinks. I think of all the pruning and prodding Foxglove did yesterday to make me a suitable match for the Sea Queen. Am I ready to face her so soon? Better yet, am I ready to face Aspen so soon?

Lorelei's mouth quirks at the corner. "You've clearly got a lot on your mind. Care to share?"

"No," I say in a rush. There's no way I'm telling her or anyone about what happened last night. Not that most in the palace don't already assume such behavior exists between me and the king. Does Lorelei know the truth? That we aren't true mates?

"Fine then. Let's get you dressed."

"On one condition." I hold up a finger. "Put me in a more modest dress today. No exceptions."

By the time we reach the balcony, the two brothers are already there. Aspen sits on one of the ornate thrones on the raised dais, the one to his right remaining empty. I hadn't paid much attention to the thrones during our mate ceremony, but now that I'm less distracted, I notice their beauty. Both are identical, constructed of twining roots and branches, gold leaves sprouting from the sides. Cobalt stands at Aspen's left, a step down from the dais. Several guards wait on each side of the balcony.

Cobalt offers me a kind smile, while Aspen lounges in his throne, barely looking at me. The king reminds me of a jungle cat, lazing in his tree. Beautiful and dangerous, even at rest.

I keep my gaze on the empty throne as I make my way forward. Today

I'm dressed in a pale blue gown. The cut of the neckline is still low, but the top is a heavy silk brocade, the skirt layers of frothy blue chiffon. An elegant necklace of bronze and sapphire circles my neck.

I take my seat in the empty throne, trying to ignore the tension rising between me and Aspen. Or am I imagining it? I glance at the king from the corner of my eye, but he's paying me no heed. His chin rests on his fist, elbow propped on the arm of the throne. His other hand sprawls across the armrest. Too close to mine. He taps his fingers in a bored way, and all I can think about is how they felt on my skin.

"Sleep well?" Aspen's voice is a cold whisper, and he doesn't face me to say it.

My eyes dart away from his fingers, straight ahead. "Yes," I say through my teeth. It's a lie, of course.

"You didn't check my bandages this morning." This time he turns his head toward me. "Do you neglect all your patients like that?"

"You were obviously feeling well enough to manage on your own."

"Oh, but I much prefer to be managed by you."

Heat flushes my cheeks, and I refuse to meet the smirk I know is waiting for me.

I'm saved from coming up with a clever reply when I catch sight of movement on the stairs leading to the balcony. Indigo hair. Dazzling blue eyes. Queen Melusine seems somehow more beautiful than she was yesterday as she slithers up the remaining steps to the balcony floor. She smiles indulgently as she approaches. "Aspen, my dear son. So wonderful it is to see you well. How is it you recovered so quickly?"

He covers my hand with his, and I resist the urge to flinch. "I had a good healer. Evelyn has many talents."

She looks down her nose at me, then returns her attention to Aspen. "Many talents, indeed. Although I heard quite the rumor yesterday. Though you recovered, you and your mate spent the night apart. Trouble in the bedroom?"

Aspen gives her a smile that doesn't reach his eyes. "No trouble, Mother, though I do appreciate your concern. Dear Evie was keeping me awake and thought it best to leave me in peace. She moans in her sleep, you see."

The way he says *moans* makes my breath catch. There was a hint of jest in his tone, and I know it was meant for me. Teasing. Tempting. I keep my breathing steady, trying not to over-think it.

Melusine's eyes dart toward me, as if she caught the jest as well. For a moment, her expression turns from haughty to worry. In the blink of an eye, her composure returns. "What a generous mate you have. In fact, I'd like to get to know her a little better. Evelyn, will you walk the shore with me tonight? See me off before I return home?"

I open my mouth, not sure what to say. I almost wish Aspen would answer for me, but he doesn't. What does she want with me? Is it safe to speak with her in private? And by the coral caves, no less. Then another thought comes to mind. *The coral caves.* Melusine is the Sea Queen. If Amelie really did run to the caves the night she disappeared, Melusine might know something. It's a long shot, but it's all I have.

"I'd be honored, Your Majesty," I say.

"You'll be leaving tonight, then?" Cobalt asks, speaking for the first time.

"Yes, dear son, but don't look so sad. If you miss me, you'll have to visit more often." With that, she turns and slithers back the way she came.

"Adjourned," Aspen says, even though Cobalt and I are the only ones in attendance aside from the guards.

Cobalt looks from Aspen to me, hesitating, then leaves the balcony. I'm tempted to do the same, but there's something I need from Aspen.

He remains seated on his throne, scowling after his mother. I shift in my seat to face him. "We need to talk."

His scowl disappears, turning to mischief as he eyes the length of my gown. "I can think of something better we can do. It doesn't involve talking at all."

I blush. "No, thank you. You are never taking advantage of me like that again."

He scoffs. "Take advantage? I'm not the one who forced secrets from my lips in a vulnerable state."

"I never imagined you could admit to being vulnerable."

"I never imagined you could kiss the way you did."

My heart races at his words. The truth is, I never imagined I could kiss like that either. Honestly, I think he did most of the kissing. I just opened to it, followed his lead. Moved the way he moved, breathed the way he breathed—I shake my head, squeezing my thighs together.

"Stop trying to change the subject. I need you to explain some things. First of all, why didn't you tell me my sister was alive? You let me believe she was dead."

His expression darkens, looking from his guards to the other end of the balcony. "Keep your voice down."

"Then answer the question."

He lets out an irritated grumble. "I never planned on deceiving you, but you seemed so convinced the body you saw was hers. I figured it might be safer that way, for everyone involved. At least until I discovered the truth."

"How in the bloody name of iron did you figure that was safer?"

"I don't know who's behind this," he says, rubbing his brow. "If the person responsible thinks we assume your sister is dead, they won't expect us to be looking for her."

"Does that mean you *are* looking for her?"

He nods. "Not that it's doing any good. There are no trails. No clues. Every day I await the ransom note, the bargain. Every day nothing comes of it. I hate dealing with assassins I can't see. They should at least have the decency to face me head on."

"Who would hold Amelie against you like that?"

"It could be anyone. Any of the unseelie who want war. Any of the humans who want the same. Any of the seelie council fae who'd prefer to see my brother on the throne. The hosting court of the Chosen is always at risk during the month following a Reaping. What I do or don't do with you could turn the tide. If I treat you badly, refuse a marriage alliance, halt compensation to your mother, any of that could forfeit the treaty. It makes me a target from all sides."

My heart does a flip at the mention of my mother. "How are you compensating her, anyway? I imagine it isn't with farm animals."

"She refused all talk of compensation. There was no bargain Foxglove could tempt her with. So I purchased her apothecary and put it under her name, in addition to leaving a heavy fund to maintain it. She will never have to worry about rent or repair. Even if she refuses to spend a coin from the fund, it will be done on her behalf."

A lump rises in my throat. My mother. She's being taken care of. Her life's passion—the apothecary—is secured. Was that Aspen's doing? Foxglove's? The council? I can't bring myself to ask.

"Regardless," Aspen says, interrupting my thoughts, "even before the Reaping, I tended to attract the disdain of seelie and unseelie alike. I have many potential enemies. Many who would like to see me lose my throne."

I remember what Cobalt had said about Aspen. How he constantly shifts sides. "Why do you do it?" I ask. "Why do you attract the rage of the council? If you just chose a side and stuck with it, they wouldn't resent you the way they do."

He lets out a cold laugh. "No, I'm sure you're right, but that's not something I'm willing to do."

"Why? You talk about maintaining the safety of the isle. Isn't that more important than childish games?"

"What I do isn't a game," he says, meeting my eyes with his steely gaze. "What I do creates balance. A balance that—if upended—could create chaos for my people."

"I don't understand."

"No, you don't."

I lean toward him. "Then tell me. I need to know what's going on."

He lets out a heavy sigh. "There's something you should understand. The seelie, the unseelie, it isn't a matter of good or bad. The seelie want the experiences the humans opened for them. To love. To feel. To hate. The power of choice and consequence. Luxury. Lack. Poverty. They want all of it. The unseelie want the old ways. They want solitude. Connection to nature. Instinct."

"That makes sense," I say.

"Since the war ended, we've maintained balance. The seelie live how they want to live, and the unseelie follow their own ways. There is give and take. Each court and ruler and citizen has the right to choose. For most of us, it's enough, but for others..."

I lean closer, entranced by his candid words, his serious tone. He's never spoken this way before, not even when he was recovering from his wound. "Go on."

"Some of the seelie see the unseelie as barbaric. Lesser. Vile, dangerous creatures that shouldn't be allowed the level of freedom they get. You've met the kelpie. Would you say he should be allowed to torment stray travelers the way he does?"

I shake my head, the memory of nearly drowning still fresh in my mind.

"But it is the kelpie's nature. Lost travelers are his prey, the same way a rabbit is prey to a wolf. The radical seelie want the unseelie ways to end. To force them seelie or destroy them. The radical unseelie feel the same way, but in reverse. They want the human influence off the isle, to free their kind from the shackles of the seelie way. Without human influence, clothes, food, the seelie would cease to exist. We would revert to our unseelie forms and the isle would return to what it was long ago. Can you see the conflict?"

"Yes, but what does that have to do with you shifting sides on the council?"

"What do you think would happen if the council shifted too heavily one side or another?"

I lift my shoulder in a shrug, even though I think I know where he's going with this.

"If one side or the other got total control, the other side would be eliminated. If the seelie ruled the council, the unseelie would be outlawed, banished, executed. Strapped into clothing, human food forced into their mouths. On the other hand, if the unseelie took control, they would exterminate the humans in their sleep, not bothering with the formalities of war. They would force the seelie to abandon all that they have come to hold dear."

My eyes widen with realization. "You're trying to prevent that from happening."

"I believe every fae has a right to choose. For that, we must maintain balance."

I sit back in my throne, feeling drained. Everything I thought I knew about Aspen is crashing around me. He may be arrogant and irritating and possibly paranoid, but he's fighting for something I can understand. For not the first time in my life, I wonder just how wrong I've been about faekind. "This is indeed complicated."

"It is," Aspen says. "Sometimes I feel like the unseelie are right. That it would be better not to feel pain or pleasure. To take my stag form forever and live on instinct in the pure radiance of my true nature. But other times," he meets my eyes, "I feel like I couldn't possibly give all this up."

"Why did you choose me?" I find myself asking, voice barely above a whisper.

"I told you the first time you asked," he says. "My words were true. I chose you because you put a knife to me."

I narrow my eyes. "When you were recovering, you said you hadn't wanted to punish me."

"No, you're right, but my words are true just the same. After the assassination attempt by the Holstrom girls, I nearly agreed to wage war on your kind. The seelie on the council talked me out of it, encouraged me to choose another for the Reaping. I could have left it to random choice, but there was a name I couldn't get out of my head. The name of the woman who could have tried to kill me but held back, even when I feigned an attack on her at the wall."

"Why was such a thing so unforgettable to you?"

He shrugs. "If you'd been an assassin, you'd have tried to kill me then. Your ferocity paired with restraint made me think you'd be strong enough to stand at my side, yet not so full of hate that you'd try to kill me."

"Oh," I say. That wasn't the answer I was expecting. "But I didn't know who you were at the wall. I didn't even see your antlers. If I'd been an assassin sent to kill you, I wouldn't have known you were my target."

"I may have glamoured my antlers and dressed in the colors of the night, but if you were an assassin, you'd have known me anyway. You'd have been expecting me."

I chew my lip, processing the information.

"Was I right about you?" he asks. "Or are you still thinking of turning that blade on me?"

I look down at my thigh and the blue chiffon hiding the dagger beneath it. I'm not ready to answer that question, so I stand. "I should take my leave, Your Majesty."

He takes hold of my hand, gently. "I meant it, Evie. It's Aspen when we're alone."

I turn to go, but he doesn't release me. I'm about to throw him a scowl, but his expression is serious. "Come back to our room," he says.

"Why, so you can take advantage of me again?"

"I'll sleep elsewhere tonight. You claim the bed." Finally, he lets my hand slip from his fingers.

"I'll consider it." I feel his eyes on me as I make my way across the floor.

It's no surprise when I hear him say my name. I turn. "I never glamoured myself in your presence but once."

I tilt my head. "Excuse me?"

"At the wall. That was the only time I've worn a glamour in front of you."

"But the day I arrived at the palace...in the dining room...you said—"

"I was teasing you, allowing you to believe I'd donned a glamour. But I hadn't."

I put my hands on my hips. "I thought you said you couldn't lie."

His eyes sparkle with mischief. "I told you no direct lie. Deception, on the other hand, is what we fae excel at."

I bristle. He just admitted to being able to deceive me without lying. A dangerous confession. But even more dangerous is the truth—that all those times I was drawn to Aspen, pulled by his strange beauty, powerless before it, I had no glamour to blame. It leaves me with a confession of my own. There is a very strong part of me that wants him.

32

That night I meet Melusine on the shore. She stands near the edge of water, waves lapping over the end of her tail. The sun is setting in brilliant shades of pink and gold, and a gentle breeze catches my hair, sending stray tendrils blowing behind me. With slow, confident steps, feet bare in the cool sand, I close the distance between us and stand before her.

"Your Majesty," I say with a curtsy.

She gives me a deep nod. "Come, Evelyn, let us stroll." She turns and slithers down the shore, away from the palace.

I follow, silence falling between us. The only sound is the crashing of waves and the occasional splash of something breaking the surface of the water. I catch sight of a whale's tail in the distance, then the leaping of a fish. Then another. Moving closer and closer to the shore.

Melusine smiles upon each visitor, each crab that scuttles from behind its rock to watch its queen.

I catch movement up ahead; seals leap upon the large rocks at the far end of the shore, then beautiful women with long, opalescent tails climb upon the higher rocks. Are they naturally drawn to their queen and simply want to see her? Or is she trying to demonstrate her power? I swallow my unease, wishing I hadn't left Aspen's guards at the other end of the shore.

"How gracious of you to meet with me tonight," she says in her melodious voice, waving a greeting at a siren with emerald green hair.

"Yes," I say, "and so gracious of you to want to get to know me better."

"That I do. You are my eldest son's mate. Soon-to-be queen of the palace that once was mine."

"I...am determined to take great care of the palace," I say, careful to avoid words like *vow* and *promise*. "And to serve the interests of human and fae alike."

"Yes, but your interests will always lie more with humans, will they not?"

I think about everything Aspen said about balance. About freedom and choice. "I'm certain I can learn to hold both my kind and yours in equal affection."

"Even the unseelie?"

I swallow hard and don a pleasant smile. "You mean like you?"

She tenses, lips peeling back from her sharp teeth.

I pretend it doesn't frighten me. "If I can walk peacefully at your side, I'm sure I can advocate for others. My mate, as I'm sure you know, often shifts his alliance to unseelie. I will have to learn to appreciate both parties."

"Spoken like an ambassador."

"Like a queen," I correct her, before I realize the boldness of my words.

"You aren't quite what I expected. Not after everything I heard about you. And your sister."

The blood leaves my face. It's a struggle to keep my voice neutral as I ask, "What exactly *have* you heard about my sister?"

"Oh, that a terrible tragedy took place here. Word has it the poor girl died. Yet, my son has said nothing of this to the humans. Could it be he fears their wrath?"

We've stopped, coming to the end of the shore where a large cliff extends over the water, giving way to the enormous rocks the selkies and sirens are so fond of. I face her, searching her eyes for truth. "You wouldn't have anything to do with my sister's disappearance, would you?"

She laughs. "What use would I have for a filthy human girl?"

"You didn't answer the question."

"I didn't take her, nor did I kill her, if that's what you're asking."

I study her words, seeking every crack she's left unfilled, every hole she's left unburied. There's a lot of room for deception.

"Now let me ask you a question," she says. "And I'll ask it directly. Will you or won't you perform the Bonding ritual with Aspen?"

This surprises me. "What?"

"A simple yes or no. Will you or won't you?"

"How do you know we haven't already?"

She slithers closer to me, sniffing the air like she did the day before. When she pulls away, she laughs, amusement dancing in her eyes. "No, you haven't. There's a distinct smell about a human who has been Bonded with a fae. You don't have it."

"What kind of smell would that be?" I ask, out of defensiveness more than anything.

"It is nothing a fae can explain to a human. Just know it's obvious to all of us that you aren't his true mate, no matter how well you lie."

"On the contrary, I am his mate. Your ambassador was here to witness the ceremony. We—"

"You and I both know that ceremony meant nothing to you." She flicks her wrist in a dismissive gesture. "To be honest, it hardly means much to the fae. Aspen could have a hundred mates if he wished. It is but the first of three steps required to fulfill the treaty, and even if you were to perform the human wedding next, you'd still be missing a vital piece."

"I don't understand." I regret the admission as soon as the words are out of my mouth.

Melusine lets out an exaggerated gasp. "You mean he hasn't told you?"

"Told me what?"

Her lips pull into a sympathetic smile, making my blood boil. "What a devious boy he's been. You see, if you fail to Bond before the timeframe given by the treaty, the pact will be considered void."

My pulse quickens at her words. "You mean we'll revert to war?"

"It's obvious that's what Aspen wants, otherwise he would have told you."

My mind is reeling for the second time today.

"Now, Evelyn, I can see you are hurt by this. I can almost promise you, my son will only hurt you more the longer you are together. End this farce and return home to your people."

"So we can go to war?"

Her tone darkens. "So we have a chance at securing the isle for who it rightfully belongs to."

"Which you think means the fae. The unseelie. You want this war."

She shrugs a delicate shoulder.

"Whatever happened to the mercy you felt after giving birth to Aspen?"

"That wasn't mercy," she says. "That was weakness. A symptom of birthing a seelie son. I made a bargain to end the war in exchange for his life. Once the human I'd made the bargain with died, my mind became clearer little by little. I was a fool to give up the isle. And I will never be that fool again."

"Why are you telling me this?"

"Because our interests are aligned. I know you don't want to do the ritual. I don't want you to either. Promise me you won't."

"I can't make that promise," I whisper.

"You can and you will. I know you don't love my son. Set him free. Otherwise, the ritual will Bond the two of you by the power of your names. It is a terrifying thing to give one's name to another, and a curse to have another's name within your control. That's just the Bond itself I'm talking about. Think of the other heartaches you could avoid by forgoing a relationship with him. Love between a human and a fae is a tenuous thing. It's intoxicating but devastating. If he leaves you for another, mistreats you, your heart will break, cutting deeper than any normal heartache. If you stay together, he will resent you for standing in the way of his true nature."

I think of Doris Mason, her lifeless eyes. Of her cousin who passed away from neglect. Is that the dark side of all human-fae pairings? And what about what Aspen said? How sometimes he thinks it would be better to give up the seelie way? Could I trust he won't eventually turn unseelie in earnest? *We'll only be allies, not lovers,* I tell myself, but it doesn't give me comfort.

She smiles knowingly. "That is no life for you. Take the mercy I am offering you. It's only a matter of time before the treaty breaks some other way. Promise me you won't do the ritual, and you will be allowed to live and return to your village. Warn your people. Take your mother to the mainland and escape the burden you now bear. Take as many of your people off this isle with you as you can."

Anxiety crushes my lungs as I consider. I could take this bargain. I could take my people to safety, free them from the responsibility of upholding the treaty century after century. Let them live in freedom, no longer in the shadow of the faewall. No longer fearing fae retribution. But in turn, everyone who escapes to the mainland would lose their homes, their land, the day-to-day lives they cherish. And it would all be my fault. I feel like my legs will give out from the weight of the burden riding on my shoulders.

"Promise me."

I breathe away the anxiety, seeking control, logic. With a deep breath, I close my eyes, focusing on the feel of my dagger against my thigh, hidden beneath my skirts. I pat it once, and my mind begins to steady. One thing becomes clear. I cannot make any kind of bargain with Melusine. "I won't."

Her fangs flash, lips peeling into a snarl. "Promise me or I will make you regret the day you denied my mercy."

"No."

She lets out an angry roar. The ocean responds, sending its waves to echo her, rising from the sea toward the sky. Shark fins break the surface, jaws snapping from the waves. The sirens begin to wail a harrowing tune.

I hold my ground, ready to meet it. As powerless as I am against the sea, I refuse to run.

Melusine's gaze locks on me, eyes like a swirling tempest as she slithers forward, arms outstretched, monstrous waves at her back ready to crash over my head.

"Mother."

Melusine freezes, head darting to the side. The waves are thrown backward, dousing me in a cold spray. I gasp, the chilling water drenching me from head to toe. In the blink of an eye, the sea is calm again.

"Aspen, dear," she hisses through her teeth.

He strolls towards us at a leisurely pace. "Didn't you know it's considered treason to attack the mate of a king?"

Her composure relaxes and her lips pull into a smile. Her tail is the only thing that betrays her, swishing wildly, erratically, in the sand. "You mistake me, my son. We had an argument that got out of hand. Nothing more. You do know how my temper can be."

"I do," he says. "Regardless, you've overstayed your welcome."

She lifts her chin. "I wouldn't call anything I received a welcome. You'll have to try harder tomorrow."

"Tomorrow?" A look of surprise interrupts his stoic expression.

"The council meeting," she says. "You didn't forget, did you?"

The calm returns to his features. "Of course not. I'm simply surprised you aren't sending an ambassador in your stead."

"Not for such an important meeting. Until then." She smiles, then dives into the sea, sinuous tail snaking across the sand until it disappears beneath the waves.

Aspen puts his hands on my shoulders and turns me to face him. "Are you all right?"

My hands ball into fists, fury roaring inside me. "*You.*"

33

———

"Me?" Aspen smirks. "What did I do to spark your displeasure this time?"

"Was she right? Did you keep the truth about the Bonding ritual from me?"

His smile fades.

I take a step away, pulling from his grasp. "She was right, wasn't she? You were going to let me break the treaty without realizing it."

"Yes."

"Why? After everything you told me about protecting the balance. How could you do this?"

"You said you wouldn't do the ritual. I wasn't going to force you."

I throw my hands in the air. "I may have reconsidered if I'd known the truth. You should have told me. You should have told me everything from the start."

His lips press into a tight line. "You weren't the easiest to talk to."

"Neither were you."

"You seemed so set in your opinion of me. I wouldn't grovel at your feet just to give you an explanation."

"Because of your pride?"

He shrugs. "Perhaps. It didn't seem worth my time when you wouldn't have believed me anyway."

"So you were just going to let me unwittingly break the pact?"

"Better you than me."

My fingers clench into fists. "How can you say that so casually when it would have meant war?"

"Because if *I* were to break the treaty, there's a good chance I'd lose my throne as well. Besides, what were my other options? I could let you make your choices based on human prejudice, resulting in war with a people who might not deserve my protection in the first place. Or I could tell you the truth and make you feel forced to perform the ritual, resulting in a Bond with a woman who hates me, a woman who could use my name against me, use it to dethrone me."

"I wouldn't have." My voice comes out small, uncertain.

He barks a cold laugh. "Not even you believe that."

"I *couldn't* have," I correct. "A human can't use a fae's true name against them. Giving me your name will do nothing. I don't have any special hormones to secrete that mess with your brain. You'd be the one with all the power."

His expression twists into a look of bewilderment. "*Hormone?* What are you talking about?"

"It's what gives you the power to glamour others. It overrides parts of our brain."

He shakes his head. "It's our magic that allows us to use a glamour. The power of giving another your true name uses a strong enough magic for even a human to use on the Fair Isle. Haven't you heard about the end of the war? The exile of the Fire King? The head of Eisleigh's council exchanged names with the Fire King and banished him. The Fire King, in turn used the councilman's name to promise he would never set foot on the Fair Isle again and would live on the mainland until his death. That's what the Bond is about. The ultimate sign of mutual fear and respect. It can be forged between friends, enemies, allies, and—yes—humans and fae."

I'm surprised to hear this part of the story, but it still doesn't mean anything. There's no proof the councilman had any power over the Fire King when he used his name. Still, I'm too exhausted to argue. "Aspen, I just want the truth. What happens next?"

"Nothing has changed on my side. I still won't force you to do the ritual. The choice is yours. If we must go to war, so be it. If you choose to give me your name, I will give you mine in return."

"I thought you were afraid I'll betray you."

He sighs. "If you were ever going to hurt me, you would have let me succumb to iron poisoning."

I feel a flash of guilt, remembering the moment I considered doing just that. "Your mother said there is a timeframe determined by the treaty. When must the Bonding ritual be performed by?"

His expression falters, almost apologetic. "The treaty states the ritual must take place no later than a week before the human wedding ceremony."

I do the math in my head. My mouth falls open, and the breath flies from my lungs. "Tomorrow is a week before the wedding."

He nods. "That's why the council is coming. I am to present you as my Bonded by midnight. If not, the treaty is broken, and the council will determine next steps."

I close my eyes and turn away from him. All I want to do is scream, to pound his chest and berate him for letting things go so long without telling me the truth. But I'm still too drained to fight or argue. Instead, I feel like I'm going to be sick.

After a stretch of silence, I hear Aspen's footfall behind me, then to the side of me. I can't bring myself to look at him. "What did you argue with my mother about?" he asks.

"She...she wanted me to promise I wouldn't perform the ritual."

He curses under his breath. "Of course she did." He goes still, studying me. "What did you say?"

I chew my bottom lip, eyes darting toward his face then away again. "I refused to give her my promise."

"Because you detest bargaining with the fae, or because you're actually considering it?"

"Both."

"For your people?" he asks.

"Of course," I say. "I'll do anything to keep the isle free from war. That's why I'm here. Why I've persevered this long."

"But you hate it here, don't you?"

"I don't *hate* it." My stomach sinks when I say it, but it's the truth. The fae may terrify me at times, and more than one has directly tried to kill me. But others—Lorelei, Foxglove, Cobalt, Gildmar, even Aspen—are showing me there's more to Faerwyvae than I grew up believing. I may not love it yet, but I'd rather not see it destroyed by war.

"What about me?" Aspen's voice comes out soft, hesitant. "Do you still hate me?"

My pulse quickens. "Not entirely."

"Is there any part of you that wants to do the ritual for...us?"

My eyes widen and find his, but I say nothing.

His expression darkens, and he turns away, shaking his head. I watch as he stalks down the beach. For an unfathomable moment, I feel cold at the sight, at the distance growing between us. Without a second thought, I march after him. "Aspen, don't you dare walk away from me."

He pauses, then turns to face me. His expression flickers between cool stoicism and the vulnerability I've rarely gotten to see.

I close the distance between us. "I said I wanted the truth."

"I never promised to give it."

"Yet you did anyway," I say. "Don't walk away from me when there's clearly more to say."

He lets out a grumble. "You really want the truth?"

I nod.

"The truth is, I've wanted you from the start. From the day I met you at the wall. I wanted you when I first laid eyes on you in the dining room, when Foxglove crushed me with the news that you would be my brother's bride. I wanted you later that night when I met you at the rail. I wanted to offer you a change of plans, to offer myself to you instead. I wanted you even after you burned me with your scorn, rejected every flirtation I threw your way. I wanted you every time we were together in a room, regardless of who else was there. I wanted you then and I want you now, and it infuriates me that you feel nothing in return."

My breaths are quick, shallow, pulse racing. He gave me the truth; I could leave it at that. I could walk away. I could tell him he's right, that I feel nothing in return. I could ignore all those times I felt drawn to him, like a fire was burning every part of me at once. For so long, I'd mistaken it for the fire of rage, and it was there. But there was another fire coexisting alongside it, something I've never given credit to. It's that thing that makes me feel breathless, out of control, and completely unlike myself. It's passion. There's no logic about it, no textbook to tell me how to cut it apart or navigate it. It's something I always swore I lacked, something only girls like Amelie have.

But if we're talking about truth, let me admit mine. I am no stranger to passion. I simply choose to ignore it, lock it up, and keep it at bay. It's something I've never let myself explore. Who would I be if I did?

I see Aspen beginning to grow tense again, his vulnerability fading behind his stony mask of pride. I could let this end here. Now. Let him walk away, allow the tension to grow between us until it solidifies into a wall.

"You're wrong," I finally say, the words flying from my throat before I can swallow them down. "I don't feel nothing."

His eyes widen, the mask slipping. "What *do* you feel?"

I can't bring myself to use words, so I reach a tentative hand toward his cheek. He closes his eyes, trembling with restraint at my touch. I run my fingers along his jaw, his sculpted cheekbone, the lobe of his ear.

When he opens his eyes, I have but a moment to bask in their color, in the desire radiating from them. After that, his lips are on mine. My arms wrap around his neck, pulling him closer, fingers tangling in his hair. His hands move down my back, and his lips trail my neck, my collarbone. I tilt my head back, gasping as he kisses behind my ear.

"I want to pick up where we left off." His voice is a low rumble, sending a shiver up my spine.

"Yes," is all I can manage to say.

"But not here." He pulls away from me. Disappointment sinks my gut, but before it can take root, he links his fingers with mine. We run down the shore, back toward the palace. At the base of the rock wall just beneath the palace, there's a cave that leads to a tunnel, a tunnel that leads to stairs, and stairs that lead to the lower levels of the palace. I'd come this way to meet Melusine.

At the mouth of the cave stand the guards I left behind. Aspen dismisses them, ordering them to wait farther down the tunnel. They obey, leaving us alone in the cool darkness of the cave, lit only by sparse orbs of light. When we can no longer hear the footsteps of the guards, Aspen turns to me, lips crushing against mine as he presses my back against the smooth, dark stone. Warmth spreads through me from head to toe, and I feel the flames of passion return. I run my hands up his chest, up the silk of his waistcoat, then to the collar of his shirt. From there, I touch his neck, his cheek, his brow. Slowly, my fingers crawl into his hair until I reach the base of an antler. Aspen inhales a sharp breath as I slide my fingers over the length of the branch.

He pulls away slightly, eyes closed. Worried I've done something wrong, I remove my hand. When he opens his eyes, his lips pull into a smirk. "You really are the most desirable being I've ever encountered," he says. "I was willing to let you go time and time again, thinking that's what you wanted. To marry my brother. To forfeit the ritual. To break the treaty."

"And now?" I whisper.

He kisses me lightly on the lips. "I can still let you go, if that's what you want. If you're going to leave, do it now. Leave before my heart realizes what's happened."

The vulnerability has returned to his eyes, more transparent than ever before. There's a sorrow in his voice that shatters me. I remember what

Aspen's mother had said, that her mercy had been a weakness. She regretted ending the war to save Aspen's life. She left him when he was likely still a child in fae years. Abandoned him to raise his baby brother on his own in an enormous palace.

Aspen's aloofness, his cold demeanor, his hard edges and sharp words—it all seems so fragile now. I put my hand to Aspen's cheek, run my thumb over his lower lip.

He shudders. "Leave me now or I won't be able to stop."

I inch toward him until our lips almost touch. "I don't want you to stop."

Our kisses return, deeper, heavier. My lips part for more of him, and I feel his tongue brush against mine. His hands move up my back, my arms, my shoulders. His fingers trail the neckline of my dress. I regret my modest clothing now, wishing my dress were thinner. Or better yet, gone altogether.

As if he can read my mind, his fingers move to the shoulder of my dress, then slide it down, revealing my naked flesh. I shiver as the cold air snakes across my skin, but his lips trace a line of fire between my breasts, then over my exposed mound of curving flesh. I shudder as his tongue lingers over the summit. He tugs the other shoulder of the dress, pulling it down until my entire top hangs around my waist. It's still not enough. I want to be closer.

My fingers find the collar of his shirt again. This time, I seek to loosen his cravat, throwing it to the ground once freed. Then I find the buttons of his shirt, his waistcoat, undoing each one with trembling fingers. He helps me with what remains, shrugging off his jacket, the open shirt, his trousers. I look him over, eyes lighting upon every muscle, every inch of golden skin. All that remains of his wound is dark bruising and several small tendrils of black. My eyes go lower, and I can't help but blush when I finally understand the truth of Foxglove's *kingdom* innuendo.

He grins when he catches the look on my face, then returns his efforts to freeing me from my dress. Hands on my hips, he spins me around to untie the sashes that secure the skirt around my waist. It falls to the stone floor in a puddle of chiffon, leaving me bare in the cold autumn air with nothing but Aspen's roving hands to warm me. Only one thing remains.

I step away from him and reach toward my thigh to undo my belted dagger, tossing it to the side where Aspen won't accidentally touch it. When I return to face him, his eyes are drinking me in.

"Beautiful Evie," he says.

"Dangerous Aspen," I whisper.

He kisses me softly this time as he reaches for my thighs. With little effort he lifts me, and my legs go around his waist. The fiery yearning pulses at my core and I feel that sense of losing control growing stronger and stronger. This time I don't fight it. I welcome it. Welcome his kisses, his hands, his fingers. All of him.

In this moment, there is no looming war, no ritual, no pact, no separation of our kind. In this moment, things are simple—he is mine and I am his. I'm teetering on the edge of passion, tasting all it has to offer me, sampling its joys and pains and moments of euphoria. But I want more than an edge, a sample, a taste.

I let myself fall completely.

34

———————

The morning dawns on us, sending streams of light into the mouth of the cave. I open my eyes, lifting my head from Aspen's warm chest. Salty air tickles my senses, blending with Aspen's rosemary and cinnamon. He wakes, and his eyes meet mine. For a moment, the silence between us feels tense, awkward.

A wave of fear runs through me. Does he regret this? Do *I* regret this?

His lips pull into the wicked smile I know so well, and he kisses me. Memories of last night rush through me in a wave of pleasure, and my body responds in turn. His hands rove my skin, slip beneath the discarded dress I'd used as a makeshift blanket to caress my back, my hips, my thighs.

"You kept your promise," he whispers between kisses.

"What promise?"

"That I'd never bed you. Luckily, you never said I couldn't *cave* you."

I smile against his lips. "I'm pretty sure I never used the words *I promise*. Nevertheless, I should have given you more credit. Turns out, any place will do."

"It will," he says. "However, bed sounds nice. Do you think you'll reconsider?"

I pull away from him and pretend to ponder. "Hmm. I suppose I can do that."

"What do you say we return to the palace, get in bed, do this all over again, and have a proper sleep on a surface that doesn't feel like cold knives?"

I want to say yes, but a more serious thought comes to mind. "What about the ritual?"

His vulnerability returns, but only for a flash. "Have you decided?"

I lay my head back on his chest, bringing my fingers to trail over his golden skin and the hard muscles of his torso. "Tell me about it."

He's silent for a moment. "At its simplest, the Bonding ritual requires only one thing—an exchange of names. I'm sure you are already familiar with the act of giving one's true name."

"Yes," I say, suppressing a shudder. I don't mention that it's something human children are taught never to do. Always be careful of your wording when introducing yourself to a fae, we're told. Never say anything like, *I give you my name.*

"Well, the Bonding ritual is nothing more than that," he says. "One party states that they give their true name to the other, and the other party states the same. That's all it takes for the Bond to take hold."

"What exactly is *the Bond*?" The way he explains it sounds so simple. If it truly is that way, why is it so taboo to talk about?

"It's just the name given for two people who've exchanged names."

"Do all mates perform the Bonding ritual?"

"No. Mate relationships are common, but Bonding rituals are rare. The ritual is performed as often by mates as it is by friends, enemies, and allies, but never without great cause. In any case, it's uncommon. It's always a component of sealing the treaty with a Chosen after a Reaping though."

"Is there really nothing more to it? No candles or flowers or oaths?"

"These extravagances can be included in the ritual," Aspen says, "but they aren't a requirement. We could do it right now, if you wanted."

My breath hitches. Am I ready for that? "Can I have a few hours first?"

He lifts my chin with his fingertips, bringing our eyes to meet. "I meant it when I said I wouldn't force you. That's a promise I'm still willing to keep."

I nod. "I just need a little more time to wrap my head around it."

"I can give you time," he says. "And I can give you another promise. I will never use the Bond to hurt you. I'll never use your true name against you."

His words send a wash of relief through me.

A flicker of worry crosses his face. "Can you promise me the same?"

My lips pull into a smile. I must admit, I like this vulnerability he's been showing me. "Yes, Aspen, I promise you the same."

He rolls, shifting me beneath him. "Then how about this." He grins and kisses my neck. "We go to bed." Another kiss, beneath my collarbone. "We get naked again." Another kiss between my breasts. "We sleep." Another. "Then we perform the ritual *if* you choose to. I'll give you candles, flowers, a sunset view, and all the oaths you could want while we exchange our names." His fingers stroke the inside of my thigh, creeping higher and higher.

Fire blazes at my core, and part of me wishes we could skip the returning to the palace part, but a comfortable bed is not something I can deny. "I can agree to that."

Getting dressed is slow going, with every move thwarted by breathless kisses and roving hands. It's a miracle we don't reenact our entire night here and now. Eventually, we dress and make our way down the tunnel, Aspen's fingers laced in mine. Farther down, we meet his guards. I'm glad they don't react to our giddy mood as they follow us down the tunnel toward the palace.

My legs feel like water as we emerge from the tunnel and begin climbing the stairs, each flight taking us higher in the palace. We're still several floors away from reaching our bedroom when I can no longer pretend I'm not out of breath. My fatigue is a combination of the endless stairs and all the energy spent over the course of our passion. I can't help but wonder how much more fatigued I'll feel an hour or two from now. The thought is oddly thrilling, although it doesn't help me walk any faster.

Aspen must see me lagging, because next thing I know, he lifts behind my knees, sweeping me off my feet and into his arms. I secure my arms around his neck, laying my head on his shoulder. I'm reveling in his seemingly effortless strength when Aspen comes to a sudden halt.

"What happened?" calls a voice nearby. Cobalt is running toward us. "Is she all right?"

Aspen's voice comes out cold. "She's fine."

"Then why—"

"My mate grew tired while climbing the stairs."

"Well, where have you been?"

"With *my mate*." Aspen's tone holds an edge that makes the prince blanch.

Cobalt looks from me to Aspen, and I feel a pinch of sympathy for him.

"If you don't mind, dear brother," Aspen says, "we'll be on our way."

"Where are you going now?" Cobalt asks.

"You sure are full of questions."

Cobalt narrows his eyes. "We're supposed to be preparing for the council meeting."

"We have time."

"The preparations have already begun, since you couldn't be found," Cobalt says, tone darkening. "Besides, there are stacks of correspondences that have been piling on your desk since before you were injured. If you'd like me to attend to them in your stead, I'd be more than happy to, *my king*." He says this last part with a hint of malice in his tone.

Aspen lets out an irritated grumble and sets me on my feet. He rubs his brow, then faces me, bringing his hands to my cheeks. "Change of plans."

"It's all right," I say. Disappointment sinks my gut, but seeing Cobalt stripped me of all desire, anyway. "Do what you need to do."

"Give me a few hours," he says. "We'll still have time to do everything we spoke of. *Everything*."

At first, I think his emphasis is meant for the ritual. However, the mischief in his eyes says something else. I grin. "I'll be waiting."

He lights a kiss on my lips, a silent promise, then joins Cobalt.

With a sigh, I make my way back to our room alone.

After the warmth of Aspen's arms, the bedroom feels cold, empty. Still, after a night on a stone floor, the bed looks inviting. I'm not sure how much time we spent sleeping in the cave, but my body tells me it wasn't long. We were...preoccupied...most of the night.

With slow steps, I make my way to the wardrobe, exchanging my gown for a nightdress and placing my dagger on the dressing table. I stare longingly at the empty tub, wondering if I should find Lorelei and ask her to have it filled. No, there will be time for that later. Right now, sleep is calling.

I climb into bed and nestle beneath the covers. My mind spins with the realization that so much has changed in a matter of days. The man who I thought was my enemy is now my lover. The land I once despised will soon be a place I help rule. And the heart I thought would never open to any man, any king, any fae, is warm with contentment. Hungry with desire. Open for new forms of passion to emerge.

With a satisfied smile, I close my eyes and drift into a peaceful sleep. It might be hours that pass, or it might be minutes, but I become subtly aware of a sound in the room, footsteps crossing the floor toward the bed. My heart flutters with anticipation, but I'm too tired to open my eyes. "Aspen?" The word comes out small and breathless.

A hand presses down hard on my mouth.

My eyes fly open, and I fight the hand that grasps me, but when my vision clears, the face overhead comes into focus. The fight leaves me. My heart leaps into my throat.

It's Amelie.

35

I struggle to say Amelie's name, but she keeps her hand clamped over my mouth. With her other hand, she brings a finger to her lips. I nod, and she releases me. I spring from the bed and wrap my arms around my sister's neck, fighting the sobs that tear through me. "Amelie! For the love of iron, you're alive."

She hushes me. "Keep your voice down."

I pull away from her. Her expression is panicked, something I've never seen on her normally serene, beautiful face. "What happened to you?"

She takes my hands in hers, an urgency in her tone. "We need to go."

"Go where? Why?"

"You're in danger. We need to leave now."

"What kind of danger?"

Her voice is a furious whisper. "I can't explain now, but you must come with me. Get dressed at once."

I hurry to obey, my fear propelling my legs to the wardrobe. The thick fur cloak Amelie wears makes me think I should be dressing warm. Instead of one of the fae dresses, I unbury my old trousers and blouse from the back of the wardrobe and pull the pants over my legs. I don't bother looking for my corset, and button the blouse over my bare chest. Next, I fetch a cloak and shove my feet into a pair of beaded slippers. Then I reach for my dagger.

"We don't have time." Amelie pulls my other arm. "Come on. Hurry."

"I need my dagger," I say as I shake from her grip. My fingers close over the sheath before she can pull at me again. I tuck it into the waist of my trousers as Amelie shoves me toward one of the crystalline walls. "Ami, what—"

Just then, she presses her hand to the wall, and a previously unseen door opens outward into darkness. Amelie pushes me through it, then closes the door behind us. I feel Amelie's hand on my arm as she tugs me forward. "Hurry," she whispers.

"Where are we going?"

"You aren't safe."

"But where are you taking us?"

Amelie doesn't answer, just leads me down endless blackness with nothing but stairs beneath my feet. It's a struggle not to trip on my slippers as she drags me down, down, farther down.

I'm reeling from the suddenness of it all. The strangeness. All I can think is that Aspen was right. There really has been a threat all along. And somehow, Amelie is saving me from it. But what about the king?

I continue to follow her, fighting the barrage of questions that rise inside me. Every word I say gets hushed by Amelie as she insists we must hurry. Danger. I'm not safe.

Finally, the stairs turn to the flat surface of a black tunnel floor, and a subtle light glows up ahead. It's a pinkish light, and with it comes the smell of salt, a rumbling echo of sound. We draw nearer to the light, and the black cave walls melt into coral. Coral all around, knitted tightly together to form walls. A spray of water seeps through now and then, and I swear the roar of waves is coming from overhead.

A chill crawls up my spine as Amelie darts into the coral cave. "Ami, where's Aspen?"

She turns around, eyes wide with terror. "Come on, Evie. Hurry."

Now that she's in the light, I can see my sister fully. Strands of kelp tangle in her copper hair, and a thin dress of seafoam silk covers her body. I look at what I'd first mistaken for a heavy fur cloak, realizing it's something else entirely. The gray-brown mass of fur isn't a cloak but a skin. A sealskin. The head is pulled back like a hood and the flippers are tied together like a clasp.

"What's going on, Amelie?"

"You aren't safe."

My shoulders tremble as I look at her, look at the panic in her eyes, the pain on her face. "You keep saying that, but I need more. What am I in danger from? Where is Aspen?"

Her face crumples. "I can't tell you."

I take a few steps closer. "I'm your sister. You can tell me anything. Whatever is happening, I'll listen. If you've gotten into any kind of trouble—"

"Just come with me."

I look from her face to the head of the sealskin. "You took the skin from the selkie woman."

Her eyes glaze with tears. "Nothing was supposed to turn out this way. I never meant for her to die. I left her my dress. She was supposed to wear it."

I take a step away from her. "Why?"

"Evie, we don't have time. Come."

I shake my head, taking another step back.

Her chest heaves with a sob. "Don't make me do this."

"Do what?"

She lets out a wail of sorrow, then takes something from her side—a pink branch of coral set above a hilt of driftwood. That's all I see before she lunges at me, swinging her blade while tears pour down her cheeks.

I dodge the coral blade, retreat from her, backing into the black cave until I slip on a pool of water. My feet fly out from under me and I sprawl on my back. "Ami, stop!"

My shout doesn't deter her. She darts at me with her blade.

I roll to my side, letting my sister crash to the floor next to me. With one hand, I push myself to my feet. With the other, I retrieve my dagger.

Amelie stumbles to stand, then faces me. We circle each other, weapons between us. Neither of us know much about hand-to-hand combat, my sister less than anyone. Her distress shows on her face, wet with tears and contorted with endless sobbing.

"You don't have to do this," I say.

"I do."

"Why? What happened?" But the answer is clear. "You've been glamoured."

"I made a bargain."

"With who?"

Her lips remain pressed tight.

Still, it isn't hard to guess. "Melusine. But why? What could she possibly offer you?"

"Just come with me," she begs. "Come with me willingly and I won't have to hurt you."

I take in her trembling limbs, her agonized expression. "I'm more worried about hurting you."

"It will hurt me more if you don't come with me. It's the only way I can save you."

I furrow my brow. "What did you bargain away?"

"My ability to lie. And my name."

My eyes go wide. "What did you get in return?"

"Love." With that, she runs at me with her coral blade.

I hardly have time to think. I spin to the side, feeling something sharp graze my ribs. She surges forward again, swinging her blade wildly. My dagger remains in hand, but I can't bring myself to use it against her. Instead, I dart and dodge, crying out when the coral meets its mark again and again. Her attack is relentless, but her skill is weak. The best she can do is cut my flesh. She has no idea how to disarm me, much less land a killing blow. But even without skill, she could get lucky. If I don't defend myself, it's only a matter of time before my strength fades, before my ability to dodge becomes compromised.

I have to fight her.

I block the next blow with my dagger, knocking her hand to the side. She comes at me again. Again. I stumble back, dodge left, swipe at her arm. She shouts as my blade makes a cut, but she isn't deterred. Perhaps it's the glamour fueling her, but she's tireless, unconcerned with every cut I land on her. I, on the other hand, feel my arms growing weaker, my side a searing ache where her blade had grazed.

This must end.

Amelie rushes at me again. I dodge, sending her reeling forward. Before she can recover her momentum, I step behind her. Raising my elbow, I meet the back of her head with a sharp jab.

Her body goes limp and she slides to the floor. I cry out as I help catch her fall, wincing as I strain the side of my body that was cut. Without bothering to check my own injuries, I hover over Amelie, testing her pulse, her breathing.

She's alive.

I let out a sigh and close my eyes, pondering the best way to bring her back to the palace. There's no way I can carry her up all those steps. Panic rises in my chest.

"Amelie."

I turn my head and find Cobalt emerging from the black cave, eyes locked on my sister. "Thank the Great Mother you're here," I say, tears pouring down my cheeks. "Help me carry her. Please."

His eyes slide to mine. "I'm so sorry Evelyn."

I'm taken aback, not sure what he's apologizing for. Does he not realize Amelie is alive?

Then he leaps forward and grabs me.

36

I wake gasping for breath, coughing water onto a small, sodden cot. My throat feels raw, and all I can taste is salt. I remember Cobalt charging me, the clasp of his hands around me. Then all I saw was water, felt it pouring into my throat and lungs. I cough again and drag my aching body to sit. All around me are coral bars, sharp and pink, woven together at the top to create a cage.

My hands fly to my waist, my thigh, searching for my dagger and finding it nowhere.

"I'm sorry I had to do this, Evelyn," Cobalt says from the other side of the bars. I know it's him even though he hardly looks like the Cobalt I've known. His skin is covered in shimmering blue scales, making his body look lithe and sinuous. A crown of red coral sits over his brow while delicate webs stretch between each finger and toe. Gone are his boyish good looks, replaced with the terrifying beauty of the sea.

This must be his nix form.

The realization startles me. When the fae talked about shifting their physical forms from seelie to unseelie, I thought it could be nothing more than a mental shift, adapting the behavior of lesser creatures. The greatest physical change I imagined was subtle, like a chameleon altering its color. At most, I thought perhaps the fae underwent animalistic metamorphoses over time, like a caterpillar turning into a butterfly. But this...this is something else. He actually *changed*. Where the bloody iron is my logic for that?

I press my lips tight and fix Cobalt with a glare. Behind him and all around my cage is a cave of coral, its walls tightly knitted. I hear rolling waves rumble overhead, feel the salt spray through minuscule fissures within the walls.

With a jolt, I recall Amelie, lying unconscious after I knocked her out. "Where's my sister?"

I see motion at the far end of the cave, stirring in the darkness. Amelie stands, looking at me through tearstained eyes, the head of the sealskin resting over her scalp. She pulls the rest of the skin tight around her body, but not before I recognize the dress she's wearing. It's the one I slipped out of this morning.

Cobalt turns to her. "Go," he says, voice surprisingly gentle. "Wait for me. We must prepare for the council meeting."

She meets my eyes, lower lip quivering, then stalks away and out of sight.

I burn Cobalt with my scowl. It wasn't Melusine that Amelie had made the bargain with, but Cobalt. "What have you done to her?"

"She won't always feel this way," he says. "She's upset that you forced her hand. Hurting you was the last thing she wanted to do."

"Because you made her do it. Didn't you? You glamoured her, ordered her to take me from the palace. To kill me if I refused."

He gives me a sad smile. "Sometimes we have to make difficult choices to do the right thing. Before now, she was happy with me. She will be happy again."

"I don't understand why you're doing this. Why capture me after everything that happened? You saved me from the kelpie, you, you..." I don't want to say what I'm thinking. *You were kind to me. You were caring. You...kissed me.*

"I thought you would trust me if I saved you from the kelpie, thought you'd ally with me if you understood the dangers of the unseelie."

My eyes go wide with realization. "You arranged the kelpie attack."

He nods, eyes full of regret.

"You told me not to do the ritual with Aspen."

He takes a few steps closer to the bars of the cage. "And you refused to promise me you wouldn't. Refused my help. Refused to heed my warnings about my brother."

"Your warnings were lies."

"No, my brother is dangerous," Cobalt says. "I tried to tell you, but you didn't believe me. You *still* don't believe me."

"No, I don't."

His brow furrows. "Why? I offered you my protection, my affection. You rejected me time and time again. Yet, I see you had no issue accepting my brother."

I deepen my glare. "Is that why you took my sister?"

His expression softens. "Your sister was much more eager to listen. All she wanted was love and I gave it to her. When she realized we could be together if only you'd marry Aspen instead, she was willing to do what was required. She came to me willingly, left the palace on her own accord, all without even a glamour. It wasn't until today that she realized things weren't going quite as she'd expected, and I was forced to use the power of her name."

"You did this before, didn't you?" I ask. Everything makes so much sense now. "You bargained with the Holstrom girls and glamoured them to try and assassinate the king. What did you take from them?"

"The same thing Amelie gave me in return for my love," he admits. "The ability to lie. All the Holstrom girls wanted was protection from the king. Unlike you, they heeded my warnings. I offered my protection in exchange for their lies. They agreed, as long as I promised to put my lies to good use against the king. Then I promised I'd have Aspen dethroned if they gave me their names. Again, they agreed. I knew sending them to assassinate Aspen would serve well whether it failed or succeeded. If they managed to kill him, he'd no longer be a problem. If he killed them, he'd show his instability as a ruler and bring the council one step closer to forcing him to step down"

"If the Holstrom girls already gave you the ability to lie, why take it from Amelie too?"

"The power of the bargain wears off after a while if the bargainer dies. I needed that power, either from you or Amelie. Like I said, Amelie was more than willing."

"Is that why you're keeping Amelie alive, to keep your ability to lie? Is that why you didn't send her on some foolish errand to kill Aspen this time?"

He opens his mouth, flustered. "There's more between Amelie and me than there ever was with the other girls. I'm keeping her alive because she's my mate and soon-to-be wife. We are Bonded."

A chill runs through me, and nausea churns my gut. They performed the ritual.

Cobalt continues. "I can't let you and Aspen Bond. That's why I sent Amelie for you this morning after I realized you and my brother had seemingly grown close. I can't have you and Aspen bringing the treaty any closer to being fulfilled."

"Why? Is it war you want?"

"No, not war. I want Aspen off the throne."

I consider his words. "If Aspen and I don't perform the ritual by midnight, we'll break the treaty."

He nods. "He'll do worse than break the treaty. I've made sure of it."

"What have you done?"

"It's not what I've done, but what Aspen is about to do. Now that he thinks you changed your mind about him and sided with our mother instead, he'll show his true nature."

"He couldn't possibly think I'd do such a thing," I say.

"He thinks you're on your way home right now to fulfill your end of the bargain with Melusine. You left him a letter, after all, saying exactly that."

"He'll see through it. He'll never believe the letter was mine."

"My brother?" Cobalt lets out a cold laugh. "The most paranoid king that ever lived? The boy who was abandoned by his own mother after she came to regret saving his life? Of course he'll believe it. He's always looking for proof that others are out to get him. That no one could ever love him."

A lump rises in my throat, but I keep my breathing steady. "He's smarter than you think. He knew something happened to Amelie. Knew the body on the beach wasn't hers."

"He may have known that," he says, "but only because the proof wasn't convincing enough."

I'm about to argue that a letter isn't strong enough proof, when a chilling realization strikes me. Cobalt is confident. Prepared. There's more to this than I know. "What other proof did you give him?"

"I put a glamour over Amelie to make her look more like you." His words are nonchalant, free of malice, as if we were talking about nothing more than the weather. "After she brought you from the palace, I sent her to steal one of your dresses. Then she snuck into the stables and stole a puca. I made sure Aspen's most trusted few saw it happen. Foxglove. Lorelei. Several of his guards. It took him a few accounts before he believed it, but it was clear when he finally did."

"No."

"He was crushed. Heartbroken. So enraged, he shifted into his stag form and tore from the palace grounds."

I blink to fight the tears, clenching my jaw. "Where is he now?"

"He's probably looking for you. Once he realizes you're nowhere to be found, the rage will consume him. He'll attack your village and draw first blood. Perhaps much of it. He'll make the slaughter at the Holstrom farm look like a picnic." He shakes his head with disgust, as if he has no hand in any of it.

"How can you say it isn't war you want, when that's exactly what will happen after this?"

He shakes his head. "We won't go to war. The treaty will not be broken, because I will be there to save it. Aspen will perform this final act of recklessness, revealing the unstable maniac he is. It will give the council the fuel they need to be rid of him once and for all and put me in his place. Aspen has been keeping Faerwyvae from the peace it deserves, and I am but one of many who feels that way."

It all makes sense now. Of course Cobalt wants to be king. All the times he talked about Aspen's faults, how he has no shortage of allies that would stand against the king...he's been planning this all along. "What about the unseelie? They couldn't possibly support you. You're seelie, aren't you?"

"I have my mother to sway them. The unseelie trust her word."

"Your mother supports all this?"

A corner of his mouth quirks. "She knows some of my plans, although she thinks I'm under her thumb. She'd always promised to support my claim to the throne if I could get Aspen out of the way. Little does she know, I won't be furthering the unseelie cause like she expects."

"No, you'll further the seelie cause," I say. "Fight for a radical seelie council. Eradicate the unseelie."

"Can you blame me? The unseelie are uncivilized. You know about my mother, how she abandoned her children. That's not rare for unseelie. They're hardly better than animals, eating their young, leaving the lame to die. And what about creatures like the kelpies and vampires and goblins? Do they deserve to terrorize their victims?"

His words make my stomach sink, but I remember what Aspen told me. About fair choice and the balance necessary to preserve it. Was he right? Or would the world be better if the unseelie were gone?

"I'm ready to make you a bargain," Cobalt says. "Go home. Return to your people. Take the ones you love most and get them out of the village tonight. I'll get you there at once, before Aspen can unleash his wrath. Hide from my brother until his dark deeds are done. I'll have guards waiting. They'll stop him before he can draw too much blood. That will be enough to lose Aspen his throne without starting a war. Then I will be made king and the treaty will remain intact. Don't you see? Amelie and I are mates. We're Bonded. She and I will marry in your and Aspen's stead, securing the treaty."

"And then what? You'll let Aspen go on his jolly way?" I let out a bark of laughter. "I doubt that. Your first order as king will be to have him executed."

"Don't let your emotions cloud your good sense, Evelyn," he says. "Aspen's removal is necessary, and yes, he will need to be disposed of entirely. But don't you understand? Your relationship with him is tenuous, even if my brother remained in power. He might marry you, and he might even make you his queen, but what about when he grows tired of you? What about when your fragile human body slowly begins to age? What then?"

I think of Doris Mason and her cousin, anxiety rising in my chest.

Cobalt shakes his head. "This is the only logical solution. Take my bargain and save your people. The seelie way will keep the Fair Isle safe. Reject my bargain and I will leave you here to die.

My heart leaps into my throat. "You're going to kill me?"

"I can't directly hurt you, Evelyn. I promised as much on our picnic. I may be able to lie, but that doesn't mean I'm immune to vows and promises. Instead, I'll leave you here. It won't be long before the tide comes in."

Panic seizes me, the taste of salt still fresh on my tongue, my lungs still raw from being filled with seawater.

Cobalt frowns. "Don't make me do this, Evelyn. It will break your sister's heart. Think of her. Think of everything she sacrificed to save you."

My heart sinks, and I do think of her. Amelie, with her fickle heart and reckless ways. Did she know what she was getting herself into when she made her bargain with Cobalt? I know he deceived her, made her believe everything was going to work out perfectly for all of us, but did she stop to think what her actions could do to me? No. When she made the bargain, she didn't do it for me. She did it for herself. For Cobalt. *For love.*

"Make the logical choice, Evelyn."

The logical choice. I could accept Cobalt's bargain and save my people from war, but in doing so, Aspen loses his throne and his life. I lose the heart of the lover I was just beginning to know and care for. And Faerwyvae will take one step closer to a radical seelie reign. The only other choice is my own death. With that, I alleviate nothing. All else will likely still come to pass, but the blood Aspen spills in my village could belong to someone I care about.

"Live or die?" Cobalt says. "Those are your only choices."

I take a deep breath and close my eyes, running through the options in my mind, piecing logic with logic, trying to formulate an answer that doesn't make me feel like my heart is being ripped in two. The options twist and blur, fueling my anxiety until it rages inside me. My head is pounding, lungs heaving. There's no way out of this. No way out.

Then something tugs at me. Not at my mind, but at something else. Something calm and quiet. My heart? I breathe away my thoughts, let my swirling deliberations cool to a simmer as I focus on the calm inside me. A surgeon's calm, the kind I felt when treating Aspen's injury. It's a strange certainty that no logic can explain. I open myself to it, let it wrap around me like a blanket.

"Do the right thing, Evelyn."

"Get out of my sight," I say through my teeth.

His expression darkens. "You're making a mistake."

I burn him with my glare. "Get. Out."

37

The tide comes in fast, as does my panic. I pull my cloak around my arm and throw my weight against the bars of the cage. The coral shards go straight through the fabric, spearing my skin. I wince, then double the fabric, triple it. Throw myself at the bars again. Again. They don't budge.

I may have refused Cobalt's bargain, but that doesn't mean I've accepted the fate he left me with.

If only I had my dagger. If only I had *anything* to get me out of here.

I aim a kick at the bars, but my beaded slippers are no match for their strength, especially with the water rising higher and higher, slowing my momentum. Before long it's around my waist.

I grit my teeth as another surge of water floods in. The echo of waves overhead is louder than before. Terror seizes me, sending memories to the surface, reminding me what it felt like to nearly drown, twice now. I remember the kelpie dragging me under the water with me powerless and stuck on his back. My fingers clench into fists. I'm even more furious now that I know Cobalt had been to blame. He likely distracted me on purpose while I ate the honey pyrus, laughed as I tumbled away from our picnic to wander alone. The forest had been silent, empty until the kelpie found me. A kelpie—*a water fae*—the only creature in the woods. There's no mistaking every moment had been Cobalt's design.

Something sparks in my mind. An idea. A dangerous idea.

The kelpie.

I remember what Amelie had said about them. They seek out lost travelers and take them to their deaths. My idea is so foolish, so reckless, it sends my pulse racing.

"Help!" I shout at the top of my searing lungs. "Help! I'm lost!"

All that answers is more water, more waves. The flood reaches my chest now.

"Help! I'm lost and I can't find my way. Please come help me. Anyone." I repeat my plea over and over, trying to ignore the water that laps into my mouth as the tide rises to my neck. I have to brace myself on the bars of the cage to maintain my footing, and its sharp edges cut into my palms. I shout again. Screaming. Begging. "I'm lost! Help!"

A dark mass enters the cave, slithering beneath the surface of the water. I swallow my shouts, terrified I've called in something worse. As the shape draws near, a horse-like head breaches the water, its mane of black swirling around it. I remember the other kelpie, how its mane seemed to flow in a wind I didn't feel. Now I know it was an invisible current it was flowing in.

"Will you help me?" I ask, coughing water as a wave douses my face.

"Come with me," it says. Its voice sounds the same as the first kelpie—ethereal and chilling.

"First, will you break me out of this cage?"

It watches me with its glowing red eyes. "Break you out?"

The words turn my stomach. I should probably be more literal. "Will you kick the bars of the cage with your hooves, but be careful not to kick me? When the bars break and I am free from the cage, will you carry me somewhere—to someone—specific?"

"Who would you have me take you to?"

"Take me to King Aspen directly, as fast as you can. Go only routes that are safe for a human to travel. If we must travel by water, keep my head above it at all times. If we travel by land, move as fast as you can."

"I could take you to King Aspen." He says it more like he's considering it than agreeing to it. He studies me, likely poring over my words. Now that I know better, I expect the part of the bargain he doesn't say. He will take me to King Aspen. Then he'll continue on to the nearest body of water to drown me. With his mane wrapped around my hands, I won't be able to stop it.

To hurry his resolve, I add, "After that, you can go anywhere you like."

"I will," he finally says. He turns around, rear facing me. I move to the far end of the cage and shield my face with my arms. The kelpie sends a sharp hoof into the coral bars, then another. After a third kick, the coral splinters and shatters, leaving a large opening near the bottom of the floor. I take a deep breath and swim through it. A shard of coral scrapes against my arm. Another grazes my ankle as I push myself off the floor. Broken bars from the cage float by, drifting in the current. My fingers clasp around one, and I don't let it go, not even as I mount the kelpie.

With my free hand, I grab his mane, and the kelpie swims forward with a speed his heavily muscled body shouldn't be capable of. True to his word, the kelpie keeps my head above water as we navigate the twisting, turning caves. Waves still crash over my face as water funnels inside, but I manage to keep my lungs clear. Finally, the tunnel floors incline slightly, and light shines up ahead. The kelpie gallops toward it. To freedom. To fresh air and open sky.

Freed from the coral caves, I'm faced with a familiar sight. The shore beneath the palace stretches before us, nearly swallowed by the tide. The last blush of sunset peeks over the horizon, sending the beach under a pink-orange glow. With a jolt, the kelpie takes off along the shore, away from the palace toward the jagged rocks. My heart leaps into my throat as it seems like the creature intends to dash us directly into them, but in a single leap, he crests the top of the nearest rock, then leaps to another, then another, more like a goat than a horse-creature.

Once clear of the rocks, another stretch of shore spreads before us. But the kelpie veers away from it and into the water instead. With a splash, he goes under, but the water only reaches my chin. If I thought the kelpie was fast on land, he is a streak of lightning in the open sea. In mere minutes the shore and the palace are nowhere to be seen.

The water is colder the farther we get from the shore, making my teeth chatter. Anxiety fights to overwhelm me, and I wonder if I left too much room in my bargain with the kelpie. Surely, taking us this far out to sea can't be the fastest way to reach Aspen. All I can do is breathe, persist. Trust the fae creature is taking me where I need to go and try not to die in the process.

～

THE SKY IS DARK BY THE TIME I NEXT SEE LAND. IT'S NOTHING BUT A BLACK shape on the horizon, growing larger as the kelpie speeds toward it. Cool night air greets me as we emerge from the sea and into the dark forest beyond the shore. I lost my cloak sometime during the swim, leaving my sodden blouse clinging to my skin, uncomfortably cold and heavy. My breaths grow shallow, coming out in ragged gasps. *Hang on, Evie,* I tell myself. *You just have to find Aspen.*

My head begins to spin, blood leaving my face as my eyes grow heavy. I bite the inside of my cheek to maintain consciousness. *Not now. Not now. Just keep going.*

Painful minutes drag on. Based on our surroundings, we still appear to be in Faerwyvae, although I swear numerous seasons have passed us by. A sprinkle of snow, bathing the night in blinding white. Autumn leaves and a reddish glow. A dense heat I've never felt before. To the left, a blanket of fog covers everything, but I think I can make out a few towering stones of the faewall here and there. Finally, the warm air cools. Flowers grow in clusters, their petals taking to the wind in the kelpie's wake.

"Your king," comes the ethereal voice.

This snaps me to attention. I lean forward, seeking any sign of Aspen. There, coming toward us in the distance is an enormous silhouette. A stag. *Aspen.* Like Cobalt, Aspen's appearance has shifted drastically. However, there's nothing human about the king as his stag hooves tear the earth beneath him. It's a chilling sight.

The distance is closing between him and the kelpie too fast, but my limbs won't move. The kelpie's mane has grown so tight over my hand, I've lost all feeling in the arm. The other hand feels dull and heavy from the cold.

We're close enough now, I can see Aspen's breath puffing in clouds from his stag nostrils.

"I brought you to your king," the kelpie says. I know what will happen next. He'll veer away, back toward the ocean or some nearby lake.

With a grunt, I lift my arm, fingers still wrapped around the branch of coral I stole from the cave. I swing it into the kelpie's mane, severing the black strands until my hand is released. No longer tethered to the creature, the kelpie's speed knocks me backward. I tumble to the ground, rolling. The kelpie speeds off into the night. I turn the opposite direction, seeking the stag. He's growing dangerously closer.

I stumble to my feet, every muscle screaming in protest. "Aspen!"

He continues forward, showing no sign of slowing.

I hold out my hand, palm streaked shades of purple and red where the kelpie's mane strangled my flesh. "Aspen, stop!"

He closes the distance, eyes wild with fury.

"It's me. Evie."

The stag snorts, mouth lathering. He'll be upon me in a matter of seconds, and I'm too weak to move. Tears pour down my cheeks. I'm too late. He doesn't know me. He's become the monster I always thought him to be.

"Aspen, I give you my true name!"

His hooves dig into the earth, and dirt sprays over me as he skids to a halt.

My shoulders are racked with tremors. The stag has stopped mere feet away, teeth bared, muscles quivering. He stomps and paws the earth, head down, antlers pointed toward me.

"Aspen," I whisper. "Did you hear me? I'm here. I came for you."

His stag eyes are locked on mine, so unlike the ones belonging to the fae I kissed this morning. Only his antlers look the same, yet much larger. I've never seen a stag so large or so majestic, so undeniably beautiful. His coat is a russet gold, hooves a glimmering onyx.

With a deep breath, I release the bar of coral, a searing pain shooting through my palm as the jagged shards release from my flesh. Keeping my other hand outstretched toward him, I take one trembling step, then another, each move almost unbearable.

Aspen remains in place watching me warily, but as I move closer, his breathing begins to even, and his lips close over his teeth.

"That's it. I'm here now." Finally, he's close enough to touch. I let my hand fall on the side of his stag face.

"You gave me your name." It's Aspen's voice, but it sounds distant, weak, as if coming from far away.

"Yes."

"You left me."

I shake my head. "No, Aspen. You were deceived by Cobalt."

"Cobalt," he echoes softly.

"He took me and locked me in the coral caves so I couldn't come to you, so we couldn't perform the ritual. He's the one who took Amelie too. It's she everyone saw riding away on the puca. She's under his control."

"You didn't leave?"

"No."

Silence falls between us. Then Aspen says, "It hurt when you left." His words remind me of those of a child. There's no wit, no banter, none of his sharp personality. I wonder if that's part of being in his unseelie form.

"I'm sorry it hurt."

"I don't like feeling like that." His tone carries a hint of anger. "I don't like to feel at all."

"I don't like feeling like that either," I say. "It hurt to be trapped in a cage, unable to tell you the truth. But I had to persevere. I had to come find you, even if it hurt."

"You humans have no choice but to feel. I don't have to."

"You mean, if you remain in this form?"

"Yes. I could stay unseelie. I could forget your face. Forget what it means to hurt or love or rage."

I bring my forehead to the side of his face, nestling into his soft coat. "Is that what you want? To forget me?"

A shudder runs through him. Then another. "No."

I stumble back as the stag pulls away, his massive shape shifting and undulating. Another shudder seizes him, and suddenly the stag is gone, replaced by a familiar figure crouching in the dirt. He wears nothing but trousers and a linen shirt, open at the neck. I kneel next to him, take his face in my hands. "Aspen."

He slowly meets my eyes. "Evie."

I bring his lips to mine, reveling in their softness, the feel of them already so familiar to me.

He pulls away. "You're crying."

I realize he's right. Sobs tear through me while tears stream over my face. "Of course I am. I thought I was going to lose you to the stag forever. I thought you would forget me and destroy my village."

"Why would I destroy your village?"

"Isn't that where you were going? To exact revenge upon me and my people?"

He shakes his head. "I...I don't remember. The rage consumed me."

"But you're free of it now?"

He nods, but his expression darkens. "Cobalt did this."

"Yes, and he's going to try to take your throne. It's been his plan to trick you into breaking the treaty all along. All these attacks, these betrayals, these mysteries. Cobalt has been behind all of them."

"Where is he now?"

"Probably taking your place on the council," I say.

He rises to his feet, helping me up with him. "I have to stop him. We need to get back to the council by midnight and prove we've done the ritual."

"Do you think we can make it?"

"It's possible if we hurry. You'll have to ride me."

"Under other circumstances, that would sound like a highly enticing invitation." I give him a weak smile, but my muscles protest at the thought of mounting another galloping creature.

Aspen must sense my resistance because he puts a hand on my cheek. "Don't worry. I'll be gentle."

"Are we still talking in innuendo?"

"I'm serious."

I let out a sigh. "All right."

"Oh, and Evie?"

"Yes?"

He smiles, thumb brushing my cheekbone. "I know it isn't candles and kisses like I told you it would be, but I give you my true name too."

We bring our lips together. Despite my exhaustion, I bask in the feel of him against me and wrap my arms around his neck. It feels like the energy is humming between us, strong and dangerous. Perhaps it's simply desire, but I can't help wondering if it's the result of being Bonded. Is this what it feels like to exchange names with another? To give another your power while making them vulnerable at the same time? Logic tells me it's impossible. The act of giving one's name is only significant to the fae. Yet, there's this odd pull between us. Like a bridge. A bridge between two cliffs with nothing but jagged shards of rock below.

Before I can explore the strange sensation more, an ethereal voice calls out behind us, "The human is mine."

38

Aspen and I pull away, finding the black kelpie before us, head lowered as he stomps his front hoof in challenge. The king leaps in front of me, hiding my body behind his. "She is not yours," he says.

"Twice she has escaped me without a taste," the kelpie says. "First, she was saved by the pretty prince. Second time, she escaped through trickery. We had a bargain."

"I only promised you could go wherever you wanted after you took me to Aspen." My voice comes out with a tremor. "I never said you could take me with you."

"Human trickery. That is why I hate your kind. You come to my home, invade my land, swim in my waters. The stupid ones have the gall to get lost, polluting everything with their stench, their recklessness. The menacing ones come with iron shackles, with traps and blades and tricks."

"She is neither stupid nor menacing," Aspen says, "but she is my mate. She is under my protection. If you try to harm her, you face my wrath."

"Wrath," the kelpie hisses, taking a step closer. "Such a human reaction."

"It will be my reaction nonetheless."

The kelpie's eyes blaze brighter, the red growing deeper. "Why should I care about your wrath? We aren't in Autumn but Spring. You don't rule here."

"I am still a king."

"I am unseelie. I bow to no king."

Aspen squares his shoulders. "The water in you is the water in me. If you won't respect me as king, respect me as one of your kind."

"Water," the kelpie hisses. "You're Autumn through and through."

"Yet water swims in my blood."

The creature cranes his neck to peek at me behind Aspen. "What about her blood?"

"Her blood is not up for discussion. She made you a bargain that you accepted, and she bested you. It is not her fault you agreed to it. Now you will let us go without further argument."

The kelpie stomps its hoof, creating a furrow in the ground beneath him, teeth peeling back. Aspen's posture grows defensive. He leans forward, hands clenched into fists as a snarl escapes his lips.

The kelpie paws the earth again, then freezes. His head swivels on his sinuous neck toward the fog in the distance and the faewall I know is behind it. I follow his line of vision and see figures moving in the mist. When I look back at the kelpie, it's gone.

I remember what Cobalt had said about sending guards to stop Aspen from killing too many humans during his rage. "We need to leave. Now."

Aspen doesn't utter a word as he shudders from head to toe and shifts back into a stag. He lowers himself for me to climb on his back, then we take off. I don't dare look behind me, terrified of what I'll see. I can only hope Aspen is fast enough to outrun Cobalt's guards. To my horror, Aspen doesn't run away from the faewall, but parallel to it. The dense fog remains in my periphery as we speed through the forest.

"How will we get back in time?" I ask him, arms wrapped around his neck as I lean into him. "In fact, how did the kelpie get me here so fast? It took nearly a full day to get from Sableton to Bircharbor by carriage. How will we get there by midnight?"

"We'll get there." His words sound far away again, but his tone is more alert, more aware. "Each section of the wall falls on a different axis. Each axis belongs to a different court. Sableton is near the Spring axis."

"What exactly does an axis mean in this instance? Is that just where a court's lands touch the wall?"

"Perhaps a better word for a human would be *portal*. These portals run along the length of the wall and allow us to travel quickly to and from courts that, without them, wouldn't be anywhere close to the wall. When you first came here, Foxglove had the carriage bypass the axis line to take you to

Bircharbor by traditional means in what's considered the long way to Autumn."

"Why?"

"To give you time to adjust," he says. "I didn't want you bombarded with interaxis travel on your first day. That's what we're doing now. We'll travel along the wall until we reach the Autumn axis."

"That must be what the kelpie did as well," I say, trying not to dwell on the missing logic and just be grateful instead. If this strange method of travel hadn't been available to me, Aspen would have crossed the faewall into my village.

"I don't think I would have hurt your people," he says as if he can read my thoughts. "I was looking for you. That's all I remember."

I stroke his neck but say nothing. There's no use wondering what might have happened if I hadn't stopped him, and there's no use holding any *maybes* against him. Cobalt is to blame for this. I'll save my anger for him.

We fall into silence, and my eyes begin to grow heavy.

"Sleep," Aspen says. "I'll make sure you stay righted on my back."

I close my eyes and let nightmares of blood and waves take me.

"I CAN SEE THE PALACE JUST AHEAD."

I jolt awake, craning my neck to look around Aspen. Soon I can see the palace too. It glows gold in the moonlight, bright against the black sky. You'd never know by looking at it that a dangerous coup is taking place inside. Once we reach the front steps of the palace, Aspen lowers himself to the ground so I can dismount, then shifts into his seelie form. I grimace as I shake out my aching limbs.

Aspen takes my hand and we dart inside. Guards stand at attention as we enter, expressions concerned. "Is the council in session?" he barks at them.

"Yes, Your Majesty," one says, brow furrowed.

"Should I carry you?" Aspen asks under his breath.

I remember how good it felt to be in his arms, head against his chest. Was that just this morning? Part of me wants to say yes. "No," I say with a sigh. "I want to stand on my own two feet when we confront Cobalt."

"And I want to tear his head off," he grumbles.

I shiver at his tone. It occurs to me I have no idea what to expect of the confrontation. How do fae handle situations like this? I've seen Aspen send his servants to the dungeon and order their execution, but will that be punishment enough for his brother? I can only imagine this ending in blood and teeth.

"Where is the meeting held?" I ask as we move higher in the palace.

"The balcony," he says.

We climb higher and higher until we reach the staircase that leads to the balcony. Before we take a step, we pause. Two figures are seated at the middle of the staircase, huddled close together in whispered conversation.

"Your Majesty!" Foxglove exclaims when he sees us. He and Lorelei all but run down the stairs. Their expressions are horrified as they look from Aspen's furious face to my bruised hands and torn clothing.

"Pardon me saying this, Your Majesty," Lorelei says, "but what in all the rotting oak and ivy is going on?"

Aspen ignores her question. "Is Cobalt sitting with the council right now?"

"Yes," Foxglove says. "He seemed most certain you wouldn't be returning for the meeting."

"And you!" Lorelei narrows her eyes at me. "You ran away."

I shake my head. "It's a long story."

"One we don't have time for right now," Aspen growls, pushing past them and ascending the steps two at a time. I follow behind at a much slower pace, with Foxglove and Lorelei at my side.

"You need a bath," Lorelei hisses in my ear. I can tell she's angry with me. I understand her feelings, considering she was one of the few who saw me—Amelie—riding away on the puca.

"I need more than a bath," I say.

I hear chattering voices up ahead, followed by Aspen's roar as he crests the stairs to the balcony. Picking up my pace, I enter behind him.

Aspen's chest heaves as he stares at the far end of the balcony where Cobalt sits in Aspen's throne, the throne at his right remaining empty. In a semicircle around him sit ten other fae in elegant chairs, including Melusine. I recognize none of them as the ambassadors I saw at the mate ceremony, which tells me these are the court rulers. Their appearances are even more unique and varied than their ambassadors had been, some wearing gowns, others in suits. A few wear nothing, their forms more animal than human. The council fae turn, and Melusine's eyes widen when she sees us. A wolf with snowy white fur and red eyes snarls, while a female fae with pale blue skin and flowing hair hisses, the sound like the wind through the trees. Cobalt, however, keeps his expression neutral.

"Brother, how good of you to return," Cobalt says. "You're late."

Aspen's eyes blaze with fury. "And you are on my throne."

Cobalt gives him an apologetic smile. "This isn't your throne anymore. The council has accepted me as king in your stead. You have proven unfit to rule time and time again. Now you have forfeited your crown."

"For what reason?"

"How much time do you have?" Cobalt says with a laugh. "First of all, how about you explain where you've been?"

"I don't owe you an explanation."

"But you owe them one." Cobalt extends his hand toward the council. A large, stout fae with curling horns, brown skin, and thick, yellow hooves nods in agreement. "You were supposed to be here, doing your duty. Instead, you were...where, exactly?"

"Yes, King Aspen," Melusine says, her tone full of musical sweetness. "I too want an explanation for why you thought it appropriate to neglect your duties."

Aspen's jaw shifts back and forth, but he says nothing. What could he possibly say to satisfy them, when all he can do is tell the truth? If there was ever a time for clever deception, it would be now. "I was misled," he finally says. "My actions were the result of—"

"Your actions were the result of instability and a volatile temper," Cobalt says. "Several witnesses saw you react to the news that your human mate had fled the palace to return to her people. Instead of handling the situation with the grace of a king, you shifted into a stag to destroy her village in retribution."

An androgynous-looking fae wearing a slim black suit lets out a low chuckle. "Tasty." The voice is smooth and feminine. Her skin is pale, hair slick, blonde, and cropped at the base of her neck. When she smiles, I see elongated canines. I've never seen her kind of fae before, but I've heard of them. *Vampire.*

"I didn't destroy her village, nor did I make it past the wall," Aspen says.

Cobalt shrugs. "But that's where you were headed. My guards reported that they saw you near the wall. If it weren't for Miss Fairfield, you'd have drawn human blood."

I can feel Aspen's rage as if it were my own. It burns every part of me, so hot I can keep it inside no longer. "He went there because of you. *You* captured me. *You* sent my sister—disguised as me—to run away and make Aspen think I left. *You* kept me in a cage and left me to drown."

The prince rolls his eyes. "The human has clearly had second thoughts about running away. Don't listen to her lies."

"You're the one who's lying." The council erupts with laughter at my words. "It's true. He can lie. He's been able to lie since the Holstrom girls arrived, took the ability from them in exchange for feigned protection. He orchestrated their attack on Aspen." More laughter at this, making my cheeks burn crimson.

"We all know humans weave fantastical tales," Cobalt says. "But let's not get off topic. Aspen left the palace at a critical time. He failed his duties as a royal on the Council of Eleven Courts. Not only that, but he failed to secure the pact by neglecting to perform the Bonding ritual with his Chosen."

"We performed it," Aspen says. "You know we did. Each of you can sense it."

Cobalt seems unconcerned. "It's past midnight, Brother."

"It was well before midnight when we performed it."

"Then you should have been here to prove it. Regardless, let us go back. Before your reckless actions tonight, you managed to lose one of the Chosen. Amelie disappeared from Bircharbor, and witnesses say she fled from you."

"You have her!" I shout.

He continues as if I said nothing. "Before that, you executed the previous Chosen without trial. Only your word is testimony to their supposed crimes. Before that, you have constantly wavered your political stance, for no other reason than to make trouble."

Some of the other fae are nodding, eyes glistening with malice as they stare at Aspen with open hostility. A fae with bright orange skin covered in delicate scales flicks his forked tongue at him, then snaps his teeth.

"You don't care about your duties as king," Cobalt says. "You are erratic, unreliable, and a danger to human and fae alike."

Aspen begins to shudder, hands clenched into fists. "Get off my throne."

"I, on the other hand, have done everything you could not. I am firm in my political standing. I am constant in my motivations. I went so far as to secure the second step in the treaty before you even made Evelyn your mate."

Melusine shoots Cobalt a surprised look.

"Come greet the council, Amelie." Cobalt waves, and a figure emerges from the staircase behind us.

Amelie is outfitted in a resplendent gown of copper and red, bringing out the fire in her hair. She still wears the sealskin like a cloak over her shoulders, yet gone are the tears I last saw on her face. Her expression is stoic, posture regal and serene as she brushes past us and makes her way to the other side of the balcony. "Greetings," she says, taking a seat in the empty throne at Cobalt's side.

My body goes cold. I'd forgotten to expect her here. The sight of her done up like a queen, all smiles and sweet grace, sends bile rising to my throat. How much of her demeanor is controlled by Cobalt's glamour over her? I refuse to believe she would stand by any of this, refuse to believe she could look at me, covered in blood and bruises and hold an unwavering smile. How much has she given away for love?

"You see," says Cobalt, "Amelie ran away from my brother, terrified of his temper, but I found her. Protected her. Kept her from my brother's rage. I made her my mate weeks ago and performed the Bonding ritual."

"Cobalt," Melusine sings, a dangerous lilt to her melody. "You told me she gave you her name, but I wasn't aware that you gave her yours in return."

Cobalt holds his mother's eyes without a hint of regret. "Ah, well, now you know."

She leans toward her son, teeth bared. "But you saved the treaty."

He smiles at her. "And you helped make me king."

A storm darkens her blue eyes as her tail swishes angrily on the floor, but Cobalt pays her no heed.

"You are no king," Aspen says. His gaze falls on each council fae in turn, burning them with his glare. "He is not my heir. You cannot give him my throne."

"They can if the king is indisposed without naming an heir," Cobalt argues. "I, as your brother, can take your place."

"You have no Autumn blood."

"Yet, this is my home. I have lived here my entire life. And when it mattered most, I stepped in where you could not."

Aspen shudders head to toe, and I think I know what happens next. "You have five seconds to get out of my seat before I rip you to shreds."

"Take one step, and you'll be committing treason," Cobalt says. "The council has already agreed. I am King of Autumn."

With a roar, Aspen's body is torn apart in a mass of fur and hooves. A flash of shock crosses Cobalt's face as the enormous stag charges him. The council fae leap from their seats, backing out of the fray. Some of the fae watch with terror, while others—like the wolf and vampire—look delighted at the spectacle. Cobalt tosses himself to the ground, and Aspen's hooves crush the arm of his throne to splinters.

Cobalt rises to his feet just as Aspen charges again. The force knocks Cobalt backward and sends him skidding into the rail at the edge of the balcony. Cobalt shudders, his princely demeanor gone. In the blink of an eye, his unseelie form takes over. His fingers come to dangerous points, webs between them like serrated knives. He stands his ground as Aspen charges again, lips peeled back to reveal his fangs.

Aspen doesn't falter, just tears across the floor at great speed.

The two collide in a tangle of scales and teeth and antlers.

"Guards!" Cobalt's shout echoes across the balcony. I whirl, wondering where the guards are, but the fae in bronze armor are nowhere to be seen. Come to think of it, I haven't seen any other guards since we arrived, aside from the two at the front of the palace. When I look back at the two royals, my breath catches in my throat.

Over the rail climb slithering bodies, dripping seawater. Most resemble Cobalt with slim physiques, webbed fingers, and gills. They wear armor of pink coral, their weapons similar to the one Amelie attacked me with. Several of them leap upon Aspen, then several more.

Footsteps sound on the floor behind me, and I feel a rush of hope. Aspen's guards—dozens of them—surge forward from the stairwell, followed by Foxglove and Lorelei. "Found them in the dungeon," Foxglove mutters to me when he reaches my side.

Aspen's guards charge the sea fae, but more of Cobalt's guards leap over the rail to face them, baring teeth, shattering armor with their coral swords and knives.

Aspen still struggles against his assailants, trying to throw them off, but all it does is allow Cobalt to dart away from his brother's reach. The sea fae pull at Aspen's ears, wrench his antlers, slick the ground beneath his hooves until he's scrambling to maintain purchase.

Finally, Aspen stops struggling. The sea fae tug him down, down, until he's sprawled on the floor.

I'm frozen in horror as I watch Aspen shift back into his seelie form, chest heaving as Cobalt's guards pull his arms behind his back. He keeps his eyes trained on his brother, fury emblazoned on his features.

"Cobalt," Aspen says through his teeth, "I challenge your claim to the throne."

39

Silence falls over the balcony.

Cobalt's lips pull into a devious grin. "Are you sure that's wise, brother?"

"The throne doesn't belong to you," Aspen growls.

"That's your opinion, and if you're offering me a challenge, that choice won't be yours to make."

"The challenge has been made," Aspen says. "Do you accept?"

Cobalt shudders and shifts back to his seelie form. "I do."

I hear a sharp intake of breath from Foxglove. "This isn't good," he mutters.

"What's going on?"

He wrings his hands. "If the council has already agreed to accept Cobalt as king, a challenge for the throne was King Aspen's last hope. But, oh, I can already see this going badly."

The sea fae release Aspen and allow him to rise to his feet, yet they maintain a tight circle around him. The council erupts in chatter.

"What does a challenge for the throne entail?" I whisper to Foxglove.

"They will have three options," he explains. "Either a battle of strength, a presentation of factual debate, or a decision of fate."

I look from Aspen to Cobalt, a spark of hope igniting within me. "Aspen will win a battle of strength."

He nods, but his expression is grave. "There's no doubt about that. But as the challenged, it's Cobalt's right to select which option they take. He'll know better than to select a battle of strength, even if he were to name a champion to fight in his stead."

"He can do that?"

"Yes. Either royal can name another to fight for them. Their champion can secure the win in their patron's name."

Cobalt walks to the other side of the balcony, then leans against the rail. He watches Aspen, a pleased smile on his lips.

My blood goes cold. "Why does he look so confident?"

"Because he's going to choose the option he knows he can win," whispers Foxglove. "A presentation of factual debate. He clearly believes his motives were just, and he already received the support of the council once. There's no doubt he can do it again."

"The council decides the winner of the debate?"

He nods.

"Then Aspen will have to stand up for himself. He'll tell them the truth." My words come out weak, and I can feel their folly before they leave my mouth. It was hard enough for Aspen to get past his pride and tell me the truth. How will he fare when facing a council that is already set against him, not to mention a brother who can lie? I feel the blood drain from my face. "Oh no. This isn't good."

"You understand now."

Aspen's eyes continue to burn into his brother as Cobalt grins back at him. "We must select the mediator," Aspen says.

"Queen Melusine," Cobalt proposes.

Aspen lets out a cold laugh. "I think not, brother. I agree the mediator should be unseelie, since we are both seelie, but our mother is not a neutral party."

Cobalt's expression falters for only a moment. "Queen Nyxia."

The vampire in the black suit steps forward with a feigned gasp as she brings her slim white fingers to her lips. "Me? I'd be honored. I'll need ink and paper, of course."

Aspen's eyes lock on one of his guards. "Go." The guard leaves, and the council fae return to their seats.

I can't help but shudder as I watch the vampire stroll to the middle of the balcony, stopping in front of the two thrones. Leaning toward Foxglove, I ask, "Should I be worried?"

He ponders before answering. "I think the Queen of the Lunar Court will serve well as a neutral party. She's never had love for either of the siblings."

"Yet she must have agreed to Cobalt taking Aspen's throne."

Foxglove adjusts his spectacles, grimacing. "That she did."

The guard returns moments later with ink, quill, and two pieces of parchment. He marches between the seats of the council and hands his materials to Nyxia. The vampire then makes her way to Cobalt's side of the balcony, where he and Amelie stand. My sister dabs at a cut above Cobalt's brow, a worried frown tugging her lips.

"She has some nerve," Lorelei says with a glower, coming up next to Foxglove and me. Hurt and rage mingle in her eyes as she watches my sister.

"Come," I say, swallowing my own hurt, "let's go to Aspen." We make our way to his side of the balcony, and I try to ignore the stares of the council watching every step I take. The guards sneer and hiss as I draw near but don't stop me as I approach Aspen. His expression softens when he meets my eyes. I want to reach for his hand, but the sharp looks the sea fae give me make me hesitate.

The council erupts in whispers, and I turn to see Cobalt taking one of the papers from Nyxia, then writing something with ink and quill. Once finished, she waves the parchment in the air to dry the ink and then folds it into a neat square. Then she turns on her heel and comes our way.

"The battle has been set in ink," Nyxia whispers as she approaches, holding Cobalt's folded sheet of parchment. She then hands Aspen a blank sheet of paper. "Write the name of your champion, if you are to use one, then sign your name."

"Think hard, brother," Cobalt calls from the other side of the balcony, tone mocking. "Are you strong enough to fight your own battles? Or will you need a champion?"

Aspen grumbles and turns toward the balcony rail. He spreads the parchment over the top of the rail, then extends his hand toward Nyxia for the ink and quill. I look from Aspen to Cobalt and back again. Cobalt looks so certain, so confident. There isn't a doubt in his mind that he's going to win. He knows Aspen would never name a champion. He knows he'll easily win over the council with a presentation of factual debate.

Ignoring the hisses of the sea fae guards, I race to Aspen's side before he can press the quill to the paper. "Choose me," I say. "Choose me as your champion."

He pauses and meets my eyes. His expression shifts from worry to resolution. "No. I won't have you involved in this. This is between me and my brother."

"But you know he's going to choose debate." My voice is a furious whisper. "The council has already accepted his word. What can you say to change their minds?"

"I have no need to change their minds," he mutters. "If they fail to see reason after I've said my piece, then the council can be damned, with all of Faerwyvae with it."

My hands ball into fists. "I can help you. You know I'm good with words. Name me your champion and we can wipe that grin off Cobalt's face."

He reaches a hand to my cheek, brushing his thumb along my jaw. "No, Evie. This is my mess. I'm going to clean it up on my own."

"But you're not alone anymore. You have me. I can do this."

He leans forward and brushes his lips to mine. "No."

I tense, and my lips don't respond to his. Anger flushes my cheeks as I glare at him. He can't just kiss me and tell me no. He can't just make this choice as if it has only to do with him. This isn't just his throne to lose. It's mine now too, and we will both suffer if this goes badly.

If Cobalt wins, Aspen dies.

I won't lose him. Not after we've come this far, fought this hard. Not when we were finally becoming something *more*.

"Aspen." The word escapes my lips, cold and powerful. Energy hums around us, as if the air between me and the king is sizzling, charged with lightning. It startles me, reminding me of the way I felt after we exchanged names. Again, I imagine a bridge, and we are the two cliffs it connects. In my mind, I cross that bridge, aware of the jagged rocks waiting hundreds of yards below. I don't know how I know to do this, but I do. "By the power of your true name, I order you to name me your champion."

His eyes widen, and it feels like an eternity that we stand locked beneath each other's gaze. Then he blinks. It's clear when he discovers what I've done, when the power of his name being used against him dawns on his realization. His face flashes with hurt, something close to fear dancing in his eyes. The expression remains for only a moment before he steels it behind a mask of indignation. "Is this what your vow is worth?" he says through his teeth. "When you promised you wouldn't use my name against me?"

"I had to," I say, trying to hide the tremors that seize me beneath his angry stare. My breath feels like it's been pulled from my lungs. *I'm doing this for both of us. Please understand.*

"Then you leave me no choice," he says with a snarl. He returns to the parchment and scrawls my name on it. He presses so hard, he pierces the paper in places. Then, below it, he signs his name. He doesn't meet my eyes when he gives the parchment to Nyxia, who folds it with her slender fingers.

With slow, elegant steps, she makes her way to the middle of the balcony and faces the council. She unfolds one sheet of parchment, then the other, reading each before holding them out for the council to see. "King Aspen has named Evelyn Fairfield his champion. Cobalt, on the other hand, will represent himself and has chosen a decision of fate."

I blink a few times, staring dumbfounded at the vampire. "A decision of fate? Not a presentation of factual debate?"

"You heard her correctly," Cobalt says, chin raised. "It's set in ink; you can see for yourself."

I round on Foxglove. "What in the name of iron is a decision of fate?"

He returns to wringing his hands, face pale. "I never thought he would choose it."

"What. Is. It?"

Foxglove's expression turns apologetic. "It's a matter of magic."

"Come, Evelyn," Cobalt says. "It's time to journey to the Twelfth Court."

40

"Twelfth Court," I echo, but no one seems to hear me. Cobalt makes his way to Aspen's throne, ignoring the shattered arm as he settles in. The council fae exchange excited whispers.

I turn to Aspen, but he doesn't meet my eyes. "Aspen, I—"

"Time to fight for my throne," he growls.

My throat feels tight at the ice in his tone. I turn to Foxglove. "What's happening? What is the Twelfth Court?"

"I told you," he says. "It's a matter of magic. The Twelfth Court isn't a true court, but a realm of magic that connects all courts. Going there is a rare thing, a sacred and dangerous excursion. Cobalt must trust his personal cause greatly to resort to such radical action."

"Don't worry," Lorelei says. "There's a chance you can win." However, the doubt on her face betrays her words.

"How?" I look from her to Foxglove. "I don't even believe in magic."

The two fae exchange an amused glance as if I've said something foolish. "You don't have to believe in a thing for it to be real," Foxglove says. "It can exist with or without your blessing, you know."

"Perhaps, but how am I supposed to win a battle using something I don't believe in?"

Lorelei shrugs. "How do you breathe every day? How do you sleep when you're tired? How do you perform surgery with your hands?"

I want to argue with her, to tell her the first two are controlled by the autonomic nervous system, and the latter is only done after years of training. But I hold my tongue, remembering the way time slowed down when I tended Aspen's wound. The way my hands knew what to do, what to feel for. There was something chilling and instinctual about it. Something I still don't understand.

"We're waiting," Cobalt calls.

I blanch, finding all eyes on me.

Foxglove gives me a gentle push toward the thrones. "Go. You can do this."

If only I knew what *this* was. With trembling steps, I make my way to the empty throne and lower myself into my seat. Foxglove and Lorelei stand next to me, a comforting presence at my side.

I take in the stares of my audience, unnerved beneath their scrutiny. Nyxia watches me with a curious expression, hands steepled at her waist. Behind her, the blue fae with the flowing hair lets out a windy hiss, while the white wolf pants, tongue lolling from between his teeth. The fae with horns and hooves scowls, and the orange fae with scales flicks his tongue at me several times. Melusine, on the other hand, refuses to look my way at all.

I shift my gaze to Cobalt's side of the balcony, where Amelie stands at the rail, looking as serene as ever. Even when she meets my eyes, her features remain unchanged. My gaze then roves to Aspen, still surrounded by Cobalt's guards. His eyes lock on mine. I try not to read too much into his expression, not sure I'll like what I find.

Silence falls over the balcony. I lean toward Foxglove. "What happens now?"

He bends toward me. "Next you and Cobalt travel to the Twelfth Court and petition the All of All."

I furrow my brow. "The All of All? Is that some god? Some deity?"

"The All of All is a culmination of all that is and all that is not."

"But what exactly is it? And how do I get to the Twelfth Court? I take it I won't find a door here on the balcony."

Foxglove shakes his head. "The Twelfth Court exists on its own axis, separate from the other courts, yet within them all at once. You can reach it from anywhere."

"How?"

"Enough chatter," Cobalt says. "Let's go."

"But I don't know—"

"If you can't figure it out, then you don't deserve to petition the All of All." With that, he faces forward and closes his eyes.

My pulse races, mind spinning as sweat beads at my brow. I can't do this. I was wrong when I made Aspen choose me as his champion. I don't know how to access an invisible court, how to petition some magical deity. I don't know what I'm doing, and I don't know how to get out of this. I messed up. Big time.

I feel a squeeze on my shoulder, Lorelei's fingers. I remember her words. *How do you breathe every day? How do you sleep when you're tired? How do you perform surgery with your hands?*

With a deep breath, I close my eyes, trying to shut out my fears, my worries, my regrets. I focus on the feel of my breath rushing through my nostrils, the sound of my blood pounding through my ears, the feel of my heart hammering in my chest. I summon my surgeon's calm, of hands that remain steady in crisis. I summon my fiery passion, the part of me that chose to open my heart to Aspen, to explore unknown parts of myself. I summon the mysteries I've yet to unfold, the instinct I felt when performing Aspen's surgery, the magic of a little girl putting her hands on the sick. I summon my mother's strength, her care, and my sister's reckless love.

My eyes flutter open, a calm warmth spreading over me. I'm not surprised by what I see, even though the vision before me looks unlike anything I've ever seen before. The balcony remains intact, but its shape is more liquid than solid, like particles of light weaving together to create a floor, bright glowing orbs of multi-hued radiance to represent the bodies in the audience. I turn my eyes to the sky, finding dark shades of violet and indigo swirling with other colors I can't put a name to.

Time isn't quite frozen, but it isn't what it was before. It's slow and fast, gentle and violent. This world is everywhere and nowhere at once. Oddly, the thought doesn't worry me. It makes perfect sense and no sense at all. I accept it.

A warm yellow light beckons me forward, and I leave my throne to follow it. I'm subtly aware that my body feels weightless, like I'm nothing more than one of the glowing orbs the council fae have become. I follow the light as it flutters away from me, down what used to be stairs, into a tunnel of swirling particles. The particles give way to darkness, with nothing to see but the light that leads me on and on.

The light stops just ahead and disappears, pitching me into a black void. My mind begins to sharpen, growing clearer. A violet speck of light begins to pulse in front of me, growing larger and larger, providing subtle illumination. I glance at my hands, aware that my body has returned to its familiar shape and density.

The speck of light becomes a violet sun. It rises overhead, beaming rays of warmth onto me. As it sets, a crescent moon takes its place and stars shoot across the sky. Violet clouds cover the moon and the sun returns, but my attention snags on something near my feet. Narrow stalks shoot from the ground and open into dazzling violet buds. The petals unfurl into flowers, then tower higher and higher. I walk through the enormous flowers, mesmerized, watching them sway in a warm breeze. The sun shines high overhead, warming my face.

When the sun sets, the flowers shiver and shake, petals dropping at my feet, each one as large as I am. I run forward, dodging the falling petals, spinning to avoid being pinned beneath them. Once the petals cease falling, the stalks begin to wrinkle and sag, then shrivel back down toward the ground. In the blink of an eye, there's nothing. Everything is smothered in a blanket of violet. Silence. Death.

A flash of panic rises inside me, and all I can think is to run. Escape the nothingness. Then suddenly, something sprouts from the nothingness. Then another. New blooms, born from death. Calm returns to me as I continue on, watching the cycle repeat around me, again and again. After a while, it no longer terrifies me when the nothingness returns.

As the petals unfurl yet again, I'm starting to wonder if this is all I'll see, if the Twelfth Court is nothing more than this endless cycle where seasons change and the sky shifts high above. Then a violent breeze sweeps by, blowing away the petals, the stalks, the ground beneath my feet, until only darkness remains. The wind swirls around me, pushing me on all sides, making me lose my balance. As I right myself, a figure stands before me. Like everything else here, she's composed of violet particles of light. Her long hair flows behind her, like the blue fae on the council. This fae, however, has the wings of a pixie.

"We get along well," she says with a mischievous grin.

"What do you mean?" My voice sounds strange in this place, like a version of me I've never heard before.

She taps the side of her head. "Thought. Intellect. You live your life in your head much of the time, yes?"

"I do, but...what does that mean?"

"It means the air in you is the air in me." With that, she disappears.

I'm left in darkness again. I take a few steps forward and see something up ahead. It's small, round. A rock? As I reach it, the rock seems to come to life. It rises on gnarled legs, then turns to face me.

A goblin. I leap back.

"I know you," he says with a snarl.

My breath hitches. Can it be? This goblin may be violet, but he looks uncannily like the one that chased Amelie and me. "You!"

"Ah, you remember," he says. "Vile beasty, you are. Why are you here? Did my claws teach you nothing?"

"They taught me to fear your kind."

"Fear. Pah! You think you know fear? You scared my children. Nearly crushed their toes with your giant beasty boots when you came to *my* land."

"Your children?"

"Did you not see them playing near the rock? No, your beasty eyes were fixed elsewhere. No respect. No caution."

I think back to our excursion to the faewall that day. When we crossed the wall to the other side, I remember seeing nothing but fog. We were hardly on the fae side for more than a few seconds, but I admit, I hadn't considered our surroundings. I was so fueled with terrified excitement at the time. "I'm sorry if I scared your children, but you scared me and my sister. You glamoured her. You nearly bit her."

"Just a nibble," the goblin says. "A price for making my babies cry."

I furrow my brow. I don't know if I can forgive the goblin for the havoc he wreaked on me and Amelie, but I can understand his motivations, in a twisted sort of way. "I know what it's like to want to protect the ones you love. To fight for them."

"Safety. Security. Family," he says with a nod. "The earth in you is the earth in me."

The goblin disappears and darkness returns. I remain motionless, puzzling over the odd encounter. What is this place? Is any of this real? I continue on through the black nothing.

I take only a few steps before warmth envelops me. A ball of violet flame emerges from the black and floats around my head. I follow it with my eyes, watching as it undulates and grows, then takes the shape of a beautiful woman. Her hips sway as she dances around me, eying me with scrutiny.

"You think you're better than me," she says, voice light and sultry. "But we know each other well."

"Passion," I say with a shudder.

She nods, then lunges forward, feminine face shifting into a beastly snarl. "And rage." I pull back, but her snarl dissipates into a trilling laugh. "That, you know well. The other, you are just getting to know."

"Yes." This time, I know what to say. "The fire in you is the fire in me."

She winks, then disappears.

I take off into the darkness again, eager to finish this strange quest. I need to find the All of All, not these mischievous fae. How do I find this deity? The thought is barely finished before something emerges from the ground. It begins as a bead of violet water and grows, rippling into the form of a hulking horse-creature.

Kelpie. Of course.

The creature bares its teeth at me. "Twice you have gotten away. You won't escape three times."

"I won't bargain with you this time."

"No? Isn't there somewhere you are meaning to go?"

I try my best to steady my nerves. None of the previous three fae were anywhere near as terrifying as the kelpie. "I am looking for the All of All."

"You are lost," he says. "Stupid human, invading places that are not your own and getting lost on the way."

"I'm not lost," I say. "Looking isn't necessarily lost. I'm simply on my way somewhere that I have yet to find."

"Sounds like lost."

I take a deep breath, remembering what the kelpie said when he confronted me and Aspen. "I'm sorry my kind have invaded your land, and I'm sorry humans infuriate you. You love your land, your water."

"Fury and love are human emotions."

"Yet you have them just the same," I say. "Admit it. You're angry that I've escaped you twice. Anger is an emotion."

The kelpie's violet eyes burn brighter.

"You are more than just an animal. You feel emotion."

"I don't."

"You do, and I understand wanting to deny that. I too have denied emotions before." I think about how I suppressed my tears after I thought Amelie had died, how I refused to recognize my attraction to Aspen.

"Humans can deny them?" His tone is curious.

"Yes, but it doesn't make them go away." I take another deep breath. "The water in you is the water in me."

I expect the violet kelpie to disappear like the others, but it doesn't. He just stands there, considering me. Perhaps I wasn't convincing enough. Finally, he lets out a slow hiss like a sigh. "I will take you to the All of All."

I hesitate. "I told you, I won't bargain with you again."

"If you are not lost, I will not require a bargain."

I watch him for a few moments, seeking hints of deception. Logic is telling me not to trust the kelpie, but my heart feels calm. "Fine," I say and climb upon the kelpie's back. Steadying my hands on the creature's neck, we take off into the darkness. Time swirls around us, racing and reversing. Hours pass. Seconds pass. No time at all has passed.

Before I know it, I am on my feet, and the kelpie is nowhere to be seen. I'm again in the black void. A voice speaks into my mind, but it sounds like no voice I've ever heard before. It's quiet and loud, powerful and meek. "You seek us."

"Are you the All of All?" My voice sounds harsh against the emptiness, returning no echo, no resonance.

"We are the All of All," the voice says. "What are you?"

"Human," is all I can think to say. "I am petitioning on behalf of King Aspen for the Autumn Court throne."

"What is it you offer us?"

My mind goes blank. No one said anything about an offering. Besides, what could I possibly have to offer all that is and all that is not? I'm nothing special, have nothing special. Cobalt has lies, words, conviction, passion. I have those things too, but how could mine compare to his? What do I have that he has not? "I...I don't know."

Silence.

I begin to tremble.

"You can offer us a look at your heart," the All of All says. "If your heart is true, we will allow your petition to pass. Do you agree?"

I swallow hard. "Yes." With a jolt, a ball of violet light escapes my chest to hover in the air before me. Images swirl inside it, memories. I see myself, Amelie, Mother. I watch myself giggle and laugh, then scream and cry. I watch as I hug Mother, then shout hurtful words at her. I see myself turn my nose at the sight of Maddie Coleman, watch as I help Mr. Meeks perform an amputation. The violet ball goes still, then shifts. It's Aspen's face I see now. I see myself shouting at him, ignoring his smiles, his jests, his flirtations. Then I watch as I fold myself into his arms, lips pressing into his. I watch as I face him as a stag, hand outstretched as I give him my name. Then I see myself on the balcony, using that very name against him.

The violet light goes still again, then lurches back into my chest. Panic seizes me. There's no way the All of All will allow my petition to pass after seeing all of that.

"Your heart has darkness," the All of All says. "It also holds light. It is smooth and rough, holds hate and love. It is both a wild beast and a tame creature."

There's no use denying it. "Yes."

"This is a true heart."

Surprise ripples through me. "It is?"

"There is magic inside it. Things you don't yet understand. Things you will explore."

I nod.

"We have made our decision." Before I can respond, the darkness explodes into thousands of particles of violet light. It surges around me, pushing me back. The breath is stripped from my lungs as I lurch through the void, feeling it rushing past me as I'm tossed backward.

With a lurch, I slam into the back of my throne. I open my eyes, meeting the astonished faces of the council. A collective gasp roars through them. I feel a hand on my shoulder and meet the wide eyes of Lorelei. Foxglove covers his mouth with his hand, gaze sliding to my brow.

That's when I feel the weight on my forehead. I reach a hand, finding something firm surrounding my skull like a...a crown.

I lift it from my head and find a gold circlet decorated with strange, swaying feathers. Or perhaps leaves. It's delicate and exquisite and breathtaking all at once. My eyes find Aspen's. His expression is equally as awed as everyone else's.

"No," Cobalt says with a gasp as he rises to his feet from the throne. "How?"

I ignore him, brushing past him and Nyxia and the dumbfounded sea fae guards toward Aspen. When I reach the king, I bow and hand him the crown. "The All of All has chosen."

He takes the crown from me, turns it over in his hands as he inspects it. I expect him to place it on himself, and for a moment, it looks like he expects the same. But he freezes, then places the crown back on my head. "I think this belongs to you," he whispers.

I rise from my bow, puzzling over his actions. His furrowed brow tells me he isn't quite sure about them himself.

Aspen turns and faces the council, raising his voice for all to hear. "The All of All has chosen my champion as the winner of the decision of fate. My challenge to the throne has been heard, judged, and decided. I am King of Autumn." He turns his gaze on Cobalt. "And you, dear brother, are charged with treason."

41

———

"No!" Cobalt shouts. He points at the crown on my head. "That crown means nothing. It's no gift from the All of All."

Aspen nods at Queen Nyxia. "As mediator, the ruling is yours."

The vampire looks caught off guard for a moment, gaze moving from Aspen to Cobalt. Finally, her eyes settle on me. "The All of All have spoken. The crown is their answer."

"She could have stolen the crown," Cobalt argues. "The All of All would never choose her over me."

Aspen lifts his hand, signaling toward his brother. "Guards, seize him."

The armored fae race toward Cobalt, swords and spears drawn as they charge him. With a hiss, Cobalt shudders and shifts into his nix form, blue scales glistening in the moonlight. He points at his sea fae. "Take them down."

The sea fae tear across the floor to meet the guards, while a few anxious council fae dart to the perimeter of the balcony, Melusine among them. Others roar to join the battle against the sea fae. With a shudder, Queen Nyxia shifts into a towering shadow with red eyes and sharp teeth. The blue wind fae floats off the floor and turns into a puff of mist as she swirls around the sea fae, lifting Cobalt's guards from the floor and tossing them off the side of the balcony. The white wolf sinks his teeth into a scaly blue leg, eliciting a shout of pain. The fae with curling horns slams his fist into a sea fae's head. The orange fae with scales stands close to the battle but doesn't join, merely watching with mild curiosity.

I hear the sound of crashing waves and turn to look over the balcony. The water is rising from the sea to impossible heights, leaping against the side of the palace, lapping over the balcony rail, catching those who've fallen.

I return my attention to the chaos of the balcony as a flash of blue darts toward the rail. Aspen follows, taking Cobalt by the shoulder and forcing his brother to face him. I see them lock in battle before the spray of a wave hits me in the face. When I open my eyes, Aspen is leaning over the rail, looking down. A flicker of movement catches my attention to the left, a mass of gray-brown fur.

"Amelie!" I run toward her, and she freezes. Her selkie skin has enveloped her body from the neck down. All that remains is her face. The head of the seal rests on her brow, and she seems seconds away from pulling it down. I close the distance between us, putting my arms where her shoulders should be. "Amelie, don't you dare leave me."

Her green eyes glaze with tears. "I have to go."

"No you don't. Shed the skin. We'll keep you safe from Cobalt."

Her expression hardens. "I don't want to be kept safe from him. He's mine and I am his."

I stumble to find my words. "That's just the glamour talking. Stay with me. Please."

"I can't." She pulls the seal's face over hers, then drops to her belly, hobbling toward the rail. I reach for her, feel my arms close around her slick fur as another crashing wave pummels me.

When I open my eyes, Amelie is gone.

I run to the rail, staring over it, but all I see is the raging ocean. Waves spray up the side of the palace, into the open windows. There's no sign of my sister. Still, I continue to watch, seeking any sign of her. I don't leave the rail, not even when the waves calm and subside. Not even when the water levels recede to normal, as if nothing had happened at all.

"They're gone," Aspen says, coming up beside me. "Cobalt, your sister, my brother's guards. All his sea fae leapt over the rail."

I continue watching the sea, not sure what I'm hoping for. Amelie left. She chose Cobalt. All I've ever wanted was to protect her. Keep her safe. Even now, I want nothing more than to save her from Cobalt's clutches. But what do I do if she doesn't want saving?

Aspen puts a hand on my lower back. "Let's go," he says. "You're shaking."

He's right. I'm racked with tremors, partially from the cold water dripping from my body, partially from my suppressed sobs. Finally, I pull away from the rail and let him guide me back inside the palace. Once we reach the hall, it's no surprise how much is flooded. I imagine the entire west portion of the palace will be a sodden mess, not to mention broken windows and damaged furnishings.

Aspen's guards flank us, the council fae walking just ahead. A few seem dazed, while others are chatting animatedly, as if they'd just returned from a fascinating play. The white wolf pads down the hall, blood dripping from his muzzle. Nyxia strolls at a leisurely pace, chin lifted as if without a care. Melusine, of course, slithers down the slick hall with ease, shoulders squared. Another fae, a female with golden-brown skin, honey-colored hair, and enormous yellow butterfly wings turns to face us. She pauses until we reach her side.

"King Aspen," she says with a bow of her head. "I will lend you my weather until Bircharbor can dry out."

Aspen nods. "Thank you, Queen Dahlia. We will accept your generosity."

She hesitates before moving on, eyes resting on the crown above my brow. Then, with an exaggerated smile, she flits away.

"Who is she?" I ask, once she's out of earshot.

"The Queen of the Summer Court," he says, a growl in his voice. "It's going to be an effort to speak to any of them like they didn't nearly strip me from my throne."

Nearly. They had, in fact, stripped him *completely* from his throne. It was only his challenge to Cobalt that won it back, and even that had nearly been thwarted. How would it have gone if I hadn't forced Aspen to name me his champion? Would Aspen have succeeded in petitioning the All of All? It's impossible to know.

Only one thing is clear. I betrayed Aspen when I used his true name like that, regardless of how things turned out. I'll never forget the look on his face when he realized I'd shattered his trust. It showed me something else too; I still don't trust Aspen. Not fully, at least. If I had, I would have let him make his own decision. I would have believed he had what it took to defeat Cobalt.

"King Aspen," says a sultry male voice, stealing my attention.

The orange fae with scales stands before us. His body is long and lean, dressed in a modern black suit, neck slightly longer and slimmer than a human neck would be. He has no hair, just more iridescent orange scales. His face is mostly flat with a lipless mouth, slits where his nose should be, and beady black eyes.

"King Ustrin." Aspen gives the fae a short bow.

The scaly king returns it, bending at the waist. "Congratulations on winning back your throne. It seems your mate here is quite accomplished."

"I'm very grateful for her," Aspen says, although the edge in his tone isn't lost on me.

King Ustrin's eyes move to me. "Might I have a word, Miss Fairfield?"

I look from Aspen to the orange fae. Would it be rude of me to say no? There's something unsettling about the lizard-like king that has to do with more than just his odd appearance. I summon my calm. "Of course, Your Majesty."

Aspen hesitates before pointing at two of his guards then at me. The guards break off from the rest and stand behind me. "We'll speak later," he whispers, but I can't read his tone. "I need to see the council fae off." Then, without so much as looking at me, he moves on, following the flock of fae.

King Ustrin regards me through slitted lids but says nothing.

Perhaps he's waiting for me to bow, so I do. After I rise, he remains silent. "Might I ask what court you rule, King Ustrin?"

"Fire," he says. His eyes slide to the crown on my brow. "A curious crown the All of All gave you. Why did the king gift it to you instead of keeping it for himself?"

Not even I know that answer. Still, I refuse to admit it. "I will be his queen once we're married, and he already has a crown of his own. He must have wanted to show his appreciation for me winning him back the throne."

"Yes, yes, that does make sense." He takes a step forward and sniffs the air, much like Melusine had done. His tongue darts in and out of his mouth. "You're familiar."

I recall the fae I encountered in the Twelfth Court, how they sought similar elements between us. "The fire in you is the fire in me."

He laughs, a low hissing sound, tongue flicking. "I suppose that's true. But there's something else. A certain...feel about you. Like that of an old enemy."

I bristle. This isn't going anywhere like I hoped. Then again, what else was I expecting? I still know very little about the fae, about their politics and biases. I'm only just now getting to understand the Autumn Court. Other courts are far beyond my familiarity.

Time to take control.

I square my shoulders and adopt Aspen's bored tone. "King Ustrin, I do thank you for introducing yourself to me, and it's been a pleasant chat. However, I've had a long day. Forgive me for cutting our acquaintance short, but I must get some rest."

He smirks, narrowing his eyes, but makes no argument. "Of course. How careless of me. You did just win a battle, after all. We'll speak again, I'm sure." With a bow, he lowers himself, then turns away.

I let out a heavy breath once he's at the far end of the hall.

A hand falls on my shoulder, making me jump, but it's just Lorelei. "Come on. You should clean up and get some sleep."

I nod, and Lorelei leads the way. The guards follow closely behind. It isn't far until we reach the door to Aspen's bedroom, and I can't help but fear it's been destroyed. The floor beneath my feet is slick with water, but at least it isn't flooded. The room itself is on the east side of the palace, so there's a good chance it might be salvageable.

The guards push open the door, and Lorelei and I step inside. The orb lights burn low in their sconces, but from what I can tell, the room has remained mostly unscathed. Water seems to reach only a quarter of the way across the floor, soaking a few rugs. But the bed, the wardrobe, and everything on the far wall appears dry.

I turn to the guards. "I'll bathe now."

"We should leave the doors open," says one of the guards.

I'm about to argue when I remember the hidden door Amelie had opened. The secret tunnels could very well connect to many other rooms like this one and were likely how Cobalt was able to get to the Holstrom girls, how he was able to sneak Amelie out of the palace the night she disappeared. For all I know, he could be lurking in those tunnels now. Watching. Waiting. I shudder. "Very well."

"We'll set up the tub behind the dressing screen," Lorelei says. I follow her to the tub, help her drag the dressing screen in front of it to hide it from the view of the hall. The tub is empty, and just looking at it makes my muscles hunger for relief. Lorelei takes a step away. "I'll put in the order—"

Before she can finish, the tub suddenly fills with hot, steaming water. Herbs and flower buds float over the top, the scent of rosemary wafting upward. My mouth falls open. All I can do is stare.

Lorelei laughs. "Your mate must have great foresight regarding you."

"You think he did this?" I look beneath the tub, trying to find the pipes and drains I've never been able to locate. "How? It came out of nowhere."

"As king, Aspen can perform minor manipulations over all the elements. But he gets earth and water from his parents. This," she waves her hand over the tub, "is easy for him. I mean, it's easy for any of the water fae employed here too, but I have a feeling he had a hand in this one."

I still can't piece it together. Aspen isn't anywhere close to this bedroom right now, nor is there any source for the water. It makes my temples throb to consider that maybe, just *maybe*, magic is real.

I think of everything I experienced today. The journey to the Twelfth Court. The crown I brought back. The way I was able to use Aspen's name. There could be a scientific explanation. The Twelfth Court could have been the result of a hallucination. Aspen's response to me using his name could have been from superstition and cultural conditioning.

Yesterday's magic is today's science.

Perhaps decades from now it will all make logical sense. Perhaps one day I'll understand what happened. Someday I'll understand how I healed Lorelei's leg, how I performed a surgery on instinct alone. Maybe someday I'll be able to explain how a crystalline tub with no plumbing can fill instantaneously with water. But today...today there's only one thing I can say about it.

It's magic.

42

———————

I jolt awake, sitting upright in bed. What woke me? Aside from the nightmares, of course. Night after night I dream my lungs are filling with water, that sea monsters are hunting me, nipping my heels as I try to swim away.

But I don't think that's what it was this time.

My heart races, body trembling from its pulse. Or is it the room that's shaking? I look at the space next to me on the bed. I'm not surprised to find it empty. It's been three days since Aspen won back his throne, and I've hardly seen him since. Every move I make to try and talk to him is brushed aside with excuses. He's too busy. He has to oversee the repairs of the palace. He has correspondences to send. He certainly hasn't stepped foot in his bedroom. Still, my heart plummets with disappointment.

Will he ever stop avoiding me?

Another tremor rattles through me, and this time I know the room is shaking. I fling myself out of bed, run to the wardrobe, and extract a robe. Pulling the robe around my nightdress, I tear from the bedroom. Aspen's guards stand at attention when they see me. "What's going on?"

One of the guards steps forward. "The king is sealing off the coral caves that connect to the palace," she says.

"How? With explosives?"

"Yes."

My eyes widen. "Take me to him."

She hesitates. "It's not safe—"

I put my hands on my hips. "Take me to him now. Please."

She leads me down the hall and stairs, then stops outside the entrance to the dining room. I round the corner and step inside. Aspen stands at the far end, looking out the open expanse, hands on the rail. He's dressed in cream and gold, but his waistcoat is wrinkled, blue-black hair tousled between his antlers. Warm summer air— thanks to Queen Dahlia—wafts through the opening, making the room stifling hot. I wish I'd brought a lighter robe.

As I approach the king, another rumble rocks the palace, and I see a spray of water shoot into the sky. "Aspen, what in the name of iron is going on."

"Destroying the caves." He doesn't turn to face me, just keeps his gaze fixed on the scene outside. I follow his line of vision and see numerous guards on the beach. The tide is out, exposing several entrances to the coral caves. Half of them appear collapsed, filled with shards of coral. The guards are filling an open cave with what looks like kegs of gunpowder.

"Isn't there a safer way to do this?"

He shakes his head. "I must be sure Cobalt has no way of sneaking into the palace. When he returns, he'll have to face me head on."

When he returns. There's no doubt in his voice that it will come to pass, and I can't say I disagree with him. The prince already went so far as to manipulate my sister, me, the Holstrom girls, the council...why would he stop now? Besides, we don't know how many council fae are his loyal allies.

Another explosion has me gripping the rail for stability, and I grit my teeth until it passes. "Aspen, we need to talk."

"I have work to do."

I cross my arms over my chest, angling my body toward him. He still won't meet my eyes. "No, we need to talk. Now. I'm tired of this wall between us. Our wedding is supposed to be in three days. *Three days,* Aspen."

"Everything has already been prepared," he says. "It will continue without issue."

"Not if you blow up the palace before then."

"I'm not going to blow up the palace."

"Are you going to use explosives to seal the tunnels between the rooms too? Blow open the walls? Put my life in danger without saying a word to me?"

He rounds on me, eyes blazing. "I'm trying to protect you."

"Protect me? You've hardly looked at me in days. Is this what it's going to be like when we're married? Are you going to hold what I did against me forever?"

He holds my gaze, and his mask of fury begins to slip. Vulnerability peeks through, a shadow of the hurt I caused him. "You broke a promise," he whispers.

I try not to tremble beneath that look in his eyes. I've been preparing for this conversation for days, but it doesn't make it any easier. With a deep breath, I steel myself. "I'm sorry that I used your name against you. I should have trusted you to win against Cobalt."

His posture begins to relax. "Yes, you should have."

"But *you* should have considered my request."

He grumbles and turns away from me. "Some apology."

I pull his sleeve, but he won't look at me. "This is what I mean. If we are going to be married, I want you to listen to me. Consider the things I say."

He faces me again. "I did consider what you said when you asked me to name you my champion, and the answer was no. Is that what life is going to be like together? Are you going to use my name against me every time you don't get your way?"

I feel a wave of fury rising inside me, but I breathe it away, finding my calm. "That's not going to happen all the time," I say. "I can promise you that. But I can't promise I'll never use your name again. Not if I think it will save you."

Aspen's expression shifts between steely and soft, eyes locked on mine.

I reach for his hands, holding them tight as another explosion rocks the ground beneath us. "I'm not going to lose you, Aspen. I thought you were going to die if I didn't force your hand. Perhaps I was being brash to make you name me your champion, but I don't regret doing it. I'll do it again if I think it will save your life. All I can do now is ask for your forgiveness."

He closes his eyes and lowers his head. "I've never been terrified of anyone the way I'm terrified of you. You have the power to use my name. The power to control me. The power to break my heart."

I let go of one of his hands to touch his face, fingers trailing his jaw. "So do you. But didn't you say that's what the Bond is about? Mutual fear and respect?"

He opens his eyes. "Yes, but I want more than that."

My breath hitches at the intensity of his stare. "What is it you want?"

He says nothing, just lowers his lips to mine in a soft kiss. I lean into him and wrap my arms around his waist. I think I know what the kiss is telling me, words we've yet to exchange. These words may not hold the power that the Bond holds, but they mean more than our names. I pull my lips away from his, but our bodies remain pressed together. "Aspen, I—"

"Your Majesty."

With a startle, Aspen and I separate and face Foxglove. His hands tremble, making the envelope he holds within them quiver as well.

Aspen darts toward him. "What is it?"

Foxglove hands Aspen the envelope. I can see the seal has already been broken. But what snags my attention more is the seal itself—an elegant scrolling *E* etched in the wax. *Eisleigh's crest.* Foxglove wrings his hands. "The human council has invalidated your pairing. You are no longer eligible to secure the pact."

Aspen tears the letter from the envelope, scans it with wide eyes. He lowers the paper and slowly meets my gaze. "The treaty is broken."

Another blast from outside shakes the ground beneath us, matched only by the pounding of my heart. My lungs feel tight, breaths shallow as I try to comprehend Aspen's words. If the treaty is broken...

I swallow hard. "We're going to war."

TO WEAR A FAE CROWN

BOOK TWO

1

———————

Every young woman dreams of wearing a crown.

Well, I never held such a frivolous desire, but I've finally come to understand the appeal. Not so much the crown itself but what comes with it. Influence. Power. Responsibility. A king at my side.

For me, it's not just any king.

It's a mate I care for, one who ignites my anger as often as he sparks my desire. And I would have been his queen.

Would have been being the operative phrase here, as that is now completely and utterly wrecked.

A hollow ringing reverberates in my ears as I stand in the dining room at Bircharbor Palace, eyes unfocused as I rock on my feet. An explosion has come and gone, one of several that have occurred this hour, but this time I don't react. It isn't that I've grown used to the work the fae soldiers are doing on the beach below the palace, sealing the coral caves with detrimental blasts of explosives. It's more that I'm too numb to care. Too shocked to do anything but stand here wishing the last minute of my life could be reversed.

A minute ago, Aspen was in my arms.

A minute ago, we still had plans to get married.

A minute ago, our alliance would have protected both the humans and fae from certain doom.

But now...

"We're going to war." It's my voice that utters the words, but it sounds distant, strange.

King Aspen and Ambassador Foxglove stand before me, but I can't bring them into focus. My eyes glaze over, the dining room shrinking until it's nothing more than a pinprick of light. The summer heat wafting in through the open expanse in the wall behind me sends waves of dizziness to my head. I take in a deep breath, then another, but I can't seem to get enough air. I'd give anything for a cool breeze. For the usual Autumn Court weather to return and dry the sweat beading my brow.

The sound of paper crinkling pulls my attention back to the present, like an anchor in my whirlpool of thoughts. I realize the sound belongs to the letter in Aspen's hand, now crushed into a ball within his fist. The letter bears the words that announced the invalidation of our pairing. The end of the treaty. Of everything I've been fighting for.

The end of me and Aspen.

My lungs constrict, and I feel like my thoughts will swallow me whole, but I refocus on that piece of paper, on the shape of Aspen's fingers curled around it. Finally, the room ceases spinning, and my breathing begins to ease. My eyes lock on my mate, taking in every curve and angle of his beautiful face as if doing so can further root me into this moment. With my study of him comes a sudden awareness of the anger written in the rigid set of his shoulders, the tick in his jaw. The sight of his rage snaps me further out of my stupor, and I feel my own fury rise to meet his. A willing partner in a fiery dance.

My anger invigorates me at once.

"No," I say through my teeth, "this isn't happening. Not after everything we've been through, after everything we've done."

"Are you honestly surprised?" Aspen mutters.

"Yes, I'm surprised. We did everything the treaty called for. Our wedding is set for three days from now—the exact date the human council gave us. We met every deadline."

"Apparently the council doesn't care about deadlines. They'll use any excuse to keep us from solidifying the pact."

"How can you say that? They can't want war any more than we do. Besides, every suspicion you had about the human council being a threat to you has proven to be misguided. Cobalt was behind every action that kept you from securing the treaty thus far."

"If that were the case, they wouldn't have sent this." He lifts his hand and the paper crumpled in his fist.

"What exactly does it say?" I look from Aspen to Foxglove. While Foxglove verbally relayed the general message of the letter, I haven't read it word for word myself. "They must have given a reason to invalidate our alliance."

"Well, they—" Foxglove cuts off abruptly at a sharp look from Aspen.

A chill crawls up my spine. "What is it? What aren't you telling me?"

Foxglove looks to Aspen in deference, lips pressed tight as if he's fighting to keep from blurting some dangerous truth.

I step closer to my mate. "Tell me what it said or let me read it myself."

He doesn't meet my eyes. "I'll take care of it."

Fury roars through me, arguments storming from my mind to my lips. Before I can utter a single one, the ground rocks beneath my feet again, forcing me off balance. From the corner of my eye, I see water shooting into the sky from the explosion.

The rumbling calms, but before I can properly right myself, another blast shakes the palace. Aspen pulls me close to keep my feet beneath me. I lean into him, and it's for more than just support. His closeness reminds me yet again how badly I wish I could erase the moment where Foxglove came in with the letter. If only we could go back to where we were moments before that, enveloped in each other's arms with tender words on our lips.

But that moment was shattered, and even this slight reprieve is stolen away as the sound from the explosion is replaced with shouts. Screams of terror.

I reluctantly part from Aspen and turn toward the rail along the open wall. Several figures limp away from the site of the most recent explosion. I can't see much else through the spray of sand and water, but I'm almost certain there are dark patches covering the beach. Blood.

My heart pounds at the sight, echoed by footsteps tearing down the hall and growing nearer with every beat. I can hardly move, can hardly tear my eyes from the scene below as I wait for the rubble to clear.

"Your Majesty."

I whirl toward the panting guard entering the dining room.

Aspen storms over to him. "What in the name of oak and ivy just happened?"

The guard's youthful face is pale, eyes wide as he explains, "It was Prince Cobalt's fae, Your Majesty. They were spotted in the caves, trying to thwart our efforts. I was sent to tell you—"

Aspen brushes past him into the hall. His voice is almost a roar. "I knew he'd be back. Where is he?"

The guard follows hard on the heels of the king, as do Foxglove and I. "The prince hasn't been spotted," the guard says, "but the fae were clearly his. They ambushed the detonation team, but your soldiers were able to keep Cobalt's fae back while they set off the explosion. Only two caves remained uncollapsed at that point, and detonation teams were sent in at once. That's when I was ordered to come to you."

Aspen's jaw shifts back and forth. "I take it from the shouts, there have been casualties."

The guard goes a shade paler, and we descend a set of stairs. "I was already on my way here when I heard the last two explosions go off, Your Majesty, but the second blast shouldn't have happened so close to the previous. Not unless..."

"Not unless it were necessary to set it off early," Aspen says through his teeth. "Have any of Cobalt's fae emerged from the caves? What about the caves leading to the tunnels in the palace?"

"Those tunnels were the first we collapsed, and I didn't see any of the prince's fae make it to the beach before I left."

Aspen is nearly running as we descend farther and farther down the palace. We must be near the bottom floor.

I quicken my pace and address the guard. "Where will the injured be taken?"

He opens his mouth, but Aspen stops in his tracks, spinning to face me. "Why are you following me? It isn't safe."

"I came to help."

He faces the guard. "Take Miss Fairfield somewhere secure."

The guard steps toward me, but I freeze him with an icy glare before turning it on Aspen. "No, I'm going to help the injured."

"You need to remain—"

"I'm going to help the injured," I repeat, louder, slower, each word pointed as my eyes burn into his. "It's what I'm trained to do."

"Fae can heal without your help."

I raise a brow, eyes roving over his torso before narrowing on the site of his former wound. A wound that would have been the death of him if it hadn't been for my intervention. I cross my arms over my chest. "Oh, can they?"

He lets out a frustrated sigh. "Fine." He returns his attention to the guard. "Take her to the east wing. That's where the injured will be. If you so much as sense a breach in the palace, take Miss Fairfield to safety."

The guard nods, and I don't dare argue with the order. Aspen's eyes find mine as his fingers grasp my palm, giving it a soft squeeze. The gesture says more than his words can, cutting through his temper to soften my heart. I can only enjoy the touch for a single breath before Aspen releases me and starts off down the hall again. As I move to follow him, the guard puts a hand on my shoulder. "This way is faster to get to the east wing." He nods toward another set of stairs. We take off, but I realize Foxglove has remained on the landing, wringing his hands as he stares at me with an open mouth. Like he wants to say something.

"Foxglove, with me." Aspen's voice echoes from down the staircase.

The bespectacled fae closes his mouth and gives me an apologetic smile. I don't want to read into what it means. But I'm sure it has to do with the letter.

I STEEL MYSELF AS I ENTER A FAMILIAR ROOM. THREE STONE TABLES ARE LINED up in the center, and upon each lies a writhing fae guard: two male, one female. They've each sustained several wounds of varying severity, blood pooling on the tabletops beneath them as uninjured guards assist in removing their bronze armor.

I shudder, remembering the last time I was here. There was but one table then and Aspen was its occupant. It's hard to believe that was less than two weeks ago. Back then I wouldn't have cared if Aspen died.

I shake the morbid thought from my mind and join Gildmar, a tiny fae with bark-like skin and leafy hair, at the far end of the room. Her small hands fly over the table as she lays out her tools—shards of shell, sharp bone, pointed sticks, swaths of spider silk, bowls of water, herbs, and wine. I'm grateful I don't have to demand wine this time.

"Are these the only survivors?" I ask Gildmar.

She nods. "The last explosion went off while they were still prepping the keg inside the cave. These three were standing nearby. All inside the cave and near its opening didn't make it."

I swallow hard, wondering if she's been informed of the true cause for the early explosion. "What can I do to help?"

"First, ease their pain." She hands me a vial. I don't need to ask to know it contains extract of honey pyrus, a psychoactive fae fruit. Its extract works like laudanum, easing pain and allowing a patient's mind and body to slip into euphoric stillness.

I move from one injured fae to the other, administering a dropperful to each while Gildmar cleans one of the male fae's wounds with an herb-infused liquid. Once all three patients have fallen beneath the honey pyrus' spell, I take one of the bowls of wine and approach the unconscious fae female. I cleanse my hands with the wine and inspect her wounds. The fae's skin is pocked with bloody gouges from shards of coral spearing her flesh where the armor hadn't covered. I peel back the linen tunic from her torso, finding severe bruising blooming over her chest, likely crushed by her breastplate. I pour the wine over her wounds. "Are they in mortal danger?"

Gildmar shakes her head, though her face remains grave. "So long as we can staunch any bleeding and keep them calm, their bodies should heal on their own. There was no ash or iron involved, so their natural abilities will remain strong. However, if they lose too much blood, their bodies won't be able to keep up with healing."

I'm relieved to hear their prognosis is good, although it's hard to believe any creature could recover after being so close to an explosion. The concussive force alone would be enough to kill a human. "What were the explosives made from? Gunpowder?"

"Marsh gas, most likely," she says, her voice like the creak of an old branch. "Most often found in the marshes where Fire and Wind courts meet. A beastly practice, if you ask me. We shouldn't be bottling up nature the way humans do, using the elements for harm. My kind didn't do that before your people came to the Fair Isle."

Her tone is more resigned than accusatory, but my stomach sinks with guilt just the same. "How long will it take for them to recover?"

"Their wounds are grave, but it won't be like it was with the king."

Again, the memory floods my mind, of Aspen near death, veins of black trailing across his skin to show how deep the iron had poisoned his blood. I had been concerned about his recovery, but only because he was my patient; I'd been nowhere near as distraught as I'd be if something like that were to happen now. Not after how close we've become.

My heart squeezes. We were growing closer even still before that letter arrived. I finally got him to express his anger over me using his name against him. We were making amends. I was so close to telling him that I...

I shake the memories from my head. Thoughts of Aspen and the mysterious contents of the letter will have to wait. For now, I have work to do.

2

———

It's midday by the time I finish helping Gildmar, my body heavy with exhaustion as I make my way from the east wing, Aspen's guard trailing behind me. Being this tired isn't a bad feeling, considering it's the result of a job well done. The three patients' wounds have been cleaned, stitched, and bandaged, and their bodies have been moved to a more comfortable room with actual beds where they can recover. All were dozing peacefully when I left them to rest in the recovery room, but before that I sat with each, resting my hands over their torsos for several minutes at a time.

Luckily, my guard remained outside the door during my visit. If anyone would have seen what I was doing, my cheeks would have blazed with embarrassment, no matter how benign my actions would have appeared to onlookers. For inside me burned the hope that my hands were doing more than just providing comfort. I'm still not positive I had anything to do with healing Lorelei's wounded leg or in aiding Aspen's sudden recovery from iron poisoning. I don't know if it was by some power of my own that helped me perform Aspen's surgery without the tools I'm used to.

If I'd considered such a notion two months ago, I would have laughed, deeming myself delirious. But now, after everything I've seen and done and experienced...

I believe in possibilities. Especially if they allow me to help others.

As we near the end of the east wing hall, a second guard awaits. She looks hesitant as she approaches us. My heart leaps into my throat as I begin to fear the worst. "Has Aspen returned?"

"No, he's involved in a skirmish with Cobalt's fae not too far from here," she says, "which is why I'm coming to you. Queen Melusine is on the beach, surrounded by our guards. She's demanding to speak with you."

"What does she want to speak with me about?"

"She wouldn't say. Only that she'd make a binding promise not to harm you and called upon the protection of *a peaceful exchange of words*. This means violence would be forbidden during your talk. If she were to attack you, each attack could be met blow for blow."

I bite the inside of my cheek. "What did you tell her?"

"Nothing. It is up to you whether to hold an audience with her. With King Aspen absent, you're in charge."

My head rushes from the weight of her words. *I'm in charge.*

The guard Aspen left to watch me clears his throat and faces me. "King Aspen wouldn't want you to meet with her without him present. He wouldn't deem it safe."

"Then you better see that no harm comes to me." I turn to face the fae female. "Take me to Queen Melusine. I want to know what she's up to."

It might not be the smartest move, but Melusine could know something about today's attack. She may have information about Cobalt, about Amelie, about the letter and the treaty—no, I'm getting ahead of myself. If she knows anything at all, she'll hide it behind a web of deception and weave it to her advantage. I should harbor no false hopes regarding her whatsoever.

I inhale a heavy breath to steady my racing thoughts and follow the guards to the beach. With the caves beneath the palace closed off, we take the long way down, skirting around the palace to a steep staircase cut into the cliff wall. When we reach the bottom, I find my unwelcome guest. Like the first time I spoke alone with the Sea Queen, Melusine perches on the shore, chin held high with a confident smirk. This time, however, she's surrounded by a circle of Aspen's guards. Luckily, she appears to be alone. Her beauty is as prominent as ever, with her dazzling stormy eyes, coral-red lips, and her long, indigo hair that flows in waves over her bare human-like upper body. Her blue-green serpent's tail props her up from her waist to where human feet should be, while the rest of her tail undulates behind her in anxious ripples across the sand.

"My, my, don't you look dreadful," she says in her melodic voice before flashing her sharp teeth in a semblance of a smile. My two guards flank me as I stop several feet away from her. Only now do I consider my state of dress. Foxglove and Lorelei always had me primped and preened with the utmost care before meeting with the queen. Now I come to her wearing a bloodstained robe and hair still mussed from sleep.

I narrow my eyes as if my appearance is the least of my concerns. That much, at least, is true. There are far more pressing matters at hand. "Why are you here, Your Majesty?"

"I wanted to know what my dear son was doing to my beautiful caves," she says with a pout.

"Your son doesn't want to speak with you." I hope she can't sense the omission in my voice—that my words obscure the fact that Aspen isn't currently here. That is, if she doesn't already know as much.

"It's clear he doesn't want to speak with me. I've tried making contact every day since the incident with his brother."

The incident. I bristle. That's a mild way to refer to Cobalt's attempt to steal Aspen's throne. "So, you decided to speak with me instead?"

She shrugs a bare shoulder. "It worked, didn't it?"

I hate that she's right. Aspen had the sense to ignore her, yet here I am giving in at her first request. My curiosity always does get the better of me. "Cut the iron-laced kelpie crap and get to the point," I say with a sweet smile. "Why are you *really* here?"

She rolls her eyes and lets out a huff. "I want you to speak to Aspen for me."

"And tell him what?"

"Tell him I want to form an alliance."

My mouth hangs on its hinge before I can speak. "An alliance? Isn't that what the council is for? Weren't you already supposed to be his ally when you sought to replace him with Cobalt?"

Her cheeks redden, lips pressing into a tight line, looking flustered for the first time. "I was wrong. I never should have supported Cobalt's claim."

I let out a bitter laugh. "Why, because he turned on you? Lied? Because you realized he was never going to be your unseelie puppet?"

"Cobalt stole lies from a human and turned them on me," she hisses through her teeth. "That is unforgivable. More than that, I respect the decision of the All of All, which he did not and will not abide by. The All of All should not be questioned. The unseelie know this in our blood."

"I'm sure Aspen will appreciate your acceptance of the All of All's verdict," I say without warmth. "Why do you seek an additional alliance?"

Again, she purses her lips as if her next words pain her to say. "I seek his protection."

"His protection? From what?"

"From my other son." Each word is punctuated with her growing rage. "He's all but taken over my court. Half my soldiers think they serve him, and that wretched human pet of his struts around in her selkie skin like she's the Queen of the Sea."

I narrow my eyes. "That wretched human is my sister."

She meets my gaze with a glower. "Then you know just how wretched she is."

My nails dig into my palms, irritation growing hotter inside me. "Melusine, you're one of the most powerful fae alive. You have the entire sea at your beck and call. What protection do you need from Aspen that you can't provide yourself?"

"I can't defend myself against my son when he can meet my powers underwater. I need somewhere on land to stay until he can be dealt with." Her shoulders tremble visibly.

I'm caught off guard by how truly shaken she seems. How can Queen Melusine fear Cobalt, her own son? He may have power over the water element, but he can't be anywhere near as fearsome as she is. Right?

As if she can sense my question, she adds, "I can't trust Cobalt now that he's ceased to be bound by fae rules. He can lie like a human and betray his allies without so much as blinking. Now that he's won over so many of my soldiers, I don't know what he's going to do next. I'd rather not wait around and find out."

My heart sinks. Unless she too has stolen the power to lie, she's serious.

She slithers closer, but Aspen's guards stop her from closing the distance between us. With a grumble, she says, "Speak to Aspen on my behalf. Please."

"You've already told him all this yourself?"

"He won't listen."

"What makes you think he'll listen to me?"

Her expression hardens. "You hold sway over him like no one ever has before."

Is she referring to my ability to use his name...or something else? She must know I'd never use Aspen's name on her behalf. It was hard enough using it to save his life. "I'll see what I can do."

"Is that a promise?"

"No."

Her lips pull into a smirk that looks close to admiration, then she nods in a semblance of a bow. "Very well." With that, she faces the ocean and slithers toward it. The guards maintain a tight circle around her, careful not to stumble over the shards of coral littering the beach. I don't take my eyes off the queen until the last flick of her tail glides beneath the water.

When I return to the palace, there's still no word on Aspen's current status. My heart races as I consider the myriad of concerns plaguing me—the skirmish Aspen's involved in, Melusine's fear of Cobalt, the letter. *The letter.* My stomach turns every time I think about it. I wish he'd left it for me to read. I need to know what it says, what it means, why the treaty has been broken, why our pairing has been invalidated. I need to pull it apart and analyze every sentence, every word, every loop and curve of the pen that wrote it to understand it. I must know...what does it mean for me and Aspen?

With nothing to do but wait for Aspen's return, I make my way to his bedroom to change out of my bloody clothes. Behind the dressing screen, I exchange my ruined nightdress and robe for a gauzy blue gown with a multi-layered, flowing skirt. When I come out from behind the screen, Lorelei enters the room. Her smile is warm as she approaches me, a shimmering swath of opalescent silk hanging over her brown arm, her petite frame swaying with every step.

"I was told you'd returned from surgery," the wood nymph says. "Did everything go all right?"

"It went well," I say, although I can't bring myself to feign a grin. "The patients are recovering."

She furrows her brow, clearly reading into my lack of enthusiasm. Still, she doesn't pry and holds out the luxurious fabric instead. "Your wedding gown is ready for its final fitting."

My eyes lock on the dress, and a shock of pain sears my heart. My emotions threaten to overwhelm me, but I force them down, force my voice to remain level as I say, "I don't know if there's going to be a wedding, Lorelei."

She lays the dress over the arm of the nearby couch and takes me by the shoulders. "Why would you say that? Did something happen between you and Aspen?"

I open my mouth and snap it shut. "I...I don't know."

"Whatever he said or did, you'll get through it. You know he loves you, right?"

That word—*love*—unravels me. Tears spring to my eyes, a sob building in my chest. "No, I don't know and I might never know."

"What do you mean?"

I squeeze my eyes shut, fingers clenching into fists as I swallow my tears and let anger replace my pain. "I'm so tired," I say through my teeth.

She takes a step away. "Then I'll leave you to rest—"

"I'm tired of living in fear of this treaty."

I open my eyes to find her nibbling her bottom lip, expression brimming with concern. "It's been hard, I know."

"It's been more than hard," I say, my anger growing, burning the anxiety from my mind, the sorrow that tugs at my heart. "We've done everything we were supposed to. We had the mate ceremony. We performed the Bonding ritual by midnight on the required date. We won Aspen's throne back from Cobalt. Our wedding is scheduled. Now we get a letter from Eisleigh's council saying our pairing has been invalidated."

Her eyes bulge as she processes my words. "Invalidated? But that would mean..."

I nod. "That would mean the treaty is broken. That we're going to war."

She shakes her head. "No, there must be a misunderstanding. King Aspen will take care of it." She takes my hand in hers. "You *must* believe he will."

I wish I could say I agree with her, but there's only so much he can do. Besides, what if Aspen was right? What if the human council *wants* war? What if they fabricated this invalidation to give them what they wanted all along? "I feel like everything is working against me and Aspen. Maybe we aren't meant to be together. Maybe there's a reason things keep coming between us."

"Don't say that. There's a genuine connection between the two of you. I can sense it with more than just my eyes. Whatever comes, you and the king will face it together."

Her words manage to stabilize some of the rage and anxiety writhing within. Yet they don't comfort me completely. There's a much darker cloud hanging behind all of this—the possibility of war. If war comes to the Fair Isle, it won't be as simple as facing the challenge at Aspen's side. At least not for me. Not when my people—my mother included—will be suffering on the other side of the wall. They'll be facing death and destruction because of a broken treaty my marriage was supposed to keep intact.

Anger returns to me in a rush. "There must be something I can do to fix this."

"There might be." Foxglove stands in my doorway, wringing his hands. "But you aren't going to like it."

3

———————

I jump to my feet as Foxglove enters the room. "What do you mean I'm not going to like it? Where is Aspen? Is he all right?"

"He's fine," Foxglove says. "The threat has been dealt with, and the king is uninjured."

I let out a sigh of relief. "Where is he now?"

"He's in his study, but that's not why I came here. I came to talk to you myself. There are...things I think you have the right to know *before* you speak with the king."

"What does that mean? Is he hiding something from me?"

"I wouldn't say that, it's just..." He sighs. "We should all sit down for this. Trust me."

I feel like my legs will give out as I lead us to the couch. I can't bring myself to sit next to the silky wedding dress strewn over the arm, so I take a seat in the chair across from it. Lorelei and Foxglove lower onto the couch.

Foxglove adjusts his spectacles, lips pulled into a grimace. "Oh, I just hate being the bearer of—"

"Just tell me."

"Very well. As you know, the human council has sent a letter invalidating your pairing with King Aspen."

I nod, leaning forward in anticipation. "Did the letter say why?"

He swallows hard. "My dear, might I ask you something? Are you of fae heritage?"

I whip my head back in surprise. "No, of course not. I'm obviously human."

He raises a brow. "Is there not the slightest chance you could have fae blood?"

I open my mouth, but too many arguments fight for dominance, making it impossible to utter a coherent word. Why would he ask me such a thing? There's no way I could be...I could be...

"I would know if I were," I finally say.

"Would you, though?" His face is full of apology.

"Yes. How else would you explain my ability to touch iron? The fact that I don't possess the sort of rapid healing the fae do? That rowan protects me from glamour?" My hand moves reflexively to my neck, seeking the feel of the red beads. I somehow managed not to lose this strand, even after being captured by Cobalt and journeying through the sea with the kelpie. However, it is by far the worse for wear, with fraying thread where beads have broken off, and haggard, lopsided berries. I can't seem to bring myself to take it off, and it isn't just because it protects me from being put under a glamour. It also reminds me of Mother. Amelie, too, for better or worse.

"The differences between the fae and part-fae are not well known," Foxglove says. "We've always assumed human-fae offspring had all the fae weaknesses and very little power. But when would they have had the need or opportunity to find out? I doubt any of the previous Chosen's children have been tested with iron. For all we know, they could be exactly like you."

"But my—" I stop myself. *My mother is human,* I want to say. She would have told me if I wasn't. Right?

But she isn't my only parent.

I shake the thought from my head. "Why are you asking me this? What does it have to do with the letter?"

"The human council is under the impression that you aren't fully human. That you and your sister are part-fae. Since the treaty requires a pair of human girls be sent to Faerwyvae..."

"Then a part-fae girl can't validate the treaty," I say under my breath, shoulders sagging. "But why do they think I'm part-fae to begin with?"

"The letter says they have proof."

"What proof?"

Foxglove shakes his head. "That they didn't say. Can you think of any way it might be true?"

I can hardly believe I'm entertaining this possibility, but I force myself to voice it. "My father, I suppose, but that's highly unlikely. Mother never gave any indication that their relationship was unusual. She never said a cryptic word about him, always said he was a decent man."

Lorelei squints as if pondering. "You never knew him?"

"I was still a baby when they separated."

"Where is he now?" Foxglove asks.

I shrug. "Still on mainland Bretton, I assume. Mother said they parted ways because he wouldn't move to Eisleigh with us. That's what doesn't make sense about this ridiculous suggestion. How could a fae, or part-fae, or whatever we're hypothesizing my father was, sire me on the mainland? Isn't being so far from Faerwyvae certain death for the fae?"

I remember the story Cobalt had told me, about the exile of the Fire King at the end of the war. They sent him to the mainland to die as punishment for being the first to engage humans in organized violence. In return, the humans agreed to the tradition of the Hundred Year Reaping. The very thing that got me into this mess.

"It is indeed death for fae to leave the Fair Isle," Foxglove says, expression grave. "Even being on the human side of the wall creates a drain on our magic. Without that magic, our lengthy lifespans are forfeit."

"So, the exiled Fire King definitely died, then?" My stomach churns. I don't want to admit the ludicrous train of thought that prompted the question.

Foxglove nods. "The exiled king lived out a mortal lifespan after arriving on the mainland. Ambassadors were sent to confirm his death when he passed."

I let out a sigh. That removes one absurd possibility. "Have there been others? Any other fae who've been exiled this century?"

Foxglove and Lorelei exchange a glance. "Not that anyone knows of," Foxglove says. "And no fae would go to the mainland willingly."

"Then it makes no sense. Either their proof is false and the human council is fabricating this excuse to break the treaty, or there's been a misunderstanding."

"I'm going to find out which of those possibilities is the case tonight," Foxglove says. "King Aspen is sending me to meet with Sableton's mayor and get to the bottom of this at once. If it is a simple misunderstanding, I'll take care of it. I'll offer whatever compensation they desire to make up for the error that led them to believe this. Then your wedding to the king will continue as planned."

Lorelei slowly turns to Foxglove. "What if it isn't a misunderstanding? Or if there's no way to dissuade them from believing their accusations?"

"Then the treaty is broken," I say, "and we go to war. Right?"

The grimace returns to Foxglove's lips, and he adjusts the bridge of his spectacles with trembling fingers. "Not necessarily."

His words should bring relief, but his expression is not one of hope. "What is it?"

"This is the part—one of many, I should say—that you won't like," he says. "The human council offered the king one final option to secure the treaty. If their suspicions about you prove correct, he'll have to accept two new Chosen and perform all three parts of the alliance at once. The mate ceremony, the ritual, and the human wedding. All of it. They've gone so far as to confirm the names of the potential new Chosen. Some Maddie and Marie Coleman. And the council insists Aspen be the one to marry, no minor cousin or other relative as has often been the practice during previous Reapings."

My stomach sinks as his words cleave my heart in two. Not only will Aspen have to marry someone else, but he'll have to marry *Maddie Coleman*. The girl I despise more than any other in my village. "Of course it's her," I mutter, a bitter smile on my lips. I remember how jealous she'd been when we met outside the Holstrom farm, how she'd boasted about being selected as backup Chosen if the Holstrom girls didn't work out. She was livid when she realized Aspen had requested me by name. Of course, I was livid too. Still...could this somehow be her doing? Her jealousy might be believable, but I can't imagine her having the power to orchestrate this new development, even with her uncle being Sableton's mayor. No, there's something much bigger behind this.

With a deep breath, I curl my fingers into fists, nails biting into my palms. "This is the only way to avoid war?"

Foxglove nods. "The mayor wants me to agree to this new arrangement when we meet tonight. If I do, I'll be leaving Sableton with the new Chosen by midnight."

I don't know what to say, so I remain quiet, eyes shifting out of focus as they fall on the wedding gown hanging near Lorelei's arm.

Foxglove wrings his hands. "King Aspen, however, has ordered me to refuse."

My eyes snap to his. "What?"

"If it comes down to breaking the treaty or accepting the new Chosen, he'll take the former."

"And bring war to us all?"

"He has his reasons," Foxglove says, "and many of them are sound. Even as an ambassador, I understand there's only so much one can take before fighting back."

I rise to my feet with every intention of storming to Aspen's study and breaking down his door. But Foxglove rises as well, palms held up facing me, as if to keep me in place. "I didn't tell you this to use as fuel in a fight with the king."

I let out a bitter laugh. "Well, I'm using it anyway."

"I told you this because it's far more personal to you than you know. The mayor has your mother. She's being detained by order of the human council. If Aspen refuses to accept the new Chosen, not only will there be war, but your mother will be executed."

4

————————

The blood leaves my face. "They're going to execute my mother? What does she have to do with any of this?"

Foxglove's brows knit together. "She's being imprisoned, charged with treason for hiding your supposed fae heritage. It's illegal for any fae to live on the Eisleigh side of the wall, much less pose as a human. She's being held responsible for jeopardizing the treaty. While Aspen's decision to accept the new Chosen should have no impact on your mother's life, I'm guessing they wanted to make it harder for him—or you—to refuse."

Rage heats my core, and it takes all my effort not to strike the nearest piece of furniture. "When are you leaving to meet with the mayor?" I say through my teeth.

"Mid-afternoon."

I'm about to say more when a shadow darkens my doorway. I don't need to face it to know it belongs to Aspen.

Lorelei comes up beside Foxglove, shoulders tense. "We should give you some privacy," she says, then pulls him toward the door. Their heads bow low as they approach the king, but his eyes burn into Foxglove.

"You told her," he says with a snarl.

Foxglove, to his credit, meets his gaze without so much as a tremble. "I'm sorry, Your Majesty. She deserved to know."

Aspen steps aside, allowing the two fae to pass, then slowly meets my furious gaze.

"Were you just going to let my mother die without telling me her life was at risk?"

He closes the distance between us. "I came to tell you everything."

"Everything? *Everything*, everything? Or just the parts you wanted me to know?"

"I wasn't going to let them execute your mother."

The fact that he didn't fully answer my question tells me plenty. I put my hands on my hips. "Oh, and what were you going to do about it?"

"I don't know yet." He throws his hands in the air. "I would have come up with something. Break her from imprisonment. Steal her to Faerwyvae. Slaughter everyone in my path until I had her safely away."

I'm surprised that he'd be willing to go so far for my mother, yet terrified at how easily he can consider taking lives to save her. Even so, it would only solve one problem, not all of them. "That still wouldn't save the treaty, Aspen. They gave you another option, and you told Foxglove to refuse."

"Yes," he admits without shame.

"Why?"

"Because I'm not going to lose you." The hurt in his eyes takes my breath away. My heart threatens to crumble at the vulnerability on his face, the fear in his eyes. But then I remember what it means, what his dedication to me would cost.

"Don't make this about us." My words come out with a tremor. "We are nothing compared to the importance of saving the isle from war."

His vulnerability fades, retreating beneath the steely mask he wears so well. When he speaks, his voice is barely above a whisper. "Nothing? Is that really what you think we amount to?"

No, we're so much more than nothing. You *are so much more.* "Yes."

He shakes his head, narrowing his eyes at me as his lips pull into a bitter smirk. "I don't believe you."

I take a step toward him, meeting his smirk with a glare. I know my next words will sting, but they're the only weapon I have. My only defense against his fierce dedication, even though I know it will kill me to use. "Why? You think you know me so well just because you took me to bed once?"

His expression hardly falters. "I do know you."

"If you did, you'd know I'd want to do anything to keep the treaty from being broken."

"Even if it means giving me to another woman?"

My stomach churns at his words, at the images they conjure. I swallow the word I really want to say and replace it with a lie. "Yes."

He turns away from me and storms over to the decanter of wine on the bedside table. "I'm not going to do it," he says, then knocks back a glass of the deep red liquid.

"Yes, you are. If that's what it takes to save the treaty—"

"Maybe the treaty isn't worth saving."

My eyes go wide. "How can you say that? If the treaty protects our people from war, then of course it's worth saving."

He lets out a shaking breath, running his hands through the blue-black hair between his antlers. "This isn't a treaty, Evie. It's a blade our councils toss from one side to the other, waiting to see who gets cut first. I'm tired of playing the game. I'm tired of watching both sides point that blade at me."

His words send a chill down my spine. I can't let myself consider whether he's right. Didn't I say nearly the same to Lorelei? *I'm tired of living in fear of this treaty.* I shake my head. "If maintaining the treaty means lives can be saved, then it is worth saving in return. So long as there's a choice that means peace, then that's the choice we have to make."

"It isn't a choice if I *have* to make it."

For the love of iron, he's stubborn. "Even if you're right about the corruption of the treaty, do you think war is going to make things better? Can you honestly live with yourself, knowing you're the cause of the destruction that will follow?"

"If it's in the name of freedom, then yes."

Heat rises to my cheeks. "Well, I can't."

Aspen pours another glass of wine and knocks it back, chest heaving as his eyes remain locked on me. "What are you saying?"

"I'm saying I can't be the reason my people suffer. You know this."

"*Your people.* You do realize war would affect both humans and fae, don't you?"

"Of course I do."

"But it's the humans you care about more."

I cross my arms over my chest. "I'm trying to protect your throne too. I didn't face Cobalt for nothing. If you refuse the human council's offer to maintain the treaty, the fae council will finish what Cobalt started."

"The All of All chose me. The council will honor that."

"The All of All chose *me,*" I argue. "If the Council of Eleven Courts thinks the treaty has broken because of me, the ruling of the All of All won't matter. They'll turn on both of us."

He presses his lips tight but makes no argument. Probably because he knows I'm right. "There must be another way."

I uncross my arms, letting some of my rage drain out with a sigh. "I hope there is too. That's why I'm going with Foxglove tonight, to see if I can prove I'm not what they think I am."

"Like hell you are. It isn't safe. If the humans consider your mother a traitor, you could be in danger as well."

"I'm not going to sit here while my mother suffers, not if there's something I can do about it."

"If anything can be done, then Foxglove will do it. There's nothing you could do that he cannot."

"I could prove they're wrong."

"And if they aren't?"

I can't consider that possibility right now. I *can't*. Not when it means...

"If they aren't," I say, "then I face the consequences."

He sets the wine glass down, shoulders slumped in defeat. His voice comes out like a growl. "I don't want to lose you."

I force my words past the lump in my throat. "If Foxglove can sort out this madness, then you won't have to. My mother will be released, the treaty will be secured, and I'll return to you."

"Promise me."

I shake my head. "I need a promise from *you*. Promise me if I don't come back, you'll marry your new Chosen."

His fingers curl into fists at his side, but he remains silent.

I burn him with a glare. "Promise me you'll do what needs to be done for the good of both our people. Promise me you'll save the treaty. If you can't do it for the sake of the isle, then do it for me."

He glares right back. "I promise."

"What are you promising to? All of it?"

"I promise if everything goes to hell, I'm going to make a decision neither of us is going to like," he says through his teeth.

It isn't the promise I asked for, but at least it's one he can keep, considering there's no solution I like. I hate all of it. The dissolution of the treaty. Aspen marrying Maddie Coleman. My mother being imprisoned and threatened with execution. Where do I stand in all of this? What happens to me?

"Fine," I say as I turn toward the door.

"Wait."

I shouldn't stop, but I do. Not daring to look back at him, I focus on his slow footsteps drawing near. A thousand heartbeats seem to pass as I hold my breath in anticipation of him. My pulse races even faster as his body presses into my back, hands wrapping gently around my waist, fingers splayed over my stomach. My body responds to his touch, a wave of desire blooming inside my chest as I breathe in the rosemary and cinnamon scent of his skin.

"Don't leave yet." His voice is deep, pleading, heavy with emotion as he nuzzles into my neck.

I close my eyes and angle my head, allowing him closer, his lips grazing the skin at my collarbone.

"We have time," he whispers. "We should make the most of it, just in case…"

He doesn't need to finish the sentence for me to know what he means. If everything goes terribly, this could be our last moment together. Ever. I might never see him again.

The thought is so crippling, tears spring to my eyes, and I feel my knees buckling beneath me.

With one hand warm on my stomach, the other brushes along my jaw, turning my face toward his. Our lips are just a breath away. "Evie."

I want nothing more than to close the distance, to feel his lips on mine. With one move, I could fold myself into him, feel the comfort of his arms, the heat of his body. What if this really is our last moment, our last memory together? My breaths are shallow as I fight the searing desire pulsing through me. I know I must fight it. Because if I give in now, I don't know if I'll ever have the strength to leave again.

I turn my lips from his and step out of his grasp. "I have to go."

This time, he doesn't stop me as I make my way to the door. But as I reach the threshold, he says, "Come back to me, Evie."

I pause for only a second. "I can't promise that." Then my feet fly beneath me, taking me as fast from Aspen's room as they can go while sobs tear from my throat.

I may not be able to promise Aspen I'll return, but I can vow that every step I take away from him feels like a knife twisting in my heart.

5

———————

I'm almost to the sanctity of my parlor when my feet are forced to slow.

A figure glides toward me, one with golden-brown skin, honey-colored hair, and yellow butterfly wings. Queen Dahlia is the last person I want to see right now. I'm in no state to entertain a guest, and her cheery smile is an infuriating contrast to my pain. I quickly wipe my cheeks dry before I pause outside my parlor door and offer the Summer Queen a curtsy. Hoping beyond hope that she'll ignore me and pass me by, I avoid meeting her gaze.

"My dear Miss Fairfield. Is everything all right? You look positively wretched."

I clench my jaw, letting my irritation overpower my anguish. Luckily, the lies flow from my tongue with ease. "There was an accident this morning, Queen Dahlia. I attended the wounded but am overcome with grief over those who perished in the caves."

"So I heard," she says with a scoff. "Serves them right, using explosives in such a manner."

I bristle at that, even though I agree that using them had been reckless. All I want is for her to leave so I can be alone, but I can't resist my urge to use words against her now that she's sparked my ire. "How much longer are we to be graced with your company? You were quite generous in lending Bircharbor your weather, but I must say it's dry now. And there is such a thing as too much sun."

She gives me a simpering smile. "Perhaps a few days more, Miss Fairfield, just to be sure. I do hope we can spend more time together. I think the sun is starting to do you good. One would almost say you don't look so drab."

I force an exaggerated grin. "Almost."

She takes a step closer, lowering her voice, although her expression remains unchanged. "I do hope nothing is amiss. I heard the king received a vexing correspondence."

The grin falls from my lips, and I don't try to remedy it. "The king's correspondences are his business, and he will attend to them appropriately."

"Oh, I know he will." She lifts a dainty hand and lights it on my shoulder. "It's just...I worry about him. He is a very, very dear friend of mine. We've known each other for many hundreds of years. I'm not much younger than he is, you know. You could say we grew up together."

I purse my lips, wondering if I'm reading too much into her words, into the purr in her tone. "Your care will warm his heart, Queen Dahlia. I'll pass it along to him."

"Oh, don't worry, Miss Fairfield. I'm sure I'll tell him myself before then." With that, she gives my shoulder a final squeeze and brushes past.

Heat blazes my cheeks as I stand frozen in place, lips immobile no matter how many clever retorts surface in my head. I know it's too late; I can barely hear her buzzing wings behind me anymore. Still, I can't shake my irritation. What was she suggesting? That she has a greater chance of seeing my mate before I do? That she...*has* been seeing him more than I do? Or does she know I'm leaving and might never return?

I might never return...

The thought extinguishes my rage, reopening the wound left by my conversation with Aspen. His pleading voice fills my mind, his beckoning touch. *Come back to me, Evie.*

My chest heaves with a sob as I dart inside my parlor and slam the door behind me.

LORELEI FINDS ME INSIDE. I'M PERCHED ON THE GROUND IN FRONT OF MY couch, knees pulled to my chest as I weep into my hands. She crouches at my side and lays a soft hand on my back. "You're all right," she whispers, her voice a soothing hum. "Just breathe."

I gasp a shaking breath, forcing my sobs to recede. I haven't broken down like this since...since I thought my sister had died.

"I brought some of your things from Aspen's room," she says.

The sound of his name sends a shard of glass through my heart, and it takes me a moment to comprehend what she means by *my things*. That's right. For my journey. I inhale deeply to steady my breathing, a sense of urgency clearing my mind. It must be mid-afternoon by now, and I'm not sure how much time I've already wasted. I rise slowly to my feet. "Did you talk to him?"

She nods, expression grave. "We should get you cleaned up and packed."

I let out a sigh of resignation and reach for one of the bags she brought, plopping it on the couch. I freeze when I see what's been laid at the top of the pile of clothing within—a crown of gold shaped into a circlet of swaying leaves. I reach for it but stop myself. "Why did you bring this?"

Lorelei shrugs. "King Aspen told me to."

"Why?"

"Perhaps he wants you to wear it to meet with the mayor. It wouldn't be a bad idea. Let the human council see you as the Autumn Queen. Let them see you aren't someone to be trifled with."

I shake my head. "I don't think posturing as fae royalty will do me any good in this instance. Not when it plays so well into their accusations about my heritage."

"Then perhaps just take it with you."

"No." My throat tightens. "It doesn't belong to me. I won it as Aspen's champion. I won it for *him*, for Autumn."

"And he gave it to you."

I take the crown in my hands, gingerly, as if it could burn me. Without so much as looking at it, I place it on the tea table in front of the couch. "If it's meant to be mine, it will still be here if I make it back." *If.* The word crushes my lungs.

I refocus on the bags of clothing, removing their contents and setting aside the most practical dresses I can find. The weather will be cool in Eisleigh, October in the human realm being nowhere near as mild as it is in the Autumn Court. Most of the fae dresses are light, flimsy, and entirely inappropriate for the human realm. The fabrics are too sheer and reveal far too much skin.

I toss the dresses on the ground with frustration until I see a familiar sight at the very bottom of the last bag—stiff, starchy, cream-colored linen. I retrieve the corset and find a pair of trousers and a blouse lying beneath.

The latter two are wrinkled but they are the only undamaged human clothing I have.

"I will return to my people the same way I left," I say, smoothing a wrinkle in the blue cotton blouse. My fingers brush a pearl-like button. There was a time when I rebelled against wearing anything but the clothes I now hold in my hands. I hated dresses. I hated corsets too, but they were a price I knew I had to pay to get away with wearing trousers in a society that frowns upon such unfeminine ways.

I stare at the clothes, expecting sentimentality to wash over me at any moment. Instead, I feel a sense of foreboding. Restraint. I've come to appreciate the freedom of a flowing chiffon skirt as it swishes around my legs, in the lightness of an unbound chest beneath nothing but gauzy spider silk.

Now I might never wear such things again.

With my corset, trousers, and blouse in hand, I make my way behind the dressing screen and peel off my silky gown.

Lorelei approaches the other side of the screen. "Do you need my help?"

I'm about to say no, but stop myself as I pick up the stiff corset. "I do, actually."

She rounds the corner of the screen, eyes widening as she stares at the undergarment. "What in the name of oak and ivy is that thing?"

"A mandatory article of clothing for women," I say through my teeth as I turn my back toward her. "I need you to tighten the laces and tie them off."

She takes up the ends of the laces, grimacing as if she expects them to bite. "Why is this necessary for human women?"

"To support our figures," I say in a mocking tone. Lorelei pulls the laces tight at the top, eliciting a gasp from me.

"Did I hurt you?" she asks with alarm.

"No, I just...forgot how uncomfortable these are."

"Is this really necessary? You could wear something else and cover your clothing with a cloak if you're worried—"

"Just do it," I say, though there's no bite in my tone. More an eagerness to get this over with. "I need them to see me as one of them."

She releases a sigh, then returns to tightening the laces. "Do I have to wear one of these too?"

I turn my head to the side to eye her from my periphery. "No, of course not. Why would you?"

"Because I'm going with you, obviously."

I'm taken aback. "Did Aspen order you to come with me?"

"I asked *him* if I could accompany you."

I sigh. "Lorelei, I appreciate your dedication, but I'll have no need for a lady's maid while I'm in Sableton."

She pauses her tightening and shifts to my side until our eyes meet. "You may not need a lady's maid, but you might need a friend."

I want to argue, to tell her Foxglove will be there, but I can't bring words over the lump in my throat. Instead, I nod and return to facing straight ahead, eyes unfocused as they well with tears. Lorelei resumes her work, and I grit my teeth against every pull.

By the time I'm finished dressing, outfitted in human clothing and my most unassuming fae cloak, I feel the same way I did when I first left home for Faerwyvae.

Like a lamb being led to slaughter.

MY HEART IS HEAVY AS LORELEI AND I LEAVE MY PARLOR. EVERY SHADOW IN the hall pulls my attention, and my eyes dart to each one, expecting Aspen at every turn, around every corner. But he doesn't appear, neither to try and stop me from leaving nor to offer me a heart-wrenching farewell. I am both disappointed and relieved.

Foxglove awaits outside the palace, standing beside the carriage led by two dark puca. The puca aren't nearly as terrifying to behold as they were when I first saw them, especially now that I've become so well-acquainted with the far more menacing kelpie. Then again, the kelpie helped me during my trial in the Twelfth Court when I fought to win back Aspen's throne from Cobalt. But had any of that surreal experience been true? Or had it only occurred inside my imagination? The crown I returned with was my only proof.

And now it sits on my parlor table. Belonging to no one.

I climb inside the carriage, taking a seat on one of the long benches while Foxglove and Lorelei take the one across from me. As the carriage begins to move, I don't dare look out the window. I don't think I can handle the sight of Bircharbor fading from view. Not because it's become dear to me —it was only just beginning to feel like home—but because I'm afraid I'll see an antlered silhouette watching me from one of the windows. The thought alone strips the air from my lungs.

It isn't until we've been traveling in silence for what feels like an hour that I finally lean forward and stare at the scenery. We're surrounded by oaks and maples with deep red leaves twinkling like rubies overhead, falling like stars to the ground where they coat the earth like a blood-red sea. I take in each crimson hue, memorizing the shape of every leaf like it's the last time I'll ever see it.

I settle back into my seat and face Foxglove, seeking a less emotional conduit for my thoughts. There's always one thing I can count on to do just that. Logic. "How are we getting to Sableton? I'm assuming we aren't taking the long way."

"Right you are," he says. "We're nearing the Autumn axis. Once we reach it, we'll be transported to the axis line along the wall. From there, we'll make our way to the Spring axis where we'll cross the wall into Sableton."

Aspen once explained interaxis travel to me briefly, but there's still so much I don't understand. "Where exactly is the Autumn axis within the court? I know where the axes are along the wall, but I've never left Autumn but by sea."

"The axis encompasses a portion of land in the forest on the southern end of Autumn near the perimeter where Autumn meets Wind."

"And it will automatically transport us to the Autumn axis along the wall?"

"If by automatically you mean as a result of me using my magic to get there, then yes."

"You have to use magic?"

"Of course." Foxglove scoffs. "We must have the option to bypass the axis and proceed the long way, must we not? So, to communicate our intentions with the axis, we must have a sort of key."

"A key."

"That's what you can imagine the magic we use to utilize the axis is."

I blink at him a few times, wishing I could make logical sense of his words. I've come to allow some suspension of disbelief when it comes to the fae and their magic. Before I came to Faerwyvae, I would have laughed at such a notion. Now that I've seen what I've seen, done what I've done...I admit there are things far beyond rational explanation. Yet, it still doesn't stop me from seeking to understand it.

"How do you use this *magic key*? Do you say some sort of incantation?"

Foxglove and Lorelei exchange a look, one that tells me they think my line of questioning is quite simpleminded. "I merely use it, my dear," Foxglove says. "It is more about intent than it is about tangible action. All magic is."

I lean back in my seat, brows furrowed as I try to pair his words with reason.

Lorelei seems entertained by my obvious struggle, lips tight to suppress a grin. "Didn't you learn about magic in the Twelfth Court?"

"I wouldn't say I learned anything," I say. Sure, it opened my mind to new possibilities, made me feel like I was drunk on honey pyrus. But if my journey to the All of All is supposed to be any indication of how magic works, I have no hope of making sense of it any time soon.

"We're entering the axis," Foxglove says.

I return to looking out the window, trying to discern any change, any flicker of magic. The forest looks the same as it did the last time I looked out at the scenery. More oaks, maples. More red leaves. I continue watching as the carriage rolls along, but there's no change.

My attention then shifts back to Foxglove. I study his face, his eyes. "Are you using your magic right now?"

He lets out a light giggle. "When am I not using my magic?"

"Are you using it for the axis?"

"I already have. We're on the other side now, nearing the wall."

I look back out the window. Still, nothing has changed. Another magical occurrence I can't decipher. It is both a frustration and an invigorating challenge to be so utterly perplexed. I shake my head, about to retreat to my seat once again, when movement catches my eye. There in the distance between the trees is a dark shape, hidden in shadows. A hulking creature with massive antlers.

My breath hitches as I study the silhouette, seeking recognition. I've seen Aspen in his stag form before. Could this be...

I can't let myself wonder. I can't.

I watch the figure until it's lost from view, swallowed by shadows beneath the setting sun. Only then do I question whether I saw the stag at all.

6

The fog that envelops the carriage tells me we're approaching the wall. We've already traveled through the Autumn and Summer axes, and when we reached Spring, the carriage turned south. Now the towering stones of the faewall emerge from the fog. We pass between two stones into a familiar forest.

Unlike the smooth transition from Autumn to its axis, the shift from Faerwyvae to Eisleigh is jarring. Night has fallen as it had over Spring, but there's a dullness to the light of the moon. The leaves don't shimmer as they drop from the trees, and unlike the Autumn Court, fall has already stripped half the branches bare. Gone are the nectar-like aromas wafting through the air, replaced with the pungent smell of decay. The sound of the wheels rolling over brown, mushy leaves brings an odd sense of nostalgia mixed with a sinking feeling.

Home. I'm home.

Less comforting thoughts chase away any sense of relief, reminding me of the confrontation I'm approaching. I don't know what to expect from my meeting with the mayor. A minuscule spark of hope whispers the possibility that I'll arrive, state my case, solve this outrageous misunderstanding, and set everything to rights. The mayor will order my mother released and I'll secure the treaty with my marriage to Aspen.

If that hope has any chance of coming about, then why does my stomach plummet when I entertain it? Because it hurts too much to hope? Or because deep down I know the hope is futile?

I grit my teeth as we continue the journey in silence.

When the carriage rolls to a stop, my heart leaps into my throat.

"We've arrived at the mayor's house," Foxglove says. His expression reflects the anxiety I feel. He opens the carriage door but hesitates, his gaze falling on Lorelei. "I think you should wait here while Evelyn and I speak with the mayor."

She meets his eyes, something like relief flickering over her face as she nods.

Foxglove's attention moves to me. "You may wait here as well, if you like. I could speak with him first and glean more information before involving you."

There's no way I'll let this situation unfold without being front and center. I want every piece of information I can possibly get handed directly to me. Forcing confidence, I lift my chin. "I'm coming."

With a sigh, Foxglove exits the carriage and extends his hand to help me out. The mayor's house looms on the other side of the carriage, an elegant manor framed with neat hedges and a manicured lawn. This is my first time seeing Mayor Coleman's house, although I've walked by his drive many times growing up. Back when my sister was friends with Maddie Coleman, we often walked with her here, leaving her at the top of the drive for visits with her uncle.

Of course, thoughts of Maddie Coleman only fill me with contempt, but at least it feels better than fear.

Foxglove and I approach the front door, where a smug doorman greets us. After a brief statement of our business from Foxglove, the doorman leads us inside the manor and into a parlor. It's clear he means to take us swiftly through to the door at the other side, but I find my feet rooted as a familiar face snags my attention.

Maddie Coleman sits on the couch in the middle of the parlor next to her younger sister, Marie. Overstuffed bags and luggage litter the ground at their feet. With a haughty grin, Maddie looks up from her needlework and meets my eyes, blonde curls bouncing with the movement. She assesses me from head to toe, although she doesn't seem surprised to see me. Her gaze moves to Foxglove. "Have you come to take me to my new husband?"

A violent heat floods me, boiling my blood as I fight the urge to lash out at her. Even my hands are hot, as if each palm holds a flame.

Foxglove inspects the girls on the couch, nose wrinkled in distaste.

Without so much as a word, he turns up his chin and meets the doorman at the other side of the parlor. I burn Maddie with a scowl before joining him, but she doesn't so much as flinch. Marie, on the other hand, goes a shade paler, mouth hanging open as if she wishes to speak.

I'm shaking with suppressed rage as we move down the hall; I only begin to sober once we stop at the end of the corridor. The doorman knocks on a door, then opens it.

Inside the room, Mayor Coleman sits at a desk with two armed guards standing on each side. It never occurred to me that the mayor employed guards, but I suppose the extra protection is a comfort when meeting with the fae, even if it's with a peaceful ambassador.

The mayor is a well-dressed man, but he looks nothing like his slim, blonde niece. He has a heavy-set build, a bushy mustache that hides his upper lip, and shrewd eyes beneath thick, caterpillar-like brows. He wears a brown jacket and waistcoat over a white shirt and cravat.

He lifts his eyes from his desk as we enter, his gaze flicking toward Foxglove before resting on me. "Miss Fairfield," he says with a reserved smile. "I wasn't expecting you, but I must admit, this makes things much easier for us all." He motions to one of the guards to lean forward, and the mayor whispers an order too soft for me to hear. Then the guard crosses the room. Toward me.

I flinch, hands flying to my thigh, my hip, but the automatic response to danger is fruitless; my iron dagger was lost when Cobalt captured me, and I've yet to replace it. A moment too late, I realize my reaction was unfounded. The guard isn't coming for me. Instead, he skirts behind Foxglove and rushes out the door.

Heat floods my cheeks in embarrassment as I release a breath and return my attention to the mayor.

Mayor Coleman eyes me through slitted lids and motions for Foxglove and me to sit. "Your king has made his decision regarding the correspondence the council sent, I presume?"

"King Aspen has considered the contents of the letter, yes," Foxglove says. I'm surprised how collected he is. I've gotten used to his often-anxious ways when dealing with unfortunate circumstances—wringing his hands, nervously adjusting his spectacles—that I nearly forgot how calm and regal he can be. This is how I first saw him, posture erect, voice high and snobbish, expression smug.

"I take it he wasn't pleased."

"That's an understatement, Mayor Coleman. I can't say Miss Fairfield and I are pleased either, and we have many questions."

The mayor leans back in his chair. "I will answer what I can, but I assure you, nothing will alter the conclusions we've reached or the final olive branch we've extended."

I grip the arms of the chair to channel my rage, my anxiety. It's all I can do not to shout my questions at him, but I know it's best if Foxglove takes the lead. For now.

"The first issue we seek clarity on is the accusation over Miss Fairfield's heritage," Foxglove says. "The letter stated she has been deemed ineligible to secure the treaty due to being of fae blood. The king's mate has assured us she knows nothing about such a possibility. Will you explain what gave your council this outrageous idea?"

The mayor purses his lips, pulling them both beneath the cliff of his mustache. "We have evidence that Evelyn and Amelie Fairfield are of fae blood and that their mother, Maven Fairfield, knew this and withheld the truth even after they were selected as Chosen. She deliberately put the treaty in danger with her omission."

I can keep quiet no longer, my body trembling from head to toe. "What evidence do you have?"

The mayor slides his gaze to me, and a flash of hatred crosses his face. "The proof we have is not up for debate and will be more thoroughly discussed at your mother's trial."

"My mother's trial," I echo. "When will that be?"

"It will be held in two weeks' time, when Eisleigh's council gathers at the Spire."

The Spire. That's the name for the prison in Grenneith, the capital city of Eisleigh. Only the most serious crimes in Eisleigh are tried at the Spire. The only thing worse would be if her trial were being held at Fort Merren on the mainland, involving the entire kingdom of Bretton as well as the king. At least her accusation of treason is being considered a territorial threat and not a national one. The thought doesn't give me much comfort.

The mayor continues. "Even though the proof we have is irrefutable, we are giving your mother a fair trial as well as allowing you and your sister plenty of time to get your affairs in order beforehand. Your presence today tells me it won't be as difficult as we'd thought to get you to comply."

"I'm here to prove my mother's innocence. My sister and I aren't fae."

"If there is innocence to prove, you may present it at Maven Fairfield's trial, as both you and your sister will be required to attend."

"That's in two weeks!" I'm nearly shouting. "You won't divulge whatever proof you have to support your claims, nor will you allow me to argue on my mother's behalf for *two weeks*?"

"Exactly," he says without remorse. "Considering your mother is being held under charges of treason, any conversations we have outside of an official trial are of no use. We are both better off waiting until then to speak more on the matter."

Foxglove puts his hand on mine for a moment, a silent request for me to regather my composure. "If the trial isn't held for two more weeks," he says, "we should delay all actions regarding the treaty until then."

Mayor Coleman shakes his head. "That won't do. Eisleigh's council has already given your king ample allowances to secure the treaty, and numerous times he's failed. This is the last chance we're giving him."

"But this most recent setback is not King Aspen's making," Foxglove argues.

"Isn't it, though?" The mayor scoffs. "Your king requested Evelyn Fairfield by name after the Holstrom girls were executed. He bypassed our selection of my nieces and received the Fairfield girls in their stead. For all we know, he could have selected them on purpose, knowing their fae heritage. He could have done it to compromise the treaty."

Foxglove doesn't argue. Even though I know the mayor's theory is wrong, I also know how the humans—and many of the fae too, for that matter—view Aspen. They see him as cruel, volatile, and reckless. They don't realize everything he does is meant to maintain balance in Faerwyvae.

But there's something else tugging at my mind. Something that doesn't quite add up. "If Eisleigh's council thinks Aspen is responsible for this newest complication, then why are you giving him a final chance at all? Why not consider it a breaking of the treaty?"

Foxglove throws me a sharp look, one I ignore as I keep my eyes fixed on the mayor.

"We don't want war, Miss Fairfield. Giving King Aspen a final offer to maintain peace is mutually beneficial to both humans and fae. We have every right to withhold this generous proposition, but we are giving him the benefit of the doubt one last time." He says this with confidence, but there's a flicker of uncertainty that crosses his face, so subtle I almost miss it.

My eyes lock on his, seeking what he's leaving unsaid. I hold his gaze, and it feels like I have his eyes in a cage of my own making, a bird trapped between my fingers. I see it in my mind's eye; his attention is that bird, and the cage is my will. The longer I hold both, the more pliant the mayor becomes. "There's something you aren't telling me," I say, my words rolling with a calm yet deadly fire. "Tell me why you're really doing this."

The mayor's face seems to have gone slack, but his eyes are still locked on mine, pupils dilated like enormous black saucers. "King Ustrin demanded our compliance. He's put us in an exceedingly difficult place."

My mouth falls open, and with it goes the image of the bird held within the cage of my hands.

The mayor blinks several times, cheeks burning crimson. He leans back in his chair, a subtle move, but it's like he wants to put space between us. Like he's...scared.

I'm keenly aware of Foxglove's stare. I meet it, but I'm not sure what it means. He seems flustered.

But why? I can't help but wonder at the strange imagery that flooded my mind moments ago when I met the mayor's eyes. One word comes to mind. Glamour. I glamoured the mayor.

Of course I didn't. All this nonsense is just getting to my head.

I focus instead on what Mayor Coleman said. That King Ustrin demanded compliance. I ponder the name and try to match a face to it. Then I recall the fae who approached me in the hall after Aspen won back his throne from Cobalt. Orange scales, lipless mouth, slitted nostrils—the King of Fire. I shudder. I don't know much about the lizard king, but our first encounter left me nothing but unsettled.

I furrow my brow. "What does King Ustrin have to do with anything?"

The mayor pins me with a chilling glare. "That is not up for discussion either."

"Mayor Coleman," Foxglove says, his light tone in stark contrast against the tension building in the room, "if the human council is willing to allow King Aspen a final chance to secure the treaty, then I don't see why another two weeks will matter. He and Evelyn Fairfield have done all but the final step in securing the treaty. If there is even the slightest chance they can finish what they've already begun, I think it's worth waiting for."

"No," the mayor says. "If your king wants to secure the treaty and prevent Maven Fairfield's execution, then he will accept my nieces as his new Chosen. You will bring them to the Autumn Court tonight. King Aspen will take the eldest as his wife and perform all acts required by the treaty in a single day by the end of one week."

"King Aspen has already made Evelyn his mate," Foxglove argues.

"That doesn't make her his wife."

"They have performed the Bonding ritual." He says *bonding* in a half-whisper, like it pains him to utter the word aloud. Considering his reluctance to tell me about it before the mate ceremony, I assume it isn't discussed with humans often.

Mayor Coleman, however, shows no sign of reverence as he says, "If Miss Fairfield never sees King Aspen again, the Bond is of no consequence between them."

His words send anger and nausea swirling inside me, a volatile mix that makes my head spin. *No consequence. Never see King Aspen again.*

The study door opens, pulling me from my thoughts. My mind sharpens as two figures enter the room. One is the guard who left earlier. The other I recognize as Sheriff Bronson, Sableton's law enforcer. There's no doubt he's here for me.

"Evelyn Fairfield," the mayor says, "you are sentenced to imprisonment."

7

———————

Sheriff Bronson takes a step toward me, and the mayor's two guards follow suit. I stand, knocking my chair over in the process. Foxglove springs to his feet a moment later, blocking my body with his. He holds his palms before him, as if they stand a chance against the swords at the guards' waists or the sheriff's revolver—*a gun!* Such a rare weapon to see in my village, or on the isle at all, for that matter. At least no weapon has been drawn yet.

"Wait," Foxglove says. "Until a trial proves otherwise, Evelyn Fairfield is a subject of the Autumn Court. You cannot harm her or hold her captive."

"Miss Fairfield is suspected of treason alongside her mother," Mayor Coleman says through his teeth. "She will be escorted to Sableton's jail tonight, and tomorrow she and her mother will be transported to the Spire to be held until the trial."

"It will be easier if you come willingly." Sheriff Bronson extends his hand, expression apologetic. I'm sure this is awkward for him. It's not that we know each other well, but he's been Sableton's sheriff since I was a little girl.

"Besides, wouldn't you rather be with your mother?" The mayor's voice is mocking, grating on my ears. But his words meet their mark, taking the fight from me as my mind fills with images of Mother alone in a dark cell.

"She's being kept comfortable, as will you," Bronson says, his tone far more placating than the mayor's. "That comfort will be extended during your stay, and I've been assured it will be maintained at the Spire."

The mayor clears his throat. "When we hear word from your sister, she will join you as well."

I lay a gentle hand on Foxglove's shoulder, wordlessly asking him to stand down. "What will happen to us after the trial?"

"Afterward," the mayor says, "the three of you will be exiled to mainland Bretton."

"Only if your suspicions prove correct," Foxglove says.

The mayor nods.

Exiled to the mainland. At least it isn't execution.

There was a time not long ago when I would have given anything to move to the mainland. But that was before the Reaping. Before Faerwyvae. Before Aspen. Now it's all over. Even if Mother is proven innocent at her trial, it will be too late for me and him. He'll already be married by then.

But my mother will live. She'll live and we'll be together. It's all I can focus on if I'm to prevent another emotional breakdown.

"I'll go to my imprisonment willingly." My voice comes out with a tremor. "Foxglove will take the new Chosen to the Autumn Court."

"A wise choice," the mayor says.

I face Sheriff Bronson as frantic footsteps sound in the hall, followed by a much slower set farther down. The familiar figure that emerges through the threshold catches me off guard.

"Do not imprison her," Mr. Meeks says through panting breaths. The aging surgeon doesn't so much as look at me as he approaches the mayor's desk. "I will host her until the trial."

Mayor Coleman shakes his head. "She must be held behind bars."

"She's just a girl," Mr. Meeks says. "She cannot be subjected to the indignity of prison."

I bristle at being called *just a girl*, but the sentiment softens my heart. My former mentor, who I apprenticed under for two years, is the one human I respect above all others. And he's here fighting on my behalf.

He continues. "Even if proven guilty of having fae blood, the fault will not lie with her but with her mother. I've known Miss Fairfield since she was a child, and can attest that she knew of no secret heritage. Do not punish her for her ignorance."

The second set of footsteps crosses the threshold, revealing an unfamiliar man. He appears to be in his thirties, wearing cream trousers and a navy-blue jacket and waistcoat. He's tall with neatly trimmed dark-blond hair, a slim mustache, and pale blue eyes that match his silk cravat.

Mayor Coleman lets out a grumble of relief. "Councilman Duveau, please speak some sense into Mr. Meeks."

Mr. Duveau scans the room, gaze roving from the mayor to Mr. Meeks, then gliding to Foxglove. Finally, it settles on me, although he doesn't meet my eyes.

Mr. Meeks faces the newcomer. "Henry, please allow Miss Fairfield this comfort. Let her stay with me while she awaits her mother's trial. I will escort her to the Spire myself when the time comes."

The mayor opens his mouth to argue, but Henry Duveau speaks first. "I don't see the problem, Mayor Coleman. Miss Fairfield can do what she pleases. She can return to the Autumn Court for all I care, so long as she and her sister attend the trial and submit to their sentence."

The mayor looks taken aback, cheeks burning. "If we don't lock her up now, what is to keep her from going into hiding?"

"She'll have ample incentive," Mr. Duveau says. "More than she has now, in fact."

I shudder as he faces me. "What do you mean?"

When he looks at me, there's no malice in his expression, no teasing. He's stoic. Confident. "You and your sister will present yourselves at the Spire by the twenty-fourth of October. If you fail to do so, your mother will be executed and a bounty will be placed on your heads."

I'm reeling from his statement, so much that I can't utter a word.

He returns to face the mayor. "See? Let her do what she will between now and then. Either way, the threat will be eliminated in the end."

What threat? I want to ask, but I still can't find my words.

"Fine," Mayor Coleman says with a sneer. "You heard Councilman Duveau. The choice is yours."

I swallow hard. "I already told you my choice. I'll stay with my mother."

Mr. Meeks faces me. "No, Miss Fairfield. Please allow me to spare you such humiliation."

"If it's humiliating for me, it can't be any better for my mother."

"But she wouldn't want this for you, dear girl," he argues. "I couldn't live with myself if I didn't do my best to protect you when she cannot."

The tender look in his eyes crushes me. I always knew he was fond of me as his apprentice, but I never expected him to care so deeply. To seek to protect me like the father figure I always wished he were. My eyes move to

Mr. Duveau. "My mother will be cared for? She won't be harmed in prison if I stay with Mr. Meeks?"

"I'll even make you a bargain," he says, "that no harm will come to your mother while she's imprisoned, so long as you promise to attend her trial. Do you accept this bargain?"

I'm caught off guard by his choice of words until I realize he thinks he's making a *fae* bargain. Because for some crazy reason no one will tell me, he thinks I'm fae. "Yes, I accept."

"Where will you choose to await her trial?"

Before I can respond, Foxglove puts a hand on my shoulder, a weak smile tugging his lips. He lowers his voice to a whisper. "There's the other option he mentioned. You could return to Autumn with me."

Autumn. I could return to Bircharbor, spend two more weeks with Aspen. A distant trill of laughter falls on my ears, muffled through the hall that stands between here and the parlor. I know who it belongs to. Aspen's new Chosen. His soon-to-be-wife. If I return to Bircharbor, it won't be to a respite. Being there for two weeks means I'll have to witness his wedding to Maddie Coleman. The thought alone sends bile rising to my throat.

"I'll go with Mr. Meeks," I say, "if I will be allowed to speak with my mother before she's taken to the Spire."

"No," the mayor says at the same time as Mr. Meeks says, "Of course."

Mr. Duveau rolls his eyes. "Let her see her mother."

"You can visit her first thing in the morning," Mr. Meeks says.

"Very well." The mayor leans back in his chair, shoulders slumped in defeat. "Then it's settled. My nieces are ready for their travels, ambassador."

Foxglove's face goes pale as he nods to the mayor.

Mr. Duveau turns on his heel, followed by Sheriff Bronson. Mr. Meeks gives me a warm smile, extending his arm to allow me to pass into the hall ahead of him. "I'm so glad I got here in time," he whispers, walking by my side. "I don't know what I would have done if I found my dear apprentice had been locked up before I arrived." Again, his care surprises me. Even after these allegations, he still considers me his dear apprentice. However, the tenseness in his posture isn't lost on me. He may be doing me a kindness, but he isn't fully comfortable about it.

"How did you know I was here?"

"I was meeting with Henry—Mr. Duveau, that is—when the mayor's guard came to inform him of your presence. Thank the stars we got here before Bronson took you away."

We enter the parlor, and Maddie and Marie rise to their feet. "Are we leaving now?" Maddie asks with a haughty grin.

"Yes." Foxglove's answer is curt as he comes up behind me. He says nothing more as he brushes past the girls and out the door, not even bothering to help them with their things.

Maddie gapes after him, then snaps her fingers at a maid. "My bags. Now."

A whimper draws my attention to the girl behind Maddie—her sister, Marie. The girl is a few inches shorter than Maddie, her hair a mousy brown, her dress far more modest and subdued than her companion. She was always the more studious of the two, kind where her sister is sharp. Practical, save for a naive sense of dreaminess about her. I've never seen her so flustered. Marie's voice comes out small. "I don't want to go."

"Grow up," Maddie mutters. "You know this is your duty."

"But I...I'm not ready." Her eyes fill with tears.

"We've been ready for this all day. All our lives, if we're being honest. You always knew this would be a possibility."

"I'm not ready to get married."

Maddie shrugs. "Perhaps a marriage won't be required of you. I'll gladly fulfill my duty for the both of us." There's more mocking than warmth in her tone.

I find myself frozen as Marie's eyes lock on mine, silently pleading. I don't know what she expects me to do. I've never been close to the younger girl, not even when our older sisters were friends. She's three years younger...

A shiver crawls up my spine. That's when I remember Marie Coleman is only fifteen years old. My stomach churns. No wonder the girl is terrified.

She may be old enough for the Reaping, but the terms of the treaty were crafted a thousand years ago. Since then, girls rarely get married that young in Eisleigh. Despite my personal pains, an ache of sympathy tugs at my heart.

But there's nothing I can do. In this—in this entire situation—I'm powerless.

I tear my gaze away from the girl and rush out the door.

Outside, Mr. Duveau enters a sleek black coach pulled by two enormous brown Clydesdales. My stomach sinks as Mr. Meeks guides me toward the door held open by the councilman's driver. "Mr. Duveau can take us to my house on his way back to his hotel. I figure you'd prefer that over riding with Sheriff Bronson."

My eyes flash toward the prison wagon parked behind Mr. Duveau. The enclosed end of the wagon is designed for transporting prisoners, not casual passengers. Yet, my stomach lurches when I consider sitting in a carriage with the brusque councilman.

"Evelyn!" Lorelei's voice has me whirling to face her as she jogs toward me. I almost forgot I left her waiting in the carriage. Her eyes are wide as she approaches me, sparing a hesitant glance at my human companion. Mr. Meeks takes a step away, giving us some privacy, and she lowers her voice to a whisper. "What happened?"

I don't have the energy to explain. I've hardly processed it myself. "It...it went the way we feared it would. There's no swaying the council. Aspen will take the new Chosen and I...I will await my mother's trial."

"When will that be?"

"Two weeks from now. After that..." Exile at worst. But what happens at best? If we can prove the council is wrong about my heritage, where do we go from there? Will we be able to return to our old lives, with Mother running her apothecary, and me acting as apprentice to Mr. Meeks, and Amelie...

My blood goes cold. For the first time, I consider a chilling possibility. What if Amelie doesn't come? What if Cobalt receives the summons for her to attend the trial but keeps the information to himself? What if he tells her about it but won't let her leave? What if...what if Amelie refuses to come?

My knees go weak, lungs constricting.

"Where are you going?" Lorelei asks.

I focus on her words to reel in my frazzled thoughts. "I'll be staying with my mentor, Mr. Meeks, until the trial. He's taking me to his home."

She visibly shudders, swallowing hard before saying, "I'll stay with you."

My shoulders slump. "No, Lorelei. They nearly imprisoned me on the grounds that I might be part-fae. There's no way you'll be allowed to remain here. Besides, why would you want to?"

"I'm not going to let you face this alone."

I'm not alone, I want to say. *I have Mr. Meeks.* But I know it isn't the same. She and Foxglove are my final tethers to the world I left behind. Proof that everything I experienced in Faerwyvae was real. Her presence is both a comfort and a painful reminder, and there's a selfish part of me that wants her to stay. But I know it isn't possible.

I open my mouth to say as much when Mr. Meeks draws near with slow, hesitant steps. "If your friend would like to keep you company, I will allow her to stay at my residence as well," he says. "Mr. Duveau will give his permission. He's a reasonable man. So long as she returns after the trial, he could have no argument against it. She can serve as an honorary ambassador until your name is either cleared or condemned."

I'm surprised at his willingness to let a fae into his house, in addition to a supposed criminal. Mr. Meeks never hated the fae as much as I did, but I never got the impression he liked them either.

"I'm staying," Lorelei says. The set of her jaw tells me there's no arguing with her.

I nod, and we follow Mr. Meeks to the black coach. Before I climb inside, my eyes snag on the other carriage, the one of gold and pearl and lustrous wood. Foxglove stands outside it and offers me a sad smile, one that makes my heart plummet. That is, until Maddie Coleman obscures my view of my friend as she saunters to the carriage door. She meets my gaze and gives me an exaggerated smile. "Looks like I get to be queen after all."

Fury roars through me, and I let it burn away my hurt, my anxieties. I shape it into a smirk, eyes burning into the girl. "Just beware of the king's antlers," I say sweetly. "He has no patience for easy prey."

8

Inside the carriage, I sit next to Lorelei while the two men sit across from us. Mr. Duveau seems unperturbed by the presence of my fae companion, his attention taken by the dark scenery outside the window. I, on the other hand, can't suppress the creeping feeling of being so near Councilman Duveau. I never met the man before tonight and only vaguely recall his name from conversation. From what I know, he's a member of Eisleigh's council, alongside Mayor Coleman and all the other mayors that oversee Eisleigh's villages. I don't think Mr. Duveau is a mayor, though, so perhaps he's one of the council's heads. Whatever the case, I find even his silence and inattention oddly domineering.

The only person who seems more uncomfortable than me is Lorelei. She watches the two men, posture stiff at my side. Considering what happened with the last human male she encountered, her suspicion is understandable. I just can't fathom why she chose to stay.

Mr. Meeks' house isn't too far from the mayor's, and before the ride grows too tense, we roll to a halt. The driver opens the door, announcing our arrival. Mr. Meeks gets out and offers his hand to assist my exit. Before I can accept, Mr. Duveau leans forward and blocks the door with his arm. A flash of red peeking from under his cuff catches my eye—a strand of rowan berries wrapped around his wrist. I reach for the strand around my neck, seeking comfort in their feel.

"Your friend may exit first," Mr. Duveau says. "I'd like a word with you."

"I'm not leaving her," Lorelei says with a snarl.

His face flashes with irritation as he assesses my companion for the first time.

My words come out calm but firm, as if I can cut the tension with them. "Mr. Meeks assured me you would accept Lorelei as honorary Autumn ambassador until the trial. If that is so, then she may be present for whatever you must say to me."

He looks at me through narrowed eyes, but he doesn't meet my gaze for long. Slowly, he leans back and straightens his silk cravat. "Very well, Miss Fairfield. I want to impress upon you what is at stake. Despite the comforts and freedoms we are allowing you, what I said holds true; if you and your sister fail to present yourselves at Maven Fairfield's trial, your mother will be executed."

I clench my teeth. It's an effort to keep my voice level as I say, "I assure you, Mr. Duveau, that my mother's life is of the utmost importance to me."

"And to your sister? Why is it you are here when your sister is not?"

I wonder if the humans know anything about what has happened with Amelie. Aspen refused to send word when I thought she'd died; I doubt anything has been communicated about her allegiance to Cobalt or even Cobalt's treachery. "My sister feels the same as I do."

"Is that a promise?"

I open my mouth but consider my words carefully before I speak. "I'll leave that promise for her to make." I shift my weight to rise from the seat, but again Mr. Duveau blocks the door with his arm.

"The council has heard nothing regarding your sister since the announcement was made that you would be marrying the Stag King and not she. Why is that?"

"Why have you not heard from my sister or why did I get paired with King Aspen?"

"Both."

I meet his eyes, holding his gaze with a glare. Shoulders square, I adopt the bearing of a fae royal. "Mr. Duveau, your curiosity flatters me, but it is getting late. I am vexed by today's news and my companion and I are tired. You will excuse us and allow us our rest."

A muscle ticks at the corner of his jaw, expression darkening. "Don't toy with me, Miss Fairfield."

"Is that a threat?"

"If I were threatening you, you'd know it."

My chest heaves as rage and terror flood me. Something in his tone, slithering beneath his words, has my skin crawling. Never would I have imagined being so terrified of one of my kind—a human. Especially after being thrust into the fae world where I was attacked by a kelpie, the Sea Queen, and Cobalt. I can't put my finger on why, but this man is far more dangerous than any creature I've ever met.

Still, I hold his gaze, my words like a growl. "Goodnight, Mr. Duveau."

He returns to his seat with a curt nod.

Lorelei and I all but tumble through the door in our rush to get away from the man. Mr. Meeks greets us with an apologetic smile. "Let's get you girls to bed."

We turn away from the carriage, but before the driver closes the door, I hear Mr. Duveau's voice. "If you're in contact with your sister, I implore you to pass along what I've said."

I refuse to turn around, refuse to do anything but dart into the safety of Mr. Meeks' house.

LORELEI AND I ARE GIVEN A GUEST ROOM TO SHARE, EVEN THOUGH HE OFFERED us two separate accommodations. With Mr. Meeks being a widower and his son once again on holiday in the mainland, he has ample space. However, Lorelei wouldn't be persuaded to leave my side, although I get the feeling she needs the comfort of my presence more than I need her protection. It's clear she's shaken by the events of this evening, her face paling from its usual rich umber to an ashen brown, a slight tremble with every move.

"Are you all right?" I ask her as we climb into the small bed piled with an assortment of quilts and blankets.

She winces as she tries to settle into the pillows, as if they pain her. "I'm fine," she says, although her tone implies otherwise. "I've just never been on this side of the wall before. Never slept in a human house, in a human bed. It's...uncomfortable for me."

"Physically? Or emotionally?"

"Both. Also, I can already feel a drain on my magic. It makes me feel unwell."

A flash of panic tenses my shoulders. "Unwell? Is the drain on your magic a danger to you?"

"Not an immediate danger," she says. "My magic won't be as strong here, but I'll get through it. It feels like when I was healing from my iron injury."

My heart squeezes. I can't imagine why she would put herself through this for me. In fact, I have a feeling there's more to her motives than she's letting on. "Why are you really doing this, Lorelei?"

"I told you. I won't let you face this alone."

"But why? I appreciate your company, but this goes above and beyond the duties of friendship, and I can tell you're uncomfortable about all of it. What aren't you telling me?"

She lets out a heavy sigh. "When you asked me if Aspen ordered me to stay with you, I answered by telling you I'd asked him if I could come. That is true, but he asked more from me. He asked me to watch over you so long as you're here and until the situation with your mother is settled."

My breath hitches at the mention of Aspen. "Why?"

"For the same reason I agreed. Because neither of us trust the humans."

"But you trust me and I'm one of them."

"You're more than just a human. You're my queen. You may not wear the crown and you may never hold the position, but until Aspen forces me to kneel before another female in your place, I will serve you."

I'm at a loss for words. It's strange to think Lorelei and I disliked each other so much when we first met. Even she and Amelie became friends before she and I began to make amends.

She continues. "If anyone tries to hurt you here, I'll protect you however I can. I've protected myself once from them before, although I failed to protect another. I won't make that mistake again with you. Aspen will have my head if I do." The last words are said in jest, but her tone can't hide the sorrow beneath.

I can't imagine how deep her pain must go, the death of her lover still recent. Now here we are in the home of the man who helped save her lover's murderer. Where *I* helped save him too. I aided Mr. Osterman's amputation, eased his pain with laudanum, comforted him. It's still difficult for me to reconcile the man I knew growing up with the man Lorelei despises, but I believe her now.

"How did it happen anyway?" I ask, my voice barely above a whisper. "Why were you at the Spring axis when Mr. Osterman found you?"

"Malan invited me to meet her parents in Spring," she says. "I'd taken a week's leave from King Aspen's court and was on my way back to Autumn. Malan had decided to walk with me from the Spring axis to the Autumn axis, but we didn't get very far. I was being careless, so caught up in our love that I didn't smell the iron until the teeth of the trap were in my leg. That's when the Butcher of Stone Ninety-Four came out from behind one of the trees near the wall. He'd been waiting for prey."

My stomach churns. "I'm so sorry, Lorelei. I hate that you've suffered at the hands of my people. I don't know how you can handle being here."

"If I didn't know there were humans like you, it would be impossible to be here. But you—and even Amelie, before everything with Cobalt—taught me that not all humans are to be feared."

"I learned the same from you about the fae."

From the light of the moon peering into the window, I see a smile form on her lips. "He won't make her queen, you know."

I wrinkle my brow. "Excuse me?"

"The new Chosen. I told you I'll serve you until the king puts another in your place. But he's never going to put her in your place. You know that, right?"

A lump rises in my throat. "It shouldn't matter to me. It isn't likely I'll ever see him again."

"It shouldn't matter, yet it does, doesn't it?"

I nod. "It does."

We fall into silence, and exhaustion quickly sweeps all thought from my mind. But as tired as I am, I can't seem to fall asleep. Even Lorelei finds slumber before I do. What she said about Aspen weaves its way into my consciousness, tickling my mind each time I'm about to slip into sleep. I toss and turn, but nothing seems to rid me of it.

So instead, I give in.

I open my heart and dig into the gaping wound where my mate should be. *Aspen.* I think his name, let it fill my mind. Like a bell, it reverberates through me and clears the fog from my head. In place of the fog lies a bridge —one I've seen before, spanning between two jagged cliffs. Last time I crossed it, the results were detrimental. What happens if I cross it now?

With hesitant steps, I make my way over the bridge, feet balancing on each precarious plank that lines the way. I don't bother looking down, for I know what's there—sharp rocks, pointed spikes. When I reach the other side of the bridge, I see not the cliff I'd been heading to but a dark room. A familiar room.

In the middle of it sits the bed I awoke from just this morning. *Was it really just this morning?* Beneath the covers lies a slumbering figure.

I approach the edge of the bed and look down at my mate. His lips are parted, face slack, making him appear more youthful than ever. His blue-black hair lies in disarray, waves curling at his neck and over his bronze pillow. His antlers make deep impressions in the pillow where they touch it, but the bulk of them hangs past the back of the mattress.

Everything inside me yearns to crawl in next to him. We've never spent the night in the same bed. We slept in the same room when he was recovering from his injury, but he had the bed while I dozed on the couch. The only other time we spent the night together was in the cave where we finally gave in to our desires. In the days leading up to now, he stayed away from our bed, either working on repairing the palace or avoiding me.

I reach out to touch his cheek, the warmth of his skin kissing my fingers. There's something about the touch that feels wrong, though, some tenuous barrier that keeps him from feeling real.

It's because I'm dreaming.

That's when I notice the violet haze that covers my vision. I'm only just now seeing it, but in the mysterious way of dreams, I know it was here all along. Even Aspen glows with a violet aura, one that pulses with every breath.

My heart sinks with disappointment. I'm about to pull my hand away when Aspen's eyelids flutter open. With a start, his eyes lock on mine and his fingers curl around my wrist. My breath catches, remembering what happened last time he woke to me standing over him. Of course, that time had been real, not a figment of my imagination.

He pulls my hand to his lips, pressing a kiss to my wrist. I close my eyes and sink to the edge of the bed, sitting at his side. "You aren't really here, are you?" he asks, voice sounding both close and far away at the same time.

"No," I say, opening my eyes to find his face. "Neither are you."

His lips pull into a crooked grin as his hand moves to my cheek. "I never knew I could dream something so beautiful."

Heat stirs inside me as his eyes drink me in, but all potential desire is crushed by the logic that permeates my thoughts. Not even my dreams are a respite from the brutal realism I hold so dear when I'm awake. "This hurts too much," I say, lip trembling. "By tomorrow, your new Chosen will arrive. You'll see that carriage and you'll have no idea whether I or they will emerge from it. I don't even want to imagine what your reaction will be."

His eyes widen, jaw clenching at my words, but he says nothing.

"I can't even warn you. I can't even say goodbye." I let out a bitter laugh. "Perhaps that's what this is. My mind's way of letting me pretend I can."

"Then pretend with me." His words come out low, and I swear there's a hint of a tremor to them. He beckons me forward. "Lay with me."

My face crumples, and I fold myself into him, burrowing into his bare chest. He pulls the blanket over us, arms wrapping around me as I breathe in his rosemary and cinnamon scent. I'm surprised I can conjure the scent within this dream, yet the certainty that this is a dream remains. Aspen's arms don't feel as heavy as they should, the blankets not nearly as warm. Yet, I enjoy it all the same.

"I'm sorry," he whispers into my hair. "I should have been with you every night like this. I never should have let my pride keep us apart."

"It wouldn't have changed anything," I say, the beating of his heart pulsing against my ear. "All of this still would have happened."

"But we would have had *this*."

"It only would have made things harder."

"Perhaps it should have been harder." His tone deepens. "Maybe I should have fought harder to keep you here."

"I would have fought back even more." We fall into silence, and I know that means the dream is coming to an end. With that knowledge, I cling tighter, willing this moment to remain frozen in time. My heart races as I wait for the dream to fizzle into nothing, for my body to jolt awake in Mr. Meeks' guest room. But the dream remains, and all I can do is revel in the sound of Aspen's heart, in the feel of his breath stirring my hair.

9

The dream is the first thing I remember when I wake. I feel hollow in its absence, wishing it had been real. I can hardly shake it, not even as Lorelei and I get dressed and prepare for our day. It isn't until the two of us are in Mr. Meeks' carriage that I finally manage to tuck the dream away. That's when more pressing concerns flood my mind.

I'm about to see my mother. I'm about to see her *in jail*.

It's a comfort that Mr. Meeks loaned his carriage and driver to me, allowing me and Lorelei privacy for our visit. The fewer witnesses to my anxious state the better. It's still perplexing to consider everything that has happened, and I'm not sure what to expect from my conversation with my mother. At least I'll know the truth once and for all—whether she truly hid my heritage or if the human council is as devious as Aspen suspects.

I'm shaking by the time the carriage comes to a stop outside the jail. The small justice building is in the village plaza on the south end of Etting's street, several blocks from the apothecary. The morning is cool with a light drizzle of rain greeting us as Lorelei and I exit the carriage. The driver gives me a nod. "I'll wait here for you, Miss Fairfield."

"Thank you." With my attention fixed on the building ahead, I hurry through the rain, forcing myself not to look around the plaza. I don't want to see any familiar faces or curious stares. By now, I'm sure half the town knows everything that occurred last night.

Sheriff Bronson meets us by the back door to the jail, expression hard.

He's a rugged-looking man in his sixties with graying hair, long sideburns, and a frizzy mustache. His sheriff's jacket looks a bit the worse for wear, his dress not nearly as refined as the mayor, Mr. Duveau, or even Mr. Meeks. I suppose such a gruff appearance comes with the job.

"Your mother is inside," he says, opening the door. His gaze finds Lorelei for only a moment, but he doesn't seem surprised. Good. Lorelei donned a glamour before we left, disguising herself as a human to prevent as much undue attention as possible. I can't see the glamour myself, but at least it seems others can despite her fears that her magic wouldn't be strong enough here to hold it. In addition to the glamour, she wears one of my most modest fae dresses I'd brought, one of pink chiffon with several layers to the skirt.

We follow Sheriff Bronson through the doorway. Inside, I find a small, dimly lit room with a bench near the door and cells lining the walls. There appear to be four cells total, each smaller than an average bedroom. Only one is occupied.

I run to the bars, finding my mother huddled on a narrow cot, a thick wool blanket over her shoulders. "Ma!"

Her eyes widen when she sees me, and she rises to her feet. She's dressed in rough, gray homespun, skin pale, hair a tangle of copper waves. Gone are her colorful scarves, her whimsical shawls and jewelry. Gone is the brightness in her eyes and the color in her cheeks. "Evelyn, what are you doing here?"

Bronson clears his throat. "I'll give you some privacy and wait right outside the door." He exits the jail but doesn't close the door behind him.

Lorelei squeezes my shoulder. "I'll give you some space as well."

"Thank you," I say. Lorelei takes a seat on the bench at the other side of the room, and I return my attention to my mother. I want to hug her through the bars, to make sure she's hale and whole, but my words are already tumbling from my lips. "What in the name of iron is going on? Why does the human council think I'm fae?"

She presses her lips tight, and I hold my breath for the answer. "Because it's true," she finally says.

There it is. Her confession. My blood feels like it's rushing from my head, and I think I might be sick. "How is this possible?" I say with a gasp. "Who is my father?"

Her brow furrows. "Your father? I told you who he was. His name was Howard, he was a good man—"

"You never told me he was fae."

She shakes her head. "He wasn't."

"Then how the bloody…" My words dry in my throat as logic pieces itself together in my mind.

"I'm the one who's fae, Evelyn."

This time, the blood really does leave my head, and I slide to my knees at the base of the cell. "I don't understand."

Mother joins me, kneeling down and reaching her hands through the bars to grasp mine. "I'm half-fae. My mother was human but my father was originally from Faerwyvae."

"So, Amelie and I…we're a quarter fae." My heart races to admit it out loud. Mother confirms my understanding with a nod. "Who was *your* father then? You told us you were born on the mainland. How did a fae male from Faerwyvae sire you?"

"I was conceived on the Fair Isle, but my mother gave birth to me on the mainland."

"She left your father?"

"I suppose you can say that, although it wasn't her choice."

"But…I remember you mentioning your father. You loved him, he was kind and strong. If your mother left him, who is the father you spoke to me and Amelie about?"

"My father didn't stay on the isle. He was exiled to the mainland."

"Foxglove said no fae has been exiled this century."

She gives me a sad smile. "Evie, I'm over a thousand years old."

Her words send me reeling, blood turning to ice. "A thousand years old," I echo.

"My father was King Caleos." She says it like it should mean something to me, but the name doesn't spark recognition. A sigh escapes her lips. "No, I suppose you wouldn't have heard of him. They consider his name taboo in Faerwyvae. You'll know him as—"

"The exiled Fire King."

She nods. "Before King Ustrin, my father ruled the Fire Court."

I close my eyes, trying to recall everything I've learned about the war, about Faerwyvae. Most of what I know, I learned from either Foxglove or Cobalt. "The Fire King had an affair with a human woman. The humans executed her when they found she was pregnant with the child of a fae."

"And he burned down her village in retribution, killing everyone who didn't flee in time."

"That sparked the war," I say.

"Yes. The war went on for decades, and my father was exiled at the end of it. That's when he was reunited with me and my mother."

"Reunited...are you saying...but his lover was killed. You just said so yourself."

"My mother was executed, burned at the stake, but she didn't die. Can you imagine why?"

"No, it's impossible."

"She didn't die because she was pregnant with me. As daughter of the Fire King, I am strengthened by fire. It was my life inside her that kept her heart beating when her flesh was scorched. It was my life that helped her slowly heal from her wounds."

My breath hitches as I look at my mother under a new light. All this time...she's been the Fire King's daughter. She's been fae.

She continues. "My maternal grandmother prayed over my mother's corpse late into the night, long after all the spectators left. It was she who discovered the healing as it began to take place. That's when she sought the first fae she could find—a lunar fae—and bargained her life for a promise that my mother and I would be taken to safety. The lunar fae took my grand-mother's life and burned her body, leaving it in my mother's place for the humans to find the next day."

I've seen a lot of blood and gore during surgery, but the images in my head are somehow far more grim. The willing sacrifice of a life to save one's child is more than I can imagine. "The lunar fae kept their end of the bargain, I assume."

"Yes. The fae took my mother to the Lunar Court, where Queen Nessina offered her sanctuary until she healed. Not even my father knew she lived, which was why he sought to avenge her death. Once Mother recovered, the queen secured safe passage for her to the mainland. I was born shortly after."

"Queen Nessina..." The name isn't familiar to me. The current ruler of the Lunar Court is Queen Nyxia, a vampire fae. "Is she Queen Nyxia's mother?"

"Yes, and she was the one who convinced the council to exile my father as his punishment at the end of the war. Very few fae know the truth, that his penance was a mercy far more than it was a death sentence. Because it reunited him with us, let him live and die at my mother's side after a human lifespan. But before the end of his life, my father took a promise from me."

"What promise?"

"That I would refuse the punishment he'd been given. That I would return to the Fair Isle and live the immortal lifespan that was my blood right."

"That's how you've been alive so long?"

She nods. "Being near Faerwyvae's magic slows my aging, but it's never been safe for me to stay in any one place for an extended period, not when my agelessness could arouse suspicion. Sometimes I returned to the mainland, living there for years or decades, which is how I met your father. There were many times I thought I would stay away from the isle for good. When I met your father, I thought I was ready to do just that, to grow old with him. But then you and Amelie were born."

Tears glaze her eyes, and I feel mine swimming in response.

She continues. "There was a light missing from the two of you, apparent from birth, and I felt it reflected inside me as well. Being on the mainland meant I was in a constant state of mental fog, of unease and illness. I had no connection to magic or healing. My existence was a flicker of life compared to the vitality I felt on the isle, and I could see my daughters were suffering the same. Amelie was a quiet, sallow, unhappy child. You were sickly and hardly did anything but cry. I realized then why my father had taken that promise from me, and why my grandmother had sacrificed her life for my mother and me; it's one thing to suffer yourself, but it's another to watch a child languish. That's when I left your father to live in Eisleigh."

"Why didn't you ever tell us?"

"I knew I'd have to tell you eventually, and perhaps I was wrong to keep the truth from you so long. You'd stop aging once you reached adulthood and we would need to move elsewhere. But the truth was dangerous. I wanted to keep the burden from you and Amelie as long as I could. By the time you were Chosen, it was too late. I couldn't bring myself to further overwhelm the two of you."

I feel a flash of anger over her excuse for not explaining things before we were taken to Faerwyvae. If we'd known the truth, at least we would have been better prepared for complications such as this. But my attention is fixated on what she said before that.

"Why was the truth so dangerous?" I ask. "I know the fae aren't allowed to live on this side of the wall, and I understand our heritage compromised the treaty, but after how lenient the mayor has been with previous mishaps with the fae, why is this considered such a serious offense?"

"It isn't just that we have fae blood," Mother says, expression grave. "It's whose fae blood we have. My father wasn't the only one included in his exile. Any possible descendants were sentenced to the same fate. My return to the Fair Isle went directly against that. And it isn't just the humans you have to fear. There are fae who feel threatened by your very existence. It's why I tried to keep you and Amelie safe from the Reaping. It's always been a precarious balance, trying to stay close enough to the wall to benefit from Faerwyvae's magic while maintaining a low profile."

"Why are the fae threatened by us?" As soon as the words are out of my mouth, I know the answer. The mayor mentioned King Ustrin last night but never explained why. I recall what the Fire King said to me when I met him, that I felt like an old enemy. "King Ustrin is responsible for this, isn't he?"

She nods. "It was he I hoped you'd never meet, as he has benefited the most from my father's exile. I wouldn't be surprised if he orchestrated his demise in the first place. Someone caught my father with a human lover and convinced the humans to execute my mother. Now that I've seen firsthand what lengths he'll go to, I'm certain he's been against my father from the start."

"How did he turn the human council so firmly against us?"

"He came to the apothecary three days ago and attacked me. I should have known his attack was a ruse. I should have known to stand down. But instinct had me returning the attack, and he saw my fire powers unleashed. As soon as he realized what I could do, he set the kitchen ablaze and disappeared." She brings her hand to her heart, rubbing her palm over her chest as if the memory pains her.

"Is the apothecary..."

"It's gone, Evie." Her voice is a hoarse whisper. "I was still trying to smother the flames when the sheriff came. And the mayor. They took me into custody before the firefighters arrived. I've been told it is nothing but a charred husk."

My stomach churns at the impossibility of what she's saying. The apothecary, her life's passion, *our home*...it's gone. "Why did you come with them? Why didn't you fight them with these fire powers you have?"

"I didn't dare make any move against them, not when there was a chance I could convince them they were wrong. I knew King Ustrin would have given my identity away, but I underestimated how far he would go. He threatened the council, saying he would tell the fae that the humans broke the treaty by giving them a fae girl for the Reaping instead of a human like the treaty demands. That's why the human council is so adamant about punishing me."

"That's the real reason they're giving Aspen a final chance with a new set of Chosen." I nearly choke on the name of my mate. "They're trying to shift the responsibility back to him."

Mother nods. "Still, I'd hoped I'd be able to sway them in the end, but I now know that was folly."

The defeat in her tone slashes at my heart, and I'm torn between guilt and sorrow. Guilt because the mayor was right. We are fae and Mother has been hiding our heritage. We've broken the law. But I feel sorrow too because I know what this is costing her. What this is costing all of us. It feels like that sorrow will open a chasm in the ground beneath me and swallow me whole. There's only one thing I can do to keep from losing my mind. Seek logic. Truth. "They say they have proof. What does that mean?"

Her face pales. "Yesterday, Henry Duveau paid me a visit."

"What is the significance of Mr. Duveau?"

"He's the descendant of the original councilman who exiled my father. I take it by now you know about the fae Bonding ritual?"

"I have some firsthand experience." I ignore the crushing pain in my chest at the confession.

"The councilman who exiled my father did so with the power of the Bond, but it wasn't just a regular Bond between them. It was a Legacy Bond, meaning it's passed on by bloodline instead of ending with the death of the bargainers. My father's Bond was extended to me, and I have passed it on to you and Amelie. Likewise, the original councilman passed it down through his family. Ever since the end of the war, Eisleigh's council always reserves a seat for a man of the councilman's blood. That's their guarantee against any of my father's descendants breaking the treaty with their return. All Mr. Duveau has to do is use my name—*all our names*—and we will be forced to obey our exile."

"So that's who Mr. Duveau is."

"Yes. He has the power of my name and can use it against me. He did just that when the mayor brought him to my cell yesterday. With the power of my name, he commanded me to take his knife and cut myself. I did. They watched me bleed. Then they witnessed my skin heal right before their eyes."

My shoulders slump, and I feel that chasm of sorrow widen, feel myself slipping into it. It's over. All of it. The council has irrefutable proof. Her trial will be nothing more than a farce. A mercy.

"There's no hope," I whisper.

Mother gives me a sad smile. "Not for me, no. But there may be hope for you."

"What do you mean, there's hope for me?" I search my mother's face for understanding. "There's nothing we can say to aid our case. We're going to be exiled."

She leans closer to the bars, lowering her voice to a whisper. "Not if you run."

My stomach takes a dive. "I'm not going to do that, Mother. If Amelie and I don't present ourselves at your trial, they are going to execute you."

"It's a sacrifice I'm willing to make."

"Well, I'm not."

Her eyes well with tears, but they crinkle at the edges as she forces a smile. "Everything I've done since you girls were born was to give you the best possible life. I'll gladly give mine if it means you get to live."

"Don't say that." My voice is a furious whisper. "You aren't giving your life for us, and that's the last I'll hear of it. Sure, it may be unfair that we're being punished for the crimes of our ancestor, but the law is the law. At least this way all three of us keep our lives. We'll be exiled, but we'll be together. We can live out the remainder of our days in peace. No compromising the treaty. No hiding from fae who feel threatened by us."

She shakes her head. "You don't know what you're giving up by leaving the isle. Life on the mainland is but a half-life for those with fae blood."

"But it's worth living. You said so yourself; you were willing to stay before we were born. And your father was given a merciful punishment by being

allowed to live a mortal life with his loved ones. I'm willing to do the same."
Despite my optimistic words, my throat constricts at the bitter taste of them.
Deep down, a spark of rage threatens to ignite.

"You deserve so much more. You deserve to live a long life, to thrive on
your own magic—"

"What magic, Mother?" I say with a glare. My anger burns brighter. Even
though I know it's misdirected, it feels better than sorrow. My hands ball into
fists. "Magic is nothing but trouble. Up until now, I lived without magic just
fine. I was happy before I went to Faerwyvae. Amelie was happy. You were
happy. I was going to go to medical school, and I would have if not for the
idiotic Reaping. If not for a chance encounter while making a pointless
offering at the wall."

Angry tears spring to my eyes as memories of that first time I met Aspen
swim through my mind. I have yet to confess to Mother or Amelie that
meeting him is what prompted all of this. My rage grows and grows, boiling
inside me like a kettle ready to howl. I rise to my feet, gripping the bars of
her cell.

"Evelyn—"

"It's my fault." The words burst from between my teeth and through my
lips, hot tears streaming down my cheeks. "It's my fault for speaking to
Aspen at the wall the night before the Reaping. And it's his fault for
choosing me after he killed the Holstrom girls. It's your fault for endangering the treaty by bringing us here. And it's your father's fault for burning
a village, and the villagers' fault for executing his lover. It's Queen Nessina's
fault for spiriting your mother away and telling no one. It's everyone's fault
including my own and it makes me so furious I feel like I'm going to
explode."

Heat radiates from my core, down my arms, and into my palms. I let out
a shout of frustration, and with it comes a flash of light followed by molten
heat beneath my fingers. I spring away from the bars, my fury evaporating
into shock as I stare at the glowing metal where my hands just were. In their
place are two bright orange prints, as if the bars were partially melted by my
hands.

Mother stands, eyes wide as she watches the glow slowly begin to cool.

"What was that?" I manage to gasp.

"Your magic. *Our* magic."

I grip my stomach, nausea turning inside me as I stare at the bars even
after the glow dissipates. Then I return my attention to my mother. "How did
I do that?"

"Rage is an element of fire," she says gently.

"Why am I only able to do this now?"

"This isn't new, my love. You've always been able to manipulate fire, although I must say, never in such a literal sense."

"What do you mean?"

"Why else do you think you have always been drawn to the healing arts, Evelyn? The element of fire is more than physical flame. It's deeper. It encompasses pleasure, passion, anger, creativity. In healing, it's the life force energy that animates living beings. I channel that life force into every tonic I make, let it flow into every spell and charm, even when working with the earthen elements I favor as an herbalist. You work with the same life force too, my dear."

My eyes search hers, a chill of understanding crawling up my spine.

She continues. "You've always held the talent to heal, to weave someone's inner fire, to strengthen their life force. You used it long before you picked up a scalpel."

My mind spins with memories. Lorelei's leg. Aspen's surgery. The silly motions I performed when I was a child, laying my hands on Mother's shop patrons. "I wish you would have told me."

"I tried, Evie. You didn't believe me."

I want to argue, but she's right. When I stopped believing in magic, I stopped believing in *her*. Started ignoring everything she had to say about magic and her craft. "I had my reasons," I say. Despite my best efforts, I can't hide the note of condemnation in my tone.

As if she can read my mind, her shoulders slump. "I know, my love, and I don't blame you for it. Magic isn't infallible, and I will regret failing your sister every day for the rest of my life."

"Why did it happen? If you have these healing gifts, why didn't you know how to help Amelie when she almost died?"

"Do you remember what happened the morning before you and your sister left to play in the woods?"

"No. Nothing out of the ordinary."

"I was caught in a downpour on my way back from delivering Mrs. Collins her draught. I caught a terrible chill from it."

"What does that have to do with anything?"

"An attack by water weakens fire, Evelyn. That's an important factor you need to know for your own good."

I'm frozen with a sudden realization. I recall how weak I felt after my near drowning with the kelpie, how it took me three days to recover. I remember how awful I felt waking up with water in my lungs after Cobalt trapped me in the coral cage. Each time I've been injured underwater, I've suffered greatly from it.

"If I'd been at my full strength, I would have known there was no curse on your sister, that her discomfort was due to a physical ailment, not a magical one. I never should have tried to rely on my powers in such a state, and I should have taken her to Mr. Meeks at once. I'll live with that guilt always."

My throat feels tight as I take in the shame on her face. I sigh. "That doesn't matter anymore."

"It matters if you can learn from my mistake."

"What's there to learn?" I let out a bitter laugh. "In two weeks, we'll be going to the mainland and I'll never be bothered with magic again."

"Despite what you think now," Mother says, "being stripped from your magic is no laughing matter. When we get there, you'll see what I mean."

"Does that mean you're done fighting me on this?" I lift my brow. "You'll go peacefully to your trial and not try to convince me or Amelie to run?"

It's her turn to bark a cynical laugh. "I don't have much of a choice, Evelyn. Mr. Duveau holds me in this cell by the power of my name. After he escorts me to the Spire, I'll no doubt be restrained with water. So, if by *go peacefully* you mean do what I'm forced to do, then yes."

"Mother, we have no right to be here." My rage threatens to return, to argue against my own statement, but I breathe it away. For good measure, I cross my arms and tuck my hands beneath my elbows. "If our presence on the isle means war, then this is a sacrifice we must make. We have to save the treaty."

I can tell she's resisting the urge to disagree. "I wish you'd reconsider," she whispers. "I won't force a promise from you, but I will implore you to take your sister and find allies who will protect you. Claim the life you deserve."

My inner fire begs to rise and meet her offer, but my good sense tamps it down. "I'm not a revolutionary, Mother. I'm a surgeon. And I'm going to stand at your side from now until death and make the sacrifice that saves the most lives."

She nods and lets out a heavy breath. "I know. This is who you are."

I lift my chin. "It is."

"What does your sister think?"

It's a struggle to maintain my composure at the mention of Amelie. Mother has no idea what has happened to her. Has no idea where she is or whose thumb she's under. The same questions from yesterday pound at my head. *What if she doesn't come to the trial?*

I force a look of nonchalance. "You know how she is, Mother. So long as a favorable marriage is an option, she'll be happy. I'm sure the sheer number of eligible bachelors on the mainland will be more than enough to keep her spirits from sinking too low."

Mother holds my gaze but gives no other sign that she can see through my ruse. "Perhaps you're right."

I approach the cell and take Mother's hands through the bars, entwining our arms. It's as close as we can get to a hug. "As long as we have you, we will get through this."

She nods.

We shed a few tears as we break apart, and I try not to crumble as Lorelei and I return to the carriage. Behind the closed doors, the two of us maintain silence, and the carriage rolls into motion. Lorelei says nothing about what I did to the bars or gives any indication she'd been listening to our conversation. But she had to have seen and heard everything. I can feel it in her silence, in her burning stare.

I lean back in my seat, analyzing the conversation with my mother forwards, sideways, and back again. No matter what conclusions I try to establish, one question repeats again and again.

Where in the blazing iron is my scientific explanation for all of this?

11

———

I have magic.

I have *fire* magic.

The concept isn't any easier to comprehend now than it was at my mother's cell. I stand at the window in Mr. Meeks' parlor, chewing a nail as I stare out at the trees surrounding Mr. Meeks' property.

Lorelei's soft footsteps come up behind me. "Are you all right?"

I shrug. "As all right as I can be."

"Do you want to talk about it?"

"What's there to talk about?" I turn to face her.

Her expression is hesitant, a look I've seen her wear around Aspen but rarely with me. "There's a lot to talk about. Your mother. Her trial." She nibbles her bottom lip. "What you did at her cell."

"You saw."

She nods. "If you want to talk—"

I skirt around her and walk to the middle of the room. "I don't want to talk."

"But I know about magic. I don't personally utilize fire, but I can help you make sense of it."

Part of me wants to smile. She's come to know me well if she understands that making sense of things is my primary aim. Still, I'm not ready to verbalize what I experienced. Not when it matters so little considering I'll be leaving the isle, magic, and these strange powers behind so soon.

I open my mouth to give her an excuse when the parlor door opens.

In walks Mr. Meeks with a tray of tea and cookies. He sets it on the tea table, then faces me with a warm smile. "I thought you might want some refreshments."

"Thank you kindly," I say, hoping my words don't carry the turmoil I'm hiding.

He nods, then turns to Lorelei. "I apologize, miss, but I admit I don't know what refreshments your kind desire."

She looks from him to the tea table. "Tea and cookies are fine." Her tone is brusque, reminding me of how she spoke to me when we first met. I bristle, hoping Mr. Meeks doesn't take offense, but he doesn't seem perturbed in the least.

He takes a few steps closer to her. "Are you implying the fae eat human food?"

"Seelie fae prefer human food, yes. We are also fond of fae fruit and wine, though, and that goes for the unseelie too."

His eyes are alight with wonder, as if her words are a gift. "That is very interesting indeed." He brings a finger to his chin, watching her with a querulous expression. Lorelei crosses her arms over her chest and narrows her eyes, but Mr. Meeks doesn't seem to get the hint.

"We thank you for your consideration, Mr. Meeks," I say to avert his unwanted attention from Lorelei.

He turns to face me, cheeks flushed. "Ah, yes, and do forgive me for my questions. It's a rare thing to chat so intimately with a fae."

"Rare indeed," I say. "I can't thank you enough for allowing us to stay."

"Of course," he says, drawing closer to me. The scrutiny returns to his face as he studies me now. "How was your mother, by the way?"

I tense, searching for words. "She seemed well-accommodated. For a prisoner, that is."

"It must pain you greatly to see her like that."

"It does."

He lowers his voice. "Did she reveal anything to you? Any explanation over these allegations?"

I consider lying to him, but what would be the point? It won't change anything. "Mother confirmed that I am of fae heritage." I watch his face, waiting for it to pale, for the fear to strike his features.

Surprisingly, he remains composed. In fact, his expression seems to brighten. "Really! Oh, that is extraordinary."

"Extraordinary is a...word for it, I suppose."

He clasps his hands together and looks me over as if seeing me for the first time. When his eyes meet mine, he blinks in rapid succession. Heat rises to my cheeks as I realize what the gesture means. I take a step back. "Mr. Meeks, I'm not going to glamour you. I don't even know if I can." My statement forces me to recall what happened with the mayor, the way I imagined holding his attention in a cage, how he spoke about King Ustrin without meaning to. So perhaps I *can*, but I most certainly *won't*. It's not like I meant to do it in the first place.

His face burns beet red, and he lets out a nervous laugh. "I know dear, I know. It was but an automatic response. However, that does pose an interesting question. How much fae blood do you have?"

"I am a quarter fae."

"I do have so many questions for you. Do you mind?"

"About..."

"About your heritage. You know how keen I am to understand the fae from a scientific perspective."

"Mr. Meeks, I only confirmed my heritage today. There's not much I can tell you."

"Still, you likely hold a great deal of answers inside you. Answers the scientific community can only guess at."

Normally, I'd be as excited as he is about such a learning opportunity. Not today. Not with mental exhaustion tugging at my mind.

Mr. Meeks flushes again as he presses his lips tight and takes a step back. "Forgive me, dear girl. I dare not press you when you are clearly in no state. However, can I request your assistance later? Would you be interested in running some...experiments of sorts?"

"Like I said, I don't know how much help I could possibly be."

He waves a dismissive hand. "You'll help me plenty. It will be like old times. Me and my dearest apprentice working side by side. You never know, we could discover something that could transform human understanding of the fae."

I let out a heavy sigh. His enthusiasm is impossible to ignore. Besides, perhaps he's right. Maybe we can learn something that will further my own understanding of myself. "I'll do what I can to help."

He turns his grin on Lorelei. "And you—"

"No." She burns him with a glare, then sidles up next to me, arms still crossed over her chest.

My shoulders tense, but again Mr. Meeks is unaffected by Lorelei's sharp edges. He lets out a nervous laugh. "Once more, I beg you to forgive my overeager excitement over your heritage. You know how I can get."

I force my lips into a smile. "I do."

"Very well. I'll leave you to it. Oh, but I have yet to mention..." He extends his arm toward the tea table. "The tea I brought is of a special nature. It's something I had from your mother's apothecary. When I bought it, she said it was a formula meant to ease the nerves. I've hardly had use for it since I much prefer laudanum, but now I find the perfect recipient of its cure."

My throat feels tight as I stare at the teapot. Only now do I recognize the aromas wafting from it. The blend is one of Mother's favorites—lavender, chamomile, vetiver, and lemon balm. Mine too, although I was always loathe to admit it before. My voice finds its way past the lump in my throat. "Thank you."

Mr. Meeks extends a hand and squeezes my shoulder, then nods at Lorelei with a warm smile. "I'll be in the surgery if you need anything."

Once he leaves, I make my way to the couch. My hands tremble as I pour the tea. Tears prick my eyes as the aroma grows stronger. I bring the cup to my nose and deeply inhale. Sipping slowly, the warm liquid dances over my tongue, soothing me with its comforting familiarity.

"I don't trust him." Lorelei's voice shatters my reverie. She walks toward me, eyes narrowed to slits. "This man is your beloved mentor?"

I furrow my brow as I look at her. "You should be kinder to him, Lorelei. He's our host. I would be sleeping in a prison if it weren't for Mr. Meeks."

"I don't like his talk of experimenting on you."

"He wasn't talking about experimenting *on* me. I'm sure he just wants to ask me some questions. Besides, of course it sounds odd to you. Healing in Faerwyvae is far different than it is here. In the human realm, we make breakthroughs in the medical arts by way of experimentation."

She shakes her head. "No. It's more than that. It's..." Her words dry on her lips, and for a moment she sways on her feet.

"What is it?"

She puts a hand over her forehead, then comes to sit next to me on the couch. "I'm not feeling well."

My stomach sinks. I haven't worried much over Lorelei's state of health since last night, but being this far from Faerwyvae can't be getting any easier for her. I set down my cup and reach for the other, then I fill it with tea and hand it to her. "Drink this. I doubt it will help much, but you'll feel calmer. It has lavender, chamomile, lemon balm—"

"Iron?" Her eyes are wide as she stares at the cup in her hands. She all but throws the cup on the table, rising to her feet. "Those cups are painted iron. That's what is making me feel ill right now."

I look at the two cups, both painted white. There's no sign that they're made from iron; before I examined them, I assumed they were porcelain. "Why would he serve us..." I can't bring myself to finish my train of thought.

Lorelei backs away from the table. "We need to get out of here."

My heart begins to race. "It can't be what we think this is. It was a mistake, an accident. An experiment, perhaps."

She darts toward the front door but pauses before it. "Someone's on the other side."

I run to her and take her hand in mine, then pull her toward the side door. It leads to the hallway and the kitchen, where we can leave out back. I fling the door open and freeze. Mr. Meeks stands on the other side, an apologetic smile on his face as I hear the front door swing open behind us.

I whirl to find Mr. Osterman in the doorway, a spear of ash and iron in his one remaining hand. His eyes burn into Lorelei. Spear aimed, he charges forward. I launch myself toward Lorelei, but an arm pulls me back.

"I'm sorry, my dear," Mr. Meeks whispers as something metal covers my nose and mouth. An inhalation cone. I recognize the familiar scent of chloroform.

Lorelei's scream is the last thing I hear.

12

───────

A subtle sound creeps upon my awareness. *Evie. Evie.*

It's my name, I realize, although the voice sounds far away. *Evie. Evie.*

"Evie." The voice becomes clear. It's Aspen's. I pry my eyes open and find myself lying on a bed in a dimly lit room. Aspen stands over me, face pale as his eyes take in his surroundings. "What in oak and ivy is this place?"

I push myself to sit, expecting to feel a head rush, but nothing more than an odd sense of mental fog comes over me. Like Aspen, I look around the room. It reminds me of Mr. Meeks' surgery, but it's far too small and cluttered, not to mention unfamiliar. Shelves line the walls full of bottles and boxes.

My heart leaps into my throat when I notice the operating tools laid out on a tray next to me. That's when I realize I'm not in a bed but on a table. An operating table.

Did something happen? Was I injured?

I try to recall the last thing I remember, but it's a blur. There was my visit with my mother. Was I hurt? No, I remember leaving. Then returning to Mr. Meeks' house. I remember the parlor, the tea, the arrival of Mr. Osterman...

Panic threatens to overwhelm me, but Aspen's presence and the violet aura around him tell me something important; this is a dream. Was my last memory a dream too? It must have been. Mr. Meeks would never...he'd never...

I refuse to consider it further until I have more proof. My anxiety lowers to a simmer, but I can't shake the wariness I feel in this unsettling environment.

"I liked the last dream better," I say, voice like a croak.

Aspen whirls back toward me, relief washing over him. "Where are you?"

I shrug. "I've never seen this place. I don't know why I'm dreaming about it."

"You need to get out of here," Aspen growls. "What happened?"

I ponder his question but can't seem to make sense of anything through the fog in my mind.

Aspen takes me by the shoulders. His touch feels the same as the last time I dreamed of him—warm but with something missing in our touch, like a barrier lies between us. "Evie, tell me what's going on."

I open my mouth, but a rumble of voices distracts me. The voices sound both near and far at the same time, but I recognize one of them. It's Mr. Meeks. I stagger to the other side of the room and through the doorway. To the right stand three shadowed figures at the end of a dingy hall, lit by the faint glow of a single light bulb overhead. There isn't a window to be seen, and only one other door occupies the hall, just across from where I stand.

Fearing I've been spotted, I pull myself back into the room, then slowly peer out again. I see the faces of Mr. Meeks, Mr. Osterman and—I suppress a shudder—Mr. Duveau. None, however, appear to have noticed me.

Aspen tenses at my side as he stares daggers down the hall. He seems far less concerned about being seen and ignores my every attempt to pull him behind the threshold with me. When sudden movement catches my eye, I stop tugging Aspen's shirt. Instead, I watch Mr. Duveau pass a pouch into Mr. Meeks' hands, expression hard. "You have some nerve bringing the Fairfield girl here," Mr. Duveau says. "I can't have her dying before the trial."

"I'm not going to kill her, Henry," Mr. Meeks says. "The girl is dear to me, regardless of bloodline."

"I can't have her talking about this...*operation*...you and Mr. Osterman have here either."

Mr. Meeks waves a dismissive hand. "Why do you think I brought her in unconscious? She will leave the same way. She agreed to help me with my scientific research. I believe once the shock wears off, she will understand quite well what had to be done. She's a sensible girl, I promise you."

"You better be right. If anything goes awry, I'm holding you responsible. If she takes word of this to the Council of Eleven Courts, the fae would consider it a breach of treaty."

"I assure you," Mr. Meeks says, "she will know nothing of her whereabouts or what we do here aside from this being a place for scientific study."

Mr. Duveau gives a curt nod. "I'll be back for the wood nymph this evening when it's time to take Maven Fairfield to the Spire."

Mr. Osterman's face breaks into a dark grin. "Can I have fun with her first?"

Mr. Duveau fixes the large man with a glare. "The patrons of the Briar House have exotic tastes, but they don't like their merchandise damaged. Do what you will, but be sure she is whole and of sound mind by the time I return tonight. You have her in iron?"

Mr. Osterman nods.

"Good. Until this evening." Mr. Duveau turns from the men and ascends a narrow staircase behind them. Daylight flashes overhead for a moment before the hall is plunged back into semi-darkness.

Mr. Meeks faces Mr. Osterman, an exasperated look on his face. "Did you have to mention having fun with the wood nymph in front of Henry?"

Mr. Osterman grunts. "He didn't seem to mind."

"Well, I do. I don't like hearing you speak like that."

"You know what happens behind my door as well as I do."

Mr. Meeks brushes his hands on the apron he wears, wrinkling his nose in distaste. "Well, do be quiet about it. I won't have you frightening Miss Fairfield while we are at work."

"I can do quiet."

"No screams."

"I'll grab rope then."

"Rope?"

Mr. Osterman's mouth twists with a disgusting grin. "I like using rope when I don't get to make them scream."

Mr. Meeks shakes his head. "Your tastes are far beyond my means to understand."

Mr. Osterman chuckles, then heads toward the staircase while Mr. Meeks starts down the hall toward us. I spring back into the room, pressing myself against the wall, chest heaving as I process everything I just heard. Aspen stands in the doorway, eyes still locked on the hall as his body trembles with rage, his violet aura writhing to match.

That's right; this isn't happening. This is a dream.

With shaking steps, I return to Aspen's side and watch Mr. Meeks approach. The man shows no sign that he can see either of us. "Why am I dreaming this?" My words do nothing to snag his attention. Mr. Meeks opens the door across the hall and peeks inside. It's too dark for me to see what lies within. His expression is grim as he closes the door and faces this one instead. Now I know for certain we're invisible. He should be able to see us.

As he enters the room, he flips a switch and the buzz of electricity hums overhead, illuminating several bulbs hanging from the ceiling. The dim room comes into full view, and I see now what lines the shelves. A vibrant, ruby-red heart is preserved in a thick green liquid encased in glass. Bones, talons, and teeth fill countless jars. A pair of enormous blue wings like a dragonfly's rest on the topmost shelf. A set of smaller green wings are set upon it.

Aspen takes my face in his hands, his terrified eyes locked on mine. "Evie, it's time to wake up now."

I pull my face away, craning my neck to see Mr. Meeks nearing the table I had been lying on. A table I'm *still* lying on. As if standing outside myself, I see my unconscious form strapped to the table by metal cuffs locked around my wrists and ankles. I've been stripped down to my corset and knickers, sending a wave of nausea through me. Even my rowan berry necklace has been removed.

Mr. Meeks approaches his table of tools and selects a scalpel. With his free hand, he gently brushes a strand of my hair off my face as he looks down at me with his kind, fatherly smile.

Aspen forces my gaze back on him. "Wake up, Evie."

My entire body is racked with tremors.

Aspen's eyes are pleading, hands warm on my cheeks. His voice rises to a shout. "WAKE UP!"

I OPEN MY EYES AND FIND MYSELF IN THE SAME ROOM I WAS DREAMING ABOUT. How can that be? My mind still feels cloudy, but it's slowly beginning to sharpen.

Mr. Meeks stands over me, just as he was in the dream. Only my perspective has changed. "Miss Fairfield, so good to see you awake."

"Where am I?" My throat feels like it's coated in cotton. Aspen is nowhere in sight.

"I'm so sorry to distress you, but this was the only way I could bring you here."

"Where. Am. I." I say it through my teeth.

"In my laboratory. It's a rare thing I get to do this kind of work, and I'm so grateful to have your assistance."

I try to sit but remember the metal cuffs around my wrists and ankles.

He follows my gaze and runs a finger over the cuff at one of my wrists, brow furrowed. "Does the iron hurt you?"

I almost say no but stop myself, some instinct urging me to lie. So I wince. "Yes, the iron burns. It weakens me."

He nods and returns the scalpel to the tray, then faces the counter behind him. I lift my head and watch as he scribbles notes on a sheet of paper. "Interesting," he mutters.

I drop my head as he finishes his notations and turns back to me. "Where's Lorelei?"

"She's fine."

"She was stabbed with a spear." Even though I didn't see it, I know it's true.

Mr. Meeks offers a comforting smile. "I'm sure it appeared that way to you, but Mr. Osterman meant her no harm. She reacted violently when she saw him with the spear and may have been injured when Hank defended himself. But she has already recovered and returned to Faerwyvae."

Lies. That is, if my dream had any truth to it. Something tells me it was more than a dream. "What's the Briar House?"

He narrows his eyes for a moment. "Nothing you should be concerned with."

It was real. Aside from Aspen being there, of course. I must have been half-awake. I must have seen this room, heard the conversation in the hall, my mind constructing it into a dream. "What are you going to do to me?"

His eyes widen as he lets out a gasp. "How could you ask such a thing as if you're frightened of me? I'm not going to hurt you, Miss Fairfield. I'm only going to gather some data like we spoke of. You said you would help me."

"I didn't say you could knock me out and restrain me."

"I'm sorry you feel like I betrayed your trust, dear girl, but I couldn't have you knowing the location of my laboratory."

"And you couldn't have asked me to come willingly with my eyes closed?"

"I never said I was a patient man." His lips pull into a grin. "This kind of work simply cannot wait. Not when you'll only be here for two weeks."

"Does that mean you plan to experiment on me for two weeks?"

"If only we had years," he says. "If only I'd known what you were when we started working together. Just think how much more the humans would know about the fae by now."

"This isn't what I agreed to."

"Which is why I had to do what I did. I do hope you can forgive me someday." He lays a gentle hand on my arm. With the other, he retrieves his scalpel.

I shout as he drags the blade over the flesh of my forearm. Once he finishes the cut, I crane my neck to examine the wound, a red line of streaming blood. I bite back tears at the searing pain. My voice comes out strained, panicked. "I thought you said you weren't going to hurt me."

"Curious," is all he says in response, brow wrinkled as he studies the wound. "You aren't healing as quickly as a full-fae would."

"I told you, I'm only one-quarter fae," I hiss through my teeth. "I may not have rapid healing abilities at all, which means this experiment is pointless."

"Not pointless." His eyes glitter with excitement. "I'm desperate to know what kind of healing can be done. In fact..." He turns toward the counter and reaches for a stoppered vial on one of the shelves above it. As he brings it to me, I see it's a deep red color.

"Is that blood?"

He nods, grinning with pride. "This one is from a brownie. I'd like to see if the blood will heal your wound. So far, fae blood has yet to show any positive effect on a human wound."

"How many fae have you killed?"

He puts a hand to his heart. "I don't kill fae, Miss Fairfield."

My eyes rove from the vial of blood to the jar of hearts, then land on the two sets of wings. "But Mr. Osterman does. You simply experiment on the ones he captures."

His expression darkens.

"Is that before or after he has his way with them?" Heat burns my core and I do nothing to extinguish it. I let it burn, radiating from my chest to my—

Mr. Meeks plunges the scalpel into my bicep, and I shout as I feel the blade dig into muscle. "Perhaps we won't experiment with healing just yet. Perhaps we will experiment with pain tolerance first." He pulls the bloody scalpel from my arm and slams it onto the tray along with the vial of blood. With a frown, he takes up a much larger knife.

I let my anger and pain burn away my fear, let it fuel the fire that rages down my arms.

Mr. Meeks moves to my other side, the tip of the knife pressed into the top of my shoulder. With a thrust, he cuts down my arm.

I scream, arching my back as the restraints hold me in place. My fire gathers hotter and hotter inside me, searing my wounds, flooding my hands.

Mr. Meeks takes a step away, eyes alight once again. "Now this is odd indeed. It seems you are beginning to heal—oh my."

The cuffs grow hot around my wrists, burning me. I close my eyes against the pain and feel the metal begin to warp. Once I can take it no longer, I lift my wrists through the molten metal, the force of my raging fire fueling me. With my wrists free, I reach for the scalpel as Mr. Meeks darts at me with the knife. I whirl toward him, thrusting the blade with a violent swipe. I don't see what happens through the blur of motion, but I feel the scalpel meet resistance. Mr. Meeks staggers back, dropping the knife and grasping his throat, ribbons of red streaming beneath his fingers.

I try not to focus on the gory sight, on the guilt that threatens to extinguish my fire. Instead, I focus on the pain of my open wounds, on the anger still burning inside me. I sit forward and press my hands over the ankle cuffs, vaguely noting that the burn marks on my wrists are beginning to heal. Once the cuffs reach a molten state, I pull my ankles from them, gasping at the pain from the blistering heat.

I push myself off the bed, landing with a cry as my ankles protest the motion. Hobbling toward the doorway, I'm suddenly aware of smoke filling my nostrils. I hazard a glance behind me to see the table linens have caught fire from the burning cuffs. Mr. Meeks still grasps his bleeding neck as he slides to the ground.

I feel another shock of guilt, but I burn it away, forcing myself out of the room, into the hall, and to the door on the other side. A soft whimper comes from within the room, and I throw the door open wide, letting the light from Mr. Meeks' laboratory wash inside. As my eyes adjust to the new environment, I see a figure against the far wall, iron shackles hanging from the ceiling, pulling Lorelei's arms overhead. A cloth gag is tied over her mouth.

I run to her and summon my rage, letting it burn through my palms as I place them over the cuffs. "I'm sorry, but this is going to hurt."

She lets out a muffled cry as the metal burns hot around her wrists. With a deep breath, I wrap my hands around the molten cuff, stifling a cry as the heat blisters my palm. Once free, she drops to the ground. I pull her up, dragging her to her feet. We cross the room just as the laboratory grows brighter, the fire blazing over the table, flames licking toward the shelves.

Knowing what kind of chemicals Mr. Meeks must have in there, it's only a matter of time before the flames set off an explosion.

"We need to hurry," I say, pulling her down the hall toward the staircase. Once we reach it, I see a door at the top. "Can you climb?"

Eyes glazed, she pulls the gag from her mouth. "Yes. Let's get the bloody oak and ivy out of here."

Smoke chases us, filling our lungs as we climb to the top of the stairs and push open the door. We scramble outside and collapse onto the earthen floor, chests heaving as we struggle to catch our breath. My vision spins but I manage to make out dense trees all around us beneath a sunset sky. I lift my head toward the smoking building we emerged from. From this vantage point, it looks like nothing more than an old-fashioned outdoor toilet, revealing no evidence of the underground operation hiding beneath it.

I think of Mr. Meeks trapped inside, fire dancing around him while ribbons of blood spill down his throat from a wound I gave him. In contrast, I recall how he sliced the scalpel and then the dagger through my arm. I think of the way he sold Lorelei to Mr. Duveau and offered her body to Mr. Osterman with nothing more than a few minor qualms.

I scoot farther from the door and lift my leg. With a kick, I slam it shut. I lay my head back in the grass, willing it to cease its spinning.

I can't stay here. I know I can't. The fire will reach the stairs, then the door, and that's only if an explosion doesn't happen first. Despite knowing this, I can't find the strength in my limbs to stand.

"Evelyn." Lorelei's panicked voice beside me prompts a rush of adrenaline. I roll onto my side and follow her line of vision.

There, between two trees, stands Mr. Osterman.

13

Mr. Osterman's eyes bulge as he stares dumbfounded at me and Lorelei. A spool of rope hangs over his shoulder, spear in hand. My body protests at the thought of moving, but I force myself to scramble to my knees, then my feet, pulling Lorelei up with me. "Run!"

As we take off, darting toward the trees, Mr. Osterman unshoulders the rope and charges after us. "Get back here!"

"We can't outrun him," I say through gasping breaths. My back tingles with the fear that any moment I'll feel the tip of his spear pierce my flesh.

"We don't have to outrun him," Lorelei says. Her voice sounds stronger now. "We're near the wall. I can feel it."

"Mr. Osterman can cross the wall, and he'll catch us before we find it."

"All we need to do is get closer to it. Just a little closer."

"Why, what will that do?" My voice is strained, the fire of my rage smothered to ash beneath my fear. My muscles scream with every move, flesh pulling at the half-healed wounds on my arms, wrists, and ankles.

Lorelei, on the other hand, looks stronger, more vital with every step, her stride becoming more and more even. A look of euphoria crosses her face.

Her confidence is of little comfort when Mr. Osterman's pounding steps and heaving breaths draw nearer and nearer. "Forget the councilman's orders," he calls out, voice taunting. "I'm going to cut you both into a thousand pieces."

I pump my legs harder, faster, stumbling over the uneven ground, ignoring the sting of branches that whip my face and arms. My lungs burn, vision going bleary. I can hardly keep up with Lorelei as she whips between the trees. I try to feel what she must feel, the call of the wall, the magic of Faerwyvae drawing her closer, strengthening and healing her. But I feel nothing. Nothing but an internal weight dragging me down.

My legs nearly give out beneath me when Lorelei holds up her hand and skids to a halt. I stumble at her side, my momentum not nearly as gracefully controlled as hers. But why have we stopped? The wall is nowhere in sight and Mr. Osterman is within range to spear us.

Lorelei takes a step toward the man as he closes the distance. He lifts his spear, an angry snarl on his lips. Lorelei raises her hands, thrusting them outward. Mr. Osterman moves as if he's about to throw his weapon when the ground rocks beneath his feet, forcing him to stumble back. A root as thick as a man's arm shoots from the earth, its tip sharp like a blade. It rears back, then barrels into Mr. Osterman, piercing straight into his chest and coming out the other side. The man convulses, blood seeping from his lips.

My stomach heaves, but I can't look away. Not until he ceases moving. Only then do I whirl around, falling on my hands and knees, and retch onto the forest floor. I retch until my stomach is empty, until hot tears stream down my cheeks. When I feel Lorelei's hand on my shoulder, I realize I'm wailing.

"You're all right." Lorelei's voice is a soothing whisper but laced into her tone is a hidden truth. I'm *not* all right. None of this is all right. I see pink from the corner of my eye and realize Lorelei is handing me a bundle of filthy chiffon. As I turn to inspect it, I see she's torn one of the layers off the skirt of her dress. That's when I remember I've been stripped to my undergarments.

I accept the fabric and do my best to tie it around my waist. "I killed someone," I finally manage to say. "I killed Mr. Meeks. My mentor. My life-long friend."

Lorelei hesitates before speaking. "There's nothing I can say to make that right for you. I can only share your burden."

A burden is exactly what this is. Will I ever be able to forgive myself? In the heat of my rage, I did what I thought I must do. I reacted. I saved myself and my friend and condemned a man to die. Of course, Mr. Meeks was by no means innocent. He may not have intended to kill me, but it was clear he had no reverence for Lorelei's life or my well-being.

But does that make it right?

"We both made difficult choices today." Lorelei's voice quavers.

I rise slowly to my feet, feeling every aching muscle in the process. When I meet Lorelei's eyes, I see conflict in them. She too killed a man today.

As if she knows what I'm thinking, she shakes her head. "I've never killed a person. Not before today."

"Do you regret it? Even though he killed Malan?"

She looks at the body impaled upon the root. "I can't say I regret it, no, but I don't feel good about it either."

"Then we feel the same."

She takes my hand and gives it a squeeze. "Come. We're close to the wall. We'll both feel better once we cross it. Physically, that is."

It's a slow journey to the wall, with neither of us pushing ourselves to the limit now that we're no longer being chased by a madman. However, we must put as much distance between us and the laboratory as we can. Mr. Duveau said he'd be back to fetch Lorelei on his way to take my mother to the Spire.

My mother.

My breath hitches. I hate to think that Mr. Duveau could punish her for what was done tonight. He warned Mr. Meeks that he'd hold the surgeon responsible if anything were to go awry. Well, awry it went, and then some. But will Mr. Duveau maintain that no harm will come to my mother until her trial? Had I allowed too much room for interpretation in that bargain? Do I even have enough fae blood to enforce a fae bargain, however that works to begin with?

The towering stones of the faewall come into view as the trees begin to thin. I don't know if it's simply relief or from our nearness to Faerwyvae, but my pains seem to lessen. My breaths come to me easier with every step we take closer. Lorelei appears to be back to full health despite her torn, bloodied dress and grave expression.

I rub my arms over my bare shoulders as we cross between two standing stones and enter the dense fog. Only when it fades to reveal a spring meadow do we stop. We fall to our knees and sink into the plush, dew-covered grass. Night has fully fallen and all is quiet around us. Pink blossoms sway in the trees at the edge of the meadow while opalescent moths flutter through the night sky.

Lorelei tilts her head to the stars, as if bathing in their radiance. My eyes rove her wrists, and I see nothing but the faintest marks where the cuffs had chafed and the molten metal had burned. A dark stain covers her torso, probably from where Mr. Osterman speared her when he and Mr. Meeks captured us.

I examine my wrists and see that my own wounds have faded, perhaps more so than Lorelei's. My eyes then move to my arms. Aside from being smeared with dirt and dried blood, it appears the cuts have sealed shut. Is that because of my heritage? Or because I used fire? Growing up, I never noticed any unusual rate of healing for whatever minor cuts and bruises I received. Could it be I've always healed quickly?

I feel Lorelei's eyes on me. "Are any of your wounds bothering you?" she asks.

"No, they feel much improved. How about yours?"

She rubs her torso where her dress is stained with blood. "Sore, but mostly healed, I believe. The Butcher of Stone Ninety-Four let my spear wound close before he put me in the iron chains. I think he liked his prey to put up a fight."

My throat feels tight as I recall his body, the root pierced through his chest. I blink the vision away. "What do we do now?"

She looks away, brow wrinkled as she ponders. Without meeting my eyes, she says, "We could go to Autumn. King Aspen will keep you safe."

I remember the version of him in my dream, the terror in his eyes when he implored me to wake up. My heart sinks to think of him, especially when I consider the truth. Aspen wasn't there. He's home safe in Bircharbor Palace with his new Chosen. Just like I said I wanted.

"No, I can't go there."

She doesn't question me or press further. Instead, she plays with a blade of grass, expression deep in thought.

"Is there anywhere safe to stay in Spring? We're already on the Spring axis. Perhaps there's somewhere I could lie low until my mother's trial."

She tilts her head as she contemplates. "Spring is a neutral seelie court, so you may be safe here. I don't dare bring you to the palace though. If word has spread about who you are and what the humans have planned for you, there could be many who would either take you to King Ustrin or return you to Eisleigh. The same goes for any seelie ruler, in fact."

"Maybe I should go back." I shudder. "I should have taken my imprisonment to begin with. None of this would have happened if I had."

"You don't belong in a prison."

"Neither does my mother."

She lets out a sigh. "If you feel you must go back, I can't forbid you. But I don't believe they will be kind if you do."

She's probably right. After what I did, locking me in the Spire would be a mercy. Mr. Duveau's bargain only stated no harm would come to my mother. He made no promise about me. There's a good chance he would force me to spend my days before Mother's trial in the care of another surgeon like Mr. Meeks, or perhaps he'd take me where he was planning on taking Lorelei.

"Do you know what the Briar House is?"

Lorelei's lips pull into a snarl. "A brothel, most likely." Her anger fades quickly, shoulders slumping. "Now that I know what the Butcher likes to do with his victims, I think Malan's fate may have been a kindness."

I remember the wings I saw on the shelves in Mr. Meeks' laboratory, the jars of hearts and blood.

"That's the only place I can think to bring you," she says. "To Malan's parents. I don't even know if they would agree to harbor you, but they're the only spring fae I know outside of the palace."

I can tell by her expression that's the last place she wants to go. "You feel the same way about Spring that I feel about Autumn."

She nods. "But I made Aspen a promise."

"You promised him you'd watch over me while I was in Eisleigh."

"*And* until the situation with your mother was settled. To me, that means until her trial. I won't leave your side."

"I can't ask you to take me to the home of your deceased mate."

She plays with another blade of grass, and we fall into silence. After a while, she freezes, her stillness drawing my attention. "There's somewhere else I can take you."

"Where?"

She grimaces, and I already know this option doesn't make her any happier. "The Lunar Court."

14

———————

"The Lunar Court?" I say with a gasp. "But they're unseelie."

Lorelei shrugs. "In this instance, that's not necessarily a bad thing."

"Why do you say that?"

"Like I said, there's a chance any seelie court will turn you in to either King Ustrin or Eisleigh's council. The radical seelie most certainly will, seeing you as a threat to the treaty. The radical unseelie will do...well, they will do far worse, if they think they can use you to purposefully break the treaty. The *neutral* unseelie courts, however, are probably the safest for you right now."

"I take it the Lunar Court is considered neutral unseelie?"

Lorelei nods. "They don't care about saving the treaty, which means they will have no qualms harboring you. However, they aren't determined to eradicate humans either."

"Are there any other neutral unseelie courts?" I try to hide my trepidation with an air of nonchalance. The thought of seeking asylum with Queen Nyxia—a vampire fae—does not sound appealing. Then again, going to any unseelie court seems like a bad idea.

"Lunar and Wind are both neutral unseelie, while Winter and Sea are radical."

"You think Lunar is the best option?"

She meets my eyes and lowers her voice. "I heard what your mother said about Queen Nessina harboring your grandmother."

"You think Queen Nyxia has her mother's sensibilities?"

Lorelei rises to her feet, brushing grass from what remains of her tattered skirt. "I'm not certain, but she's our best chance right now. Besides, she owes me." She extends her hand and pulls me to my feet. "Come. The Lunar axis is the next one west of here. If we start walking now, we'll get there before morning."

I take a step, surprised to find that my muscles have stopped screaming. "Why does Queen Nyxia owe you?"

She nibbles her bottom lip. "Let's just say we have a history."

My curiosity is burning, but I force myself not to pry. If she feels like clarifying, I'm sure she will sooner or later. In the meantime, I can only hope she's right about her.

ALL RELIEF I FOUND FROM REST IS WASHED AWAY AFTER HOURS OF WALKING. The only thing that keeps me going are my occasional bursts of anger. Each time I feel it rise, I allow it to grow, to burn away my exhaustion, to fuel my healing. That healing is all that keeps me on my feet, prevents me from succumbing to the torturous pain the earth causes my bare feet. I'm still not sure what to think of this newfound power with the element of fire and can't help wondering what else I might be able to do.

Of course, such thoughts take me down a dark path as blood and smoke and flames fill my mind.

We keep the fog of the faewall within our periphery at all times to help us navigate within the confines of the axis line. It feels like we'll never find anything but spring grass, sparkling dew, and delicate blossoms. Even in the dark of the night, it's clear we are traveling through Spring.

Luckily, due to our proximity to the wall, we cross no fellow travelers, save for several rabbits, a doe, and countless squirrels. Whether these creatures are regular animals or fae in their unseelie forms, I do not know. In Faerwyvae, is there even such a thing as a *regular animal*?

The sun is just beginning to rise, illuminating the early morning, when our scenery finally changes. At first, it's a shift in the light. The blush of the sunrise dims, throwing our surroundings under a hazy filter. It reminds me of the sky before a lightning storm or the eerie quality of light that falls over everything during a solar eclipse.

Lorelei lets out a sigh of relief. "We made it to Lunar."

The feeble hope that we can now rest sparks within me, but it's quickly dashed to bits when Lorelei quickens her pace and shifts direction. With a deep breath, I try to connect to my inner fire and follow her.

We move away from the wall and deeper into the Lunar forest. Even the trees look different here, with tall, slim trunks that disappear high overhead where dark branches in shades of deep indigo and violet mingle with the more familiar browns and greens. Clusters of elegant brambles blanket the forest floor while dark vines of ivy snake up the trees.

There's no obvious season, just a moderately cool temperature and the smell of night-blooming jasmine. As the sun rises higher, the forest grows somewhat brighter, but the eerie quality of light doesn't diminish.

We continue on, going deeper and deeper into the forest. It's quiet, as if most of the creatures here are asleep. In fact, I spot several animals in the midst of slumber. Tiny bats cling to branches, dozing upside-down, wings wrapped around their bodies like blankets. A feline purr rumbles behind a patch of flowers with glowing, bell-like blooms, revealing nothing but two black, pointed ears. Owls doze in the beams overhead, occasionally opening an eye to study us. Surprisingly, a few fully awaken when we pass, launching from their branches to take flight.

"Messengers," Lorelei says under her breath. "Nyxia will know we're here."

I suppress a shudder. "Are we nearing the Lunar palace?"

She nods, the movement revealing the tenseness in her posture. Her eyes are narrowed as she stares into the distance, attention fixated on the path ahead. "We've crossed the axis and have been transported about an hour's walk from the palace."

My pulse begins to race. While our arrival will mean relief from walking, I feel only trepidation about everything else regarding the visit. Meeting the Lunar Queen, in particular. My only experience with Queen Nyxia was her involvement with Aspen's challenge for his throne when she acted as mediator between Aspen and Cobalt. Even though she ultimately decided in Aspen's favor, before that, she'd supported Cobalt's claim. I'm not sure what to make of her. I swallow hard, preparing to keep my voice level. "Is there anything I should know about Queen Nyxia before we arrive?"

Lorelei seems uncertain of what to say. "She's very powerful." Her tone doesn't reveal whether that's a good or bad thing.

"Powerful in what way?"

"She's quite...dominating in both her seelie and unseelie forms."

I remember how she shifted into a towering shadow with red eyes and terrifying fangs when the fighting began after Cobalt lost. "What exactly is she in her unseelie form? I mean, I've surmised she's a vampire, but what does she become when she's a shadow?"

"In her unseelie form, she takes the shape of fear and can delve into others' minds, finding their darkest thoughts and bringing them to the surface. That's how she feeds. While she can terrify a victim any time of day, she specializes in feeding off nightmares."

I want to know if she feeds off more than fear—blood, specifically—but I can't bring myself to ask. What little I've heard about vampires always includes some tale of bloodlust and the sinking of fangs into an unwilling victim's flesh. I rub my neck reflexively.

Lorelei grimaces. "I'll warn you now that you might have odd dreams while we're there."

"That's comforting."

She halts, posture rigid as she holds an arm out for me to stop as well. "Someone's here," she whispers.

With my thoughts swarming with blood and vampires, I can't suppress the shiver that crawls up my spine. A sound rustles in the brambles up ahead before a dark shape launches into the trees. I let out a heavy sigh. "A raven."

Lorelei doesn't seem nearly as relieved. She turns her gaze to the branches overhead, lips pulling into a frown.

"Well, Lorelei, don't you look like the wrong end of a centaur." A low, drawling male voice trickles down from somewhere above us, but I can't locate its source. Is the raven talking? "And what is with that dress? I don't think I've ever seen you in pink. I do like how you've decorated it, though."

My eyes move to the blood staining Lorelei's torso, then to the layer of grime coating my corset and makeshift skirt.

Lorelei crosses her arms and bumps her hips to the side. "Did Nyxia send her dog?"

I hear a gasp. "Now that's plain rude."

"Rude? You just called me the wrong end of a centaur."

"But I don't even like dogs."

"And I like centaurs?"

A dark shape falls to the ground. As it lands, shadows unfurl, revealing a male figure. His frame is lean and tall, skin pale, eyes the most shocking shade of silver-blue above chiseled cheekbones flushed the palest rose. His hair is a silver blond that falls in silken wisps past his pointed ears. He wears a black silk waistcoat and trousers, both patterned with silver threaded designs, but he wears no jacket. His white shirt is unbuttoned at the neck, free of cravat or tie. There's something frighteningly seductive about his state of dress.

He leans against the trunk of the tree behind him, posture casual as he waves a hand toward Lorelei. "You have that...earthen magic. You're practically related to a centaur."

Lorelei scowls. "I'm a wood nymph, and you are clearly trying to get on my nerves."

He tilts his head, lips pulling into a sultry smile. "I didn't realize I had to try so hard."

She rolls her eyes. "Is your sister at the palace?"

"Why, is she back in your good graces? Come to rekindle that spark?"

"There's no spark, but I seek an audience with her. You'll take us to her."

His eyes fall on me for the first time, assessing me from head to toe. "Us? Is this your new plaything? I thought your heart was truer than that. Darling Malan has hardly been dead for—"

Lorelei lifts her hand, and a pointed root erupts from the earth at the fae male's feet. He can hardly flinch before it rises and hovers an inch from his throat, the sharp tip vibrating as if it begs to dart forward and sink into the fae's flesh. "Don't you dare speak of Malan or so much as utter a word about me being untrue to her memory. If anyone knows about being untrue, it's your sister."

His wide eyes are all that betray his composure. He holds up his hands in casual surrender. "My apologies."

With a violent sweep of her hand, the root burrows back into the ground.

He straightens his waistcoat and extends his arm. "To Selene Palace."

Lorelei brushes past him. Before I can take a step, he faces me and folds into a graceful bow. I can't tell if he's mocking me. "Prince Franco at your service. And you are?"

"Evelyn," I mutter through pursed lips.

"Evelyn. Is that your true—"

"Don't even start." With a scowl, I rush after Lorelei.

Prince Franco matches my pace, eyes burning into me. "I like you."

"Excuse me?"

He smiles, revealing the tips of elongated canines. A vampire. "You smell like violence. That's my preferred vintage." With a nod of approval, he streams to the head of our small retinue and leads the way.

With a shudder, I force my trembling legs to keep moving.

15

Queen Nyxia is a sight to behold, as is the lush palace that surrounds her. Upon an obsidian throne, she sits with such confident authority, you'd think she's the queen of the world. Walls of moonstone and opal make up the throne room while the ceiling ends in enormous domed glass, giving an open view of the sky above.

My eyes linger on this feature as Prince Franco leads us toward his sister. "You should see it at night," he whispers in my ear.

I avert my gaze without a reply, focusing on the Lunar Queen instead. Lorelei and I drop into curtsies. As we straighten, Nyxia rises from her obsidian throne and steps down from the dais to approach us while Franco sprawls on an elegant chair at the base of the throne.

My eyes are locked on Nyxia, stunned by her eclectic clothing. At the council meeting, she wore a slim black suit. Now she wears dark silk trousers with a top that is somewhere between a jacket and a dress. The material is a blue so dark it's almost black and shimmers indigo and violet when she moves. The collar is enormous, its stiff fabric lifting from the neck to frame her face at an angle. The front is cropped above her hips like a waistcoat, but the back is like an open-front skirt, trailing the ground behind her.

Like the first time I saw her, her short silvery hair is slicked back, and her smile reveals pointed canines. She assesses me from head to toe. "What an odd surprise. If it isn't Miss Evelyn Fairfield."

I force my words past my lips, hoping I can manage them without a stutter. "I come seeking your hospitality for a short period of time."

"Now, what would King Aspen's mate be doing seeking hospitality with me? Aren't you his beloved champion?" Her voice is laced with sarcasm. "Then again, he sure is collecting his share of mates these days, isn't he? I believe I'm supposed to witness yet another grand spectacle with a Chosen in a few days from now."

My breath hitches and I find my throat stripped of words.

Fortunately, she doesn't wait for a response, instead turning her attention to my companion. "And you, Lorelei. How wonderful to see you again. I didn't realize we were on speaking terms. You hardly said a word to me at Bircharbor." Her rosy lips pull into a pout.

Lorelei crosses her arms, throwing out all sense of formality. "Trust me, we wouldn't be on speaking terms if I didn't need to call in that favor you owe me."

She lets out a trill of laughter. "I can't believe you're still upset about what happened at Summer Solstice."

"Still upset? Solstice was less than four months ago."

"A silly accident."

Lorelei narrows her eyes at the queen. "You gave Malan traumatic nightmares. About *me*. She could hardly look at me for a week."

Nyxia shrugs. "I don't create the nightmares from nothing. They come from existing fears."

"And you fed off hers."

Another casual laugh. "I was jealous. You know how protective I am over you."

"If you wanted to be so protective, you would have tried harder to keep me around in the first place."

"If I recall, you were the one who ended things with me."

Lorelei grinds her teeth. "And if *I* recall, you cheated on me. With seventeen other fae. At once."

Nyxia waves her hands in a dismissive gesture. "It was Beltane."

My cheeks grow warm, and I wish I could shrink on the spot. This is not the kind of conversation I feel like I should be present for.

Franco watches me through slitted lids, then slides lazily from his seat. Nyxia and Lorelei are still arguing by the time he makes it to my side. "Come. They'll be at this for a while."

Lorelei whirls toward us, eyes furious as they lock on Franco. "Don't you dare take her anywhere."

"Don't worry about it," Nyxia says. "Until I make a formal decision about whatever you've come here for, she's under my protection. Franco can take her to the baths. Speaking of, you could use one yourself. Why don't we get you out of those filthy clothes."

Lorelei rounds on the queen. "Oh, that's just so like you. Turn every serious topic into a seduction—"

"Told you. Come on." Franco waves his hand forward. "I'll take you to the moon baths."

He starts toward the door, but I hesitate, eyes flashing from the prince to the arguing pair. With a sigh, I give in and follow Prince Franco.

The prince winks as I catch up to him. "Bet you didn't know you were in for that treat."

"Can't say that I did," I mutter.

"Don't worry, they'll cool off in an hour or so. Although, I doubt they'll be making up in the same fashion as they used to."

We continue down the moonstone halls in silence. My heart races with every step, both from the unfamiliar territory and my unsettling companion. I feel his eyes burning into me more often than not, and I wish he'd just keep his gaze to himself.

"So, you're the Evelyn Fairfield I've heard so much about."

I suppress an irritated grumble. "What exactly have you heard?"

"That you're King Aspen's mate."

"I am." The statement is a barbed defense against his unwelcome stare, but as soon as the words are out of my mouth, I realize their futility. I might be Aspen's mate, but it means nothing now. Not when I'll never see him again. Not when he's about to marry another. "I mean, no. Not really."

His lips quirk into a grin. "Not really. How interesting. Are you too proud to share him with his new Chosen? Or is it King Ustrin's venom against you that has you running to Selene Palace?"

"It's none of your business."

"It might be, if you are to stay here for a time. Selene Palace is not just my sister's home. It's mine too."

I keep my lips pressed tight as we continue through the palace. Finally, we come to an ornate sliding door. As the prince pushes it open, wafts of steam spiral into the hall. We enter, and I find three enormous pools inside the room. The ceiling is domed glass like the throne room, with that eerie light bathing everything in a dusky glow. The smell of jasmine and gardenia beckon from the calm waters.

Franco faces me. "Welcome to the moon baths. This is another place I recommend you come at night. I'll keep this room private and have a servant bring fresh clothes. In the meantime, make yourself at home." With that, he shudders and transforms into a black raven. I jump, hand to my pounding heart as I watch the raven prince fly into the hall.

Alone in the bathhouse, I stare at the pools. The size of the room and the vast sky above make me feel vulnerable. Even though I'm the only one here, I feel exposed, but the thought of cleanliness is too tempting to ignore.

Before I can change my mind, I hurry to peel off my filthy clothing. Luckily, my corset has been torn enough that I can remove it without aid. Then I slip beneath the soothing waters.

ONCE CLEAN, I FIND MY PILE OF CLOTHES HAVE BEEN REPLACED WITH A THICK towel and a dress in a lightweight shimmery fabric the color of fire opals. I pull the dress over my head, relieved to return to the freedom of fae clothing after the confines of my corset.

Unsure where to go now, I take a few hesitant steps past the sliding door and into the hall. Lorelei leans against the far wall, arms crossed. She appears to have gotten cleaned and changed as well, all blood and grime wiped from her brown skin, a long, silky, black dress clinging to her form. Her expression looks relieved when she sees me. "Oh good, Franco didn't drown you."

"You should be surprised I didn't drown *him*."

"True." She gives me a halfhearted smile, then nods toward the other end of the hall. "Come. Nyxia has rooms for us so we can rest."

I follow her eagerly, the word *rest* like a tantalizing prize. The bath was merely a precursor to what my body truly needs after everything it's been through in the past twenty-four hours. But first, there are questions that need answers. "Did you explain my situation to the queen?"

Her expression darkens. "I did. She'll provide you hospitality so long as you need."

"You don't seem happy about that."

"I'm happy that we've found a safe place for you to stay."

"But you aren't happy that you have to see her because of it."

"Exactly."

"So...you and Nyxia?"

"Yeah," she grumbles. "We were a thing. Two years. She wasn't into settling down like I was. She was even less into seeing me move on to someone else. Hence her petty revenge on Malan."

It's hard for me to imagine my friend in a relationship with the domineering Nyxia. However, it's clear Lorelei can hold her own against the queen.

"That's why she owes me a favor," Lorelei says. "I nearly tore her head off, queen or no, after what she did to my lover. Like I said, prepare yourself for some uncomfortable dreams while we're here."

"Will do."

We come to a small room with walls of onyx and silver. The ceiling hosts not a dome but a glass window in the middle where faint light streams through. A bed with indigo velvet blankets beckons me from inside. Lorelei puts her hand on my arm. "You should get some rest. Do you...feel comfortable staying in this room alone? I can stay with you."

I try to offer a reassuring smile. "No, Lorelei, I'll be fine here by myself."

"Very well. I'll be in the room next door if you need anything."

She slips down the hall, and I enter my room, legs nearly puddling to liquid as I head straight for the bed. My head hardly hits the pillow before sleep overtakes me.

The nightmares begin without warning. I'm trapped in the underground laboratory again, and Mr. Meeks stands over me with a knife, the gaping wound at his neck trailing blood down the front of his apron. He cuts into my arms, my legs, my skull. I scream, but my lips are sealed shut. Fire roars around us, but instead of strengthening me, it burns the flesh from my bones. Mr. Meeks doesn't cease his operation, his knife digging into my very soul as flames char him from man to skeleton. The fire obscures my vision, but before it burns my eyes, I see the silhouette of a stag charging through the room.

Aspen.

I repeat the name like a soothing melody. The more I focus on it, the dimmer the terrifying visions become. Finally, the nightmare fades, blood and fire drifting to smoke as I follow the safety of the name. No longer is the dark lab surrounding me. Instead, a bridge spans before me, and I don't hesitate before crossing. At the other end, I find myself in the dining room at Bircharbor Palace, the sound of waves falling upon my ears.

Aspen stands at the rail near the open expanse, back facing me as he stares out at the night sky. My heart leaps at the sight of him, at his messy hair, his towering antlers, the wrinkled waistcoat that tells me he hasn't been sleeping well. Like before, a violet aura glows around him.

"Aspen." I say the word out loud this time.

He whirls, freezing when he catches sight of me. For endless moments we do nothing but lock eyes. Then his swift stride carries him across the room. His hands frame my face as his lips press into mine. My body responds to his, arms wrapping around his waist, moving up his back. Our kisses are hard and urgent, as if fighting against the strain, that discrepancy between what our touch feels like and what it *should* feel like if this were real.

It's the only thing that reminds me this is just a dream.

As if the realization comes to us both at once, our kisses slow. We separate our lips but our foreheads remain touching. "You're all right," Aspen whispers. "What happened to you?"

I swallow hard. "I don't want to talk about it."

"I wish you were really here."

"I wish I was too."

He pulls his head back, eyes swimming as they drink in mine. If only the evening light were brighter so I could better make out his beautiful eyes, the dark brown flecked with green, gold, and ruby. Eyes I should have done a better job at memorizing when I had the chance. His thumb trails over my bottom lip, then along my jaw. I take a hand from his back and place it over his chest, feeling the steady thrum of his heart beneath my palm. My breath hitches, eyes locked on his lips, ready to taste them again.

Before I can claim them, he speaks. "Where are you? I need to know you're safe."

"I'm safe. I'm—"

"Aspen." The voice that shatters the moment grates on my ears with nauseating familiarity. Maddie Coleman strides into the dining room draped in a robe—one of *my* old robes. "I thought you might show me the selkies like you promised."

Aspen stands at the rail again as if he never left it. Come to think of it, I can't recall him leaving my side. One moment he was in my arms, the next he was gone. He's no longer looking at me but at Maddie. His jaw is set, but I refuse to read more into his expression.

Because, of course, this is a dream. No. A nightmare. And if this nightmare is as visceral as my last, I can only imagine what I'll be forced to witness next.

I take one last look at Aspen. His expression falters as his eyes meet mine before I close my eyes and try to remember where I am—where I *really* am.

The Lunar Court. The bed.

I jolt upright, blankets tangled in my limbs as I blink into moonlight. My head pounds. I look around the room, expecting a dark shadow to be hovering nearby, red eyes glowing as it drinks in my nightmare. But there's nothing. No one.

I let out a shaking breath and shove the blankets off me, forcing away the dream-images that linger in my mind. As much as I enjoyed the part about Aspen, it's Maddie's smug expression that prevails. The vision of her wearing *my* robe and speaking to *my* mate with such familiarity sends a wave of burning rage through me.

I nearly let it consume me before I remind myself that Aspen isn't my mate anymore. He's about to be *hers*, and there's nothing I can do about that. Not if I want Aspen to save the treaty.

With a grumble, I get out of the bed. There's no getting back to sleep now.

16

―――――――

I find a small wardrobe in the room filled with an assortment of clothing. From within, I retrieve a midnight-blue velvet robe embroidered with stars and crescent moons. My dress is slightly wrinkled from sleeping in it, so the robe should hide that as well as warm me from the slight chill in the air.

I open my door, expecting to find darkness and quiet in the hall outside. What I don't anticipate is the bustle of activity that greets me. Dark has fallen over the hallway, but orbs of light that resemble moonlight hover along the walls. Fae float by in pairs and triplets, speaking animatedly. And I say *float* literally, as most of the fae appear to be sprites and specters, their bodies hovering above the ground like wisps of flame or smoke. Some are tiny, about as tall from the ground as my kneecap, while others are of average human height. A couple glance my way, but most are too distracted to pay me much heed. I can only guess they must be servants.

I scurry to the room next door and tap a light knock. "Lorelei."

A dark shape dives down from the opalescent beams of the ceiling, materializing as Prince Franco by my side. I lurch back. "Could you not do that?"

He leans lazily against the wall next to Lorelei's door. "I wouldn't wake her. She's sleeping deeply, and it wasn't easy for her to find restfulness."

"How do you know?"

He shrugs. "I can sense her dreams."

I bristle, wondering if he's to blame for my uncomfortable nightmares. "Are you like your sister then?"

"Not exactly," he says. "I'm not nearly as powerful."

I pull my robe tighter around me, then cross my arms over my chest. "What is it you do then?"

"I can sense dreams and feed off their energy in a similar way that Nyxia can. But she can do more. She can enter another's dream space, prompt fears and memories to the surface that she can use as nourishment. She can't control the dream, but she can give the dreamer a nudge in the direction she'd like them to go."

He flashes me a smile, revealing his pointed canines. It brings to mind a very specific concern I have yet to find clarity on, one I know I should handle with some delicacy. Which, of course, is not my specialty. "Is it always fear you and Nyxia feed off of?"

"Fear is one of the strongest emotions to use as nourishment as well as one of the easiest to elicit from another, but we feed off any emotion that offers an enticing taste."

Perhaps I was too delicate. "Is there...anything else you feed on?"

He looks at me through slitted lids, the corners of his lips revealing his amusement. "I take it you're hinting at something. Perhaps you should ask me directly."

Heat flushes my cheeks. "Do you drink...blood?"

He smirks. "Depends whose blood and how tempting it is to taste it."

Great. This is just great. It's a struggle not to bring my hands up to cover my neck.

Franco lets out an amused chuckle. "No, I don't drink blood. I'm a psy vampire, not a sanguine."

I can't tell whether I'm more relieved at the truth or annoyed at his teasing. My eyes flash to his teeth again. "Then why do you have elongated canines?"

"Can you think of no other reason to have such a feature aside from drinking blood? What do other creatures use them for?"

I refuse to answer.

"To spear their prey, of course. I may not drink blood, but I'm not above a good hunt."

This time, I can't help but cover my neck, resting my hand over my collarbone. "And what exactly do you hunt, Prince Franco?"

He leans closer and winks. "Beautiful human-fae hybrids like you, of course. But only if I want them badly enough." He straightens and offers me his arm. "Now that that's settled between us, will you allow me to show you the beauty of the palace at night?"

I take a step away from his leering stare, arms crossing tighter over my chest. "You just named me your prey. Whether it was in jest or truth, I have no desire to be alone with you."

"I only named you my prey if I were to want you badly enough."

I burn him with a scowl. "And just how badly do you want to eat me, Your Highness?"

His lids grow heavy, eyes falling to my lips. "How badly do I want to eat you? Now that is a loaded question."

My heart hammers in my chest. I whirl toward my door. "I'm going back to sleep. I prefer my nightmares to this."

He intercepts me before I can reach my door, expression jovial. "I'm joking, Miss Fairfield. I'm not going to eat you. Unless you ask me nicely and we aren't talking about dinner at all. In that case..."

"Can you be serious for once?"

He gives me a mock bow. "My apologies. I admit, I enjoy getting a rise out of you, testing your response to fear and flirtation. I like the taste of the energy you emit. Most of it tastes like fire."

"What is it with aggressive males testing my resolve?" I mutter.

"It's the Old Ways in us. Our instincts make us want to determine who's alpha, who's omega. It's in our nature."

"Well, it's getting old."

"Spoken like a woman who has clearly had much experience with the follies of aggressive males seeking her attention."

My mind goes to Aspen, to the nightmare. To the kiss we shared. To Maddie Coleman taking my place. My heart clenches.

He offers me his arm again. "Let me give you an intermission from your worries. I promise I'll be less of an ass. I'll even show you Selene Palace's finest feature."

I roll my eyes. "Don't you dare say it's your ass."

His eyes widen as he gives me an approving grin. "I can't believe I didn't think of that myself. We're going to get along just fine."

I let out a grumble before placing a hand at his elbow. My other hand seeks to pat my thigh until I remind myself my dagger is long gone. If only I'd been of sound-enough mind to steal one of the knives from Mr. Meeks' laboratory.

As we move through the halls, we encounter more and more fae. Many are like the ones I first saw, sprites, wraiths, and specters in various shades and forms. Others appear more like Franco or Nyxia, and there are several nocturnal animals that scurry about the halls. Each fae bows to the prince as we pass.

I've been determined to say as little to the prince as possible, but my curiosity gets the better of me. "Why is the palace so busy right now? There was hardly a soul out and about earlier."

"Selene Palace is the liveliest at night," he explains. "This is the Lunar Court, you know. Most of our residents, servants, and guests are nocturnal."

"And you?"

"I prefer a nocturnal lifestyle as well. In fact, I was sleeping soundly until a rather rude owl came hooting about two foreigners covered in blood traipsing through the woods. That's when Nyxia sent me out to find you."

We reach a staircase and continue up several flights in what seems to be a wide spiral. When the summit is in sight, cool night air greets us. The staircase ends at a circular balcony that rings an enormous glass dome. The night sky opens overhead, speckled with countless stars in such unfathomable quantity I've never witnessed from any other viewpoint.

Franco points at the bubble of glass before us. "That's the roof of the throne room. And this," he pulls me forward until we reach a platform that juts out from the balcony, "is the observatory."

My mouth falls open, hand slipping from Prince Franco's elbow. Upon the platform stand several telescopes in varying sizes and designs. "Are these for viewing the moon?"

He approaches the largest telescope, a hulking device constructed of gold and crystal. "This one is for viewing the moon. And other planets, of course. You'll find only one telescope to rival it in Faerwyvae, and it belongs to the Star Court. Come see what it has to offer."

My intellectual hunger is too ravenous to do anything but obey. Prince Franco adjusts the dials on the telescope, then extends his hand for me to take a look. I place my eye to the viewing glass, which reveals the waxing moon in such detail that I've never seen. The sight makes my throat feel tight, awed over the beauty and terror of seeing such a fixture of the night sky as if I were floating before it. "It's beautiful."

"You'll have to see it again in a few days when it's full."

It's almost painful to force myself away from the sight. "What do the others show?"

"Whatever its previous user was looking for. Go ahead and see."

I move from telescope to telescope, greeting different planets, stars, and nebulae. I haven't felt this happy and alive since...since...well, probably since the night in the cave with Aspen.

The thought dampens my joy, and I pull away from the final telescope. With a sigh, I walk to the edge of the platform and look out at the landscape around the palace. I wasn't in the best state to care about my surroundings when we first arrived, so I can hardly recall what it looked like during the day. But the moon illuminates plenty for me to see, revealing lush meadows, towering trees, glittering lakes and streams. To my right, I see a marsh upon which tiny blue lights glow.

Franco comes up beside me, shoulder brushing mine as he follows my line of vision. "Wisps," he says. "They used to live more often in the Fire Court, but they've taken a liking to Lunar. However, don't rely on them to guide you if ever you are lost at night. They like to cause more mischief than good, although they aren't harmful."

The heat of his body next to mine is an unexpected distraction, sending my pulse racing just the slightest bit faster, but I do my best to ignore it. Instead, I squint deeper at the blue lights. "Wisps? But I've seen this phenomenon back in Eisleigh. Are the lights not a result of combustible marsh gases?"

"Perhaps where you're from. I assure you the wisps are more than a trick of light and gas."

I leave Franco's side to reach for one of the smaller telescopes and swivel it until I have the marsh in sight. I adjust the dials until the blue lights come into focus. To my surprise, the light has some semblance of form—swaying arms and legs, a hint of eyes and mouth. I know I shouldn't be surprised, but I can't help it. Now I wonder if the strange blue lights I saw in Eisleigh had been fae after all. "You say they used to live in the Fire Court?"

"Wisps are related to fire sprites, making the Fire Court a decent home. However, they are nocturnal. In Lunar, all night-dwelling fae are welcome, as well as lovers of the moon. We are also home to many fae who are shunned by other courts, especially the unsightly or ghoulish varieties. They feel safer here beneath the cover of night."

I shudder. "You mean like banshees and harpies?"

"Banshees, harpies, lycanthropes," he flashes me a toothy grin, "and vampires."

"Aren't they dangerous?"

"About as dangerous as I am. Or you."

"I'm not..." I can't bring myself to finish the sentence, knowing it would be a lie. I may not be as dangerous as the fae male before me or the monstrous creatures that lurk in the dark, but I killed a man and burnt his laboratory to a crisp.

"Look!" Franco points over my shoulder, a welcome diversion from my thoughts. "The kitsune are gathering at the Wishing Tree."

I turn around and seek where he's pointing. All I find is an enormous willow tree with flickering orange lights beneath it. Again, I reach for the telescope and bring the tree into focus. My heart leaps at the sight. Dozens of lithe, white foxes gather around the trunk of the tree, balls of flame hovering at their mouths or tails. They appear to be speaking with one another, but I can't hear a word from here.

"Another type of fae that once held their allegiance to the Fire Court," Franco says. "Most kitsune choose Lunar as their home these days. Actually, thousands of unseelie fae have migrated from Fire to other courts as King Ustrin grows less and less patient with them. Not when his radical seelie ways keep him in such good standing with the council."

"King Ustrin is radical seelie?" I remember his orange, scaly skin, his slitted nostrils, and forked tongue. "I would have thought King Ustrin was unseelie based on his appearance. He seemed more lizard than anything."

"The fire lizard has always been a powerful type of fae in the Fire Court. Retaining similar features when in seelie form is another way to show his power. It doesn't impact his political affiliation, however."

A shadow falls over us, and I find my attention drawn to the sky where a black silhouette passes over the glittering stars.

"A moon dragon," Prince Franco says. "Yet another type of fae that fled Fire to live in Lunar. Many of the fire lizard's draconian cousins have moved to other courts." He lowers his voice. "Rest assured, you are far from being the only one who isn't a fan of King Ustrin."

I tense. "The more accurate statement is that he isn't a fan of me. I couldn't care less about him."

"Even though he's responsible for orchestrating the charges against your mother?"

My head whips toward him. "You know about that?"

He nods. "My sister filled me in on the details Lorelei shared."

A question rises to my mind, another that requires much decorum. "Is your mother the same as Nyxia's?"

"Yes. Why do you ask?"

"Do you know much about Queen Nessina's involvement with the war? Were you alive back then?"

He shakes his head. "Nyxia and I were born centuries after the war ended and Mother didn't tell us much."

That might mean he knows nothing about his mother harboring my grandmother. Did Lorelei share that part with Nyxia? With Franco? I don't want to ask directly, in case the secret isn't safe with him. "Where is your mother now?"

"She is no longer with us."

"She died?"

"Not in the way you're imagining," he says. "Fae rulers tend to remain at court until they pass the throne to the next in line. For most unseelie, that means when an heir proves their worth as alpha. It didn't take long for my sister to demonstrate her alpha status after she reached maturity, and I didn't dare challenge her. She's the strongest alpha the Lunar Court has seen in generations. Anyhow, after my sister became the new queen, Mother left court and sort of...reverted to the Old Ways entirely."

"You mean she took her unseelie form indefinitely?"

He nods. "It is our way."

My eyes meet Franco's, and I find myself fascinated by his words. Everything he's said about the lunar fae, the unseelie, the Old Ways—it's intriguing. *He's* intriguing, when he isn't being annoying. That alone is worth my awe. Even a day ago, I would have thought befriending an unseelie fae was out of the question. Now, here I am genuinely enjoying my time with an unseelie prince.

A flash of guilt seizes my chest, and I avert my gaze.

A pair of light footsteps approach from the balcony, and Nyxia comes into view. "I thought I might find you here, Miss Fairfield." She offers me a grin before her gaze moves to her brother. "Thank you for showing our lovely guest such kind hospitality."

"It was my pleasure," he says, adding a wink for me.

"I have no doubt about that. May I ask for my turn to speak with her?"

Prince Franco nods, then takes my hand in his. Before I can react, he pulls the back of my hand to his lips, brushing a light kiss over my skin. "I do hope we can speak again soon." With that, he shudders and shifts into a raven, taking off into the night sky. I follow his silhouette until it's out of sight. Only then do I force my gaze to return to Nyxia.

Alone with the most powerful lunar alpha in generations, I suppress a shudder.

17

Nyxia approaches me with slow, confident steps. She's changed out of the elaborate outfit she wore earlier and now has on a pair of black silk slacks and a matching tunic. "Let's take a stroll," she says.

Falling into step beside her, we walk the circular balcony ringing the perimeter of the dome. I force my breathing to remain even, natural.

"My brother seems quite taken with you," the Lunar Queen says.

I let out a bark of laughter before I can stop myself. "We've hardly spoken."

"I think you've learned by now that the fae know what they want quite quickly."

I press my lips tight, refusing to follow the train of thought that I know will lead me to Aspen. To the gaping wound left in his absence.

"Regardless," Nyxia says, "he wouldn't be a terrible mate to make an alliance with."

My head swivels toward her. "What are you implying?"

"I'm implying that I understand the precarious position you are in. You're considered a criminal by the humans and would be used as a bargaining chip by many of the fae, if given the chance. Unless you can secure your position in Faerwyvae, you'll be exiled to a slow death on the mainland."

I stop in my tracks. "I'm not staying in Faerwyvae. That would be trea-son. It would break the treaty."

Nyxia halts, then slowly spins on her heel to meet my gaze with a delighted grin. "Then let's break it."

"That will bring war."

She shrugs a delicate shoulder. "I guess we should try to win it then."

I shake my head and continue walking, quickening my steps as if I can outpace her treasonous suggestion. "That's not why I came here. I came to seek refuge while I await my mother's trial."

She matches my hurried stride with little effort. "Yes, but there's another option open to you. If you were my brother's mate, you'd be Lunar royalty. You'd have a shot at earning enough respect to take the throne that is right-fully yours."

I round on her. "The Fire Court isn't rightfully mine. My ancestor was exiled. The treaty states his descendants cannot live in Faerwyvae ever again."

This time, she's the one who walks ahead, and I'm forced to race after her. "The treaty was made with human rules. King Ustrin likely never would have become king according to the Old Ways. As cousin to the exiled King Caleos, Ustrin claimed the throne based on human traditions of male blood-line succession, but he never proved himself the alpha blessed by the All of All."

I have no idea what she's talking about, so she must be referring to some unseelie custom. "It doesn't matter what King Ustrin did or didn't do. A fae Legacy Bond keeps the treaty in place and forbids me from claiming the throne. A man named Henry Duveau will put a bounty on my head if I try to stay in Faerwyvae."

She waves her hand dismissively. "Don't you understand? If the treaty is broken, so is the Legacy Bond. Besides, if this human wants to place a bounty on you, I'd like to see what great fool would try to claim it. A human bounty hunter will get himself killed before he so much as crosses the axis line. And no fae would turn on you if you were a respected leader."

"Oh, you mean like when Cobalt stole King Aspen's throne?"

She shrugs. "King Aspen was challenged and came out the victor. With your help, of course. Your success in the Twelfth Court is exactly what makes me think you have what it takes to claim the Fire Court throne according to the Old Ways."

Her words send my heart racing, both from the fear and excitement they generate within me. There's a part of me that rises to meet her words with a spark of hope, igniting a fire of indignation against those who would stand against me. I hate it. I hate the part of me that wants her to say more.

She continues. "I'll be honest with you. I don't like King Ustrin or any of the radical seelie. I don't like the Council of Eleven Courts or how much they seek control over the unseelie. The very name of the council is blasphemy against the Old Ways. You cannot be fae and disregard the Twelfth Court. I'll support any effort that puts an unseelie queen on the Fire Court throne."

My mouth falls open. "Unseelie," I say with a gasp. "What makes you think I'd be *unseelie?*"

She seems unperturbed by the bite in my tone. "You'd have to be unseelie to go against the treaty. I suppose you could call yourself seelie, but it comes down to this: you don't want to be controlled. You don't want your true nature suppressed or for your freedoms to be taken away. That's what being unseelie means."

Again, that secret part of me stirs and rises. It wants to shout in agreement, to wail a battle cry and fight for what is mine. *No. Not mine. Nothing in Faerwyvae is mine.* "You know nothing about what I want," I say through my teeth.

Her voice takes on a soothing, ethereal quality. "I know your dreams. Your fears. I can see them even when you're awake. They float around you like specters."

I shake my head, crossing my arms over my chest. "This conversation is pointless. I will not break the treaty nor will I stay in Faerwyvae. I'm going to my mother's trial, and there I will face my fate."

"You will choose death."

"I will choose my mother. I will not abandon her. If I do, she will be executed."

"But you would live. I'm sure she'd want that, wouldn't she?"

I open my mouth to argue but snap it shut. There's no way I'll admit Nyxia is right, but I can't deny the truth in her words either. Finally, I say, "Just because I'm here, and just because I'm part-fae, doesn't mean I've turned my back on the humans."

We've reached the other end of the loop where the staircase opens beneath the balcony. Nyxia faces me, looking down her nose. "When you're ready to take a side, let me know. A crown awaits."

"I don't want a crown forged from blood."

"All crowns are forged from blood."

"Then I never want one."

She lets out a trilling laugh. "What about the one the All of All gave you?"

The gold crown of swaying leaves. If it's where I left it, it remains on the table in my parlor. "It was never mine. Aspen's new wife can have it for all I care."

"She'd look awfully silly wearing a crown of flame, don't you think?"

A crown of...flame? My breath hitches as the swaying leaves emerge in my mind's eye. What if they weren't leaves after all? What if they were flames?

I shake the questions from my mind. What does it matter now?

Nyxia takes a step closer. "I think Aspen knew exactly what he was doing when he placed that crown on your head."

THE FOLLOWING DAYS PASS WITH FAR LESS EXCITEMENT, BUT MY CIRCADIAN rhythm is totally thrown off. Nightmares plague my sleep, and I find myself most often awake at night. When this happens, I visit the observatory, watch the moon, the stars, and the unseelie fae that play about the landscape. Few fae pay me much heed, aside from the occasional attentions from Franco, which I must admit I'm beginning to grow more and more comfortable with. His lighthearted persona has its charm, and even his irritating moments tend to rouse a secret smile from me. Nyxia, however, seems preoccupied most of the time, which I'm grateful for. I have no desire to continue our conversation from before.

During the day, I spend idle time with Lorelei. She, however, seems perfectly capable of sleeping at night, so there are times when I'm left without her company. Whether alone or with my friend, I try my best to keep busy, forcing myself not to consider the upcoming event...

Aspen's wedding.

Every time I think about it, nausea churns inside me. I wish I could burn the thought of him and his soon-to-be wife from my mind. I wish I could feel anger at him instead, fury that he's really going through with this. But I can't even drum up the ghost of my rage. Not when I was the one who made him promise to marry her. Not when I know it's for the best. Not when it's the only way to stop a war.

It's the eve before the dreaded occasion when I wake from a string of unpleasant nightmares involving none other than Aspen and Maddie. My only relief is that tonight's dreams were not the visceral kind like the one in

Bircharbor's dining room; those are far more difficult to decipher between dream and reality.

Sweat soaks the sheets as I finally give up on sleep and force myself out of bed. I dress in a cream gown and pace my room. There's only one matter I can count on to distract me. A matter of life and death...and a certain unseelie prince.

I retrieve the prepared sealed envelope from my dressing table and stuff it beneath the sash around my waist. I've been working on the letter for two days now and only settled on my final draft earlier this evening.

When I enter the hall, I'm greeted by the bustle of nocturnal activity. With slow steps, I make my way down the corridor, eyes flashing to the ceiling, seeking black feathers hidden in the shadows of the beams overhead. However, all I find are wraiths and owls. If only I knew where the prince's bedroom was.

The thought stops me in my tracks, a barrage of unanticipated images flooding my mind as I picture myself showing up at his private quarters unannounced. He would only be too pleased. And I...how would I feel about that? I shake my head to clear it.

As I continue down the corridor, a black shape catches my eye from a beam just ahead. With careful steps, I approach it, craning my neck to see if it might be—

"What are you looking at?"

I startle, finding Franco at my side, matching my posture as he stares up at the ceiling. A blush heats my cheeks as I'm forced to recall the discomforting visions I had of him just moments ago. I square my shoulders and steel my expression. "Do you take pleasure in scaring me each time?"

"I take any pleasure you'll give me. But why were you so fascinated with the soot sprite?"

"A soot sprite?" I return my attention to the black shape, part from curiosity, part to obscure the fire that I'm sure still shows in my cheeks.

Franco lets out a whistle. In response, the sprite moves, opening a pair of glowing red eyes that lock on mine. Now I can clearly see it is not a raven at all but an orb of soot, motes of black swirling as it hisses in irritation before scurrying across the beam and out of sight.

Franco turns to me, brow lifted, mouth open in mock surprise. "Wait, did you...were you looking for *me*?"

I roll my eyes. "Don't flatter yourself. I have a favor to ask of you."

"A favor? I can only imagine—"

"Can you get a message to another court without drawing attention?"

The grin slides from his lips. "I think you have me confused with a messenger fae."

"Not you personally, but someone in your employ."

"I suppose," he says. "What court are you trying to infiltrate? If you're intending to reach your beloved mate, I'm sure Nyxia could deliver the message herself. She'll be leaving for Bircharbor at dawn."

I ignore the pressure in my chest, the wave of sorrow that threatens to drown me on the spot. Crossing my arms over my chest, I dig my nails into my arm, the sharp sensation a welcome point of focus. "It's not King Aspen I'm trying to reach. It's an unseelie court I need to get a message to, and I need it to reach someone specific."

He looks surprised by this. "Which court would that be?"

"Sea."

His expression darkens. "Queen Melusine is a keen-eyed ruler. Not much gets past her."

"Yes, well, she won't be at court during the wedding, will she?"

"Ah, so you would like this message delivered while Queen Melusine is distracted."

I nod. "And if the recipient isn't at the Sea Court, I need her found as soon as possible. This message must get to her at once."

"It sounds like you need a spy more than a messenger."

I uncross my arms to put my hands on my hips. "Do you have someone in mind or not?"

He leans lazily against the wall, a smirk playing over his lips. "I may have someone who will perform this duty, but it won't come free."

"How much will it cost?"

He eyes me from under his lashes. "Your company. Tomorrow night. At the full moon revel."

"My company?" My pulse quickens, but I manage to keep a straight face. "I'm not going on a date with you."

"You can call me a chaperone if that makes you feel better. The Lunar Court can get quite...rambunctious on the full moon. With my sister away at Bircharbor Palace for the wedding, you'd do well to keep close to me."

"Or perhaps I should stay in my room and avoid such rambunctiousness altogether."

He shrugs. "Suit yourself. However, that is my price."

"Fine," I growl. I pull the letter out from under my sash. "But this isn't a date."

"I dare not dream of it." He accepts the letter, then turns away and stalks down the hall, but not before whirling back around and shouting, "Wear something scandalous."

I purse my lips and shoot him a glare, but as soon as I face ahead, it turns into a half-hearted smile. I'm left with the smallest comfort—that if I must endure the night of Aspen's wedding, at least I won't have to do it alone.

18

———————

Lorelei isn't too pleased when she learns of the promise I made to Prince Franco. "You agreed to do what? To go to the full moon revel? Do you have any idea how these celebrations tend to end?"

Her raised brow tells me it isn't fear I should feel, but a heated blush. "Well, no," I confess.

"Every moon revel in Lunar might as well be Beltane."

I lift my chin to hide my trepidation and make my way to my wardrobe. "Then you better come with me and make sure the prince keeps his hands to himself."

"Or we could skip it altogether," she says.

"I sort of…owe him," I say as I begin rifling through the dozen or so dresses in the wardrobe. The first is black, which I immediately deem too dour before flipping to the next. Pink? No, reminds me too much of Amelie. Blue chiffon? No. Reminds me too much of Aspen. My heart plummets, and I'm forced to consider what's happening at this very moment. Queen Nyxia departed for Bircharbor at dawn, and now it's nearly evening. Surely the treaty has been sealed with a wedding at this point. I swallow the lump in my throat and blink the tears from my eyes as I bite the inside of my cheek until I taste blood. Only then can I breathe again and return to examining the dresses.

Lorelei puts her hands on her waist, oblivious to my moment of pain, and bumps her hip to the side. "Are you telling me you made a bargain with Prince Franco?"

I pause my search to meet Lorelei's eyes. When Franco offered me his terms to deliver my letter, I knew it was a bargain of sorts. But the weight of that fact didn't strike me until now. I'm suddenly aware of how careless I've become ever since Mother told me I'm part-fae. Somehow, the knowledge has made me grow less wary around the fae, less guarded.

Having fae blood doesn't make me invulnerable, though. In fact, I still have nearly all the human weaknesses and very little fae power. I can still be glamoured or tricked into a bargain. The incident long ago with Amelie and the goblin is proof that a part-fae can be glamoured. Although, whether her relationship with Cobalt is additional proof is impossible to know. Is the Bond the only reason he controls her, or did he glamour her into the Bond to begin with?

I return to sorting through the dresses. Gold? No, it's too scandalous. Prince Franco would be all too happy about it. Purple silk? Another heart-sinking reaction. *Definitely not.*

"Perhaps it wasn't the best idea," I admit, keeping my voice level, "but I needed him to do something for me. I needed him to find Amelie. He agreed to send a spy to deliver my message to her discreetly while Queen Melusine is at Bircharbor. I must know if she's coming to Mother's trial."

"Why would you ask Franco? I could have handled it for you. I could have gone and done it myself."

"I needed it to be done in secret. Your presence at the Sea Court would certainly arouse suspicion. Besides, can you even visit the Sea Court? Is it not underwater?"

She rolls her eyes. "I would have sent someone. I have my own contacts, you know."

I sigh. "I know. I'm sure you would have done it, but I didn't want to wake you. Also, I don't think Franco is so bad. His flirtations irritate me to no end, but I can't say I despise his company." My eyes flash to Lorelei. "You know him better than I do, though. *Should* I despise his company?"

Her posture relaxes. "No, he's not despicable. I hate him, of course, but it's more like the disdain for a little brother. He was basically that to me when Nyxia and I were together. We were at each other's throats with teasing more often than not. Still, I wish you would have let me help you instead." She places a hand on my arm. "I feel just as useless as you do, you know. I want all of this to work out, and I hate that nothing is going the way I wish it would."

I bite the inside of my cheek again as my lungs constrict. I hardly trust myself to speak. "How do you wish it would go?"

She gives me a sad smile. "I wish you would decide to stay. I wish you would storm over to Bircharbor right now and stop Aspen from sealing the treaty with his new Chosen."

A wave of shock runs through me. "That would mean—"

"I know what it would mean. Sometimes I agree with King Aspen about the treaty. Sometimes I question whether it's worth saving."

I clench my jaw. "It is, Lorelei. That's one thing I know. If it saves lives, it's worth it."

"Is it truly saving lives? Or controlling them?"

Heat floods my veins with the effort it takes not to argue. My anger is a welcome alternative to the sorrow that threatens to crush me, but I'm in no mood to affirm my stance yet again. Instead, I let my rage burn away my pain and change the subject. "Come with us tonight. The prince may not be the worst fae in the world, but I don't want to be alone with him."

"I suppose I could go. If it's a moon revel, there will be wine. But there better be Midnight Blush or I'm out."

"What's Midnight Blush?"

"It's a wine made from night blooming jasmine and obsidian pyrus—a cousin of honey pyrus. Don't worry, there are no dreadful hallucinations to go with it. And it's the only thing that's going to allow me to endure hours of Franco's company."

I force an emotionless laugh and return my efforts to sorting through the dresses. My fingers fall on the one I first dismissed as being too dour—a black dress with silver moons stitched at the hem of the skirt. The sleeves are a sheer spider silk draped with strands of pearls. The neckline is lowcut and lined with white feathers. Best of all, it doesn't remind me of autumn, Bircharbor, Amelie, or Aspen.

I hold the dress against my figure. "Does this look scandalous to you?"

She quirks a brow. "No. Definitely stunning, but not scandalous."

"Perfect," I say. "Scandalous was not the bargain I agreed to."

At midnight, Prince Franco arrives at my room to claim his bargain.

He stands in my doorway, looking like a storybook vampire indeed, with his black leather trousers and a white linen shirt unbuttoned to the middle of his chest. His silver hair is slicked away from his face, revealing the hard planes and angles of his jaw and cheekbones. A long strand of hematite beads hangs around his neck, drawing my eyes to his chest. For the first time, I notice dark ink tattooed on his skin, crescent moons and other geometric symbols peeking from beneath the open collar.

"Lovely females." He extends both arms, not seeming at all surprised by the presence of my companion. I place my hand in the crook of his elbow, while Lorelei takes his arm with a grimace.

Franco's eyes drink me in. "Nice dress."

I ignore his compliment even though it sends a flutter of pleasure through me. "Where is this revel taking place? The observatory?"

"Not a chance. Moon revels are far too crowded for the observatory to accommodate."

He guides us through the dark halls lit by the warm glow of the moonlight orbs to the lawn outside the palace. The moon is full and bright overhead, enormous and near-blinding with its glow. In the distance, the sound of laughter and voices and animal noises mingle with the beat of a drum. The latter reverberates in the ground beneath my feet. As we near the source, an enormous tree comes into view with hundreds of glowing lights surrounding it. The lights are from wisps, wraiths, sprites, and dozens of other kinds of fae I have no name for.

Franco points at the tree. "Do you recognize it?"

It takes me a moment to realize it's the same tree we saw from the observatory, the Wishing Tree. At its base stands a fae with pearlescent skin, silver hair, and a flowing gown of white gossamer. She speaks a language I don't recognize, lifting her arms to the moon, then lowering them over a silver cauldron of water. The water reflects the moon as if the fae holds the celestial entity before her.

"Priestess Dionna," Franco says. "She performs the moon rituals at every revel."

I'm entranced by the flowing motions of the priestess' arms as she lifts and lowers, bends and sways. Her movements seem sacred and ancient. I'm surprised to find not everyone is watching her. A crowd of reverent onlookers surrounds the priestess, but most of the fae are elsewhere, dancing, drinking, running, flying. The freedom I see is both terrifying and exhilarating.

"Where's the wine?" Lorelei asks in a bored tone.

Franco guides us away from the ritual to a long table made of white quartz edged with gold. I certainly never noticed this enormous piece of furniture in all my views through the telescopes over the last few days, so it must have been transported for the revel. I don't bother wondering how. Surely some impossible feat of magic is responsible.

Upon the table are trays of fruit and flowers and hundreds of bottles of different colored liquids. Lorelei paces the length, eyeing the bottles with heavy scrutiny before she finds the one she's after. It's a pale blue that shimmers in the moonlight. Franco finds three glasses and Lorelei fills each nearly to the rim. Once we each have a glass in hand, she raises hers. "Midnight Blush. Drink up."

"In honor of the full moon." Franco gives me a wink and knocks back his glass, swallowing the liquid in a single gulp.

I stare at the contents of my glass, knowing I shouldn't risk even a sip of the fae wine. But there's a void inside me, one that wants nothing more than to forget, even for a time. I raise my glass in a silent toast. *To forgetting what I'm missing and enjoying what I have while it lasts.* I take a deep breath and down a hearty sip.

Franco takes my hand in his and pulls me away from the table. "Let's dance."

19

The night wears on and the wine continues to flow. I find my sorrows are swept away, leaving me with the most luxurious ecstasy. Lorelei was right; the effects of Midnight Blush are far less troublesome than honey pyrus. There are no psychoactive properties, only intoxicating relaxation and a calm euphoria.

My two companions and I sway to the beat of the drums while the priestess continues to chant. All kinds of fae surround us; wisps bounce and undulate with every pound of the drum, bats swoop overhead, humanoid fae dance with graceful motions, cats pounce and claw their way up the Wishing Tree, dark shadows writhe as they expand and contract with the tempo. Even banshees, harpies, and dragons soar through the night sky, joining in the revel, but I can't find it in me to be bothered by their presence. Instead, I let my body loosen, let my arms swing as if they're made of air. This dance is unlike any I've ever witnessed.

Only one other dance compares. One with ribbons, masks, and vows, and a fae male with a sensuous smirk...

No. None of that tonight. This dance is everything I need.

I close my eyes, feel deeper into the drums. A new kind of fire floods me —a mixture of my life force and unfurling passion. I follow it, become it, let it rise. When I open my eyes, a purple haze falls over my vision, blanketing everyone beneath an ethereal glow. It reminds me of my journey to the Twelfth Court, and—more recently—my dreams. Again, unwelcome thoughts threaten to shatter my peace, so I push them away, focusing instead on the joy and passion, on the beauty of the purple haze.

"You're glowing." Franco's voice sharpens my mind, and the violet begins to dim. After a few moments, the scenery returns to what it was. Still beautiful, of course, but no longer filtered through the strange vision. My eyes meet the prince's, finding them alight with wonder. He repeats his words. "Evelyn, you're glowing. It's like flames."

I slow my dancing and examine my hands. He's right. My body has taken on a golden, shimmery aura. It's enough to surprise me and snap me even further from my daze. In a blink, the glow is gone.

Perhaps Lorelei hadn't been entirely correct about Midnight Blush after all. It obviously elicits some psychoactive effects.

Still, it isn't enough to worry me, and before long, I return to my dance. Lorelei takes my hands and we begin to spin. When we stop, we fall into fits of laughter and tumble onto the grass. It reminds me of being with Amelie.

Another thought I quickly smother. I'm not thinking of Amelie tonight. Not Amelie. Not Aspen. Not—*Oh look!*

I let out an unrestrained squeal of delight as a pair of sleek white kitsune dart by, the first with a glass of wine over its muzzle, the second chasing the orb of flame on the other's tail.

Franco chuckles as he offers me a hand to help me rise to my feet. "I knew you'd have fun." Once I stand, he turns the same hand to Lorelei, but she bats it away, shoulders slumping as her expression crumbles.

"I miss Foxglove," she says with a pout. "He's supposed to be my drinking partner."

Franco and I exchange an amused glance. "This is what happens when you drink too much Midnight Blush," Franco says, then lowers his voice so only I can hear. "We should take her back to her room."

My heart sinks at his suggestion. All I want to do is dance and drink and drink some more. All I want is drums and rhythm and the feel of my body moving without care. But a rational part of me remains intact, and it can understand the reason for his concern. Lorelei looks like she's on the verge of falling asleep, and it can't be safe for her to doze in the middle of a dance floor.

Franco bends to lift her, which is a struggle as she fights him. Once she's righted, he pulls her arm over his shoulders and helps her walk. It's slow progress as we make our way from the revel to the palace, but I don't mind. Every step I take carries the rhythm with me, and I continue to feel the drum, even once indoors. My hips bounce to it as Franco lays Lorelei on her bed. My arms sway to it as he walks me to my room, his hand on my lower back. I can feel the heat of his touch even through my dress.

Too soon, we reach my door. I face him and our eyes lock, trapping us in a bubble of silence. The wine still spins inside me, burning my blood with euphoria. I don't want to move from this moment. I don't want any of this to end. All I want is to stare at the beautiful fae male, to avoid sleep for as long as possible. To avoid the reality that awaits me with the coming dawn.

He grins, his sharp canines glinting in the glowing light of the hall. This time, they don't make me flinch. Like Foxglove's pointed teeth, the prince's now seem charming somehow, safe, even as he steps closer. "Did you enjoy yourself tonight?"

"I did. Thank you."

Again, silence falls between us, making the distance separating our bodies feel too vast. I crave to return to the revel, to throw my arms around his neck and resume the dance right here in the hall. With the beat of the drums still pounding inside me, my body proceeds to move and sway. It's only natural when that beat brings me toward the prince, draws our lips together to continue the song. His lips are tantalizingly soft, our kisses slow and lingering. The brush of his tongue against mine is like fuel for the Midnight Blush, renewing its ecstasy as heat ignites in my core, tingling between my thighs.

A word comes to mind, one that encompasses the desire that has taken over. Only it isn't a word, exactly, but a name. *Aspen.*

I pull away, my pleasure drowned in a shocking sense of sobriety. My eyes fill with the prince's face, with the hunger in his eyes. It isn't the face I wanted to see.

Franco is beautiful and seductively alluring, but one problem remains. He isn't Aspen.

A string of expletives runs through my mind ending with *bloody iron*. No matter how much I try to deny it, my feelings for Aspen run deeper than I can contain. Yet, at this very moment, he's likely in bed with his new mate, his new Bonded, his new *wife*. And here I am with a gorgeous male who stirs my passion, yet all I can think of is *him*.

Rage courses through me at the unfairness of it all. Aspen is certainly enjoying the pleasures of the flesh with someone new. Why shouldn't I?

Franco's brow furrows. "Is everything all right?"

If I close my eyes, I could pretend it's him.

No, that's disturbing.

"Yes." I force my lips into a smile.

"Do you want me to stop?"

Yes, yes, yes. A million times yes. Stop this at once. "No."

He leans in to kiss me again, but not before something catches my eye at the end of the hall. Blue-black hair. Narrowed eyes. Antlers.

As Franco's lips meet mine, I turn my head, and his lips graze my cheek. "Aspen?" This time I say the name out loud. But the hall is empty. There's no sign of the Autumn King, or of anyone, for that matter. Most fae are likely still at the revel. My chest heaves as I blink at the place I thought I saw him. Of course, I *hadn't* truly seen him at all. I'm thoroughly drunk on Midnight Blush. My dreams are beginning to weave into reality.

Without me realizing it, Franco has taken a step away from me, his expression wounded when I meet his eyes. An embarrassed flush heats my cheeks. I put a hand to my forehead as I lean against my door. "I'm sorry," I say breathlessly. "I'm clearly not in the right state of mind."

Franco's face shifts into a smile, but his eyes retain the hurt I caused with my outburst. "I should let you get some sleep." He offers me a low bow, which gives me a chance to better compose myself. When he rises, he studies my face for a moment before reaching a hand to my cheek. He gives my skin a soft brush of his fingers, then leaves.

I hurry into my room and strip off my dress, not even bothering to toss on a nightgown. All I want to do is disappear beneath my covers, and I do just that. My mind reels from the events of the night, from the beauty of the dance, to the ecstasy of the wine. To the unfathomable fact that I danced alongside unseelie fae and never once feared for my life. Perhaps my chaperone was to thank for that, or maybe it was the Midnight Blush. Whatever the case, I truly enjoyed myself. That is, until that strange kiss. I mean, the kiss itself was delightful. But how it ended...

Thoughts of Aspen threaten to sober me further, but I refuse to let it happen. In the morning I know my sorrow will return, but until then I seek the beat of the drum, still heavy in my veins. I let it rock me, soothe me, and pull me into the deepest, dreamless sleep.

20

In the morning, the drums continue to pound, but it isn't the beat of the revel that carries the thrum. It's a pulsing headache that has me wincing against the morning light. Even with the muted quality of the Lunar Court's daylight filtered through the single glass window in the ceiling, it's too much. I groan, realizing I can't have slept longer than four hours.

I should have known better. Of course drinking that much fae wine—or any wine—would leave me with a hangover. At least it isn't nearly as bad as I felt after eating honey pyrus. And at least it was the very distraction I needed to get through the night.

Even if it ended in such an odd manner.

I pull myself out of bed, surprised to find I'm naked before I recall the haste in which I'd gone to bed last night. My black dress is a crumpled heap by the wardrobe. I obviously couldn't be bothered to hang it up last night. With a shake of my head at my former intoxicated self, I hang the dress in the wardrobe and slip into my velvet robe. Every movement sends a shard of glass through my skull, but I manage to make my way to the dressing table where a pitcher of water sits. I down one glass, then another, until my throat no longer feels like sand. Only then does the pounding in my head begin to lessen.

My thoughts then turn to Lorelei; if I feel this awful, she can't be faring much better. Then again, being full-fae could be in her favor. Still, she was quite indisposed.

I straighten my robe, pulling the sash tight around my waist to hopefully conceal all traces of my nudity underneath, and leave my room. When I reach Lorelei's door, I'm surprised to find it open. Animated voices come from within. One of the voices sounds like...

I rush inside. "Foxglove?"

He grins when he faces me, then pulls me into an embrace. When we separate, he studies me, his smile shifting to a grimace. "Evelyn, dear, what in the name of oak and ivy have you been doing with your hair? It looks terrible."

I run my hand over it, finding tangles. If I'd been expecting to find anyone but Lorelei next door, I would have brushed it. However, that is the least of my concerns. "Foxglove, what are you doing here?" I look from him to Lorelei.

Lorelei seems to be in full health, seated on the arm of her couch with bright eyes and a glowing smile. She's obviously thrilled to see her friend, but when her eyes meet mine, there's trepidation in them. She bites her lower lip. "We were just talking about that."

"We arrived before dawn," Foxglove says. "It's been a whirlwind, I tell you. I haven't slept a wink."

"We," I echo. "Who's *we*?"

"Aspen and I, of course. And a few of his soldiers."

"Aspen's here?"

"Yes," Foxglove says.

"Right now? He's been here since before dawn?"

He nods, a sympathetic frown pulling his lips. "I'm sure he would have come to you at once if there wasn't so much to attend to. I only just left the throne room myself."

My legs turn to water beneath me, my hand flying to my chest as my breaths grow shallow. Foxglove is wrong. Aspen did come to me at once. He came to me and saw me...

"You said you just left the throne room? Is he there?"

"He is, but—"

I don't wait to hear another word. On flying feet, I tear down the hall. The palace layout isn't entirely familiar to me, but I know I can find the throne room without guidance. I've visited the observatory plenty of times on my own, and the throne room is just beneath it.

After a few wrong turns, I finally find a set of enormous double doors. Two shadowy wraiths stand before them. Guards. I'm taken aback, realizing this is the first time I've seen guards at Selene Palace. This can't be good.

I address the two wraiths. "May I have permission to enter?"

They say nothing.

"I am Evelyn Fairfield, guest of Queen Nyxia. Might I speak with her?"

Again nothing.

A lump rises in my throat, desperation mingling with frustration as my palms grow hot. I'm about to do something reckless, although I'm not sure what, when one of the doors opens.

Queen Nyxia squints at me. "I thought I tasted violence."

I'm surprised by her appearance. Her black suit is wrinkled and torn in places, her silver hair no longer smooth and sleek but sticking out at odd angles. I blink a few times and open my mouth to speak. Although, now that the queen is before me, I'm not sure what to say. I should bow, offer a formal greeting, ask an intelligent question. But I can only say one thing, and it comes out like a croak. "Aspen."

She rolls her eyes and opens the door wider. Inside the throne room, a group of fae are huddled around a table. I recognize them as fae royals—the white wolf from Winter, the fae with curling horns from Earthen, and the blue fae with flowing hair from Wind. All are in similar states of disarray as Nyxia—wrinkled clothing, messy hair, skin covered in grime or blood. But my eyes seek the figure standing at the end of the table.

Aspen's eyes meet mine. His hair falls in disorderly waves around his face, and his russet waistcoat is unbuttoned, gold cravat hanging loose around his neck. I want to run to him, to fold myself in his arms like I did in my dream. His eyes, however, keep me at bay. There's no warmth in them. It confirms my fears—Aspen really was there last night. He saw me kissing Prince Franco.

My voice comes out with a tremor. "May I speak with King Aspen in private?"

The wolf lets out a low growl. Aspen silences him with a shake of his head. "It wasn't her," he says, although I'm not sure what he's referring to. He says nothing to me, though.

Queen Nyxia speaks, her tone casual and exasperated at once. "We are in the middle of a very important discussion."

"I need to speak with him."

She crosses her arms and stares daggers at Aspen. With a grumble, he turns away from the table and stalks toward me. I expect him to stop when he approaches, but he brushes past me and out the door. I give Nyxia a belated bow before following Aspen into the hall.

I find him leaning against a wall, expression bored. He watches me through narrowed eyes, taking in my appearance from head to toe. "You look like you had a fun night." There's no mirth in his tone as his gaze lingers over my chest.

My hands fly to the neck of my robe, where I find it has slipped in my haste to get to the throne room, exposing a little too much skin. That's when I realize what this looks like. I'm dressed in a robe and naked underneath. I take a step toward him. "Aspen, nothing happened last night. It's not what you think."

He averts his gaze, and his voice comes out with a lazy drawl. "It's none of my business. You are free to choose any mate you desire."

"It's not like that." A thousand arguments, justifications, and questions soar through my mind. *I was drunk. I was upset you were marrying someone else. Wait, did you marry someone else? It was just a kiss. I wanted it to be you.* But nothing makes it past my lips.

"Nyxia told me about her offer," Aspen says, punctuating each word with clear disgust.

I shake the cacophony from my head. "What offer?"

"That she'll support your claim to the Fire Court throne if you take Prince Franco as your mate." His jaw shifts back and forth, but vulnerability tugs at his carefully curated facade. "I wouldn't blame you for accepting."

My mouth hangs open. "I'm not taking Prince Franco as my mate. And I'm certainly not bidding for the Fire Court throne."

He furrows his brow, posture stiffening. "Then why are you here?"

"To await my mother's trial. I needed a safe place to stay until then, and I..." I can't finish what I was going to say. *I couldn't come back to Autumn and watch you with your new Chosen. The new Chosen I told you to accept.*

Aspen pushes away from the wall, anger twisting at his features. "You're going back to the humans? After everything they've done to you?"

I take a step back, surprised at his sudden rage. "I'm not going to let my mother die for me."

His hands curl into fists. "They had you strapped to a table, Evie. You cannot go back to Eisleigh."

I blink at him a few times. "How do you know about that?"

"For the love of oak and ivy, I was there. Do you not recall?"

I shake my head. "That's impossible. It was a dream." Even as I say it, I know my words are folly. If he remembers, then it had to have been more than that. Memories flash through my mind, awakening every instance I've dreamed of him, the more visceral experiences blending with the horrible nightmares I've had of him and Maddie.

That brings up a vital question. "Wait, why are *you* here? What happened last night?"

"I left Bircharbor."

"Why?"

"There was a fight."

"Obviously." I wave a hand at his unkempt appearance, at the blood staining the collar of his tattered linen shirt. "For the love of iron, Aspen. Tell me what happened. Did you break the treaty?"

"I did not fulfill it."

I swallow hard. "Did you refuse to marry Maddie Coleman?"

"Yes."

Relief and anger wash over me at once, followed by terror for my mother. If Aspen broke the treaty, will Mr. Duveau maintain his bargain not to kill her before the trial? Will there even be a trial? Rage prevails, and my words come through my teeth. "You promised me."

"I promised you I'd make a choice neither of us would like. I was never going to marry the new Chosen."

"By breaking the treaty, you put my mother's life at risk. She could be dead right now for all I know!" I realize I'm yelling, but I don't care. Let the entire palace wake from my fury.

Aspen's lips pull into a snarl. "I may not have fulfilled your precious treaty, but as far as the humans are concerned, it isn't broken."

"How is that possible?"

"My brother fulfilled it."

My mind goes blank as I process his words. "Cobalt...fulfilled the treaty? You mean..."

"He is now King of Autumn, according to the council."

"You gave up your throne after everything we did to save it?"

He shrugs. "It is but a partial loss. I have every intention of remaining King of Autumn."

"How? If the council has determined Cobalt has the throne—"

"I am claiming Unseelie King of Autumn according to the Old Ways. The rulers of Earthen, Wind, Winter, and Lunar support me. When Cobalt is defeated, I will once again be the only King of Autumn."

What he's saying shouldn't be possible. Since when is there both a seelie and unseelie ruler in one court? The question is quickly overshadowed by what it suggests about Aspen's allegiance. *Unseelie King of Autumn.* My blood goes cold, even as flames lash my palms, begging to be unleashed. "You're turning unseelie? What about the balance of the council?"

"All hope of maintaining balance on the council has been lost. I've had enough. The only thing to do now is to break the council completely."

My rage grows to a fiery inferno at his matter-of-fact tone. "If you destroy the council, what is left to secure the treaty?"

He throws his hands in the air. "Why not ask a better question? If we destroy the treaty, what is left to enforce your exile? Evie, if the treaty breaks, you can't be forced to leave. The Legacy Bond breaks with it."

My voice comes out barely above a whisper, shoulders trembling as I fight to suppress my fire. "They have my mother, Aspen. Without the Legacy Bond, the promise to keep her alive until her trial will be nullified. The humans will execute her on the spot."

His expression alternates between stoic and wounded as silence falls between us. Finally, it settles on steely. "If you are so determined to return to your vile human world, we won't make our stance known until you and your mother are safely on the mainland."

"Your actions will still condemn all the people of the Fair Isle to war. All the people I'm trying to protect with my exile."

"Once you leave the isle, it won't be your problem anymore." His words hold a bitter edge.

"It *is* my problem. This ruins everything. Everything I care about!" Hot tears spring to my eyes, a sob building in my chest.

Aspen's face falls, eyes turning down at the corners. He lifts a hand as if to bring his fingers to my face but stops himself halfway. He lowers his arm, tensing as he pins it stiff at his side. "Maybe it's time to reevaluate what you think you care about and make a different choice."

"What's that supposed to mean?" I say through my tears. "Are you insinuating I don't care about the right things? Are human lives not worth saving?"

He lets out a low grumble. "*Human* lives. Even with proof of your heritage, you still care more about them than the fae."

My breath hitches when I realize what I said. I didn't mean to say *human* lives. I meant to say lives in general, but the word came so naturally. In all honesty, I've been growing more and more enamored with the fae, even the unseelie, as of late. I still don't trust them, especially outside a controlled environment, but I've seen for myself how amiable they can be. How wild, beautiful, and unrestrained.

Before I can say any of this, Aspen takes a step away, shoulders rigid. "I must return to the meeting." His eyes lock on something behind me, narrowing as his lips raise into a snarl. "Perhaps Prince Franco can see you back to your room. He's quite adept at that."

He stalks back behind the double doors, leaving me feeling empty in his wake.

21

———————

When I turn around, Prince Franco stands in the middle of the hall. He smirks at the closed doors of the throne room until his eyes meet mine. His expression softens, cheeks flushing to a pale rosy hue.

With hesitant steps, he approaches me, lips flickering between a frown and a wary smile. "I should apologize."

"It's not your fault." *It's everyone's fault. Everyone's including mine. Everything is ruined.* White hot rage continues to burn after my argument with Aspen. I let it sear away my sorrow and pain, let it char the remnants of my hangover-induced headache to nothing. The result is a sharpening of clarity. Strength.

"I said I *should* apologize, but that doesn't mean I'm sorry. Causing you pain was never my intention, but I don't regret kissing you."

I'm at a loss for words, surprised by his candor. I, however, don't have any honest words to meet his. Do I regret kissing him? Do I regret the fun and freedom I had last night? I regret that Aspen is under a false impression about my involvement with the prince, but it's hard to be sorry when my anger at the king is stronger.

The *unseelie* king. The king who is plotting war at this very moment.

"Anyhow, I came to give you this." Franco holds out an envelope.

My heart leaps into my throat as I take it. The envelope holds no seal, no address, and I tear the letter from inside with trembling fingers.

Franco doesn't say a word as he leaves me to read the letter alone.

I'm grateful for the privacy because I'm quickly undone by the words I read.

Dear sister, I thank you for your concern. I assure you, I have received word of the allegations against our mother and the summons for my presence at her trial. However, as Faerwyvae is my home, I will not leave it to attend.

The letter ends there, unsigned. However, the script is familiar and written without haste, Amelie's elegant loops and swirls intact. Could she have written so neatly under duress? Were these words forced from her by Cobalt's demand through the Bond? Or are they entirely her own?

Anger and sorrow clash as I fall to my knees. My sob is accompanied by a shout as I slam my fist into the opalescent floor. The ground rocks beneath me, and I feel a wave of heat burst from my palm. I'm so startled, my emotions drain in an instant. When I turn my attention to the floor, I find several fissures darting from where my hand made contact. The damage isn't deep, but it's obvious. With a gasp, I leap to my feet and run from the scene of my destruction.

I don't realize where I'm going until I find myself outside Lorelei's open door. She and Foxglove rush toward me, taking in my blank expression. My tears have already dried with my violent outburst in the hall. I'm not sure what to say, so I hand Foxglove the letter.

He and Lorelei read it in tandem, then their wide eyes meet mine.

"I'm so sorry," Lorelei whispers. She puts a hand on my shoulder and guides me into her room until we reach her couch. "Here, sit."

I do as I'm told, finding a glass in my hands a moment later. As I bring it to my lips, a familiar aroma sends my head spinning. "Midnight Blush?"

Lorelei grimaces. "I might have smuggled a bottle under my gown from the revel last night."

I don't hesitate a moment longer before I take a drink, letting the wine slide down my throat and warm my stomach. With eyes closed, I savor the way it eases my breathing and slows my racing heart. It helps me find a sense of calm amidst the chaos in my mind. Once I've managed to regain some semblance of composure, I say, "Tell me everything. What happened last night?"

Foxglove takes a seat on the couch next to me while Lorelei perches on the armrest. "It was madness," Foxglove says, adjusting his spectacles. "We knew it would be messy, of course, but things went far worse than the king expected."

"What did Aspen expect?" I say, forcing my words to come out evenly. "How long had he been planning on refusing to marry his Chosen?"

"I doubt he ever planned to marry her at all, so long as he could guarantee his actions didn't put you or your mother in danger. When Queen Nyxia informed him in private that you were safe in Lunar, he was confident in his decision to refuse the marriage alliance. However, I do believe he was under the impression that if you were in Lunar, you were resigned to stay in Faerwyvae."

That explains why he seemed surprised when I told him I still planned to attend my mother's trial. "Did Nyxia not tell him the truth? That my stay here is a temporary one?"

Foxglove frowns. "Omission is a great form of deception when one can't lie. Especially when the result suits one's needs quite well."

Of course Nyxia wanted Aspen to compromise the treaty. Her omission helped hurry his resolve.

Foxglove continues. "Once the king made his stance clear to the council, the majority reacted as he anticipated. The unseelie supported him, but most of the seelie were in an uproar. The king even expected what happened next, although it was a surprise how it came to pass."

I sit forward in my seat. "What?"

"Queen Dahlia suggested the council allow Prince Cobalt to secure the treaty and strip Aspen from his throne."

"Queen Dahlia made that suggestion? Why am I not surprised?" I knew there was something about her I didn't like. Well, aside from the grudge I've carried against her for not taking better care of Faerwyvae's only other living Chosen—the aging Doris Mason, a lonely woman spending her miserable final days at Queen Dahlia's Summer Court. After my most recent unsettling conversation with the queen, I thought perhaps it was Aspen's affection she wanted. I wouldn't have guessed she was after his demise.

"I always thought she was fake," Lorelei says with a sneer.

"Aspen had his suspicions about her as well," Foxglove says. "It's unclear whether she was in contact with Cobalt during her entire stay, but it can be assumed the betrayal was set up from the start."

"What happened when she petitioned for Cobalt to take the throne?" I ask.

"Well, it certainly put the council further at odds. Arguments were made that Cobalt had lost his right to rule Autumn when the All of All chose Aspen. But other council fae insisted the ruling of the All of All encompassed that incident alone, and that Cobalt could still be considered an eligible heir now that Aspen was compromising the treaty yet again. The debate went on and on without resolution as the council was split half-and-half. You see, one ruler was missing from the festivities up to that point."

His grim expression sets me on edge. "Who?"

"Queen Melusine. Queen Dahlia got the council to agree that the Sea Court would have final say over the ruling. And that, my dear, is when Cobalt came waltzing into the palace like he owned it."

Lorelei mutters a string of curses.

A rush of indignation heats my core. "How did Cobalt have the nerve to show his face before the ruling was made for or against him?"

"He was protected," Foxglove says, "by his claim that he was now King of the Sea Court."

"Wait, did Melusine...give her throne to Cobalt?"

His voice lowers, tone grave. "Not willingly. He made his apologies, stating he was late because he'd spent all day dealing with the murder of his mother."

My throat goes dry. "Murder?"

"He went on to claim she was found dead in one of the collapsed underwater caves near the shore with an iron blade buried inside her. *Your* iron blade, to be exact."

"Mine?" The room begins to spin around me, the blood leaving my face. I remember what Aspen muttered to the wolf king in the throne room. *It wasn't her.* "The council actually believed it was I who killed her?"

Foxglove wrings his hands. "It was a devious accusation, one that served several purposes. Not only would your guilt weaken Aspen's position, but your innocence would reveal your whereabouts to King Ustrin. You see, neither Aspen nor Nyxia could provide you an alibi without giving away your location."

I shake my head, wondering how long this plan has been in motion. All this time, Cobalt had my missing blade, the one I lost when he captured me in the coral caves. He's likely been waiting for the perfect opportunity to use it as revenge, and what better way than to condemn me and his brother while earning himself a new crown? Then again, the iron blade should have made my dagger impossible for him to wield...

A chill runs up my spine. *But not impossible for Amelie.*

My heart races as another chilling thought creeps upon my awareness. Melusine knew this would happen.

I put my hand to my heart as I sink into the back of the couch. "It's my fault," I whisper.

Foxglove and Lorelei exchange a glance. "Why would you think that?" Lorelei says.

"The day the letter came, after the explosion and the attack on the coral caves, she came to me while Aspen was still fighting Cobalt's fae. She told me she feared for her life, begged me to petition Aspen on her behalf. With everything that happened after, I never gave her request a second thought. I...never said a word to Aspen."

Foxglove's eyes turn down at the corners. "That doesn't make it your fault."

"I may not have killed her like the council thinks, but her death is on my hands."

Without a word, Lorelei refills my glass with more Midnight Blush.

I down it as quickly as I can. "Let me guess what happened next," I say, voice hoarse. "Cobalt ruled in favor of himself on behalf of the Sea Court and became King of Sea and Autumn in a single day."

Foxglove nods. "It created a violent divide between the council. The unseelie held their stance that making Cobalt King of Autumn was the worst kind of blasphemy against the All of All and deemed the council disbanded. The meeting ended, as you might imagine, with bloodshed."

"Was anyone fatally wounded?"

He returns to wringing his hands. "Guards, mostly, but none of the royals. Aspen made the call for his allies to retreat, although it pained him greatly to leave his household staff behind. But with Cobalt ruling the Sea Court, Bircharbor had become too vulnerable for him to try and stay. We fled in the night and came here to Lunar."

"Are those in the throne room Aspen's only allies?" I ask.

"For now," Foxglove says. "They were the royals firmly against Cobalt. However, some of the neutral seelie might be persuaded, like the Earthen King was. It will be a challenge to convince all the neutral seelie to join the rebellion, though, when it would mean fighting for the Old Ways to return, for with that comes the end of the treaty and the dissolution of the Council of Eleven Courts. And war."

The final word chills me, but my attention snags on something else. "I've heard the term the *Old Ways* before. What does it even mean?"

"The Old Ways were how Faerwyvae operated before the war began. The

Council of Eleven Courts was only established to mirror the humans' efforts at the start of the war. When the treaty was forged at the end of it, the fae council was solidified in turn, and the Old Ways fell out of favor."

"And the Old Ways state Aspen can rule as Unseelie King of Autumn even though Cobalt has claimed power?"

"Yes," Foxglove says. "Long before there was ever a fae council, the All of All chose its rulers by blessing an alpha during a show of dominance. When humans came to the isle and fae started taking on seelie forms, there were often two rulers in each court, a seelie and an unseelie. Of course, that was when seelie and unseelie lived in balance and both agreed to follow the Old Ways. But simply declaring a return to the Old Ways isn't enough to bring that balance back. Not with the remaining council fae determined to maintain their authority at all costs. The rebels must overthrow the council. Aspen will have to take down Cobalt."

"It sounds like the fae are at civil war."

His expression turns bleak. "They are. Not everyone knows it yet, but there's no turning back now."

Anxiety tickles my chest. "What does this mean for the treaty? Do we know for sure that Cobalt secured it? Are the rebels considered a threat to it?"

"As far as the humans are concerned," Foxglove says, "the treaty is secure. Nyxia's spies have confirmed that Cobalt performed all three steps to secure the pact. The spies say the humans are aware of the unrest amongst the fae royals but have been assured the threat will be dealt with."

"So, my mother might be safe," I say under my breath. *For now*, I add, the contents of Amelie's letter hitting me like a blow to the heart. "This is a mess," I whisper. "Not only are the fae at civil war, I have my own personal matters of life and death to deal with. If Amelie doesn't come to the trial, my mother will be executed. I doubt my willingness to attend will count for much, as Mr. Duveau assured me my sister's presence is vital. Even if I show up, they...they'll kill me alongside my mother."

Lorelei puts a soothing hand on my shoulder while Foxglove leans in close. "You have one option," he says. "I know about the offer Nyxia gave you."

My eyes go wide. "You think I should make a bid for the Fire throne? Nyxia will have me paired with her brother for it." I say this last part with disdain, although that doesn't reflect my true feelings about the matter. In all honesty, I like Franco. As a friend, at least. But do I like him enough to make him my mate? I can't imagine the term *mate* belonging to anyone but Aspen. Then again…

My chest squeezes as my argument with Aspen echoes through my head.

"Evelyn," Foxglove says, tone gentle, "you don't have to do anything you don't want to do. Nyxia is a clever fae. She will support her own cause in any way she can. In this, she is simply trying to secure an alliance between her court and yours. I have no doubt she would support the Unseelie Queen of Fire regardless of mate, and if so, those allies you saw in the throne room would be your allies too. I wouldn't underestimate that kind of backing."

Unseelie Queen of Fire. I shudder. "How would that help my situation?"

A spark of excitement lights his eyes. "If you were queen of your own court, you would have a say alongside the other royals. You could use your influence to temper the most violent whims of the unseelie. Your position would give you the means to protect those you love and shape the future of the Fair Isle. If you wanted, you could strive to maintain the treaty after the rebels win the war against the council fae."

My pulse races at the last part. If what he's saying is true, there's a chance I could prevent a second war with the humans. Still, there's something missing. "I don't see how that saves my mother."

His expression falters. "It doesn't, honestly. I hate to say so, but saving her might be a lost cause. At least this way, you can save your own life and secure your place in Faerwyvae. You said so yourself; if you attend your mother's trial without Amelie, they will kill you."

"There must be another way. Please, Foxglove, you must have some idea how I can fix this."

He lets out a heavy sigh. "There's only one last hope."

I sit straighter, heart pounding.

"Make the humans a bargain they can't refuse."

22

"How do I make a bargain with the humans?" I ask. "One so tempting they can't say no?"

Foxglove squints, then rises to his feet and begins to pace. "Give me a moment," he says, shaking out his hands and stretching his neck right then left. "Creating bargains to appease the humans is what I excel at, but this is a complicated matter."

I watch him eagerly, and Lorelei leans forward with keen interest.

Finally, he stops and faces us. "There is a loophole in the treaty. You know how the council has been able to adjust the timelines required by it? And how the humans were able to offer Aspen a final set of Chosen before deeming the treaty broken?"

I nod.

"That's because the treaty allows for changes to be made. The exact wording is lengthy and complex, but it basically states that mutually beneficial concessions that support the treaty can be created. These amendments are rare, however, and never so drastic as what I'm about to propose."

My heart leaps into my throat. "And what is it you're suggesting?"

"That they amend the treaty and remove the clause that forbids King Caleos' descendants from living in Faerwyvae."

I'm stunned into a moment of silence. "Can the humans even do that without permission from the fae council?"

"Technically," Foxglove says with a wary grimace. "Considering the humans were the ones who requested King Caleos be punished for the human village he burned, they have the right to revoke the agreed-upon term concerning his exile."

Hope flutters in my heart for a moment before it's crushed by reason. "If this were possible, wouldn't you have suggested this option to begin with?"

He adjusts his spectacles, a frown tugging his lips. "If I thought it had a chance of working, yes. Considering this proposal is highly unlikely to pan out, I'm only voicing it as a last resort."

I deflate and lean back into the couch. "Well, that's comforting."

"At least highly unlikely isn't impossible. Would you like me to go on?"

With a sigh, I nod.

"So, I know King Ustrin has the council wrapped around his finger." He nods at the fae next to me. "Lorelei filled me in on the situation earlier. Here's the thing; if you want to get the humans to amend the treaty in your favor, you first need to compel them to abandon their allegiance to King Ustrin and convince them to place it in you."

I shake my head. "This is sounding more impossible by the minute."

Foxglove ignores me. "To do this, you'll need to promise them something better than anything he can provide. What exactly is he offering them?"

I shrug. "Threats, as far as I know. If the humans don't exile my family, they will be blamed for breaking the treaty."

He shakes a forefinger. "Then it will need to be something bigger than a threat, something only you can provide as a queen. It must be tempting enough to encourage them to look past their fear and see opportunity instead. This will be a challenge because their fear will be strong regarding you. The terms about King Caleos' descendants are woven tightly into the treaty. The humans know that if you claim the throne, the act alone will break the pact."

"I can't break the treaty, Foxglove."

"I know. Which is why you need to convince them to amend the treaty *before* you claim rule as Unseelie Queen of Fire."

I ponder for a moment, collecting my thoughts. "All right," I say, nodding to myself. "I attend the trial, plead my case, and present some tantalizing bargain to win their allegiance. In exchange, they will remove the clause in the treaty that requires exile of King Caleos' descendants. Then Mother and I go free."

Foxglove nods, but his expression isn't optimistic.

With a furrowed brow, I ask, "What am I missing?"

"Nothing dear. It's just...you must follow up with claiming your place as queen."

I take a deep breath. "With Nyxia's support, I think I can do that."

"And you must defeat King Ustrin according to the Old Ways."

"Defeat...King Ustrin," I echo slowly, hating the taste the words leave in my mouth.

"Well, yes," Foxglove says. "Even if the treaty were amended to allow you to stay, he'd never acknowledge your right to rule. He'll put up a fight."

What he's saying is obvious, but hearing it stated aloud highlights the ridiculousness of this entire plan. "This really is crazy, isn't it?"

Lorelei leans in closer to me. "It's not impossible to defeat him, Evelyn. I know it sounds that way, but all you need according to the Old Ways is the All of All's blessing. The fact that you already petitioned the Twelfth Court and were blessed with a crown shows you have an advantage over King Ustrin. He never faced the All of All for his throne. It was given to him by the two councils."

"What makes you think he won't gain the All of All's blessing just because I unwittingly managed to?"

Foxglove and Lorelei exchange a glance. "There's no way to know for sure," Foxglove says, "and I can't say it won't be a huge risk."

I shake my head and rise to my feet. Now I'm the one who's pacing. "I can't do this."

"You could at least try," Foxglove says.

"Or give up this whole idea," I say under my breath.

Lorelei approaches me, taking me by the shoulders to halt my steps. Her expression is fierce, though not unkind. "What's the alternative? Are you going to beg Mr. Duveau for your life? Plead with him to exile you?"

My skin crawls at the thought of begging Mr. Duveau for anything. I force my words past my teeth. "If I must."

"And where will that get you?" She gives my shoulders a light shake as if she's trying to stir my anger. I almost wish it would ignite. Anything is better than this overwhelming despair. "I know you'd never forgive yourself for leaving the Fair Isle on the brink of chaos without at least trying first. You're better than that. Fiercer. You're above begging scum like Henry Duveau for your life."

Finally, her words meet their mark, like flint striking steel. The fire of indignation burns inside me, forcing my posture to straighten. However, the intangible odds continue to batter my resolve.

"I don't know what to do," I say, surprised at the heat in my tone. "I need to save my mother, the treaty, and the fates of two races. Oh, and if there's time, I'd like to save my life too. To do so, I'll have to bargain with a council that hates me, defeat a fae king who hates me more, and once that's all taken care of, I'll have to help the rebellion win a civil war. For the love of iron, how the hell am I to accomplish all this?"

Foxglove's lips pull into a frown. "I agree with what you said. This is too much. If you don't take a side, you spread yourself too thin. But if you're determined to try and do everything at once, then this scheme is the only way."

Tears spring to my eyes, the sheer impossibility of the task at hand threatening to crush me back into despair. This time, I refuse to buckle beneath its weight. Lorelei's right. I'm fiercer than this. Things may have swung far out of my control, but there's still a way for me to gain an upper hand. There's an option that might make everything right...or as right as it can be.

If I do this, I could save the treaty.

I could save my mother.

I could prevent bloodshed.

I could protect fae and humans alike.

There's another benefit to this scheme, one that takes me by surprise.

I could be with Aspen.

It's the first time I've considered our relationship since this conversation began. Of course, after the words we exchanged in the hall, I'm not sure we even have a relationship. Still, I can't deny the way my pulse races at the idea that, if we wanted to, we *could* have one.

Maybe. If this works.

"I'll do it," I finally say. "With all things considered, the worst that can happen is I die trying. At best...well, at this point, I'm not sure if there is an at best. But at least this way, I'm part of the fight *and* the solution."

Lorelei lifts her chin, giving me an approving smile, while Foxglove claps his hands.

"We don't have much time," I say. "The trial is in less than a week. I know I must come up with an offer compelling enough to convince the humans to bargain with me, but what can I do in the meantime?"

"First step is," Foxglove says, "you need to gather supporters."

23

After night falls, I meet Queen Nyxia outside the palace. Lorelei insisted on coming along, but Nyxia arrives alone. The queen spots us hidden in the shadows of a moonstone column on the southern end of the palace, and when her eyes find mine in the dark, a smug smile spreads across her face.

"I almost didn't believe Foxglove when he arranged this meeting," she says in her smooth voice. "Please tell me this isn't an ill-constructed assassination attempt." Her eyes flash toward Lorelei, her smile turning a hint seductive.

Lorelei tosses her a seething glare but says nothing.

I pull my cloak close to my body and take a step toward the queen. "Have you told anyone else about this meeting?"

"Like your mate?"

"Like anyone." While Aspen certainly is on the top of my mind in this regard, I'm not ready for word of my plans to spread just yet. Not until I'm far more certain of its possible success. At this point, anything could go wrong. For now, I don't want the pressure of others' hopes riding on my shoulders.

Nyxia rolls her eyes with an irritated sigh. "No, I didn't tell anyone."

"Promise me you won't say anything. Not until I'm ready."

Her fingers flutter dismissively in the air. "Sure. Silence on this matter benefits my cause as well, you know. I don't want to present you to the rebel leaders until your footing is more secure."

"That wasn't exactly a promise."

Her tone sharpens. "If you want a solid promise, you're going to need to be a little more direct in your wording. If I must tell no one that you plan on taking the Fire Court throne, how am I to introduce you to the fire fae? Perhaps you should trust that, in this matter, our interests are aligned."

Despite her often-indifferent air, I'm reminded of her terrifying power. This is not a fae to anger. I square my shoulders. "Very well."

Nyxia's smile returns. "Come along then."

Lorelei and I follow the queen away from the palace. At first, I think we might head where the full moon revel took place, but instead, she leads us into the forests beyond. My pulse quickens as we move deep into dark trees, bleak shadows punctuated by clusters of glowing mushrooms and towering, bell-shaped flowers that emit near-blinding luminescence. It's breathtaking and terrifying all at once.

We continue in silence until Queen Nyxia speaks. "Now that you have accepted my offer to support your claim to the Fire throne, I do wonder if that means you've also accepted the terms I'd presented alongside it?"

I clench my jaw. I was wondering how long it would be before she brought up a mate alliance with Franco again. However, broaching the subject in the dark of the woods is not ideal. Not with so many convenient places to bury my body.

"Honest but tactful," Lorelei whispers in my ear. "And strong," she adds.

With a deep breath and careful consideration over my choice of words, I construct my reply. "Queen Nyxia, I appreciate your support of my claim to the throne and am honored—"

"Don't pander to me," the queen says. "It's unbecoming."

Lorelei emits a low growl, but I place a hand on her arm to still her.

"Fine," I say. "I understand you want our alliance made formal by pairing me with your brother, but I cannot accept. If you believe in my right to rule the Fire throne, then I claim that right alone. My choice of mate will be mine to make and shall have no bearing on my rule."

Nyxia watches me out of the corner of her eye, then lifts her chin. "Spoken like a true unseelie queen. I will continue to support your claim."

I exchange a look of relief with Lorelei.

Nyxia continues. "It would be hypocritical of me to condemn your desire to claim your throne by yourself when I too have yet to take a mate." She glances at Lorelei, her seductive smile tugging her lips. "Although it isn't from lack of trying."

Lorelei scowls. "Oh, I'd say those seventeen fae at Beltane would disagree."

She shrugs. "It was a mere slip in judgment. You know I was never good at being monogamous before. It was a difficult adjustment…"

And the bickering begins.

~

By the time we reach the mouth of a cave, Lorelei and the queen have already cycled through several rounds of verbal assaults and steely silence. I tuned them out long ago for my own sanity.

The queen stops outside the cave's opening, her mood unflustered, while Lorelei's irritation wafts like a tangible essence as she stands at my side with her arms crossed. "Here we are," Nyxia says in a sing-song voice. She enters the cave, and Lorelei and I follow.

"The fire fae are gathered inside?" I ask, trying to hide the tremble in my voice as the damp cave walls seem to close in on me.

"Yes. Those who received my summons in time, that is."

"How did you gather them so quickly?" Foxglove couldn't have requested this meeting more than a few hours ago. I was surprised when he told me it would happen tonight.

"Owls." She says it like it should be obvious. "They are the most astute messengers and spies my court has."

As we venture deeper into the cave, a faint light begins to glow up ahead. It soon proves to be from more glowing mushrooms protruding from the walls of the cave, joined by the luminescence of enormous crystals.

"Where are we?" I say with a gasp.

"Oh this? It's Venitia's house."

"Venitia?"

"A moon dragon. You'll meet him."

I swallow hard. The light grows brighter as we continue on, and soon comes the sound of voices, growls, and yips. We come to a wide chamber, its walls lined with more glowing fungi and crystals. Throughout it, various fae are gathered including several kitsune with their orbs of fires hovering over their mouths or tails, blue wisps, a black dragon, and something I at first took for an overgrown fungus but now see is some kind of crustacean-mushroom hybrid with curious eyes peeking beneath its shell.

The fae grow quiet as we enter the chamber, eyes falling on Queen Nyxia. She addresses them with a smile. "Thank you for gathering to meet me on such short notice and being so willing to greet my guest." She flicks a finger at me, and I come up beside her.

My mouth dries up as all eyes lock on me, some with boredom, others with keen interest, and a few with open hostility. "I am pleased to meet you," I manage to say.

Nyxia frowns at me for a moment before returning her attention to the fire fae. "It is my great honor to introduce to you King Caleos' granddaughter, Evelyn."

Gasps and yips emit from my audience. Some of the expressions have now turned reverent while others seem a bit more fearful.

Nyxia continues. "With King Ustrin growing more and more militant in his rule as the centuries pass, your kind have sought shelter in other courts. You've always been welcome here in Lunar and will continue to be. However, I ask you to consider what it might be like if an unseelie ruler were on the Fire throne. Not just any ruler, but the blood of the great King Caleos."

Whispers, grunts, and other animal noises rumble throughout the cave. When they subside, a kitsune steps forward on graceful paws, a ball of flame hovering in the air above its muzzle. Its eyes move from me to Nyxia. When it speaks, the words come through like Aspen's had in stag form—not from its lips but from somewhere inside it. Or inside my mind. "I see the blood of King Caleos, but I see no unseelie ruler but you."

Nyxia extends her hand toward me. "Evelyn plans to stake her claim as Unseelie Queen of Fire according to the Old Ways. Once she defeats King Ustrin, she will be the only ruler of Fire and the unseelie will be safe to return to the Fire Court if they wish."

The kitsune doesn't look convinced, nor do the majority of the fae in the crowd. "What is her unseelie form, then?"

Several voices echo their support of the question. A blue wisp bounces forward, her ethereal voice slow and smooth as she says, "Yes, I too want to see her unseelie form. I want to see she's truly one of us."

The blood leaves my face. Do they honestly expect me to be able to *shift forms*? Surely, they must know I'm not full-fae.

Queen Nyxia gives the crowd a placating smile. "She will show you her unseelie form when the time is right." I shoot her a look of surprise, but she ignores it. "This is but an introduction so you can spread the word that hope is coming to Fire. That an unseelie rule is soon to return."

Voices rise, calling out demands to see me shift. I feel like I might be sick.

"Why doesn't she speak for herself?" the crustacean-mushroom says in a low, gravelly voice. A rumble of agreement moves through the crowd.

Nyxia gives me a pointed look before nodding.

My palms grow hot as, once again, all eyes fall on me. I want to run, to forfeit this entire plan and forget I ever thought I have what it takes to do this. This is what it would mean to be queen. I'd be required to give speeches, to represent a people I hardly understand.

I take a step back to catch my bearings, but my heart leaps into my throat as my lungs constrict.

"Breathe," Lorelei whispers. "You can do this."

I close my eyes, the cave spinning around me.

Lorelei's whisper takes on a harsh quality. "Would you rather beg Henry Duveau for your life?"

Her words ignite a ripple of fire, and with it comes a sense of clarity. I connect to the fire, let it burn away my fears. *All I can do is try,* I remind myself.

With a deep breath, I step forward and meet the eyes of my audience —*my people.* They don't truly feel like my people, not only because they are fae but because they are unseelie. However, that must change. If I am to become Queen of Fire, I will have to consider the term *unseelie* without fear or disgust. I will have to fight for them as strongly as I fight for the humans.

"Your kind are suppressed by the radical seelie like King Ustrin," I say. The hesitation in my tone is obvious, but I call forth more fire to burn it away. Thoughts of King Ustrin allow my anger to rise. I think about what he did to my mother, to the apothecary. Until I can fight for the unseelie without forcing it, I can at least fight against *him.*

"King Ustrin maintains his power by turning his back on the Old Ways." I'm not even sure what I'm saying, but my voice is stronger now. "He betrays his own kind to keep a throne he never earned. The council he supports grows more and more seelie every day. If allowed to fall too far into the hands of the radical seelie, the Old Ways will be eliminated entirely. The unseelie will be eliminated. You'll be forced into clothes, forced to obey laws that strip you from the traditions you've held onto for countless centuries."

Even though my words only echo what I learned from Aspen, I find myself feeling the truth in them. My audience seems intrigued, their gazes intent upon me. I continue. "The Council of Eleven Courts has been broken and a war between the fae is coming. The radical seelie seek control while the rebels seek freedom." I put my hand on my heart. "I am part of that rebellion. As Unseelie Queen of Fire, I will fight the forces that threaten your way of life. I will fight against King Ustrin and win us back the Fire Court. I will win back our home."

A kitsune lets out a bark that sounds like approval, while other encouraging sounds emit from several other fae.

Nyxia looks almost impressed.

Movement at the back of the crowd snags my attention and the masses return to quiet. The black dragon uncoils, extending its lithe neck toward me. "You are of human blood." The voice is part hiss, part whisper. "You may promise to fight for us, but how do we know you won't fight for them more? How can we trust you won't be worse than King Ustrin?"

My confidence falters. To say I won't fight for the humans would be a lie. Am I ready to promise I'll at least fight for them equally?

Nyxia seems to sense my loss of momentum and takes a step forward. "Like I said, dear ones, this is but an introduction. We know it will take time for you to trust what Evelyn has to offer. In the meantime, I ask you to trust *me*. Trust me when I say that I believe Evelyn is the answer to tipping the balance in our favor. Spread word of what you learned tonight, but do it discreetly. Rally the unseelie fire fae and anyone who seeks an end to King Ustrin's reign. We will gather again when Evelyn is ready to make her move against him."

"Will she show us her unseelie form then?" asks an orange sprite.

Queen Nyxia plasters an exaggerated smile over her lips. "Yes. Until then, do as I've requested."

The cave erupts with commotion, and the three of us turn to leave. All I hear is the pounding of my heart in my ears as we exit the cave, my feet flying beneath me. Once we return beneath the forest trees, I halt and round on Queen Nyxia. "You lied."

"I cannot lie."

"You told them I would show them my unseelie form next time I meet with them."

"And you will."

My eyes bulge as I stare at her. "You don't understand. I don't have that kind of power. I can't shift like the full-fae can."

"Sure you can." She walks on ahead, leaving me gaping behind her.

I turn to Lorelei, silently begging her to argue some sense into the queen.

Instead, she says, "She's right."

"How do you figure?"

"You've already proven yourself capable of using fae magic," Lorelei says. "That's all you need to shift. It's simply a matter of knowing how, which you have yet to learn."

"How can you be so sure? I'm only one-quarter fae."

She shrugs, and we hurry to catch up with the queen. "The half-fae children of the Chosen have always been able to shift, and none of them seem any more adept with magic than you."

This takes me by surprise. "They can?"

Nyxia turns to look over her shoulder at me. "Yes, and so will you. It is your only hope of winning over the unseelie fire fae completely."

I rub my temples. "Great. Let me just add that to my list of unrealistic things I'm supposed to do to save the isle."

"Evelyn, you've been to the Twelfth Court," Lorelei says. "That's all it takes. That, magic, and intent. All magic stems from intent. You'll learn."

I open my mouth to argue, but Nyxia comes to a sudden halt, forcing me and Lorelei to stop as well. An enormous owl swoops down from the sky and lands at the queen's feet. "Urgent," the owl says. "Unwelcome guests have traveled through the axis. They're heading for Selene Palace."

24

———————

"Who do you think it is?" I ask Lorelei as we hurry back through the woods toward the palace. Nyxia already took off in her shadow form as soon as the owl delivered its message.

"I don't know," Lorelei says, "but it can't be good."

We continue on as swiftly as we can. The forest remains eerily silent, as if the message has every creature in the woods on high alert. I'm hyper aware of every snapping twig, every rustling leaf.

"Evie." The sound of my name has me nearly leaping out of my skin. I draw back as a figure materializes seemingly from nowhere. A scream builds in my throat and I nearly release it until the moonlight illuminates a pair of antlers.

"Aspen! What are you doing here?"

He takes me by the shoulders. "For the love of oak and ivy, where have you been? Are you safe?"

All I can do is nod, startled by the concern written over his expression.

His eyes leave me to scan my surroundings. "Why are you in the woods?"

I blink a few times, confused by the question. Then I recognize that familiar purple aura around him and realize he isn't really here. I take a deep breath to steady my nerves as I consider how to answer his question. I'm not ready to tell him the truth about what I've been doing. Besides, the longer he stands in my presence, the more I recall I'm still mad at him over our argument in the hall. I don't owe him an explanation. Not yet. "I'm with Lorelei," I say curtly.

He purses his lips, hands sliding from my shoulders as if he's suddenly uncomfortable with the physical contact. In the absence of his touch comes a sting of regret. "Stay there," he says without warmth. "Do not come back to the palace."

"Why? What's happening?"

"King Ustrin is coming."

My throat goes dry. "What does he want?"

"Just stay where you are." With that, he's gone.

When my vision adjusts to Aspen's sudden disappearance, I find Lorelei in his place. Her hands are on her hips, head cocked to the side as she watches me with a raised brow. "What the bloody oak and ivy just happened?"

"You didn't see him?"

"See who?"

I almost don't want to explain, but her expression tells me she won't let me off that easy. "Aspen was here."

She lifts a brow. "Aspen? He was here just now?" Her tone is flat, full of skepticism.

I let out a sigh. "It's something that's been happening since I left Bircharbor. At first, I thought they were dreams, but they're...something else."

Her posture relaxes. "Wait, you're serious?"

I nod. "I don't understand it, but there are times when we're able to see each other. It...might be linked to the Bond." Since finding out my dreams were true occurrences, I haven't given the phenomenon much thought. But now, it's beginning to make sense. "I think we've been using the Bond to visit each other somehow. When I use his name and think of him in a certain way, I can see where he is. And when he uses mine...likewise. That's why he knew I was in trouble in Eisleigh. Lorelei, he was there in the underground laboratory."

"That's a lot to take in," she says. "But all right, I think I understand what you're saying. Although, I don't believe that's a common feature of the Bond."

"Well, whatever the case, there's something far more pressing. He told me King Ustrin is coming and urged me to remain hidden."

She gapes. "He's coming? Where, to the palace? That's who Nyxia went to confront?"

"That's what it sounded like."

Lorelei darts forward, then hesitates. "No, he's right. You need to remain in hiding."

"Like hell," I say. "I need to know what's going on."

"A lot of good that will do if he kills you."

I feel the blood leave my face, but I refuse to back down. "Even so, what if he already knows I'm here? What if he's coming to threaten Lunar for harboring me? I can't let anyone get hurt for me."

"What are you going to do? Sacrifice yourself?"

"If I must."

She rolls her eyes. "What is with you and the constant need to put others before you? Is your life not worth more?"

The question catches me off guard. I've always wanted to help others and save lives. That's why I wanted to become a surgeon. But her words bring to mind an unsettling question; what is my own life worth? I shake my head. "If there's anything I can do to keep others from getting hurt, I have a right to do it."

"Fine. But I'm making you invisible."

"Invisible? How?"

She lifts her hands. "I'm putting a glamour over you."

I step away, blinking furiously as a flash of betrayal ignites within. "You're going to glamour me?"

She clenches her jaw. "No, Evelyn. You can stop blinking now."

I take a deep breath and force my eyelids to stop fluttering.

Her hands remain raised. "I'm putting a *physical* glamour over you. It's different from a mental one. A physical glamour doesn't interfere with a person's mind."

"All right," I say slowly. "You think you can really make me invisible?"

"I'll try," she says. She remains still for a few moments before lowering her hands with a shrug. "Well, let's hope it works."

"What do you mean, let's hope? You can't tell if it worked?"

"It's my glamour. Since I know it's there, I can see through it. You look as clear as day to me."

I sigh and start back down our path. "Good enough."

Lorelei shakes her head. "King Aspen better not have my neck for this."

MY FEET ACHE BY THE TIME WE REACH THE EDGE OF THE FOREST OUTSIDE THE palace lawn. Despite my glamour, we remain hidden behind the trunk of a tree while Lorelei scans the landscape. She tenses, and I follow her line of vision. Outside the southern end of the palace, where Lorelei and I had met Nyxia mere hours ago, stand dozens of armed fae, mostly wraiths and ghouls with weapons as ethereal as their forms. Their bodies are angled away from us as they face the distant tree line.

We creep forward, crossing the lawn toward the palace. Once we reach a row of towering hedges near the building, we make our way forward until the retinue comes further into view. We slip beneath shadows until we reach the nearest column. There we peek around it for a better vantage.

Before the soldiers stand Nyxia, Franco, and Aspen, as well as the rulers of Wind, Winter, and Earthen. Their postures are tense as they stare ahead at what appears to be nothing. Endless moments of chilling silence pass until movement flickers in the distant shadows. Three figures approach, and as they near, I recognize the middle as King Ustrin. He wears a red suit, its color dim against the radiance of his orange scales glinting in the moonlight. The fae on each side of him look like guards. They have scaled bodies like the king, but their coloring is pale yellow. The one to Ustrin's right seems to be trembling, his steps slower than his companion's.

The three figures stop several yards away from the gathering before them.

I hardly breathe as I strain to hear over my pounding heart.

"Queen Nyxia," Ustrin says, his voice quiet but loud enough to carry to us. "How good of you to greet me with such a charming welcoming party. Although, when I requested my right to a peaceful exchange of words, I didn't expect so many soldiers to take part. Did your owl not make my intentions clear? I did not come for a fight."

Nyxia gives him a toothy smile, her canines conveying the hidden threat in the gesture. "Why are you here? You were not invited."

"That's no way to speak to a fellow council fae."

"You and I both know I am no longer considered a council fae. The same goes for the rulers who stand beside me."

"Ah, well I did want to hear it from your lips before I assumed too much," King Ustrin says, a false smile on his lipless mouth. "Then my next order of business can commence. By order of the Council of Eleven Courts, I hereby deem you, Nyxia of Lunar, stripped of your right to rule. The same goes for you, Aspen of Autumn, Aelfon of Earthen, Minuette of Wind, and Flauvis of Winter." He nods at each of the rulers in turn. The tension in the air is palpable, and even I bristle at this blatant omission of their royal titles.

The wolf fae—King Flauvis, that is—lets out a deep growl. King Aelfon, the stout fae with curling horns and deep, brown skin, pounds his hooves into the grass beneath him. The ethereal Queen Minuette lets out a windy hiss with her blue lips.

"You don't have that kind of power," Nyxia says, unperturbed by the threat. "We have deemed the council disbanded. Nothing you say has any weight over our actions, decisions, or rights to rule."

King Ustrin narrows his beady eyes. "We'll see what tune you're singing once you're outnumbered on a battlefield. You see, the council is electing seelie rulers in each court." His eyes flash toward King Aelfon. "A *new* seelie ruler, in some cases."

A snarl rips from the Earthen King's lips. I'm surprised he can manage not to launch for the Fire King's throat. With only two guards, King Ustrin could easily be overpowered.

"Go ahead and play at being in power while you still can," Nyxia says. "You won't be much longer."

I feel a chill at her words, sensing the double meaning. Not only does she mean the council, but him personally. King Ustrin seems to sense it too, the smile slipping from his face. "Now onto my next order of business. I'd like to offer one of your subjects an alliance with the council. Prince Franco, the council offers you the position of Seelie King of Lunar."

Nyxia visibly tenses, shadows curling from her fingertips. "Excuse me?"

Franco's eyes bulge, but he says nothing.

"Now, now," Ustrin says, "there's no need to get your shadows involved, Nyxia. This is a peaceful exchange of words, remember? If Prince Franco would like to accept the offer, he should be free to do so. Or is all that talk about freedom of choice simply...talk?"

Nyxia snarls, but it's cut off as Prince Franco takes a step forward, then another. She watches in horror as her brother closes the distance between himself and King Ustrin.

The Fire King greets the prince with a triumphant grin.

"That slimy, son-of-a-harpy," I say under my breath. Rage burns inside me, turning every fond memory of the Lunar Prince to ash.

Ustrin extends a hand, which Franco accepts. In a blink of an eye, the prince pulls Ustrin toward him, and his free hand collides with the Fire King's flat nose. "That's what I think of your offer," he says, arms wide as he sweeps into a mocking bow.

All right. I take it all back. Prince Franco is—

One of the guards, the one who was trembling earlier, unsheathes his sword and buries it in Franco's stomach. I let out a shout echoed by Nyxia as the prince falls to his knees. Nyxia's shadows unfurl and her soldiers begin to surge forward. The guard convulses before releasing the hilt and falling to the ground motionless. The second guard takes his place, gritting his teeth as his fingers stop inches from the hilt.

"It's iron." King Ustrin's voice halts the oncoming melee. "One more step and I'll have the prince beheaded with it."

Nyxia's shadows disappear, and she motions for her soldiers to take a step back.

"Think about the rules, Nyxia," Ustrin says. "In a peaceful exchange of words, violence is forbidden. It can only be met blow for blow. As of now, equal blows have been exchanged and it can stop here. But if you attack me, it will be my right to end his life."

"Let him go," Nyxia says through her teeth.

Franco moans in pain, head lolling to the side.

"I'll let the prince go if you let me speak with Evelyn Fairfield."

A hush falls over the crowd, punctuated only by Franco's whimpers.

"Oh, let's not play dumb," Ustrin says. "I know she's here. As my final order of business, I ask only that I speak with her. The rules made by the peaceful exchange of words will be extended to her, and she will not be harmed tonight. I give my promise."

Aspen burns Nyxia with a glare, but Nyxia keeps her lips pursed tight.

I look from King Ustrin to Prince Franco. "Release the glamour," I whisper to Lorelei.

"No," she argues. "He may have promised not to harm you today, but once he knows you're here, there's no stopping him from returning tomorrow."

"I'll give you a count of five," King Ustrin shouts. "If you don't reveal Miss Fairfield in that time, I'll be the next to deliver a blow, and it will cost your prince his life." His guard's fingers flinch toward the sword. "Five."

"Release the glamour," I hiss at Lorelei.

"Four."

"I'm not letting Franco die."

"Three."

"Damn it, Lorelei—"

She lets out a frustrated grumble and lifts her hands toward me. "Fine."

"Two."

I dart from my hiding place.

"One."

"I'm here. Let the prince go."

Aspen whirls toward me, expression unreadable. He takes a step forward as if to stop me from approaching. I meet his gaze with a subtle shake of my head, hoping I can convey my meaning through the gesture. *Do nothing, Aspen.* His chest heaves with suppressed rage, but I can't tell if it's for me or Ustrin.

King Ustrin faces me with a feral grin. "The rumors are true after all."

"Let. Him. Go."

He waves his hands dismissively. "Once we're done speaking, he's all yours." He nods at his guard, who takes a step away from the prince.

I cross my arms over my chest to keep them from shaking. "What do you want?"

His forked tongue flicks toward me. "I simply wanted to know what your intentions are. After I learned of your escape from imprisonment, I wanted to be sure you weren't doing anything...unwise."

"I didn't escape from imprisonment," I say, my words walking the blade's edge between truth and lie. "The human council gave me permission to await my mother's trial wherever I pleased."

"So you chose Lunar? How quaint."

I shrug.

"And you still plan on attending your mother's trial?"

My mind races as I weigh the impact of my words. "I'm considering it."

He hisses. "What is there to consider?"

"I want a bargain from you."

He erupts with a violent laugh. "A bargain? From me?"

"It will serve us equally."

"What terms do you offer?"

"I want my last days in Faerwyvae to be peaceful ones. That's all I ask. I want you to promise that neither you nor any ally of the Council of Eleven Courts will engage the rebel alliance in violence so long as I remain on the Fair Isle."

His slitted nostrils flare. "What do I get out of this promise?"

"In return, I promise to attend my mother's trial and accept my exile without argument if the human council allows us to leave unharmed."

"And that you will never return," King Ustrin adds.

I swallow hard, preparing the words that could seal my fate. "In addition, I promise that once I leave the Fair Isle, I will never return."

The Fire King's expression shifts with a pleasant smile. "That's all I ever wanted. For your grandfather's ilk to be gone for good. You see, I am not a violent man. I could have you, your mother, and your sister executed, yet I am giving you this mercy."

"Mercy indeed," I say through my teeth.

He lifts his chin. "I agree to this bargain." With a flick of his fingers, the standing guard pulls the sword from Franco and shoves it into the sheath at the incapacitated guard's hip, then hefts him off the ground. The three retreat behind a line of fire that springs from the earth, stretching out in a wide arc behind them.

I run to Franco as does Nyxia. Some of her soldiers pursue Ustrin, breaking through the wall of fire, while the rest set up a perimeter around us. I kneel at the Lunar Prince's side and call for wine and clean cloth. His shirt is soaked with his bright red blood, his face even paler than usual, a gray tinge beginning to creep up his neck. I know what happens to fae who sustain iron injuries. I can only hope the sword wasn't embedded in his abdomen long enough to do severe damage.

I grasp the collar of his linen shirt and tear it open. Black patterns cover his chest and stomach, mingling with the blood. With a shock of relief, I realize the black is not from veins of poison but from his intricate tattoos. I let out a sigh, the tension smoothing from my shoulders. His wound is deep, but with his abdominal cavity free from poison, he will heal much faster than Aspen did.

With the thought of his name, comes the awareness of his proximity. Aspen stands near Franco's head, his presence heavy in the space he occupies. I meet his eyes for a moment, finding a flicker of confusion in them. Then they go steely, and he turns away. Before I can consider him a moment longer, a wraith's gray hand comes into view, bearing a bottle of wine. I quickly pour the liquid over the wound and my hands, then get to work.

25

With every move, I call upon my fire, let it tingle my fingertips as I pour all my intent into Franco's healing. In a matter of minutes, the wound is cleaned and the bleeding is staunched by the remnants of Franco's shirt. Only then do the guards lift him and transport him to his bedroom. That's when I'm finally able to seek out a splinter of bone and spider silk thread to stitch his wound.

In the prince's room, I'm joined by three petite fae with enormous black eyes and pale moth-like wings. I quickly learn they are Lunar Court's healers. They flutter around me, helping where they can. Like Gildmar, they aren't adept at handling injuries from iron or any kind of human weapon. Luckily, Franco's affliction proves to be minimal. I assess internal damage and find that a lesion in his small intestine is already knitting back together before my very eyes. With no further surgery needed, I finish cleaning his wound and begin stitching him back together.

One of the healers hands me a cluster of silky green moss. "Moon moss," she says. "Use it beneath his bandage once you finish his stitches."

I take it from her. "Thank you, but what does it do?"

"It will speed his healing. It only grows near the Wishing Tree when the moon is full."

I finish my ministrations with the help of the fae. Prince Franco begins to rouse by the time I finish tying off his bandage with the moss packed beneath it. His eyelids flutter open, accompanied with a groan of pain. He tries to sit, but I place a hand on his shoulder to steady him.

The moth fae flutter about, and one darts toward the door. "I'll tell Queen Nyxia he's awake." Another pours a cup of Midnight Blush and hands it to me.

"Drink this." He takes the wine from me, and immediate relief crosses his face. Midnight Blush might not be as effective as honey pyrus extract, but considering the mildness of his injury, it should suffice.

He takes the cup and drinks the liquid down, then meets my eyes with a furrowed brow. "You...saved me. With a bargain."

"So you were conscious during that."

He shakes his head, silvery hair sticking out at odd angles. "Sort of. I hope you didn't bargain away anything too vital."

I purse my lips. "So do I."

He studies my face. "Why did you do it? Nyxia would have taken him down before he managed to kill me. Her shadows would have wrecked his mind and each of his guards before they made another move. That's if he had any intention to follow through with his threat to begin with. You know he was baiting you, right?"

At the time, it didn't occur to me that Nyxia would have saved her brother or that Ustrin might be bluffing. In retrospect, of course the powerful alpha would have saved the prince. King Ustrin's threat was a trick for me alone. And it worked.

I try for a nonchalant shrug. "Maybe I wanted to make the bargain."

A corner of his mouth quirks. "For me? Or for some devious plan of yours?"

I blush. Even with the presence of the moth fae, I'm still painfully aware of my proximity to a shirtless Franco in his bedroom. It hadn't seemed improper when he was unconscious. Now all I can see is his heated expression, his bare, inked chest. I clench my jaw and take a step away from his bed where I can more easily maintain my composure. "If I had a devious plan, I wouldn't tell you about it."

"Then I'll pretend you did it for me."

"Pretend all you like, but don't leave this bed for the rest of the night."

His lips pull into a mock pout. "That will be so boring. Unless you plan to stay in it with me."

The sound of buzzing wings and stifled giggles deepens my blush. The prince certainly has no shame. I cross my arms and give him a pointed look, although I can't hide my amusement. "I'm a medical professional, and you are my patient. You are going to stay in this bed *alone* and try to get some sleep. Iron injuries are no joke."

He rolls his eyes. "Fine. You sure know how to take all the fun out of a near-death experience."

I shake my head and pour him another glass of wine. "Drink this, then go to sleep."

He accepts it, and I watch him down it in a single gulp. He winces as he returns the glass to me, then settles back on his pillows. His lids grow heavy and his expression turns serious. "Thank you," he says, "for what you did for me."

"You're welcome." I place a hand on his shoulder to give him a comforting squeeze. Just as I'm about to pull away, he lifts his hand to rest it over mine. Our eyes lock the way they did outside my bedroom after the revel. I can't help but think of the kiss we shared that night. But, of course, that kiss is impossible to consider without thinking of Aspen. About the hurt it caused. About our fight, about the passion and fury I still carry for the king.

My heart sinks, and I gently pull my hand from under his.

Maybe in another life, Franco and I could have been something. Or even in another time. If Aspen and I are unable to mend the rift between us...

I can't finish that train of thought. Instead, I smile at the prince. "Goodnight, Franco."

He returns the grin, blinking slowly as the Midnight Blush begins to take hold. "Goodnight, Evelyn."

I move away from the bed, and one of the moth fae flutters over to me. "We'll watch over him tonight," she whispers.

I give her my thanks and continue to the door, only to come to a halt. In the doorway stands Foxglove, expression forlorn as his eyes rest on the sleeping prince.

"Oh, were you coming inside?" I ask, nodding toward my patient.

He shakes his head as if to clear it. "No, I came to find you."

I join him in the hall, but as we turn away from the door, his attention snags once again on the room.

"Are you sure you didn't want to—"

"No." A blush creeps up his neck as he pushes the bridge of his spectacles.

I can't stop the grin from stretching over my face. "You fancy Prince Franco, don't you?"

His expression turns wistful. "He's just adorable, Evelyn, how could I not?"

"Are you...well acquainted?"

"We've hardly spoken a word. I doubt he knows I exist. Besides, I can admire him from afar, can't I?"

I chuckle. "Yes, I suppose you can."

"Now, enough about that beautiful prince. I came here to talk about you and what happened with King Ustrin."

"Did you witness it?"

"I watched everything from the observatory and nearly died when I saw what that guard did to the prince. It is a crime most foul for a fae to use iron against another."

"I was shocked to find a fae could use iron at all."

"As was I. It's nearly debilitating to so much as touch iron. I'm certain even sheathed, it leeched strength from that guard. I hope he was gravely afflicted." His words carry venom, and I can't help but feel the same. The guard went immobile after he stabbed Franco, making me wonder if he survived the act at all.

"How did King Ustrin come to own an iron blade anyway?" I ask.

"It's likely a relic from the war. We stumble across such weapons, often buried in some forgotten area. You can usually tell by the dying earth surrounding it. However, with all the deserts in Fire, it may have been easier to go undetected for much longer."

I nod, but my mind lingers on Foxglove's mention of the desert. I've never seen desert lands and always imagined them with equal parts fascination and terror. If I take the Fire Court as my home, that desert will belong to me.

"More pressingly," Foxglove says, interrupting my thoughts, "we should talk about the bargain you made. I couldn't hear the words spoken from the observatory, but Lorelei told me what was exchanged. How you sacrificed our great plan to save the prince. I can't say I blame you. I'd have been tempted to bargain for the fair prince's life, but...we came so far." His shoulders sink, expression crumbling.

"I'm not sure I did sacrifice our plan, Foxglove."

He furrows his brow. "How do you figure?"

"Well, I'm not clear on how this all works, so you must correct me if I'm wrong. When I made the bargain, I told him I'd attend my mother's trial. I have every intention of fulfilling that promise as stated."

"But you told him you'd accept exile too, did you not?"

"I told him I'd accept exile without argument if the human council allowed us to leave unharmed. Well, I can't accept my exile if it isn't offered, and if the council agrees to my bargain, then they won't offer exile."

Foxglove's eyes widen. "Well, now, aren't you clever!"

"There's more. I don't know if I did this correctly, but I tried to use the power of intent. When I said I'd accept my exile if the council allowed us to leave unharmed, my intent for the word *us* was myself and my mother. That way, if it comes to begging Mr. Duveau to allow her and I to leave the isle, Amelie's absence from the trial will have no bearing on the bargain."

Foxglove's lips pull into a wide grin.

"Did I do it right? The power of intent?"

"Yes, I believe you did. Very well done. However, you also promised you wouldn't return if exiled."

"And I'm willing to keep that promise," I say. The thought alone makes my heart sink. "But, most importantly, was his side of the bargain. I agreed to all this in exchange for his promise that he and the council fae wouldn't engage the rebels in violence so long as I remained on the isle. If all goes according to plan, and I'm able to stay in Faerwyvae forever, we'll have an upper hand. The council won't be able to attack us...ever."

His mouth falls open. "Brilliant, Evelyn. Simply brilliant."

"You think it will work? Did I leave too much room for interpretation?"

He tilts his head one way and another, as if weighing the various scenarios in his mind. "Depending on the exact words used, I don't think that will stop the civil war from breaking out between the rebels and the council, but it will prevent them from engaging us first. They will only be able to attack on the defensive."

"Then that's enough for us to have an advantage, right?"

We arrive at my bedroom door and stop outside it. Foxglove grins. "My dear, I think you're right. I could hug you if you weren't covered in blood. Instead, I will have to settle for a goodnight. Will you be ready to leave in four days' time?"

The blood drains from my face. It's both too soon and not soon enough. I'm far from ready to face the council at the trial, and yet I'm eager to get this over with. To free my mother. To face my fate.

He continues, "You should arrive the day before her trial so you can get settled in. Well, I should say so *we* can get settled in. I'm most certainly going with you."

The statement surprises me from my frazzled thoughts. "But you represent Autumn, Foxglove. Why would you attend Mother's trial with me?"

He squares his shoulders. "You will be Queen of Fire, my dear. It's time you start acting like a royal. No fae queen would face the humans without an ambassador, and until you have one of your own, I am more than happy to play the part."

"But...will Aspen even let you?"

He lets out a tittering laugh. "I assure you, I won't have a choice in the matter. He'll think it was his idea."

I furrow my brow. "I'm not so sure. Things have been...strained between me and the king."

His expression softens. "I know things aren't exactly comfortable at the moment, but King Aspen cares for you unlike he's ever cared for anyone. Trust me. You'll work out whatever is amiss between you."

My heart yearns to feel the optimism of his words as if it were my own, but I don't allow myself to dwell on it. Instead, I shift the subject to more practical matters. "You're certain you can manage not to tell him about our plan?"

"So long as he doesn't ask, I don't have to tell the truth, although," he twists his fingers together in a nervous gesture, "I implore you to tell him the truth. If he had hope—"

"I don't want his hope." My tone comes out sharper than I intend. "I don't want anyone's hope right now. Not until I think this might actually work. If I can get the council to agree to my terms, then I'll make our plan known. Until then, it's folly."

"Hope is never folly, Evelyn."

I swallow hard, steeling my expression. "It is when it could break your heart."

26

———

The next four days pass in a blur of anxious preparations. I hardly see a soul as I spend most of my time in my room going over every word I've prepared to say at Mother's trial. Only Lorelei and Foxglove come to visit, and I try not to read too much into Aspen's absence. Even the few times I've left my room to seek him out, he's nowhere to be found. The doors to the throne room remain firmly closed throughout most of the day, and Foxglove tells me Aspen and the rebel allies are busy plotting their first move against the council fae.

Perhaps it's for the best I haven't spoken to Aspen. I'm still not sure what I intend to say when I finally do. Should I apologize? Yell? Force his lips onto mine until that spark returns between us?

Only one thing is clear: we're running out of time. If I don't see him soon, there's a chance I might never see him again.

～

On the day we are to depart on our journey to Grenneith, I'm an anxious mess. With pacing steps, I cross my room, rehearsing the terms of the bargain I'll be presenting. I try to anticipate every argument the council could counter my proposal with, and plan out answers to those as well. It's maddening and hopeless, and I just want this to be over already.

As a hazy sunset throws my room beneath a dusky glow, I discard my mental preparations in favor of physical ones. We'll be leaving by nightfall to arrive in Grenneith by tomorrow morning.

My hands tremble as I pack my bag, wishing I had more to bring, if only to keep my hands busy. Yet, all I'll need is a nightdress, undergarments, and extra shoes. I don't bother trying to dress in human clothing this time, considering not even my corset was salvageable after my arrival at Selene Palace. However, Nyxia did loan me some cream silk trousers and a blue linen blouse, which I'm wearing now beneath my velvet cloak.

A knock sounds on my door, almost too quiet to hear, as if the visitor is unsure of their intent. When I open the door, I'm speechless to find Aspen on the other side. My breath catches in my throat as our eyes lock. Silence envelops us, leaving nothing but a tense hum of energy I can sense down to my bones. The energy feels wrong, the air too thick. Does he feel it too?

He clears his throat, the sound so loud it startles me. "Can I come in for a moment?" His tone is cold, formal, catching me off guard.

I blink a few times, realizing we're still standing under my threshold. "Of course," I say, hating how my formality matches his.

He enters, striding to the center of my room, back facing me. He wears russet trousers, a white shirt, and a bronze waistcoat—wrinkled again. It's an effort not to reach for him, to place a hand in the middle of his back and soothe whatever has him so rattled. But I can't touch him, not when everything about this is wrong—his posture, his formality, the way he's been avoiding me. I get that we've yet to reconcile our grievances toward each other, but the way he's acting has my stomach in knots.

This can't be just about my stolen kiss with Franco. Surely anger would suffice his feelings over the matter. Rage, I can handle. Rage, I can counter with my own. But this distance, this strain...I know neither how to confront it nor how it's come to lie between us. There must be something else I've done to deserve his coldness.

I run through our last few interactions and consider everything that's happened between leaving Bircharbor and now. So much has changed but—

Then it dawns on me. His mother died and it was my fault. Does he know? Did Foxglove or Lorelei tell him what I admitted to? Does he realize I could have prevented her death if I'd mentioned her plea before I left? The blood leaves my face, sweat beading over my forehead.

Finally, he speaks, attention fixated on the empty wall in front of him. "I want to come with you to the Spire."

My mouth feels dry as I search for words. The way he refuses to look my way tells me the offer to accompany me pains him greatly. But why? "All right," I say, my voice tenuous.

He remains facing away from me, each heartbeat tugging on the air between us. When he speaks again, it's drowned out by my own words. "I'm sorry about your mother."

He whirls toward me. "What?"

I swallow hard. "I said, I'm sorry about your mother. I heard about her...murder." My unspoken question echoes in my head. *Does he know the truth? Does he know it's my fault?*

He nods but says nothing in reply.

Another stretch of silence. Aspen opens and closes his fists, a nervous gesture I've never seen him do, one that makes the air in the room feel suffocating. I can't help but feel that this marks the end. That nothing will ever feel right between us again.

I wish he'd yell. I wish *I'd* yell. I wish anything were happening but this painful quiet.

Tears spring to my eyes as the room begins to spin. There's only one thing left to say. "It's my fault."

His expression softens. "Excuse me?"

"Her death. It's my fault."

"I don't understand. You were here when she was murdered. Nyxia vouched for you. I know Cobalt had your dagger, he—"

I shake my head. "I could have prevented it." I inhale a trembling breath, preparing my confession. "She spoke with me the day I left Bircharbor, telling me she feared Cobalt. Feared for her safety. She begged me to speak to you on her behalf, to form an alliance. She wanted your protection. And I...I never said a word."

He closes the distance between us, stopping a few feet away. His hand lifts toward my face, and my heart races in anticipation of the touch. A flicker of hope rises inside, as if everything will be set to rights with this one caress. But it doesn't come. Like he did in the hall, he pulls his hand away before he can touch me, curling his fingers into fists as he purses his lips. "It isn't your fault." His words come out with a tremor, as if filtered through suppressed rage.

My throat feels tight, seeing his repulsion in the set of his jaw, in the fists balled at his sides. I call upon my fire to steady me as I fix him with a glare. "Obviously you don't believe your own words," I say through my teeth.

"How can you say that? You had nothing to do with her death. If anyone is to blame, it's me. She came to me with the same request, the same fears. I didn't trust her." A flash of pain crosses his face. "But you, Evie. You're innocent of blame."

My mind reels to comprehend him. His words sound so genuine, but his body betrays the truth. If he isn't upset about that, then why does he find it so hard to be in the same room with me? Why does he look like he'd rather be anywhere but at my side? I'm about to give voice to the questions when footsteps sound outside my room. My eyes flash to the open door where Foxglove emerges from the hall.

Aspen takes a step away from me, and the hum of that unsettling energy shatters. "What is it?" he asks, voice gruff.

Foxglove's expression flashes with surprise, as if he hadn't expected to find Aspen here. "Queen Nyxia has prepared her carriage for our journey. It's time."

My hands tremble at his words. "I should finish readying my things."

"I'll meet you at the carriage," Aspen mutters without looking at me. With that, he leaves my room.

Foxglove gives me a knowing grin. "See, I told you things would be better between you soon enough."

I open my mouth to argue but can't find the words to express the truth of what just occurred. Because honestly, I have no idea what any of it meant.

A ROUND, WHITE, OPALESCENT CARRIAGE AWAITS US OUTSIDE THE PALACE. At the front are two skeletal equine creatures, thin and white with lipless mouths and red eyes. Instead of a mane, each creature has a set of sharp ridges that run from their heads to the middles of their backs.

Nyxia stands before one of the creatures, hands framed on each side of its face as it nuzzles her. The queen's expression is delighted, as if she's playing not with a terrifying beast but a puppy. Lorelei leans against the side of the carriage, arms crossed, but straightens when she sees us.

When we meet, she pulls me into a hug. I'm surprised by the gesture—I never knew Lorelei was the hugging type—but I wrap my arms around her petite frame without hesitation. "Stay safe," she whispers.

We pull away, and her arms wrap around Foxglove next. Seeing their worried expressions as they embrace reminds me just how dangerous this journey is. Not only are we traveling to the human lands, we're going to Grenneith, the capital city of Eisleigh. The most densely populated human location on the isle. There won't be familiar faces or childhood friends—neither of which I have reason to trust anyway.

My beloved mentor betrayed me.

What could strangers do?

When Foxglove and Lorelei separate, she eyes us each in turn. "Good luck with everything. I *will* see you again." She says the last part for me alone, then leaves toward the palace.

We turn to Nyxia, who is still showering affection on her creatures. Her gaze meets mine as we approach. She gives a final pat to the horse and kisses its bony nose. "Sylvia and Mernog are well-fed and ready for the journey. They'll make it to the Spire without needing to rest and they won't need to eat again until they return."

I'm about to ask what they eat, but I don't think I want to know the answer.

She continues. "If you need to stop for any reason, Franco will communicate with them. They listen to him almost as well as they listen to me."

Foxglove and I say the same thing in unison. "Prince Franco's coming?"

"But he's wounded." As soon as I say it, I know my argument is feeble. Four days is plenty of time for a fae to heal from such a wound.

"He's fine," Nyxia says. "He's fully healed as if nothing even happened. Besides, if you want to get to the Spire quickly, you'll have to take the moon mares. We don't employ any other carriage-drawing creatures in Lunar but them."

"And that has to do with the prince...how?"

Nyxia glares, making me immediately regret my tone. However, the thought of Aspen and Franco together in one carriage...it gives me no small amount of trepidation.

Foxglove elbows me. "What she means is, for what reason do you give us the great honor of his presence? Surely such a task is beneath the sweet prince."

She gives a casual shrug. "Like I said, the moon mares listen to him."

I squint at her, wondering if there's more to this plot than she's letting on. Is she still hoping she can get me to take Franco as my mate?

Nyxia ignores my scrutiny. "Go on. My brother's already inside the carriage."

"What about Aspen? Has he come yet?" I ask, scanning the grounds.

"Why am I not surprised he's going too?" she says with a roll of her eyes. "I'll have someone fetch him."

Foxglove and I move toward the carriage, and I step inside first. Franco greets me with a warm smile. "Evelyn, I'm so pleased I get to be your chaperone once again. We had such a nice time before, did we not?" His grin is suggestive, making my pulse race. I look from the empty seat next to him to the unoccupied bench on the other side of the carriage.

"I'm grateful for your generous offer to accompany us," I say and take the bench across from him.

Foxglove's cheeks flush pink as he enters with an audible sigh. His expression is dreamy as he takes the seat next to me.

"Are you sure you're recovered enough for the journey?" I ask, giving the prince a pointed look.

Without warning, he lifts the hem of his shirt, exposing far more flesh than necessary. "Not a scratch. You have a real healing gift."

I blush and look away from his lean stomach, while Foxglove emits an awkward giggle.

The carriage sways as a new figure enters. I meet Aspen's eyes before they shoot toward Prince Franco and the only empty seat at his side. "Why are you here?"

The prince gives Aspen a charming grin. "King Aspen, what a pleasurable journey this will be. Cramped, but pleasurable."

With a grumble, Aspen lowers himself into the seat, his antlers snagging the white silk roof above him. I look from one male to the other, noticing for the first time how much taller Aspen towers over the prince, and that's not including the extra height his antlers provide. Franco doesn't seem intimidated in the least, his eyes resting on me.

I feel Aspen's burning into me as well and avert my gaze to the window.

The carriage lurches and rolls into motion.

"King Aspen," Franco says, "I was just telling Miss Fairfield how grateful I am for her healing gifts. She has the gentlest yet most powerful hands."

Aspen lets out an irritated grunt while Foxglove erupts with another giggle.

I shake my head at the window and grit my teeth. This is going to be a very long ride.

27

The capital city of Grenneith is unlike any place I've been before. I watch out the carriage window as we roll over the cobblestone streets. Even though it's barely past daybreak, the streets are already busy with commotion. Towering factories clutter the skyline behind endless rows of merchant shops, townhouses, and elegant city manors. I gasp as I watch an automotive vehicle roar across the cobblestones like some mechanical beast. Such contraptions are far more common on the mainland, but even there they are considered a rare luxury.

Once the vehicle is out of sight, I study the people, their fine dresses and stylish suits, the way they carry themselves almost like royalty. My stomach takes a dive as I realize how out of place I feel. And it's more than just the fae carriage drawn by skeletal moon mares that makes me feel that way.

Luckily, no one seems to notice our passing as we make our way down the bustling streets.

"Are we beneath a glamour?" My voice cuts through the silence that's fallen since we entered the city. The mood has gone from tense to frightened.

"We are," Franco says, brow furrowed as he stares out the window. After a while he meets my gaze, his face pale and tinged with green. "I've never been in a human city before. There's a lot of iron."

"Not even I have been in such a place as this," Foxglove says, covering his nose with his hand. "I think I might faint."

"We're only here until tomorrow," Aspen says, stoic as ever. He doesn't so much as glance out the window, as if our surroundings are far beneath his care. "We'll manage."

Our eyes lock, and his expression softens, but we don't exchange a word. We've hardly spoken to each other at all during the entire journey. With so much left unsaid after our last conversation, it's hard to believe any words could suffice.

I move away from the window and settle back into my seat. The deeper we move into the city, the faster and faster my heart races. "What's the plan now that we're here?"

"We'll need to find somewhere to stay the night," Foxglove says. "Beneath a glamour, of course. Then I'll act as your ambassador and go to the Spire to sort out all the details for your mother's trial. All communication I've exchanged so far has assured me trials at the Spire begin at noon. However, if there are any others scheduled for tomorrow, your mother's may not be the first."

I inhale deeply to steady my nerves. "Will I be able to see my mother beforehand? I want to speak with her before the trial."

"It isn't safe to go anywhere near the Spire before the trial," Aspen says. "If anyone sees you, there's a good chance they'll lock you up."

"I'll take you," Franco says. "A raven can infiltrate many places. I should be able to orchestrate a visit with your mother without a hitch."

"You don't know that," Aspen says with a growl. "It could be more danger than it's worth."

"I think it's worth anything if it's the last time she sees her mother before the trial," Franco argues.

I look from Aspen to Franco, wishing they'd stop opposing each other at every opportunity. "I'll do what it takes," I say. "Even if I get caught and thrown into prison with her, I don't care. I want to see her tonight."

Franco leans forward and places a hand on my knee. "I'll make it happen."

Aspen clenches his jaw, eyes burning into Franco's hand until the prince pulls it back to his lap. "We'll all make it happen," Aspen says through his teeth, "if you're so keen to squander your last night of freedom."

My last night of freedom. Considering the chances of my plan's success are slim to none, he very well might be right.

~

WE FIND A DECENT HOTEL ON THE OUTSKIRTS OF THE CITY, FAR ENOUGH AWAY from the bulk of the crowds yet not too far from the Spire. Foxglove covers me with a mild glamour to help me blend in better with the other humans —I'm assuming that means he's made my clothing look a little less fae—and my three male companions don their own. I, of course, can't see the effects of their glamours, but the looks we receive as we enter the hotel are ones of curiosity, not terror.

We each get a room of our own, which I'm grateful for. Part of me expected I'd be forced to share a room and be put in a position to choose my sleeping companion. At this point, I most likely would have chosen Foxglove over the two other males. I still can't get over Aspen's odd behavior in my room before we left. It infuriates me each time I recall how he nearly reached for me before snatching his hand back, as if he couldn't bear to touch me.

If it isn't blame over his mother's death that has him acting in such a way, then is it truly my kiss with Franco? Surely such a misunderstanding isn't worth this level of disgust on his part. It's not like I thought I'd ever see my mate again. In fact, I thought he was married when I kissed Franco. *Married,* for the love of iron.

I pace inside my tiny room at the hotel, teeth clenched. Now that I'm alone, I can let out my irritation, although it doesn't really get me anywhere. It provides no answers. All I know is before Mother's trial, I will force Aspen to speak to me, even if it ends with a fight. Maybe a fight would do me good. A fight. A fiery kiss. A final night of reckless passion before I meet my fate.

My fate.

The thought sobers me quickly, and I sit on the narrow yet well-made bed, shoulders slumped with sudden fatigue. The daunting task ahead sets my head spinning. My eyes dart to the single window in the room, one which showcases a view of the sprawling city and smokestacks reaching high into the sky, puffing black smoke.

To the right of my view stands a tall, stone building, its central tower reaching dozens of floors high. The Spire. I remember learning it's one of the oldest architectural structures in Eisleigh, built as a castle when humans first settled here. Considering its ability to withstand not only the war with the fae but the tests of time, it's no surprise the building has been converted into a prison. From what I know, the top of the tower hosts the prison cells, while the bottom floor houses the courtrooms. My eyes lock on the highest point of the tower, wishing I knew how my mother fared.

Foxglove has already left for the Spire. Soon he will gather all the information we need. Her courtroom location, her trial time. Meanwhile, Franco will fly to the tallest portion of the building and find my mother.

Then tonight, we infiltrate the prison.

28

———————

Night covers the city streets in a blanket of shadows as we reach the Spire. The bustle of Grenneith has been laid to rest for the evening, save for the occasional shouts of merriment floating on the air from the nearby taverns.

Aspen stalks close to my side while Prince Franco flies overhead in raven form. When we reach the side of the building, Foxglove steps out of the shadows and greets us.

"Everything has been settled," he says, although the wringing of his hands doesn't make me feel too confident in his words.

I raise a brow. "Is there anything I should be worried about?"

He sighs. "What's not to worry about? The iron in this building is making me feel like I'll melt into a puddle at any moment."

I'm reminded of how difficult it must be for my companions to be here. Although, Franco seems to have recovered at least partially from his initial response to our arrival. You'd never guess by the smooth motions of his wings that he or his magic was suffering from the city's ill effects. Aspen too seems to be managing well. It makes me wonder about the power of the two royals compared to fae like Foxglove or Lorelei. Perhaps the stronger fae are less impacted by being so far from the faewall.

"What are the details?" Aspen asks.

"Maven Fairfield's trial is set for noon tomorrow, the first trial of the day. I was given the location of the courtroom as well. We'll be able to arrive promptly before it begins."

"And my mother?" I ask. "Where is she now?"

The black raven begins his descent in slow circles until Prince Franco materializes next to me. He rocks unsteadily on his feet before he catches his bearings. "This place is the worst. I never get dizzy from flying."

"Where's Evie's mother?" Aspen asks, a hint of irritation in his tone.

"Cellblock four, room seven," the prince says. "She's the only prisoner on that floor and the guards make their rounds on the hour. Once the clock strikes eleven, we'll wait ten minutes before I fly Evelyn up to the cellblock. We'll be out again before midnight."

Aspen tenses next to me, while I remain struck by something he said. "What do you mean by *fly me up*?" I ask.

"I'll shift into my winged form, but only partially so I maintain my size. Then I'll carry you up and fly you through the window in the hall outside the cellblock. The windows are old and glassless in the tower hall."

"You're going to fly. With me. In your...arms."

"That's reckless," Aspen says, taking a forbidding step toward Franco.

Franco meets his glare with a nonchalant grin. "I've never dropped anyone yet."

"There must be another way inside."

Franco points to the top of the Spire. "You mean, up through the central tower of the building, past several cellblocks, and nothing but a hope that we bypass the guards without notice?"

"What about an invisibility glamour?" I ask.

His eyes widen. "Invisibility glamours are hard enough in Faerwyvae. I can't maintain one over the both of us in a building filled with iron."

Aspen throws his hands in the air. "Oh, but you can maintain your winged form no problem."

Franco takes a challenging step toward Aspen. "Shifting is in my blood. I don't have to use much magic to do it. Even you know that, Stag King."

Aspen looks like he's on the verge of showing the prince exactly what he knows about shifting, but instead, he clenches his jaw and faces me. "It's your choice, Evie. I know you want to see your mother, but I'd rather you didn't risk your life with *him*," he tosses the prince a scowl, "as your only lifeline."

When his eyes return to mine, I see the concern in them, rendering me speechless. Just then, chimes sound from the city center, and I don't need to count to know there are eleven. Once the echo recedes, I square my shoulders with resolve. "I'm willing to take the risk."

At that, Franco shudders and spouts a pair of enormous black wings from his back. A few stray feathers protrude from his neck and shoulders, but the rest of him remains unchanged. He winks and extends his arm. "Let's do this."

"You said you'd wait ten minutes," Aspen growls.

"Yes, but I'm not going to wait *here*. We need to get deeper into the shadows before someone spots us."

Aspen's jaw shifts side to side. "Fine. I'll keep watch here and make sure no one heads your way."

Foxglove wrings his hands. "I suppose I should stand guard around the front of the building."

Aspen nods, then leans against the building's wall, arms crossed over his chest, but his gaze remains on me. My eyes are glued to his for several breaths until I force myself to take Franco's arm.

We round the back of the building and wait beneath the boughs of a well-manicured tree, my pulse racing with every minute that passes. Finally, Franco leans in and whispers, "It's time."

I let out a shaking breath and Franco pulls me close, wrapping his arms around my waist. I don't look at him as I put my arms around his neck.

"Ready?"

I nod.

We launch into the sky, Franco's enormous wings beating at the cool night air. I suppress a shout as we rise higher and higher, shutting my eyes against the ground falling farther beneath me. My stomach dips in a way that makes me fear I might be sick.

It only takes a few seconds for us to gain enough height before I feel our weight tip to the side. Franco tucks his wings around us, and I open my eyes to see us dart through a window and into a long, narrow hall. With a lurch, he brings us to a skidding halt, just in time to avoid smashing us into the wall at the other side.

"I'm glad that worked," he whispers while I put a hand to my spinning forehead.

Franco nods toward an unmarked door. We enter it into a dim room lined with cells. Musty aromas of dirt and unwashed bodies flood my nostrils, but like Franco said, there's only one prisoner on this cellblock.

Franco gives my hand a squeeze. "I'll stand guard outside the door."

Once alone, I make my way to the occupied cell to find my mother sleeping on a cot. Like Mr. Duveau promised, she seems to have been given decent amenities. Trays of half-eaten food and a cup of tea rest on a simple table, while Mother's sleeping form is draped in thick wool blankets.

A sudden presence at my side makes me jump. Aspen stands next to me, and it takes me a moment to understand how that could be. He's only here through the Bond, his violet aura rippling around him. "I'm not going to leave you alone," he says, his voice a casual drawl. However, his expression betrays the true concern that his tone tries to mask.

"I thought you wanted to stand guard?" I whisper.

"I'm getting better at doing...whatever this is. I can sort of see both places at once now. This way, I can actually warn you if I notice anything concerning from my vantage on the ground."

I nod, his nearness a steadying comfort. It's almost enough to help me forget the strain of the last few days.

His eyes flash from me to Mother. "I'll give you your privacy." He hesitates as if he wants to say more but makes his way to stand by the door.

I return my attention to my mother and press myself close to the bars. "Ma."

She stirs, blinking at me with a furrowed brow before she springs to her feet. "Evelyn! You're all right."

I can't stop the tears that flow as she approaches the bars. It breaks my heart to have bars between us, twice now, but knowing she'll soon be free serves as a minor comfort. In a matter of hours, she'll be out of here.

Then one of three options will prevail: we'll either be allowed to return to Faerwyvae, exiled, or...dead.

"You really came back," she says. There's a note of disappointment in her tone. "Part of me hoped you wouldn't. That you'd return to Faerwyvae and never look back."

"You know I couldn't abandon you to be executed."

She sighs. "I know." Her eyes leave my face to look around me. "Where is your sister?"

My lower lip trembles at the hope in her eyes. A hope I'll have to crush either with truth or a lie. I think it's time she knows the truth. She'll find out tomorrow regardless.

"Amelie isn't coming."

Her eyes widen for a moment. "Why? Did she choose freedom...or is it something else?"

I grip the bars of the cell to stop my hands from shaking. "Shortly after we arrived in Autumn, Amelie bargained her name to a fae male in exchange for his love. I don't know if she refused to attend because he forced her to do so, or if..."

"Or if it was her choice." Tears glaze Mother's eyes. "Either way, it doesn't matter, I suppose."

"No, I suppose not. The fact remains that she's not coming, and Mr. Duveau will use that as means to execute us both."

She puts a hand to her heart, but I reach through the bars to grab the other.

"I'm not going to let that happen."

Her eyes widen with surprise. "What are you going to do?"

I glance at Aspen from the corner of my eye, wondering if he can hear us from where he stands. "Whatever it takes."

She lifts her chin. "That's the fire I wanted to see in you."

Her look of pride fills me with a greater sense of accomplishment than I've ever felt—greater than Mr. Meeks' praise or any compliment I've ever received regarding my intellect. In this moment, my mother sees me for who I am, and I finally understand that she's seen it all along. I was the one who never saw it. I was the one who refused to acknowledge the truth.

In what may be one of the final hours of our lives, we understand each other. It makes my heart ache, wishing she'd been honest with me and Amelie from the start. Would that have changed anything?

It's too late to wonder.

"Do you think she's happy?" Mother asks. "Was the love she bargained for worth it?"

Again, I debate truth or lie. "I'm not sure, Ma. I wouldn't say the cost was worth the kind of love she got in return, but only she knows for sure. And she won't speak to me. I don't think...I don't think she's the same Amelie she used to be. I think the bargain and the Bond changed her."

Mother nods, face drooping with sorrow as her gaze falls to the floor. Then her eyes snap back to mine. "What about you? Were you happy in Faerwyvae? Or did you despise it as much as you thought you would?"

I'm taken aback by her question. This, at least, I can be truly honest about. "I hated it at first, but after a while, I came to find...something very unexpected."

Her expression brightens, lips pulling into the ghost of a smile. "And the fae you were forced to be with? Did he treat you well?"

I can feel Aspen's eyes burning into me from across the room, perhaps more so due to his presence through our Bond. Part of me wants to keep my lips pressed tight on this matter just to spite him, but there's a truth I can't keep hidden. Mother deserves to know. Maybe Aspen does too. "He was that unexpected thing."

Tears glaze her eyes, and her voice comes out with a croak. "Did you find happiness with him?"

A lump rises in my throat, and for several moments I'm paralyzed, still wondering if Aspen is paying as close attention as I imagine he is. My words don't seem to come, so all I give her is a subtle nod.

"Love?"

The word destroys me, crumbling my walls, dousing the anger that I've kept burning between me and my mate, the only thing that has prevented me from falling apart over the strain between us. My expression plummets, which seems to be answer enough for Mother. She reaches her arms around me and pulls me close. Even with the bars between us, we find a way to embrace, and I let myself cry. I cry for the words I never got to tell Aspen, words I still might not get to say. I cry for my uncertain future, for my mother's precarious fate.

Mother's hands smooth my hair, her soft voice hushing my tears. After a while, I manage to regain my composure, although I can't bring myself to let go of my mother.

"What's it like?" she asks in a whisper.

I pull away enough to see her face. "What do you mean?"

Her tone takes on an air of wistful wonder. "Faerwyvae."

It suddenly dawns on me that after all this time she's been alive, coming and going from the isle to the mainland and back again, she's never been beyond the wall. She has no idea what the different courts are like, what it feels like to travel through different seasons and climates. She's never seen the vibrant orange leaves of Autumn or the moon and stars the way they look in Lunar.

So I tell her.

29

———————

Mother's lips curl into a smile of contentment as I express the delights and terrors of Faerwyvae. I tell her about the puca, the kelpie, and the Twelfth Court. I relay my experiences with honey pyrus and fae wine, describe the fae food and dresses. I'm so immersed in my stories that I lose track of time.

It isn't until I hear a noise in the hall that I begin to wonder how near we are to the next hour, the next round the guards will make. I look toward the door, surprised when I find no sign of Aspen. When did he leave? I could have sworn I felt his presence during most of my conversation with my mother. Perhaps some of what I said made him uncomfortable. Maybe he didn't like the feelings I implied I still have for him.

I frown at the door before I turn back toward my mother. With a jump, I find Aspen materializing next to her, my name on his lips.

"What—"

"Someone's coming," he says. "Foxglove saw several figures enter the front of the building. He says one is a man named Henry Duveau."

Aspen disappears as suddenly as he came, leaving me reeling over what the councilman's presence means. He's here? This late? It's almost midnight!

The door swings open to reveal Franco charging forward. "We have to go. Now."

Mother's eyes widen as they take in the fae prince. I cling to Mother's hands, words pouring from my lips. I don't know why I feel compelled to say them now, but I do. "I hope you know how much I love you. I'm sorry for every grief I caused. I'm sorry I never listened to you. I'm sorry I didn't respect you and your craft. I'm sorry I rebelled."

"Evelyn, we must hurry." Franco circles his arms around my waist, but I cling tighter to Mother's hands.

"I'm not sorry," she says, smiling through a sheen of tears. "Your rebellion taught you independence. It taught you about fire before you even realized it."

She swims inside my vision as tears flood my eyes. Franco gives me another tug, and this time, I let him pull me away. "I love you," I shout. "I'll see you tomorrow."

I hardly hear her echo the sentiment before we speed out of the room and into the hall. We race to the far side, and Franco grips me tighter. He takes off, sprinting us toward the window. I see guards racing up a set of stairs before he jumps out the window with me pressed close. We fall for endless seconds and I'm sure it will be to our doom. Then I hear Franco's wings beating the air, and our momentum shifts.

My heart hammers in my chest as I cling to Franco, the Spire shrinking as he flies us away from it. The city clock strikes midnight, and we stop in the shadows of an alley several blocks from the Spire. If it's the same place we agreed to meet earlier in the case that anything went wrong, then we're between a milliner and a baker. I can almost smell the remnants of stale bread in the dumpster nearby.

Franco sets me on my feet, and I lean against the alley wall, head spinning as I gather my bearings. I'm not even worried about rats or the overflowing canisters of garbage further down. All I can think about is filling my lungs with air. Slowing my pulse.

When I can finally form a coherent word, I ask, "What happened? Why did the guards make their rounds so early?"

He shakes his head. "I don't know. I watched them for most of the afternoon today. Not a single round was made before the hour, and no guards came outside these scheduled rounds aside from delivering meals or to escort prisoners to their trials. Neither of those occurrences should be happening this late."

I can't help wondering if it had anything to do with the presence of Henry Duveau. "Did anything else happen?"

"Nothing that I saw."

A dark silhouette enters the mouth of the alley, but I know at once that it's Aspen. He rushes to me, hands framing my face. I'm surprised by his touch, and he seems to think twice about it as well. He straightens, pinning his arms to his sides, but remains close. "You're all right."

"Do you know what happened?"

"No, but Foxglove had me worried. He seemed to think the presence of the man he saw was something to be concerned about."

"It might be worth some distress," I say. "The guards made their rounds too early. They may have seen us escaping before we fled."

"At least you're safe."

My eyes lock on Aspen's, the words I said to my mother about him ringing in my mind. Did he understand what I hinted at? What my tears meant to convey to her? Who knows what he actually heard. How long he was there.

Franco clears his throat. "I'm going to fly back and see if I can figure out what triggered the guards. Wait here. I'll let you know if there's anything we should be concerned with."

"Good idea," Aspen says.

The prince shifts into his full raven form and flies off, leaving me alone with Aspen. I avert my gaze away from his face. "Is Foxglove all right?" I ask.

He nods. "He took a different way back to the hotel. I told him I wanted to find you first."

"I'm worried," I say. "Mr. Duveau is the councilman who holds the Legacy Bond with my family's names. He's not a good man."

"Do you think he'll hurt her?"

I shrug. "He made me a bargain that I could do whatever I wished before her trial, so long as I vowed to attend. He promised he wouldn't hurt her in the meantime."

Silence falls between us, and with it, the energy between me and Aspen hums like it did in my room. His posture stiffens, fingers twitching and closing into fists.

When he speaks, his voice is quiet. Strained. "Did you mean what you said to her?"

My eyes flash to his, breath hitching. "About what?"

"Finding happiness with me."

I swallow the lump in my throat and give him a hesitant nod. "Does that bother you?"

His brow furrows, a pained expression. "Why would it bother me?"

A blush of anger rises inside me, heating my cheeks. I'm so tired of this discomfort, this divide between us. "I don't know, Aspen, why would it? Why do you seek to protect me, take comfort in my safety, then act revolted whenever you're alone with me?"

"I'm not revolted."

"Then what is it? Why do you keep doing that?" I point to his trembling fists.

His words come through his teeth. "I can't stand to be around you because it feels impossible to do so without having you in my arms."

I study his face, reconciling his words with his posture, his tense shoulders. "And that's a bad thing?"

"Yes, it's a bad thing when the effort to keep away from you feels like a blade in my chest."

A thousand questions pound through my mind. *Why do you want to keep away from me? Why am I causing you so much pain? Why do you sound like you want me, yet act as if you despise me?* But no words make it to my lips. Nothing comes but tears and tremors as I try to gather my thoughts into something coherent.

Aspen closes his eyes and lets out a sigh. With it goes some of his rigidity. "It's a bad thing when this is your last night here."

I almost argue, almost reveal my plan. My fear over its improbability keeps my lips pressed tight.

Aspen continues, voice breaking. "It's a bad thing when I'm not sure if there's someone else you'd rather be with."

A tear rolls down my cheek, and I hardly know why I'm crying. My words come out a breathless whisper. "There's no one else."

His jaw shifts. "No one? No one you'd rather spend your final moments on the isle with?"

My flash of anger ignites again, and I take a step toward him. "No, Aspen, there's no one else. There's never been anyone else and there will never be anyone else."

His expression flickers with a hint of vulnerability. "Not even the Lunar Prince?"

Irritation sends another wash of ferocity through me. "No. How can you ask me that?"

"You kissed him," he says through his teeth. "I saw the two of you together. Then I saw how you bargained for his life, trading every last chance of your freedom for him. I watched you run to him when he was injured like he was the only person left in the world. Then you brought him here."

"I didn't choose for him to come here," I say. "Nyxia did. But he has every right to be here because he's my friend. When I bargained for his life, I did it because it was the right thing to do. I treated his injuries with care because he was my patient."

"And the kiss?"

Guilt seizes me, and I have the overwhelming urge to defend myself, to tell him all the misconceptions and mistakes that led to that moment. I want to beg for his forgiveness, to convince him how badly I wanted that kiss to have been with him. But there's a calm warmth beneath my guilt, something that feels far truer. "Yes, Aspen, I kissed Prince Franco. I kissed him because in that moment and in that situation, I wanted to."

His eyes narrow, but I refuse to shrink beneath that look.

I continue, fighting the quaver in my voice. "I thought you were married. Even though I made you promise me you'd do it, it crushed me. Killed me inside. The fact that I found the will to smile or dance or kiss anyone that night is a miracle. I can't regret that I managed to find joy on your wedding night, even if it hurt us both in the end. Regret doesn't change what happened, and the truth is, I don't owe you an explanation. The same way you wouldn't owe me an explanation if you'd gone through with marrying Maddie Coleman. We aren't each other's property."

"Is that how you see me?" he growls. "As someone who wants to own you?"

"No, and that's exactly why I'm not going to debase myself before you. I've never wanted to be another male's property, nor have I wanted someone else to be mine. You and I have made our choices in the past, but our relationship—if we have one—is in the present. I'm sorry things haven't felt right between us since I used your name against you, but I can't apologize for the snippets of peace I've found between then and now, even the ones I found with another male when I thought we were over."

My truth sizzles between us, and the hard look on his face makes me wonder if I should have gone with my first instinct to beg. *No,* I tell myself. *I do not beg for love.*

Finally, he takes a step closer to me, his chest a mere inch from mine. Even beneath the pale moonlight, I can see the full color of his eyes, the browns, rubies, emeralds, and golds. "You're terrible at apologies," he says.

"I know. That I'm very sorry for."

His lips pull into a tentative grin and the sight of it fills me with more comfort than I think I've ever felt. He lifts a hand to the side of my face, and this time he doesn't snatch it back. With trembling fingers, he brushes a strand of hair away from my forehead as he stares deep into my eyes. The gesture is gentler and more heartwarming than any kiss could be in this moment. But a kiss is what I yearn for. My lips tingle with their craving as my gaze falls to his full mouth.

"The day you left Bircharbor, you wouldn't let me hold you," he says. "You pulled away from me when I asked for more time together. Do you still feel the same? Or will you allow me this before the end?"

Another truth is on my lips. One I've been fighting not to tell him for days. Do I dare give him hope? Give *us* hope? "This might not be the end."

His eyes widen. "What do you mean?"

I open my mouth, but I don't want to talk. I just want to feel his lips on mine already. My fingers reach for the collar of his shirt, and I pull him down to me. He pushes me against the alley wall as a furious passion unleashes between us. We gasp for air as our lips lock together. His tongue brushes mine with tangible need, each stroke a plea for more. My hands twine in his hair while his move to my lower back, my hips. I arch against him, needing more of his warmth, his strength.

"I don't mean to interrupt," a voice calls overhead. Aspen and I pull away, breathless, to find Prince Franco perched on the roof of the bakery.

"What?" Aspen growls.

"I have bad news. The trial is happening now."

30

I furrow my brow, staring up at the prince. "What do you mean the trial is happening now? How is that possible?"

"I don't know," Franco says, "but I watched the guards escort your mother down from the prison to a courtroom."

"But it's midnight. Her trial isn't supposed to be until noon."

He shrugs. "You'll have to tell them that. The trial has already begun."

My heart pounds in my chest as my mouth goes dry. All the pleasant feelings conjured by my kiss with Aspen have evaporated.

"Take her," Aspen says. "Take Evelyn and fly her back to the Spire at once."

The prince leaps from the roof of the bakery and lands in a crouch with surprising ease. His wings spout from his back as he rights himself and extends his hand.

I reach to accept but hesitate for a moment. There's still so much left unsaid between me and Aspen. So much I wanted to tell him before the trial. "Aspen—"

"I'll be there," he whispers. "I'll be with you the entire time. Now go. Hurry."

With a nod, I allow Franco to pull me close. In a matter of seconds, we're high above the alley and flying toward the Spire.

When we land, we dart toward the front doors of the building. "I know where the courtroom is," Franco says. I pull open the doors. The lobby of the

Spire is quiet and empty, with not a soul in sight. Franco shifts fully into a raven and darts down one of the halls. My feet fly beneath me as I follow, pulse pounding with every step.

He stops outside a closed door, then circles in the air in front of it, cawing wildly. I push it open and find a courtroom in full session. On one side of the room sits a gathering of men in black robes. Jurors, I can only assume. On the other side are men in black suits. I recognize one as Mayor Coleman. These must be the men of Eisleigh's council.

At the center of the room stands Henry Duveau, outfitted in a black robe like the jurors wear, but upon his head rests a black cap. A judge's cap.

He's the judge? Fury sparks within me, but only for a moment. My attention is quickly diverted to what's behind him—my mother.

Flanked by several guards, her arms are extended to each side of her, wrists strapped in iron cuffs which are secured to two marble columns. The lower half of her is submerged in an iron tub of water. By the way she shivers and the blue tinge of her skin, I can only assume the water is ice-cold.

A black shape swoops past me—Franco—then disappears high in the rafters overhead. The confused jury and councilmen stare from the raven then back to me.

Mr. Duveau greets me with a cold smile. "Miss Fairfield, how good of you to attend."

I stride into the courtroom, each step echoing on the marble floor beneath my feet, pounding in a fraction of my heart's racing tempo. "What is the meaning of this? My mother's trial was scheduled for noon."

Mr. Duveau seems unaffected by my rage. "We have every right to change times of trials."

"And when were you going to inform me?"

"You were given the proper notice as required by law. We sent a message to the hotel the Autumn ambassador said you'd be staying at when he came to inquire earlier on your behalf. If you weren't there to get the message, then perhaps you should have stayed put." His last words are punctuated with venom.

I grit my teeth. It's impossible not to suspect this was part of the ultimate plan all along. No wonder the guards came when they did. They weren't alerted of our infiltration; they were coming to take Mother to her trial. All to make it difficult for me to meet the terms of the bargain and serve King Ustrin's whims.

"It comes down to the fact that you're late," Mr. Duveau says. "You were supposed to attend Maven Fairfield's trial, otherwise her sentence—and yours, mind you—would be execution."

I lift my chin. "The bargain never stated I had to attend from the start of the trial. I'm here now. Her trial is still in session, is it not?"

The councilman narrows his eyes, a tick at the corner of his jaw. "Very well. We will allow you to be present for the remainder of her trial. Have a seat." He extends his arm to an empty chair next to my mother. One with iron cuffs on the arms and legs.

With trembling steps, I make my way to the chair, bristling as I sense Mr. Duveau following in my wake. Once seated, the councilman closes the cuffs around my wrists and ankles, then returns to the middle of the floor. I try not to recall the last time I was locked up this way, ending in fire and smoke and blood. My eyes find Mother's, and I force a smile. She forces one in turn, but it's nothing more than a flick of her lips as she continues to convulse from the chilled water.

"To catch you up to speed, Miss Fairfield," Mr. Duveau says, "the council has presented their evidence of your mother's treason and the jury has determined her guilt."

I toss him a glare, although the ruling doesn't come as a surprise.

"I'm going to tear out his throat." A gravelly voice comes from beside me, and I turn my head to find Aspen has materialized, violet aura shimmering as his eyes burn into Mr. Duveau. I say nothing, not wanting to look like I'm talking to an invisible specter before the council and jury.

Mr. Duveau's attention turns to the men. "Let us continue, shall we?"

A round of "Aye," is uttered from the jurors and councilmen.

"The punishment for Maven Fairfield's crime is exile," Mr. Duveau says. "However, that merciful punishment was only to be extended if Amelie and Evelyn Fairfield attended this trial and accepted their exile with her. Considering only one daughter is present today," he waves a hand toward me, "that mercy has been made void. Agreed?"

Another round of ayes.

"Then it can only be surmised that Maven Fairfield and her two daughters are sentenced to death. The two present will be executed immediately following the conclusion of this trial, and a bounty will be placed on Amelie Fairfield for her life to be claimed as soon as possible."

Mother and I exchange a glance, while Aspen lets out a roar only I can hear. A furious caw echoes from the rafters, eliciting gasps and mutters from the jury.

"All in favor—"

"Wait!" I shout. "You haven't given me permission to defend myself."

Mr. Duveau turns slowly on his heel, expression both haughty and amused. It's as if he'd been waiting for me to speak up. "I don't believe allowing you the chance to speak on this trial was part of our bargain."

"But it is my right," I say. "As a citizen, I have a right to defend myself."

He turns toward the jurors. They hesitate, exchanging whispers before the majority utters their agreement that I may speak.

"Very well," Mr. Duveau says, taking a few steps toward me. "What do you have to say for yourself?"

"I came here as requested. I did everything that was asked of me."

"I daresay you did that and more." The councilman narrows his eyes, expressing what he's left unspoken. He knows that I'm responsible for the fates of Mr. Meeks and Mr. Osterman. He knows I broke into the Spire and visited my mother.

I refuse to falter, forcing my posture straighter despite my bindings. "I did what I had control over, and even went so far as to try and ensure my sister's compliance. Her refusal to be present today should bear no weight on either my or my mother's fates."

I'm relieved to see a few nods coming from the jurors.

"So, you would like me to show you and your mother mercy and allow the two of you to go into exile?"

I could say yes. I could say it and this could all be over now. At this point, there's a chance he and the jury will allow us to leave. I almost give in and take the easy route. But there's another path, one I'm already resolved to try. Even if it kills me.

I take a deep breath. "I ask that you leave my sister out of your considerations regarding me and my mother, but I do not ask for our exile."

Gasps erupt from the room.

Mr. Duveau pins me with his cold stare. "Is it death you want then?"

"No," I say. My heart pounds as I deliver my next words. "A new bargain."

Nervous laughter emits from some of the men, but Mr. Duveau does not seem amused. "What kind of a bargain?"

For days I've rehearsed these words, memorized them. That doesn't make them any easier to say. "I want you to let my mother and me remain on the isle and return to Faerwyvae."

More gasps. Mayor Coleman rises from his seat, expression twisted with malice. "You cannot be serious. The treaty states that any descendants of King Caleos are to be exiled. If we fail to do so, we will break the treaty. Is that what you want? Is this some fae trickery?"

I'm painfully aware of Aspen's eyes burning into me, expression full of shock and hope. I can't meet that hope with my own. Not yet.

Mr. Duveau waves a hand at Mayor Coleman, urging him back into his seat. He returns his attention to me. "Explain yourself, Miss Fairfield."

"I want to save the treaty just as much as anyone in this room," I say. "War is the last thing I want, both for the humans and the fae. I may be both, but as far as I'm concerned, I was human for far longer than I've been fae. I will always have the humans' best interests at the top of my priorities." I force myself not to look at Aspen, knowing I'll find hurt in his eyes if I do.

"How do your *priorities*," Mr. Duveau says the word mockingly, "prevent war when your very presence demands it?"

I dig my nails into the arm of the chair to keep my hands from shaking. "If you allow me to stay and claim the Fire Court throne, I will replace King Ustrin as ruler. From my position as Queen of Fire, I will represent the humans amongst the fae and ensure an ally for you in Faerwyvae. A *true* ally, not a bully with nothing but his crown to care for. Can King Ustrin offer you that? Or does he only offer threats and demands for your obedience? Wouldn't you rather ally yourselves with a true patriot of Eisleigh?"

The councilman takes a step closer. "Your words might be pretty, but they still do nothing to explain how you will claim the throne and stay on the isle without bringing war. Do you not comprehend this simple fact? You taking the throne will break the treaty."

His sentiment is echoed by the council and jury. I wait for their mutterings to subside before I speak again. "I have a solution to that. My taking the throne will not break the treaty, for you will amend it to allow me and any of King Caleos' descendants to stay. Every other term can remain intact. The threat of King Caleos has passed. His violence against humans does not run in my blood."

Mr. Duveau smirks. "Is that so?"

Heat rises to my cheeks, knowing I walked into that one all on my own. I steel my expression. "It is. However, I will defend my life and my honor if forced."

Mayor Coleman speaks again, words heavy with skepticism. "Let me get this straight, Miss Fairfield. You want us to amend the treaty before you so much as challenge King Ustrin? How can we trust you?"

"The fact that I didn't challenge him yet should show you exactly how much you can trust me. I know taking the throne would break the treaty and I'm not willing to do that. I'm not even asking you to change it right this moment. All I'm asking for is time to prove my allegiance and abilities.

The treaty may say I must be exiled, but it doesn't say when. If you let me and my mother go today, you won't be breaking the treaty if we agree that you plan on exiling me at a future date. And that's only *if* I fail to prove myself."

"How will you prove yourself?" Mr. Duveau asks.

"I will do anything of reasonable means that supports the peace of the isle. Once I prove myself, only then will you change the treaty. After it is officially changed, I will defeat King Ustrin and claim the throne. I already have followers who support me." That last part is only partially true. Or perhaps it's a full lie. *There are followers I intend on convincing to support me,* would be more accurate. Lucky for me, I'm not full-fae. My lies go undetected.

"We should take a brief recess and then deliberate Miss Fairfield's offer," one of the jurors says.

A wave of hope rises inside me as several other jurors affirm their agreement. They're taking me seriously. They're—

"No." Mr. Duveau's voice silences the room. With slow steps, he approaches me. Once he's in front of my chair, he leans forward and lowers his voice. "You seem to forget something, Miss Fairfield. Changing the treaty to allow you to stay may keep most of the treaty intact, but it will sever the Legacy Bond. Why would I agree to that?"

My shoulders tremble with suppressed rage. "You would put your own love for power over the benefits I offer our people?"

"There's more to it," he says with a malicious grin. "I don't think you have what it takes to beat King Ustrin."

My words come between my gritted teeth. "Then give me a chance. Amend the treaty stating the changes go into effect only if I beat him."

"No," he says again. "The council will not accept. *I* will not accept. You have no right to ask in the first place. You have no right to defy me. You have no right to even beg. As a human, you are nothing but a Chosen, a sacrifice made for the good of the isle. As a fae, you are the illegal descendant of a criminal."

Fire heats my palms, and it takes all the restraint I have not to set the arm of my chair ablaze. "It's not for you to decide. The jury—"

"In matters of the treaty, I am the legal judge and executioner. My word is final."

All hope drains from me at once, and with it goes my fire.

He takes a step away, voice rising for all to hear. "Our original terms stand. You, your mother, and your sister were offered exile or execution. Your sister didn't come today, so the punishment is death."

Aspen shudders at my side, chest heaving. I can feel his anger, his help-lessness at not truly being here in physical form.

Franco lets out several angry caws, while the jurors exchange furious whispers. The councilmen, on the other hand, seem perfectly composed.

It's over. Mr. Duveau will never let me stay. He's sentenced us to death. There's only one thing left to fight for.

31

———————

"Please," I say, tears springing to my eyes. "Please reconsider. I told you, I tried to get my sister to come. Just...just let us leave the isle. At the very least, let my mother go free."

Mr. Duveau grins. "Oh, now you beg for my mercy? Now you ask me to allow you to take exile?"

Mother tries to speak, but all she can make is a pained moan.

I nod. "Please."

"I want to see you beg." The room returns to silence as Mr. Duveau takes a key from the pocket of his black robe. He places it inside a lock on the arm of my chair. With a turn, the cuffs at my wrists and ankles spring open. He steps back and motions me forward. "I want you to plead on your knees."

Mother's teeth chatter as she says my name, but I pay her no heed. With shaking steps, I rise from my chair and move toward the councilman.

"Don't dare try anything clever," he says, pulling his robe to the side. A flash of silver catches my eyes. A revolver, like the one Sheriff Bronson had. I swallow hard. Since when do councilmen carry revolvers? "Iron bullets," he says with a smirk.

"Don't do this," Aspen says, voice thick with fury. "Do not beg from this monster. We'll find another way."

I ignore him as I lower to my knees and press my palms together. "Please show us mercy."

"Beg me to exile you."

"Please exile me and my mother." My words are flat, toneless.

The councilman responds with icy silence. "Perhaps I'll consider exiling your mother," he says. "You, however, will serve a different fate before you meet your exile. You made a good point about the treaty. I can exile you without sending you away right now."

I don't know what he's carrying on about, as all words have lost meaning.

He continues. "Before you take your exile, you will serve in the Briar House."

My eyes shoot to his.

"That is the only way I will agree to grant you freedom from execution."

My mouth is too dry to say a word, so I give him a jagged nod.

"Beg," Mr. Duveau says through his teeth. "Beg me to take you to the Briar House. Beg me to be your first patron."

Aspen darts toward the councilman, lips pulling back from his teeth as he roars in his face. Mr. Duveau, of course, can't see him, nor can he feel my mate's antlers making their futile attempts to tear into the man.

I open my mouth to do as told, but this time it's fury that holds me back. Anger builds in my core, snapping me out of my daze. I'm frozen, suspended between words that will condemn my mother and words that will destroy my honor.

An unexpected voice shatters the silence in the room. "You will not beg." Mother's words are said through chattering teeth, but they're stronger than I expected them to be. "You will not utter a single one of those words, Evelyn. You do not plead for this scum to defile you. This ends now. I will end my life myself before I see you on your knees before this filth a minute more."

Mr. Duveau shoots my mother a glare before turning his eyes back to me. "This is your last chance, Miss Fairfield. Beg now or die."

All I hear is my mother's words, her fire sparking with mine, creating an inferno in my heart. My mind becomes clear. My mother is right. I cannot grovel before this man, even if it's for my life or hers. I'm not merely a human Chosen or an illegal fae. I'm so much more. I'm a lover and a daughter and the descendant of a king. I am the Unseelie Queen of Fire.

I turn my head to meet my mother's gaze. Her eyes have grown clear, swimming with flames. We exchange no words, but a silent understanding passes between us. If this is the end, so be it. Mother gives me a subtle nod.

I rise to my feet on strong legs. "No."

"Seize them." Mr. Duveau's shout brings two guards toward me, while the others close in on Mother. A sudden blast of light halts all movement for a split second. I look toward Mother. Despite the icy water soaking her bottom half, fire erupts from her palms, melting the iron cuffs. She yanks them hard, and they break, releasing her. She presses a fiery palm to the chest of the nearest guard, and he shouts in pain.

"Maven Fairfield." My mother's name bursts from Mr. Duveau's lips, carrying the undeniable weight of magic. "Do not move."

To my horror, Mother freezes where she stands, and the guards wrest her arms behind her back. Mr. Duveau retrieves his revolver from beneath his robe and points it at her.

I look from him to Mother, then back again. That's when I remember my final weapon against the councilman. One I didn't want to use unless absolutely necessary.

"Henry Duveau." I say it with the same power I touched when I used Aspen's true name. I await the vision of the bridge, the cliffs, but it doesn't come. Only a flicker of a vast chasm obscured by fog. Perhaps the vision of the bridge is unique to me and Aspen. I refocus on the power of the councilman's name. "You will let my mother go. You will allow us to leave this trial unharmed and will not pursue us for as long as we live."

My eyes lock on Mr. Duveau's, his expression unreadable.

Then, to my horror, his lips pull into a wide grin. "Did you really think I've made my birth name public? Did you honestly believe *you* had the power of my true name?"

He pulls the trigger.

My world shatters at the sound of the gun firing, then narrows to the point of a bullet. All sound is hollow in my ears as I watch the bullet strike between my mother's eyes.

There's no moment of hope, no opportunity for Mother to fight against the iron that burrows into her forehead and ends her life.

A scream that is mine yet sounds so far away bursts from my chest as Mother's body topples into the tub, the water quickly running a bright shade of red.

I'm vaguely aware of a raven's caw as Mr. Duveau shields his head, shouting as a black beak seeks to peck out his eyes. A few of the guards leave my mother's lifeless form to charge the bird, while others close in on me.

Anger burns inside my heart, sharpening my mind. The raven shifts into Franco, but he's unlike any version of him I've ever seen. He's tall, lithe, cloaked in shadow, fangs lengthening in his terrifying maw as he intercepts the guards. The guards shrink back with horrified shouts, and I watch as shadows are leeched from them, being pulled in by the prince.

The councilmen and jurors begin to shout, clambering out of their seats.

Mr. Duveau stumbles back from the dark prince, and my eyes lock on him. Heat floods my palms as I pursue his retreat. When his attention meets mine, his composure stiffens. He turns the barrel of his gun on me. "Evelyn Fairfield."

I'm too enraged to fear that he's using my name. All I feel is fire and pain and a burning need for revenge.

"Don't move," Mr. Duveau says, the power of my name heavy in the command.

I freeze, hating the lack of control over my own motor functions. His fingers find the trigger, but before he can pull it, I say his name again. He may have kept his birth name secret, but the Legacy Bond means I should have power over it regardless. So this time, I seek the power of intent. *His true name, his true name.* I repeat it like a mantra, seeking it beneath the fog that blankets the chasm. There's still no bridge, but a thin rope-like tether connects us and is growing clearer by the second. I imagine his hands stiff and immobile, frozen like ice, unable to fire the gun.

The councilman's hand begins to shake, and I can see the effort it's taking him to try and pull the trigger. His gaze intensifies, and I feel his attention on my name. I still can't move, but neither can his trigger finger.

Sweat beads at my brow, but I maintain my focus, gripping that tether with everything inside me. From the corner of my eye, I see Franco still fighting with the guards, most of whom are cowering on the floor, convulsing wildly.

Mr. Duveau blinks a few times, his face growing red. Finally, a gasp escapes his lips and he lowers the gun. In that same moment, an enormous creature barrels between me and the councilman. My heart leaps into my throat. It's Aspen. The real Aspen, not the ethereal version of him that was here before.

In stag form, Aspen charges Mr. Duveau, antlers striking the man's midsection and sending him sprawling across the floor. I'm about to chase after him, my palms yearning to burn his flesh to a crisp, but Aspen steps between us. "Get on," he says.

Mr. Duveau struggles to rise, blood seeping from his abdomen. Everything inside me wants to finish the job. To do to him what he did to my mother.

"Get on!" Aspen repeats, louder this time. That's when I see the flood of soldiers enter the room. Without a second thought, I pull myself on Aspen's back. He carries us toward the startled soldiers before they can react, swinging his antlers to clear our way. In seconds, we're racing out the front of the building, Aspen's hooves pounding the cobblestones.

"Get Foxglove and meet us at Lunar," Aspen says.

I know he must be talking to Franco, but I don't bother looking for the raven prince. All I see is blood and flames, my mother's lifeless body in a tub of crimson water. Sorrow threatens to unravel me, so I seek my anger instead. It burns easily, searing me from the inside.

I lose all sense of time as we race through the night, Aspen's stag mouth lathering as he carries us from city streets to the quiet forest. Even beneath the cover of trees, he neither slows nor rests. My anger refuses to slacken as well and only seems to grow with every minute, every hour that passes. The heat becomes tangible, uncomfortably warm as sweat drips from every inch of my skin. I'm only half-aware of the bright glow that emanates from my body.

Aspen's voice comes out strained. "Take it to the Twelfth Court."

I don't know what he means, nor can I find words to respond.

Instead, I burn, burn, burn.

32

My next coherent thought is a sudden awareness that I'm surrounded by water from the waist down.

As if waking from a dream, my mind grows sharper, my vision clearer. Up until this moment, all I saw was smoke and flames. Blood. My mother's corpse.

Fire threatens to consume me again, but the water seems to quell it, returning me to neutral.

I blink several times as I take in my surroundings. The domed ceiling overhead is familiar, as is the quality of moonlight streaming into the room and sending the surface of the water glittering.

I'm in the moon baths at the Lunar Court, half-submerged in one of the three pools.

Something soft brushes against my back, a soothing touch. I crane my neck to find Aspen behind me in the pool, a sponge of silky moon moss in his hands as he runs it over my shoulder. I wince, eyes roving to where the sponge made contact. All along my arms are bright patches of raw skin, surrounded by darker charred flesh. The sleeves of my shirt are nearly burned entirely off—or perhaps they were torn by Aspen in order to do what he's doing.

He dips the sponge in the water and returns it to my shoulder, letting the water trail down my arm. Each trickle of water and brush of the moss eases a pain that I'm only just growing aware of.

"What happened?" My throat feels raw, my words coming out hoarse.

"You were burning." His voice is quiet, gentle, although it carries a hint of strain.

"How long?" I'm barely able to finish the sentence as I choke on the last word. My lungs feel like they're filled with smoke.

"Hours. It's just before dawn at Lunar."

I'm surprised it's so quiet, considering this is when the palace is most active. "Where is everyone?"

"Queen Nyxia ordered the moon baths and the hall outside vacated when I brought you here."

"Why?" I wheeze. "Why are we here?"

"In Lunar, or in the bath?"

"Bath."

"Like I said, you were burning. You burned the entire way here."

That explains my scorched skin. I remember how I erupted with fire, how I burned relentlessly until I slipped out of awareness. If it took us several hours to get here, I must have been unconscious for most of the journey. "Why did my fire burn me?"

He dips the sponge in the water again, then trails it lightly over my burns, easing my wounds some more. "Your powers got out of hand. Fae magic can hurt even its wielder if one knows not how to control it."

"Could it have killed me?"

"Your own fire can never kill you, but when allowed to consume you that way...it's debilitating."

I watch as he dips the moon moss again and returns it to my arm. "I thought water was harmful to fire."

"An attack by water, yes," he says. "However, your fire got out of balance. An opposing element can bring it back to healthy levels without harming you. It's helping you heal."

That much is obvious, but I thought perhaps it had more to do with the moon moss.

"These pools are more than just for daily cleansing," he explains. "They are constantly purified by the light of the moon and stars, charged with energy when the moon is full. This was the only place I could think to take you." His voice sounds pained, expressing an undercurrent of worry beneath his composure.

Aspen pauses, and I realize he's finished soothing my arm. In fact, he must have already tended the first arm, because both seem unmarred save for their deep pink hue. I turn to face him fully but freeze, startled by what I see. He wears no jacket, no waistcoat, and what remains of his shirt is nothing but charred tatters. His chest is covered with what looks like mild burns, and an angry red color marks his neck...as if...

I try to circle behind him, but he's faster. Not so fast that I don't glimpse a flash of red and black puckered skin. I gasp, tears springing to my eyes. "Aspen! Is that from me?"

"I'm fine," he says. "I'm already beginning to heal."

"But I...I did that."

"You didn't know."

"You carried me here on your back in stag form and I burnt you the entire time." This is the first time I've been forced to consider what features fae carry between forms. If even his clothing has been destroyed, then I can only imagine his stag fur and flesh burnt to a crisp.

My stomach churns and I reach for the sponge of moon moss. He lifts his hand over my head, snatching it out of my reach. "You aren't healed yet." His eyes flash over my torso, covered only by the remnants of my burnt blouse.

I try to stretch for the moss, but wince as the motion sears my side. Hoping he didn't notice, I say, "Let me tend to your wounds, damn you."

"No, Evie." His voice is firm yet gentle. "For once in your life, let someone else put your wellbeing above their own."

His expression has me swallowing all argument. Instead, I offer a compromise. "We'll take care of each other then."

He releases a sigh. "Fine."

I glance again at my chest, then start to undo the buttons. Aspen averts his gaze, shifting from foot to foot. It reminds me of how awkward he was before our conversation in the alley. Before our kiss. I hope what's happened since then hasn't pushed us a step back again.

What's happened since. Flames and smoke fill my mind, and the image of my mother falling from an iron bullet. Sorrow washes over me, threatening to drag me into a black void of endless grief. The feeling is so terrifying, I reach for my quickest defense—my fire. Anger ignites, but instead of fueling me, it increases the sharpness of my wounds. I cry out in pain, my legs collapsing beneath me.

Aspen catches me before my head goes beneath the surface of the water. He pulls me close, hand on my cheek as he tilts my head toward his. "Just focus on me right now."

I breathe away my pain, my anger, and focus on his face, the color of his eyes, the angle of his jaw. Facts. Shapes. Logic. It settles me.

"There will be time to grieve and rage after your body is healed," he says.

Once the strength returns to my legs, I pull away from him, but only slightly. This time, he reaches for the buttons of my blouse himself. I shudder as the fabric falls away, then I reach down to slip off my tattered trousers. He brings the moon moss toward me, but I shake my head. "You too."

With a grumble, he allows me to pull the scorched linen off his chest, separate it from the burns on his back. My stomach roils as I examine the full extent of the damage I've caused.

Freed from our clothing, I finally allow Aspen to tend to the burns on my torso. I keep my eyes locked on his, emptying my mind of the terrors that lurk behind every thought, every breath. When all traces of stinging pain leave my chest, Aspen hands me the moss and turns his back to me.

I have to extend my arms to reach the top of his shoulders, but I'm relieved to see the immediate effects of the moss and water taking place. His skin seems to repair even faster than mine, which I'm assuming must have to do with his heritage. Being the son of Queen Melusine gives him an advantage over the water element.

I watch as the charred skin falls away, revealing new pink skin in its place. His golden coloring has yet to emerge, but his healing is promising. Blisters shrink and dissolve, returning the smooth planes of his back, the strong angles of his shoulder blades. A tender feeling stirs inside me, breaking through the chaos that I'm somehow able to keep at bay. Even after Aspen's skin has fully healed, I linger over him, letting my hands trail up and down his back as I study the curve of his spine, the muscles in his arms and shoulders. The silence of our bated breaths speaks louder than any words we can say.

Aspen shudders at my final touch before turning to face me, hand moving to the back of my neck. With gentle fingers, he pulls my damp hair over one shoulder, a wordless signal for me to turn around. As I do, he takes the moss and brings it to my back. With my pains nearly gone, every touch feels like a welcome caress.

My mind begins to wander to the dangerous territory of blood and fire, and I quickly force myself to focus on Aspen's touch. But a memory remains, one neutral enough for me to consider without much harm. I break the silence around us. "When I was burning, I remember you telling me to take it to the Twelfth Court. What did you mean by that?"

Aspen runs the moss over the back of my neck, my upper shoulders. "If you'd taken your rage to the Twelfth Court, you would have been able to more evenly distribute your fire, use it for transformative purposes."

His words do nothing to clear my confusion. "What does that mean?"

"That's how the fae shift into our unseelie forms. It's one way, at least. Most of us can shift at will, but strong emotion or an overuse of our power can shift us without effort. Sometimes, that can be detrimental, but in your case, I think it would have helped."

"You really think I could have...shifted forms?"

"I'm not sure, but I think so."

"How would it have helped? Would I not have felt the same rage?"

"You would have been more in control of it on an instinctual level," Aspen says. "You would have used most of your excess fire in the act of physically shifting. It takes magic to shift forms, and you had a dangerous amount to spare."

I furrow my brow, pondering Aspen's words. Nyxia hadn't told me this when I relayed my doubts about having the ability to shift. From how he describes it, it makes a sort of logical sense.

If magic and logic can ever coexist, that is.

The realization serves to relieve some of the darkness hanging over me. However, there's still so much I know I need to face. That rage I felt on the journey here hasn't diminished. The water is merely keeping it dormant. But now I'm starting to see how I can utilize it in a logical manner. Pieces of a puzzle fall into place before me, and only a blush of anger comes with it.

I return my attention to the feel of Aspen's fingers, the silky moss against my now-soothed skin. Turning my head slightly to the side, I catch Aspen's eyes from my periphery. "You were right," I say.

He pauses his ministrations, then runs the moss down my spine. "About what?"

"The treaty being a broken thing not worth saving. You were right all along."

"I don't revel in being right about this. I never wanted any of that to happen."

I turn to fully face him, shutting out violent images in my mind and replacing them with firm, rational facts. "It has to end," I say. "The treaty, the Reaping, and both councils. I have to take the throne from King Ustrin."

His jaw shifts back and forth, and I remember how little he knows about the plan I tried to enact. "How long were you planning to do what you did at the trial?"

Again, I have to skirt around my pain to seek the facts. "A few days. I'm sorry I didn't tell you. Things were strange between us and I...I couldn't bear the pressure of your hope or mine."

He releases the moss, letting it float away on the surface of the water. "I wish you would have told me. I could have supported you better, long before the trial."

I shake my head. "I can't deal with regrets right now. All I can focus on is what to do next."

He brings a hand to my cheek, moving closer to me until my breasts are a breath away from brushing his chest. I ache to pull him against me as his thumb caresses my jawline. "What will you do?"

"Whatever it takes to make things right," I say. "Not just for one people but for all of them. The fae, both seelie and unseelie. The humans."

His expression brightens, and I realize it's the first time he's heard me voice such care for the fae. Perhaps it's the first time I've admitted it out loud. "You're going to stay?"

I bring one hand to his hip, the other slides up his torso to rest over his beating heart. I tip my head back and lock our eyes. "I'm staying. Faerwyvae is my home. The Fire Court is my throne. And you are my mate."

He brings his lips to mine and I eagerly receive them, the heat we had to abandon in the alley returning at full force. But before we fall too deep, there are words I need to say. Words I'm no longer willing to hold onto. With so much that can still go wrong, I can no longer keep it to myself.

I separate my lips from his, but our foreheads remain touching. He sinks low into the water, and I wrap my arms around his neck until only our heads are above the surface. I pull away to take in the autumn colors swimming in his hungry eyes. "Aspen, I love you."

He trembles against me, then brushes his lips lightly against mine. Silence stretches between us, and for one terrifying moment I fear I've said the wrong thing. Do the fae even exchange sentiments of love? Then his lips pull into a smile. Not the smirk I adore, or the seductive grin that makes my knees weak. A pure, authentic smile. "I love you too, Evie."

When our kisses return, they are gentler, softer. His tongue caresses mine as a burning need hums at my core. I run my hands through his hair, eliciting a deep moan from him as I bring my fingers to dance along the beam of an antler. He tenses against me. One of his hands grips my bottom while the other explores the crest of my breast. Our breathing rises in tandem, a furious melody playing the tune of our growing desire. I feel weightless as he lifts me off my feet, pulling me close until my hips are pressed against his.

My core burns to deepen the connection, to move further into my passion. I let it rise to illuminate my entire being. I'm glowing with the need to feel every part of him.

That's when I realize I really am glowing. Like the night of the full moon revel, a violet haze has clouded my vision. Even though I can feel this glow radiating from my inner fire, this kind isn't painful like the one caused by my blazing rage. This one is gentle, glittering, and pleasurable unlike anything has ever been before.

Aspen whispers my name, and I whisper his in turn. Beneath the light of the rising sun shining from the domed ceiling overhead, we move to the tune of our love.

33

Hazy sunlight brushes my eyelids, and the smell of rosemary and cinnamon floods my senses. I open my eyes to find Aspen sleeping next to me. His face is slack, head turned slightly to the side as his antlers hang over the back of his mattress. We're in his bedroom, where the bed is in the middle of the room to accommodate his extra assets.

Speaking of extra assets.

I find my leg is sprawled over his hips, bringing to mind our early morning passions, the moon baths, the way he carried me to his room for us to sleep. Or *try* to sleep for several hours until we finally fell into a heap of exhaustion. It must be midafternoon by now.

I extract an arm from beneath his and bring my fingers to his face. Brushing his golden skin, I drink in the sight of him, so youthful and beautiful in slumber. He stirs at my touch, eyes opening to find mine. The smile that greets me makes my heart flip.

"We managed to sleep in a proper bed for once," he says.

"We did."

He moves closer to me, bringing a hand to my lower back. "Was it better than it was when you visited me in your dreams?"

"It was. In those moments, there's a discrepancy in physical sensation. Is it the same for you?"

His brow wrinkles as he considers. "Yes, I think you're right. That didn't stop me from enjoying it though. I wished so badly that you'd really been there that first night."

His words send a flicker of pain inside me. "I did too."

"And in the dining room at Bircharbor. That's when I knew the visions were more than fantasy. You appeared out of nowhere while I was wide awake." He lets out a light laugh. "You should have seen the terror on that fool girl's face when I roared at her and ordered her back to her room. She hadn't the slightest idea she'd just interrupted a much-desired kiss."

"That kiss was everything I wanted," I say. "Although, at that point, I still thought I was dreaming. In fact, I thought I was having a nightmare, certain that any moment the dream would shift into something I wouldn't want to see. It wasn't until you came to Lunar that I realized those visions had been real." My heart sinks, the words I omitted screaming in my mind. *It wasn't until you caught me kissing Franco.* Now that we've fully reunited, I feel like my apology to him in the alley could have been better.

He moves his hand to my face. "You were right, Evie. You don't owe me an explanation and you are not my property. You are my mate. You are free to seek pleasure with whomever—"

I sit upright, cheeks blazing with indignation. "I only want you, Aspen. You damn well better know that."

Amusement shines in his eyes as he props himself up on his elbows. He quirks a brow. "Only me?"

"Yes. I'm like Lorelei. Monogamous, that is. This is not...this isn't a Nyxia at Beltane situation." Blood drains from my face as I consider something I never have before. Not all fae love the same way I'm used to. Does he love the way I need to be loved? "Wait, do you prefer...taking other lovers?"

A smirk pulls at his lips and I want to slap it off his face. Or kiss it off. No, definitely slap. "I feel the same as you," he finally says, his smirk shifting back to a genuine smile. "It's just us, Evie. You're all I want."

I let out a shaking breath, posture relaxing as I let him pull me to his chest. His heart beats against my ear as his breath stirs my hair.

"You're all I love."

My heart skips a beat, and I lift my eyes to meet his. Love. It's still so new to me, both the feeling and the word. It feels fragile and precious and terrifying all at once. With a soft brush of our lips, we seal our unspoken vow with a kiss.

∼

It's almost painful to separate and force ourselves out of bed, but the outside world doesn't stop to cater to my stolen moments of peace. There's still much to attend to. The humans will want retribution for my escape. King Ustrin will want revenge.

And I have a throne to claim.

I return to my room, my body aching with every step—a combination of my leftover strain from the journey and the exhaustion of pleasure. Once dressed, I go to find Lorelei.

She opens her bedroom door and wastes not a moment before throwing her arms around me. "I heard you returned last night, and not in the best state. I was terrified for you."

We pull away, and she looks me over. "I'm all right, I promise. Aspen took care of me."

She raises a brow. "You actually let someone else take care of you for once?"

I roll my eyes. "I know, I know."

Her expression turns serious. "How did it go?"

A shard of glass pierces my heart as an iron bullet shoots through my memory, followed by blood and smoke. Sorrow drags at me, and I feel like I'm being buried beneath mounds of stone. It's so painful, I can hardly breathe, can hardly stand—

I seek my inner fire, transforming my sorrow into rage. This time, the fire doesn't sear me. Instead, it clears my head, my heart, returns my composure.

Tears swim in Lorelei's eyes. Her words are a gentle whisper. "You don't have to say anything. Not until you're ready."

I steel myself and let out a heavy sigh.

"What happens next?" she asks.

"I must meet with the fire fae again to secure their support in claiming Unseelie Queen of Fire."

She bites a corner of her lip. "I won't pressure you to say more than you are ready for, but can I ask...did the humans agree to change the treaty?"

I force the darkness away, keeping my mind trained on facts alone. "No."

"Then you know claiming rule in Faerwyvae will officially break the treaty, right?"

I square my shoulders. "I'm ready to break it."

Her eyes widen, lips pulling into a sad smile.

"However, the bargain I made with King Ustrin keeps war at bay for now," I say. "A fight between the fae council and the rebels will come to pass, but in the meantime, they can do nothing. I think we should use this time to come up with a solid plan."

"Let's do this," she says with a nod. "Have you told Queen Nyxia?"

"No, but I need to speak with her. I want to meet with the fire fae tonight."

She's already moving to the door. "Then let's find her."

We head toward the throne room, plans and ideas buzzing through my head. One question plagues me again and again. I turn to Lorelei. "When I do face King Ustrin, must I make a formal challenge for the throne like Aspen did with Cobalt?"

She shakes her head. "No, those formalities were created by the Council of Eleven Courts. Once the treaty is broken, the rules of the council need no longer apply. With the rebels already claiming a return to the Old Ways, it will be in accordance with the Twelfth Court that you will face him."

"How does it work, exactly?"

She shrugs. "You need to prove you are the alpha blessed by the All of All."

"You say it like it's simple, but I don't understand how that comes to be. Do I engage him in physical combat? Will it be a fight to the death?" My stomach turns at the thought. There's no way I can beat King Ustrin in physical combat. If only I had an iron blade...

"It's impossible to know ahead of time," Lorelei says. "Sometimes it's simply a matter of facing each other in the Twelfth Court, like you did as Aspen's champion. The win may still be shown with a token, like the crown you were given. Other times it's won by submission to the alpha, like with Nyxia and her mother. But yes, there are times when only death can decide the victor. In those cases, the All of All gives their champion strength."

My heart races. It sounds impossible no matter how she puts it. Luckily, my bargain with King Ustrin will give me enough time to prepare.

We are almost at the doors to the throne room when the sound of commotion draws my attention.

Lorelei and I exchange a glance before we take off down the corridor toward the noise. Once we reach the entry hall to the palace, we find dozens of bedraggled fae streaming inside, two of which are Foxglove and Franco. Lorelei runs to Foxglove while Franco offers me a tired wink. Both seem flustered but none the worse for wear. The fae surrounding them, however, look as if they just returned from battle. Their clothing is stained and torn. Those who have hair wear it disheveled, and those with fur appear matted. My heart leaps in my throat when I recognize a figure.

"Gildmar!"

The old fae's bark-like face stretches into a relieved grin as I approach her. "You're here," she says.

"Yes, but what are *you* doing here?"

She extends her arms toward her fellows. "We are who remain of King Aspen's most loyal household. Not everyone chose to come." Her lips twitch into a frown. "And not all made the escape."

My heart sinks at that. I return my attention to the fae continuing to file inside, finding another familiar face—one of Aspen's handsome servants, Vane. The next figure is even more surprising.

Marie Coleman meets my eyes, face crumpling as she rushes to me. The girl wraps her arms around my waist and sobs into my shoulder.

I almost forget how to move. What in the name of iron is Maddie Coleman's little sister doing here?

"Oh, Evelyn, I can't believe I made it. I thought I was going to die."

I'm torn between surprise and utter confusion, flustered at how she says my name with such care. We never were friends before. The most familiarity we ever exchanged was when she wordlessly pleaded with me in Mayor Coleman's parlor. My mouth goes dry, remembering her tears of distress, how her eyes begged me to help her.

I thought I was powerless then.

My arms return the embrace, even though my mind still whirls to comprehend what is happening. She heaves a heavier sob as she pulls away from me, her attention snagging on something she sees over my shoulder.

"Aspen!" Marie runs to my shocked mate, his eyes taking in the swarm of fae and the girl who clings around his waist. He takes a tentative hand and pats her heaving shoulders.

A flicker of jealousy flutters through me, but it dries before it can ignite into something more. There isn't anything sensual in their embrace. The way Marie holds onto Aspen isn't like a lover but a friend. And his consoling touch is more fatherly than anything, although he seems hesitant to give it.

Marie seems to compose herself, pulling away and wiping the tears from her ruddy cheeks. "I'm so sorry, Your Majesty, Miss Fairfield." She gives us each a trembling curtsy. "That was very unbecoming of me. You just have no idea how relieved I am to be here."

"Please don't take this the wrong way," I say, "but why exactly are you here? Is your...sister here too?"

Her expression darkens. "Of course not. Maddie is quite comfortable with her new arrangement, despite the questionable ethics she's embroiled in."

I raise a brow at Aspen, still bewildered.

He takes my hand and gives it a squeeze. "Marie expressed to me her reservations about Faerwyvae from the start."

Marie nods eagerly. "I begged him to send me home. I thought for sure he was going to kill me for my insubordination, but instead, he was kind." She lifts her chin. "He promised I wouldn't have to marry—*ever*—if I didn't want to."

I flash a grin at my mate. "That's quite good of him."

Marie crosses her arms. "It's the first time in my fifteen years of life that option has ever been given to me."

I look away from Marie to take in the rest of the refugees, seeing the exhaustion tugging their features. "It must have been a difficult journey."

"One I didn't expect any of you to make without aid," Aspen adds. He seems hesitant, anxious almost, before he says more. "The rebels and I had plans to send spies to help you escape."

Then I realize the source of his conflict; he's fighting not to show how touched he is that his household came. They followed him before he even sent anyone to assist them. For a king who keeps his truest, kindest nature behind a mask of stoicism, it must surprise him to find so many loyal to his reign.

It's my turn to give his hand a squeeze, and we exchange a smile.

"We were stuck near the border between Solar and Lunar for two days," Marie explains, oblivious to Aspen's internal struggle. "There were soldiers patrolling the area. It wasn't until Ambassador Foxglove and the Lunar Prince came along that we were able to make it the rest of the way. Some of us were smuggled through the carriage, while the prince flew others across the border one at a time."

That explains why it took Foxglove and Franco so long to arrive.

"Are there more of you?" Queen Nyxia's voice comes from over my shoulder as she approaches us.

Marie pales at the queen's domineering presence. Belatedly, she sinks into a clumsy curtsy. "Yes, Your Majesty. We left Autumn in three separate groups. The second caught up with us when we were stuck in Solar, but the third is still unaccounted for."

"I will inform my owls," Nyxia says. "I'll have them on high alert with orders to allow them safe passage."

"Thank you," Aspen says.

She raises a brow. "I suppose you'll want me to house all your refugees until you get your palace back?"

His jaw shifts back and forth. "Please."

She tuts. "It won't come free. I'm already hosting you and your mate. What will you give me in return?"

I step forward, fingers balled into fists. "We're giving you what you always wanted. A broken treaty."

"*You* are giving me a broken treaty, but what is Aspen providing?" She extends her hands toward the fae cluttering her entry. "A fragmented household? Exhausted soldiers?"

"His household is my household. If you ally with me, you ally with them. Once Aspen and I have our thrones, our people will be out of your way."

Nyxia studies me through slitted lids. After a few tense moments, she says, "You've chosen a side after all."

I maintain my composure beneath her scrutiny. "Will you send word to the fire fae to meet me tonight?"

Her lips pull into a devious grin. "It would be my pleasure."

34

———————

After nightfall, Nyxia, Aspen, and I make our way through the forest toward the same cave I visited before. The waning moon is bright, but the forest is oddly quiet, making the glowing mushrooms and bell-like flowers that light our path seem almost sinister.

It makes me grateful I accepted the presence of my two companions. My first instinct was to refuse. I wanted tonight's meeting with the fire fae to speak volumes, to show them I stand on my own, that I am no one's puppet, and that I don't see them as a threat. However, Nyxia made the compelling point that there are other creatures to fear besides the fire fae. Going to the meeting alone would be foolish.

At least the three of us are under the same agreement. Tonight, I represent myself. Nyxia and Aspen will support me as my allies, not my protectors.

We reach the mouth of the cave. From here, it's black and soundless, giving no hint that anything awaits deep within. A chilling thought comes to mind. What if there really is no one waiting within? What if my first meeting was enough to convince them never to follow me?

Sensing my hesitation, Aspen reaches for my hand. "Are you sure you're ready to do this?"

The touch soothes me. "Yes."

Nyxia lifts her brow. "That...issue...we spoke of last time still stands. Are you prepared to follow through with what I told them?"

I know what she's asking. *Am I ready to show them my unseelie form?* That's an additionally perplexing obstacle, one I've given much thought to but no answer. I tried several times throughout the day to take my anger to the Twelfth Court, like Aspen had described. It did nothing. My anger wasn't nearly as strong as it had been after my mother's death, but that intensity is hard to reach without giving way to sorrow first. And I'm afraid if I give in, not even my rage will be able to save me from it.

I try to put on a convincing face for Nyxia. "I will do what I can."

She flashes me a glare. "I told them you would show them your unseelie form next time you met with them."

A spark of anger stirs within me. "You also told them I'd meet with them when I was ready to make a move against King Ustrin. I'm ready to do that and I'm ready to fight for them. If that isn't enough, then perhaps I'm not enough to be queen. If I'll have their support, I'll have it for who I am. For all I know, this," I wave my hands over the length of my body, "is also my unseelie form."

She rolls her eyes. "Fine. I hope you're ready for this."

"So do I," I mutter. Not an hour has gone by without me questioning whether everything I'm about to do isn't absolute insanity. I escaped the Spire. Eisleigh. Mr. Duveau. I escaped exile. If I wanted, I could lay low, go into hiding. Avoid Mr. Duveau's bounty hunters and the seelie fae who would turn me in.

The very thought ignites my indignation. No matter how many times these doubts creep in, I remind myself why I'm doing this. Because it's the right thing to do. Because the treaty must be broken. Because men like Mr. Duveau and males like Cobalt and Ustrin don't deserve to be in power. Because I deserve a whole life, not one spent in hiding. Because I'm the only one who will fight for both the humans and the fae.

Nyxia enters the cave and I follow behind her. I feel Aspen's steadying hand on my lower back, a silent exchange of his support. His touch lowers my pulse and sends calming warmth through my heart.

After a long stretch of darkness, the glowing mushrooms and luminescent crystals begin to light our way. Soon sounds fall upon my ears, proof that at least someone is waiting within. Finally, we reach the inner chamber.

Like before, a variety of fae are clustered inside, eyes full of scrutiny as I enter. What surprises me is how many more there are this time than the last. There are new kitsune in various colors. Wisps in blues, reds, oranges, and violets float through the air. A second moon dragon with opalescent scales is coiled next to the black one I met last time. There are also several other kinds of fae I've never met before—sprites of dust and ash and odd-looking flames, birds with bright, fiery wings, glittering snakes and salamanders. There are also fae who appear barely different from an average animal, although none I've seen anywhere but encyclopedic reference—fennec foxes, desert rodents, scorpions. Their keen eyes are all that give their true natures away.

With a deep breath, I walk forward and stand before them. Aspen's hand brushes my back one last time, a gesture hidden from view, before he takes a step away to stand near the wall of the cave. Nyxia does the same, although her resistance is obvious. I can see her struggle not to speak on my behalf written all over her expression.

"You again, and in human form," says the crustacean-mushroom I remember from before. "I thought you'd only come back when you were ready to prove you were one of us."

A rumble of agreement moves through the crowd, and to my disappointment, several fae break away from the group and stream out the cave before I can say a word. The others shuffle, as if eager to follow.

"Wait," I call out, my tone weak and pleading. I take a moment to gather my nerves, reminding myself I'm supposed to be a queen. With a deep breath, I force my voice to ring out with authority. "Give me a chance to speak before you make your decision about me. I will respect your choice, but I will be heard."

The fae go still, and not another tries to exit the cave. Glowing yellow eyes lock on me from the back of the chamber. It's the opalescent moon dragon. "I want to hear what she has to say," says a hissing feminine voice. "I wasn't here last time, if you recall. If we don't like what she offers, she'll make a pretty snack."

Tittering laughter comes from the crowd, but I'm not sure if it's sinister or meant to be cajoling. Whatever the case, I came here for a reason and I can't falter now.

I steel myself, throwing back my shoulders as I try to feign confidence. "Last time we met, Queen Nyxia introduced me as the figure who would fight King Ustrin. Today I come to you as Unseelie Queen of Fire."

Gasps and yips and growls answer. Again, I'm unsure how to translate the sounds. The clamor could be supportive, shocked, or angry for all I can tell. I continue. "I am claiming Unseelie Queen of Fire according to the Old Ways. When the time comes, I will face King Ustrin and the All of All will bless their alpha. I intend to win."

An orange wisp bobs forward, her high, feminine voice floating on the air. "How do you intend to beat him? You are but a human with the blood of a former fae king. King Ustrin has lived much longer than you and he's been king nearly his entire life."

I'm prepared for that question, my voice ringing out clear and strong. "King Ustrin rules without respect for the Old Ways or the All of All. I may not be full-fae and I may not have the experience he has. But I have the heart. I care about the lives of the fae, and that includes the unseelie. King Ustrin cares about his own power and he'll shun your kind to keep it. I believe the All of All cares about the seelie and unseelie in equal measure—the way I do."

"So you believe the All of All will bless you as their alpha?" asks an indigo kitsune with a pale blue flame on its tail. Both his words and expression are heavy with skepticism. "Why you and not another? Why should we support you and not someone else who would fight against him?"

I feel the blood leave my face. That's a question I never considered. Not once have I wondered if there were another eager to take the Fire throne. I exhale a deep breath to steady my nerves and clear my mind. The words that come are from deep within, and I hardly know what I'm saying before I say it. "Because the fire in you is the fire in me. I feel it burning in every vein, in every ounce of my blood. I may not be full-fae but King Caleos' legacy is my legacy. I am the result of his deep love for a human woman. His love should have created unity between the humans and the fae. Instead, it brought war and destruction and ended with a corrupt treaty based on lies. I have every intention of restoring the balance that should have been there from the start."

I see a few nods, but there are just as many hisses. A bright yellow salamander scoots forward. "You speak of love like that should mean something to us. We are unseelie."

"So was King Caleos," I say, "and he fell in love. I know love doesn't always look the same, but its essence is universal. We all love our families, our children, our homes, and our freedoms. We may show it in different ways, but it's the same love."

"How will you fight for us?" asks a swirling dust sprite. "Will you help us eradicate the humans? Will you return the Fair Isle to the fae?"

I'm caught off guard by talk of eradicating humans, but I maintain my composure. All I can offer is the truth. "I don't have all the answers, but I'm committed to hearing all voices and make the decisions that support the highest quality of life for all fae. I may be claiming unseelie queen, but I will not claim to be radical. I will fight for what the unseelie truly represent.

Freedom. And that freedom starts by destroying the treaty. My very rule breaks it irreparably."

"What will that even get us?" asks the white dragon. "War will come. The last war wiped out several thousands of fae. Back then, we fought for control over the isle. What will we be fighting for this time?"

"Like I said, I don't have all the answers yet. I don't know what the end result will be. But I do know we'll be fighting for a better world. A better life for all beings on the isle. We'll be fighting for freedom from prejudice and hate amongst fae and humans. We'll be fighting to rid the isle of corrupt leaders and oppressive rules. We'll be fighting for a world where fae aren't captured, experimented on, and sold for parts. Where females aren't sent to brothels."

Fire heats my core, fueling my words. "We will fight for a world where the unseelie are free to be who they wish without sacrificing their ways, their homes, or their land. A world where seelie may keep the lives they cherish without diminishing the rights of the unseelie. We will fight for a world where human girls aren't considered expendable, where they will not be groomed as brides to the fae for a Reaping that never should have been created. We will fight as one. I will fight at your side for all of you. I will defend both humans and fae, and I will fight both humans and fae. Our allies are not those who look like us but those who dream of the same world. I ask you to consider if you want to be part of that vision."

Silence answers. Countless eyes stare back at me, some wide, some hopeful, others narrowed with hostility.

The crustacean scuttles forward. "You'll fight for us, but are you one of us? How can you understand the unseelie if you can't even show us your form?"

Echoes of agreement rattle through the chamber.

"Yes, show them," a malicious voice hisses from the shadows behind me. I whirl toward it, hearing footsteps echo through the cave walls. Someone followed us. Or found us.

King Ustrin steps into the chamber. In his wake, trails Mr. Duveau.

35

The sight of the councilman hits me like a punch to the gut. He meets my eyes with a stony expression, no remorse, no smile. He's stoic, the way he was when I met him at the mayor's. I can't see his face without imagining the revolver, the bullet, my mother's blood streaming into the water below her. A chasm of sorrow opens beneath me, but my anger burns alongside it, keeping me from falling to my knees. I allow it to grow but keep it at a simmer.

Aspen steps forward with a low growl while shadows curl from Nyxia's fists. The two royals come up beside me, facing our unwelcome guests.

Aspen's gaze burns into Mr. Duveau. "I thought I gutted you."

The councilman shrugs, the hint of a teasing smirk playing over his mouth. His stiff posture is all that betrays the underlying wounds he's hiding. "You tried. Merely got one solid gash in. Better luck next time."

Several guards file in behind Ustrin and Mr. Duveau, while a small brown rodent, one I'm fairly sure I saw flee the cave when I arrived, circles the Fire King's ankles. Ustrin looks down at it in disgust, then opens his scaly orange palm. A yellow flame ignites over his hand, then disappears. "Your family has been released," he says with a sneer. "Thank you for your service. You may go."

The rodent emits a squeak before scurrying back out.

A violent shudder ripples through my mate as he lowers into a half-crouch, ready to charge.

Ustrin's eyes whip toward him. "I wouldn't do that if I were you. Not if you want your precious refugees to live."

Aspen bares his teeth, chest heaving. "What are you talking about?"

The Fire King takes a casual step closer. "My soldiers stumbled upon them days ago trying to cross Fire in secret. When Mr. Duveau contacted me with the results of Maven Fairfield's trial, I realized the refugees would provide the perfect cover to infiltrate Lunar and coax a meeting from Miss Fairfield."

"Where are they?" I ask. I remember Marie saying one more group remained unaccounted for. If there are even half as many as those who came this morning, there could be dozens.

"They won't be anywhere unless I make it back to them by midnight," Ustrin says. "My guards have orders to kill them if I don't return by then. Therefore, we should hurry on with our business, yes?"

Aspen emits a growl, shoulders trembling. "What's to stop me from torturing you to an inch of your life until you tell me where they are?"

"Do you think I'd give you the chance?" Another ball of flame, orange this time, ignites over his palm. "I can also send a message. With a snap of my fingers, this flame will leave my palm and transport to my guards. Another sign that they may proceed with the execution."

I burn him with a glare. "What do you want?"

"I only want to talk," he says, a false smile plastered over his lipless mouth. He holds out his hands in a sign of surrender, the orange flame shrinking back into his palm until it's nothing.

"What does *he* want?" My eyes flash to the councilman.

"He's here to force your hand should you fail to comply, but I promise we will give you every opportunity to act on your own."

"Then let's talk."

"Tell your mate to either leave or stand down."

Aspen and I exchange a glance. His muscles ripple with agitation, but he gives me a subtle nod.

I return my attention to Ustrin in time to see him close his eyes with a violent tremble. He rolls his neck, then faces Nyxia. "Stop that already."

Nyxia gives him a devious grin, shadows thickening around her. "Why? Afraid of the dark?"

Ustrin continues to tremble as he turns his palm to the ceiling. This time, a blood-red flame emerges. With a snap of his fingers, it disappears.

Nyxia falters, eyes widening. "What was that?"

"That one went to your palace. If it doesn't find you there shortly after it arrives, it will set your home ablaze, starting with wherever your dear brother can be found. I'd hurry if I were you."

Her shadows retreat, eyes locking on mine.

"Go," I whisper.

With a nod, she transforms into her shadow form and streams from the chamber.

King Ustrin lets out a long breath, the tremors gone, and straightens his cravat and jacket. "What about you, King Aspen? Care to leave or stay?"

"I'm staying," he says through his teeth, body pressing close to my side.

"Will you let his people free once we're done talking?" I ask.

"So long as I am unharmed. If I were you, I'd make no move against me." He gestures to his guards. I flinch, but they don't come for me. Instead, they move further into the chamber to form a ring around the fire fae.

Ustrin looks from the crowd to me, a sneer on his lips. "I must say, I was quite affronted when word spread throughout the forest tonight that you sought a meeting with *my* citizens. Did you really think you could steal my people?"

"They are living in Lunar," I say. "They are no longer your people."

"That's where you're wrong. I've been given new rights by the Council of Eleven Courts. It is my duty to bring the fire fae back to the Fire Court. There they will be tamed and taught to free themselves from their savage ways."

Growls rumble through the chamber. A fennec snaps at one of the guards, earning a swift kick. My heart twists as the tiny fox yelps, then falls on its side.

I round on the king. "You're one to talk about savage ways."

He ignores my scorn as well as the increasing growls and threats and flames coming from the fire fae. "They're armed with iron," he says. The crowd falls into stunned silence. "Each guard carries stone grenades filled with iron shards. Step out of line and I will order their detonation."

Iron grenades. The very thought churns my stomach. I saw what kind of damage explosives can do to the fae, and those didn't contain iron. But wait. The explosion would...

"Won't that hurt you too?" I ask. "And your guards?"

"I will be safe from its radius," King Ustrin says, keeping his voice low.

I don't lower mine to meet his, allowing it to carry. "But you'll sacrifice your guards."

He clenches his jaw. "They understand the risks. They know what they are fighting for."

I cross my arms and take a bold step forward. "So do we."

He lets out a burst of laughter. "Who's this *we*? Do you honestly think you've won their allegiance?"

I purse my lips to keep from saying something foolish. The truth is, he's probably right. The meeting didn't go anywhere near how I wanted it to go.

King Ustrin's posture relaxes. "Speaking of, that's why I came here to speak with you. It's time for you to remove yourself from the isle like you were supposed to. Your presence is a threat to the treaty—"

"You mean a threat to your rule."

His eyes flash dangerously. "—And it prevents the Council of Eleven Courts from engaging the rebels in combat. I can see your bargain with me was far cleverer than I gave you credit for. I should make you pay for your deception. Instead, I offer you a private escort off the isle."

I raise a brow. "A private escort? With Mr. Duveau? Please. I'll take the alternative."

He bares his teeth. "The alternative is he uses the power of your true name to force you to come. What about this don't you understand?"

"What I don't understand is why you're even here. Why go through all this trouble bringing Mr. Duveau to try and get me off the isle yet again? What game are you playing?"

"I'm trying to spare your life."

"Why?"

"I won't kill you." He says it slowly through his teeth, expression twisted as if the statement pains him.

That's when I realize the truth.

"You *can't* kill me. You made a bargain."

He says nothing, confirming my suspicion.

"That's why you've been pushing for my family's exile when you really couldn't care less if we live or die. What was the bargain?"

He lifts his chin. "It was a promise. Before my fool cousin Caleos left for his exile, he made me vow that if it ever came to pass that his progeny found themselves on the isle, I would see that they were treated fairly and given every chance to live well. To avoid stirring suspicion regarding my involvement with his demise, I made the promise. He left it loose enough for me to navigate, but not loose enough to be anything but a thorn in my side since I learned of your existence. He must have known even then what awaited him on the other side of exile. He knew his lover and child had survived."

"Treated fairly?" Aspen growls. "Live well? I don't see how you've fulfilled either of those terms."

"I've fulfilled it enough that I'm still alive, aren't I? Not that every deviation hasn't caused me enough pain to wish for death a time or two. Do you have any idea the suffering Maven Fairfield's death caused me?" He shoots Mr. Duveau a look of contempt.

The councilman, surprisingly, manages not to wither beneath his scorn.

I puzzle over his words, a ripple of shock moving up my spine. Is that what the punishment is for breaking a fae promise? Excruciating pain resulting in eventual death? Before I was willing to accept magic, I thought fae vows and their refusal to lie came from cultural conditioning. Now...I fully believe his punishment is tangible.

Ustrin returns his attention to me. "Let me fulfill my vow and get you off the isle so I can be rid of you once and for all. Not that I'll be truly free until your sister manages to show her face." He says the last part with no small amount of venom.

My heart leaps into my throat at the mention of Amelie. "You don't know where she is?"

His fingers clench into fists. "King Cobalt insists he doesn't know—"

At the words *King Cobalt*, Aspen's growl rumbles in his chest.

"—But he's hiding her from me. I'll deal with him next. He may have the council convinced, but I see through him. Even as an ally, he has much to learn about earning his place."

I take in every word, filing them away in the back of my mind. I'm not sure what it means, but it must be significant that he thinks Cobalt is hiding Amelie from him. While I doubt it suggests noble intentions on Cobalt's behalf, it could mean Amelie's refusal to come to Mother's trial wasn't her choice after all. *Not that it changes anything. Her actions still led to Mother's death.* My simmer of anger rises to a boil. I let it grow, let it burn hotter.

"Let's get this over with," Ustrin says, voice rising an octave. "Otherwise I can hurry your resolve. Mr. Duveau can force you immobile while your ears flood with the haunting melody of the Autumn refugees' dying screams." He turns his gaze to Aspen. "Would you like an invitation to the symphony as well?"

I freeze. His words suggest the refugees are close enough that I'd be able to hear them scream from here. That means we can likely find them without Ustrin's guidance.

"No," I say. Fear floods my body for what I'm about to say, but I call upon my fire to burn it. "We'll get this over with, but I'm not leaving the isle unless you plan on shipping my corpse. We face each other in accordance with the Old Ways. We let the All of All choose their alpha. And we do it now."

Aspen tenses beside me. "Evie, don't—"

Aspen, I say his name in my head, seeking that connection through our Bond. *Please trust me. Make no move against what I'm about to do.*

His eyes search mine, wide with terror. I hear his voice in my mind. *I trust you.*

King Ustrin stares at me for endless moments until a sudden burst of laughter erupts from his lips. "Stupid, stupid girl. You dare challenge me? You dare refuse my offer for mercy? Fine." He shakes his head with bitter amusement. "I gave you your chance. I fulfilled my vow. If you won't come willingly, then you will come by force. And you won't enjoy it."

King Ustrin steps to the side, allowing Mr. Duveau to take his place and face me. Only now does his stoic expression shift into a chilling grin. "Evelyn Fairfield." The name reverberates through my mind, my blood, my bones. "Follow me. Use your mate's true name and order him to remain here until daybreak."

He turns on his heel and takes a few steps away. I stay rooted on the spot, trembling as the command writhes inside me. Ustrin lets out a hiss, making the councilman whirl back around. His face pales, a look of shock in his eyes. He regathers his composure and speaks through gritted teeth. "Evelyn Fairfield."

I hear the name, feel its power, but I'm focusing on something else. Every part of me is fueling my intent—my mind, my heart, my very soul. It grows and grows until it becomes so solid in my mind's eye, I feel like I could touch it.

Mr. Duveau takes a step closer. "Follow me. Now."

I pour my intent into every word. "You have my name wrong."

"Excuse me?"

"My true name isn't Evelyn Fairfield."

"That's a lie. Your mother gave you the name Evelyn Fairfield at birth. It is your true name, and it's a name I've memorized since the day you were born."

"I may have been born with that name, but my name has since changed. It is now Evelyn, Unseelie Queen of Fire."

His face goes blank, but only for a moment. His lips pull into a devious smirk. "Is this your true name you've given me?"

I smile sweetly. "Yes."

Mr. Duveau squares his shoulders. "Evelyn, Unseelie Queen of Fire—"

"No!" King Ustrin's shout roars through the chamber, but it's too late. Mr. Duveau steps back, hand to his forehead as if to stifle a terrible pain.

A roil of nausea washes through me, followed by the feeling of something ripping—something *inside* me. With it comes a searing agony, and I call my fire to combat it. In a flash, it's gone. Like it was never there to begin with.

I open my eyes to find Mr. Duveau panting, face pale and covered with a sheen of sweat.

King Ustrin lunges toward him. "Do you have any idea what you've done? You've broken the treaty!"

The councilman steps back, unsteady on his feet as he shakes his head. "The Legacy Bond should have—"

"The Legacy Bond was destroyed the moment you named her queen," King Ustrin says through his teeth. "The treaty is broken if King Caleos' descendants claim rule. And you, with the breath of the Bond, spoke that very thing into being."

Aspen takes my hand, and we step back from the pair. There's nowhere to go. Behind us are the fire fae and King Ustrin's guards. Ustrin and Mr. Duveau block the exit.

Ustrin's chest heaves as he pins the councilman with a vicious scowl. "Which means our arrangement is over." He lunges for Mr. Duveau, his fingers stretching into claws as he swipes at the man.

Mr. Duveau reaches beneath his jacket and pulls out his revolver. The movement makes him wince, and he brings his free hand to a place below his ribs. That must be where Aspen wounded him. The arm that holds the gun, however, is steady. Firm. Ready to shoot.

Ustrin recoils at the sight. The two are frozen, eyes locked. Slowly, Mr. Duveau takes a step back. Then another. Ustrin hisses, body shaking as if fighting his instincts to attack the man. When the councilman moves far enough into the tunnel, his form is swallowed entirely by shadows. A moment later, I hear his pounding footsteps fleeing from the cave.

King Ustrin points at two of his guards, nodding his head in the direction of Mr. Duveau's hasty exit. The guards obey, streaming past us.

Aspen and I take another step back.

Ustrin faces me head on, fingers curling and uncurling as flames dance between them. "You get your way. We will fight for the Fire Court throne after all."

36

————————

Ustrin's chest heaves with rage as he storms over to me, fire climbing from his fingers to his shoulders. The blood leaves my face. This is what I asked for, but it doesn't mean I'm ready. Still, I don the bravest face I can, throwing back my shoulders as I take a step closer to him. Aspen's fingers cling to mine, and I can feel his reluctance to let me go. To let me fight. To stand down. But he does.

I'm right here, he whispers in my mind.

King Ustrin burns me with narrowed eyes as he removes his jacket and cravat, throwing each to the ground with force. "You must make the first move," he hisses. "Our bargain keeps me and the council from engaging the fae rebel royals in violence. Even according to the Old Ways, a bid for alpha status is considered an attack. Since you have sided with them, I cannot engage you."

My pulse races, and my mouth goes dry. "Very well."

His fire grows, dancing over the scales of his face and scalp, creating a blinding shimmering radiance around him. "Come get me."

I make no move as I seek my fire, allowing it to rise from my core and burn down my arms, my hands, my legs. Doubt creeps in, so heavy it threatens to dampen my fire. I hardly know what I'm doing. I'm not ready for this. I can't do this.

What exactly is this anyway? I know we must stand before the All of All. We must prove which of us is the alpha. Do I really have what it takes to do that? I'm not Queen Nyxia, the most powerful lunar alpha in generations. I'm not even close in power to the weakest fae royal I've met.

My mind spins with anxiety. What in the name of iron convinced me I should do this? Shouldn't I have taken death? Exile?

My fire retreats, pulling back from my arms and returning to my core where it remains a white-hot ball of flame.

King Ustrin lets out a hiss of laughter. "You can't do it, can you? You're weak. Nothing more than a pitiful human woman. A girl. A child. You know nothing about rage or warfare. You know nothing about ruling a kingdom or wearing a crown."

A crown. For some reason, the word stills me, my golden crown of flames appearing in my mind's eye. The All of All gave that to me when they could have given anything. They could have given a maple leaf or a robin's feather. Instead, they gave me a crown of fire. That must mean something.

I focus on the arrogance in King Ustrin's face, reminding myself of everything he's responsible for. I remember how it felt to be torn from my mate, to be told we could no longer fulfill the treaty. I think of the burnt apothecary, imagining it as nothing more than a charred husk with all my mother's herbs and jars burnt to ash. Portraits gone and books and spells and recipes lost forever. Then all I see is Mother. Mother. Mother.

Sorrow rips through me, but my rage is hotter. It fills my body in a flash, igniting my skin in a white glow, brighter than King Ustrin's.

The look on King Ustrin's face is priceless. However, the expression is momentary, a flash before he steels it behind a sneer. His glow increases to match mine.

Heat surrounds me, searing my flesh. A jolt of panic racks my core, but I breathe it away. Aspen's voice fills my mind. *Take it to the Twelfth Court.*

I close my eyes.

WHEN I OPEN THEM, VIOLET COVERS MY VISION. MY SURROUNDINGS ARE LIKE what they were before, but there's no movement, save for the swirling particles of violet light that make up all matter. It's as if time stands frozen.

My mind has gone still, and my only sensations are a calm warmth and the sound and feel of the energy humming through my body. This return to the Twelfth Court feels both new and familiar at once. I feel welcome, yet at the same time, I feel like an invader.

A black tunnel opens beside me, and without hesitation, I enter it.

Inside, it's like I'm floating, even as my feet touch what seems like solid ground. I see nothing, hear nothing. Only my body remains, although it's nothing more than violet particles. My observation prompts a memory—no, a reminder. I came here for a reason. To find my unseelie form.

My mind begins to clear, and as it does, the black tunnel reveals shimmering purple far ahead. I run toward it, keeping my goal firmly in my mind so I don't lose track of my awareness. My destination comes into focus the nearer I get, and I find myself standing before a mirror. At least, it seems like a mirror. It's an oval of swirling light with a black void in its middle shaped like a human silhouette. My silhouette.

I squint at it, looking for my features, but they aren't there. Particles of light. A black void. Endless nothingness. Endless everything. Comfort. Terror.

With a shake of my head, I refocus on my mission. *What is my unseelie form?* I think to myself. *How do I shift into it?*

Words float upon my awareness, chilling and ethereal. "You showed us your heart once before. It was a true heart."

I shudder. "I remember," I say, my voice harsh on my ears after the melody spoken by the All of All.

"You will find your unseelie form there."

I stare deeper into the black void that is my silhouette. "What does my heart look like?" I whisper.

The darkness swirls with the shimmering violet. I feel lost in the movement of the particles as they shift and swirl. I see what looks like a blustering wind move in the mirror. Its every move is sharp and quick and effective. A word forms in my mind. *Intellect.* The images in the mirror shift again, showing deep black water, so vast it should be terrifying. Instead, it feels comforting, warm. Like Mother's arms. Again, a word comes to me. *Love.* The water turns to waves, then form the peaks of trees. At the base of the trees is solid earth, rock, stone. It's strong and steady and calm. *Logic.* The leaves of the trees begin to fall, floating to the ground like heart-shaped jewels. The Autumn Court comes to mind, and thoughts of Aspen follow, making my chest feel light and open. A burning heats my core. *Passion.* As the leaves fall, they grow into beautiful flames. The fire rises higher and higher, and as it grows, I become breathless, enamored with its dangerous beauty. *Rage. Anger.*

The mirror goes still, returning to my silhouette against humming violet particles. I think that might be all it will show me, until the silhouette begins to dissipate and is replaced with golden pinpricks of light piercing through the purple. It reminds me of the sky as seen from Lunar, filling me with that same sense of wonder. Words come to me again. *Mystery. Darkness. Magic. Discovery.*

"You are all of this," the ethereal voice of the All of All says. The mirror returns to stillness. This time, my reflection isn't a black void. It's...something, although I can't see it clearly, like there's a film over my eyes. I blink and stand closer. Colors emerge, and I'm surprised to see something other than violet or indigo. Still, it's difficult for me to understand what I'm looking at. Then finally, I realize it's flames. Beautiful dancing flames. But not like a normal hearth fire. This fire shifts and sways in the most stunning pinks, purples, and aquas. It's like the Aurora Borealis, something I've only read about and seen in paintings.

My heart races as I watch it—watch *me*. I stare deeper into the flames, seeking shape. Two blue eyes look back at me, keen and clever and curious with a hint of darkness in them. A flash of teeth warns me of a quick temper and a fierce determination to protect the ones she loves. Her posture shows me there is logic behind her motivations and that she doesn't react in violence without just cause.

I take a hesitant step back and she does the same. Because she is me. With a small, elongated muzzle, two pointed ears, she—*I*—stand on four tiny paws beneath slender legs.

There's only one word I can think to explain what I've become.

I'm a firefox.

Unlike the lithe kitsune with their slim bodies and their balls of flame hovering near their mouths or tails, my tricolor flames lap over every inch of my fluffy, white fur, rippling around me like waves.

And upon my fox head rests a golden crown of fire.

37

I shudder, torn between terror and awe. I've done it. I've truly shifted forms. And I wear the blessing of the All of All. My crown. The one I left behind at Bircharbor.

A roaring hiss comes from behind me, and the mirror disappears like a violet puff of smoke. I'm back in the cave, although the purple haze remains. Time, however, has unfrozen, revealing King Ustrin towering before me as an enormous orange fire lizard. His beady black eyes are narrowed, nostrils flaring with rage as his tongue lashes out of his mouth.

Gasps and grunts and growls come from the fire fae. I hear whispers uttered, first too quiet to hear. Soon I realize it's one thing repeated. *Unseelie Queen of Fire.*

I meet Aspen's eyes. For a moment I'm scared of what I'll find in them. I've seen him as a stag, but...can he accept me like this? His voice comes through the Bond. *You're beautiful, Evie.*

My heart swells, burning away the remainder of my doubts. I turn my attention to Ustrin.

With slow, slithering steps, he moves toward me until he's positioned between me and the cave's exit. "Fight me," he taunts. "Prove your worth, fool girl."

I know what needs to be done, but I can't do it here. Not where the fire fae—my fae, my people—could get caught in the crossfire. I feel a calm warmth in the back of my mind. Something tells me to turn myself over to it. As I do, my vision becomes clearer, my sense of awareness sharper. Information streams through me at once—every angle of the cave walls, my own weight, size, and shape. But I don't have to think about it or even process it. I just know it in an instant.

I lower into a crouch, springing off all four paws. I soar over Ustrin's scaly shoulder and land on an outcropping of the cave wall next to him. Scrambling to maintain purchase, I feel a weight sliding from my head. The crown. I try to right myself, but the crown clatters to the floor. I look from it to the fire lizard. Before I can make a move, hot orange flame shoots from his mouth, incinerating the crown.

I can do nothing but stare in horror as the gift from the All of All glows red, melting and shifting until what remains is a pile of shapeless molten metal. "No," I gasp.

"There goes your gift from the All of All," Ustrin says. "It was never a sign of their favor. You were never worth their blessing. Now submit to me!"

My heart sinks, eyes still locked on the melted crown. Is this my answer? Am I truly not the alpha blessed by the All of All? How did I ever think I could be?

You are more than that crown. The words shatter my stupor and I meet Aspen's eyes from over Ustrin's shoulder. *Do not accept defeat, Evie. The crown was gifted to you from an intangible realm. It exists outside physical form.*

I don't think I can beat him, I reply. *He's too strong.*

He isn't stronger than you are. You're the Unseelie Queen of Fire.

His words strengthen me, and I stand firmer on the stone.

"Submit to me," Ustrin says, oblivious to my silent exchange with Aspen.

Wear the crown, Aspen says.

Returning my attention to the cave walls, I launch over the fire lizard to another outcropping that places me behind him. He hisses, whirling around as I launch again, landing on the floor of the tunnel. I take off, my flames lighting my way. Even if they weren't, I have a feeling I'd be able to see in the dark regardless. Ustrin's claws scrape the stone as he tears out of the chamber, hard on my heels.

I know he can't attack me until I attack him first, but I'm not willing to risk him getting too close. As I clear the mouth of the cave, I keep running, my mind processing risk and reward as I seek favorable ground. A clearing ringed by enormous trees comes into view, and I spring toward it, my four paws pounding the earth with ease as if I never had only two legs before. As

I reach the other side of the clearing, I skid to a halt and whirl to face the fire lizard.

Grass and earth turn beneath Ustrin's claws as he enters the clearing, flames dancing over every scale. His movements aren't as graceful as mine, his thick limbs slow and lumbering. "Tired of running? Ready to face me?"

I assess the clearing, calculating the arrangement of trees, the grass, the glowing mushrooms. I note every rock and branch, pinpoint which smells belong to which animals lurking nearby. I'm still without much of a plan, but something inside me knows all of this is important. I take in Ustrin's size compared to mine. Even though he's slower than I am, his size makes up for my upper hand in agility. There's no way I can win by dominance of strength. And he'll never concede to me the way Nyxia's mother conceded to her. What other ways can I prove myself the alpha?

Ustrin's voice bellows through the night. "Fight me!"

I shudder at the rage fueling his tone. It's now or never. I may not be able to win by physical attack, but it's the only thing that can start this. Lowering into a crouch, I let my fire curl around me. Then I dart forth, paws pounding the earth as I charge the fire lizard. As I approach, he doesn't so much as flinch. Before I collide with him, I turn to the side and swipe out with my back legs. My claws make contact with his scales, but all they meet is firm resistance. I tear back toward the opposite end of the clearing, spinning to face him in a defensive posture.

Ustrin remains where he is. His tongue flicks in and out of his mouth, then hissing laughter fills the air. "That's all you have? A swipe of your dainty little paws?"

"We're just getting started," I say. It's the first time I've attempted to speak out loud in this form. I'm startled to realize I didn't form the words with my mouth. I've witnessed many unseelie who communicate without the need to move their lips, but it's still jarring to do it myself, no matter how natural it comes. However, the surprise only lasts a moment before my instincts prevail over all else.

"You're right about that." Ustrin opens his maw, and an orange glow surges forth. The ball of flame barrels toward me, almost faster than I can react. I roll to the ground, but the fire skims my side, extinguishing my flames where it touches and replacing them with scorched fur and blackened flesh. The pain feels the same as the burns I caused myself after Mother's trial. At least these wounds seem to quickly subside, as my own flames return, pink, purple, and aqua lapping over my ribs, repairing the flesh and restoring my strength.

I right myself but scramble along the ground to avoid his next blast. This time, the fire skims my fluffy white tail, most of the blast hitting the tree behind me. I speed across the clearing, blasts of heat soaring close enough to feel, one right after the next. I pause behind the wide trunk of a tree. My eyes flash to the clearing, finding patches of burning grass, charred trunks of trees, scorched stone.

Again, that calm warmth pulls me in, and my attention sharpens. I hear several mice burrowing beneath the earth, desperate to flee from what's happening above ground. I hear the fluttering wings of a moth in the tree overhead as it draws near a patch of flame. I hear Ustrin's claws tearing the dirt as he plods toward the tree I'm hiding behind. Even before he opens his mouth, I know what's about to happen, the sound of the fire stirring in his throat now familiar to me.

I try not to flinch as flames lap toward me, burning the trunk of the tree I'm hiding behind and searing the tips of my ears, my tail, the edges of my fur. With a breath, my fire repairs the damage to my body, and I dart out of my hiding place to another tree. Again, I focus on the sounds, the sights, the smells. A patch of earthy mushrooms glow nearby, but there's a stronger aroma to my left. It's pungent like the mushrooms, but mingling with it is the scent of decay. I look toward the source, finding an enormous tree nearby. From sight alone, it looks just like any other tree. But as my eyes seek the boughs overhead, I see it bears no leaves, no fruit. I hear termites scurrying inside the bark, sense the hollowed patches within the trunk.

Another ball of flame soars my way, but this time I sprint out from behind the tree before it strikes it. I seek the dying tree, circling around it a few times to snag Ustrin's attention. He tears across the clearing, mouth opening wide as he prepares to launch another ball of flame. I skirt around the tree just as the flame hits it. However, he doesn't stop there. Ball after ball strikes the tree, the heat searing me. One misses the tree and sets the grass aflame near my feet. I dance away, then peek around the trunk. Ustrin is now only several feet from the tree, tongue lashing in and out of his mouth.

"Stop hiding," he hisses. "Give me a real challenge, fool girl. Let me show you what a true alpha looks like." Another blast of flame surges forth. When it strikes the trunk, I hear the melody I've been waiting for. A hollow creaking.

I launch onto a large rock and from there leap onto the nearest tree, my paws springing off its trunk as they make contact. The momentum sends me higher, and I soar to an enormous boulder. Once again, I launch away as soon as I touch the surface and find myself even higher now as I leap toward the burning tree. Heat sears my paws as I touch the bark, but I press off with all my strength. As I do, I leave behind a burst of my own fire.

I tumble to the ground, my muscles screaming at the impact as I roll across the dirt. Ustrin tosses his head left and right, seeking where I've gone. Finally, he spots me.

The burning tree creaks louder, then a sound like lightning ripping overhead tears through the night.

Ustrin rushes toward me. But he isn't fast enough.

The rotted tree comes tumbling down, pinning Ustrin beneath its flaming trunk in a tangle of rotting branches. His orange flames burn its base, but where I made contact, my tricolor fire glows and expands, creeping to where Ustrin is trapped.

I stand frozen as I watch, certain I'll see Ustrin rise at any moment.

When I see no movement, I creep forward on silent paws. I find Ustrin in his seelie form, writhing beneath my flames as he tries to combat them with his own. The enormous trunk of the tree crosses his midsection, while his shoulder is speared into the earth below by a thick, sharp branch.

He catches my eye and lets out a laugh. "You think this means you've won? I can heal, remember? You can toss your pretty little flames at me all night, but you'll run out of power long before I do. I'll continue to heal and regenerate, and when I overcome your flames, I'll kill you."

"Submit to me as alpha," I say, voice even.

He laughs again. "You're out of your mind. I just explained I'm stronger than you. I can defeat you."

"Submit to me as alpha," I say again, louder now.

"You aren't the alpha. That was nothing but a clever accident. I am far from defeated."

"Submit."

All amusement flees from his face, and he bares his teeth. "I will never submit to you. Even if you had the upper hand, I would rather die than submit."

I study his face, contorted with effort as he continues to combat my fire lapping upon him from the tree. Just how his flames managed to damage me, my fire seems to do the same to him, blackening his bright scales.

My eyes then fall to his throat, the scales there still unmarred by my fire. In seelie form, I can only imagine his internal anatomy must be humanlike, the same way Aspen's was when I performed his surgery. If that's the case, I know exactly where to find his jugular vein.

I must admit Ustrin is right. He's stronger than me. He'll never submit to me and he will fight so long as he has breath and strength. The truth of what must be done is chilling, but the calm warmth in the back of my mind promises to carry the brunt of the burden. "That leaves me one choice," I say.

With a lunge, I sink my sharp teeth into his scaly throat.

38

Sitting back on my haunches, I stare down into a moonlit stream, eyes locked on the white fox's face staring back at me. Her flames have dissipated to a glow, leaving the blood coating the fur around her neck in clear view. Even her muzzle is smeared with it despite countless attempts to cleanse herself in the rushing waters. At least she managed to wash the taste of blood from inside her mouth.

My mouth, I correct myself. *Me. That fox is me.*

Something large appears on the other side of the stream. I heard it coming minutes ago, knew it was a stag before it appeared from behind the trees. My keen hearing is attuned to my surroundings, yet I can't find it in me to care about a thing.

"Are you all right?" Aspen's voice asks through the stag.

I keep my eyes trained on my reflection. "Did you find the body?"

Silence. Then, "Yes."

Bile rises in my throat. If he found the body, then he saw a fae with its jugular torn out, left to bleed until his heart stopped beating. Bleed as my beautiful flames lapped over him.

"We must find your refugees," I say.

"I already found them." His voice is quiet, careful. Like it's walking on glass.

"You found them?" I allow my eyes to flash up to him, grateful he wears his stag face. I'm not ready to see how his seelie form looks at me.

"When Ustrin's guards took off from the cave, I knew their master must have been defeated. I came to find you straight away. When I saw you here like this, I figured I'd give you some time."

His words make sense. Now that I think about it, I remember a stag coming to this stream half a dozen times before now. A raven visited a time or two as well. I return my gaze to the flowing waters.

He continues. "That's when I sought out the refugees. They weren't far from here. The guards had fled the site there as well. Nyxia joined me after the threat to Selene Palace was extinguished. She brought my people back with her."

"The guards fled? And the flame too? No one put up a fight?"

"The guards likely felt the dissolution of their vows to their king, and the flame he ordered to the palace no longer needed to obey orders either. There was no reason to fight us."

With a single nod, I say, "No reason because Ustrin is dead."

"Yes."

"Because I killed him."

"Yes."

My muzzle twitches, and it reminds me of a human lower lip quivering. "Will he heal from his wounds?"

Aspen hesitates before answering, but I already know what he's going to say. I remember what Gildmar had told me when we treated our patients after the explosion at Bircharbor. If a fae loses too much blood, their bodies can't keep up with the healing. And I left him with more than an open throat. I buried him in my fire.

"He's gone, Evie."

A tremble goes through me. It had been so easy to snap my teeth over Ustrin's throat. My human training told me where to bite. My fox instincts knew exactly how to angle my mouth, how to sink my canines beneath the shingle of scales where I could puncture his flesh. After the deed was done, all I could do was stare. When I could look no longer, I retched, then took off for the nearest source of water.

My stomach turns at the thought, and I try to retrain my focus on my reflection. But now all I can see is the blood still matted in my fur.

From the corner of my eye, I see Aspen shudder, then two legs replace his four. My reflection becomes distorted as feet splash through the stream. When the water returns to its calm flow, I see Aspen at my side in his seelie form. He's gazing at me. Me, the firefox. Me, the killer.

I can't bear to look at him, so I stare at the earth beneath my paws.

A warm, gentle hand falls on my back. I want to pull away from the touch, but I can't find it in me to move.

Aspen brushes his hand along my fur, safe from my flames now that they've diminished to a harmless glow. "I've felt exactly how you feel now," he says, voice thick with emotion. He sounds so different from his stag's voice. I try to remember what my seelie voice sounds like, but I can't. He continues. "This is how I felt after I killed the Holstrom girls. Then again after I slaughtered their animals. It isn't an easy feeling."

"But the act of killing...that part was *too* easy."

"Yes."

I swallow hard, the lump in my throat feeling out of place in my fox's body. "I've killed two people. Torn open two throats without a second thought."

His hand stills, then returns to stroking my fur. "It won't get any easier. But what you did was necessary. Unlike me, you didn't fall victim to your rage. You protected yourself. Stood up for what needed to be done."

"How do you know? You weren't there when I left Mr. Meeks to burn alive. You weren't there when I sank my teeth into King Ustrin's neck."

He angles himself closer to me, but I still won't meet his gaze. "I know because I know you. I know how calculated you are. How calm under pressure. How precious you consider life."

"You are one of us." A new voice fills the air, one I only half-noticed in my distracted emotional state. It's the crustacean from the cave, and he's scuttling toward me from between the trees.

In fact, several dozens of figures stream from the shadows, lighting the night with their balls of flame, their bright bodies, their glowing eyes and fiery wings. "You're one of us," the fire fae echo.

A white kitsune steps forward and lowers down on its front paws, eyes closed. "Unseelie Queen of Fire."

A blue wisp bobs at the kitsune's side. "No. Ustrin is defeated. There is but one ruler of Fire now." She flourishes a glowing, blue hand and bends into her version of a bow. "Queen of Fire."

The rest of the fire fae perform their own bows, echoing the wisp. "Queen of Fire."

I stare wide-eyed at the fae surrounding me. My fae. My people. The daunting task of ruling them falls heavy on my shoulders.

After what feels like an endless silence, the fire fae rise. Some stream off into the night, but a few step closer to me, as if awaiting instruction. The kitsune who first bowed taps anxiously from paw to paw. "Can I eat him?" he finally says.

I'm caught off guard. "Eat him?"

"The dead king."

The other kitsune nod, pleading to join the feast. A fire sprite flies overhead. "Can I burn him?" she asks. "That is, if Your Most Gracious Majesty hasn't consumed all of him with your flame."

A firebird swoops down from the trees. "May I harvest any remaining scales? They will insulate my nests and keep my young warm."

My stomach churns at the eagerness in the eyes around me. My human side shouts from the back of my mind, *No, absolutely not. This is not how we treat our dead.* But a new part of me admits the chilling realization that I know very little about the unseelie.

Both sides confess I'm in way over my head.

Finally, I turn to Aspen. Without reading his expression, I give him a questioning glance. In return, he offers a subtle nod.

"Do what you will," I say, hoping my voice doesn't quaver. "Harvest him, burn him, and consume him as you wish, but do so without argument amongst each other. You may have your requests in the order I received them, and not one fight will break out amongst you. When you are finished, I want no sign of him remaining."

Another round of bows follow, and after thanking me, the fire fae disappear into the night. A few remain close; some retreat to the boughs overhead, others burrow in holes nearby, and a few sprites and wisps float about the trees.

Aspen and I are left mostly alone in silence.

After a while, he asks, "Do you know how to turn back?"

I shake my head. "I'm afraid to."

"Why?"

The lump rises in my throat again. I can't give voice to my feelings, my fears. In truth, I'm afraid that once my fox side falls away, I'll crumble. I'm afraid I'll taste blood in my mouth, feel it on my flesh and never be able to face myself again. And I'm afraid how Aspen will look at me. He seems to accept the vicious firefox. Can he accept the violent woman?

"You can't stay in this form too long," he says. "At best, you'll be putting off the inevitable. At worst, you'll forget who you really are."

"What's the inevitable?"

"You must face what you've done and accept yourself. You must feel. For one with human blood, I can only imagine it's going to be far more painful than anything I've experienced. But it's the only way."

I'm pulled between two terrors: the fear of emotions that will surely cripple me, and the fear that I could lose myself completely. "How do I do it?"

"Someday it will be effortless to shift between forms," he explains. "For now, strong emotion is the easiest. What helps me find my seelie side when I'm trapped in a rage is tender feelings. Anything sad or painful or joyful. Do you remember when you stopped me in my stag form when I was on my way to your village? You helped me remember. You made me feel."

I nod, recalling how he'd calmed and returned to his seelie form. "But you were stuck in a rage. I'm stuck in...I don't know what this is."

"You're in between," he says. "You're trying not to feel one way or another, but you must give in at least a little. You must let yourself feel something."

The resistance is like a solid wall. Fiery anger stands on one side while debilitating sorrow stands on the other. I'm perched on the top of the wall, balance tenuous as I teeter on a blade's edge.

Aspen's hand rests on my shoulder. "You can fall, Evie," he whispers. "I'll catch you."

With that, I close my eyes, a sob lurching over the lump in my throat, tears streaming from beneath my eyelids. I shudder, again and again. Then a ripple of pain tears through me from my head to my toes. My body feels like it's grown unwieldy, heavy, lumbering, enormous hands where dainty paws just were, clawing into the dirt. My eyes catch those looking back at me in the stream. Wide and wild, auburn hair like a tangled nest around my head, blood splattering my cheeks. I slap the water with my hand, disrupting the reflection, then take my damp fingers and smear them across my face, furiously rubbing.

Hands grab my shoulders, warm and strong. I freeze, finding Aspen's eyes. I'm locked in his gaze, unable to move or look away. It's the moment of truth. The woman in the reflection was more of a crazed animal than my firefox form was. Is that what he sees too?

He studies my face, and I study his. I've never been more aware of our contrast. His golden skin is pure and flawless, his eyes swimming with color. The angles of his jaw and cheekbones look as if they were carved by a master craftsman. And his hair; even in disarray, his blue-black tresses fall in elegant waves around his antlers. But me? I'm...I'm...

"You're so beautiful, Evie." A hand leaves my shoulder and lights on my cheek, thumb brushing away the dampness of tears and water from the stream. "In every form, you're beautiful. In every form, I'm here for you. In every form, I love you."

His face swims before me as more tears obscure my vision. My shoulders slump, and Aspen pulls me close. I nestle into his chest, clinging to his shirt as his warm arms wrap around my back. The dam breaks from within me, unleashing the sorrow I held back after my mother's death, releasing my agony over the two lives I've taken. I let it all out, let myself break and crumble, break and crumble.

Throughout it all, Aspen maintains his silent vigil, holding me like a vessel for the pieces of my shattered soul.

39

———————

A warm light touches my face, and I turn away from it, burrowing my head into Aspen's chest. I inhale his scent deeply, his rosemary and cinnamon helping to clear my mind. We must have slept by the stream last night after I sobbed for hours. I don't remember falling asleep, but my body feels rested. Invigorated. A buzzing sound flutters by my ear along with an odd warmth.

I turn my head and open my eyes, expecting to find the light of dawn. Hazy morning sunlight has fallen over the woods, but that isn't the light that first woke me. A fire sprite hovers over my face, head turning one way then another as she smiles.

My eyes widen, and she darts a few feet back. "Forgive me, Your Majesty," she begs, her tiny voice quavering. "I came to thank you for your gracious gift last night. Then when I saw you, I couldn't help but look upon my queen. You're so…" she lets out a dreamy sigh, "pretty."

Aspen stirs next to me, and he lifts himself onto his elbows, brow furrowed as he takes in our little interloper.

I pull myself to sitting, and the sprite dances in the air before me.

"I didn't realize how pretty you were before," she says. "Truly, I didn't like you much at all, but then you were a firefox with those lovely flames, and then you defeated Ustrin. Then you let me burn him." She lets out another sigh, this one contented. "I feel quite invigorated this morning. I've never burned a royal before."

"He was delicious." I whirl toward the voice, finding a kitsune sitting on the other side of the stream. He runs his tongue over the side of his muzzle as if savoring the memory.

My stomach churns, and I suppress a shudder. I've yet to utter a word and am still befuddled over what I could possibly say.

Before I can come up with a coherent reply, a firebird lands nearby. "His scales will keep my hatchlings warm. Thank you, Your Majesty." She bows, and the other two fae follow suit.

I manage to find my voice. "You're welcome."

"Will you be taking us home?" the kitsune asks.

"Home?" I echo.

The sprite clasps her hands together, expression wistful. "To Fire. I haven't been since I was a wee spriteling. Now that Ustrin is gone, you can have his palace!"

I'm overwhelmed by their forward nature, by thoughts of going to the Fire Court and claiming a palace. But these are my people. These strange, unsettling creatures that feed off carrion and harvest the dead are whom I now rule. They are whom I must care and advocate for. I plaster a forced smile over my lips. "Yes, we will return once I have settled the details of my travels."

The sprite flutters closer, head tilted to the side. "Might I travel at your side? I can light your reading materials and I promise not to burn your gowns."

"I'll consider it," I say.

"And may my tribe light your travels at night?" the kitsune asks. "Do not allow these duties to fall on the wisps. They will take us miles off course each night. They have no sense of direction, despite what they will tell you."

"Another thing I'll keep in mind."

The firebird flaps her wings. "And will you—"

I hold up my hand to silence her. Squaring my shoulders, I adopt a regal bearing. "Let us discuss travel once I am prepared to hold a formal audience. You may petition me then."

The three fae bow, uttering, "Most Esteemed Queen of Fire."

When they make no move to leave, eyes still trained on me, I rise to my feet and extend a hand with a nod. "You may go."

Once they're out of sight, I hear Aspen snickering behind me. I round on him. "Stop that. I have no idea what I'm doing, and you know it."

His lips pull into a smirk. "You're doing fine."

I try to match his grin, but my lips falter. All at once, the crushing sorrow

I felt last night returns in a rush. My knees buckle beneath me, but I clench my fingers into fists to steady myself. Sorrow and rage go to war within, but I neither fight them nor encourage them to grow.

Aspen's face softens as he offers me a hand. "It will get better."

I'm tempted to follow my rage, to take it all to the Twelfth Court and shift back into my firefox form. I could run free, with only a fraction of the burden I feel now. Perhaps it would be easier to rule the unseelie in that form as well.

I shake the thought from my head, reminding myself I have more than the unseelie to fight for. There's a war coming. Two, most likely. The seelie council will discover what I've done and they'll come for me. They'll come for all the rebels. We'll be forced to fight, fae against fae. The humans will come next. Without a treaty, what's to stop violence from breaking out? What's to stop the humans from crossing the faewall with iron swords, guns, and grenades? What's to stop the fae from crossing the wall to slaughter innocents in an attempt to reclaim their land?

Me. I'm the only one who can temper the destruction. I'm the only one who cares enough about both sides to fight this war without letting the Fair Isle fall into chaos.

War will come. It's already here.

I sparked it. I'll fight it. And I'll end it.

I don't know how, but I know that I will.

With a sigh, I take Aspen's outstretched hand, and we make our way through the forest together.

By the time Selene Palace comes into view, an imposing figure is halfway between us and the front doors. Queen Nyxia closes the distance, expression twisted with irritation. "Look who finally decided to show up. The good Queen Evelyn."

I furrow my brow, taken aback by her scorn.

She puts her hands on her hips. "As if I didn't already have enough unwelcome guests."

My mouth falls open and snaps shut as I search for words. "If I'm no longer welcome—"

"Not you." She flutters a dismissive hand. "Your...*sister*." The last words come out more like a hiss.

The blood leaves my face. "My sister? She's here?"

"Yes. She claimed the protection of a peaceful exchange of words and said she'd speak to no one but you."

"Did she come alone?"

Nyxia nods. "Thankfully, otherwise I wouldn't have spared the girl's life."

"Where is she?"

She lifts her chin and purses her lips, as if preparing for reproach. "The dungeon."

I start off toward the palace again. "Take me to her."

My heart pounds in my chest as Nyxia leads me through the front door, then down a hall I've never been to. We descend a flight of stairs that end in a corridor carved from obsidian. My mind is whirling to comprehend what Amelie's arrival must mean.

I feel Aspen's hand graze my elbow. "Be careful," he whispers. "We don't know what to expect."

I nod. Every part of me assumes this is some sort of trick, and I don't fault Nyxia for choosing to lock her up.

The dark corridor widens, and two wraiths in flowing black translucent robes stand guard before what must be the dungeon. Nyxia nods to the guards, and they stand apart, allowing us to enter. Beyond, everything is carved from the same glossy, black stone as the corridor, and the bars of the cells are blanketed in writhing shadows. The only light comes from a few sparse orbs along the walls, keeping the occupants hidden from view.

Nyxia stops before a cell, gesturing toward it before she steps away. Arms remaining crossed, she takes up post along the empty wall opposite the cells. Aspen does the same.

Only I approach the cell. I step closer, squinting into the dark. A figure shifts inside, but I can't see clearly. I lift my hand.

"Don't touch the bars," Nyxia says, making me jump.

I look back at her, taking in the warning her eyes are trying to convey.

"The shadows will incapacitate you," she explains.

I swallow hard and return my attention to the cell. Hand still raised, I turn my palm upward. My motions are almost automatic, as is my intention for light. As soon as I think it, a blue flame ignites above my hand. Only then does a wave of shock move through me.

"Evie." The voice comes from within the cell. The figure steps closer to the bars, as do I. My fire illuminates my sister.

Rage and tenderness and sorrow fight for dominance as I take in her haggard appearance. She looks worse than I did last night—than I likely still do now. Her copper hair is matted with dirt, tangled around her shoulders.

There's no sign of her selkie skin, only filthy flesh and a thin, torn dress that ends above her knees.

She smiles, eyes swimming with tears. "You're making fire," she says with a gasp. "Are you queen now?"

My eyes narrow, suspicion creeping over me. Is that why she's here? To fight me for my throne? She's the eldest. It never occurred to me that she would fight me for the crown. That she might have a stronger claim to it than I do. I lower my hand, extinguishing the flame as my fingers clench into fists. "Why are you here?"

She takes a step back, as if surprised by my cold tone. "I escaped him. I finally did it, Evie."

I steel myself to voice my next words. "Our mother is dead."

Her hands fly to her lips. "No."

"They killed her because you refused to attend her trial." I know I'm omitting more than I'm saying, but in this moment, I want to wound her. I want to punish her for everything she's done and for everything she intends to do now.

She slides to her knees, wailing. Her hands reach for the bars but flinch away before they make contact with the writhing shadows. "He did this," she cries through her teeth, slamming her fists on the obsidian floor.

"Who?"

"Cobalt." The name escapes her lips with more wrath than I've ever witnessed her demonstrate. "He...he destroyed me. You have no idea the things he made me do. The things he made me say and suffer through."

My heart squeezes, but I refuse to fall for her words. He could have sent her here, could have planted every reaction and every word into her. He could be lurking near the border, waiting for some sign from Amelie that he and the council can make their move against us. She could be here to poison me, to take my crown. "Why are you here?" I say again, more forceful this time.

She looks at me through glazed eyes, cheeks wet with tears. "I came to see you."

"What do you want from me?"

"Your protection."

I let out a bitter laugh. "You had your chance and you refused my help. Why should I protect you now? After everything you've done—"

"I want to kill him." She says it like a growl, face twisting into a hateful mask I've never seen her wear. "I want your protection. Then I want to help you kill Cobalt."

I study her, seeking signs of Cobalt's manipulation. "How would you help me do that?"

"I have the power of his name," she whispers.

"You're Bonded, so he has the same power over yours as well," I argue. "He could be ordering you to do this, to be here and say everything you're saying at this very moment."

She shakes her head. "I made sure I waited until all his orders that could possibly harm you faded. He had to give me new orders daily to ensure he always covered all his bases with me. But with his new wife," she says this with clear disdain, "he became easily distracted. Stopped renewing my orders as often. Left me alone in the undersea palace for longer and longer. When I felt no current command to keep me there, I fled. I crossed lakes, rivers, and streams to get here. Ran until my feet bled."

I can feel my resolve to hate her beginning to lessen, a sure sign I need to cling to it more. "How can I trust you?"

She rises to her feet on trembling legs. Tears continue to stream down her cheeks. "Evelyn Fairfield," she says, voice quavering. "I give you my name. I give you the power of my true name."

A hum of energy buzzes toward me, feeling like both a lightness and a weight at the same time. It isn't like the mutual hum between me and Aspen. This one only moves one way. Rage soars through me, revulsion at this one-sided power she's bestowed. I never asked for this burden. All I ever wanted to do was protect her. Now I control her.

Angry tears swim in my eyes, but I blink them away. I square my shoulders to hide how shaken I am and burn Amelie with a glare. My voice comes out cold. "Thank you, dear sister."

Without another word, I turn on my heel and march from the dungeon, letting my sister's sobs follow me long after the sound of them is gone.

TO SPARK A FAE WAR

BOOK THREE

1

———

No one dreams of starting a war.

A revolution, maybe, but never a war. Personally, I've never been one for revolutions or warfare, preferring to fight death and illness in the surgery room. Instead of a sword, I once favored the scalpel. Laudanum. Chloroform. All essential weapons against threats to mortal lives.

But that was back when I thought I *was* mortal. Human.

Before my mentor betrayed me and I used a scalpel not to save a life but to end one.

Before a human shot my mother with an iron bullet and tried to turn the gun on me.

Before I tore out the throat of a fire lizard to take his throne as my own.

After all that, I think I understand warfare. The pursuit of justice.

With the blood of fire fae and ruthless kings flowing through my veins, I admit I was born to inherit a legacy of violence.

I carry that legacy now, feeling it rushing through my blood and veins as I walk down the darkened street—a human street, in the same city my mother was killed. The night is blanketed with smoke and shadows and sounds of evening merriment. I'm in the pleasure district of Grenneith, where brothels, taverns, and gambling halls cluster side by side.

I keep my head held high, trying my best to exude confidence as I walk by a particularly rowdy-seeming pub where several men loiter outside the door. They leer at me, whistling. I pat the obsidian dagger—a gift from Queen Nyxia—strapped around my waist beneath my coat. The blade isn't iron, like I once carried in the past. But it isn't iron I need for what I'm about to do. Still, blade or no, I'd rather not deal with any interruptions to my night's plans.

One of the men breaks off from the group and comes toward me, sending my heart racing. The swagger in his steps tells me he's clearly had more than his share of drink tonight. I allow my fire to flood my palms, but only enough to keep my mind clear without burning my kid gloves.

The man smirks as he looks me up and down, eyes trailing the modestly high lace neck of my gown to the black and white striped satin hem that brushes the cobblestones at my feet. "What's an elegant lady like you doing walking the streets unaccompanied this late at night?"

For the love of iron, perhaps I should have come dressed as a man tonight. I wasn't sure I could pull it off once I reached my destination, but I hadn't accounted for the perils on my journey there. Now what to do about it? I could brush past him, ignore him, hurry my pace, but that would show fear. Instead, I look him straight in the eyes. "Same as you."

"Oh, I doubt that, miss."

I put a hand on my hip, an innocent gesture, if not for the blade sheathed and hidden within reach. "Am I close to the Briar House?"

The man draws back in surprise before a crimson flush rises to his already ruddy cheeks. "The Briar House? You?"

I keep my eyes pinned on his and flash him a dangerous smile. "I have exotic tastes."

He seems encouraged by this, taking a bold step closer, hand resting on the waistband of his trousers. "I have something exotic you could taste."

"I doubt that." A surge of fear leaps in the back of my awareness, but I burn it away. I focus on his eyes on mine, drawing his attention deeper until the imagery of a bird in a cage floods my mind. His face goes slack, and I know that I have him. This is only the third time I've glamoured someone, and only the second time I've attempted it consciously. The first was an accident with Mayor Coleman, and the second was earlier this morning when I —well, let's just say *borrowed*—this dress.

I keep my voice low and even as I speak to him. "You will tell me where the Briar House is."

He doesn't hesitate to answer, his tone flat. "Next block over. Right side of the street. Second building from the corner."

"Thank you. Now, you are going to return to your friends and pay me no heed as I continue on with my business. You will allow none of your companions to harass me either."

He nods, pointing a thumb at the group of men eyeing us from near the pub door. "I'm going back to my friends."

"Wonderful." Now the true test begins. He takes a step back, then another, and turns. Our eye contact is severed. My breath hitches as I watch him walk in the opposite direction. Any moment he could turn back around. As far as I know, most glamours end when eye contact is lost. However, I gave him an active order. Will the glamour last long enough for him to do as he was told? I didn't stick around the dressmaker's shop long enough this morning to find out what happened once I left with my borrowed goods.

I remain in place as I watch his unsteady progress back to the group. Only when he rejoins them and lets out a casual laugh do I feel I can breathe again. With a turn on my heel, I continue on my way.

To the Briar House.

I'VE NEVER BEEN INSIDE A BROTHEL—NOR OUTSIDE ONE, COME TO THINK OF IT —and I've never wanted to be. Not until I learned Henry Duveau, the councilman who shot and killed my mother, brings unfortunate fae females to this particular pleasure house after illegal capture. Over the last week since Mother's death, I've thought mostly of two things: killing Mr. Duveau and taking down the Briar House.

If I'm lucky, I'll do both tonight.

The brothel's foyer is a mass of scarlet silk, maroon velvet, and gold lace as far as I can see. The lights are dim; no electricity, only several lanterns with red or gold glass covers. Plush couches line the walls, strewn with pillows bearing an ungodly number of tassels. Partitions that look like dressing screens separate certain corners and alcoves, and I can hear tittering laughter behind at least two.

I try not to allow discomfort to show on my face as a stately woman in a dark pink gown steps into the foyer from one of the halls. The cut of her dress is modest like mine, her gray-streaked brown hair arranged in a neat pile on the top of her head. My auburn tresses, on the other hand, are hidden beneath a wide white hat decorated with black peonies. Anything to keep me from being immediately recognized should I come into contact with Mr. Duveau. Hence my human state of dress.

"I am Madame Rose," the woman says. A false name, obviously, considering it fits a little too neatly in with *Briar House*. Nonetheless, she's whom I came here to see. Her posture is confident, her eyes are keen, and her smile is welcoming. "What can I do for you? Have you come seeking companionship tonight?"

"I have, Madame." I take a step closer to her, lowering my voice. I repeat the same thing I said to the drunk man outside, use the same term I once overheard Henry Duveau use when mentioning the Briar House. "I have... exotic tastes."

She nods, a knowing twinkle in her eye. "And might I ask how you came to know of my wares? I do not recognize you as a regular patron."

I know she's testing me, but I have my lie prepared. "I was referred to your establishment by a colleague of my father's. We are visiting from out of town, and I needed to sate my unusual appetites, if you know what I mean."

She eyes me with scrutiny, although her smile remains on her lips. "How did you sate these...*unusual* appetites before? The Briar House is the only of its kind in all of Eisleigh."

It takes no small effort to hide my giddy relief. If this is the only brothel peddling fae females as merchandise, then what I'm about to do will be far more satisfying than if I'd learned there were several more establishments like this. I hide my relief behind a conspiratorial grin and lower my voice further. "I have my ways."

She gives me an approving nod and extends her hand toward a velvet divan strewn with gold satin pillows. "Then tell me more about your tastes and I will see if I can find something to satisfy you."

We take a seat on the divan and I pretend to ponder. "I like them to have a tendency to put up a fight." My voice remains steady as I say it, but my words make acid churn in my stomach. I can't help but recall how similar they are to what Lorelei had said about Mr. Osterman. *I think he liked his prey to put up a fight.* Mr. Osterman was one of the two men who'd captured me and Lorelei and tried to do unspeakable things. The other man was my mentor, who I apprenticed under during my training to become a surgeon. Both men are now dead.

Good riddance.

"You like a fight, do you?" Madame Rose's lips quirk at the corners.

"A little," I say. "I prefer if you have someone who has remained a bit... untamed, shall we say? Feisty."

She assesses me from head to toe. "Now, you are a surprise, aren't you? Who did you say referred you to me?"

I lean in, my voice a whisper. "I dare not say his name, but he is a well-respected councilman. You do know who I speak of, do you not?"

"Ah," she says. "Yes, I know exactly who you mean. He is my establishment's prime patron. One would even call him a partner in my business. Although, I'm hurt he's never mentioned you to me before."

Is that suspicion I'm sensing? I hardly falter, continuing my feigned conspiratorial air. "Like I said, my father and I are on business from out of town. Father's acquaintance with the councilman is new, but I must say it has grown quite intimate. This won't be the last you see of me here." I end that with a wink.

"I should think that's the case, for I'm confident once you sate your appetite, you will hardly be able to keep away."

"That's what I'm hoping for."

Madame Rose rises to her feet. "I think I have the perfect specimen in mind. Give me just a moment and I will prepare her for you."

"One more thing," I say, standing before she can turn away. "Father was under the impression his colleague would be here tonight. He has an urgent message he'd like me to pass on to him. Could you arrange a meeting for us?" I have no grounds to assume anything I've just said. No intel that Mr. Duveau is here, only the barest hope.

She cocks her head slightly to the side. "The man you speak of is not here tonight, so I apologize that I will not be able to satisfy that request."

Damn. Still, there's one more chance. I lock my eyes on hers, pulling her attention to me, drawing that imaginary bird into the cage of my hands—

Nothing. There's no give in her attention, no sway in pulling her gaze. I adjust my hat as an excuse to break eye contact and glance at her wrist. There I see what I should have sought before: a hint of red beads around her wrist, barely visible beneath the lace cuff of her gown. Of course she wears rowan. In a brothel full of enslaved fae, it would be idiotic not to. Still, I had to try.

Try and fail.

Even though I went into this knowing the chance of finding Mr. Duveau was slim, I can't stop the crushing disappointment. However, my mission is far from over.

I plaster a false smile over my lips. "Never mind that. I'll seek him out myself."

That's a promise.

2

Madame Rose leaves me in the foyer for several minutes. When she returns, she guides me into one of the halls that branch off from there. The carpets are plush and red, the walls papered with red and gold designs of roses and vines. Before I went to Faerwyvae, I might have considered the decor luxurious. Compared to fae luxury, however, this place is hideous.

We walk past several doors as we make our way down the hall, and I try not to blush at the sounds of pleasure that emanate from behind them. I constantly summon my inner fire to keep my nerves at bay until Madame Rose pauses outside a door at the end of the hall. "Your merchandise awaits."

I give her my thanks and enter the room. Inside is a modest accommodation with more gaudy crimson satin and papered walls. A vanity and wash basin peek from behind a dressing screen next to a narrow wardrobe. The only other furnishings in the room are a high-backed chair and a small bed. Upon the latter rests a petite female with lavender hair and pale green skin.

"Enjoy," whispers Madame Rose before she closes the door.

"Welcome," the fae female says without warmth. She lies on her side wearing a sheer nightgown, head propped up by one arm while the other hand is draped over her hip. Her pose would be seductive if it weren't for the scowl etched over her face that no false smile could hide.

With slow steps, I approach the bed. She tenses as I near her, violet eyes trained on me, burning me with their hate. "Finally, I can take this off," I say, pulling the enormous hat from my head and tossing it on the ground. With a sigh, I lower myself into the chair and adjust my bone-crushing corset to no avail. I can no longer stand restrictive human clothing, and corsets are the worst offenders. Another reason I should have come dressed as a man today.

But would Madame Rose have bought my disguise? I've barely begun to test my fae powers over fire, and glamouring others is a gamble. There's no way I would have been able to conjure a physical glamour over myself.

Still, what's done is done, and there is more yet to do.

The fae courtesan looks visibly alarmed by my behavior as she watches me from the bed. "Do you...want me to come to you?"

"No need." I wave my hand dismissively. "We can talk as we are."

She furrows her brow. "Talk?"

"Yes. Go ahead and make yourself comfortable. There's no need to sprawl out for my sake."

Her eyes widen, and she makes no move to change positions. Meanwhile, I fiddle with the pins in my hair until half of it comes down from its achingly tight updo. For some reason, this seems to set the fae at ease. Slowly, she folds in on herself and moves into a seated position, shoulders hunched. "May I put on a robe?"

"Do what you will," I say without looking at her. However, as soon as she stands and turns her back to me, I take the opportunity to study her. She's smaller in stature than Lorelei, with narrow hips and dainty limbs. Thin iron cuffs circle her wrists and ankles, the skin beneath them visibly red. She approaches her wardrobe and retrieves a colorful robe. I'm about to look away as she drapes it over her shoulders, but my attention is snagged on something I can barely make out beneath the sheer back of her gown—two jagged marks over her shoulder blades. Scars.

Bile rises in my throat as I recall the sets of wings I saw in Mr. Meeks' underground laboratory. Did any of them belong to her?

The fae returns to the bed, sitting at the edge. She leans back halfway, chest arched slightly forward, before she seems to reconsider. Straightening upright, she crosses her arms over her torso and fixes me with a glare. "I don't understand what you want me to do."

"Let's start with your name."

"Mikaela," she mutters.

"Pleasure to meet you, Mikaela. I am Evelyn, Queen of the Fire Court."

She rolls her eyes with a grunt of irritated laughter. "Right. So that's the fantasy you came here for."

I ignore her. "Are you a pixie?"

Her expression hardens. "I'm whatever you want me to be," she says through her teeth.

"But what are you really?"

Another eye roll. "Yes, I'm a pixie."

"What court are you from?"

"Summer."

"I see. How many of your kind are there in the Briar House? Not pixies, exactly, but fae."

She shrugs. "Seven, unless you count the children."

The blood leaves my face. "Children?"

"There are two who haven't been taken from their mothers yet."

"Are these half-fae offspring born from relations had here?"

She scoffs at the word *relations* but nods.

"What is done with the children who are taken from their mothers?"

"Madame Rose sells them," she says, and her fury is written on her face. I'm sure it's reflected on mine as well, because my gloves are growing dangerously hot. "Rumors mention experiments."

A chasm of grief threatens to open up beneath me, pulling me under as the slice of a scalpel flashes through my mind. I channel my pain into rage, let my fire burn it away until I can breathe again. I curl my fingers into fists. "So, Madame Rose is complicit in everything that happens here?"

"Yes."

There goes my final doubt that Mr. Duveau could be the sole offender in this operation. Madame Rose must not be spared from my wrath. I lean forward. "If there were to be an emergency here, what would happen?"

She lifts a brow. "An emergency?"

My lips curl into a smile. "A fire, let's say."

"Chaos, I suppose. Everyone would fight to flee out the front door, and hardly a man would be wearing pants."

"Is there a back door?"

"Yes, outside the kitchens, but it opens into an alley. Not the best escape in the event of a fire."

"I see." I ponder this for a moment. "When would be the worst time for such a tragic emergency to occur here? Meaning, when might it be the most difficult to escape?"

Mikaela's green skin goes a shade paler. "Is this really what gets you going?"

"Just answer the question honestly."

She pulls her arms tighter around her. "I would have to say around three in the morning. The last patron has left by then and everyone is asleep."

"Does Madame Rose retire by then as well?"

She nods.

"How much time would you need to ensure your fellow courtesans knew to escape through the back door during a fire?"

Her body goes still as stone. "Why are you asking me this?"

I rise to my feet and take a step closer to her, summoning every ounce of regal air I can find. To be honest, it isn't much. I haven't been Queen of Fire for more than a week. At least I know how to fake it. I repeat my question, slower, firmer. "How much time would you need?"

Her answer comes out in a whisper. "A few hours, I suppose. I would circulate word during our nightly bathing hour."

"Good. See that it's done. Discreetly." I retrieve my hat from the floor and begin pinning my hair back up under it. I can feel her eyes on me, her expression dumbstruck. "I must confess I cannot pay you. When are you required to pay your mistress her dues?"

"You mean give her everything?" Her voice is heavy with venom. "At the end of each Sunday."

"Good. Since that's the case, may I borrow some coin from you? If I must remain in town until three in the morning, I should probably have dinner."

She eyes my gown. "*You* need money? From *me*?"

"I don't have any of my own."

"You don't understand. Madame Rose requires I give her every last coin—"

I round on her, leaning in close. "No, *you* don't understand. You won't be here by Sunday to pay her. Nor will this building be left standing by morning."

Her mouth falls open. "Who are you really?"

"I told you who I am," I say flatly. "Now do what I've asked of you. Speak to your fellow courtesans. A fire will occur at three in the morning. Anyone who wishes to escape must flee to the alley in secret by then and meet me there. Must I make it clear Madame Rose is not to be privy to this information?"

She shakes her head.

"Good. Will you do it?"

Her lower lip quivers. "If this is part of your game for pleasure, it is cruel and I beg you not to play it with me."

My first instinct is to lay a comforting hand on her shoulder, the way

Lorelei often does with me. However, knowing the unwanted touch the pixie is forced to tolerate, the gesture seems inappropriate. Instead, I turn to my fire.

I pull the glove off my right hand, let my rage burn to my fingertips until a ball of fire ignites there, swirling purple, pink, and aqua. "This is no game, Mikaela. I am burning down the Briar House. Now I will ask you one more time. Will you do as I've requested?"

She swallows hard, hopeful tears swimming in her eyes. "I will."

3

―――――――

The city clock chimes three times, its bells echoing through the otherwise silent, sleeping city. With bated breath, I fix my eyes on the back door of the Briar House, the view clear from where I lurk in the shadows farther down the alley. Unwelcome thoughts threaten to shake my resolve; the chimes recall memories of the first time I heard them in the city and the fate that visit led me to. The alley, on the other hand, reminds me of Aspen's lips on mine, the weight of him pressing me into the wall behind my back. One memory fills me with terror while the other teases me with joy. Both are distractions I can't afford right now.

I refocus on my anger, my mission at hand. As the echo of the third chime fades, panic rises within me. What if something went wrong? What if Mikaela got caught or needed more time to spread the word? What if she didn't take me seriously? There's no way I can stay in this city any longer than I already have. It's taken nearly everything I have not to succumb to the grief Grenneith stirs within me, and I know from experience I can only ride the wave of my rage so far before I suffer for it.

Just as I'm tempted to storm inside and drag each courtesan out of the building by force, the door swings open. My hand moves to my obsidian blade, ready to strike should danger be revealed behind the door. I release a heavy sigh as the figure emerges and moonlight illuminates a hint of lavender hair and green skin. I'm even more relieved when I see several other figures file into the alley behind her.

I move from my hiding place and approach the growing crowd. There are far more than seven, but not all of them appear to be fae, and more than a few look like servants. The pixie must have warned all the courtesans and staff, not just her own kind. I'm relieved to find this to be the case, for I don't want to consider what I would have done if I knew anyone but Madame Rose was left inside to handle their own fate.

Mikaela's eyes widen upon seeing me, as if she never truly expected I would follow through with my plan.

"Is this everyone?" I whisper, scanning the crowd. Mikaela nods, the fae huddled close to her, eyeing me with suspicion. Two of the females hold wrapped bundles in their arms, which I can only assume are their sleeping babies, and I'm surprised to see one of the fae courtesans appears to be male. Their human comrades hesitate only a moment longer before taking off into the night.

"What do we do now?" Mikaela asks.

"Now you run," I say. "Get at least three blocks from here and wait for me to find you."

One of the fae mothers—one with enormous black eyes and a squirrel-like face—squints at me through slitted lids. "Why should we even trust you? Why shouldn't we run off on our own like the humans did?"

My gaze slides to the iron cuff around her wrist and the puckered red skin around it. "Do you have means to get that cuff off?"

She purses her tiny lips. "No."

"Then you'll need someone who can touch iron. Someone like me. Now go. I'll find you."

Mikaela turns toward the group and ushers them toward the mouth of the alley. I, on the other hand, turn away from it toward the Briar House.

With slow, silent steps, I creep into the open door and find myself in a dark kitchen. Aromas of rotting food and pungent perfume assault my senses the farther I step into the room. I remove my gloves and toss them to the ground. Raising a palm out before me, I shape my intent into a need for light. With that, a pale blue flame hovers over my hand, lighting my way as I leave the kitchen to enter a hall. I follow that hall until I find my destination: the foyer I was in mere hours ago.

My blue flame throws the crimson room under an eerie glow. I glare at the pillows, the privacy screens, the papered walls, recalling Mikaela's scarred back, her mention of half-fae children being sold for experimentation. Such a thought can't occur without memory of Mr. Meeks' laboratory, the severed wings, Mr. Osterman's dark room, the iron chains he had Lorelei strapped into. Lastly, for no more than a second, I allow myself to remember an iron bullet lodged between Mother's eyes.

Just like that my blue flame turns a pink so dark it's almost red.

I stalk the perimeter of the room, hand outstretched as my fire-laced fingertips brush the seat of the divan, the tassels of the pillows, the paper of the privacy screens. In a matter of seconds, the room has fallen beneath a beautiful, rosy inferno. Turning my back on my work, I exit the same way I came and return to the alley. Keeping my anger burning hot inside me, I close my eyes and take it to the Twelfth Court.

I wish the effect were immediate, the way it seems to be for fae like Aspen, Franco, and Nyxia. But quarter-fae that I am, and new to the ability to shift forms, I'm stuck seeking for a frustrating stretch of time. Violet fills my inner vision, turning the alley into swirling particles of light. I continue to turn ever inward, seeking my inner firefox, my instinct, my wild birthright.

Finally, calm settles over me. My body shrinks in on itself, while my senses grow sharper. Slim legs replace my four human limbs, each ending in dainty white paws. Sound becomes louder, the night more alive now that I can hear the bats fluttering in the sky, the distant hoot of an owl. Smoke tickles my nose, even though it has yet to enter the alley.

Fully in my firefox form, I sprint away from the Briar House and into the streets beyond.

As a fox, I find the fae with ease and guide them to the outskirts of the city just as the first siren begins to wail. Ignoring the sounds of alarm, I focus on the distant smell of dew-soaked grass, of towering trees. The woods. I traveled through them with Aspen, Foxglove, and Franco the first time I came to Grenneith, but even if I hadn't, I'd be able to find them now. They call to me, with their sounds and aromas, with the sense of peace left in the absence of human houses and bustling cities.

Only once we are safely beneath the blanket of trees do we rest. That's when I return briefly to my human form to melt the cuffs from each fae's wrists and ankles. Without the iron bonds suppressing their powers, a few of the stronger fae are able to shift into their unseelie forms and head north to find the faewall on their own. The remaining four, plus the two babies, stay with me. This includes Mikaela and the fae male, who I think must have had his wings shorn as well, considering the way he absently rubs his shoulders.

I know I should let them rest. I should let them sleep. They cannot keep up with a fox, and being this far from the faewall cannot offer them the ability to heal from blistered feet and torn heels. The two mothers need to nurse their babies and rest their weary arms from carrying their charges so long already.

But we must keep moving.

Shifting back into my fox form, I prod them onward.

PROGRESS IS SLOW AS MORE THAN A FULL DAY OF TRAVEL PASSES. IN MY FOX form, I fight the urge to race on without my companions. Although my instincts tell me I'd reach my destination much faster on my own, a part of me remembers that this journey means nothing without those I lead.

By the time we make it past the faewall, the sun is lowering in the sky and creeping toward evening. Just as planned, I've brought us to the Lunar axis, where I know we'll all be safe. The dusky light is a welcome respite from the glaring sun combined with the unforgiving late-October cold of the Eisleigh side of the wall.

I return to my human form, although my ribs protest at being back inside my corset. I should have had the foresight to keep the fae clothing I'd discarded when I borrowed this stupid dress. Although, when I first set out to do this, I didn't exactly have a plan. Just a need. A need to run, to flee, to seek vengeance on *something* before the empty void inside my heart swallowed me whole.

The four fae fall to their knees. Mikaela sobs into her hands while the male stares blankly ahead, shoulders slumped. The squirrel-like mother rocks her child with tears streaming over her round cheeks, and the other, a petite fae with gnarled brown skin, begins to wail a mournful song in a language I don't understand.

I remember feeling this way when Lorelei and I made it past the wall after the incident at the laboratory. It was the most agonizing grief mixed with solace I'd ever felt. The main difference between myself and the fae before me is that none of them were forced to become murderers tonight.

That burden lies on my shoulders alone.

With a sigh, I sink into the grass, letting my satin skirt pool around me. What remains of my inner connection to my fox form slips away, leaving nothing but aching limbs and a pounding headache. I breathe the pain away, too tired to even summon my flames for relief. There's nothing left to do but let the magic of Faerwyvae do its work.

"Do you have homes to return to?" My voice comes out small, revealing the truth behind my feigned confidence. The broken girl is showing beneath the mask of the unseelie queen, and I've exerted too much energy to keep her hidden a moment more.

Only the male nods, but his expression isn't hopeful.

"You are all free to stay in Lunar," I say. "Queen Nyxia will welcome you. And when I claim my palace in Fire, you will be welcome there as well."

Mikaela's gaze whips toward me. "Are you truly Queen of Fire?"

I nod.

"How is this possible?" the squirrel fae asks. "King Ustrin has ruled Fire as long as I've been alive."

"And you—you can touch iron." The male rubs his wrists, the red welts left by the cuffs only now beginning to fade.

I open my mouth, but again exhaustion drags me under. "It's a long story, but King Ustrin is dead and I have taken his place."

With that comes an image of orange scales covered in tricolor flame, of my teeth sinking into a scaly neck. Blood in my mouth. Smeared on my fur. I can almost taste it all over again, as well as the bile that rose in my throat afterward. My eyes unfocus as the moment I ended his life replays over and over in my mind.

I'm so lost in the memory that when I return my gaze to the fae, they're gone. I barely recall them leaving, but now that I think about it, I remember each one offering at least a parting glance, if not a distinct farewell. Whether they continued on through Lunar or went to their home courts, I do not know. I can only hope they're safe. And that the ghosts of what has been done to them will cease haunting them one day.

I wish the same for me.

As I rise to my feet, I expect to feel a surge of triumphant pride over doing exactly what I set out to do. I took down the Briar House and put an end to one of Henry Duveau's disgusting operations. I set seven fae free and just as many human courtesans who were probably also kept there against their will.

I may not have claimed my vengeance against the councilman who killed my mother, but I did something. Something good.

Good? The word strikes a painful chord inside me. *Is ending yet another life good?*

My stomach lurches as Madame Rose's face flashes through my mind. As much as her actions disgust me, the weight of what I've done to her hits me for the first time. Without the fire of rage burning away my fears and pain, I am defenseless against my own cruelty. My own violence.

Was it really me who set that fire, condemned a woman to die?

Or was it the fox inside me?

Is there even a difference?

Something builds in my throat, something enormous and painful. It's a sob, and with it comes stinging tears and an agonizing guilt so vast, I think my vision will go black from it.

I sink to my knees with a wail, and suddenly all I can think about is Mother. Mother at the trial. Mother in chains. Mother in a tub of freezing water. Mother shouting to defend my honor. Mother fighting the guards. Mother with a bullet between her eyes.

And between all that lies every cruel thing I've ever said to her. Every right thing I've ever dismissed. Every eyeroll. Every instance where I denied her magic and spouted off about how superior Mr. Meeks was.

Burning down the Briar House was supposed to make me feel better. It was supposed to alleviate this pain that continues to plague me. I thought I'd faced the full depth of my grief when I cried in Aspen's arms the night I defeated Ustrin. I thought I'd at least begun to recover from my mother's loss.

But I haven't.

My cheeks grow hot, breaths too shallow. My lungs feel like they're shrinking into nothing. All around me spin images I cannot bear to face. For if I do, I'll be buried beneath them forever. Instead, I seek my fire, let it burn my pain, my regrets. I let it build within me, let it light my way from the bottomless sorrow I've fallen into.

With a deep breath, I turn it into rage. Then I take it to the Twelfth Court.

4

———————

The fox's feet are almost silent.

She stalks over the forest floor, padding over grass and brambles on quiet paws, ears attuned to the sounds around her. Right now, all her senses are focused on what awaits on the other side of the brambles.

The fox crawls closer, peering through a gap in the tangled thorns to her unwitting prey.

A blackbird, some strange part of her notes.

Meal, says another part.

The plump bird pecks the damp earth, seeking its own sustenance. The fox watches as it moves closer and closer to her hiding place, salivating in anticipation of the kill. She hasn't eaten anything but berries since she can remember; it's as if she woke up this morning with the sudden realization there were other things in the forest to eat. Why hasn't she noticed before?

The fox's prey inches closer.

Her body quivers as she prepares to pounce.

"A bird, Evelyn?" The voice startles both the fox and her prey, resulting in a flutter of wings as several blackbirds take off into the sky, chirping with alarm. "I resent that, you know."

Familiar, the fox assesses about the voice. She whirls toward the source and finds a slim male on two legs leaning against a tree. He watches her without fear.

He's too large to be prey, but his presence is a threat, considering how easily he drove away her meal. Her fur bristles along her back, and she emits a warning growl.

To the fox's surprise, the male doesn't seem even remotely alarmed. Instead of backing away, he crouches down before her. "Aspen sent me to find you."

Something about the name makes her mind go still. *Aspen. Aspen. Aspen. What does it mean?*

"He's worried about you."

The fox is still trying to place the name, while another part of her argues that names don't matter to her. In fact, she should bite his hand. His pale fingertips are only several inches away—

"Hey, Evelyn."

The fox's eyes dart toward the male's face just as he pulls his lips from his pointed teeth. His face contorts with a terrifying snarl, eyes going black, skin nearly translucent as purple veins bulge beneath the surface. The monster lets out a shrieking hiss.

The fox's shock is so strong, she's left blinking several minutes. No, *I'm* left blinking. *I'm* the fox. Wait, not a fox. A...person. Oh, for the love of iron, what just happened?

I'm sprawled on my back, suddenly aware of rocks and twigs digging into my palms. I glare up at Prince Franco—the familiar Prince Franco, not the nightmarish glamour he donned to frighten me—smiling over me with his hand extended.

"I thought that might do the trick," he says.

At a loss for words, all I can do is take his hand and allow him to pull me to my feet. Vertigo seizes me as I adjust to the feeling of standing on two legs. As my vision returns to normal, I glance around. I'm in the forest. Based on the muted quality of light, I'm in Lunar. Have I been here since I crossed the faewall? Finally, I manage to shape my burning questions into words. "How long have I been away from Selene Palace?"

Franco shrugs. "Five days, I think."

My eyes bulge. "Five?" It shouldn't be possible. I was only in Grenneith for a single day, then another day or two of travel back to the faewall. After that—

I shake my head, finding my mind oddly blank aside from flashes of images. Trees. Underground burrows. Berries. The bird.

"I don't understand. I shifted into my unseelie form, and..."

"You got stuck," Franco finishes for me.

"But why? I was starting to shift faster and faster between forms."

"You must have lost touch with your seelie side."

I suppress a shudder. Aspen warned me about the possibility of forgetting who I am in fox form, but I never thought it would be so easy to do. What would have happened if Franco hadn't found me? Would I have stayed a fox forever? Surely, I would have remembered who I really am.

I recall one of my last coherent thoughts before I shifted forms.

Was it really me who set that fire?

Or was it the fox inside me?

Is there even a difference?

Anxiety rushes through me, but my fire is ready to burn it away. I don't let it burn too hot; just enough to keep my mind clear. Then I recall what Franco had said before he scared me out of my fox form—something that makes my heart flip. "Aspen sent you?"

"Yes, and it's a good thing I found you. Do you have any idea how hard it is to find a fox in the woods? Luckily, you glow."

"I...glow?" I furrow my brow, and Franco nods. I haven't given much thought to what I look like in my firefox form. When I first glimpsed my reflection in the Twelfth Court, I noted white fur rippling with pink, purple, and aqua flame. After I killed Ustrin, I remember looking at myself in a stream and saw my flames had died down to a harmless glowing light. If that's always the case with my fox appearance, it's a wonder I managed to sneak up on that bird at all.

"Why didn't Aspen come himself?" I ask, keeping my voice casual despite the way my heart tightens at the question.

"He said he made you a promise that he wouldn't use the Bond to look for you, whatever that means."

I snort a laugh, his answer relieving me of my momentary tension. "So he sent you to find me. A clever way to work around a promise."

He lifts his chin with a smug grin. "I'm sure it also had to do with the fact that my power of flight has an advantage over his unwieldy hooves."

I roll my eyes, but a more serious question drains my mirth. I bite my lip. "Did you tell him where I went?"

"How could I? It's not like I knew myself."

I avert my gaze to stare guiltily at the ground between us. "I'm sure it isn't difficult to guess. You're the one who flew to the Briar House to gather intel on the brothel at my request. Surely, you must have guessed what I was planning on doing with the information once you gave it to me."

"When I saw for myself what went on inside that brothel, I thought you might set off on some heroic mission to rescue the enslaved fae there," he says. "However, I never would have guessed you'd go alone or that you'd burn the entire building down once you did."

My eyes flash to his, a spark of alarm running through me. "You know about that?"

"Where do you think I first flew to look for you?"

I turn my gaze to my skirt—the stolen human gown that serves as further evidence of my guilt. Surprisingly, the dress has held up during my travels as a fox, although the hem is coated in black. My obsidian dagger remains at my side as well.

"Thank you, by the way," I say. "I honestly can't remember if I said that when you gave me the information about the brothel."

He lifts his chin. "I don't believe you did thank me. Turned a fiery shade of scarlet, I think was your response. Not an hour later, you were gone from Selene Palace. On that note, it seems I've done quite a bit more for you than you've done for me, and I've yet to be repaid for that *errand*, as you called it."

I put my hands on my hips and give him a pointed look. "I think saving your life after an iron injury should count as payment for several favors, don't you think? Besides, I don't recall promising you anything in return."

"A fae never does anything for free," he says with a teasing smirk.

"Well, a *smart* fae shouldn't perform a favor without requesting a bargain beforehand."

"And only the most ruthless fae would deny fair compensation." He takes a step closer. "Better late than never, though. Worry not, I can think of several things you could do to pay me and none of them would take too long." He looks at me from under his lashes.

I bark a laugh. "Wouldn't take too long? Now that's a ringing endorsement."

"You'll find I'm long in the ways that matter the most."

"If you haven't noticed, Franco, King Aspen is my mate."

At that, the laughter is leeched from his expression. His voice comes out quiet, hesitant. "I have noticed, actually."

Guilt drags my stomach as the air grows heavy between us. I could ignore it, I could laugh it off and change the subject. But Franco is right about one thing: he's done far more for me than I've ever done for him. He deserves candor from me. Even so, I can't stop the blush that warms my cheeks before I even say a word. "Franco, I know we had a moment before Aspen came to Selene Palace. Unless I imagined it, there was something between us. But...Aspen is..."

Words dry in my throat as I struggle to express my love for my mate without hurting Franco.

To my relief, his lips pull back into a smile, although it doesn't quite reach his eyes. "You don't need to explain, Evelyn. You did not imagine what was, for a time at least, between us. Even now, I confess you give me a thrill. Much of what I say to create a rise out of you is said in jest, but only partially so. No part of me would deny you if you wanted me. But in matters of the heart, I knew you belonged to another long before I kissed you. I could taste it in the air around you. I still can."

Tears prick my eyes. "I love him," I whisper.

Somehow, his smile grows both wider and sadder at the same time. "I know you do. I hope to find a love like that myself someday."

"Have you never loved anyone?" My breath hitches in my throat as I imagine with terror what would happen if he says he feels that way about me. *Please, don't say it...*

His eyes grow distant as he averts his gaze. Finally, he says, "I've felt it. Tasted it from others. But experienced love myself? No, I don't think so. When you can taste the emotions of others, it leaves a lot to be desired when your own feelings are lacking."

My heart sinks at that. I never imagined such an unfortunate downside to being a psy vampire. "Well, I do hope you find that person who makes you feel that way. Better than that, in fact."

"So do I. In the meantime, if you and the Stag King find yourselves on the outs, come to me for a revenge tryst." He winks.

I shake my head with a chuckle. "Are we friends, then?"

"Yes, Evelyn. We're friends. I didn't risk my wings for you at your mother's trial because I thought I stood a chance at winning you from Aspen. Same reason why I flew to the Briar House for you without question. I did it because we're friends. I like you and I always will."

I tilt my head. "Are you sure you don't just like the violence that seems to trail in my wake?"

"Well, there's that too," he says. "And don't think for a minute that this means I'll stop baiting your mate. I can't help it, nor will I give it up. He emits the most delicious emotion when it comes to you." His expression turns wistful, as if savoring the memory of the last time he got under Aspen's skin. "Speaking of violence, did you get what you were looking for? At the Briar House?"

I cross my arms over my chest to keep my mind from spinning down the wrong path. "Not exactly," I say. "I thought my mission would make me feel better, but it didn't. Perhaps if I'd been able to find and kill Mr. Duveau as well, it would have felt more meaningful."

"Are you sure even that will make you feel better about losing your mother?"

I swallow the lump in my throat and replace it with fire. "It has to. We're at war. I can't have my grief distracting me."

"Why is that?"

"Grief makes me weak."

He furrows his brow. "I don't think anything could make you weak. If you let it, I have a feeling it could make you stronger."

His words tug at my heart, but I don't let them pull me far. I can't afford where they might take me if I do. Instead, I give a casual laugh and bat him playfully on the shoulder. "Since when are you one to get serious? Are you aiming to become some great fae philosopher next?"

He winces. "I don't like the taste of your teasing at my expense. Remind me never to be serious with you again."

"Agreed."

Another wince. "Well, actually, I have one more thing to be serious about. It's why I was sent to find you in the first place."

"I thought Aspen was worried about me."

"Oh, he was. Stalking around the palace like a caged bull for days. However, I think he would have let you frolic around the woods a while longer if it weren't imperative that you return at once."

Despite his casual demeanor, I can't help but shiver with dread. "Why? What's happened?"

"The rebels have called an emergency meeting. It's about you."

5

———————

By the time Franco flies us to Selene Palace and sets me on my feet outside the palace doors, my stomach is a roiling mess. And it isn't just from soaring terrifying heights in the sky; my panic stems more from anxious anticipation. Anything could have happened in my absence. Anything could have prompted this mysterious meeting, and none of my imagined causes are good.

As soon as the doors open, Nyxia is standing before us, arms crossed over her chest. Like always, she's dressed in a way that is stunning, eccentric, and elegant all at once. Her top is like a waistcoat, but it's composed entirely of small, black beads, and she wears nothing underneath. Her trousers are skintight silk that show off every curve and muscle of her long, slim legs. As she stands there staring daggers at me, I can't help but wonder if one of her owl messengers announced our arrival or if she's been waiting here endlessly for dramatic effect. I wouldn't put the latter past her.

"And hello to you too, sister." Franco greets the queen with a crooked smile, but she ignores him, her eyes fixed on me.

"Look who decided to show up," the Lunar Queen says, running a hand through her hair. That's when I realize her short silver strands are wet, as if she's recently stepped out of the bath. "Where in the name of iron have you been?"

I open my mouth, but all air is stripped from my lungs as I glimpse the figure strolling down the hall toward us.

My heart lurches, first from the joy at seeing Aspen. Even though I was unconscious of the passage of time when I was stuck in my fox form, my absence from him suddenly comes crashing down on me, the space between us a painful and tangible thing I want to destroy at once. I dart toward him, but my steps falter, my heart lurching a second time as I take in his appearance.

Aspen's face is splattered with what looks like dried blood, smears of dirt crisscrossing his forehead. His russet shirt is filthy and torn, the sleeves rolled up to his elbows to reveal bloodstained forearms. Only his hands appear clean. I finish closing the distance between us, my throat tight as my fingers reach his face, seeking signs of injury.

Before I can prod him further, he stills my fluttering hands with his. "I'm fine." His tone is gentle as his eyes drink in mine. I can feel his relief at seeing me surging through the Bond between us.

I lower my hands and rest them on his chest, over the caked dirt and blood. "What in the name of iron happened?"

"There was a skirmish at the border between Solar and Lunar," he says. "It was nothing."

From his state of dress, I highly doubt that's true.

"It really was nothing," comes Nyxia's airy voice. "Just like every other minor skirmish they've attempted this past week. Do they honestly think they're intimidating us, sending their pathetic soldiers to feign an attack only to flee at the first draw of blood? The royals don't even have the decency to show their faces and fight us themselves."

Aspen ignores Nyxia, eyes still locked on me. "Are you all right?"

"I'm fine—"

"What in the name of night are you wearing?" Nyxia has come up beside me and my mate, gaze burning into the length of my gown. Franco trails behind her, lips pulled into a grimace. "Is that..."

Aspen pulls away slightly, just far enough to study my dress. Guilt burns a hole in my heart as Aspen's eyes turn steely. "Human clothing," he mutters, and the scorn laced into those two words can only be met with my fire.

"So what if it is?" I say, lifting my chin in defiance.

"That's my cue to leave," Franco says under his breath as he inches away from us. After an exaggerated bow, he shifts into his raven form and takes flight down the hall.

Nyxia beams at me and Aspen. One would think she was oblivious to the tension rippling between us, but I know she's probably relishing the energy we're emitting. She almost sounds disappointed when she says, "I suppose I should make sure everyone is ready for the meeting. Don't take too long."

Aspen's eyes don't leave mine as Nyxia exits the corridor. I force myself not to waver beneath his glare, knowing if I do, he'll see all the guilt I'm hiding inside.

"You promised me you'd stay safe," Aspen finally says. "In turn, you made me promise not to seek you through the Bond. You said you needed time to be alone. Time to heal. You lied."

I lift my chin. "I didn't lie."

"Since when is setting foot on human soil while we're at war considered *staying safe*?"

I feel a ripple of hurt through the Bond, and it isn't mine. It's enough to extinguish some of the fire in my veins. My shoulders slump, and I break his gaze, eyes resting on his chest. "I'm sorry."

He runs a hand over his face, smearing the dirt and dried blood. His expression softens. "We'll talk later." There's only a hint of resignation mixing with the frustration in his tone, telling me this conversation is far from over. He turns away and motions for me to follow. "Let's join the meeting."

"What's this about?" I ask as I hurry to his side.

"We'll find out," is all he says.

Icy silence falls between us, but I walk with my head held high.

We enter the throne room, and my attention is immediately drawn to the large table at its center. Around it stands Nyxia and three other fae rulers I've grown somewhat accustomed to seeing at Selene Palace: King Aelfon of Earthen, King Flauvis of Winter, and Queen Minuette of Wind. The first two are in equal states of disarray as Aspen, smeared with grime from the battle they too must have joined. But there are two additional fae I only vaguely recall seeing before. One is a tiny pixie who resembles a brown stick with a pair of pink, fluttering wings and a cherry blossom for a head. The other is a tall female figure—which I only know because she's without clothing—composed of particles of shimmering white light from her toes to her hairless, humanoid head.

All eyes fall on Aspen and me as we join the fae around the table. I realize this is the first time I've been present at a meeting of the rebels, the first time I've confronted these rulers as a queen myself. Without meaning to, I've inched closer to Aspen's side for comfort. I go still as I feel his pinky wind around mine, our linked fingers hidden behind the folds of my dress.

The touch of his flesh, despite the current grudge we hold between us, helps steady my nerves.

"Queen Estel." Nyxia nods at the shimmering fae, then faces the winged one. "Queen Tris. I present to you Queen Evelyn of Fire."

I freeze, unsure if I'm supposed to curtsy. I'm still so uncertain what customs are universal to faekind and which are adopted only by some as preference. Besides, I'm a queen now. Am I ever expected to curtsy? When both offer me only nods of acknowledgment, I do the same for them. "Have you joined the rebellion?" I ask.

Flauvis, the wolf king, lets out a growl that sounds more like a laugh. "I'd like to know that answer too," he says, gaze locked on Queen Estel.

"I gave you my answer days ago," Queen Tris says in a minuscule voice. She shudders, and suddenly the pixie stands as tall as Queen Nyxia. Her skin remains brown and bark-like, decorated in elegant whorls. Her hair is composed of brambles and bright pink cherry blossoms, her dress like woven branches laced with pink petals. Translucent pink wings fold down her back. I suppress a rush of nausea as I'm reminded of Mikaela's scars where wings should have been. Queen Tris gives an audible huff and crosses her arms over her chest. In this form, she looks much more familiar as one of the rulers I recall seeing at the council meeting where Aspen fought Cobalt for his throne. She must be Queen of Spring.

"And my presence here today is my answer," Estel says. Her voice is light and musical, like the tinkling of distant bells or wind chimes. The particles shift and sway over her face, rearranging until they form the semblance of a smile. I can only imagine she's Queen of Star.

"It took you long enough." If a wolf can scoff, Flauvis certainly does now, an expression I can't even imagine on a common canine.

Estel remains composed, giving no reply.

I glance from Estel to Flauvis when I'm suddenly aware of a pair of eyes burning into me. I look across the table at Queen Tris, who stares as if seeing me for the first time. However, if I recognize her, she should damn well recognize me. I was certainly hard to miss when I was presented as Aspen's champion before the entire fae council. Regardless, her scrutiny feels invasive as her eyes bore into me, lingering on my dress. I wonder if that's the primary reason she shifted from her smaller form into this one—to unsettle me with her glare. Her upper lip lifts in clear distaste. "*You* defeated King Ustrin?"

I meet her eyes without falter, lips pursed. Indignation dances down my arms to my fingertips. I lift a hand, let flames flicker over my palm. "I tore out his throat with my teeth. Would you like to scrutinize them too? You might still find one of his scales if it's proof you're after."

Tris pales to a lighter shade of brown, pink eyes locked on my menacingly pleasant smile.

Aspen chuckles next to me.

"We aren't here to discuss the virtues of oral hygiene," Nyxia says in a bored tone. "We're here because Queen Estel has important information to share with us. It's about our enemies."

"Or she's a spy," Queen Minuette says with a dangerous, airy hiss, her blue hair rippling behind her on an invisible wind.

"She has a point." Aspen narrows his eyes at Estel.

"Estel *is* a spy," Nyxia says. "She's been spying for *me*." Her eyes move from one fae to the next until she's burned us all into silence.

"For you?" King Aelfon's voice is low and gruff. He stomps a yellowed hoof, shaking his curled horns. "Why is this the first we're hearing of it?"

"Because I wasn't sure I trusted her yet," Nyxia says through her teeth.

"But you do now?" Aspen asks, tone skeptical.

"Enough to let her speak," Nyxia says pleasantly.

The Star Queen steps closer to the table, the particles of her face dispersing and rearranging until they form a stoic expression. "Queen Nyxia is correct; I agreed to spy for her. It is why I have yet to officially join your alliance. But the actions I must take next will pit me firmly against the opposition, and I will not be able to spy any longer."

King Aelfon crosses his thick, brown arms over his barrel chest. "What is this special information you have, then?"

"As you know," Estel says, "Irridae Palace has been vacant since Ustrin's death. He left no heir, which meant all who were loyal to him were displaced upon his death, including his household."

She's right; this information is known. Within a day of me defeating Ustrin, Nyxia urged me to send a pair of moon dragons to Irridae Palace—Ustrin's former home—to investigate the grounds. When they returned, they reported that the palace was empty, all entrances sealed, the grounds protected by some strange magic. I ordered them back to Irridae to remain nearby and report any changes, but I haven't heard a word since.

Estel continues. "What you don't know is that Queen Dahlia has been adamant that we hunt down members of Ustrin's former household for intel. She wouldn't say why at first, at least not in front of me. I think she suspected my hidden motives from the start. But she called a council meeting yesterday and told us what she's discovered."

Aspen runs a hand through his blue-black hair, sending a good portion of it spilling into his eyes. It takes all my restraint not to reach up and brush it off his brow. "What is it?" he asks.

"Dahlia told us she'd suspected Ustrin had a weapons stash hidden in his palace," Estel says. "She claims the informant she questioned confirmed it exists and that they aren't just any weapons. They are iron, the same ones Ustrin tried to use against his own kind."

I shudder, remembering how Ustrin's guard carried an iron sword during a peaceful exchange of words, then used it against Franco. He later threatened his own fire fae with iron-filled grenades, a weapon that would have obliterated his own soldiers in the process if used.

Estel continues. "With this new information, she set forth a petition to send the council's newly appointed seelie king as Ustrin's replacement to take over Irridae Palace at once. She said it was to weaken Queen Evelyn's claim, but I know that isn't the real reason the Renounced are suddenly sending someone to occupy the abandoned palace. They want those weapons."

Flauvis mutters a curse-like growl, while Minuette lets out a low whistle.

"When are the Renounced sending the new pretender king?" Aelfon asks.

My attention snags on the word *Renounced*, having heard it twice now, but I'm more concerned with hearing the answer.

"I was supposed to escort him tomorrow evening. Instead, I'll be escorting Evelyn, solidifying my stance against the Renounced and with the Alpha Alliance."

"Wait," I say. "Renounced? Alpha Alliance?"

Nyxia lets out an irritated sigh. "We can't very well continue calling our enemies *the council*, can we? Not when we've deemed the Council of Eleven Courts disbanded."

"And we can't keep calling ourselves the rebels when we aren't in the wrong," Aelfon grumbles.

"The former fae council is now the Renounced, as far as we're concerned," Nyxia explains, "and we are the Alpha Alliance."

"Not that that's a much truer name," mutters Flauvis. "How many of you were appointed by the council as opposed to proving yourself the alpha blessed by the All of All?"

"That's not what matters right now," Aspen says, raising his voice. "What matters is that Irridae Palace contains dangerous weapons. We need to get to the palace first and make sure those weapons don't fall into the wrong hands."

"Exactly," Estel says in her soothing voice. "Queen Evelyn, it's time to claim your new palace."

6

My new palace.

Even though I've known I'll have to eventually claim Irridae Palace as my own to demonstrate the seriousness of my stake as queen, I've dreaded the thought. I can't imagine how something that once belonged to Ustrin could be considered my home. Not to mention, I've never set foot in the Fire Court. Never felt its desert heat.

But Queen Estel is right. The Alpha Alliance is right. If Irridae harbors iron weapons that could harm the fae I'm sworn to protect, I must do whatever it takes to keep the palace out of enemy hands. I'll get there first if it's the last thing I do.

As the meeting comes to a close, the fae royals begin to file out the door of the throne room. I'm about to follow suit when I notice Aspen hasn't budged from his place at the table. His body is tensed, eyes fixed on the obsidian surface before him. I groan internally. So this is where it will happen. This is where we'll have that dreaded talk he promised.

I cross my arms and lean my back against the table, watching the rest of the fae exit. The last is Nyxia, although she lingers by the door for a moment. Beneath the threshold, she glances at me over her shoulder. "A little owl told me the most delicious piece of news," she croons. "It seems a certain brothel in Grenneith burned down earlier this week. A brothel that has since been revealed to have housed fae merchandise." She looks me up and down, a knowing glint in her eye. "Well done, little foxy."

Aspen tenses even further, and I can already hear the growl building in the back of his throat. As Nyxia closes the door behind her, I whirl toward him. He does the same toward me.

Before he can open his mouth to speak, I say, "Aspen, I have something very important to discuss with you."

"As do I," he says through his teeth.

I ignore his venom, doing my best to feign a nonplussed air. "This is important. Timely, considering what's about to happen tomorrow."

Some of the fire seems to go out of him, which was my very intention. He furrows his brow. "What is it?"

"As I'm going to claim Irridae Palace, it's time I get serious about appointing my household staff. Primarily, I'll need an ambassador."

"I am sure Foxglove will be happy to serve you until—"

"No, Foxglove is your ambassador, and he's already done so much for me. I'd like to officially appoint someone to the position."

"And you'd like my advice on whom you should appoint?" Aspen almost looks pleased, which makes my heart sink.

"No," I say slowly. "I have someone in mind, but I need your..."

I hesitate. What exactly is it I need from him? Permission? His blessing? Honestly, this whole tangent was meant mainly as a distraction, despite the truth of the matter. I square my shoulders. "I want to make Lorelei my ambassador."

For a moment, he appears dumbstruck. "Lorelei?"

"Yes. And since she's employed by the Autumn Court, I figured I'd run it by you first."

He rubs a hand along his jaw, then shakes his head. "I don't think it's a good idea."

My mouth falls open. "Why? Do you think she should toil away as a lady's maid the rest of her life? Surely, she's worth more than that."

"She is," he rushes to say. "It isn't that at all, it's more...it isn't a good idea to appoint your friends as your staff. Especially to such powerful positions."

"Why not?"

"It makes things difficult," he says. "When your subordinates are your friends, it makes it harder to be firm with them."

I bristle. "For one, I don't consider Lorelei my subordinate but my equal, and for another, why should I ever need to be firm with her?"

"See, this is exactly why this is a bad idea. You don't understand—"

"No, *you* don't understand. I didn't bring this up because I wanted your opinion. I brought it up simply to inform you of my intention to remove her from your employ and into mine."

Aspen rolls his eyes. "Why did you even bother asking, then?"

"I thought you might support me," I say, "but clearly you don't trust me to make my own choices."

"Like I trusted you when you said you only needed space? That you promised you'd stay safe?"

I scoff. "Oh, here we go."

"As soon as I saw you in that human dress, I knew you'd lied. I knew you'd done something reckless. But never could I have imagined you'd do something so stupid as to return to Grenneith. Nyxia was right, wasn't she? You burned down that brothel, the one Henry Duveau tried to send you to."

I take an angry step toward him. "I put an end to fae torture. You don't know what it was like there. They had them cuffed in iron, forced to pleasure whoever came to pay them a visit. Some of the fae had their wings shorn. Worst of all, the brothel's madame sold half-fae children to be experimented on." A lump rises in my throat, but I burn it with fire. "I only saved two children."

His expression softens. "I'm not saying what you did was wrong, but doing it alone was reckless. You should have mentioned this was something you wanted to do. We could have brought it up to the Alpha Alliance. We could have taken the brothel down as a formal demonstration to the humans."

"I wanted to do it alone," I say softly. "I *needed* to do it alone."

"I understand you felt like you had to seek vengeance. Do you think I don't know what it's like to feel helpless when those who've wronged you are free? My own brother is living in my palace and I've yet to have the means to move against him."

My rage returns in a flash. "It's not the same. My mother died right in front of me."

"I know, Evie, and I'm so sorry. But what if Mr. Duveau had found you while you were in Grenneith?"

"I wanted him to find me!" I shout. "He was half the reason I went there. I hoped Madame Rose could be glamoured to tell me his location."

His eyes bulge. "Don't tell me you tried to glamour someone."

"I did, Aspen, and it worked. For the dress, at least." I purposely omit mention of glamouring the man who harassed me in the street. "And it would have worked on Madame Rose too, if she wasn't wearing rowan."

He throws his hands in the air. "This is what I'm talking about! That is reckless. That is the opposite of staying safe."

My fury rises higher and higher, and I let it burn around me. Let it melt my pain and emotions away. "You need to get it through your head that you don't control me. I am queen of my own court. I am ruler of my own actions. I will make my own decisions in all things, and that includes seeking vengeance where I please and making Lorelei my ambassador. You don't get to stand over my shoulder and operate me like a puppet."

His expression falls, wounded like I've never seen before. His words come out quiet, strained. "Is that what you think I'm doing here, Evie? Controlling you? I confess, I cannot help but try to keep you safe. I love you more than I can say, and it kills me to watch you run from your grief and instead put yourself in danger. And when it comes to your rule, I only gave you my advice because I thought you respected my opinion. I thought we were ruling together. As mates. Did you not mean what you said to Nyxia? That my household is your household?"

Something breaks inside me, and guilt swarms my heart. Suddenly, I feel the barbs of the words I said to Aspen pricking my chest. That was my fire talking, not me. And yet, I can't bring myself to reply when every truth I want to say teeters on the brink of the emotions that could destroy me, that could pull me into that black chasm of sorrow.

Aspen misreads my silence, eyes going steely. He takes a step back from me, then another, shaking his head. "No. When it all comes down to it, you're just a lying human."

He turns on his heel and stalks toward the door.

Agony, rage, and terror surge through me. "You don't mean that," I call after him, painfully aware of how my voice trembles. "Don't walk away from me."

He reaches the door without a second glance.

No, I can't bear it. I can't let him leave. "Aspen." The name rings out with power, and that bridge spans between us in my mind's eye.

He whirls back toward me, his gaze as sharp as a dagger's edge. "Don't you dare," he says through his teeth.

I burn him with a fiery glare. "By the power of your true name, don't walk away from me. Come back to me right now."

His shoulders tense, arms rippling with rage, but he's powerless against the command. With pounding footsteps, he returns to me, stopping just inches away. "How dare you use my name like this. I thought we—"

I crane my neck to look into his eyes. "I don't want to be mad at you."

"And this is supposed to help?"

I tilt my chin up. "Kiss me."

He narrows his eyes. "This is hardly the time for that."

Magic dances on my lips, emitting the power of our Bond. "Kiss me," I repeat, louder this time. "That's not a request. It's a command."

His mouth presses hard on mine, almost painfully so. I can feel his anger as if it were my own, and I meet it with mine, kissing him equally as firm until we both break away with a gasp for air. Then his lips are back on mine, the pressure still fierce, but with a more yielding quality. His hands slide down my shoulders, helping me shrug out of my coat. I tear the belted obsidian blade from my waist as one of his hands moves into my hair, the other down my back. After tossing the belt on the floor, my arms wrap around his waist, pressing him hard against me as if we could melt into one another.

His kisses are like fire, my lips an inferno as he burns against me. My mouth parts, and his tongue moves against mine, sending a wave of pleasure through my core, igniting heat between my thighs. His lips part from mine only to carve a trail of fire along my jaw and down my neck where they pause at the high lace collar of my gown.

"Evie," he whispers against my neck, the feel of his breath making me shudder against him. I can't tell if there's a command in the word or not, but I don't care either way. "Take off your dress."

I rake my fingers through his hair, paying no heed to his unwashed state. I press a kiss to his forehead, then his temple, until I reach the lobe of his ear. My teeth graze it, before I say, "Take it off for me."

At that, he spins me around. I brace my hands on the table as he rips the buttons free at the back of the gown. "I hate this dress," he says as the back opens. He slides the dress down my back and over my hips, and I step out of it. He gathers the black and white satin in his hands and tosses it onto the table. Then his fingers skate over the laces of my corset. One hand moves over my stomach while he brings his lips to my shoulder. I close my eyes and turn my head to let his kisses move to my neck, his body pressed close behind me. "How do I get you out of this thing?" he whispers.

I brace my hands steadier on the table as my knees threaten to give way beneath me, his breath on my skin unbearably pleasurable. "The laces in the back," I manage to say.

The hand on my stomach moves up the front of the rigid corset and over my chest where the tops of my breasts strain against the starchy linen. "I don't think I have the patience for that."

"Then rip the damn thing off already," I say. "I never want to wear it again."

That's all the permission he needs before both hands come to the bodice of the corset and tear it in two. I gasp with relief and can't help but laugh. "It's just like in the novels." I reach an arm behind me to grasp the back of Aspen's neck.

"What kinds of novels have you been reading?" His hands move over my bare skin, his palms warm against my naked flesh. I arch my back as he teases the crest of my breast with his thumb.

"The wrong kind, apparently," I say. In all honesty, it was Amelie who read the romantic stories, and I laughed at the few I tried to read. I was always more interested in academic literature. But why am I thinking about books when the real thing is right here? Aspen's thumb continues to elicit the most delectable sensations, while his free hand moves down, over my hips, my thighs, then to the place between them.

I return both hands to the top of the table, a moan escaping my lips. Despite the desire stirring inside me, I need more of him to fully quench it. I whirl toward him, dragging his mouth to mine, my fingers reaching for the waistband of his trousers. Before I can free the top button, his hand moves to my waist, lifting me until I'm propped on the table. With agonizingly slow kisses, he leans me back until my bare skin is fully upon my discarded dress he'd tossed there. I reach for his trousers again, but he intercepts my hands, pinning them over my head as his lips leave mine to trail down my neck. Then his mouth moves lower, across my chest, his tongue trailing over each mound, then further down to my ribs, my stomach, my hips.

I gasp as his lips continue even farther down, resting at the apex of my thighs. My body tenses at the unexpected caress of his tongue. As he elicits the most euphoric pleasure, the tenseness leaves every muscle and I succumb to the devious spell Aspen has put me under. The sensations reach an impossible crescendo. I arch my back and gasp. I'm limp and shuddering by the time Aspen's lips return to mine.

He pulls away, and our eyes lock. He brushes my hair from my sweat-soaked forehead as he catches his breath. "I love you, Evie. You devious, reckless creature."

My stomach sinks despite his passionate words, considering they seem to hint that our pleasure is over. "Not so fast," I say, voice trembling. "I'm not done with you yet."

Again, I reach for his trousers, but this time it's a sound that stops me—the throne room door opening.

"Is this what I left the two of you alone to do?" calls Nyxia's exasperated voice.

Aspen goes still over me, and I'm suddenly grateful one of us has kept their clothes on, as well as the fact that I'm fairly certain I'm hidden mostly from view by Aspen's form.

"I know from experience that this table works wonders for such activities," Nyxia says, voice dripping honey, "but it's mine. Go spread your passions all over your new palace and get off my damn furniture."

At the sound of the door shutting, Aspen and I burst into stifled laughter. "I suppose we should get you back in that dress." Aspen caresses my cheek with his thumb, which only reminds me of what his thumb was doing not minutes ago.

I find my hips moving beneath him, the heat returning to my core. "Can't we—"

The door opens again, just long enough for Nyxia to say, "Now."

My cheeks are warm as Aspen walks me to my room. We stop outside it, and I turn to face him, back pressed against my closed door. Aspen steps closer to me, one hand braced on the doorframe, the other winding around a strand of my tangled hair. The energy between us sizzles, and it takes all my restraint not to pull him inside my room and push him onto the bed so we can pick up where we left off.

I bite my lip as Aspen lifts his hungry eyes to meet mine. There's no doubt he's thinking the same thing. He lets out a sigh that almost sounds like a groan. "I should probably get cleaned up and changed."

With a reluctant nod, I force my fantasies to subside. "As should I. I must meet with the fire fae tonight and tell them of the plan to go to Irridae."

A cloud falls over his face, reminding me of our fight. He drops my strand of hair and straightens his posture.

I reach for his hand before he can take a step away. "I didn't mean what I said," I say in a rush. "I let my fire take over. I've been...doing that a lot lately."

"It's all right," he says. "A lot of what you said was true. I can't control you, and I need to give you the space to make your own decisions as queen."

"That doesn't mean I don't want you at my side. I really did mean what I said to Nyxia when your refugees came here. Your household is mine, and I want them to come to Irridae. I want my home to be their home. Even once you defeat Cobalt, I want us to continue to rule side by side, if we can."

His expression brightens, lips pulling into a crooked grin. "Does that mean you want me to come to Irridae too?"

I lace my fingers through his, squeezing his palm with mine. "I thought that went without saying from the very start. I need you, Aspen. I love you."

He leans in and kisses me lightly on the lips, soft and slow. Too slow, for it gives me enough time to crave him again. I'm about to suggest we get cleaned up together, perhaps perform an encore of our time in the moon baths, but he pulls away. "I'll let you get on with your tasks."

My heart sinks, but I let him go. I turn toward my door and am about to push it open when Aspen's voice drags my attention back to him.

"It's a good idea, Evie," he says. "Making Lorelei your ambassador. She deserves the promotion, and you deserve someone you trust at your side." With a wink, he turns away and continues down the hall.

My eyes sting as I watch his back until he's out of sight. Although I would have gone forth with my plans regardless of his approval, hearing him vocalize his support moves me in a way I hadn't expected. Despite his stubborn streak—and mine, for that matter—I think we make a decent pair.

So long as we don't burn anything down when we're at our worst.

Then again, I burn things down when I'm at my best.

ONCE I'VE CLEANED AWAY THE GRIME OF MY TRAVELS AND CHANGED INTO A gauzy indigo gown, I knock on Lorelei's door. Her eyes widen as she opens it and then throws her arms around me. I return the embrace, no longer surprised at Lorelei's warm affection. For someone as sharp as she is around most people, I'm honored by how freely she shows her care for me.

"You're back!" She pulls away to scan me from head to toe, as if checking for damage, then lowers her voice. "Nyxia told me what you did. Or at least what she suspected you did. Is it true? Did you burn down the Briar House?"

She steps to the side so I can fully enter her room and leads us to a set of chairs. She sits in one, and I sink wearily into the other, not bothering to maintain a regal countenance around her. "I did."

She lifts her chin approvingly. "Well done. Although you don't look too pleased yourself."

I sigh. "I am, it's just...I'm..." I consider telling her everything; the fae I rescued, Mikaela's scarred back, the fire, the escape, the way I got stuck in my unseelie form. But the thought alone exhausts me. Instead, I sit straighter. "Actually, I came to speak to you about something specific."

She leans forward, brow furrowed. "What is it?"

"I'll start by saying I've spoken to Aspen and he approves." Of course, I leave out the part where he at first *didn't* approve. "That is, if you agree. You may remain in his employ if you prefer, but—"

"Wait, I'm losing my job?"

"No. Well, yes, but..." Why am I so nervous to ask? "Lorelei, will you be my ambassador?"

Her mouth falls open as she leans back in alarm. "Me? Your ambassador?"

"Yes."

My stomach drops as she does nothing but stare at me for a few moments. Then finally, she says, "Are you sure? I'm not a fire fae."

"Is that important?" I ask, and my uncertainty is genuine. Now that I think about it, most of the ambassadors I've seen were easily distinguishable as belonging to a certain court based on their appearances. But is that simply due to clothing and style choice, or their actual heritage? "Must all ambassadors be native to the court they represent?"

"No," she says to my relief, "but I thought perhaps you'd want to establish a connection with the fire fae. This is an opportunity to elevate one of your own people and show your respect for them. Elevating me might...well, it won't be seen as a negative thing, but it will remove that possibility to connect with others you'd want to keep close."

My eyes unfocus as I consider what she said. She has a point, one I hadn't considered myself. Still, there's no one I can imagine doing a better job than Lorelei. "See, this is why I need you. What you're saying makes perfect sense. However, I don't know or trust any of the fire fae enough to make any appointments just yet. As my ambassador, you can help me navigate my relationships with them and find other opportunities to honor them."

"I could." The word comes out slowly.

"Will you do it?"

I wait with bated breath as she considers. For a moment, I worry that the offer has somehow offended her. Perhaps she prefers being a lady's maid or considers it a step down to work for a less-established royal like me. Then her lips pull into a wide smile. "Yes, of course I will. You know I am already loyal to you. I love Aspen, but I will follow you anywhere."

I can hardly contain my joy, and before I know it, we're embracing again.

When we separate, she puts her hands on her hips and smirks. "Besides, now I can finally get away from Nyxia." Despite the exaggerated relief in her tone, I can tell there isn't the same venom that used to be present when she'd speak about Nyxia. It makes me wonder if her heart is softening in regard to the fierce queen. I know her grief over her deceased lover will likely never fully disappear, but I can't help hoping there might be a second chance at love waiting in the near future for my friend. Perhaps even another shot with Nyxia.

"Do you think you can begin your ambassador duties tonight?" I ask.

She squares her shoulders with a confident grin. "I'm ready."

"Good. Then we'll visit the fire fae together."

"If you truly want me to start my duties now," she says, "then I have a better suggestion. You won't be *visiting* the fire fae. You will hold court and your people will come to you."

I flash her a smile. "I knew you were the one for this job."

AFTER EVENING FALLS, I MAKE MY WAY TO THE WISHING TREE AT THE EDGE OF the lawn outside Selene Palace. Lorelei arranged everything to accommodate my makeshift outdoor throne room, including an elegant moonstone chair to act as my temporary throne. With the long skirts of my indigo gown flowing around my legs, I lower into the chair with as much grace as I can muster.

"Your people should arrive shortly," Lorelei says, standing at my right. "They have been briefed on your travel plans, so you won't have to go into much detail regarding that."

I'm surprised she informed them already, only because I hardly know the details myself. All I know is that Estel will be escorting me and a small retinue to Irridae. I get the feeling the Star Queen won't be acting simply as a guide, but using some sort of magic to take me there. "Do you know anything about Queen Estel's powers? Does she have control over travel or something?"

"Pretty much," Lorelei says. "The Star Court's magic is deeply connected to time and space. All courts are represented by some combination of the elements. Star magic has an affinity for air, which makes it easy for the most powerful star fae to utilize their magic for swift travel. Queen Estel specifically excels at travel through time and space. Her technology created the axis line and the axis points in each court when the wall was built."

A chill runs up my spine. I had no idea a single fae could have such significant power. What other strange magics have I yet to learn about? "So when she said she's escorting me to Irridae Palace…"

Lorelei nods. "What she means is she will use her magic in the form of a portable travel device called a Chariot. It's hard to explain. You'll see it for yourself."

"Wow. All right. I had no idea that was possible."

"Her magic is rare, as are the devices she creates," Lorelei says. "That's why the Renounced wanted her to escort their fire king pretender. Taking you instead will be a huge slap in their faces."

"How many do you think Queen Estel can transport at once? I was told I should bring only a small retinue."

"I've never known the Star Queen to transport more than eight. We already know your retinue will include you, me, Aspen, and Foxglove, and I can guarantee the king will insist on bringing at least two guards. So that leaves two—"

"And Amelie," I rush to say before I have a chance to take it back.

Lorelei pauses, mouth hanging open. "You want to bring your sister with you?"

My pulse quickens. Talk of Amelie is dangerous territory, as I can't think of her without considering everything she's done. Betraying me for Cobalt. Missing Mother's trial which resulted in her death. Arriving at Lunar without warning, giving me the power of her name as the only tether to trust her by. My fingers curl around the armrest of the chair as I squeeze the cool moonstone. The distraction stabilizes me, helps me maintain even breathing as I say, "I can't leave her here."

"Can you trust her?"

"Of course I can't," I say, "but she's my responsibility. If she truly came here on some nefarious order from Cobalt, I can't leave her at Lunar to draw danger in my absence."

"What if this is exactly what he wants?" Lorelei's eyes are wide with fear. "What if he ordered her here, knowing you'd eventually take her to Irridae, to the weapons stash?"

I shake my head. "If that's the case, I'd like to see her try so I can catch her in the act and be done with her for good. Besides, I'd rather lead my enemies straight to me than put another court at risk." Lorelei opens her mouth to argue, but I speak first. "I'm sorry, Lorelei, but in this, I can't be persuaded otherwise. If Amelie is my enemy, then I must keep her close. And if she isn't…" I was going to say, *then I can protect her*, but I can't bring myself to voice it out loud. There's still too much fire in my veins when it comes to my sister. It will take a miracle for me to trust her again. To go out of my way to protect her when she already denied me once.

For *him*.

I squeeze the arms of the chair again, forcing my breathing to calm.

"Then you will have one opportunity to show favor to a fire fae," Lorelei says. "Appoint whomever you think you can trust most to travel at your side."

DOZENS UPON DOZENS OF FIRE FAE BEGIN TO GATHER BEFORE ME, SCREECHES, yips, and yowls filling the air as they settle in. Once it seems everyone has arrived, I'm surprised to find there are even more now than there were in the caves. I see two more moon dragons, a few more varieties of kitsune, an entire family of the mushroom-crustacean fae, multiple flocks of firebirds, and all the others I remember from before—fiery sprites, glowing wisps, snakes, salamanders, and desert rodents.

These are my people.

I'm still intimidated by that fact, by the unseelie ways I'm still mostly a stranger to. But I'm no longer afraid of them.

As easy as it is to get lost in my curious study of the fae, I remind myself that I must present a regal facade. By now I've grown adept at adopting the regal bearings of the fae I've come to admire—Aspen's cold stoicism, Nyxia's powerful authority, even Lorelei's intimidating stare. I wear it all like a glamour. The mask of the Fire Queen.

I sit tall in my chair and lift a hand in greeting. "Thank you for coming to our makeshift court," I say, allowing my voice to carry over the lawn. "This will be the only one like it, as the next time I hold court, it will be at Irridae Palace."

The response seems positive, if I'm reading the wagging tails, barks, and slithering bodies correctly.

I continue. "As you have been informed, Queen Estel will be transporting me to the palace tomorrow afternoon. Those of you who prefer to remain in Lunar will continue to be welcome guests under Queen Nyxia's rule. However, for those of you eager to return to your native court, you will now be safe to do so."

More wags, yips—and even a few human-like shouts of excitement—come from the crowd.

A blue wisp bobs forward, sinking into the semblance of a bow before hovering several feet before me. Her voice is light and airy. "I offer the services of my fellow wisps to guide our travelers to the palace."

A white kitsune with a blue flame over his tail pads forward. "No," he snaps at the wisp, "everyone knows you have a terrible sense of direction."

The wisp whirls around. "I do not. I am an excellent navigator. Ask any of my brethren."

"I offered the services of my tribe first," the kitsune argues.

"I witnessed no such offer."

"You weren't there!"

The two continue their argument while Lorelei leans close to my ear. "The kitsune is correct. Wisps should never be allowed to guide travelers anywhere, unless you're trying to sabotage them."

I nod to her, then address the crowd. "Be silent," I order, forcing my voice to be firm. As uncomfortable as I am with enforcing my new power, it's time to take control. "You," I say to the kitsune. "What is your name?"

"Dune, Your Majesty."

"Dune, I recall you did offer me the services of your tribe and I will grant you that honor now. You will be responsible for guiding all who wish to return to the Fire Court, taking them safely through the Star Court. You will not take the route through Solar, as they are considered my rival at present and cannot be trusted to allow safe passage."

Dune taps excitedly from paw to paw. "It will be done, Your Majesty."

The wisp pouts, bobbing low toward the ground.

"You," I say to her, "will seek out any fire fae who did not come to court tonight and relay the details they have missed."

She floats higher, her blue a shade brighter. "It isn't as fun as travel, but I will do as you say."

It takes no small effort to hide my amusement, but I remain the gracious queen as the two fae return to the crowd. Lorelei leans toward me again. "You should select your traveling companion now before anyone else tries to come forth."

"If only I knew who to choose," I whisper back, a flash of panic rising.

"Has anyone demonstrated budding loyalty?"

I scan the crowd until my eyes fall on a deep red flame. It's a fire sprite with a female figure, slightly larger than the blue wisp—about twice the length of my palm. She lets out a girlish gasp as she realizes she has my attention. Her eyes are wide as she fights to hide the squeal building in her throat, her tiny hands framing her face. I'm almost positive I recognize her, based on her unrestrained enthusiasm alone. "What is your name?" I say to her.

"Breeda, Most Esteemed and Beautiful Majesty!" Her voice trembles with her effort to keep her composure.

"Breeda, you will accompany me to the palace tomorrow afternoon. You will keep watch over me when we arrive and light any dark places." I don't actually know if there will be such dark places for her to illuminate, but I hope it sounds like an honorable job. And if she's the same sprite I remember, she'd asked to journey with me to Fire anyway.

She spins in a circle before facing me again. "Most Glorious Queen Evelyn, this is a great honor. I won't let you down."

I glance at Lorelei, seeking her approval. All she gives me is a subtle shrug and a slight grimace. "If you say so."

"You said budding loyalty," I mutter.

"That's more than loyalty," she whispers back, but I can hear the laughter in her voice. "That's more like idolatry."

She's right, but maybe that's exactly what I need. If I can hardly accept that I'm now queen of an entire court, the least I can do is surround myself with those who believe in me enough to make up for the faith I lack. And maybe—*just maybe*—my rule as queen will come to feel more than just an act.

Until then, idolatry will have to do.

8

____

The next day, I follow Nyxia down the dim obsidian halls beneath Selene Palace toward the dungeon. Shadows writhe up and down the bars of the dark cells that line the walls, each occupant hidden from view, likely cowering far away from whatever debilitating power said shadows contain.

My throat feels dry as Nyxia stops outside one of the cells—one I haven't visited since the day my sister arrived. I squeeze my hands into fists at my sides, relishing the sharp sting as my nails dig into my palms; it's a welcome distraction from the anxiety that builds in my chest at the thought of facing Amelie.

One of the dungeon guards, a wraith in flowing black robes, slides open the barred door. I uncurl my fists and shake out my hands, turning up a palm with the intention for light. After a few seconds, a pale blue flame sparks above my hand where it hovers steadily as I steel myself to enter.

"Are you sure this is wise?" Nyxia says, stopping me in my tracks before I can step inside. Her tone is laced with irritation, but I can sense what lies beneath it—fear. The Lunar Queen, the powerful alpha capable of summoning one's deepest terrors to the surface of their mind is *afraid*. But I don't think she's afraid for herself; she's worried for me.

If I wasn't feeling so on edge, I'd be honored knowing Nyxia cares enough to consider the distinct possibility that Amelie could still be working under Cobalt's orders and will kill me at her first chance.

"Isn't that how the saying goes?" I whisper to the queen. "Keep your enemies close?"

She shakes her head dismissively and steps back to lean against the wall opposite the cells. Despite her casual posture, I can see her shoulders are tensed, body poised to leap to my defense if needed.

With the comforting assurance of the Lunar Queen's protection, I enter the cell with slow, cautious steps. It isn't until I'm at the center of the tiny room that my blue light falls on a form huddled in the corner of the far wall. Amelie appears to be sleeping, curled in on herself, back facing me. My chest squeezes as a wash of guilt tugs at my heart. When I first came to see her, I hadn't noticed how sparse her accommodations were. Now I see there's no bed, no chair, no table. Nothing but a few blankets, a chamber pot, and cold obsidian from floor to ceiling. *What have I done? How could I have kept her like this?*

I reach for my inner fire to steady me, calling forth my anger. *Remember what she's done. Remember what happened to Mother.*

My guilt burns away, and I square my shoulders. With the tip of my shoe, I nudge Amelie in the shoulder. Once. Twice. Harder. "Wake up."

Finally, she stirs. Back still facing me, she shifts to her hands and knees, then sits back on her heels. She looks one way and another, then at her hands. Her shoulders begin to tremble and heave, and a wail escapes her throat.

"Amelie," I say.

She pays me no heed as she hunches forward, bringing her hands closer to her face. Her wail builds higher and higher until it's a shout. Only then does it shape into words. "What have I done?"

"Amelie!" I say again, taking her by the shoulder with my free hand and forcing her around to face me.

She tumbles to the side as she whirls around, but her eyes are still on her hands. "Whose blood is this?" The flame in my palm illuminates the terror on her face, pupils dilated as her fingers quiver before her. "What did I do?"

My gaze flashes to Nyxia, who watches my sister with a furrowed brow. "Are you doing this?"

The queen shakes her head. "Don't get me wrong," she says in her smooth voice, "her fear tastes delicious, but it needs no help being conjured forth by me. Whatever she's seeing is entirely her own making."

I have a hard time believing that, considering what I was told about the shadows blanketing the cell bars. Perhaps the human side of my sister has made her more susceptible to whatever mental powers this dungeon has over its prisoners.

I turn back to my sister and crouch before her. Again, I take her by the shoulder, shaking her forcibly until her eyes meet mine. "Amelie, wake up!"

Her chest heaves as she blinks several times, body still convulsing. A look of recognition crosses her face, followed by relief. She lunges forward, arms outstretched.

I lurch back, holding the fire in my palm between us while my free hand flies to my obsidian dagger. Before I can slide it from its sheath, I realize Amelie's arms were reaching for an embrace, not an attack. At least, that's how it appears now.

Hurt replaces the relief in her eyes, but she seems to steel herself as she rises to her feet and pins her arms at her sides. "Evie, it's you," she says, her soft, familiar voice like a knife to my heart. How many times has that voice been my comfort, my companionship? "Are you taking me somewhere?"

I consider not answering her at all, but there wouldn't be much point, since she'll find out in a matter of minutes. "Yes."

"Are you punishing me?" Her voice comes out small, but there's a flash of something unexpected on her face—anticipation, perhaps. Whatever it is, it's a profane contrast to our topic of conversation. "Am I to be executed for my crimes?"

"Not yet. Come with me."

Just as I take a step away, she retreats toward the corner. "You should give me commands first. To protect yourself from me."

A hint of the terror I saw in her eyes returns, sending a chill up my spine. "Why? I thought you said you waited out any of Cobalt's commands that could hurt me."

"I did." She moves farther into the corner, as if she could disappear into it, posture rigid. "But I don't know where you're taking me. If we're going to... if we see...if it's *him*, I..." She squeezes her eyes shut as her chest returns to heaving.

I'm rendered speechless as I take in her growing discomfort. How much of this is an act? All? None? Is this still the fear generated from the dark magic of the dungeon? Whatever the case, she's probably right. It would be stupid to let her leave this cell without commands.

"Amelie Fairfield." I let my voice fill the cell, waves of magic rolling off my tongue. "By the power of your true name, I order you not to hurt, harm, sabotage, or incapacitate me in any way."

My sister sighs, shoulders sagging as her breathing returns to normal.

With her eyes still closed, she says, "If you're going to give me more commands than that, which I suggest you do, you should provide a time period in which I'm required to obey. Cobalt renewed my orders daily."

I remember her mentioning something about that the first time we spoke after her arrival here. "Why is that?"

She opens her eyes, and from the light of my flame, I can see her pupils have returned to a normal size. "He once gave me several long-standing orders at the same time and the results were debilitating for me. A single lifelong command will do, or several short-term commands. I suggest the latter to cover all your bases, and that you extend them to twenty-four hours."

"How convenient it is that you have such specific parameters for me to go by." My tone is flat, eyes narrowed as I study her for any hint that she's manipulating me.

"If you don't believe me, you may try and do what you wish." She says it without taunting or malice. It's more like resignation that fills her toneless voice. "You can see for yourself."

"Fine," I say through my teeth. "You will follow my commands for twenty-four hours—"

She shakes her head. "In order for it to work properly, you must specify that you are altering your first command. And then provide the time frame for each separate command you give me."

I curl the fingers of my free hand into a fist, jaw clenched tight as I consider whether she's doing this to stall me or sabotage the commands. Then again, I did command her not to sabotage me. "Amelie Fairfield, by the power of your true name, I alter my first command. I demand you will not hurt, harm, sabotage, or incapacitate me in any way for the next twenty-four hours. I demand that you remain by my side and in my sight at all times for the next twenty-four hours. I demand that you not hurt, harm, sabotage, or incapacitate anyone I consider a friend, ally, or subject for the next twenty-four hours." I pause, searching my mind for any other potential threats to protect against. "And you will not attempt to run away or communicate with anyone I consider an adversary, threat, or enemy for the next twenty-four hours."

"As you think of more, you may add them throughout the day," Amelie says.

I give her a pointed look. "Thanks so much for your permission," I say with venom, then turn on my heel. We exit the cell, Amelie remaining close to my side. Nyxia throws my sister a scowl, then starts down the dungeon hall. We follow in her wake, the wraith-guard trailing close behind.

After a few minutes of silence, Amelie edges closer to me. My body goes on high alert, fire flooding my veins as I prepare for any attack. "Don't hate me, Evie," she whispers to me. "I hope you can come to trust me again."

Her fingertips brush against my palm, and she inches closer, curling her fingers around mine. I flinch at the touch, the feel of her flesh conjuring images of Mother's hands grasping mine through the bars of her cell at the Spire. A bullet. Blood. Flames. A shiver of revulsion runs through me, and I snatch my fingers away to fold my hands at my waist. I can't bring myself to meet her eyes as I say coldly, "So do I."

            9
         ——————————

After we leave the dungeon, I allow Amelie a short visit to the moon baths. My eyes don't leave her as she washes away the grime of her captivity, wrings the dirt from her hair, and attempts to smooth her matted tresses. I try not to focus on how her shade of copper looks so much like Mother's. Instead, I attune myself to the potential threat she poses.

Every muscle in my body is tensed, poised for attack. Part of me expects my sister will whirl around to face me wearing the head of her selkie skin— even though I know the skin is gone; Nyxia informed me it was disposed of as soon as Amelie arrived at Selene Palace. Still, I don't know if I'll ever forget the way she looked at me on the balcony at Bircharbor Palace, the way she told me she didn't want my protection, the way she pulled the sealskin over her face and leapt off the rail and into the waves below, leaving me for *Cobalt.*

His name is like a curse, even in my thoughts.

I force the memories from my mind, tapping my foot impatiently for her to hurry up. Once she's done taking her sweet time, Amelie changes into a simple black gown borrowed from Nyxia, one to match my own plain, gauzy black dress. Considering our next destination will likely host temperatures hotter than I've ever felt before, I figure we should dress appropriately in simple, lightweight attire.

After she's dressed, I lead us to the throne room. That's when my stomach starts to roil. In a matter of minutes, I'll be transported to a new court. A new palace. My new home. The concept is still impossible for me to reconcile.

For the love of iron, I own a *palace!*

As we enter the throne room, I see everyone else has already gathered. Aspen grins at me, and my lips tug upward to mirror his, warmth stirring inside my chest. With all the arrangements that needed to be made last night, my mate and I have yet to finish what we started in this very room. I blush as my gaze snags on the table at the edge of my periphery.

I missed you last night, he says through the Bond, and with it pulses his desire. His eyes flicker to the figure at my side, and all heat is extinguished from his expression, gaze turning to steel. The same goes for Foxglove and Lorelei, who'd been engaged in animated conversation until we walked in.

I hazard a glance at Amelie, watching her face brighten when she sees her former fae friends. She opens her mouth as if to speak, only to shrink in on herself as Lorelei shoots her a seething glare. I almost feel bad for my sister. Almost.

A girlish squeal cuts through the tension in the room as a red flame flutters over to me. "Your Most Incredible and Beautiful Majesty," Breeda says, folding into a bow before spinning in a circle. "I am so honored to serve you."

"I am grateful to have you at my side."

Her tiny mouth stretches into a wide smile, and she floats above my shoulder between me and Amelie as I join the others. Aspen stands at my other side and Queen Estel stands next to him. Two fae I recognize as Aspen's guards flank the group. Even Nyxia is here, although I know she won't be traveling with us.

"We should make haste," Estel says. "I want us to arrive well before the Renounced expect me to come to them. Once they realize I have shifted my allegiance, I don't know what they will do. We must all be on alert for any retaliation."

"They would be idiots to retaliate," Aspen says. "They've already lost Spring. Once they realize they no longer have Star, they'll see they're outnumbered."

"That may be the case," Estel says, "but they find it all too easy to replace those who've joined the Alpha Alliance with pretender kings and queens."

"Those pretenders have yet to prove competence or power," Nyxia says, lifting her chin.

While that may be true, there's an unvoiced concern I can't help but confront. What if Queen Estel can't be trusted? What better way to sabotage a threat to the Renounced than this? Our enemies could be waiting exactly where she takes us. She might not take us to Irridae Palace at all, but to a nest of blades and adversaries. Then it would be easy to overpower me and Aspen, taking out two rulers at once. My heart races at the terrifying thought.

But fae can't lie, I remind myself, trying to steel my nerves. I pat the dagger at my waist for good measure, only this time, I wish it were iron like my old one. Iron, at least, would work on my enemies amongst the Renounced. Like Dahlia. Cobalt. Maybe even Estel.

That's when another nagging thought creeps up on me. There *is* a way for fae to lie. Cobalt discovered it. What if that's Amelie's true purpose? What if she gave a piece of herself to more than just him? What if she made similar bargains with all the Renounced and gave them the ability to lie?

Aspen's voice comes through the Bond, shocking me from my racing thoughts. *What's going on in that head of yours?*

I consider brushing him off, but if there's a chance I'm right...

With a sigh, I quickly relay my fears through our Bond. *Do you think it's possible?* I ask.

I watch his brow wrinkle as he considers the question. Part of me expects him to tell me I'm just being paranoid. If anyone knows about being a paranoid ruler, it's him. But instead of dismissing my concerns, he turns to Estel, interrupting her conversation with Nyxia. "Queen Estel, do you promise you are taking us to Irridae Palace and that no Renounced know of this plan?"

Silence falls over the throne room, a blanket of unease settling over us. The particles on the shimmering queen's face disperse and shift into a frown, but only for a moment. With grace, she faces my mate. "I promise I am taking you, your mate, and your companions straight to Irridae Palace and that none of the Renounced know of this. I promise my allegiance is to the Alpha Alliance."

Aspen gives her a nod of respect. "Thank you."

A weight slides off my shoulders. I remember Cobalt confessing that he was still bound by direct promises, even with the power to lie. That should make me feel better. Shouldn't it?

Estel's gaze falls on me. "Are you ready?"

I swallow hard, shoulders tense. "Yes."

Queen Nyxia takes a step away from our gathering. "Good luck claiming your new palace," she says to me. "Try not to get yourself killed if things go badly, all right? If there really is a stash of iron weapons at Irridae, we need you alive to defend it."

I give her a wry smile. "I'll try not to inconvenience you with my death."

We exchange nods, and I watch as Nyxia makes her way to the door of the throne room. There I see a slim figure with silver hair leaning against the doorframe. Franco. The sight of him warms my heart, and I flash him a smile. He winks at me, then turns and enters the hall at his sister's side.

I return my attention to my companions, and Estel instructs us to form a circle around her. Breeda can barely contain her squeal of excitement, while Amelie trembles next to me, eyes on her feet.

Estel opens her shimmering palm, and a silver, hexagonal disc appears over it. With a flick of her thumb, two halves separate on a hinge. One half appears to be nothing more than a cover while the other is inlaid with several facets of quartz surrounding a small orb of golden light at the center. The light is so bright it looks like a miniature star. Estel's eyes meet mine. "This is the Chariot. It will take us to your palace."

I return my gaze to the disc, hardly able to blink. I'm so fascinated by what I see. *That's* the mysterious Chariot Lorelei told me about? That tiny object is a device to allow instantaneous travel? As I continue to stare at it, sifting through all the scientific knowledge I have to explain how even the concept alone could possibly work, the light at the center begins to glow brighter and brighter, spanning in a radius until it surrounds us all. Then it grows taller, encompassing us in a bright golden bubble.

The skin prickles up the back of my neck, and I'm forced to admit this goes beyond everything I know about science. It's beyond everything I know about *magic*, even. This is so unlike the magic of the axis line. There, the transition is subtle, imperceptible. Here, the power at work is unmistakable. The light seems to vibrate to my very core, humming in my bones as the throne room disappears, swallowed by the light. The humming increases, and for a moment I think it will tear me apart, as surely, I am no longer a solid being. Am I?

And then it's gone.

The golden light is absorbed back into the tiny orb, and Estel closes the cover over it. The next thing I'm aware of is a stifling warmth, a heat unlike anything I've felt before. It's different from the scorching glow of my fire; this comes from all sides with a weight that immediately makes sweat bead at my brow.

"We're here," Estel says.

Aspen's guards break from the group, unsheathing their swords as they flank us to investigate our environment. I turn in a slow circle, hand on the hilt of my dagger as I eye an enormous courtyard surrounded by a tall sandstone wall. The sun beats high overhead, blindingly bright with its glow. Peaks of mountains in shades of brown and gold hover in the distance far beyond the wall while fluffy green palms and spiky cacti decorate the sandy landscape.

Next, my attention turns to what's inside the walls of the courtyard, glimpsing the perfect symmetry spread before me. Two rows of palms stand sentinel along each side of the courtyard, lining two rectangular, crystal-blue ponds that flank a red tile walkway—and that's when I see what the walkway leads to.

A set of immense blue double doors decorated in gold filigree await at the opposite end of the tile floor, surrounded by a breathtaking palace that spans from one side of the wall to the other. Its base is of brown sandstone that gives way to slender white towers ringed with circular balconies. Some towers are peaked with tiled turrets while others end in bulbous white marble domes. Three larger domes are clustered over the center portion of the palace, each carved with intricate flames and floral designs.

My mouth falls open as I study the structure. If I thought Bircharbor and Selene were incredible feats of architecture, this puts them both to shame. I've never seen such beauty, such craftsmanship that defies the norms and seems to favor art over function. "It's beautiful," I say under my breath, shoulders relaxing as my hand finally leaves my dagger.

Amelie whirls to face me. "I've never seen anything like it!" Her expression is so bright, so much like the sister I grew up with, that I forget for a moment the tension between us. Without realizing it, my grin has mirrored hers, and I'm about to grasp her hands excitedly in mine.

That's when I remember the wall I must keep firmly in place. I can't grow lax in my trust, not until I know the truth about her.

I clench my fingers into fists and avert my gaze, returning my attention to the palace. From the corner of my eye, I see Amelie lower her head, her disappointment at my rejection so palpable, it makes my heart clench.

Remember what she did to Mother, I repeat in my head, allowing my fire to replace my guilt.

A flicker of red hovers at my shoulder, and Breeda lets out a squeal. "We're home, Your Majesty! Do you just totally and completely love it?"

I stand tall and give her what I hope to be a regal and composed nod. "It's quite adequate."

Aspen snickers at my poorly concealed awe, and my lips curl into a smirk. He opens his mouth to speak, but movement near the front doors of the palace catches my eye. The others notice too, and silence falls over our group as one of the doors swings open.

Aspen's soldiers rush to the front of our retinue, standing between us and whatever is coming out to greet us.

Once the door opens fully, a bronze haze funnels outside. All I see is a vicious face and two gigantic hands thrusting forward before everything is replaced with a cloud of dust and sand. It builds before the door, growing higher, higher, blocking out the light of the sun.

Then it speeds straight for us.

10

I close my eyes and spin away from the dust cloud as it crashes into me. Gasping for breath, I fall to my knees, feeling sand barrel into my back. My first thought is that I was right. This really is a trap. Queen Estel betrayed us after all.

But it's her voice I hear, shouting over the din of my companions' coughs and the swirling of dust and sand beating relentlessly overhead. At first, her words are incoherent, but then I hear, "Stop! Queen Evelyn of Fire is here to claim Irridae Palace. Stand down before your queen!"

To my surprise, the dust storm abates. Once I no longer feel the sand pelting me, I rise to my feet, coughing through gasping breaths. I try to open my eyes, but grit stings them so badly, I dare not attempt to rub it away for fear I'll simply irritate my eyes further. Instead, I allow my tears to well, allow them to push the grains away. But it's no use. There's too much—

I'm struck by a sudden splash of water that drenches me from head to toe. From the gasps I hear around me, I take it I'm not the only one. When I'm finally able to open my eyes, it's to Aspen's face, concern written in the crease between his brows as he takes me by the shoulders. His blue-black hair hangs limp around his antlers, dripping brown, sandy water.

"Are you all right?" he asks.

I nod. "What happened? Where did the water come from?" I glance around us. Everyone but Estel and Breeda—who were apparently immune to the attack, likely due to their less-corporeal forms—are covered in a mixture of sand and water. Amelie is slumped on the ground, blinking rapidly while Foxglove and Lorelei take turns brushing debris off each other's faces.

"I pulled water from the ponds to clear the dust," he says. "Can you see?"

"Yes," I say, looking from him to the two ponds flanking the palace, a sense of awe washing over me. Even though I know my mate holds power over water, I've never seen him use it before. It's a chilling reminder that there's still much about him I don't know.

"Which one of you is this supposed queen?" a voice calls out from near the palace, filling the courtyard with its deep, echoing resonance. I face it, finding Aspen's guards already edging forward, swords pointed at the figure standing before the doors. He wears no shirt, only loose, brown trousers that reveal a wide torso, broad shoulders, and thick arms roped with muscle. His skin is a deep bronze, his eyes dark and deep set below thick black brows. Strands of long, wavy black hair brush his shoulders. From this distance, I can't tell exactly how tall he is, but he appears even taller than Aspen.

Foxglove nearly trips in his haste to rise to his feet, grasping Lorelei's wrist for balance. "For the love of oak and ivy," he mutters, his tone full of fear...or is it awe?

I take a few hesitant steps forward, squaring my shoulders as I force myself into as regal a posture as I can, despite how haggard I'm sure the dust storm has made me. "I am Queen Evelyn of Fire."

The domineering fae crosses his arms over his chest. "Is that so?"

"Who is he?" I ask, quiet enough so only my companions can hear.

"He's a djinn," Lorelei says.

"He's quite angry," adds Breeda.

As one of the guards creeps forward, the djinn's face clouds over with a snarl and he lifts his hands. Dust and sand begin to rise at his feet.

Foxglove whirls toward me and Aspen. "Tell the guards to stand down or he's going to attack again."

"Then why should they stand down?" Aspen says through his teeth.

Foxglove wrings his hands. "He's clearly Bonded to the palace and trying to protect it. We must speak with him."

Two orbs of dust have gathered in the djinn's hands and are growing larger by the second. His eyes flash from one guard to the other.

Aspen lets out a grumble, then shouts at his guards, "Stand down!"

The guards falter, freezing in place. The djinn doesn't lower his arms, keeping the enormous orbs of sand hovering over his palms.

Foxglove swallows hard. "I'll go speak with him."

Lorelei whips her head toward her friend, burning him with a glare. "Why you? I'm her ambassador. I should speak with him."

He flushes. "My dearest Lorelei, while I respect your new position and am confident in your abilities, this situation must be handled with care."

She puts her hands on her hips. "What's that supposed to mean?"

"You aren't the friendliest with strangers," he says with a grimace.

She pops a hip to the side, narrowing her eyes. "As ambassador, I will be...*friendly*...just fine."

Foxglove raises a brow. "Really? Can you honestly say you're planning on going up to the very male who just attempted an attack on your queen and speak to him with courtesy and calm?"

The two are locked in an icy standoff, neither saying another word. For a moment, I worry my decision to appoint Lorelei as my ambassador may have created an unforeseen complication—pitting the two friends against one another. I'm about to intervene when Lorelei's lips pull into a smirk. "Good point."

Foxglove nods triumphantly. "Well, then—"

"Actually, I should be the one to speak with him," says Breeda, bobbing toward foxglove. "I am a fellow fire fae. He'll listen to me."

Before another argument can erupt, I say, "You both should go. Now." I then raise my voice and address the djinn. "I am sending an ambassador and a fire sprite to speak with you in a peaceful exchange of words."

For a tense stretch of silence, the djinn makes no move to lower his threatening orbs of sand. Then finally, he returns his arms to cross his chest and the sand crashes to his feet. "Very well."

Foxglove sighs and removes his spectacles, rubbing them on his burgundy jacket before replacing them. His efforts seem to have done nothing but smear a layer of dust over the lenses. With trembling fingers, he runs his hands through his damp, dirty, brown tresses, which only makes his hair stick up at odd angles. "How do I look?"

The hope in his eyes catches me off guard. "You look..."

"Flustered," Aspen finishes for me and grunts a laugh.

"Well, do you see his arms?" Foxglove says. "He could completely crush me in them." Despite his words, I'm almost certain there's wistful excitement in his eyes, not terror.

Realization settles over me; I've seen that expression before. "You fancy the djinn, don't you?"

Foxglove blushes, a sheepish grin tugging his lips.

"But I thought you fancied Franco."

He waves a dismissive hand. "Forget Franco."

"A motto to live by," Aspen mutters with a smirk.

I roll my eyes. "Just go."

Foxglove flashes me an anxious smile, then he and Breeda begin their slow approach toward the djinn, stopping several feet from him and the palace steps. Breeda speaks first. "Your Most Large and Powerful Servant of Irridae Palace, I represent your new master, Queen Evelyn of Fire."

Foxglove takes a hesitant step forward. "You may not have heard, but Queen Evelyn has defeated the former King Ustrin. She has been blessed by the All of All and has come to claim the palace that is hers by right."

The djinn's eyes flash over their heads to pin me beneath his stare. "I will allow her to approach. If she truly is the new Queen of Fire, she may take my hand and let the palace decide the validity of her claim. If she is unworthy of the palace, she will burst into flame and burn until her bones are nothing but ash."

I suppress a shudder at the not-so-veiled threat. The blood leaves my face as I consider all possible scenarios. What kind of magic is at work here? Is it the magic of the All of All? Will I once again receive the proper blessing? Or is this some trick, some vile defense Ustrin had woven into the palace should his reign fall? Worse than that is the thought that the magic he speaks of is real and I will be deemed unworthy. Ever since I defeated the Fire King, part of me keeps waiting for everything to blow up in my face. For my people to turn on me, for them to realize I'm just a pathetic human—

Relax, Evie. Aspen's voice comes through the Bond like an invisible caress. It's then I realize how tense I've grown, my jaw clenched and hands balled into painfully tight fists. *You will pass this test. Just like you did in the Twelfth Court.*

I can only hope he's right, that he understands whatever ritual I'm about to participate in. With a deep breath, I call out to the djinn. "I will take your hand and prove to you my right. Allow me to approach with my guards and companions."

"Very good," he says. "The easier for me to kill them should you prove to be false."

I purse my lips to hide my snarl. *No, the easier for them to kill you should you make one wrong move against me,* I think to myself.

As we make our way to join Foxglove and Breeda, I notice how Amelie lags behind, nearly dragging her feet with every step, eyes wide with fear. She's clearly struggling against the compulsion of my command that keeps her at my side at all times. In the presence of our foe, I can hardly blame her. Is this proof that my commands truly work as she claimed they would?

We pause once we reach the palace steps, and I make my way to the front of the retinue, the two guards crouched in defensive postures just a step behind me.

The djinn extends his hand. "Place your palm in mine."

I meet his eyes, summoning all the confidence I can muster. Now that we're close, I can see he is in fact nearly a head taller than Aspen, which places him significantly taller than me. I try not to notice the sheen of his bronze skin over his rippling muscles as I grasp his enormous hand.

At the touch of his flesh on mine, fire roars through my blood, rushing down my arms, my legs. Pink, purple, and aqua flames lap over my skin, adding to the unbearable heat from the sun. My flames, however, don't scorch me. Not like they did when Aspen carried me from the Spire, resulting in me burning the both of us in my unrelenting rage. This time, they are nothing but a warm glow.

My eyes remain locked on the djinn's, and his widen as my flames grow higher, extending toward him.

In one swift move, the djinn drops my hand and falls to his knees before me.

My flames extinguish, leaving me feeling invigorated and strong.

The djinn lifts his head to find my gaze. "Forgive me, my queen. My name is Fehr, and I am your humble servant. Welcome home."

11

———————

My new home is even more breathtaking on the inside than it was on the outside.

Fehr leads us through the entrance hall to a grand foyer with towering ceilings and thick marble columns. The walls are made of sandstone interspersed with white marble panels carved with as much intricate detail as you'd expect from a painting or a tapestry.

"Soooo pretty," Breeda squeals, hands framing her tiny face as she flits from one wall to the next.

Our footsteps echo as we make our way across the tile floors. The hollow reverberations sing of how empty the palace is. There's no bustle of busy servants, no mutterings from guests and residents.

It's just like the moon dragons had reported; there's no one here.

Fehr comes up alongside me. "I pray you forgive me for the attack. I will take any punishment you see fit." His rich baritone is devoid of fear or remorse. In fact, I'm almost positive there's a hint of indignation laced into his words, as if he's speaking out of rote necessity.

I suppose I can't blame him for neither trusting nor liking me. The feeling is mutual. Distrust aside, logic has me recalling Foxglove's assumption regarding the djinn's motives. I adopt a formal bearing as I say, "I assume your actions were taken to protect Irridae Palace."

"You are correct. I was Bonded to the palace as its lifelong steward long ago by King Caleos."

A ripple of surprise runs through me at the mention of my grandfather. "Why?"

"A punishment for my darkest deeds. A way to control my power." That hint of resentment returns, clearer now, but it doesn't linger. "I am loyal to the palace and am bound to serve the one who rules it. As steward, all household matters of importance may be given to me."

"And how does the palace know who the true ruler should be?" I can't help but think of the pretender king the Renounced had planned to send here. Would he have passed the test? Or burned to a crisp?

Fehr lifts his chin, expression turning haughty as he eyes me with a condescending smirk. "It is simply the palace's magic, Your Majesty. Ever mysterious, even to me." The last part is said somewhat under his breath, revealing more of his poorly hidden disdain. It's clear he's surprised I passed the test. Then again, so am I.

We reach the end of the foyer where it opens to an enormous atrium. At the center is a large circular table carved from fiery pink, orange, and red sunstone. On each side of the table are wide staircases; one leads to the upper levels of the palace while the other descends below. Several halls branch off from here, leading who knows where.

Aspen's hand brushes my arm. *Now that's an adequate table,* he relays to me.

I press my lips tight to hide my grin and wonder if my sudden blush is visible through the layer of grime that coats my cheeks.

"Do you know of a stash of iron weapons hidden within the palace?" Estel asks, facing Fehr.

Fehr's eyes narrow with suspicion, his expression hard as he assesses the Star Queen. "I do not answer to you."

I'm about to tell him it's all right, that he may answer the question. But again, I'm plagued with doubt. Estel gave us our promise that she is on our side, but now that I've experienced the trial required to enter the palace, I wonder if the Renounced needed me to come here, to reopen the palace, to show someone where the weapons stash is so they could be led straight to it.

I shudder, as Amelie's proximity feels heavy. What if Lorelei was right? What if *this* is why my sister is here?

"It's all right," Estel says, shaking me from my thoughts. "I will ask you something else. Will you protect Queen Evelyn and the palace until sufficient guards and household staff can be appointed?"

Fehr's jaw shifts back and forth, hand flying momentarily to his chest before he composes himself. "I will protect the queen and Irridae with my life now and even after she has proper guards. It is my duty, which is not to be questioned."

Breeda flashes the djinn a scowl, then mirrors his posture. "I will guard Our Most Beautiful Queen Evelyn as well. None will dare creep upon her while my light shines."

Estel's face shifts and rearranges into a look of amusement, then settles on a more serious expression. "I must return to my court in case there's any retaliation from the Renounced. I will return tomorrow with more of King Aspen's guards."

I furrow my brow, the thought of retaliation sending a shiver up my spine. What happens if our enemies retaliate *here*? Can Fehr truly protect us? As begrudging as he obviously is to serve me, his declaration of loyalty does little to strengthen my confidence in him. My only consolation is that what little tales I've heard about djinn have always told of their immense power. "Must you wait until tomorrow to bring more guards?"

Estel opens her palm, the silver disc that brought us here flashing beneath the light streaming in from the high windows of the atrium. "The Chariot only works twice before it must be charged by starlight. I've already used it once, which means I can only use it to take me to my palace."

It's strange that something so powerful would require a period of rest. Then again, I suppose even the strongest magic must have its limits. If the fae could travel through time and space at will and in unlimited quantity... the power is almost too incredible to imagine. The fae would be unstoppable.

Perhaps Estel's device was created with limitations on purpose.

The hair rises on the back of my neck at the thought. I hope, despite my doubt and suspicions, the powerful Star Queen truly is on our side. I'd hate to see her power in the hands of our enemies.

Once Estel leaves, I order Amelie to remain with the guards while I speak with Fehr out of earshot. I square my shoulders and force myself to ignore the way he narrows his eyes when he looks at me. "About the question Queen Estel asked," I say, keeping my voice level. "I need to know that answer myself. Is there an iron weapons stash?"

His lips curl in disgust at the mention of iron. "There is a vile room in the lowermost level of the palace, below the dungeon. It reeks of iron, strong enough to keep prisoners weak, although I've never been able to get close enough to the room to witness what is inside."

"Can you take us to it?" My eyes flash toward my sister, and I add, "After stopping at the dungeon first, perhaps?"

"It will be done," he says with a low bow.

We rejoin the others and Fehr leads us down one of the staircases. The lower we go, the cooler the temperatures become as open windows disappear and are replaced with solid mud-brick walls. Fehr conjures an orange flame over his palm to light our way, but it begins to shrink the farther down we go. His pace, too, starts to slow, and the breaths of my companions grow ragged.

I glance at my mate, seeing the sheen of sweat that now covers his brow. Even with only the light of Fehr's flame, I can tell he's grown pale. However, the others seem to be faring far worse—Breeda has dulled to a pale pink glow, the guards struggle to maintain their postures, Foxglove looks like he's on the verge of retching, and Lorelei appears worse than she did when Mr. Meeks used iron teacups against us. It seems only Amelie and I are immune to the iron we must surely be nearing.

The staircase opens to a narrow hall, where the mud-brick walls melt into a more natural formation, with curved walls pocked with tiny holes, like the lava caves I've only seen documented in encyclopedic sketches. As we leave the final stair to enter the hall, my companions slow to a halt. Fehr's flame all but sputters out. I open my palm and ignite my own light, blanketing us in a blue glow and revealing rows and rows of barred caverns. This must be the dungeon.

I turn toward the djinn, who sags against the uneven wall, glaring into the corridor. "Are there any prisoners currently kept here?" I ask.

"All were expelled along with the household," he says, voice hoarse. His eyes flick from me to Breeda, and his expression softens for the first time. "Although I doubt you would consider many of them a danger, if you keep company with the unseelie. Most were like her. Sprites. Wisps. Any who refused to take seelie form at his command."

My eyes widen. "He kept unseelie fae down here?" Fehr nods, and I step farther into the hall to examine the cells. Each room is small and rounded, providing no flat surface to lie down, not to mention the rough texture of the curved walls. The doors and bars of the cells are of dark green malachite. I see no additional defenses like Lunar's dungeons, no dangerous enchantments or writhing shadows. Then again, considering the degrading state of my companions, I doubt any added protections were needed with an iron store so close.

Fehr comes up beside me, his steps slow and lagging. "Was there a reason you wanted to see the dungeon first?"

I look over my shoulder where Amelie stands nearby. Her head is lowered, but she eyes the cells, shoulders trembling. When she suddenly lifts her head and meets my gaze, her expression goes slack. She gives me a subtle nod, as if to relay her resigned acceptance over why we're here.

I look from her to the cell, hating the way my heart lurches at the thought of her inside that cramped room, unable to stretch out or lie down. But why do I care? *Remember what she's done. Remember Mother.* Fire floods my veins, and I know I must make the command. If the commands truly work, then she can't leave my side unless I give the order. I open my mouth to do just that, but I stop myself as a slew of questions invades my mind. What if she can easily break free? What if there's an unseen tunnel hidden behind the cells, like the ones leading from the coral caves at Bircharbor? What if leaving her alone is exactly the opportunity she needs to escape?

My sister isn't weakened by iron, so if there's a way out, she can find it.

Evie, Aspen says into my mind, cutting through the chaos of my thoughts. His voice comes across barely louder than a whisper, expressing just how weakened he's becoming. *You don't have to leave her in there if you aren't comfortable with it.*

I bristle at that, even though I know my irritation isn't meant for him. I'm more annoyed at myself for wearing my internal debate so clearly that he could see it.

I sense Aspen's approaching presence before I feel the brush of his hand on my lower back. It soothes me, steadies my mind.

I turn to Fehr. "Thank you for showing me the dungeon. I think it will serve me quite well should anyone give me a reason to utilize it." I enunciate this last part, flashing my sister a warning glare.

Her eyes widen, and I'm not sure if it's from fear or surprise that I'm not locking her up. I hold her gaze, letting the veiled threat hang heavy between us so she understands what I'm trying to convey. I'll give her a chance to prove me wrong, but I'll be watching her every move, waiting for the moment she tries to betray me. And if she does, I'll be ready.

Fire burns inside me, so hot it helps drown out the hidden truth I refuse to acknowledge—that maybe I'm not keeping her close just to catch her in the act of betraying me. Maybe I'm doing it because, somewhere deep down, I want to trust her.

~

THE FIRST TEST OF THE STRENGTH OF MY COMMANDS COMES WHEN I ORDER
Amelie to remain in the dungeon hall with the guards and Breeda while the
rest of us make our way downstairs. Foxglove and Lorelei only make it to the
bottom of the final stair before the scent of iron overcomes them. Fehr's
flame has completely extinguished, leaving only my blue fire to light our
way as the djinn, Aspen, and I make our way down the black hall. Our pace
is agonizingly slow, considering the weakened state of my two companions,
and only adds to the eerie quality of our surroundings. The hall is made of
the same volcanic rock as the dungeon, but there are no caverns or corridors
along the way. There's nothing but a winding black tunnel that makes my
skin prickle amidst its eerie quiet.

"You're sure it's at the end of this hall?" I ask, my whispered voice
creating an unsettling echo.

"Like I said, I've never been able to get close enough to see it for myself."
Fehr's voice is even weaker than it was upstairs, for once devoid of its bitter
edge. "I've glimpsed a door though. Also, I know this tunnel is where Ustrin
often took his human allies."

His human allies must refer to Mr. Duveau, who I'm sure is responsible
for providing these weapons in the first place. They'd formed a secret truce,
one I'm not sure I entirely understand. They both seemed united by the
need to maintain the treaty for the sole reason of hoarding the power it gave
them. What exactly had they bargained?

With a grunt, Aspen doubles over. My heart races as I whirl toward him
and bring my free hand to his cheek. A sheen of sweat coats his entire face,
expression twisted in agony. My throat feels tight, and a sudden stab of pain
comes through the Bond, pain that isn't mine. "I'm sorry," I whisper,
although I'm not sure what I'm apologizing for. He insisted on coming with
me as far as he could, and we agreed it's imperative to confirm the location
of the weapons stash.

"It's all right," he says with a gasp. "This is as far as I can go."

"I won't be able to go much farther either," Fehr says, "but I can at least
make it to the point where I can see the door."

A rush of fear goes through me at the thought of approaching the end of
a dark tunnel alone. All I can do is seek my inner fire to burn away my trepidation and hope Ustrin hadn't left me a trap to waltz into.

Fehr and I continue on farther down until he too doubles over and sags against the wall. With one hand grasping his chest, the other points down the hall. "You should see it," he mutters. "The door."

With a deep breath, I take a step away from the djinn and hold out my ball of flame. There's only a slight bend in the tunnel, and as my eyes adjust, I see the edge of something flat and metallic. With the door in sight, I hurry forward. Just like Fehr had assumed, the tunnel ends in an enormous wooden door. The metal I'd glimpsed is a bar that crosses it. I slow my steps as I approach, eyes flashing left and right for any sign of hidden threats. Finally, the door is within reach.

I brace my free hand beneath the bar, which appears to be solid iron, and lift.

Nothing.

I touch my flame to the ground, willing it to remain in place. Luckily, it obeys, illuminating the door as I struggle to lift the bar with both hands now.

It doesn't even budge.

With a grumble, I retrieve my flame and storm away from the door.

"Well, that was disappointing," I say to Fehr once I reach him. "The door is barred with iron and I'm the only one who can get close enough." Well, aside from Amelie, of course, but I don't say so. Besides, I'm not even sure the both of us could lift it together if we tried. "How was Ustrin able to use this room at all?"

"His human allies were the only ones who could enter the room itself," he says, pushing off the wall to right himself on unsteady feet. "I believe his use of these weapons was contingent upon compliance with them."

That explains why Ustrin only used iron weapons twice, to my knowledge. At least this serves as proof that none of the Renounced could reach the weapons room. If not even Aspen and a powerful djinn can, then I doubt there's any fae alive that could fare much better.

Then again, the Renounced aren't our only enemies, and our other foes have no problem with iron.

12

———————

Night has fallen by the time we make it back to the atrium upstairs. Fehr snaps his fingers, bringing orbs of light over the sconces on the walls and throwing the area under a warm glow. The color seems to be coming back to my fae companions' faces, although the mood is significantly subdued. Conversation shifts to talk of meals, baths, and bedroom accommodations, which Fehr leaves to arrange for us. Breeda trails after him, insisting she must have final say over the best room for me.

As our guards move to stand watch at opposite ends of the atrium, and Foxglove and Lorelei leave us to lounge by one of the windows, I realize this is the first opportunity I've had all day to be somewhat alone with Aspen. As if he can sense my thoughts, he catches my eye with a grin. It pains me to see the effort he puts into the expression after so much strength was expended downstairs. I'm only glad the iron store doesn't affect him or my friends up here.

"Amelie," I say with the power of her name, "I allow you to leave me momentarily, only to remain where you are until I return to you, whereupon your order to remain at my side will recommence."

She nods, eyes downcast, and I take Aspen's fingers in mine. We make our way to stand by the table near the stairs, which is far enough from the others that we can speak privately. He faces me, bringing a hand to my cheek and brushing a thumb along my jaw. "What do you think of your new home?"

My heart feels warm as I luxuriate in the feel of his simple touch. Placing my hands on his waist, I tilt my head to meet his eyes. "I think it's only home because you're here."

He brings both hands to my face, cupping my cheeks. "I am here. For everything you need, the good and the bad."

For some reason, his words stir shame inside me as I recall how easily he saw through my inner turmoil over keeping Amelie in the dungeon. It also brings to mind something I hadn't previously thought of, something that makes my heart sink. And once again, he must be able to see my mood written clearly over my face.

"What is it?" he asks, brow furrowed.

"I can't stay with you tonight," I say with a grumble.

His concern melts off his face, replaced with a look of understanding. "You want to stay with your sister."

I groan. "I don't *want* to at all, but I should. At least tonight. I doubt I'll be able to sleep no matter where she is in the palace, not until I'm certain the commands will hold her in place. But tonight I want to keep her in plain sight."

"I understand."

"Is that because you're just as paranoid as I am?" I say with a teasing grin.

"No, it's because you're clearly just as smart as I am." His tone is smug, reminding me of how I perceived him when we first met. It's funny how easy it is to see through it now, how that vulnerable side of him is never far below the surface anymore.

"Your Majesty!" Breeda shouts, becoming a stream of red as she circles me and my mate.

I force myself not to roll my eyes in irritation as I separate from Aspen. "Yes, Breeda?"

She stops her circling to hover in the air before me. "You will never believe how beautiful the room I've picked for you is. It's the royal chamber!" Her words dissolve into a delighted squeal.

Fehr steps onto the landing from one of the staircases and offers a bow. "The bathing chambers and bedrooms are prepared."

"Ugh, delightful," Foxglove says as he and Lorelei saunter up to join us. "I haven't wanted a bath so badly in my life."

Fehr's eyes rove Foxglove as if seeing him for the first time. Beneath the djinn's stare, Foxglove blushes and looks sheepishly at his feet. I can almost hear the giggle he's sure to be suppressing.

"What about clothes?" Amelie's voice is so small and unexpected, it takes me a moment to realize she'd spoken. She remains where I left her, lifting the hem of her filthy black skirt, a grimace twisting her lips. Considering today is the first she's been allowed a bath and change of clothing after a week in a dungeon, I'm surprised she even cares. Then again, her preoccupation with fashion is so befitting the Amelie I once loved that my chest tightens.

I tear my eyes from my sister and return my gaze to the djinn. "Yes, Fehr, we will all require clean clothes, especially ones appropriate for this climate."

"In each bathing chamber, you will find towels and robes to change into," he says. "While you bathe, I will ensure each room is properly stocked with clothing. However, King Ustrin kept no concubines or female mates of status. There likely won't be much suitable for a queen."

"It will have to do," I say. Unlike Amelie, I have never been overly concerned with style, although that has changed much since coming to Faerwyvae.

"For now," Aspen adds, as if he finds my response lacking. "Once the new household staff has been appointed, see to it that Queen Evelyn has a royal wardrobe made up at once."

Fehr's gaze slides slowly from me to Aspen. "Am I to listen to his orders, Your Majesty?"

Aspen tenses, hands clenching into fists, but says nothing in reply.

"Yes," I say to Fehr. "King Aspen is my mate. His household will arrive here shortly, and you will allow them entrance onto the palace grounds. Same goes for the fire fae who will arrive from Lunar."

"Very well," Fehr says, expression hard as he bows to Aspen. "I will see that Queen Evelyn's wardrobe is made a priority by the palace seamstress. Shall I show you your rooms now?"

"Give me one more moment to speak with my mate."

Without a word, he returns to the bottom staircase, where Foxglove and Lorelei join him. Even Breeda seems to get the hint and joins the others, where they spark up casual conversation. All but Fehr, that is, who stands composed and slightly away from the group, unaware of how Foxglove's eyes flicker admiringly at him every few seconds.

I turn my attention back to Aspen. "I'll miss you tonight," I whisper. "I'll stay in a guest room with my sister. You take the royal chamber—"

"Just like that?" His lips pull into a devious smirk, making my stomach flip. "The woman who all but kicked me out of my own bedroom the night we became mates is forfeiting her right to the royal chamber?"

I put my hands on my hips, lips quirking up at the corners. "Were you hoping for a fight?"

"Why would I expect anything less? Especially when our last one ended so favorably."

Heat stirs in my core, and I tilt my head to the side. "Maybe I will fight you for the royal chamber after all."

His arm snakes around my waist and pulls me to him, then he presses his lips to mine. Not even the grit covering our faces or our nearby spectators can keep me from deepening the kiss, and I once again debate if I shouldn't just throw Amelie in the dungeon so I can take Aspen to bed here and now.

Too soon he pulls away, leaving my lips tingling for more. "You win," he says with a mock sigh. "Take the royal chambers tonight." With a wink, he turns away and joins the others at the staircase.

Unable to suppress the grin on my face, I go to retrieve my sister.

"So, it's true," she says as I reach her side. Her awestruck tone shakes me from my giddy daze. "You've truly come to find love with the Stag King."

Her words wipe the smile from my face. I try not to read too much into the tears that glaze her eyes. If I did, I might think she's genuinely happy for me.

THE ROYAL CHAMBER IS A SIGHT TO BEHOLD; NOT EVEN ASPEN'S BEDROOM AT Bircharbor is this breathtaking. Its ample spaciousness contains all the accommodations I've come to expect from a palace bedroom—bed, bathing chamber, wardrobe, desk, dressing screen, sitting area—but the style is unlike anything I've seen. The walls are white stucco painted with intricate designs in gold, blue, and red, with orbs of pale yellow light hovering above red clay sconces. Arched windows line the expanse of the far wall, each with intricate gold shutters left open to invite the night air. The bed is draped in layers of cool linen sheets and topped with a heavy brocade blanket. Overhead, a canopy of gauzy chiffon hangs from the ceiling, tied off to the side on all four corners of the bed. Everything from the sheets to the canopy is a deep orange color.

The only thing that spoils my awe is the icy tension hanging between me and my sister. We've gone through the motions of washing and changing into robes without saying more than a word here and there to each other.

Now we stand on opposite sides of the bed, sorting through piles upon piles of bland, brown dresses Fehr has brought us.

"You could have locked me in the dungeon," Amelie says, breaking the silence.

I purse my lips, tossing a dress that looks more like a shapeless sack to the floor. I must admit Fehr was right about Ustrin not having anything appropriate for a female royal to wear. The staff here must have been dressed quite plainly indeed.

Amelie seems to have given up on the dresses altogether and instead fiddles with the swaths of bright cloth the djinn brought from the former seamstress' room. Unsatisfied with my refusal to respond to her statement, she adds, "Why didn't you lock me in there? I expected you would, but—"

"I wanted to keep my eye on you," I say, tone firm as I toss yet another dress into the *absolutely not* pile.

"I can't disobey your orders," she whispers. "You can leave me by myself."

I lift my eyes from the dresses to study her with narrowed eyes. "Is that what you want?"

She shrugs. "I can tell you don't want to be near me. You'd rather be spending the night with your mate, would you not?"

"That's none of your concern."

"If you gave me commands to stay in my room all night, I would be bound to follow."

"You sure are keen on convincing me to leave you alone."

She meets my eyes for a moment, then lowers them back to the saffron spider silk in her hands. "I just don't want you to feel like you must watch my every move. I know I'm a burden to you, but I don't want to keep you from enjoying what should be a wonderful experience. You have an entire palace, a mate you love—"

"We're at war," I snap. "There's no such thing as a *wonderful experience* right now."

She gives another shrug, one that makes my blood boil. I burn her with a glare, studying her every move to see if I can decipher any hidden agenda written on her face. But she gives nothing away, her attention fixated on the length of russet chiffon she holds up to her chin, as if she's imagining it as a dress. Her brow furrows as she shifts it this way and that, the tip of her tongue visible at the corner of her mouth. In this moment, she bears a chilling resemblance to Mother hard at work on a new tincture or tisane.

My chest tightens at the sight, my throat constricting. I whirl away from my sister, eyes unfocused as I try to burn the dueling images that plague my mind. Amelie. Mother. Amelie. Mother.

How can I love one and hate the other?

Remember what she's done. Remember what her betrayal cost Mother.

I reach for my inner fire, let it burn the conflict from my mind until it clears, dissolves into nothing. The heat warms my insides, but I'm left realizing the skin on my arms has begun to prickle. I cross my arms over my chest and rub my shoulders, frowning at the open windows and the cool air they welcome into the room. At first, it was a relief to feel a drop in temperature, but now I almost wish we had a fire going in the hearth.

That's when I recall the red clay fireplace that lines one of the walls. I approach it, finding it empty of any source to burn. For a moment, I consider calling in Breeda from the hall to have her fetch something. I'd ordered her to stand guard to give me a break from her chatter, and she's likely still out there doing her due diligence as if it were the most important job of her life. However, this might be something I can solve myself.

I extend my hand and think of heat. A spark of blue light flickers over my palm, then grows into an orb of flame. I'm about to reach inside the fireplace to set the flame down like I did by the weapons room, but I stop myself. I've seen both Aspen and Fehr summon light over sconces in an instant; surely, I can do something similar with a hearth fire. I narrow my eyes at the orb of flame, willing it to transport from my hand to the hearth. All it does is flicker in my palm.

I clench my jaw. How in the name of iron do I move a flame from one space to another, without simply transferring it by touch?

I'm suddenly reminded of Queen Estel and her power over time and space. Lorelei had explained it's the Star Court's affinity with the air element that gives her such an ability. Ustrin must have mastered at least a portion of air, considering he was able to send an orb of flame straight to Selene Palace. But how can I use the ability myself?

I close my eyes, recalling what little I know of the air element. I remember my first visit to the Twelfth Court, the ethereal, windblown pixie I met there. *We get along well,* she'd said. *Thought. Intellect.* How do I use either of those things to move my flame? Surely, I can't *think* it into moving.

What else do I know about air?

An instinctual nudge calls my attention to my firefox form. As soon as I give in to the train of thought, my body relaxes. Through my unseelie form, everything comes so much more naturally. My intellect is bound to my instincts, data is filtered at rapid speeds and turns into usable information. I call upon my inner firefox, ask how else she relates to air, aside from what goes on in her head. She shows me an image of me running through the woods, my paws taking me across vast stretches of land. Smooth, swift travel. Then she shows an image of me leaping from a tree to a boulder, then to another tree, gaining height with my momentum.

In that moment, it's clear to me. I can see how it all connects, how the elements weave together in everything I do. The way air meets earth in a strange and magical dance that creates gravity, acceleration, travel, motion.

With this awareness filling every part of my being, I will the fire to leave my hand and light inside the hearth. A sudden burst of heat pulls my eyes open.

There it is. My fire.

I watch the flame as it shifts from blue to orange, roaring quietly inside the fireplace. Sweat beads at my brow, dripping into my eyes, but it isn't from the heat. It's from the feat of concentration I just pulled, although I hardly realized I was doing it until it was done.

"You've grown so powerful with your magic," Amelie says, startling me from my awe.

A blush creeps up my cheeks. I shouldn't have let her see that. My gaze turns steely as I return to the bed where Amelie appears to have constructed several makeshift dresses from the bright fabrics. How she managed to do such a thing without a single stitch is beyond me.

She lifts a gown of flowing silk in a deep golden hue. "This one is fit for a queen," she says. My breath catches as she rounds the bed and approaches me with it. "Let me show you how it's worn."

I tense with every step she takes. Part of me wants to refuse to allow her close enough to help me dress, but I doubt I'll be able to figure out how to don the strange garment myself. With a sigh of resignation, I strip off my robe, and she drapes a swath of long, golden silk over my shoulders to drape over each breast down to the floor. Then she takes a separate piece of the same cloth and wraps it around my waist, tying it off just above my hips to form a skirt. The end result is light, breathable, and surprisingly elegant.

Amelie steps back to admire her work. "You make it look even more beautiful than I imagined." With a grin, she returns to the bed to pick out her own dress.

"How did you do this?" I ask, unable to suppress my curiosity as I stare down at the smooth silk. "You've never made a dress in your life."

"I examined the style of the others and made one like those, but more regal," she says. I'm about to return to sorting through the dresses, but after seeing what Amelie created, it seems futile. Silence falls between us again as I mindlessly push the dresses from one side of the bed to the other. Then Amelie says, "How do you make fire? Do you simply wish for flame and it happens?"

I press my lips into a tight line, debating if I should remain silent. Somehow though, this dress she's made has softened something inside me, for better or for worse. "I can conjure many forms of fire through intent, but the first time was an accident." There's much I leave unsaid with that statement, primarily the fact that I was with Mother when it occurred. "I was angry, and it just happened."

She meets my eyes with a curious gaze. "Is that what helps you create fire? Anger?"

"Anger, rage, passion. There are many emotions that can spark it, but those are most natural for me."

Her expression turns to steel, hands wringing around the cloth she holds, lips pursed so tightly, they turn white. "I've felt more rage than I can stand, and I've never summoned so much as a spark, accident or no."

A flash of heat goes through me. I doubt she's felt anything close to my rage. Still, I keep that to myself, my own curiosity taking over. "You've been underwater, correct?"

"Cobalt had me locked in our bedroom in the coral caves." Her tone is cold, and I think I hear a hint of a tremble.

"An attack by water weakens fire," I explain. "There's a possibility that your proximity to water stifled any chance of recognizing your power."

She furrows her brow. "So, you think I could have the same gifts you do?"

I give a halfhearted shrug. "It's possible."

She lifts her palm, eyes narrowing to slits as she examines it. A hateful grin, one so unlike anything I've seen her wear, pulls at her lips.

My body is frozen as I watch her, trying to make sense of—

A red flame bursts over her open hand.

13

With a gasp of delight, she turns to me with a glowing smile. "Evie, look—"

"Amelie Fairfield," I say in a rush, the power of her name ringing in my voice, "I forbid you from using the power of fire."

The flame extinguishes along with her smile, all hope and pride draining from her eyes.

"For the next twenty-four hours," I hurry to add. My chest heaves, shoulders trembling. The terror of seeing my sister conjure flame like it was nothing strikes me harder and harder with every second that ticks by. It had been so easy for her. *Too* easy. How could that be?

"I'm sorry," Amelie whispers. "I never should have even thought of trying it."

I grit my teeth and stalk over to the sitting area. With my back to my sister, I sink into one of the chairs. "Put the dresses in the wardrobe once you're finished."

The tension in the room is so heavy, it makes my skin crawl, and my mind continues to spin from the shock of what I just witnessed.

"Did Mother hate me?" Amelie asks, breaking the silence. Her words don't diminish my discomfort, however; they add to it. How dare she mention Mother? How dare she even ask?

I turn in my chair to burn her with a glare.

Of course she doesn't so much as flinch at my stare. She never was one to read a room, always saying the wrong thing in her sweet, naive way. Her next words come out tremulous. "Did she...die...hating me? Did you tell her the awful things I did?"

The air leaves my lungs as her words open a chasm of grief beneath me. I return to facing forward in my chair, fingers clenched tight around the armrest. I should silence her. I should forbid her to speak. But before I know it, my response is tumbling from my lips. "I told her the truth," I say through my teeth, tone dripping venom. Then, against all reason, I soften the blow. "But I didn't give her the details. I said you bargained away your name for love."

"Love." She scoffs the word like a curse. "I only bargained my ability to lie for love. We didn't exchange names until after I left Bircharbor."

Again, I clench the armrests. This time, it isn't grief I'm fighting against but the rage that threatens to explode out of every pore in a fiery inferno. "So, you're saying you gave him the ability to lie of your own free will? That he didn't compel you with magic?"

"Exactly." She says it as if she were speaking about someone else, a response to some juicy gossip regarding a foolish peer. From the corner of my eye, I see her carry an armload of dresses to the wardrobe where she begins to hang them. She's changed into one of her makeshift gowns, a pale orange.

But all I can see is red. "So, you betrayed me from the very start, and yet you wonder why I can't trust you."

She turns to face me, taking a few steps closer. "It wasn't supposed to be like this, Evie. He still had the power to lie back then. It was fading fast after the Holstrom girls' deaths, but he had it and he used it on me. I'm sure he used it on you too."

She's right. He did use that power on me, well before he stole my sister. "How is that supposed to make a difference? You still did what you did."

"I was misled." There's no pleading quality to her tone, only bitter resentment. "He said everything was supposed to be perfect. He and I would be together, as would you and Aspen. The four of us were supposed to be happy."

Another flash of rage heats my veins, and it takes all my restraint to breathe it away. "Does anyone look happy to you?"

Amelie returns to the wardrobe and continues hanging the dresses. Once finished, she approaches the sitting area with slow, hesitant steps. I can't bear to look at her as she lowers onto the couch nearby. "You looked happy," she whispers.

My gaze flashes to hers, a scowl burning in my eyes. "Excuse me?"

"When I saw you and Aspen together today. You shared a moment that was so potent, even I could feel it."

"You know nothing about me and Aspen."

She laces her fingers together, then smooths them over her legs, an anxious gesture. "I knew he cared for you from the start. While you were unconscious after the incident with the kelpie, I saw a side of Aspen during our daily chats. It only came out when we talked about you."

"Is that when you began your secret tryst with Cobalt?" I don't bother hiding the malice in my tone.

"Yes." Her confession comes without hesitation. "All along, I knew it was wrong for me to desire your fiancé. I was selfish and cruel to do what I did, conspiring with him to find a way for us to be together. He promised me the four of us would be paired with the mates we were best suited with. He said as long as I did everything he told me to and followed his plan, everything would work out perfectly. Seeing how Aspen cared for you fueled my justifications that it was the right thing to do, even if I had to keep the truth from you. Now, I regret the day Cobalt ever looked upon me. I curse the moment he declared his secret affection." Her hands clench into fists at her sides, posture stiff as her eyes unfocus.

Her words weave conflict in my heart, reminding me what may have happened if she *hadn't* betrayed me. I could be the one in Amelie's position, and she could be Aspen's mate. There's no way I can regret what brought me and Aspen together. Right?

"Everything was supposed to be perfect," she whispers, tone wistful as she stares at her lap. "He promised me it would be, over and over. I believed him."

Fire turns in my stomach. "Shouldn't you have realized you were wrong when you abducted me from the palace and attacked me in the coral caves? How about when Cobalt had me trapped in a cage? Or when he stole the throne from Aspen?"

Her eyes are filled with tears when they meet mine. "I wasn't myself during any of those instances. You have no idea how many of my words and actions were controlled by Cobalt."

"I offered you my help. I told you I would protect you from him and you denied me."

Our eyes lock in an icy standoff, fury radiating from each of us. I can tell she wants to argue, wants to defend herself, but she purses her lips and returns her gaze to her lap, another agonizing silence blanketing the room. As heat prickles behind my neck, I regret lighting the fire in the hearth.

"Remember you love me." Amelie's words are so quiet, I question whether I heard them at all.

"What?"

"That's the only clear memory I have before everything becomes clouded beneath the haze of his commands. The last thing I remember him saying is this: 'In everything you do today, you will remember how much you love me. No matter what questions or angers or worries arise, you will brush them aside. You will return again and again to your love for me.'" A tear rolls down her cheek, but her expression isn't one of sorrow; it's anger etched across her face.

The image she portrays is like looking in a mirror. All that rage, all that fury—I never could have dreamed I'd see it on my carefree, confident sister. But is it true? Something in the deepest recesses of my heart tells me it is, that that kind of fury can't be faked. That same part of me begs to reach for her, to take her hand in mine and tell her I understand.

Yet I can do no such thing. Just considering it is dangerous territory. In this moment, it feels so easy to give in and pity her. But what if she's lying? What if it's Cobalt who controls her emotions now, even in this confession? What if her Bond with him is the same as mine is with Aspen? What if he can travel in spirit to see her, the way Aspen has been able to do with me? He could be here right now. Watching everything. Hearing everything. Perhaps he's waiting to attack until Amelie can confirm the contents of the weapons room.

My stomach lurches as I jolt to my feet and rush to the door. I don't know where I'm going, but I know I need air, to get away from my sister and the tangled emotions she weaves inside me, at least for a minute. As I reach the arched doorway, I say her name.

Her eyes meet mine.

"Don't leave this room or speak to a soul until I return."

With that, I flee.

14

Breeda greets me in the hall as I rush out of the room, but I order her to remain outside the bedroom to guard my sister. My legs tremble as I make my way through the palace and out the front doors. I don't stop until I reach one of the rectangular ponds within the courtyard. There I collapse to my knees, gasping for breath as my conversation with my sister strikes me even harder. Free from her gaze, I can fully process the emotions she stirred—fear, pity, fury, sympathy, rage, love.

As fast as I try to burn it away, it grows and grows, rolling over me in waves, gathering momentum with thoughts of Mother, of iron bullets, blood, and flame.

Guilt floods me next, followed by crippling shame. How can I be queen if I can't even keep my emotions under control? How can I lead an entire court when a talk with my sister unravels me? How can I rule both seelie and unseelie when my seelie side is weak but my unseelie form threatens to trap me?

Every inch of me ripples with anxiety, the burden of everything I've faced and done burying me beneath its weight. I sink deeper into the ground beneath me, the cool sand digging into my knees and shins.

"Are you all right?" Aspen's voice snaps me to attention.

I face him, watch as he approaches from the tile walkway. The sight of him returns me to the present, reacquaints me with this moment, the feel of my breaths, so shallow in my compressed lungs. On trembling legs, I rise to my feet, sucking air deep into my diaphragm. I close the distance between us, pressing my face into his chest once I reach him. Strong arms close around me, holding me tight. "I had to get away from Amelie for a time," I say, my voice breaking on my sister's name.

"I sensed you through the Bond." His voice rumbles deep in his chest, a soothing reverberation against my ear. "Your pain was so strong, I could feel it as if it were my own."

We say nothing else for endless moments while he holds me, his rosemary cinnamon aroma filling my senses, calming my heart. The warmth of his bare chest pressed against my cheek helps drain the remnants of my anxiety until my breathing returns to normal. My fire returns, and I reach for it, let it flood my arms and legs with its steadying heat. Only then do I pull away to study him.

I quirk a brow as I take in the golden planes of his chest left bare where his cream linen shirt hangs open and unbuttoned. My eyes trail down to the loose brown trousers he wears, much like Fehr's. They aren't quite as neat and tailored as what he usually wears, but I must admit, he looks good in them.

"I like your outfit too," he says with a smirk.

My lips pull up at the corners, but my smile wavers when I'm reminded who made my outfit.

Aspen furrows his brow. "Are you sure you're all right? What happened?"

I release a heavy sigh. "It's just...hard being around Amelie right now."

"You don't have to stay with her. You can keep her in the dungeon tonight, or have Lorelei watch over her."

I bite my lip. Yet another conflict stirs in my heart. What is it I want from Amelie? To love her or hate her? To trust her or suspect her? Am I waiting for her to prove me right or prove me wrong?

With a shake of my head, I take Aspen's hands in mine. "I don't want to talk about her right now."

"Fair enough," he says, although his rigid shoulders can't hide his lingering concern. "Is there anything else you want to talk about?"

I force a grin as I grasp for a distraction. "Has there truly never been any other Bonded pair that can communicate the way we can?"

Some of the tenseness leaves his muscles. "Not that I've ever known. If there has, the pair has kept it a secret. But I have a theory why ours exists as it does."

Even though this tangent began as a diversion from more serious matters, I find my interest genuinely piqued. The word *theory* tends to do that to me. "You do?"

He nods. "You know how I told you that the Bonding ritual is performed as a sign of mutual fear and respect, most often used to forge alliances? That it's rare to be done in mate relationships? Well, I think that's why ours works the way it does. Because we are more than just allies Bonded by name. We love each other."

My heart flips at the word *love,* and with it comes a warmth spreading through my chest. Could he be right? Could only Bonded pairs who love one another form such a deep connection? A darker thought comes to mind: if that's the case, does it work that way with Amelie and Cobalt, just like I fear? Is there...love between them?

I shake the question from my mind. This is supposed to be my respite from thoughts of Amelie. This is about me and Aspen.

"I sensed you when you were away from me earlier this week too, after you went to Grenneith," he says. "Just like tonight, I sensed your pain. Even though I promised I wouldn't seek you through the Bond, my awareness of you and your emotions was strong."

His words toe the line before dangerous territory, the kind that could have me gasping for air and fighting back tears again. I have yet to give him the full details of my trip to Grenneith and the journey back to the wall with the freed fae courtesans. Eventually, I'll tell him all about it. Perhaps when I'm in better control of my emotions. But not today.

Needing yet another shift in subject, I tilt my head back and step closer to him, a wide grin on my lips. "You know what else is strong? Your ability to use water like you did today. I had no idea you could do that."

He says nothing for a moment, and I wonder if he'll let me get away with evading serious subjects twice now. Then his grin mirrors mine. "I suppose you haven't seen me use my magic much, have you?"

"Lorelei told me you had the power to fill the baths at Bircharbor at will."

"I may have done that for you a time or two," he says with a smirk. "Anything to encourage you to get naked."

A welcome heat warms my core, and I wrap my arms around his waist. "Is that so?"

"Can you blame me?" He leans down and presses his lips to mine. His warm mouth is like nourishment for my flesh. I yield to him, allowing our kiss to gently linger. When we pull away, I rest my head against his chest, letting my ears fill with the lullaby of his steady heartbeat.

"You can learn to wield water too," he says, returning to our previous conversation. "As a queen, you have access to all four elements now. It's only a matter of learning how to manipulate them."

I tilt my head to meet his eyes, a flash of excitement running through me as I recall the feat I accomplished with the fireplace. "I think I used air today." I tell him all about it, and of course, he exaggerates his pride in me.

"Combining two elements doesn't come easy," he explains. "Even the fae who've inherited more than one element tend to favor one as their primary. I take after my father's side and am much stronger with earth. And, as you know, I can also control water to a degree. I combined water with air to lift the water from the pools today and transport it to us after the dust storm. That's also how I was able to fill the tubs at Bircharbor. And Ustrin, like you've learned for yourself, used fire and air to transport flame."

"You really think I can learn earth and water too?"

"Of course I do. I know how capable you are. Not only are you a queen, but you were strong enough to steal my cold, dead heart. If you can do that, you can do anything." His tone is teasing, his crooked smirk such a wicked sight it has my heart racing.

More aware now of the heat of his body pressed so close to mine, my thoughts turn devious as a much more enticing distraction comes to mind. "Do you realize this is the first time we've been completely alone since yesterday?"

He runs his palm down my hair, then trails up the length of my arm until his warm hand settles over my bare shoulder. I close my eyes at the sensation of the slow caress. "I'm aware of it."

I open my eyes and drink in the brown, gold, green, and ruby shades swirling in his irises. I run my hands up his chest, then grasp his collar firmly between my fingers. "You and I have unfinished business."

"What about your sis—"

"She can wait."

His eyes sparkle as his smirk matches the mischief in my heart. I tug his collar, and his lips are on mine again. My arms wind around his neck, pressing him closer to deepen the kiss. His hands rove the bare skin left exposed by the dress, then begin to explore every inch the sheer silk covers. My fingers tangle in his hair, then move to the branch of an antler, teasing a tine with my caress. He emits a hiss of pleasure, then moves his mouth down my neck. His fingers feel like fire through the silk of my gown as they trail the neckline. He tugs the neckline aside, and I arch against him, his warm hand full against my naked flesh.

My hands move down his back. When I reach the bottom hem of his shirt, my fingers lift it so I can feel the heat of his skin. Our breaths grow ragged and our kisses move deeper, his tongue moving against mine, conjuring images of what his tongue did last time we explored our passions together. My legs nearly give way at the thought, and I move against him, rocking my hips to sate the craving for a deeper feel of him.

Then suddenly, Aspen tenses, and it isn't from desire. Completely still in my arms, his lips press into a tight line as a low growl rumbles deep in his chest. I pull away, brow furrowed. I study his face, but his eyes aren't on me. They're locked somewhere behind me.

Don't move, he says through the Bond.

But it's too late. I'm already whirling around.

At the center of the courtyard stands a shadowed figure. Dressed in a dark hooded cloak, all it reveals is a flash of teeth glinting in the moonlight, followed by the gleam of a blade.

15

Faster than I've ever seen Aspen move, he shifts his body in front of mine and lets out a hiss just as I hear a thud come from behind me. I whip my head to find a dagger stuck in the trunk of the nearest palm tree. Aspen slaps a hand over his shoulder where he was struck by the blade. My attention is torn between him and the menacing figure standing at the center of the courtyard.

The assailant reaches beneath his cloak, drawing another blade. I reflexively reach for my obsidian dagger, but I come up empty and recall I never put it back on after my bath. Still, I brace myself for the attack, preparing to dodge the assailant's next throw, but he falters as a roaring sound comes from near the palace doors. There, a funnel of sand begins to whirl and rise. I can vaguely make out Fehr's face at its center. The cloaked figure shifts his stance to face the djinn, and the glint of his dagger speeds across the court-yard, straight at the cyclone. It strikes its center, just below Fehr's face. I stifle a shout, but the djinn disappears, sand storm and all.

The assailant takes the opportunity to dart toward the palace. He obviously didn't come for Aspen and me. He came for something inside Irridae, and it isn't hard to guess what it could be.

I circle Aspen, seeking the site of his injury. "Are you hurt?"

"I'm fine," he mutters, already rushing toward the palace. "I'll go after him." Without another word, he shudders and tilts forward, as if he'll fall on his hands, but by the time he makes contact with the ground, his hands have become hooves and his body has been replaced with his stag form. The assailant races up the palace steps, retrieving the dagger he'd thrown at Fehr before charging through the doors.

Aspen tears across the tile walkway, hard on the figure's heels.

I spin back toward the palm tree, bracing one hand against its rough trunk while the other wraps around the hilt of the dagger. As the blade comes free, I note its composition. Iron.

That means the attacker must be human.

"Your Majesty." Fehr materializes before me, hand rubbing his chest, although I see no sign of injury. "The man has entered the palace. Shall I guard you or—"

"The weapons room. Now."

He nods and disappears in a puff of bronze smoke, leaving me alone in the courtyard. With the dagger in hand, I part my flowing skirts to trail behind me and pump my legs as hard as I can to race inside the palace. Once I reach the atrium, a moment of disorientation stalls me. Which staircase leads to the weapons room?

I need my instincts, I realize. My fox.

Tucking the dagger beneath the waist of my overskirt, I close my eyes and give in to my fox form. With the fire of urgency roaring through my veins, it takes little effort to shift, body shrinking as my hands become paws. Almost as soon as the transformation is complete, my senses sharpen, and I become hyperaware of distinct aromas calling me to the staircase on the right. My mate passed by here, as did the human attacker, made clear by the smell of human sweat.

I take the stairs several times faster than I could on human legs, following the data that reaches me through my eyes and nose. Before I know it, I'm racing down a familiar hall of volcanic rock, the malachite bars of the cells, and then—

My heart leaps into my throat, threatening to shock me out of my fox form, as Aspen comes into view. He's no longer a stag; in his seelie form, he's hunched on the floor, head thrown back in agony as the hilt of a blade protrudes from his upper thigh. His hands frame the hilt, just inches from it, quivering with the resistance he's trying to fight in order to grasp it.

"Aspen." My voice wavers, and again I'm close to losing my unseelie form, yearning for human hands to grasp the dagger to free him from it.

"No." His voice is firm, and in his eyes is a command. "I'll be fine. Go."

I falter for only a moment, but my fox side swallows my fear, my pain, telling me the assailant must be nearing the weapons room, if he isn't there already. "I'll come back for you," I promise, and take off down the hall to the end of the dungeon and down the final staircase that leads to the winding hall. I speed down it, only slowing when I catch sight of Fehr. Several blades litter the floor at his feet, but he appears unwounded. His fight seems mostly with himself as he drags his body along the wall, struggling against the iron that keeps him at bay.

Fehr's eyes widen with momentary surprise as his eyes lock on me, seeing me in my firefox form for the first time.

"Where is the human?"

"He's already inside," Fehr gasps.

That's all I need to hear to surge onward, the door of the weapons room in sight. As I approach, I see the door is indeed thrown open, the iron bar that had kept it shut now on the ground. The figure stalks the room, shoving crates aside, prying open wooden lids, and tearing through dozens upon dozens of stands that hold iron swords, daggers, maces, and axes. I swallow my horror at seeing so many weapons, but the human doesn't seem to have eyes for them.

He's looking for something else.

This close, I can make out his face, his stature. He's tall and muscular, built like a warrior, his jaw set as he continues his frantic search. It's then I realize why I can see so clearly; at the center of the room, perched upon a wooden crate, rests a silver disc with a bright, golden light at its center.

A Chariot.

What this means, I have no time to consider, for the man's face brightens as he lifts a small, wooden crate. He brings it next to the travel device and opens the lid. Whatever is inside illuminates the room like the sun. It's so bright, it's nearly blinding, and I'm forced to avert my gaze.

I blink rapidly, willing my eyes to adjust while I run through every scenario I could use to take him down.

The dagger.

For that, I need hands. Again, the urgency of the situation sends the fire rushing through my veins, burning away my firefox form and sending me stumbling as I rise on two human legs. The light coming from the box is still painfully bright, but it's dulled now. Terror seizes me when I realize it's because the light is no longer at the center of the room. It's muted by the man's fingers, the light cradled in his hand as if it's a solid ball he holds in his palm. His other hand reaches for the Chariot.

My fingers close around the hilt of the dagger as I lunge forward. With a flick of my wrist, the blade spins end over end. It doesn't meet its mark, which I'd intended to be his chest. Instead, it grazes the wrist that holds the Chariot. His eyes flash toward me, lips pulling into a sneer as the travel device goes clattering to the ground between two large crates.

With the orb of light still in his other hand, he dives to his knees. But I'm faster. I don't know when I shifted back into my firefox form, but paws are what reach the Chariot and send it skittering out into the hall. I dart after it, but the man clambers over the crates, leaping over my head, his cloak trailing after him. I snap my teeth, grasping the edge of his cloak and locking it in my jaw before he can escape. He whirls toward me and reaches his free hand toward his hip, but his eyes widen when he comes up empty. No more daggers.

Fire roars through me, and I let it rise, let my flame dance over my body, extending from my ears, my face, and the tip of my muzzle. Purple, pink, and aqua fire lights the edge of his cloak. I release him and my flames leap higher. He stumbles back, struggling with his free hand to release the clasp of his cloak, but I circle his ankles, igniting the hem of his trousers, the laces of his boots.

His cries assault my ears as he begins a frantic dance to stamp out the flames. It's no use. My fire is growing by the second. In a final bid to save his own life, he releases the orb from his hand. The fur stands up along the ridge of my spine, and everything inside me screams danger, even as the light of the orb blinds me once again. And yet, even without seeing it, I can sense the orb. The energy it emits hums through the corridor, a tangible weight against the air around it.

I close my eyes and leap forward. My paws make contact just as I realize they won't do the trick.

Once again, I need hands. Hands. Hands. It's all I can think.

My back slams into the hard floor, thrusting the air from my lungs. They're human lungs. And clasped between my human hands is the glowing orb.

〜

Energy buzzes between my fingers as I return to the weapons room. With trembling hands that beg to be rid of the chilling power radiating from the object, I return the orb to the small box and shut the lid. Only when the room returns to dark do I feel I can breathe again.

It takes me several breaths to compose myself before I can approach the man. He's gone still, and my flames have died down to a subtle flicker, seeking flesh and cloth that have yet to be charred.

I swallow the bile that rises in my throat as I look down at the man. His skin is blackened, chest rising and falling in shallow bursts. I crouch at his side, trying not to focus on his wounds—wounds I caused with my terrifying power.

"Who sent you here?"

His lips peel back from his teeth, the movement splitting the skin at the corners of his mouth, but he says nothing.

My mind reels to find a way to extend his life long enough to get the answers I need. He's most certainly near death. Then I remember the power I've hardly given much thought to ever since I learned I could wield flame. It's a power I've used many times without knowing it, something Mother and I were both able to utilize to help others heal—life force.

Ignoring my revulsion at the damage I've caused, I place my hands over his burnt chest. A gentle fire flows from my heart and down my arms, tingling my palms. "I will heal you if you answer my questions. Who sent you and what is the significance of that orb?"

He snarls again. "Don't touch me, vile half breed."

My entire body goes still. "So you know of me." Although, technically, I'm a quarter breed, but this isn't the time for asserting facts.

"Are you working with the Renounced? Queen Dahlia?"

"Fool," he mutters.

I clench my jaw and feel the halt in the flow of energy from my hands. "I will heal you if you tell me," I say through my teeth, "but you must tell me something."

"He will ruin you," he finally says.

My pulse races. "Who? Cobalt?"

The semblance of a grin stretches over his blackened face as his eyes roll back in his head. "He will ruin all of you."

I move my hands from his chest to his shoulders, shaking him. "Who? Tell me and I will heal you, you idiot!"

"The mainland army comes even as we speak. Warships by the dozen. The time of the fae is at an end."

My blood goes cold. I don't need to know the name he refuses to say. It could be but one person.

He grins, opening more fissures at the corners of his mouth. "Mr. Duveau sends his love."

I stare down at him, no longer able to feel the fire running through my palms. His eyes slide away from mine, his grin fading, lips going slack. That's when I realize the man is gone.

Another life taken by me.

16

My mate.

It's the only thing that snaps me out of my stupor, drawing my attention from the charred, lifeless body before me to recall the iron blade Aspen had stuck in his thigh. I turn away from the body, retrieving the human's Chariot and tucking it into the waist of my overskirt as I rise to my feet. I find Fehr slumped against the wall farther down.

"I failed you, Your Majesty," he gasps through his teeth. "You may punish me."

"Maybe later," I mutter. There's more ice to my tone than I intend, but all I can think about is Aspen right now. "The thief is dead and he's given us vital information. Come."

I don't wait to watch the djinn rise; instead, I race down the hall, up the stairs, and to the dungeon.

Aspen is where I left him, but this time, Foxglove and Lorelei are there too, faces full of concern. I brush them aside as I kneel before him, eyes locked on the dagger hilt, mind trained on nothing but the task at hand. My heart races, but I force my surgeon's calm to steady my hands.

"Tear a piece of cloth from my skirt," I command, voice level.

Lorelei rushes to obey. As soon as the cloth is in my hand, I pull the blade out with the other. Aspen bares his teeth but doesn't make so much as a sound as I throw the dagger to the ground and bind his leg with the cloth.

I wait for the pain to subside from his face before I allow him to stand.

Foxglove and Fehr take up posts on each side of my mate as he favors his injured leg. With slow progress, we make our way up the stairs. Once we reach the atrium, we don't bother going any farther. All I need is to be far enough from the weapons room for Aspen's natural healing to kick in, so one of the couches near the windows will have to do.

"Bring wine," I tell Fehr, hoping the food stores weren't emptied when the household was expelled. After he brings a bottle of deep red liquid, I request cloth, needle, thread, and any other helpful tools from the seam-stress' room.

My fingers fly as I go to work, ignoring the ache in my chest that burns at every wince on Aspen's face, every groan he suppresses while I clean and stitch the wound. Only a few tendrils of black branch off from the lesion, but his blood has yet to be tainted.

He will heal. He will heal.

The mantra keeps me sane, fuels my fire as I lay my hands over the bandaged wound, attempting to do what I failed to do for the human.

By the time I make it to my bedroom, my sister is already tucked into the bed, sleeping soundly. It was a struggle to leave Aspen's side, but he assured me he was well. He even managed—with the help of Fehr and Foxglove—to limp from the couch to the bedroom next to mine where he's staying. Still, I laid next to him for nearly an hour, hand resting over his steadily beating heart until I was satisfied with his condition.

Only then did I come back to my room, remembering my promise to myself that I would watch my sister's every move and renew her commands at my first chance. After the events of the night, my suspicion over my sister's anticipated treachery feels weak in comparison to the real dangers I faced.

Not bothering to change out of my dress, I crawl under the covers next to Amelie. The fire I created in the hearth still burns steadily, and the shutters have been drawn over the windows, blocking most of the chill. Never would I have imagined nights could be cold in the desert. Although perhaps the ice I feel is on the inside, left by the thief's chilling words.

The mainland army comes even as we speak.

Warships by the dozen.

The time of the fae is at an end.

I roll toward Amelie, burrowing deeper beneath the blankets as I try to shake the terrifying visions from my head. Seeing my sister's sleeping face, my mind goes still. Her expression is so soft and innocent. So much like the girl I grew up with.

If I let myself, I could pretend we're back home at the apothecary, young girls snuggled up in the same bed after a nightmare. Back then, we sought comfort in each other, taking turns stroking the other's hair, depending on who'd had the bad dream.

It takes all my restraint not to nestle against her sleeping form.

When I wake, it's to screaming.

Amelie thrashes in the bed, fighting the blankets, a blood-curdling wail tearing from her throat. It's just after dawn, meager light spilling in through the golden shutters to illuminate the terror that rips across her face. "What have I done?"

I bolt upright as she scrambles out of the blankets, backing away until she comes up against the headboard. She brings her hands toward her face, eyes wide as she stares at them. "Whose blood is this?"

A chill runs through me. This is how she was when I awoke her in the cell at Lunar. I'd attributed it to the terrible power of Selene Palace's dungeons, but now I can't fathom what could cause such a state of distress.

"What have I done?" Another wail escapes her lips.

I crawl toward her and grasp her shoulders in mine, shaking her the way I did before. "Amelie, wake up."

"No. No. This isn't happening. It wasn't me."

I shake her again, harder. "Wake up!"

She shudders, then her eyes meet mine. Her body trembles, but she sags as recognition crosses her face. Sweat coats her brow, and she brings her hands to cover her face and quietly cries into her palms.

I'm frozen in place as I watch her, uncertain of what to do. My hands leave her shoulders. Part of me wants to turn away and let her pull herself together on her own. But another part of me recalls the childhood memories I'd conjured last night, ones that make me want to reach for her, to brush the hair from her sweat-soaked brow and embrace her in a comforting squeeze.

Instead, I sit back and settle on words. "What happened just now?"

Silence answers, and I wonder if she'll ignore me. Then slowly, she lowers her hands and pulls her knees to her chest. Her eyes are distant as she subtly rocks back and forth. "I didn't know where I was. Or when I was. Maybe even who I was."

My heart lurches at the ghost of horror that lingers on her face. "What do you mean?"

"It's always like this." Her voice is small, breathy. "Every time I awaken from sleep. There's so much I don't remember. So much that plagues me."

"You remember nothing when you wake?"

She shakes her head. "I remember too much and nothing at all, all at once. My mind has grown addled ever since Cobalt first used the power of my name to glamour me, to force me to obey his commands. All I have left are snippets and images, and they haunt me. Today, I barely remember yesterday beneath the cloud of your commands. Tomorrow, I'll feel the same about today. The next day, I'll feel the same about tomorrow."

A lump rises in my throat, skin crawling at the thought. "How can you live like that?"

She meets my eyes, although hers are still haunted. "It's the only way I *can* live. You won't trust me without the commands, nor will I trust myself. Not until Cobalt is dead and the Bond breaks."

Again, I want to reach for her, comfort her until this stranger before me disappears and returns the sister I once loved.

Her gaze goes steely. "Don't feel sorry for me. Just promise me you will let me kill Cobalt." Like last night when I looked at her and saw my own rage reflected in her eyes, the fury in her tone feels like a mirror to mine.

It leaves me speechless.

"Promise me!" she shouts, making me jump. "Promise you will let me kill Cobalt!" She trembles with the anger coursing through her, so hot, I swear flames are dancing just below the surface of her skin.

My answer comes out a whisper. "I promise."

Then, with the power of her name, I trap her beneath another day's worth of commands.

As soon as I'm cleaned and dressed in another one of Amelie's makeshift gowns, I race to the room next door to see Aspen. I'm amazed to find him on his feet, standing before a mirror while he buttons a cream-colored linen shirt over his chest, similar to the one he wore last night. He wears another pair of loose trousers, these ones a deep burgundy, that hide all sight of the wound.

His eyes meet mine in the mirror, and a corner of his mouth quirks up.

The golden color has returned to his skin, making him look very unlike a fae who suffered an iron injury mere hours ago.

My heart flutters with relief and I run to him. As he turns to face me, I throw my arms over his neck and draw his lips to mine. Fearing I'll hurt him, I don't let the kiss linger. "Are you all right?" I ask as I pull away.

He has the nerve to roll his eyes at the question, arm circling my waist to press me closer. "I'm fine, Evie. I told you I would be."

I put my hand on his chest to force distance between us. "Go lie down so I can change your bandages."

He takes my hand in his, removing it from his chest so he can place a kiss on the inside of my wrist. "I already took the bandages off myself," he says against my skin. "The wound has healed."

My eyes widen, although I shouldn't be surprised. The iron wasn't embedded inside him long, which means his own healing powers would have been free to do their work. "Then let me at least examine the site of the wound. I want to see for myself."

A wicked smirk plays on his sensual mouth. "Are you just trying to get me out of my trousers?"

My breath hitches as desire stirs inside my core, mind swimming with images of his body pressed against mine, his hands slipping beneath the layers of my skirt. Twice now, we've been interrupted from fulfilling the passion that's never far from the surface whenever we're together. Unfortunately, that thought reminds me of how we were interrupted last, bringing about an onslaught of sobering facts that must be attended to. I bring my lips close to his, and my words come out a little breathless. "I have every intention of getting you out of your trousers, Aspen."

He groans at the sound of his name and I take a few moments to bathe beneath the hunger in his eyes, knowing I'm about to shatter it all with what I say next. "But there is much to do this morning, and there is much I need to discuss with you."

His next groan is one of disappointment. "Why must you be so intelligent?"

"Well, one of us must be if we're to win a war," I tease, taking a chaste step away from him, pinning my hands at my sides to keep from wringing them. "Has Breeda returned?"

He shakes his head. "I'm sure she'd have gone straight to you if she were back."

He's probably right. As soon as I saw her last night, still obediently guarding my bedroom like I'd commanded, I ordered her to go immediately to Lunar with a message for Nyxia. I bite my lip, eyes going unfocused.

Aspen's expression turns serious. "Why? What's wrong?"

I let out a heavy sigh. "I didn't just send her to relay what transpired last night. I also had her request that Nyxia call an emergency meeting of the Alpha Alliance at once."

"That's probably a good idea. Now that we've confirmed the weapons room exists, we must find a way to protect it."

"That's not all." My stomach sinks. He hadn't been in the best state last night for me to tell him everything that occurred. All he knows is that the human was able to enter the room and that I killed him before he could use the Chariot to escape. He has no idea about the strange orb, the final threat he made about the humans coming to destroy the fae.

He has no idea this is so much bigger than we'd thought.

So I tell him.

17

It's terrifying how quickly the charred husk of a human being burns entirely to ash beneath my powerful flames. Almost as fast as the assailant's life was snuffed out, all that remains of him is contained in a bucket. My stomach churns as I haul it from the weapons room. Even once I reach the stair past the dungeon, the stench of burning flesh lingers in my nose, tickling the back of my throat. In addition, every step I take is haunted by what I left behind—the mysterious golden orb the human had tried to steal.

I'm so wrapped in my thoughts when I reach the atrium, that I almost miss the figures lingering at the far side. I pause, catching Fehr and Foxglove deep in conversation. Foxglove stares up at the much taller djinn, his smile brighter than I think I've ever seen it. They're too far for me to hear what's being said between them, but Foxglove laughs in response, covering his mouth with a demure hand. I've rarely gotten to see Foxglove so sweet and uncomposed, but more surprising is Fehr. Not only is the djinn rapt in their talk, but his eyes are crinkled at the corners, all traces of the resentful servant gone.

I feel like my heart might melt out of my chest, and I'm unable to tear my eyes away from the contented couple. However, I'm very much aware that this moment isn't meant for my eyes and my presence could shatter—

Fehr's eyes flash my way, and just like that, their sweet exchange is over. As they both straighten and offer stiff bows, I feel not like a queen but an interloper. I hide the heat that warms my cheeks as Foxglove excuses himself and scurries away.

Fehr approaches me, expression returning to its hard, familiar state. "Your Majesty, might I take your burden and dispose of it?"

It's then I remember the bucket of ash I carry. I extend it toward him, trying not to wrinkle my nose as the ash shifts with the motion. "You may."

He takes it from me and moves to step away, but I stop him with a word. "Fehr." Seeing him interacting with Foxglove has softened my heart, and I'm eager to be on better terms with my new steward. Or, at the very least, to understand him better.

He narrows his eyes. "How may I serve?"

"Why did my grandfather, King Caleos, bind you to the palace? You said it was a punishment, but what was the crime?"

The djinn purses his lips, jaw shifting side to side before he answers. "It was long ago. Long before humans came to the isle. Long before we knew humans existed. Our world was bigger then. Vast. My kind—the djinn—sought to control it."

His words send my mind reeling to comprehend what he could mean. There are so many new questions, so much fuel for intellectual debate, but I still my eagerness and force myself to focus on the singular question I began with. "The djinn tried to take over the entire realm of the fae?"

He nods. "We were the most powerful of the fae, and we were tired of sharing rule with lesser kings and queens. We fought to overthrow those who tried to wrestle power from us. We refused to acknowledge those who'd obtained the blessing to rule over us by the All of All, so in essence, we fought the gods as well."

"And...you lost?"

He lets out a bitter laugh. "Indeed, we did. Very few of my kind remain, and those who survived were punished with eternal slavery."

"Even after all this time?"

"To the fae, time isn't forgiving, regardless of how long." He squints at me. "But you know so little of time, human that you are."

I know he means it as an insult, but I lift my chin higher. "I am part human, but I am also part fae, not to mention your queen."

He glowers, eyes locked on mine for an uncomfortable, endless moment. Then he averts his gaze with a resigned sigh. "Yes, the palace recognized your power. You are my queen and I am here to serve you."

"You aren't happy about that." It isn't a question.

"My happiness is of no concern. I do my duty without fail." He winces.

"And yet, I failed to protect the weapons room last night. You may punish me."

I recall him saying the same thing last night. "Thanks for the reminder." My words come out with a sarcastic bite. "How might I best punish you?"

"Death is suitable, although I'm sure you will deem such a punishment too kind."

My breath hitches at that, at the raw yearning in his eyes. "Do you truly find life so unbearable?"

"I have lived long and have lost much of what most consider a good and proper life." He states it not to evoke pity, but as a fact.

"What do you mean? Don't you have friends? Lovers?"

His expression softens, but only for a moment. "I can have no lovers without permission, and King Ustrin forbade me from getting too close to anyone, friend, foe, lover, or stranger."

My heart clenches, remembering the joy I saw on his face when he was chatting with Foxglove. As much as Fehr's disdain for me irks me, it probably isn't too different from how I felt about any of the fae when I first came to Faerwyvae. And despite the betrayal against his people, does he deserve an immortal life devoid of comfort and friendship?

The question sends my heart racing, as it evokes thoughts of my sister. *That's different,* I tell myself. She betrayed me personally.

I clasp my hands before me. "Fehr, I give you my permission to take however many friends and lovers you desire."

His eyes go wide, then harden with suspicion. "Aren't you afraid?"

"Afraid of what? That you'll actually enjoy your life beneath my rule and serve me out of respect rather than duty? Why, yes, what a terrifying thought."

He squints, studying me for a few moments. "King Ustrin ruled through fear."

"If you haven't noticed, I am not King Ustrin," I say, my inner fire heating my words. "I am not even my grandfather. That doesn't mean I am soft, however. I may be part human, but fire roars through my veins as hot as it did in my predecessors. I am my own queen, and I am dedicated to the Fire Court and the fae I now serve to protect. That includes you, Fehr. You'd do well to remember that."

He furrows his brow, as if puzzling over me and my words. "I will, Your Majesty," he finally says. His gaze moves to the bucket in his hand before returning to me. "I should inform you that this man has not been the first to try and invade Irridae Palace since Ustrin's death."

My pulse quickens, surprised at the sudden admission. "He isn't?"

"There were four other occurrences, all of them human, all using a Chariot. None were able to enter the palace, for its magic sealed it shut. Last night's assailant was the first who was able to enter."

"Because you opened the palace to me," I say under my breath. "Was it always the same man?"

"I believe so. The first time, however, he came with another, but they both disappeared almost as fast as they arrived. Ever since, there has been only one. We would battle in the courtyard, but he would always disappear before I could severely wound him."

I suppress a shiver as I prepare to ask the next question. "The first time, when two arrived...was it Queen Estel who brought the attacker?"

He shakes his head. "Both human."

I let out a sigh of relief. Even though the Chariot is clearly one of the Star Queen's devices, it makes me sick to consider she could be involved, that she could have been behind the attack to begin with. Not to mention, the chilling similarity the orb has to the much smaller light held within the Chariot. Until she explains how a human could have gotten one of her devices, my suspicion only hardens. Especially since she has yet to arrive with more of Aspen's guards like she promised.

"So long as you have the Chariot," Fehr says, stealing me away from my frantic thoughts, "the humans can't return."

"Unless there are more devices."

"They are rare, as far as I know," he says. "Only Queen Estel has access to them."

"That's what I'm afraid of," I mutter.

Fehr grimaces. "I should also add that, should the humans have more Chariots, and should any assailant manage to make it inside the palace without being apprehended, they will have the ability to return to any place they have already been in person. That is how the devices work."

A chill runs up my spine. Is that what would have happened if the attacker had gotten away? Would he have returned directly to the weapons room with a host of companions, only to storm the palace and turn their iron blades on everyone inside?

"We should destroy the iron," Fehr says, tone darkening. "So long as it remains, I cannot properly protect the palace."

I open my mouth to reply, but before I can consider his suggestion, a flash of red streams into the atrium and circles around my head before appearing as Breeda. She folds into a bow as she floats in front of me. "Your

Most Beautiful Majesty," she says, sounding somewhat out of breath. "I have returned from my very important mission."

"You delivered the message to Queen Nyxia?"

"Yes! I told her exactly what you ordered me to. Then I rushed right back. Well, first I stumbled upon your retinue of loyal subjects on their journey here through Star. So, of course I had to make sure Dune was doing his job, for their progress seemed terribly slow. If *I'd* led them, they'd be here by now, but—"

"What did Queen Nyxia say?"

She spins in a circle. "Ah, yes. She said she has sent out notice to all the Alpha Alliance to come here for an emergency meeting. They will arrive by nightfall."

Nightfall.

My pulse quickens, anticipation mixing with equal parts dread. For who knows what this meeting will bring.

18

Just as Breeda said, the royals of the Alpha Alliance all arrive by nightfall, which thankfully includes Estel. Knowing her guilt would be proven in her absence, I'd spent hour after hour of tense waiting, wondering if she'd even show up.

She was the first of the royals to arrive, and just as she'd said, she came with eight of Aspen's guards. One by one, the rest soon followed, and now the entire Alpha Alliance stands around the sunstone table in my atrium.

Aspen remains close at my side, and I feel his warm hand light upon my lower back. Warmth floods my chest with a steadying calm. *Are you ready?* he asks through the Bond.

Am I ready to tell them a fleet of warships is on its way to destroy all of faekind? Sure, can't wait. I wonder if my tone comes across as sardonic as I intend.

I'm here too, Evie. We're doing this together.

I nod, his words helping me keep my composure as I watch my guests settle in around the table. Nyxia, looking elegant in a black suit, stands slouched to the side with a hand on her hip, a casual posture that hides the tenseness I see in every muscle. Aelfon lowers into a chair, crossing his enormous arms over his chest as he watches me through slitted lids. Flauvis leaps onto a stool, tongue lolling from his panting muzzle. Minuette sways side to side, feet inches off the ground while her hair and the skirt of her thin blue gown blow behind her. Tris stands tall in her seelie form, lips pressed tight while her pink wings flutter against her back in clear agitation. Then there's Estel, looking as serene as ever, the particles on her face shifting and reforming, each expression as content as the last.

It's an effort not to let my suspicious gaze linger on the Star Queen, but I can't help wondering how she'll react when I confront her about the Chariot. My heart races, but I slow it with a deep breath. *One thing at a time.* With all eyes turning toward me, I greet the royals. "Thank you for gathering to meet me here."

"Yes, now will you tell us what this is about?" Nyxia asks in her smooth voice. Her expression reads a mixture of boredom and indignation, but her eyes are hard, keen. She knows I wouldn't have requested a meeting if it wasn't vital. She knows my vague message meant secrecy and tact were required.

"I too would like to know," Tris says, her impatience not feigned like Nyxia's. "I have a kingdom to run. I can't be called away on emergency meetings every other day."

"We're at war," Flauvis says with a growl. "If such things inconvenience you so, then perhaps you don't belong on our side."

Tris' lips peel back, the beauty of her tree-like face transforming into a monstrous snarl that should belong only in nightmares.

"Yes, Flauvis, we are at war," Aspen says in his lazy drawl, "but not with each other. Cut it out so we can get on with it."

Flauvis runs his tongue over his muzzle, but begrudgingly averts his gaze from Tris. The Spring Queen pouts with a huff, eyes snapping to me.

"I summoned you here today for many reasons," I say. "Firstly, to say we have found and confirmed the existence, location, and contents of the weapons stash. There is indeed a room full of iron weapons here at Irridae Palace. My steward, Fehr, confirmed Ustrin had made a private alliance with the humans, particularly Councilman Duveau, which granted him access to these weapons. To what end, I am unsure."

"We know to what end," Minuette hisses. "To use them on his own kind. Disgusting."

"But what did the humans get in return?" Aelfon asks.

"That's what I'm not entirely sure about," I say, "but it leads me to my next piece of information. A human infiltrated the palace last night and went straight for the weapons stash."

Nyxia's eyes go wide, and Flauvis lets out a rumbling growl.

Tris scoffs. "Oh, so now that Ustrin is dead, they want their weapons back?"

"Not the weapons," I say slowly. "The assailant paid the weapons no heed. He was coming for this." I wave my hand at Fehr, who had been standing near the guards at the perimeter of the room. He steps forward and brings the small wooden crate I'd brought him just before the meeting and sets it on the table in front of me.

Gingerly, I remove the lid from the box, letting its contents fill the room. Even within the enormous atrium, the light is blinding. Squinting against its luminance, I grasp the orb of light in my palm. Considering my hands are much smaller than the assailant's had been, I'm only able to mute a minor portion of the light, but it should be enough to let the fae glimpse its shape. I hold it out for several silent moments before returning it to the crate and shutting the lid. Then I reach beneath the sashes tied around my waist to retrieve the Chariot and place it on the table next to the box. My tone sharpens as I pin Estel beneath a glare. "The human came here with this."

My indignation immediately dims as I take in the horror on her sparkling face. Her expression shifts again and again, eyes not on the Chariot but on the crate, and each new countenance she wears is only more terrified than the last.

Nyxia's face whips toward the Star Queen, rage heating her cheeks. "You have some explaining to do."

Estel brings a shimmering hand to her lips, the particles that compose her body buzzing faster than I've seen before. She takes a step back, and Aspen stiffens at my side. The nearest guards reach for the hilts of their swords and shift their spears. But she doesn't try to flee, eyes still trained on the crate. "It was supposed to be destroyed," she whispers.

"What was?" Aspen says through his teeth.

Estel's chest heaves. "The Parvanovae."

"*That's* the Parvanovae?" Nyxia's tone is shriller than I've ever heard, her composure shaken as she points a trembling finger at the crate. "The thing Queen Evelyn was just holding in her *hand*?"

Even Flauvis is unnerved, his hackles raised along his back. "It can't be."

Tris throws her hands in the air, shaking her head of cherry blossoms in confusion. "What is a para...parva..."

"It's a star bomb, Tris," Nyxia snaps before burning me with a glare. "A tiny, living star encased in crystal, and it could have killed us all, should it be dropped."

My mouth goes dry as the implications wash over me. I recall the chilling instinct I had to catch it when the assailant nearly dropped it. And I *held* it. A bomb. In my hand. "Blazing iron," I mutter.

Aspen runs his hands through his hair, shifting from foot to foot. "So, the humans are after a bomb."

"But what exactly is it?" Aelfon asks. "You say it's a star bomb, but why does it even exist? It isn't a human creation."

"No," Estel says with a breathy sigh. "It's fae. My sister created it."

"Queen Estora?" Aspen says, eyes incredulous. "She *made* this abomination?"

"You never knew my sister well," Estel says, her tone calm despite its defensive edge. "She was a brilliant inventor, even more talented than I am. She worked not only with time and space, but on the cutting edge harnessing the power of the stars. When the war with the humans began, she put all her efforts into creating something that could defeat our enemies. Just before the war ended, she invented this, the Parvanovae. It wasn't meant to be an abomination; it was meant to save our realm. It was…a mistake."

"My mother told me about it," Nyxia mutters, eyes fixated on the crate, shoulders tense as if she expects it to burst open at any moment. "The final, desperate move the fae were prepared to take before the treaty was made."

"This was the final motion the council was going to pass?" Aspen asks, mouth twisted with disgust. "The one to rid the isle of humans forever?"

Estel nods, expression grave as the shimmering particles tug her lips into a frown. "The very same. The council had gotten word that the mainland king was now involved and was preparing to send in armies to invade. Their weapons were said to be far more destructive than anything we'd seen used on the isle yet. The Parvanovae was our final defense."

Nyxia's eyes are glazed. "It would have killed everyone. Including the fae."

"Almost everyone," Estel corrects. "Some of the fae could have survived, but yes, most would die. Worse, the isle would take centuries to recover, leaving even the survivors with little to live off of."

Nausea churns in my stomach as I envision the carnage, the damage. If this star bomb can cause such detrimental effects, it must be far more powerful than any human explosive that exists today. The fact that the fae were willing to use it chills me to the bone. It's no wonder even the cold, cruel Melusine was willing to stop it. Despite the terrible mother she eventually became, my heart aches with the understanding that she alone saved the Fair Isle. Or perhaps I should say it was Aspen alone. For his birth was what swayed her heart, convinced her to shift to the seelie side and forge the treaty with the humans.

My gaze slides to my mate, taking in the distress on his face. I wonder if he's thinking about his mother too.

"It was supposed to be destroyed," Nyxia says through her teeth, eyes burning into Estel. "Why is it still in existence?"

Estel shakes her head. "Estora said—"

Her words cut off, and she closes her eyes. When she opens them, her expression looks puzzled. "No, I suppose she never did outright say it was destroyed. Only hinted that it was. Hinted it was no longer a threat to us."

"Did she give it to Ustrin, then?" I ask.

"I don't know," she says. "Even when I took her place as queen, she never said a thing about it. However, she was never the same after the war ended. She was bitter and weak, which was why I challenged her as alpha. She must have sided with Ustrin before she left us for the stars."

I furrow my brow. "Left you for the stars?"

"She died." Nyxia doesn't bother with any pretenses of sympathy.

"So, Ustrin has had the star bomb this entire time. But what about this?" I point at the Chariot. "It looks just like yours."

Estel opens her palm, revealing her own Chariot that she arrived here with. Setting it next to the other confirms they are nearly identical, aside from the scratches and signs of age on the one the human brought. "Yes, that is one of the first I ever made."

I bristle. "How did a human come to have it?"

She seems unconcerned by the suspicion in my tone. "When the war ended, one of my Chariots was given to the councilman who exiled King Caleos. It was an additional gift to ensure the balance established by the treaty. He never used it, nor any of his descendants, to my knowledge."

"That likely changed with Mr. Duveau," I say. "He must have used it to meet with Ustrin, to transport the weapons here with ease and without any of the other fae royals knowing about it."

"Estel," Aspen says, "is there a chance the Renounced know about the bomb? Is that what Dahlia truly was after?"

She considers this for a moment. "I don't think so. All who know of the Parvanovae know how dangerous it is. The seelie would never approve of using it."

"Perhaps they want it so it can be destroyed," Tris says.

Estel shakes her head. "Even if that were the case, not even the Renounced would be so careless as to send a human to retrieve it."

I bite my lip, eyes going unfocused. "Then that means Mr. Duveau is acting alone."

Minuette lets out a low whistle. "The humans want to blow up the isle."

Flauvis shows his teeth in a wicked snarl. "I say we use it to destroy the mainland. That will put the humans in their place."

My heart leaps into my throat. "What? No!"

"That is not what I joined this alliance for," Aelfon says, springing to his feet and stomping an enormous hoof.

"But Flauvis has a point," Nyxia says, and I burn her with a glare.

"I didn't come here to blow up humans either," Tris says, putting a hand on her hip. "I joined you to stand against the Renounced. Even though we must bring back the Old Ways, I remain seelie."

"As do I," Aelfon agrees.

"Pitiful." Flauvis shakes his wolf head with a canine grin. "We are gifted with the one thing that can silence our enemies forever, and you get cold hooves, Aelfon?"

Aelfon raises an enormous clenched fist and the wolf king crouches into a defensive posture, ready to spring off all four paws—

"Enough!" Aspen's voice rings through the atrium. "We did not call this meeting to divide our alliance."

Flauvis makes a muttering sound that mimics Aspen's tone in a high-pitched whine, but returns to his place at the table. Aelfon too stands down and lowers onto his chair.

Aspen continues. "We called you here because the threat from the humans is far more imminent than we originally thought." He turns to me, drawing the attention of the others.

"He's right," I say. "According to the assailant, the mainland has already sent warships. Even if we can keep the Parvanovae out of their hands, they're coming for us."

19

———

Shouts and arguments roar across the table, so chaotic it makes my head spin.

"This is just like the last war, isn't it?" Tris puts her hand to her forehead, expression panicked.

"It's worse," Aelfon says. "The humans have far more terrifying weapons than they had back then."

He's right, but I can't bring myself to say so out loud. I've read about the latest weapons the mainland army has begun to manufacture, seen sketches in the broadsheets of tanks, rifles, machine guns, and mortars. Airships that soar through the sky like monstrous birds, dropping explosives on enemy soil. All things that make the swords, spears, and the occasional gun I've glimpsed on the isle seem like children's toys.

"All the more reason to use the star bomb," Flauvis says.

"No," Aspen argues. "We need more information before we can consider using the Parvanovae."

Heat rises to my cheeks. That wasn't the argument I'd expected him to make. Fury radiates through my blood as I whirl toward my mate. "Are you seriously entertaining this idea?" I say in a furious whisper.

He doesn't meet my eyes as his response comes through the Bond. *I'm sorry, Evie, but we must discuss every possibility we have. Not only in terms of winning the war, but to make the Alpha Alliance fair.*

I continue to burn him with my scorn, fists clenched so tight I can feel my nails slice into my palms. It takes no small effort to wrench my gaze away, back to the arguing royals while tears sting my eyes. I'm surprised how protective I feel over the humans after everything they've done to me. But the truth is, for every corrupt councilman, soldier, or mayor, there are thousands of innocent lives. They don't deserve to die in a war they hardly understand. A war no human is ever taught the true history of. Until recently, not even many fae knew the truth—that the descendants of King Caleos had survived the very execution that sparked the first war.

Without realizing it, my voice leaps from my throat, quavering despite the fire that roars through it. "We cannot continue to perpetuate the same corrupt violence the humans began. If we annihilate their people, we are no better than the townspeople who burnt my grandmother at the stake."

"That's all very sunny and idealistic of you," Nyxia says, "but if a human army truly is on its way, we have no other choice but to meet that violence with greater violence."

"There must be another way," I say through my teeth.

"There is." Estel's voice is raw, quiet. All eyes turn to her. "We shift our tactic from violence to protection."

Nyxia cocks her head to the side, skepticism clear on her face. "And how do you suggest we do that?"

Estel sighs. "Before my sister shared her plans to destroy the Parvanovae, she'd had ideas to transmute the energy of the bomb to fuel an enchantment that would make the wall between Faerwyvae and Eisleigh impenetrable, keeping all humans from crossing over to our land. That, of course, went against the treaty."

Flauvis scoffs. "She should have done it anyway."

Estel ignores this. "If she discovered a way to use the Parvanovae to protect the wall, then I can figure it out too."

Aelfon stomps a hoof. "What good is a wall when warships could surround the isle and attack by sea?"

"We extend the wall around the perimeter of Faerwyvae as well," Estel says.

Nyxia rolls her eyes. "Yet another idealistic suggestion that sounds pretty but lacks execution."

"Nyxia's right," Aspen says. "Even if we could get the strongest earthen fae to begin construction at once, we can only do so in our own courts. How are we to ensure the wall gets built around the courts belonging to the Renounced?"

"I have a better idea," Flauvis says. "We destroy the wall, free our magic to flow over the entire isle. Then we kill all the pathetic humans and bomb the mainland."

I open my mouth to argue, but Tris speaks first. "How many times must I remind you I am seelie? I will not condone annihilating the humans on the isle!"

Flauvis ignores this. "In fact, Evelyn should leave for the mainland at once to detonate it."

"Excuse me?" I shoot the wolf king a scowl, hand on my hip. "You do know that would kill me too, right?"

"It's for the greater good." A malicious, teasing grin lifts the corners of his muzzle.

"It could kill more of our kind too," Estel argues. "The Parvanovae is untested technology. There's no saying how far the damage could reach, even if detonated solely on the mainland. If the blast radius reached the isle, only the fae with ethereal forms could survive."

"Then the rest of us burrow underground, just in case," Flauvis says.

Aspen puts his hands on the table and leans toward the Winter King. "Evelyn is not sacrificing herself to use the bomb."

Flauvis shrugs. "Then do it yourself."

Aspen growls, but Nyxia lifts a hand, shadows writhing around her shoulders and darkening the room for a split second. "This conversation is getting way off course." The royals quiet, but Aspen and Flauvis don't take their eyes from each other. "Estel understands the Parvanovae more than any of us, and if she says it isn't safe, then we cannot rely on it as our first course of action. I agree we must keep it as a last resort, at the very least as a potent threat to hold against the humans, but let us first consider the idea of extending the wall." She turns her gaze to Estel. "What is your plan?"

The particles on her face rearrange, shifting from worried to composed. "I'll need at least a few days to go through my sister's old blueprints. I know she recorded her original findings regarding the Parvanovae and the wall. In the meantime, Aelfon will organize builders to erect the stones around our courts."

"That still only gives us a partial wall," Nyxia says. "What do we do about the Renounced?"

Flauvis reveals his teeth in a chilling grin. "Let's turn those vile iron weapons on them. If they want them so badly, let's deliver them. We'll bury them right in their hearts so we need not concern ourselves with them any longer."

"No," I say. "We'd have to sacrifice our own—"

The wolf king bursts into maniacal laughter. "*Our own*, the human queen says!"

Aspen takes a forbidding step toward the wolf. "Evelyn is fae. She has proven herself worthy to the All of All."

"Ah, something not even you have done, little king."

Aspen clenches his fists, tensing as if he might leap across the table, but again Nyxia stops them with a flash of her shadows. "Enough with the alpha ego measuring contest. We can see they are both large indeed."

Aelfon snickers, but Aspen and Flauvis again stand down. I'm starting to think the wolf king lives for baiting others. He's worse than Franco.

I steel my nerves and take my opportunity to finish what I was trying to say. "I've seen what it's like when the fae are forced to use iron weapons. It's cruel and we cannot stoop to that level."

Flauvis mutters another high-pitched mockery, but I ignore him.

"But I agree something must be done with the Renounced before we face the human threat. We cannot fight two enemies at once, and we need their cooperation to extend the wall around Faerwyvae."

"Then what do we do?" Minuette asks, her blue hair fluttering around her head.

I ponder for a moment, pieces of a puzzle coming together in my mind. "We need to convince them to agree to a ceasefire until the wall is complete and the human threat is dealt with."

Tris nods her agreement. "They may be our enemies, but they deserve to be warned of what's coming."

"Will that be enough to get them to stand down?" Aelfon asks. "We can't tell them about the Parvanovae, in case they get any clever ideas, which means they can't know our plan for enchanting our proposed wall."

"We can tell them Estel has created the technology to protect us," Tris says with a shrug. "That's simple enough."

"If they were that easy to reason with," Flauvis says, "we wouldn't be at war in the first place."

"True," Nyxia says. "I doubt they'd even agree to hear us out. How can we convince them we're sincere? How do we get them to meet us for a peaceful exchange of words in the first place?"

Aspen shakes his head. "We'll have to offer them a compelling bargain."

"But what?" Tris asks.

My eyes unfocus as ideas shift and reassemble in my mind. A bargain. We need a compelling bargain.

Then I see it.

"I know what we have to do." All eyes turn to me, burning with curiosity, disdain, hope, fear. "Flauvis is right. If it's the weapons they want, we should deliver them."

Flauvis grumbles. "Why do I get the feeling it doesn't involve the best part of my suggestion? The part about shoving them through their hearts?"

Aelfon shakes his horned head. "We cannot give them weapons they could use against us."

"We won't," I say. "Not exactly, at least."

Aspen turns to face me, brow quirked. "What are you thinking?"

"If they agree to a ceasefire, we will agree to deliver the weapons once the battle with the humans is resolved. What they won't know is that the weapons will be unusable by the time they receive them."

Aspen narrows his eyes, then his lips quirk into a devious grin.

I lift my chin and meet his approving gaze. "The weapons won't be usable because I'm going to melt them."

20

———

Apparently, talk of fae deception was exactly what the Alpha Alliance needed to forge unity, for the rest of the meeting goes smoothly. Plans are finalized and our message to request a peaceful exchange of words with the Renounced is drafted. Nyxia promises to send it with one of her owls as soon as she returns to Lunar. By the time the meeting is adjourned, the mood in the atrium is far less grim.

As the royals begin shuffling toward the hall to exit the palace, Aspen turns to face me, taking my hand in his and bringing it to his lips. As he lowers my hand, his mouth quirks into a crooked grin. "You truly are a brilliant queen," he says. "Or perhaps it's your devious human side that is so wickedly clever."

His confidence in my plan makes my chest feel warm, but I can't keep my mind from spinning up the worst possible scenarios. I bite the inside of my cheek. "Do you think the Renounced will buy it? Do you think they'll even agree to meet?"

"The Renounced are losing allies by the day," he says. "They won't be able to refuse any chance at regaining the upper hand."

"I hope you're right," I say with a sigh.

He leans in and kisses my cheek, then trails his lips to mine. The nearby sounds of the royals chatting at the other end of the atrium keeps me from deepening the kiss, and too soon he breaks away. "I'll see the others out." His eyes flash to the side, a suspicious gleam in them, before he steps back and makes his way to join the royals. That's when I realize what—or whom—he'd glanced at.

Estel remains at the table, eyes trained on me while Aspen leads the others down the hall. Fehr comes up beside me, gaze shifting from me to the Star Queen. "Shall I wait with you or join your mate?"

I study my guest, her folded, shimmering hands, her serene expression. There's no threat in her lingering presence, only a silent request for privacy. Besides, she was the one most firmly on my side about not using the Parvanovae. "You may join my mate and see that the others are safely on their way," I tell Fehr.

With a bow, he follows Aspen.

Once we're alone, Estel slowly rounds the table to approach me. As she closes the distance between us, I'm forced to crane my neck to meet her eyes. As I do, the particles on her face shift into a somber expression, lips pulled down at the corners. "Thank you for supporting my stance regarding the Parvanovae," she says.

"I'm thankful for you as well. I agree with everything you said. The technology is untested and could have detrimental effects we can't even begin to imagine."

"And I agree that not all humans are our enemies."

I quirk a brow. "You're neutral unseelie, then?"

She nods. "My sister was not, but in the end, even she regretted creating the Parvanovae after the war ended."

"Then why didn't she destroy it like she said she'd planned?"

"I don't know. Perhaps she never was able to find a way to unmake it, only to transmute it like she'd planned with the wall."

"Do you really think it will work? Moving the wall and infusing an enchantment with the energy of the star bomb?"

"Once I find my sister's blueprints, I'll know for sure." Her gaze shifts from me to the crate on the table. "I will take it off your hands if you believe it is safer with me. However, I hate to admit I fear it being anywhere within reach of other fae. *Any* other fae."

Her words skirt around the truth, but I can read beneath what she's left unsaid. She's afraid of what would happen if even one of our allies got hold of it.

"I'll keep it here," I say, despite the nausea that turns my stomach at the thought of the bomb being in such close proximity for even a minute longer. "So long as you're certain no other Chariot is in possession by the humans."

She tilts her head at the two travel devices—hers and the one the human had—still resting next to the crate. "That was the only one. But are you certain humans won't try to take it another way?"

I bite my lip, considering that. As unlikely as it is that humans would try to infiltrate my court and palace on foot and without means of immediate travel, the possibility exists. And with all those iron weapons...

An idea forms in my mind, a way to prevent humans and fae alike from getting to the weapons room. Even better, it ties in so well with the deception we've planned for the Renounced. My lips pull into a tight smile. "I think I know what to do about that."

"Very well," Estel says. "I shall leave it with you." She reaches across the table and takes up the two Chariots, brow furrowed as she studies them. After a few moments, she extends a hesitant hand, palm up to reveal the slightly more beat-up Chariot, the one that had belonged to Mr. Duveau. "I think you should keep this as well."

My fingers tremble as I take it from her. "Why?"

"It was gifted to forge the treaty," she says. "It makes sense it should now belong to the one who has broken it."

I study the silver disc, flipping open the cover to reveal the golden light of the orb and the crystals surrounding it. "I don't know how to use it," I say as I snap it shut and try to hand it back to her.

She gives a dismissive shrug, making no move to take it back. "Like all magic, it's fueled by your intent. Simply open it and think of a place you've already been that you would like to go." Her face shifts into a smile. "Accept my gift, Queen Evelyn. I've come to trust you. I hope you trust me too."

As loathe as I am to trust much of anyone right now, I must admit this meeting has changed my suspicions about her. She might be the only one on the Alpha Alliance, aside from Aspen and Nyxia, that I trust at all. I match her smile and close my fingers over the Chariot. "Thank you, Estel."

I OPEN THE DOOR TO THE ROYAL CHAMBER, SURPRISED WHEN I FIND IT EMPTY. Before the meeting, I'd left my sister here with Foxglove, Lorelei, and Breeda. I hadn't ordered Amelie to remain in the room, only to stay at Lorelei's side. They must have found elsewhere to await the end of the meeting.

Just as well, I suppose, considering what I hold in my hand.

Safe from prying eyes, I stalk the perimeter of the room, looking for a place to keep the Chariot. When I accepted the gift, my first instinct was to hide it in the weapons room with the Parvanovae, but I remembered what Estel had said about it needing to be charged by starlight after it's used. If there's ever a chance I want to operate it, I need to place it somewhere beneath the open sky. But where won't it be in danger of being stolen?

I move to the windows and open the golden shutters. Leaning slightly over one of the ledges, a terra cotta window box catches my eye. I look down the row of other windows and see each hosts a similar rectangular box, all filled with tiny green succulents and miniature cacti with orange and purple blooms. I hadn't noticed them last night, but their inconspicuous design makes them the perfect hiding place for the Chariot. Carefully tucking the disc beneath a spiky, green limb—

"Oooh, what's that, Your Majesty?"

I jump back, sticking myself on several spikes in the process, as Breeda hovers before me. "Do not sneak up on me." My words come out much harsher than I intend, and I bring my tender finger to my mouth to soothe where I'd been poked.

The little sprite's expression falls, her red flames dimming to a pink. "Oh, Most Beautiful Gracious Majesty, I truly didn't mean to! I saw the meeting was over and came to find you."

I sigh, forcing the fire to retreat from my veins. "It's all right, Breeda," I say with more composure. "Next time, state your presence if I've yet to acknowledge you."

Her color returns, as does her grin. "Yes, Your Majesty." She spins in a circle, then lifts her chin, eyeing the window box. "Is that a Chariot—"

"Please, Breeda, do not speak of it. You must tell no one. In fact, make it your duty to guard it." I curse myself inwardly, knowing I'll have to move it once I get the chance.

She nods. "I won't let you down."

"Where are the others?" I ask, mostly to change the subject. But also, I should relieve Lorelei from her charge. It can't have been fun to babysit someone she so thoroughly dislikes. I'll have to thank her with a bottle of Midnight Blush, if I can get my hands on some.

"I know just where they are," Breeda says. "Shall I take you to them?"

"Please." I follow the sprite out of my room and into the hall. She leads me away from where I know the sleeping quarters to be and into a part of the palace I don't think I've seen before. The doors are sparser, the hall wider. She pauses before an ornate pair of golden doors beneath an arched doorway.

I open one of the doors to reveal an enormous room, almost as vast as the atrium. The ceiling towers high overhead beneath a marble dome, moonlight streaming in through the long, wide windows. Orbs of light illuminate the room, their reflections dancing over the shimmering sunstone floor.

"Evie!" My sister's voice calls my attention to the perimeter of the circular room, where she, Foxglove, and Lorelei lounge in a sitting area near the wall. As I approach, I see evidence of half-filled glasses and decanters of wine. My sister rises to her feet, cheeks blushed pink, eyes alight like I haven't seen in such a long time. "It's a ballroom," she says, smile stretching from ear to ear. "*Your* ballroom. Isn't it incredible?"

"It is." My words come out stiff, despite the awe the room instills.

Foxglove lifts an empty glass. "Shall I pour you some? It's a Fire Court specialty. Agave Ignitus wine."

"It's so good." Lorelei's words are slow and slurred as she swirls the amber liquid in her glass. "You've got to try it."

Breeda flits in front of me. "It really is, Your Majesty."

I stare at my fae friends, the sprite, my sister, stripped of all words. A weight has settled into my stomach, and it takes me a moment to understand why. Then my gaze settles back on Amelie, and I understand.

Amelie is smiling, happy, as are her companions. Gone is the disdain Foxglove and Lorelei had first shown her when I brought her from the dungeon, as if it was never there at all. It's just like it was when we first arrived at Bircharbor. My sister, in her sweet and ever-likable way, has won their hearts all over again.

When I left my sister under Lorelei's care this evening, the wood nymph had grumbled. I hadn't expected to return and find them drinking amiably in a ballroom.

For reasons I can hardly comprehend, a lump rises in my throat, a feeling of betrayal sending fire through my veins. Before I can think, those flames are leaping from my lungs, weaving into my words. "I don't recall giving any of you permission to wander my palace or get drunk off my wine stores."

The smile slips from Amelie's lips. Foxglove and Lorelei stiffen, placing their glasses on the table. Lorelei rises to her feet, eyes wide and full of a trepidation I've never seen her wear for me. For Aspen, maybe, but never for me.

It's enough to cool my rage. Blazing iron, maybe Aspen had a point about the difficulties of appointing friends to positions of service when you're a royal. I hate the opposing forces that swarm inside me—anger at seeing them so at leisure, shame at the look in Lorelei's eyes.

With a deep breath, I do my best to compose myself. "Lorelei, can I speak with you for a moment?"

She nods and approaches me. Amelie follows, seemingly against her will.

Then I recall the order I gave her to remain at Lorelei's side. "Amelie, you may wait with Foxglove while I speak with Lorelei."

My sister nods and returns to her seat, while Lorelei closes the rest of the distance between us. She meets my eyes with hesitation. "Your Majesty?"

"I'm sorry," I say in a rush. "I didn't mean to react like that. I was just...worried."

Her shoulders relax, the frown smoothing from her face. "About what?"

My eyes flash from her to Amelie. "About..."

She turns to follow my gaze, then lowers her voice. "I owe you an apology too," she says. "I was wrong to be so firmly against you bringing your sister here. I think you were right about her. She...she seems sincere."

My throat feels dry at those words. I was *right* about her? No, this is all wrong. That's not what I'd intended to happen. I wanted to watch her, investigate her. Not open her to friends and dresses and ballrooms.

A life devoid of comfort and friendship.

My conversation with Fehr echoes in my head, creating a swarm of conflict in my heart. Again, I'm plagued by the same questions that fought inside my mind last night. *What is it I want from Amelie? To love her or hate her? To trust her or suspect her? Am I waiting for her to prove me right or prove me wrong?*

I still don't know the answer.

With a shake of my head, I burn the questions from my mind and return my attention to Lorelei. "She didn't say or do anything suspicious while she was with you?"

Lorelei shrugs. "No, she was silent. I admit, Foxglove and I gave her the cold shoulder until about an hour ago when we found the wine and decided to explore the palace." Her expression falls again. "I'm sorry we did that."

I wave a dismissive hand. "It's fine. But you're certain you found nothing suspect about her?"

She shakes her head, eyes turning down at the corners. "I think she's been through a lot more than I've given her credit for."

I grit my teeth, gaze trailing to my sister, who has already fallen back into casual conversation with Foxglove.

"Be careful," I say, my attention snapping back to Lorelei. "I may have been right to bring her here with us, but she's still a suspect. Do not let your guard down around her again."

The trepidation returns to her eyes at my stern tone, but this time I don't take it back.

If my sister wants my trust, she'll need to do a lot more than charm my friends to earn it.

21

———————

The next day, I stand at the end of a river composed of molten iron. It spreads out before me, spanning one side of the hallway to the other, where the weapons room is. The room remains empty aside from the small crate containing the Parvanovae and the few weapons— explosives, primarily—that I wasn't able to safely incinerate.

I've spent the best part of my morning and afternoon melting nearly every sword, axe, dagger, spear, and mace the room contained. All but a minor selection of blades I've decided to keep for myself, of course. Everything else has now become a flowing stream of red-orange iron, kept in its molten state by my faintly glowing flames that dance over the top. At each side of the river, my flames are absent, leaving hardened metal to act as a barrier that keeps the river from entering the weapons room or from extending too close to the stairs at the other end.

I smile at the job well done. A tiring job, I must say, but one that will keep both humans and fae alike from getting to the Parvanovae. No fae could make it down the stairs to get to this hallway with how much iron now flows into the hall, and no human could brave a river of molten metal and flames. Only I can call my fire back. Considering my hearth still glows steady with the flame I conjured two days ago, it's clear my fire will obey my will and remain for as long as I intend it to.

That's my theory, anyway.

The heat of the fire is oddly comforting, despite the sweat that soaks my brow. I crouch down, balancing on the balls of my feet as I watch the beauty of my dazzling, tricolor flames. There's something hypnotizing about the way they dance and sway over the molten river's surface, making me feel an odd sense of calm. Or perhaps it's exhaustion I feel. Whatever the case, I can't help but admire my work. My fire. My magic.

Extending my hand, I reach for the nearest flame, letting its heat tickle the tips of my fingers. I open my palm, turning it upward, and the flame climbs over it, swirling until it shifts into a tiny orb. I let it dance and undulate, watching it until my eyes grow heavy.

Indeed, I should probably get some rest.

I lean forward again, about to return the flame to join the rest, when another thought crosses my mind, one that sharpens my senses and makes me feel suddenly awake.

Instead of rest, perhaps I should practice my magic.

I lift my palm again and focus on my orb of fire. Then, without touching it, I will it to rise.

It shifts and sways, moves and undulates. But for the most part, it remains an orb hovering just over my palm.

With a sigh, I close my eyes and try to summon the same elemental connection I felt when I lit the hearth—the dance between air and fire. I created my river of melted weapons through touch, but now I want to hone the skill I've yet to master. With human armies coming our way, not to mention the meeting we hope to have with the Renounced, sharpening my fire magic as well as I can is more important than ever.

I breathe in, letting the dense, hot air fill my lungs, then breathe out, letting air whistle between my lips. Calm settles over me. I conjure thoughts of running, leaping, air brushing against my fur when I'm in my fox form, whipping my human hair the same way it constantly dances through Minuette's.

Eyes still closed, I focus on the heat of the fire brushing my skin, seeing the orb in my mind's eye. I envision the flame lifting, rising, sensing the balance between air and fire, the way it feeds it, raises it, encircles it, pervades it.

When I open my eyes, my orb hovers several inches above my hand.

Pride swells in my chest, but I try not to let it overcome me as I focus on the next feat. With my intention firmly in my mind, I will the flame to move away from me. I maintain my connection to the air and fire elements, watching as the orb floats higher, moves down the hall, following the river. Once it reaches the far end, I will it to lower.

As my flame disappears to join the rest, my chest bubbles with excitement. I did it! I moved my fire through space. Not just once, not just in a single flash of motion. I controlled its speed, trajectory, height, distance. My success should be enough to satisfy me, but it only fuels a deeper yearning for mastery. What if...

"Metal is earth, right?" I mutter as I squint at the river. "Earth is an element I should be able to control."

Again, I close my eyes, igniting my inner fire, reconnecting to air, and gathering all I know about earth. Rocks and plants are obvious. Logic and facts feel like they fit in here well. But I also remember what I learned from the goblin I met when I first visited the Twelfth Court. *Safety. Security,* he'd said. I wrap it all around me, picturing my fox paws padding over soft dirt, solid rock, lush grass. I see myself in the operating room, assessing facts and figures, using logic to dispense the proper amount of laudanum and chloroform. Then I imagine the halls of this palace, the walls of the apothecary that was my home, the composition of metal and stone that make up the weapons I've used to defend my sense of safety.

Once again, I lift my palm, and this time I picture it shaping an orb of the metal. My fire dances inside it, air envelops it, lifts it, helps it rise.

With a deep breath, I open my eyes. Just like the hovering flame, my orb of molten iron drifts above the river. My mouth falls open at the sight.

"You really are mastering the elements, aren't you?"

I startle at the sound of Aspen's voice so close to my ear, but I manage to maintain my focus on the orb. At once, logic tells me it isn't possible he could be here, not with the iron so close.

But as I turn my head to take in his form, the way he crouches at my side, studying my deadly river, I see the telltale violet aura that surrounds him. He's here through the Bond.

I grin, returning my gaze to my floating orb. With control, I will the orb to slowly lower and return to the river. "I wouldn't say I'm *mastering* them. Not yet at least."

He faces me, eyes drinking me in. "No, I suppose you aren't."

I meet his gaze, brow furrowed. "You aren't supposed to agree with me."

"Then you shouldn't be so self-deprecating," he says with a smirk. He leans closer. Even though he's only here through the Bond, my awareness of his presence, his closeness, is as strong as if he were truly here. The energy sizzles between us just the same. "Besides, I meant it. Compared to how you've mastered my heart, that hovering orb is nothing."

I blush beneath his stare. "I don't know if I should swoon or roll my eyes at that."

His eyes fall to my lips. "I suggest you kiss me."

I place a hand on the side of his face, aware of the usual discrepancy of touch that exists between us when we visit through the Bond. Still, it's enough. Bringing our lips together, I luxuriate in the pressure of his mouth, the caress of his tongue. It stirs desire in my heart, in my core, and I want nothing more than to leave this hall to find him.

I gently pull away. "Where are you right now?"

"The bedroom next to yours," he says. He bites his lip, hunger heavy in his eyes. "Will I be joining you tonight? Or do you want another night with your sister?" There's no malice or judgment in his voice. Just a question.

Mention of Amelie sobers some of the passion heating my blood. I groan, considering what to say. So far, all evidence has proven her compliance with my commands, both with her own willingness and through the power of her name. Still, I hesitate to leave her alone at night. There are so many more what-ifs—what if I'm wrong? What if she isn't following my commands at all, but some lingering command of Cobalt's, forcing her to act as a spy? What if he comes for her in the night and takes her away again? What if I lose her again?

The last question catches me off guard, and I shake it from my head before I can analyze it too deeply. "One more night," I whisper. "That's all I need."

The disappointment is clear on Aspen's face, but he hides it with a crooked smile. "You can have as many as you need."

"But in the meantime..." I lean in and place a kiss at the corner of his jaw, sliding one hand behind his neck while the other moves up his chest, his torso, down his stomach to the waist of his trousers. He lets out a gasp as I slide my hand over the front of them. "I should come to you," I whisper, "so we can do this in person."

"Or," he says, snaking a hand around my waist and lifting me as he rises to his feet. My legs wrap around his hips, and seconds later I feel the warm volcanic stone wall press into my back. His lips crush into mine and I eagerly receive them, the caress of his tongue lighting a fire at my core. It feels so much like he's really here, but I crave every part that's missing. The heat is there, energy humming between our bodies. The rosemary cinnamon scent of his skin mingles with the smell of hot iron, and even his form feels solid. But there's something just slightly off about the pressure between our lips, the feel of his hands cupping my backside as I pull him closer.

It's enough to make me crave him harder than I ever have before.

Then again, there's something new and exciting about this, something enticing about the thought of being intimate across time and space. Perhaps in my normal state of mind, the idea would be unsettling, but right now, with him feeling so close, with his violet aura invading my senses...

"Aspen," I gasp as his lips trail down my neck. "Take me now."

With a groan, he presses me harder against the wall, lips returning to mine as one hand leaves my backside to grasp my knee, then trails up my thigh. Heat burns hot at my core, tingling at the apex of my thighs. I move against him, hating the linen of his trousers that creates a barrier between us. Unable to handle it a moment longer, I reach between us and slide them down—

I find myself suddenly on my feet, all warmth stripped from me as Aspen's body is no longer against my own. My chest heaves as I fight to catch my breath. Brow furrowed, I stare at the empty space where my mate just was.

There's no way I imagined all that.

"Well, that was incredibly awkward," comes Aspen's stilted voice. I whirl to find him standing next me, hands on his hips as he stares unfocused at the floor in front of him. His shirt and trousers are wrinkled but the latter are no longer pulled down. His golden cheeks are tinged with red and a sheepish grin seems to be hiding behind his pursed lips.

"What happened?"

He rubs his brow, his grin finally breaking through. "Foxglove has informed me our people have arrived at the palace. My household and your fire fae from Lunar."

I've never seen him so uncomposed; it's almost comical. And when I imagine what strange sight the ambassador must have just walked in on, I can't stop the laughter that bubbles in my chest and bursts from my lips.

He meets my gaze, trying unsuccessfully to look stern. "You think this is funny?"

"It is. Besides, I think you may have made one of Foxglove's lifelong dreams come true?"

He crosses his arms over his chest, lips quirked as he pins me with a teasing glare. "And what exactly would that be?"

I can hardly form the words through bursts of laughter. "A glimpse at your magnificent kingdom."

22

───────────

Aspen has regained his composure by the time we meet in the atrium. The only thing that betrays him is the embarrassed smile that continues to tug at his lips, and when he winks at me, part of me considers pulling him up the stairs to lock ourselves in the bedroom.

The thought doesn't linger long before Breeda soars into the atrium and hovers between us. "Everyone is here!" she squeals. "They're waiting in the courtyard for you to greet them."

"Fehr won't give permission for any to enter without your word," Lorelei adds, approaching from the hall that leads to the palace entrance. Foxglove follows just a step behind, cheeks crimson as he adjusts his spectacles, clearly avoiding Aspen's gaze.

My heart sinks as we close the distance between us and the ambassadors, and I'm worried that the awkwardness between my mate and Foxglove might not be easily undone.

"They're just outside," Lorelei says with an easy grin, oblivious to the tension. "Aspen's household too." She waves a hand forward, then pauses as if she's reconsidering her actions. Pursing her lips, her eyes flick to mine before she bends into a humble bow, arm extended for me to pass ahead of her.

Some of the day's mirth is stripped away from me at the sight, reminding me of the conversation we had yesterday. Instead of walking in front of her, however, I link my arm through hers. "Let's go."

Her eyes widen with surprise, but her lips pull into a grin. As we make our way down the hall, I hazard a glance behind me. Foxglove's neck is nearly swallowed by his shoulders as he shuffles at Aspen's side. My mate glances from me to Foxglove, then gives a resigned shake of his head. Slinging his arm over the ambassador's shoulders, he gives him a cajoling smile. "Did you like what you saw, my friend?"

Foxglove blushes deeper, eyes flicking up at Aspen as a grin stretches across his face. "I think it would be a treasonous lie to say I didn't, Your Majesty."

Aspen barks a laugh.

Foxglove's gaze meets mine and he lifts his brows, the tension seeming to melt from him as his shoulders relax. "Queen Evelyn certainly is a lucky lover."

Aspen squeezes the ambassador to his side. "As are yours, Foxglove."

Content that the awkward rift has been smoothed over, I return my gaze straight ahead.

"What was that about?" Lorelei whispers.

"I'll tell you later," I say under my breath, stifling my giggle. "If Foxglove doesn't tell you first."

Outside, the courtyard is filled with fae too numerous to count. All of Aspen's refugees that had escaped Bircharbor are here, as are most of the fire fae from Lunar. Dragons dart across the sky, wisps bob in clusters, kitsune explore the paths and plants, and an entire family of the crustacean-mushroom fae settle in by one of the rectangular ponds. I catch sight of Dune amongst the crowd, tapping anxiously from paw to paw as he barks directions at some of his comrades, clearly trying to maintain order over his traveling companions. But the fae seem too relieved to have arrived at their destination to pay him much heed, as they continue to flit about the court-yard, awed by what they see.

Fehr watches them all through slitted lids, bronze arms crossed over his chest. "Do you approve of their presence here, my queen?"

I find myself momentarily taken aback. That's the first time he's ever referred to me as *my queen*, and not just Your Majesty. "I do, Fehr. Any who seek shelter indoors may also be permitted inside the palace. Those who would like to apply for positions within the palace may take it up with you and Lorelei. Same goes for all of my mate's household. All of his people will need rooms and positions in the palace."

He nods. "It will be done."

I scan the crowd again, which has begun to quiet now that most have noticed my presence. Then silence falls completely, and the fae—both Aspen's and mine—lower into bows. Our names are uttered, creating a wave of sound before they rise.

A tiny figure with brown skin hobbles toward us. "I hope you are still in need of a healer," Gildmar says.

Aspen and I make our way down the stairs to greet her. "Of course," Aspen says.

"You and all of Aspen's household are welcome here," I add, "and will be given appropriate positions."

She looks from me to my mate. "What will happen, Your Majesty, when you defeat Cobalt? Will you rule from Irridae together or reclaim Bircharbor?"

We exchange a glance, neither knowing how to answer. That's something we've hardly discussed. "We have two wars to win," Aspen says. "Only then will we finalize such plans."

Gildmar nods, her smile wide.

"Evelyn!" A familiar voice steals my attention as a human girl comes charging up the stairs. Marie Coleman, dressed in trousers and a linen tunic, stumbles into a last-minute curtsy before taking my hands in hers, a dreamy look falling over her face as she gives an exaggerated sigh. "Your palace is more beautiful than anything I've seen so far."

I stare at her, blinking rapidly before I find my voice. "Thank you, Marie, but...what are you doing here?"

She furrows her brow, her smile wavering. "I came with King Aspen's household. Did you not expect I would come?"

"No," I say. Then, lowering my voice, I add, "I thought you would go home as soon as you learned the treaty was broken."

Her expression continues to fall. "Why would I go home? This is where I belong now."

I shake my head. "Without the treaty, the Reaping is over. There's nothing keeping you here."

She studies me as if I've grown two heads. "I know that. I'm choosing to stay."

It's my turn to look at her in disbelief. "But why? We're at war with your kind."

"*Our* kind," she corrects, "and I'm well aware."

"Then you should also be aware how dangerous it is for you to be here. We don't know what's going to happen."

"Do you honestly think it's any safer back in Sableton?"

"Yes! Here, if things go poorly, there are fae who wouldn't treat you well."

She lifts her chin. "I've already dealt with plenty of prejudice from the fae, trust me. I can handle myself."

"It's more than prejudice." I sigh, searching for words that will help her understand the very real threats she could be facing. "Not all unseelie are kind and playful. There are some that will literally eat you. And there are others who could hurt you, if they think it would help their position in the battles that are to come."

She tilts her head to the side and gives me a pointed look. "How is that any more terrifying than returning to human parents who groomed you from birth to be a bride to a stranger?" I open my mouth to argue, but she continues. "Look, Evel—*Your Majesty*, I mean—this is the first time I've felt alive in all my life. Back in Sableton, every moment of my life was planned. All I ever wanted was to sail the seas on Father's merchant ships, but instead, I was forced into dresses, taught how to play the pianoforte, and how to snag a wealthy husband. In my free time, I was told how to please the fae, should I ever be chosen for the Reaping."

"Marie, Faerwyvae isn't a place for some lighthearted adventure."

She shrugs. "That's not how I see it."

"You are in very real danger. We are at war."

"We're at war in Sableton too," she argues. "Please, Your Majesty. I understand your fear for me, but don't send me back there. I'd rather live a short and dangerous life here where I can be free than a long one acting as a slave to my parents and husband."

My shoulders slump. I don't know why I should care. Before she came to Faerwyvae, Marie Coleman meant nothing to me. She was only Maddie Coleman's younger sister. And Maddie Coleman is lower than dirt, in my mind. Still, I can't help but feel responsible for Marie. Her words conjure something that makes my heart ache—a comparison between the meek, plain girl she was back home and the bold, reckless creature she's become here. Would sending her back to Sableton truly be in her best interest?

Her eyes are pleading as she brings her clasped hands to her heart. "Please, Your Majesty."

I purse my lips, jaw shifting side to side. "Fine," I finally say with a groan. "But don't say I didn't warn you."

She throws her arms around my waist and crushes me in a hug before abruptly breaking off and tumbling into an awkward curtsy. "Sorry. Thank you. I can't tell you how much I appreciate you."

With a flick of my wrist, I wave her away, but not before giving her a warm smile that expresses all that I wasn't able to say out loud...

That I completely understand her.

She skips back to the courtyard to join the others, the joy bursting from her face as she relays something to a companion—one I recognize as Vane, one of Aspen's handsome servants. Then she turns to another familiar figure, Ocher. Both males grin at her as she chats, and by the way her lips move, I can only imagine she's speaking a mile a minute. Her attention flips from one male to the other, totally oblivious to the way they look at her as if mesmerized by a fascinating painting.

I turn to Aspen, who has just finished speaking with a group of his soldiers. When he catches my eye, he comes to me and circles his arms around my waist. "Your empty palace just got very, very busy," he says with a smirk.

"Perhaps we should have savored our temporary privacy more."

"Not that it did us much good when we did." The blush I saw earlier returns to his cheeks, making me love him even more than I did before. It's funny the little things I discover about my mate that make my affections grow. Like the fact that he's easily embarrassed.

Aspen's irises glitter with their shimmering autumn color as they lock on mine. Then they leave me to light on something overhead. I follow his gaze, just as the sound of flapping wings beats the air. A white owl with black spots lands at our feet, quirking its head at us. Aspen and I separate, and my mate's expression turns to steel. "What is it?" he asks.

A male voice comes from the owl. "Two messages from Queen Nyxia. First, her owls have confirmed sightings of warships heading toward the isle. Second, the meeting with the Renounced is tomorrow."

THAT EVENING, I STAND BEFORE MY MIRROR IN MY BEDROOM, THE BLUSH OF A pink and orange sunset lighting the room. Eyeing the length of my freshly donned gown, I shift side to side to see if any of my movements reveal the weapons I've concealed. My obsidian dagger is strapped to my thigh while an assortment of iron blades—the few I didn't melt—circle my waist.

The dress I wear is a deep red, another one of Amelie's designs. It covers my front and back from my neck to my ankles but remains open at the sides and is tied loosely at the waist. The dagger belts at my thigh and waist are covered by the design of the dress while still providing easy access for me to reach. I practice a few times, sliding my hand behind my back to retrieve an iron dagger from beneath the dress, then unsheathing my obsidian blade from my thigh.

"Are you going to tell me what's going on?" Amelie appears reflected in the mirror, coming up behind me as she wrings her hands. It's the third time she's asked since I came to add new commands that hinted at the need for travel.

I turn to face her, returning my weapons to their hidden sheaths. "I'll tell you when you need to know. If ever."

Her eyes are locked on my gown, as if seeking the invisible blades beneath it. "I'm worried about you," she whispers. "Whatever you're about to do..."

"Worry about yourself," I snap, turning away from her and moving to the bed where I stuff a few necessities into a bag.

"I'm worried about myself too," she says, following me. "You aren't...you aren't giving me back to *him*, are you? Please don't do this. Not unless you can guarantee me the means to kill him."

I pause and meet her eyes, surprised at the terror on her face. "That's not what we're doing."

"Then what is it?"

I ignore her and return to packing my bag. The Alpha Alliance will be meeting with the Renounced at midday tomorrow on the border between Fire and Solar. Fehr is in the process of allocating the best candidates to pull the coach Ustrin left behind so we can leave at once. My heart sinks at the thought of leaving the palace overnight, especially when Aspen's household and my own just arrived. However, we want to set up a proper camp and scope out the meeting place well in advance of the Renounced arriving. At least I trust the palace will be protected by Fehr, and the Parvanovae will remain inaccessible to anyone.

"Where's your bag?" I ask without looking at my sister.

With a sigh, she retrieves it from the sitting area, then places it on the bed next to mine. "Please." Her voice comes out with a stifled sob, stealing my attention to the anguish on her face. "Please tell me what's about to happen. I'm going out of my mind wondering if this is the end for me. If it is, just—"

"It's a meeting," I say through my teeth.

She furrows her brow. "What do you mean?"

I clench my jaw, hands on my hips as I shake my head in irritation. "I don't have to explain anything to you."

"If you're taking me too, it must have something to do with me."

I narrow my eyes. "Amelie, not everything is about you. I'm taking you because we won't be back by morning, perhaps not even by tomorrow night. It could take days to come to an agreement."

Her shoulders sag, relief ironing out the furrows on her brow. Then her gaze turns suspicious. "What's the meeting about?"

"What is it you don't understand? I don't have to explain a damn thing—"

"You can trust me, Evie. I've done nothing to show otherwise since I've returned to you."

Heat rises to my cheeks, a fiery rage flooding my veins. While she may be right, nothing will make up for what she's done. Still, there's that part of me that I hate to recognize. The part that softens with every day that goes by, the part that sees the sister she used to be. I let out a grumbling sigh. "We're meeting to establish a ceasefire."

"With whom?"

"Who do you think? With the Renounced."

Rage ignites on her face, transforming it in an instant. "You can't!"

I take a forbidding step toward her. "Is that so? Are you in any position to tell me what I can and can't do?"

Angry tears glaze her eyes. "The Renounced are our enemies. Cobalt is our enemy, and you promised me I could kill him."

"The ceasefire is temporary, only until we can defeat the human army that comes our way."

She doesn't seem surprised by this latter part, which tells me she's already heard about the oncoming threat. I'm sure I have Foxglove or Lorelei to thank for that. She throws her hands in the air and turns her back to me. When she speaks, her voice comes out quiet. "Every day Cobalt lives is like a knife twisting in my heart. Not to mention what the ghost of his commands do to my mind."

My heart squeezes, a lump rising in my throat at her anguish. I find my walls unraveling around me, and I shudder at how vulnerable it makes me feel. How weak and small. "We will kill him, Ami."

She slowly turns to face me again. "You won't make me see him, will you?"

I shake my head. "During the meeting, you'll remain behind where we make camp. He won't even know you're there. Unless..." My blood goes cold, a question that I've yet to ask burning in my throat. "Can Cobalt...sense you through the Bond? Can you feel each other? See each other?'

She tilts her head back, perplexed at my words. "Of course not. That's not how it works."

I bite back my arguments that it very well *can* work that way. Maybe Aspen is right. Perhaps only Bonded pairs who deeply love each other can connect the same way my mate and I do. "You truly don't love Cobalt?"

A shadow darkens her expression. "I did, once," she says, tone flat. "That was before I realized what was going on. Before he started using my name to control me." Once again, her rage is a mirror to my own, as seen in her clenched fists, her steely gaze.

"How will you do it?" I ask.

She shakes the cloud from her face to meet my eyes. "How will I do what?"

"How will you use the power of his name to kill him?"

Her eyes widen for a moment, revealing fear and perhaps a hint of guilt. "I...I don't know yet."

Heat rises to my cheeks. "What do you mean, you don't know? When you first came to me, you said your power over his name could help us kill him."

"It can," she says in a rush, then lowers her eyes. "I just haven't sorted out how. I've never tried using his name like that before."

I shake my head with a roll of my eyes. "Great. A lot of use you'll be."

Indignation hardens her features when she lifts her head. "It's not like I had a chance to try. Once he began giving me daily commands, that was always one of the first. That I couldn't use his name or act out against him in any way. But trust me—"

"Trust you," I echo with a bitter laugh.

"Yes, Evie. When I get the chance, I will use Cobalt's name. I don't care if I have to force him to peel every inch of skin from his own body. I will do whatever it takes to watch the life fade from his eyes."

Her words send a shudder up my spine. One that tells me, perhaps her rage isn't as dark as mine. Perhaps it's darker than anything I've ever felt.

23

The sun beats high overhead as we make our way across the sandy dune to the stretch of land on the other side. The heat is so heavy in the air that I can see it, blurring the landscape in the distance. Still, I can make out rolling hills at the edge of the horizon. I'm surprised to see so much green beyond the invisible divide between Fire and Solar. I'd expected Solar to have more desert land like my court.

Aspen and I walk side by side with the rest of the Alpha Alliance, trailed by several guards. Each royal has brought two guards to the meeting, leaving another dozen or so at our camp to come to our aid in the case of an ambush. Amelie waits there too, with commands not to leave our tent. I wish there were more of us. I wish Foxglove, Lorelei, and Fehr were here. But our ambassadors remained behind to organize our newly arrived households, and Fehr of course can't leave the palace.

Aspen's hand lights on my back, and I turn to meet his gaze. A sheen of sweat covers his brow, and I can feel the same on my own face, as well as the gritty sand that seems to attach to my skin whenever I'm outdoors in the Fire Court. My mate gives me a reassuring grin, and I do my best to match it. I hate the thought of meeting the Renounced without absolutely obliterating them, but this ceasefire was my idea, after all.

It's necessary, I remind myself. *We have to do this.*

Our group slows its pace until Estel comes to a full stop at the head of our retinue. "This is it," she says. "The divide between Solar and Fire is just ahead. We will hold back and send my ambassador to meet theirs when they arrive."

My nerves only increase now that we've stopped, and the sun feels hotter. Oddly, I'm beginning to get used to the heat of the Fire Court, but I imagine not all the fae feel the same. While Estel and Minuette seem as content as ever, Flauvis looks downright miserable, panting rapidly. Nyxia glares up at the sky on occasion, as if she thinks it holds a personal grudge against her. Tris continues to shift between her tiny pixie form and her seelie form, as if she can't decide which one helps keep her cool.

Now in her larger form, her cherry blossoms seem to wilt beneath the heat. "Is it noon yet?" she whines.

Estel turns her shimmering face to the sky. "Not quite, but they should arrive—"

Something falls from the sky not too far away. When it lands, it takes the shape of a female figure rising on strong, heavily muscled legs. Her hair is golden with curls that rest above her shoulders, and she wears a gauzy white dress with gold trim that reaches just below her hips. Enormous golden-brown wings span out behind her. My heart races as I recognize her as one of the royals. I hardly noticed her at the council meeting where Aspen fought Cobalt for the throne, but now she's a formidable sight to behold. "Queen of Solar?" I whisper to Aspen.

He nods, his eyes narrowed at the figure. "Queen Phoebe."

The Solar Queen remains where she landed, arms crossed over her chest as she assesses us from afar. Movement behind her snags my attention, and I see a group marching to meet her.

"They're here," Aspen says under his breath.

My pulse races the closer they get, but as they come into full view, my nerves begin to calm. Their gathering is almost as large as ours, but not quite. The only other royal I recognize amongst the bunch is Queen Dahlia of the Summer Court. Her enormous yellow butterfly wings stretch out behind her as she joins Queen Phoebe. The rest of the fae are an assortment I can only imagine are their pretender kings and queens, some guards, and an ambassador or two. However, the only sea fae is a slender female with blue scales and coral-pink hair.

I whip my face toward Aspen. "Did Cobalt leave the Renounced?"

He studies the opposing crowd through slitted lids. "I can't imagine why he would have."

I return my attention to the sea fae. She stands next to Dahlia and the other supposed royals. Has Cobalt been replaced by a new royal? If so, why?

The question is stripped from my mind as Estel turns to face us. "I will send my ambassador now."

A fae who looks much like the Star Queen—an androgynous figure made of the same shimmering particles of light—bows low. "Your Majesty," the ambassador says in an airy, genderless voice, then turns away from us to make their way to the stretch of land that stands between our two groups.

Another figure—one I think I recognize as the Summer Court ambassador—does the same. The two ambassadors stop when they come within several feet of each other. From here, I can see their mouths move, but I hear nothing. My hands clench into fists, my anxiety returning in a rush. I'm desperate to hear what's being said, what arguments are made—

Then, just like that, the meeting is over. At least, it seems to be, for the Star Court ambassador is already making their way back to us. Aspen stiffens at my side. "It shouldn't have been that easy," he says under his breath.

I can't form a word as I wait with bated breath for what the ambassador will say. When the star fae reaches our group, their glittering eyes pin on me. "Queen Dahlia's ambassador claims her queen requests a one-on-one conversation with you, Queen Evelyn."

My throat goes dry. "Why me?"

The ambassador shakes their head. "She wouldn't say."

My gaze turns to my mate, then to the others. But wait. Why am I seeking permission? Validation? This was my plan to begin with and this is my decision to make. I steel my nerves, squaring my shoulders as I lift my chin. "If there is no argument from the Alpha Alliance, I will meet with her."

No royal speaks against my statement, so the ambassador nods and returns to the summer fae. When they finish speaking this time, both ambassadors return to their separate parties. I see Dahlia step to the front of the retinue, her gaze trained on me.

Aspen's fingers find mine. "Are you sure you want to do this?"

I tilt my head. "Am I sure I want to call a ceasefire, or am I sure I want to speak with Dahlia and try not to rip her head off her shoulders?"

He quirks a halfhearted grin. It's clear he's nervous for me; I can feel it rippling from his palm into mine. "Both."

I let out a heavy sigh. "It must be done." Returning my attention to our opponents, I give Aspen's hand a final squeeze and step away from our group. Dahlia does the same, mirroring each step of mine. Every inch we close between us feels like a mile, and my rage grows hotter the clearer she comes into view. It's impossible for me to forget everything she's done, starting with her poor treatment of Doris Mason and her cousin—the last two Chosen from the previous Hundred Year Reaping—and ending with her betrayal of Aspen, when she petitioned for Cobalt to take Aspen's place as king when my mate refused to marry Maddie Coleman.

We come to a halt several feet from each other, and my eyes narrow to slits, jaw clenched tightly as I fight the fury that radiates down to my fingertips. Every inch of me begs to release my fire, let it dance over my palms.

I could end this, I realize. I could attack Dahlia now, set fire to her pretty little wings. My allies could join me, and we could take down the Renounced before they even know what's happening. Now that I'm closer, the pretender kings and queens are in clearer view. They look meek compared to my allies. The only formidable opponents would be Dahlia and Phoebe.

That's all they have left.

Excitement rises within me at the realization, and I can feel my flames licking the surface of my palms.

Dahlia looks down her nose at me. "Whatever devious thoughts are running through your traitorous human mind, you can stop now," she says in her irritatingly smooth voice. "Phoebe's soldiers are on watch."

The queen glances up, and I follow her gaze. High in the sky, I catch sight of what appear to be birds. But I know better. They are winged fae like Phoebe. I return my attention to the Summer Queen, fire flooding my veins at the sight of her simpering smile.

"They could put an end to your pathetic life in seconds, should you try anything," she adds.

I grind my teeth, fighting the seething retort that begs to spring from my lips. However, I force my rage to calm to a simmer. This is a peaceful exchange of words. If I break it and everything goes poorly, it will be my fault.

Plastering an exaggerated smile on my face, I adopt a similar tone to hers. "Queen Dahlia, I will ignore that threat and instead tell you how lovely it is to see you again. You must feel the same about me to request such a close meeting between us."

She huffs. "It's only because I want to hear whatever nonsensical lies you've prepared straight from your lips."

I hold her gaze while I mentally prepare everything I must relay to the Renounced. Obviously, I hadn't planned on explaining it myself. It was agreed from the start that Estel's ambassador would be the one to do it. But now it must be me.

Clasping my hands before me, I begin. "We have received intel that a human army has been sent from the mainland with the intention to wipe out faekind."

Dahlia pales, her eyes flashing with alarm before she steels her composure. Her words come out hesitant. "When you say you've received intel, does that mean you have proof?"

"Nyxia's owls have confirmed sightings of several warships."

"That could mean anything," she says.

"We've had an additional witness demonstrate the humans' desire to obliterate the fae as quickly as possible." I fill my words with enough emphasis to mask what I'm hiding—that the witness was a human who attempted to steal a bomb that could kill us all.

"Why should I believe you?" She gives a shrug, but the tenseness of her shoulders betrays how shaken she is.

"They're coming," I say. "If you don't believe me, let any of my allies confirm my statement."

"Am I supposed to believe this meeting is all an act of goodwill? A kind warning?" She scoffs. "I doubt that."

"No, it's to discuss the necessity of a ceasefire between us."

She barks a laugh, mouth falling open. "Why would we ever agree to that?"

"Because it's a matter of survival. We can't face a human army if we're divided, distracted by our civil war."

Dahlia's lips pull into a sneer. "Just because you and your pathetic allies will be distracted, doesn't mean we will be."

I bristle and force myself to keep my fury at bay. It takes all my control to hold my voice steady. "We'll be stronger together. Then as soon as the humans are dealt with, we can return to sorting out our grievances."

She doesn't even give it a second's thought. "I appreciate the warning, but no. We will not agree to a ceasefire."

I clench my jaw. Time to step up negotiations. "I have something you want."

Again, her composure falters, expression going blank. Her words come out clipped. "What would that be?"

"The very thing that made you try to take my palace," I say with a grin.

She studies me in tense silence before saying, "I don't know what you're talking about."

I put my hands on my hips, aware of their proximity to my hidden blades. "I think you do, Dahlia. Iron weapons. If you agree to a temporary ceasefire that lasts only as long as we must fight the human army, we will deliver the weapons to you once the army is defeated."

She pops a hip to the side, wings buzzing in agitation. "We do not agree," she finally says, although I swear there's a hint of regret in her tone.

Fire heats my cheeks at her easy dismissal. It wasn't supposed to go this way. I haven't even brought up the wall yet! No, this can't be how this ends. I must regain control over this conversation at once.

My gaze flashes to the gathering behind her. "I suggest you reconsider. Your allies are dwindling. All you have are pretenders. Without a united front, your little *council* won't survive the oncoming attack."

"That's what you think," she says with a grin that doesn't quite reach her eyes.

I study her, analyzing every tense muscle, the tick in her jaw, seeking the truth beneath her feigned casual demeanor.

"How about this," she says, her mask of confidence regaining its hold over her features. "We will agree to a ceasefire, but we will not trade it for weapons. Instead, we will trade for something else, something we will claim at once. Otherwise, we will make no deal."

Dread sinks my gut, every instinct telling me whatever she has in mind can't be good. "What is it you propose we trade?"

"We will agree to this temporary ceasefire," she says, lips pulling into a devious smirk, "in exchange for you."

24

———————

I stare blankly at the Summer Queen, blood draining from my face. When I regain my composure, I pin Dahlia with a glare. "What do you mean you want to trade for *me*?"

She looks at her fingernails, as if I'm no longer worth her attention. "It's exactly as it sounds. Give up your claim as queen, surrender to us, and we will agree to a ceasefire."

My fingers clench into fists as fire roars through my shoulders, my arms, my palms. "Why in the bloody name of iron would I surrender to you?"

She puts a hand on her hip, a scowl twisting her lips. "It's because of you that we're in this mess to begin with, Evelyn. You've already caused enough trouble, breaking the treaty and all. It's your fault this human army comes in the first place. Don't you think you owe it to your allies? To all fae? To the humans, even? For all we know, you stepping down as queen could be the very thing we need to repair the treaty or forge a new one."

My fire falters, draining from me at her words. Guilt sinks my heart, making my legs feel heavy. I feel how I did when I first learned my pairing with Aspen had been invalidated, then later when I learned my heritage was putting the treaty in jeopardy. All I wanted to do then was sacrifice myself. To do whatever it took to prevent war and bloodshed. The treaty was the only thing that stood between peace and war, and I was the only one who could stop it.

In this moment, it's like that all over again. Once again, I alone am responsible for the threat, and this one storms across the sea from the mainland. I feel like I'm the one at the helm of each of those warships, and only I can call them back.

It's just me. My life. My throne.

If I give it all up, the isle could be safe. All I've ever wanted was to save lives. That's exactly why I wanted to become a surgeon.

I can't deny this final chance for peace.

I open my mouth, my pulse racing at the words that nearly climb up my throat. But something tugs at my mind—a memory, one strong enough to give me pause. It surges through me with the echo of a voice. It's my mother's voice, fierce and strong and full of fire as she orders me not to make a deal with Mr. Duveau. Next, I hear Aspen's voice, posing the question of whether the treaty is worth saving at all. Then, it's my voice I hear, telling Aspen that Faerwyvae is my home, that I will sacrifice myself no more. Finally, I hear the words I said to the fire fae in the cave at Lunar, promising I would fight for the unseelie and to end the corrupt ways of both human and fae councils.

My fire returns to heat my blood as I remind myself who I am. I do not cower, I do not beg, and I certainly don't sacrifice my own life for my enemies.

I am Evelyn, Unseelie Queen of Fire.

"You had your chance," I say sweetly, "but I will agree to no such deal. Goodbye, Queen Dahlia." I turn my back on her and take a slow step away. I'm confident she'll call out for me to stop, to cave in and try to backtrack to my previous offer for the weapons.

But the words that come out of her mouth are not what I expect. "You won't agree? Not even to be with your sister?"

I freeze. I know she's bluffing, acting like they have Amelie even though I know better. But there's something about the bravado in her tone that chills my blood.

That's when I see it. Movement to the right.

I whip my attention toward it and see two figures skirting around the far end of the sand dune. They're far enough away from my allies that they haven't been noticed by the Alpha Alliance yet, but the direction they're coming from...

My blood goes cold. The camp.

I turn back to Dahlia, who wears a triumphant grin. "You think we didn't know your sister had returned to you?"

This is it. The moment I've been anticipating with both resignation and dread. The moment I get confirmation that Amelie truly has been lying to me, poised at every moment to betray me. Was every word planted by Cobalt from the start? Or was it her will all along?

Someone appears at my side, giving me a start before I realize it's Aspen. He's wreathed in the violet aura of the Bond, eyes trained on the two figures that cross the stretch of land from Fire to Solar.

"What the bloody oak and ivy," Aspen curses between his teeth as Cobalt comes clearly into view.

I burn the traitorous male with a glare for only a moment before turning it on my sister. Cobalt grasps her around the waist, lifting her while her legs drag behind her. She's conscious, but the way she walks looks as if her legs have turned to lead, fighting gravity with every step. Her head lolls, face twisted, mouth open in a silent scream. It's enough to wipe the scowl off my face.

"This is a peaceful exchange of words," I say to Dahlia.

"And Cobalt has done nothing to compromise it," she says smoothly. "He simply reclaimed what was rightfully his. As Amelie is one of his mates, he has every right to take her back."

"She is not property."

She barks a laugh. "Oh? Is that why you kept her out of sight?"

I press my lips tight together, eyes flashing back toward Amelie. She truly appears to be in excruciating pain. That's when I remember the command I left her with: *do not leave this tent until I return for you.*

I reach for my fire to burn away the pity that sinks my heart. She may be in pain, but that doesn't mean she didn't betray me. "We're done here," I say. "You can have her."

"You're going to give her up that easily?" Dalia lets out a tittering laugh, then leans in, lowering her voice. "Cobalt may think we allowed him to seek her out for his own satisfaction, but he's wrong. His actions to harbor your sister when the treaty demanded both of you be exiled to the mainland is unforgivable. You may be the primary cause of the broken treaty, but he must pay a price for keeping her. And if it succeeds at punishing you too..." She doesn't clarify what she's hinting at, but her malicious smirk tells me enough.

I no longer know what to think, what to believe. Just moments ago, I was so certain Amelie was the traitor I'd always thought her to be. But now...

My hand moves slowly to my hip, fingers desperate to reach for the hilt of one of my iron daggers. Then my gaze moves to Aspen, still present through the Bond. He watches me knowingly.

If I react with violence, this peaceful exchange of words is at an end. Phoebe's winged soldiers will descend and chaos will break loose.

With a sigh, I begin to lower my hand.

"No," Aspen says, stilling me. His lips twist into a cruel grin that he pins on Dahlia. Of course, she can't see him, but the invisible threat fuels my inner fire. "I've already sent a guard back to our camp. If Cobalt didn't kill them all to take your sister, they'll be here any moment."

"Are you reconsidering my offer?" Dahlia says.

My fingers flinch toward my waist again. I send my words to Aspen through the Bond. *Are you sure? There will be no chance of a ceasefire.*

"There obviously never was to begin with," he says through his teeth.

I give a subtle nod. *Tell the others.*

In the blink of an eye, Aspen disappears. In that same moment, I reach for the nearest dagger on my weapons belt and lunge for the queen. Before she can react, I plunge the blade into her stomach. She calls out, eyes wide as she takes in the iron weapon protruding from her gut. I'm about to withdraw the dagger when I reconsider. The wound will only be fatal if it remains inside her long enough to poison her blood.

Footsteps pound behind me, the sound of the Alpha Alliance charging in. The Renounced surge forward as well, and I unsheathe two more iron daggers from beneath my gown. I advance toward Dahlia as she retreats from me, doubled over, face twisted in pain. Teeth bared, I prepare another strike of my blade, but a shadow swoops overhead, followed by the sound of flapping wings.

Winged fae descend from the sky, and one grasps long, curved talons beneath Dahlia's arms and lifts her high above me. In a matter of seconds, she's flown safely beyond my reach and out of sight.

Another set of talons is suddenly before me, and I have just enough time to lean back to avoid the deadly swipe. My fae opponent has a feline face with a mane of golden hair and wings like a falcon. She lets out a deafening roar before swiping out again. I duck under her reach and slice both blades across her ribs. She whirls back, hissing at the searing iron, but it only holds her back for a second before she charges again. This time, one of her claws grazes my left arm, opening the flesh over my bicep. I grit my teeth against the pain, fighting against the urge to drop the dagger from that hand.

Blood pours down my arm in rivulets of crimson, but I keep my eyes trained on my opponent as we circle each other. Sights and sounds of fighting surround us, but I don't let it distract me as I assess her height, her build, seeking weaknesses. Her talons seem to be her only defense, as she wears no armor, carries no weapon. Her body is composed of soft flesh covered in short golden-brown fur. If I strike her several times with iron, she'll eventually succumb to its effects. Grow weak. Heal slower. Even so, I hate to admit I'm at a disadvantage. Smaller. Shorter. Fleshy from head to toe.

But that's without my flames.

I let my rage fuel every part of me, let it surge through my veins, ignite my palms, and dance over my fingertips. It crawls up my arms, burns down my back. I feel it knitting the skin back together where I've been sliced open, stopping the flow of blood. The heat blankets me, but my flames cause me no pain. They feel comforting, strong. Like form-fitting armor made just for me.

My opponent's eyes widen at the sight of my tricolor flame, but she quickly replaces it with a glower. I fight my yearning to shift fully into my fox form, knowing human hands are needed to wield my iron blades.

"Is that all you have, human?" the fae teases. "Pretty little flames?"

I let my body form my reply, darting toward her with my daggers raised. As expected, she lunges with her talons, but I spin to the side, ducking under her arms, and grazing her forearm with the tip of one of my blades in the process. She hisses, and the momentary distraction gives me the opportunity to reach for one of her wings, letting the flames dancing over my arms ignite on contact. She swipes again, but I'm already retreating. She takes a step to close the distance but falters, her attention drawn to the fire crawling up her wings. The smell of singed feathers fills my nostrils, and as more of her wings are engulfed in flames, I suppress the wave of nausea that hits me. She begins to shout, spinning wildly to swat at the fire, but it's no use.

I'm frozen in place, torn over what to do. She's so distracted, I could charge in to make my killing blow. For a moment, I consider it a mercy, compared to the possibility of burning to death. Still, I find myself unable to move at all, consumed by a sudden horror at the thought of killing my opponent. I know I've killed before, but the others were personal or an act of self-defense. For the most part, I knew their crimes, their dark deeds. But this fae...

I retreat a step backward as my flames climb higher and higher up her back. My pulse races as I try to remind myself she's my enemy, but it's no use. Because the truth remains: for all I know, she could be like Foxglove or Lorelei. She could have been my friend or ally if the situation were different. It is only the queen she serves that pits her against me, not anything she's personally said or done.

I call back my flames, willing them to extinguish from her wings. As soon as they're gone, she falls to her knees in a wail of pain. I don't bother waiting to see the extent of the damage. All I can think to do is run, dodge the fighting pairs that surround me. Run from this field of growing carnage.

But there's nowhere to go. Nowhere safe from blood and blades.

Nothing to see but the bloodshed I've sparked.

25

When I resigned myself to break the treaty, I knew we'd go to war. I knew there'd be battles. Lives lost. But it's one thing to know and another to actually see it.

All around me the Alpha Alliance engage in bloody combat with the Renounced. My breathing is labored as I whirl around, daggers still clenched in my fists as I struggle to keep my wits about me. Half my attention is focused on preparing for oncoming attackers while the other half seeks a pair of antlers and blue-black hair amidst the chaos. Finally, I spot my mate in his stag form, fighting Queen Phoebe. The Solar Queen swings a gold-tipped spear in furious swipes, but Aspen meets each thrust and jab with his antlers. My heart lurches, seeing his fur matted in places with red, but my view of him is cut off as another fighting pair—King Flauvis, tearing his vicious fangs into the leg of the female sea fae—moves in front of them.

The sight chills my bones, but not because of the blood that streams down the sea fae's scaly leg; it's because it reminds me of someone else.

Clenching my jaw, I steel my nerves and seek signs of Cobalt. My fire returns with every step I take, so strong I hardly register the soldier who charges me. It's another one of Phoebe's winged fae, this one far more humanlike, aside from his elongated beakish nose and tufts of feathers on the tips of his pointed ears. When he swipes out with his sword, I dodge back, blocking the tip with my crossed daggers. As he prepares another strike, fire encases my hands, dancing over my blades.

My intention wraps around the flame, shaping it to my will. Fire. Air. Movement. The fire leaves my daggers, hovering above them in a fiery, pink orb.

In a flash, I send the flame shooting to the curve of brown wings folded over the fae's shoulder. As it ignites the feathers, the soldier falters, slapping his palm in an attempt to stamp out the flame. I use the distraction to leave the fae behind, once again seeking Cobalt. I take hardly five steps before I'm forced to halt behind a writhing mass of bodies, groaning in agony. Above them, Nyxia, in her shadow form, reaches smoky black tendrils to each of their heads. She seems to grow larger and darker with every beat of my racing heart.

Keeping a wide berth, I skirt around the moaning fae to the edge of the battlefield. Finally, I see what I'm looking for.

Cobalt stands in the distance at the crest of a nearby dune, my sister locked in his arms. She still looks as if she's in pain, face twisted as she sags against him. I pump my legs and race toward them. Cobalt has the sense to look startled, stiffening as I draw near. He retreats a few steps, dragging my sister with him, then seems to think better of it. Instead, he stands his ground.

"Stop, Evelyn!" he shouts. "Can't you see she's being tortured?"

He doesn't say it like a threat, but his words slow my attack nonetheless. Keeping my daggers clenched tightly in my fists, I shift to a jog, only coming to a stop when I'm a dozen feet away. Everything in me wants to keep moving, keep closing the distance until Cobalt's neck is wrapped in my fiery hands. But even though he's refusing to join the battle, I must remember he's fought Aspen before and came out of it alive. He isn't harmless.

And now he has my sister.

"Did she give you her name?" he asks, pulling her tighter to his side. "Is that why she struggles to get back to your camp?"

I purse my lips, but it seems to be the only answer he needs.

"Renounce your command," he says, and there's a pleading quality to his voice. "Every moment she's forced to struggle against it is torture for her. You can't imagine the damage it could cause if it continues too long."

My heart squeezes as I go over the exact wording of the command I gave her. *Do not leave this tent until I return for you.* I gave no other expiration but my return. Is it possible her obedience would be enforced forever? I breathe in deeply to maintain my composure. "You should just let her go then."

"I will," he says, raising his free hand in a gesture of surrender. "Revoke your order and I promise I will let her go."

My eyes move from him to Amelie. She seems completely unaware of all that's transpiring around her, eyes squeezed shut, face turning crimson as she screams soundlessly. He must have ordered her not to make a sound.

My hands begin to tremble. I can't let her suffer like that. I can't.

"Amelie." My voice fills with the power of her name. "I have returned to you. You are no longer required to wait in the tent for my return."

Just like that, her mouth snaps shut, tortured expression relaxing. As promised, Cobalt lets her go, and Amelie slides to the ground, limp, weak. Her copper hair hangs around her face and her shoulders heave as if she's sobbing.

When I return my attention to Cobalt, he's smiling. "Amelie," he says, dropping something onto the ground before her. It only takes a moment for me to realize it's a coral-bladed dagger. "Kill Evelyn."

My sister reaches a quivering hand to grasp the hilt and rises slowly to her feet. When her hair parts, her tortured expression returns. This time, tears stream down her cheeks, and her mouth moves, forming the word *no* over and over. With a heave, she lunges forward, movements wild and erratic.

Before I can consider it, the words leap from my lips. "Amelie, kill Cobalt!"

She halts mid-step, shoulders sagging as she whirls back toward him. His eyes widen for a moment before he points at me. "I gave the order first, kill your sister!"

Again, she turns to me, but she doesn't take another step. She begins to tremble from head to toe, subtly at first, then rippling into full-body convulsions. Her eyes roll back in her head and a stream of scarlet blood trickles from her nose, over her lips and chin.

"Revoke your commands," Cobalt says, eyes flashing from Amelie to me. "Revoke them now, or she dies!" Again, there's no threat in his tone, only mad panic.

"You revoke them first!" I shout back.

Amelie falls to the ground, convulsing in the dirt.

Cobalt puts a hand to his chest, his breathing labored as he watches my sister. Part of me knows this is the perfect time to attack Cobalt, catch him unaware, but the rest of me can't take my eyes off my sister. More blood continues to pour from her nose, her face turning a chilling shade of blue.

"Amelie, I revoke all orders." Cobalt's words come out strained, choked on a sob.

Amelie sucks in a deep inhalation, her convulsions calming back to a mild tremble, but she doesn't open her eyes.

Cobalt's gaze flashes to mine, his expression accusatory. "You must revoke yours too," he says with a sneer. "She's been overcome. She will not recover if you don't free her from your orders."

He could be lying. I know this. And yet, despite everything that's happened, every doubt I still hold about my sister's allegiance, I can't take the chance that my actions could be killing her.

"Amelie, I revoke all orders," I say.

Finally, she gasps again and goes still, the blue pallor already receding from her face.

"I'm so sorry." Cobalt steps toward Amelie, arms outstretched, but I leap forward, daggers raised.

"Don't touch her," I hiss.

His expression hardens, lips peeling back from his teeth as he meets my glare. "You could have killed her."

"Why do I get the feeling that would have been a mercy compared to everything you've done to her?"

"You know nothing! I love her."

My lips quirk into a cruel grin. "Well, she doesn't love you."

As if my words had been forged of barbed iron, he roars, head thrown back in agony as if struck by a fatal blow. He shudders. Once. Twice. Before my eyes, he shifts into his nix form, blue scales covering his body from head to toe, a crown of coral resting over his brow. His chest heaves with rage. "I will make her love me once you're dead." With that, he charges forward, sharp fingers outstretched with serrated webs in between.

I shift into a defensive posture, one dagger ready to swipe out in an arc, the other prepared to plunge straight into him, flames dancing over my body, hungry for his scales.

A flash of brown charges between us, knocking Cobalt down in the process. Aspen slashes his antlers into his brother. Where Aspen is ferocious, Cobalt is fast. He manages to roll out from under Aspen's enormous hooves, swiping a gash in the stag's leg in the process. Aspen doesn't falter, charging his brother with every retreat, pursuing him on and on until they take their fight to the other side of the dune.

My heart lurches, begging me to follow and see that Aspen is unharmed, perhaps even help him end Cobalt for good. But my attention snags on my sister's lifeless form. I return my blades to their sheaths and run to her side. Kneeling next to her, my fingers rush to check her pulse, finding it slow but steady. Then, taking her face in my hands, I slap her lightly on the cheeks. "Amelie. Amelie, wake up." There's no command in my voice, only urgency.

Finally, she begins to stir, eyelids fluttering open as she gasps for air. She mumbles, movements unsteady as she attempts to sit. It takes me a few moments to understand what she's trying to say. Then her words become clearer. "Where is he?"

"Cobalt? Aspen is fighting him. Are you all right?"

She succeeds at pushing herself up to sit and wipes the back of her hand across her mouth, smearing the blood that had dribbled down her face. Her chest caves in as she struggles to catch her breath, eyes unfocused. Then, with a snarl, her gaze narrows on me. "How could you do that to me?"

For a moment, I'm caught off guard. She's hardly shown an ounce of anger toward me since she first arrived at Lunar. I furrow my brow. "I'm sorry. I should have been the first to revoke my orders, but I didn't trust that he'd do so after I did."

"Not that," she says through her teeth. "You ordered me to kill him."

I lean back, fury heating my cheeks. "You're upset with me because of *that*? Because I ordered the very thing you've been begging me to let you do?" I rise to my feet and stare down at her. "After everything you said, you love him, don't you?"

"I *hate* him," she snaps. "And you had no right to rob me of the right to kill him with a clear mind. I told you, I want to see the life leave his eyes. I want to remember it forever. How can I do that if I'm trapped beneath the haze of your commands?"

My fury cools in the shadow of hers. In this moment, her rage is chilling, making her look so unlike the Amelie of my childhood. She's a feral creature, one hungry for blood and vengeance. It's enough to make my heart plummet. When I speak, my words come out strained. "Ami, this isn't the life for you."

"What do you know about it, Evie?" She rises angrily to her feet to face me eye-to-eye. "You've killed in self-defense. You've ended lives of terrible people. I've been *forced* to kill. For once, I want to kill of my own free will."

I shake my head. "It won't make you feel better."

"Is that why you tried to hunt down Mr. Duveau after Mother died? Why you burned down a brothel when you couldn't find him? Because it *didn't* feel good?"

A rush of guilt turns in my stomach. "How did you hear about that?"

She lets out a bitter laugh. "I may have lost half my mind, but I'm not stupid."

I clench my jaw, wondering if this is yet another piece of information shared by Foxglove or Lorelei. "Mind your own—"

"Oh look, you found each other," says a haughty, feminine voice.

I whirl to find Queen Dahlia, sauntering up to us, a tiny purple pixie hovering at her shoulder. The pixie carries a bright yellow flower that's almost as big as her, but my attention is pulled to the wound I gave the queen. The hilt of the iron blade I buried in her gut has been removed, the lesion bandaged. Her complexion is a little green, but she seems otherwise unharmed.

A rush of surprise washes through me. Who would have been able to tend to an iron wound so quickly? I figured the fae would have enough trouble removing the blade in the first place.

I reach inside my dress to retrieve a dagger, but a sudden puff of yellow dust obscures my vision. Gripping the hilt of my weapon, I blink rapidly to clear my eyes, seek out Dahlia. When the dust finally settles, everything around me begins to blur at the edges. Dahlia's pixie companion hovers before me, a mischievous smile on her tiny lips, flourishing the yellow flower in her hands.

That's the last thing I see.

26

I jolt awake into a world of agonizing pain. My mind feels slow, heavy, and all I can sense is cold. It burns my skin worse than any fire could, chilling me to my bones, my blood. My very soul.

My vision blurs as I pry my eyes open, blinking into whatever nightmare I've awoken to. When my sight begins to clear, adjusting to the semi-darkness of the room I'm in, I find the lower half of my body is submerged in icy water. It's contained in an elongated tub, like the troughs I've seen on the farms in Eisleigh. Ropes tie my ankles together and bind each of my wrists to handles on opposite sides of the tub. Panic surges through me as I whip my head from side to side. All I see are solid walls, a barred door, and my unconscious sister in the same predicament as I'm in, her tub just a few feet from mine.

It's clear now that we're trapped in a prison. A dungeon. And the ice-cold water tells me our captors have every intention of suppressing my powers.

My teeth chatter as I yank my wrists as hard as I can. It's no use, of course. I hardly have strength in my limbs to move, and the bindings are tied tight.

To my horror, my movement seems to stir a previously unnoticed presence, a dark silhouette leaning against the wall. I bite back a scream until my eyes fall on the shape of antlers. A sob of relief crawls from my throat as Aspen pushes off the wall and races to my side. "For the love of oak and ivy, you're awake." Warm hands move to my cheeks, and I nearly moan at the comfort they bring me.

"Get me out of here." My words come out weak, jagged through my chattering teeth.

His expression darkens, shifting between rage and sorrow as he brushes a damp strand of hair off my face. "I've tried. I can only touch you. Nothing else is affected by me."

Of course. Why didn't I see the violet aura before? Aspen isn't really here. "Did they take my daggers?" Not that they'd do us any good if Aspen's touch can only affect *me*. Still, I'd feel a lot better if I knew they were there.

Aspen leans in closer and slides his hand beneath one of the open sides of my sodden dress, running his fingers along my cold flesh. In any other situation, his touch would feel seductive. Right now, it only crushes me with disappointment. For if I can feel his hand flat against my back, then that can only mean my weapons belt has been taken. Damn.

"How long have I been..."

"Two days," he says, pulling back and moving his hands to my shoulders to warm them. "Do you know where you are?"

"The last thing I saw was Dahlia," I say. "There was a pixie with a flower. Some yellow dust. I'm guessing I'm in the dungeon at either Solar or Summer."

He shakes his head. "I've been to both palaces and seen both dungeons. This place is nowhere I've ever been."

A shudder runs through me that isn't from the cold. Where in the name of iron am I?

Aspen looks me over, taking in my violent shivers, my bound wrists, my damp cheeks, and pain lashes his face. Clenching his jaw, he rises to his feet with a roar. He stalks toward one of the walls and slams a fist into it. It makes no sound, creates no reverberation. "I can't stand to see you like this. I'm going to kill them all."

"What happened after I was taken?" I ask, each word a struggle while I fight the tremors that seize me. "Was anyone on our side injured?"

He leans on the hand that punched the wall, head low in defeat. "Not mortally. It was as if the Renounced were all waiting for something. Waiting for you to be taken." His eyes find mine, his gaze so full of rage and sorrow all at once. "Hardly any time had passed at all. One moment you were there with your sister, and I was fighting Cobalt. The next, a whistling call was made overhead, and the Renounced retreated."

"Cobalt?" I ask.

His eyes unfocus, a sneer pulling his lips. "He got away, taken to safety by one of Phoebe's winged soldiers. But not before I slashed out one of Cobalt's eyes."

"Where are you?"

"I've remained at the camp, along with Estel and Nyxia. The others returned to their courts. As soon as we know where you are, we'll come for you."

I furrow my brow. "What about Estel's Chariot? Can't you use it to come here now that you've seen where I am?"

"I tried." His voice trembles with suppressed rage. "So many times I've tried. Visual reference of a place isn't enough if you don't actually know where it exists in the world. I need to know for certain where you are for my intent to fuel the device."

I mutter a curse under my breath, but mumbled words pull my attention to my side, where Amelie begins to stir. Her mumbles turn to moans and moans turn to screams. I lean as far toward her as I can within the restraint of my bindings. "Hush, Amelie!"

She pays me no heed as she thrashes in her tub. "What have I done?"

Aspen leaves the wall and darts toward us, eyes wide as he takes in the terror on Amelie's face, but of course there's nothing he can do. "What's wrong with her?"

"She always awakens like this," I say under my breath. Then, to my horror, the sound of footsteps pounding somewhere beyond the cell begins to draw near. "Amelie, quiet!" I hiss.

Her screams dissolve into sobs, head lolling to the side. The footsteps are closer now, just beyond the cell door.

I sharpen my tone, raise my voice just a little louder. "Amelie!"

At that, she goes still, blinking into the dim light of the room. She stifles a cry as she stares down at the water she's submerged in, the ropes binding her wrists and ankles. When her gaze turns to me, her breathing goes shallow, expression turning to panic. "Evie—"

A figure arrives at the door, cursing under his breath while he fumbles with the lock. "I leave for hardly any time at all…" The voice is unfamiliar, and I can't make out his face with the light coming from somewhere down the hall casting him in shadow.

Amelie's eyes flash from the figure to me. Her words come out in a whispered rush. "Order me not to obey any commands Cobalt might give me."

I don't give it a moment's thought. "Amelie, I command you to ignore any and all commands Cobalt might give you." I'm about to add a time restriction, but she shakes her head, making my mouth snap shut.

The figure enters the cell with an irritated sigh, every move stalked by Aspen, whose hands clench into fists at his sides. I can see his desire to pummel the male etched in the tic of his jaw, the fury in his eyes.

As the figure draws near, I make out his features. Tall, slim, with long white hair slicked back behind his pointed ears and falling far below his shoulders in silken sheets. He wears a long blue robe with silver embroidery, like something from a long-forgotten century. His eyes are slanted with pale blue irises, lips pursed with irritation. I think I recognize him from the meeting with the Renounced—one of the pretender kings. His appearance makes me guess he's from Winter.

"Where are we?" I force out, voice tremulous as my shoulders continue to shake from the chill.

The fae wrinkles his nose. "Some gods-forsaken place I've never desired to be," he mutters, then holds out a hand toward each of us.

I gasp in shallow breaths as the water grows noticeably colder, a thin sheet of ice coating the surface.

Aspen slams a fist through the winter fae, but of course it's no use.

My words are even more of a struggle to bite out now. "Why...are you... doing this?"

"Why am I babysitting you when I'm supposed to be a king?" He seems to be speaking more to himself than either of us. "We're a joke. And two humans in exchange for thousands is supposed to make up for it." He lets out a bitter laugh.

Two humans in exchange for thousands. What's that supposed to mean? My mind spins to comprehend the implications, but all thoughts are stripped away when another set of footsteps sounds down the hall.

A whine comes from Amelie. She shakes her head, the sudden terror in her eyes telling me she recognizes those footsteps. It's no surprise when Cobalt's silhouette appears in the doorway.

What is surprising, however, is his appearance as he steps into the room; a leather patch covers one eye, so similar to ones I've used with Mr. Meeks when treating ocular damage. When Aspen said he'd slashed out one of Cobalt's eyes, I assumed it would heal and grow back. Then again, it makes sense that full removal of vital limbs and organs are unable to grow back. The evidence being the scars on Mikaela's back where the courtesan's wings had been shorn.

Aspen crosses his arms and glares at Cobalt. "It looks good, brother." His voice is thick with venom; I only wish Cobalt could hear it.

Cobalt falls to his knees before Amelie's tub, lips pulling into an agonized frown. "Amelie."

"Get away from me!" my sister shouts.

He blinks at her a few times, as if he can't comprehend her scorn. "I'm sorry, my love. They won't let me take you from here."

Amelie's lips peel back from her teeth. "Don't you dare use that word around me. *Love.* I am not your love and you are not mine. I hate you and you know it."

He puts a hand to his heart. "Dahlia deceived me. I never thought she'd trap you too."

I analyze his words backwards and forwards, hating how slow the ice-cold water is making my mind. What he's saying suggests he knew all along the Renounced were planning on capturing me.

"I promise you," Cobalt says, "I will get you out of here. I will free you and we will be happy—"

"Cobalt," Amelie hisses as she burns him with a glare. Even with the shivers that rack every inch of her body, her fury is palpable. She says his name again. Then again. "Cobalt. Cobalt." With every repetition, her pitch shifts, changes.

Her mate shakes his head. "What is it, Amelie? Why do you..." He freezes, face going pale.

"Cobalt." She says his name one more time, and this time, the hair on the back of my neck stands on end. I recognize the power wrapped in his name, her fury woven through each syllable. Even Aspen seems to notice, shoulders tense as he stares at my sister with wide eyes.

In a flash, Cobalt lurches away from her, scrambling to rise to his feet. His single eye bulges with terror as he backs away, tripping over his own feet. Before Amelie can say another word, he's gone.

Amelie screams, thrashing against her bonds, sending water and shards of ice splashing over the sides of the tub. "Come back here!"

The winter fae, unaffected by the tense exchange, lets out a bored sigh. "Quiet down." He approaches my sister, hand outstretched. The icy surface of the water in her tub begins to crack and ripple. I don't understand what's happening until I notice the orb of water in the fae's palm, growing larger and larger until it's the size of his head. Then it floats toward Amelie, which is threat enough to quiet her shouts.

Aspen stiffens and starts toward the fae, even though there's nothing he can do.

"What are you doing?" I ask, pulse racing as the ball of water hovers above her scalp. Then, with a snap of his fingers, the ball loses shape and douses Amelie, coating her hair, her face. She gasps for air, her shuddering more intense.

The winter fae turns a cruel grin to me. "Might as well teach you both a lesson."

Before I can react, a second orb of water crashes over my head, its icy shock turning my vision to black.

27

The cold. The cold is all I feel. Time loses meaning as I slip in and out of consciousness. The winter fae returns now and then to chill our water every time it grows even remotely comfortable. I only feel the slightest bit warm when Aspen visits through the Bond, rubbing his hands over my cheeks, my shoulders. Even if he were truly here, I doubt his actions would do much good.

For the love of iron, will this cold be the death of me?

Several times now, I've experienced what Mother once referred to as *an attack by water*. First, was when the kelpie took me under and Cobalt feigned his rescue. I must have come very close to losing my life by drowning, for I was unconscious for three days. Not long after that, Cobalt held me in a coral cage after pulling me underwater. I was sick and miserable afterward, but it wasn't nearly as bad as the first time.

This, however, is far worse than both combined because the attack is unrelenting.

And now I know how my mother felt.

This thought pursues me into wakefulness as I come out of my cold slumber. My nightmares were plagued with memories of Mother trapped in the icy tub at her trial, and now I wake finding that same fate cursed upon me. I blink into the dark, the only light coming from that same illumination from somewhere down the hall. I find no sign of Aspen or the winter fae. It's just me and Amelie, who sleeps in her tub, skin pale and tinged slightly blue. My heart squeezes at the sight, and a wave of terror writhes through me. Surely, this will kill her. Is it only our fae heritage that keeps us from succumbing to frostbite and death?

Again, I think of Mother. Mother trapped in a tub just like this one. Mother shaking and trembling at her trial. Mother with a bullet between her eyes. My breathing grows painfully shallow as a lump sears my throat as if barbed with razors.

I cry out, but it's stifled by another memory that ripples through me, one shocking enough to dispel my pain at once—Mother, flames dancing over her fingers despite the water that holds her. Mother melting her iron cuffs, fighting the guards with her fire.

It's the part I never recall. The part that always gets swallowed by the memory that follows this one. A bullet. Blood. Death.

This time, I push this latter away and linger on the former. Despite all odds, my mother was able to summon her flames to fight for her freedom. Could I possibly do the same?

My mind feels thick and heavy, but I seek my inner fire, searching for it buried beneath the depths of ice that tamp it down. Still, no matter how far I seek, it isn't there. For a flicker of a moment, I feel rage or anger, but it doesn't last. Each time a shiver runs through me, it's gone. Only cold remains. Water. Ice.

If only I were like the winter fae—

The startling realization is enough for me to feel a momentary warmth heat my core. I *am* like the winter fae. I may not have a natural affinity for ice or water, but I am a queen, which means I have access to all four elements. I've already proven my competence with fire, air, and even earth. Water can't be out of reach for me.

I shake my head to clear my mind, steel myself against the bitter chill that threatens to snap my bones. With the deepest breath I can take, I close my eyes and focus on the water that surrounds me. It hits me harder than before, as if I can feel the weight of every drop, every particle of ice that brushes my skin, that clings to my dress, the ends of my hair.

Focus.

I summon what I know about water. Hydration is obvious. Rivers, lakes, and streams. But if there's anything I've learned about the elements, it's that each contains layer upon layer of deeper meaning.

I recall my first visit to the Twelfth Court, and my meeting with the ethereal kelpie. He'd expressed his disdain over me and my kind, over our thoughtless invasion of fae land and sea. How did that relate to water?

My mind grows cloudy again, the chill threatening to drag me back to unconsciousness, but I bite the inside of my cheek to sharpen my thoughts. The pain brings me back into focus, and I home in on my memory of the kelpie.

Now I remember. We debated over whether the fae could feel emotion.

Emotion. That's it. That's the water element.

I sink into that, and an immediate rush of sorrow comes to greet me, swallowing me whole. The breath is stripped from my lungs as the moment Mother died plays over and over in front of me.

A bullet. Blood. Death.

It was over so fast, and it was all...

It was all...

It was...

"Evie?" Amelie's voice pulls me from the endless chasm of grief, returning me to the present. To my cold tub and the oppressive walls of the cell. It's then I realize I've been sobbing.

I swallow my tears and turn my head toward my sister to see her watching me with hazy concern, her lips a terrifying shade of blue. Memories of the sorrow that consumed me threaten to pull me back down, but I refuse to slip into them. Instead, I seek my rage, which slowly complies. No fire accompanies it, but it's enough to harden my heart, thrust the dangerous emotions away.

"Evie, what's wrong?" Amelie asks, voice weak and trembling.

I turn my anger—the only thing that makes me feel warm—on her. Narrowing my eyes to burn her with a glare, I speak through chattering teeth. "It was all your fault."

Her shoulders heave as a violent tremor rips through her. "What?"

"All of this. Everything." I swallow hard. "Getting caught. Mother's death. It's all your fault."

Her eyes widen for a moment, then she nods and turns her face forward. "You never told me how she died."

I let my rage grow, building a wall against her words. Even with the cold combatting all heat it could bring, the intangible barrier is an immediate comfort. "Yes, I did. Mother was sentenced to death because you refused to attend her trial."

Her shoulders sag. "I know. But how was she executed?"

My lips pull into a snarl. "Mr. Duveau shot her with an iron bullet and ended her life."

Silence stretches between us, and I wonder if she'll cry. Beg for forgiveness. But she does neither of those things.

"You're right," she whispers, lower lip trembling. "I don't think I ever admitted it out loud, but I am now. It's my fault. I killed Mother."

At that, I shudder, her unexpected confession far more chilling than the tub.

"I may not have had a choice in refusing to attend," she says. "I tried. I really did. I tried to get a letter to you after the one you sent me. Cobalt showed up just as my orders not to communicate were beginning to fade. I had a pen in my hand and ink had already begun to flow, but he stopped me. And yet, that's not when it began, is it?"

Her eyes meet mine, and I shake my head.

She continues. "It began when we arrived at Bircharbor. When I had my heart set on your fiancé. When I agreed to do whatever it took to be together. When I was stupid enough to fall for his lies and extend the very ability that allowed him to deceive me in the first place. To continue to deceive you."

Slowly, I nod, but my malice is beginning to fade. I can't help but recall the thought I've had many times now. If she hadn't betrayed me, I might be in her position right now. I might not be with Aspen.

Amelie's gaze turns to steel. "I did it. I killed Mother. And when this is all over, when I've killed Cobalt, I want you to take your final revenge on me. I want you to punish me. I want to feel every inch of pain you can give me until my dying breath."

Her face contorts, shifting from the sister of my childhood to the feral creature who lashed out against me for robbing her of the chance to kill Cobalt with a clear mind. The one who wants to watch the life fade from her mate's eyes, force him to peel his own flesh from his bones. I told her this isn't the life for her, but it's clear it's the life she's chosen. She wants revenge.

And not just on Cobalt. She yearns to have revenge on herself.

My heart feels like it's shattering in two.

Seeing the hatred in her eyes tells me she's already punishing herself more than I ever could. The realization unwinds me, melts my anger, freezes it in place like the water that surrounds me. Her permission to kill her makes me understand something else: I don't *want* to kill her. I don't want to hate her. Not really. Maybe I never did. I only want to hate her because it helps me hide the truth. That it isn't her I hate. It isn't her I blame. It's me.

It's *me*.

She is my mirror. We are one and the same.

The lump returns to my throat and with it comes a searing truth. It breaks through the shadows in my mind, battles the chains around my heart, and rises to the surface. A truth I despise more than any other.

"It isn't your fault," I say with a sob.

Amelie burns me with a glare. "Stop, Evie. I don't want your pity."

I shake my head, feel words rising from my gut like bile. Words I can't keep from either of us a moment longer. "You may have started this, but you never acted alone," I say in a rush. "You alone didn't kill Mother. At the very end, I had a choice that could have saved her life. A bargain was offered, one that would have defiled my body and shattered my pride. She told me not to accept it. She wanted me to fight. She wanted us to fight together. But even knowing what she wanted doesn't make it better, for the choice still rested with me. In the end, I refused the bargain, and it resulted in a bullet in Mother's forehead. That was me. I killed her."

I expect another lash of pain, for that chasm of grief to return to finish the job, for endless black to consume me until I'm nothing more than dirt and ashes. Instead, I feel empty. An emptiness that feels an awful lot like peace.

Amelie remains silent, her gaze neither accusatory nor pitying. There's only a dawning understanding in her eyes. I stare back at her, waiting for her to speak. When she does, her words are quiet. Weak. "Mother had a choice too. We all had choices. Some of them might have been wrong, but her choice not to let you sacrifice yourself wasn't a wrong choice."

"But I still must live with the part I played. I don't know how to get over that."

She attempts a shrug despite her bonds. "Do we ever get over the choices we make that lead to another's death? Will I ever be able to look at my hands and not see Melusine's blood? What else can we do with our grief but let it eat us alive?"

The answer comes to me right away. It's what Aspen would say if he were here. *Take it to the Twelfth Court.*

My breath hitches, and I repeat it out loud. "Take it to the Twelfth Court."

Amelie furrows her brow. "What does that mean?"

I ignore her. Closing my eyes, I throw my head back with equal parts gratitude and irritation. Why didn't I think of this before? My flames may be thwarted but that shouldn't stop me from shifting. The Renounced don't know about my unseelie form; only Ustrin did, and he died before he could share what he knew. My unwitting captors put nothing in place to stop a fox.

The Renounced underestimated me.

Now I'll make them pay for it.

28

It takes longer than usual to seek my fox form, like grasping water, only to find it shapeless and running through your fingers. I know it's there. I know I can reach it. If both Aspen and Franco were able to shift in Eisleigh, where the wall weakens fae magic, then I should be able to from this predicament as well.

"Evie, are you all right?" Amelie asks.

"Stay silent." My words come out harsher than I intend, but I can't afford the distraction right now.

I ignore my sister's worried protests and steel myself against the cold, trying to imagine the burning chill feels more like fire than ice. I let it wrap around me, ignite my rage. Focusing my mind's eye on the faces of those who've put us here—Dahlia, Phoebe, Cobalt, that infernal winter fae—I seek my inner fire, even just a spark.

There.

The flame is tiny, just an ember at the center of my core, but it's enough. Closing my eyes, I take that minuscule fire to the Twelfth Court.

At first, nothing happens. No violet haze, no buzzing particles of energy to swirl around me, shifting my form. I let my disappointment turn to fury, let fury turn to flame, let flames grow brighter, hotter.

Then it happens.

Violet falls over my vision, and just like that, my fox form feels near. I summon her forth, feeding her all my rage and sorrow, giving her the energy she needs to transmute it into physical change. I feel a buzzing in my hands, like flames dancing over my skin as my wrists grow narrow. The ropes that bind me begin to feel loose as my hands shrink to paws. A momentary pain shoots through me at the unnatural angle my fox limbs are being stretched, but as I shrink smaller, smaller, I slip from my bonds altogether.

Amelie cries out in alarm as I'm plunged beneath the icy water on my back. In a swift roll, I right myself and break my head above the water. As a fox, the chill is far more bearable, but I still can't call it pleasant. Lacking much grace, I scramble out of the tub and shake the icy water from my fur. I'm panting by the time I'm freed from as much of the water as I can, but the warmth that envelops me outside the tub is more pleasurable than anything could be in this moment.

"Evie?" The word is strangled, quavering.

I turn my attention to my sister, finding her startled expression fixed on me. "Time to go," I say to her and dart toward one of the tub's handles where her wrists are bound. Grasping the rope between my teeth, I gnaw, feeling each fiber snap as I work my way through the thick coil. When it comes loose, I run to the opposite side and free her other wrist.

Amelie shakes out her hands, eyes locked on me. "Is that really you, Evie?"

"Yes, Ami," I say. "Now hurry and untie your ankles. We need to get out of here."

Her gaze lingers on me only a moment longer before she leans forward to work out the knot binding her ankles together. When her cold fingers don't seem to obey, I have her swing her legs over the edge of the tub so I can chew the ropes apart.

Fully free, Amelie rises on unsteady feet, her dress dripping water on the floor of the cell. I run to the barred door, my heart sinking at the next obstacle that awaits. My fox form is slim enough to squeeze through the bars, but what about Amelie? I assess the length of the door, seeking a solution. It's then I realize the bars are steel.

Steel. An iron alloy. In a fae prison?

Even though iron alloys are only harmful to fae who have been weakened by pure iron, I can't imagine the fae would ever utilize something like steel. I remember how unbearable Aspen and Lorelei had found my steel surgery tools when they were recovering from iron injuries.

I shake the thoughts from my mind and refocus on my task. There's only one solution I can think of. But for this, I'll need hands.

Shifting back into my seelie form, I extend my palms toward the bars.

"Stand back," I tell Amelie. I can feel her wide eyes burning into me, but she obeys. I seek my inner fire again, horrified that it remains hardly a flicker. Shifting forms seems to have dried most of the icy water from me, but still, my connection to my magic feels weaker than ever before. I know the detrimental effects an attack by water can have, but...

Steel bars. Weakened magic.

My stomach sinks at what these implications must mean, but again I train my mind on what needs to be done. Closing my eyes, I summon my rage and fury, my sorrow and grief. Cobalt's face flashes through my mind, then Dahlia's. Ustrin's. Duveau's. I recall Maddie Coleman's smug expression when she taunted me over taking my place as Chosen. I return to Mr. Meeks' underground lab, feel the searing pain as his knife cuts through my arm. Mr. Osterman's vile hungers. Madame Rose's cruel brothel.

I let my anger grow, let it rush through my veins until an inferno roars inside me, begging to be released. Finally, I allow myself to think of Mother. But not the moment of her death. The moment she produced flame when it should have been impossible. The moment she told me to fight.

In a flash, fire ignites over my palms. Its heat warms me like a lover's caress, soothing me, healing all remnants of cold and ice. I open my eyes, taking in the pinks, purples, and aquas of my flames before I return my attention to the barred door.

Air.

I breathe in deeply, feeling the air flood my nostrils, imagining it moving through my body and down my hands to join the flame. It surrounds it, moves it, sways it. I see where I want it to go, and the air obeys. My flames leave my hands to dance over a portion of the door. In seconds, the bars glow orange, reaching a molten state before my eyes. As the metal begins to drip and pool on the stone floor, I realize my plan is far from complete. While I may be able to leap over a pool of molten steel if I shift back into my fox form, Amelie cannot.

Earth.

Just like with my river of melted weapons, I connect to the liquid steel through the element of earth. Logic. Safety. Mixing with air, I lift what has spilled onto the floor, shaping it into an orb. As my flames melt what remains of the door, I gather the rest of the molten steel into my orb, letting it hover before me, my outstretched hands guiding it where I want it to go. I shift it from beneath the door, moving it into the hall.

"Come on," I whisper to Amelie. Slowly, we step out of the cell and into the corridor, following the orb. Once on the other side, I guide the orb back into the cell, preparing to set it down near the tubs. Before I do, I separate a smaller piece and call it back toward me. The larger portion I allow to dissolve into a molten puddle.

Amelie gasps. "How are you doing this?"

"Not now," I say, returning my attention to the hall. It is long, dark, and narrow with no windows. One side disappears into darkness, while the other ends with light—a single torch set in a sconce. We make our way toward it, past rows of black, empty cells. I keep my small molten orb before me, let it illuminate the shadows in the absence of torchlight. As we continue, the hall curves to the right, on and on. At first, I think it's going to bring us back around in a circle, but as the cells come to an end, the floor takes on an incline, then stairs. The walls are empty stone now, with only the occasional torch along the way.

Finally, one last torch illuminates the end of the hall. A door. And a slumbering figure dozing against the wall.

The winter fae.

I motion Amelie to stop, but it's too late. Our footsteps have woken him, sent him lurching upright. He blinks several times, as if he can't believe his eyes. Then he raises his hands, long, sharp icicles forming in each fist like knives. Maintaining focus on my molten orb, I move air around it, let it shape the metal into an elongated point. Pulling back my flames, the steel begins to cool until a red-orange dagger remains.

His eyes widen and he swallows hard, looking from me to the threat that hovers in the air between us. The icicles tremble in his hands.

He's scared. Of *me*.

As he should be.

I could kill him. With the flick of my wrist, I could direct the makeshift dagger straight to his heart. Even if I missed, I could still strike him, disable him, melt the steel and embed it so deep no fae healer could remove it. But just like with the winged soldier I fought on the battlefield, I hesitate. Why do I hesitate? Why is it sometimes so easy to defend myself and other times I'm weak?

But am I truly weak? Or is there a difference between self-defense and cold-blooded killing? A difference between justice and cruelty?

I take a deep breath, keeping my weapon hovering in place. "I don't have to hurt you," I say. "You can let us go."

He barks a laugh, but it doesn't diminish his obvious fear. "Let you go? Why should I do that?"

I recall the bitterness he's shown, the way he tended to us as if the duty were an insult to him. "Because you're fighting for the wrong side."

"I'm fighting for the side that would make me king."

"And how's that going for you?"

He shakes his head with a sneer. "It's a joke. This is all a joke. Two humans for thousands. It's a disgrace."

There it is again. *Two humans for thousands.* "Let us go." I inch my dagger closer, my eyes locked on his. "Or I will have to hurt you."

Sweat beads at his brow as his gaze flashes to my blade. Silence wraps around us. One of us will have to make the first move, and it looks like it will be me.

"Fine," he says through his teeth. Lowering his hands, the icicles disappear. "Go ahead and leave."

I eye him through slitted lids, watch as he leans against the wall, arms crossed over his chest. The tip of my dagger remains trained on him with every move we make. Amelie and I inch forward, my sister pressed close to my back. Keeping a wide berth, we skirt around the winter fae to the door. When we reach it, I give him a reluctant nod of thanks.

He doesn't bother looking at me. "Letting you go isn't a mercy," he says with a smirk. "Wait and see. I've just had enough of this pathetic *council.*" With a shudder, he shrinks, replaced a moment later with a sleek white ermine with a black-tipped tail.

Amelie bites back a startled squeal, and I push open the door. The ermine darts between our legs, disappearing into the night. We don't wait long to follow suit, rushing up the short staircase that opens onto a stone walkway. We pause once under the open night sky, the moon bright overhead. Grasping the hilt of my dagger, the metal still warm to the touch, I begin to turn in a slow circle to gather our bearings. Amelie's fingers grasp my free hand. I squeeze her palm.

The first thing I see is a towering structure. A lighthouse. Ancient and built from weathered stone, an undeniably human building.

My stomach sinks. The steel bars. My weakened magic. The reason Aspen has never seen the dungeon we were held in. It's because we aren't in Faerwyvae. We're in Eisleigh. But where? Why?

The next thing I see is the crumbling wall that extends to either side of the lighthouse—an old fortification. The sight is so familiar, although it's nothing I've ever seen in person. Perhaps in a history book? A painting? The smell of salt tingles my nostrils, followed by the rhythmic sound of waves.

Then it dawns on me. I know where we are. This is Varney Cove.

During the first war with the fae, the humans used Varney Cove as a naval base to defend against the sea fae, and the lighthouse was repurposed as a fort. But why in the name of iron are we here?

Amelie gasps, her grip on my hand growing suddenly tighter. I whirl to follow her line of sight. Behind us stand rows and rows of tents. Military tents, the kinds I've only seen depicted in the broadsheets.

I feel like my throat will close up from the effort it takes to suppress the scream that builds in my chest.

I can only think one thing. *They're here. They're here. They're here.* The mainland army is here and we're too late.

Aspen, I whisper down the Bond. *Aspen, I know where we are.*

I continue to take in the rows of tents, my eyes falling on the one at the far left bearing the scrolling *B* crest of mainland Bretton alongside a second symbol—the winged staff denoting a place of medical practice.

Now I know how Dahlia received such quick care from the iron injury I gave her. The Renounced have allied with the humans. And not just any humans. Soldiers from the mainland, sent by King Grigory—the King of Bretton—himself. But to what end? *Two humans for thousands.*

Movement catches my eye, sending my heart hammering against my ribs, but it's just Aspen, violet aura rippling around his form. He heard my summons.

Storming over to me, he grasps my shoulders in his warm hands. "Where are you?"

"Varney Cove in Eisleigh," I rush to say.

He repeats it under his breath, then looks around, as if committing each sight to memory. When his gaze falls on the army camp, he mutters a string of curses. "I'm coming for you, Evie." Without another word, he's gone.

I'm left blinking at the place he was, hoping against hope that he now has all the information he needs to use the Chariot. Then again, perhaps I should have waited until I got us farther from the camp. If Aspen comes here, it will be to the heart of a viper's nest, surrounded by a human army with human weapons. Weapons that could end his life in an instant.

At least the camp is asleep, I remind myself, willing my quavering breaths to go silent.

Amelie trembles at my side. "We should run," she whispers. "Why are we still here?"

"Aspen's coming for us." Before the words finish leaving my mouth, another flash of movement enters my periphery. My pulse races, fueling a spark of hope. But it isn't Aspen that's returned. It's a human guard, marching along the inside of the wall, a rifle held against his side.

I grip the hilt of my makeshift dagger tighter, wishing I knew the first thing about creating an invisibility glamour. Perhaps another kind of glamour could work. If I can lock his gaze when he sees us—

There's no time. Before I can react, his rifle is leveled straight at us. "Prisoners escaped!" His voice rings out, shattering the silence of the night. Movement erupts in the camp, soldiers rushing from their tents while more guards close in from their previously unseen posts. Footsteps pound the stone behind me, spilling out from the lighthouse tower. I flash my dagger toward one threat then another while Amelie presses in closer. Closer. The barrels of countless rifles form a ring around us.

One dagger against an army. Not the best odds. Even if Aspen were to suddenly appear, even if he brought all the fae the Chariot could transport, could we even make it out of this alive?

"Evie," Amelie cries.

"I know," I bark under my breath. "I'll—"

"Who is that?" She nudges my left side, prompting me to whip my attention toward the lighthouse. There the soldiers have parted to reveal a smug-faced Queen Dahlia. But that's not who Amelie was inquiring about. For standing before the Summer Queen is my greatest foe.

Mr. Duveau.

29

"Evelyn Fairfield," Mr. Duveau says, taking a step closer.

Heat courses through my body at the sight of my mother's murderer. I grit my teeth against the urge to lunge for him, to plunge my blade into his heart. As much as the thought fuels my fire, I know I wouldn't live long enough to see it through. Not with all these rifles and armed soldiers surrounding us.

Instead, I burn him with a scowl. "Hearing you say my name doesn't quite have the same ring to it anymore. Do you know what I mean?"

His expression darkens, but he maintains his composure. He seems somewhat changed since I last saw him, as evidenced by the dark circles beneath his lower lashes, his bloodshot eyes, the slight dishevelment of his hair. Even his formerly slim mustache has grown unruly, stray hairs brushing the snarl of his upper lip. Keeping his eyes on me, he speaks to Dahlia through gritted teeth. "I thought you said she was contained."

"She was," the Summer Queen says, tight lipped as she eyes me with clear disdain. "How did you get out, girl?"

I turn my glare on her. "Wouldn't you like to know."

She opens her mouth, but a human guard rushes up the stairs from the underground cells and whispers something in Mr. Duveau's ear. Dahlia's eyes widen at whatever she overhears, but the councilman only looks amused.

"It seems you're up to your mother's tricks," he says to me.

"My apologies, Councilman Duveau," Dahlia says, a pleading quality in her tone. I'm shocked to see her debase herself even slightly before a human. "I will have her returned to her bindings at once—"

"No need," Mr. Duveau says sharply. "I know how to make her obey."

I brace myself, squeezing the dagger tighter as he reaches beneath his jacket and withdraws a familiar weapon. My eyes lock on the barrel of the revolver as he cocks the hammer. I've faced this weapon before, but without the power of his name under my control, I know I can't still his hand the way I once did. My heart races as I assess the distance between us, trying to calculate how fast I could throw my makeshift blade before he can fire the gun. Perhaps if I wield air to direct its momentum, ensuring a direct hit to—

My thoughts go still as he moves the gun. Not to fire it. Not to bring it closer to me. He aims it at Amelie.

My sister bites back a squeal, her fingers digging into my forearm as she grabs me.

"Don't move," Mr. Duveau orders. "Either of you."

Every inch of me is frozen, aside from my raging heart that pounds in my chest. With his gun trained on my sister, every reckless idea I have loses viability. I hate that he's using her against me. I hate that he was right.

I know how to make her obey.

Threaten someone I love. That's all he has to do. That's all anyone has to do.

And after everything I admitted, both to Amelie and myself when we were trapped in the cell, I can acknowledge that I do in fact love her. For the love of iron, I love her fiercely. I can't let anyone take her away from me again.

"What do you want?" I ask, feigning as much calm as I can. Surely, he can see the way my shoddy weapon trembles in my hand.

"First, release the dagger."

I hate to leave us defenseless, but what else can I do? The barrel of the revolver is aimed at my sister's head. Even if I could dive in front of her, she's taller than I am. He'll kill her just like he killed Mother. My fingers feel stiff as I open them one by one. Then, with a thud, the metal falls from my grasp to the ground at my feet.

Duveau nods to a nearby soldier, who rushes in to retrieve the discarded dagger. The soldier wrinkles his brow once he has it in his hand, clearly unimpressed by my workmanship. Mr. Duveau's eyes flash toward it, just long enough to see what I made. His gaze returns to me, a smirk on his lips. "Really, Evelyn? You thought you could take us down with that?"

I press my lips tight to avoid saying something I'll regret.

"You," he says, expression turning serious as his attention moves to my sister. "Take a step away from her." When Amelie makes no attempt to obey, he waves the gun, emphasizing the direction he wants her to move.

With trembling steps, she inches away from me. Her fingers release my forearm, leaving my flesh cold in their absence. It takes all my restraint not to reach for her.

"Guards," Mr. Duveau barks. The soldiers shift, each step sure and calculated as some back away and others move in closer, until about a half-dozen men form a tighter circle around us. Revolver still trained on Amelie, Mr. Duveau's attention returns to me. "You will come with me willingly. Otherwise, these men pump you full of iron bullets. And that's after you watch me kill your sister. Agreed?"

I burn him with a glare. While I don't refuse, I don't argue either. "Where are we going?"

Duveau ignores me, motioning forth a soldier outside our ring of guards and whispering a string of orders. I hear the words *tub* and *water*, which tells me he plans on returning us to our former captivity. But when next he speaks, it isn't to order us back to the dungeon. "Turn around and walk," he says, nodding in the opposite direction, away from the lighthouse.

Dahlia's brow furrows as she eyes Mr. Duveau. "Where are you taking them?"

"You know where," he answers without looking at her.

"But...how? How will you get them there?" There's no worry for me and my sister in her eyes. It's something else that has her suddenly so flustered.

"On my new ship," Duveau says through his teeth.

Crimson rises to the Summer Queen's cheeks. "I thought that was supposed to be *my* ship."

"You thought wrong."

Her fingers clench into fists. "What about our deal? I have a war to win. We're giving you the girls. We promised you a new treaty."

Finally, he leaves my gaze to pin Dahlia beneath a scowl. "And I'm giving you an army."

Two girls for thousands. There's my answer.

There's still so much I don't understand though. All those dozens of warships the human assailant mentioned...they were coming to aid Dahlia? How can that be? The assailant said *the time of the fae is at an end.*

The fae. Not just the Alpha Alliance.

He will ruin all of you.

"We agreed to more than this," the Summer Queen says, an edge to her tone. "Not just a single garrison."

Duveau lowers his voice. "You will get more as soon as I send word to the rest of the fleet. Once I'm on the ship with the girls, I'll know you're worth your word."

Her eyes flash dangerously, but she makes no further argument. Finally, with a begrudging nod, she takes a step back. Mr. Duveau's eyes immediately find mine. "Move!" he shouts, thrusting his revolver at my sister.

Amelie jumps, and I whirl around, nudging her with my elbow to follow suit. We begin to walk in the opposite direction toward the other end of the crumbling wall. Progress is slow as each step is mirrored by our circle of guards, who maintain an uncomfortable proximity at all times. The only benefit to our pace is that it gives Aspen more time to find us.

Then again, do I even want him to find us? Now that we've awoken the entire camp, there's no way he could make it out of here alive.

Aspen, I send down the Bond. *Don't come here.*

I hear nothing in response, filling my heart with dread.

As we reach the end of the wall, the ground shifts to a decline where old stone steps lead the way down the side of the cliff beneath the lighthouse. With the morning sun beginning to rise, I get my first glimpse of the sea. It spreads out below us, beneath the cliff. And not too far from the beach is a massive black shape. A warship. Additionally, dozens of soldiers pace the beach, some guarding a smaller sea vessel while others offload the crates it carries, crates of what I can only imagine are weapons.

I nearly trip on the next step and force my eyes to return to the crumbling stairs.

"What's going on?" Amelie whispers.

"No talking," comes Duveau's voice from behind. Even though I can't see his revolver, I can feel its presence all the same, nipping my heels, dragging invisible black claws down my sister's spine.

Once the stairs meet sand, I catch yet another sight of the warship, a hulking mass far more terrifying than the broadsheets depicted. Its body is long and angular, smoke billowing into the air while impossibly tall, slim towers pierce the sky. The deck is lined with turrets armed with enormous guns, ones I never wish to see fired.

I shudder at the sight. War on the mainland always seemed like a faraway thing, something that could only ever involve the larger landmasses and countries, never the Fair Isle. But here it is, lurking outside my isle. My home.

We continue forward, our guards ushering us toward the smaller boat. A pair of soldiers offload the last crate, leaving the sea vessel mostly empty, aside from two men who stand at what must be the helm. The levers and mechanical panels tell me this boat is unlike anything I've seen before; its technology is likely closer to that of the warship. At a nod from Mr. Duveau, one of the boat's operators turns to the controls, and the vessel roars with the deafening sound of a motor coming to life.

"Get on the boat," Mr. Duveau orders.

My heart races as Amelie and I obey, my mind spinning to find a way out of this. But every move I can think to make only ends in Amelie's death. And my own.

Once we reach the center of the boat, Mr. Duveau orders us to face him. I steel my nerves as we slowly turn around. Fury rushes through my veins at Duveau's triumphant grin.

"What will you do with us now?" I ask. To my credit, my voice somehow manages not to shake.

"You're coming with me back to the mainland," he says. "And don't even bother with fantasies of escape. Unlike your little friends, you'll find your new guards far less lax." Another reminder of the rifles still pointed at us, unwavering in the hands of the soldiers.

"What then?" I ask, if only to keep him talking. Anything to give me more time to think of something. Anything. I still have my fire. It may be weaker than I'd like, but it's there, hovering just below the surface of my skin. I know how to shape it with air. Know how to manipulate the metals of earth. That's got to be worth something, right?

Mr. Duveau hazards a quick glance behind him. My eyes flash over his head, where I see two sets of guards heaving our tubs down the steep steps below the cliff. He's waiting for them before we depart.

Good. That means I still have time.

"There I will present you and your sister to King Grigory, show him I alone was able to apprehend the two girls who put the treaty in jeopardy."

Half my mind analyzes his words, while the other half assesses our surroundings, the space between me and Amelie and our armed guards. I quirk my lips in a teasing grin. "Trying to save face for the blunders you made?"

His expression darkens. "Those weren't my blunders. Those were yours. You nearly ruined everything."

I bat my lashes, shaping my next words carefully. I know they'll put me on thin ice, but I need to rattle his confidence without inviting deadly reproach. "Sounds like *your* blunders, if a single girl could upend your standing with the King of Bretton so easily."

"Shut up," he says through his teeth, face flushing crimson. "You know nothing. I tried to fix everything a different way, but those attempts proved fruitless."

The memory of the thief sent to my palace comes to mind. "You mean the weapon you tried to steal? How was that going to fix anything?"

He purses his lips, studying me for a moment. "You do have it, don't you? It's still at Irridae just like I thought, isn't it?"

Heat flushes the back of my neck as I consider it may not have been the wisest to bring up the Parvanovae. A quick change of subject is in order. "And now you're making a deal with the fae in order to make up for your failures? How's that going to work?"

He regathers some of his composure. "Your enemies are my allies because we want the same thing. Peace on the isle."

I bark a laugh. "Peace? Is that what you call giving power-hungry fae the means to destroy their own people?"

"I don't care what the fae do to each other, so long as it serves the greater good of Eisleigh."

I study his face, the tick in his jaw. "There won't be a treaty with the fae, will there?"

"What are you talking about?"

"I wonder...does Dahlia suspect you plan to betray her? Will her gifted soldiers turn on her as soon as the other warships arrive, or after the armies have killed her enemies?"

He refuses to rise to my bait. "I have no idea what you mean."

I'm right. I know it. He didn't forge a deal between the King of Bretton and Queen Dahlia. He just found a convenient way to get human soldiers on fae soil without a fight.

"I don't know who disgusts me more right now," I say with a sneer. "You, for obvious reasons. Or Dahlia, for being a big enough fool to trust you."

His eyes blaze as he takes a step forward. "Watch your mouth. Don't forget whose life is at stake."

That silences me, but my mind remains active, fire coursing through my veins, gathering at my core in a fiery orb. It glows so hot with my rage that it takes all my restraint to keep it beneath the surface of my skin. I can't summon it forth for the others to see. Not yet. Not until I connect to the other elements, figure out how to send my flames outward in all directions at once—

Mr. Duveau takes a sudden step forward. All fire drains from me as he presses the barrel to Amelie's forehead. "Stop!" he shouts at me. "Whatever you're thinking, whatever you're doing, stop. I can see the calculations in your eyes."

"Evie," she cries, voice strangled.

I raise my hands in surrender, force my words out as calmly as I can. "I'm not doing anything."

Revolver still pressed firmly against Amelie's forehead, Mr. Duveau calls out to the soldiers still making their way across the beach with our tubs. "Hurry up! Fill them with the coldest water you—"

"Get away from her." The voice that rings out from the beach isn't one of the soldiers. It's Cobalt. Shimmering blue scales cover every inch of his nix form, chest heaving as he pins Mr. Duveau beneath a glare with his single eye. His empty eye socket remains hidden behind the leather patch he had on before. The soldiers on the beach turn their rifles on him, but he pays them no heed.

Keeping his gun in place, he whirls to the side to eye Cobalt. "What are you doing? We're in an alliance," he calls out.

"Amelie wasn't supposed to be part of it."

A guttural sound comes from my sister, and I turn my head to catch the hate twisting her face. She no longer seems to care about the revolver kissing her skin. "Cobalt," she mutters, then changes her tone, her pitch. "Cobalt. Cobalt."

My blood goes cold. This may not be the best time for Amelie to focus on vengeance. I hush her, but she continues to say his name again and again, her voice growing louder each time.

Luckily, Duveau seems too distracted by Cobalt to notice. "You're wrong," Mr. Duveau says. "This is indeed vital to my agreement with your people."

As the soldiers on the beach inch closer to Cobalt, he extends his sharp fingers, curling them as if he's preparing to swipe.

"Stand down or die," Mr. Duveau says. "I doubt your friends will be too upset if I kill you, considering they've all agreed what must be done."

Cobalt pauses, gaze locking on Amelie. His brow furrows as Amelie continues to speak his name.

Mr. Duveau whirls back to her, finally aware of her mutterings. "Why are you doing that?" He pulls back the gun just enough to tap it against her forehead. Fire lights the tips of my fingers, the orb reforming at my core. When

Amelie doesn't stop, Duveau swings the gun away from her, as if preparing to strike her with it.

"Cobalt!" Amelie shouts, the power of his name ringing through her voice. "Kill these men."

At the same moment, calls of alarm come from the lighthouse, followed by gunfire.

Cobalt spins into action in a whirl of blue, darting toward the nearest set of soldiers. Gunfire rings out all around, both above and below the cliff. From here, I can't see what's going on at the lighthouse, but I can feel it. I can feel my mate's proximity. He actually came.

Which means those bullets above the cliff are for him.

My heart lurches over Aspen's unknown fate, but I force my attention back to the scene before me. With the chaos of gunfire, the beach falls under a haze of disrupted sand, leaving only a vague image of the action taking place, of several dark shapes and one blue. The human shouts I hear are far more telling.

Amelie's smile is vicious, eyes fixated on the beach. She takes a step forward as if to join the mayhem, sidestepping Mr. Duveau's revolver while his attention is drawn away.

"Stop!" one of our guards shouts, and Mr. Duveau whirls back around, stopping Amelie in her tracks. Some of the fight leaves her eyes as she seems to remember the very real threat before her. Slowly, she lifts her hands in surrender and takes a step back.

"Go!" Mr. Duveau calls above the din.

Vertigo seizes me as the boat lurches into motion. Amelie grabs my arm as we both struggle to keep our feet beneath us.

"Get away from each other," Duveau orders, and we rush to separate.

With my legs somewhat stabilized against the motion, I return my attention to the beach, feeling my heart sink at how far away it already is. My eyes flash to the lighthouse, watching it shrink with every second. *Aspen, please tell me you're alive,* I think to myself, not daring to use the Bond in case it distracts him from protecting his life. I squint, wishing I could see what was going on up there.

Something above the lighthouse snags my attention, a small, dark shape making lazy circles in the sky.

A raven.

Do I dare think...

Its circles spread out farther, over the beach, over the sea. Then the bird suddenly changes course, heading straight for us.

I suppress a smile.

Mr. Duveau flashes a glance over his shoulder, trying to glimpse what has me so amused. When he whirls back to me, he snaps his fingers with his free hand, eyes wild. "I'm getting tired of you girls not taking me seriously."

I curl my lip in a mock pout. "Aww, you poor thing."

He shakes his head with a smirk, then nods at the nearest guard. "Knife."

The soldier lowers his rifle, exchanging it for an iron blade.

"Take one of her fingers," Mr. Duveau says, tilting his head toward Amelie.

The blood leaves my face as the soldier lunges forward, grasping my sister's wrist between his fingers. "No!" I shout.

"From this point on, she'll lose one for every smart retort you make," Duveau says. "And for every instance of even mild disobedience, I'll have one of her toes. Until I have your full compliance, I'll continue to carve up your sister until there's nothing left."

I should stand down, I should beg for Amelie's safety, but my rage is so hot, flames return to my core, reforming the fiery orb. I can feel my skin growing hot, fire tickling my palms, begging for release.

The soldier lifts Amelie's hand as she screams and struggles to pull away. Gone is that reckless girl who used Cobalt's name to order him to kill, replaced with the sister I always swore to protect.

"Stop struggling, or he takes two," Duveau says in a bored tone, thrusting the barrel of his gun at her to remind her just how many dangers there are. "And don't worry. This will be very, very slow, considering we don't have a proper chopping block."

Amelie lets out a wail, tears streaming down her cheeks.

The soldier singles out Amelie's forefinger and brings his blade toward it.

My eyes flash to the sky, to the dark shape hovering just overhead.

The orb of flame burns hotter at my core, and I begin to shape it with air, preparing to send it flying outward.

The soldier with the knife looks to Mr. Duveau, who nods. "Do it," he says. The edge of the blade bites into her skin just as a dark shape drops into the boat, landing near the motor's controls.

"Hey beautiful," says a familiar voice.

Our guards whirl toward it, leaving Franco in full view, perched on the control panel in his seelie form. Two dark, smoky tendrils spiral from his fingers to the heads of the navigators, holding them immobilized while their mouths are open in silent screams. Shadows are leached from them, flowing into the prince.

Mr. Duveau starts forward, but Franco burns him with a scowl. "I wasn't talking to you," Franco says, then lifts his chin with a charming smile, eyes on me. "Hey there."

"Fire!" Duveau shouts.

"Bye now." With a flutter of his fingers, Franco leaps to his feet and shifts back into his raven form. But not before he kicks out against two of the levers on the control panel. The rifles fire just as the boat's momentum is thrust back by the sudden loss of power, making the soldiers' aim go wild. Several bullets strike the boat's controls.

The man with the knife loses balance and releases Amelie from his grip.

I reach for her, pulling her close to my side as I unleash my flame, letting it shoot out in every direction from my core, lashing the guards in a fiery inferno. Flames erupt from my skin, and it's an effort to keep them from scalding my sister. Screams roar along with my growing fire, and I charge the nearest guard, who spins in a circle, desperately trying to beat the flames from devouring his uniform. Lifting my knee, I aim a kick at his gut, sending him curling inward. I shove him to the side and pull Amelie forward as we rush to the edge of the boat. With every step I take, I leave fire in my wake, coating the floor of the boat, raging up soldier's legs. I hear splashes as soldiers jump from the other side. I exchange a glance at Amelie. She nods, knowing what must be done.

Squeezing each other's hands, we take a deep breath and jump.

Waves pull me under at once, swallowing me into a world of cold and darkness. Sound is muted in my ears while pressure builds in my head, my lungs. I open my eyes, feeling the sting of salt as I struggle to orient myself in the raging current. Spreading my arms, I realize with horror that Amelie's hand is no longer in mine. I whirl one way then the other, my movements painfully slow, but I see no sign of her. All I see is dark water with no indication which way is up or down.

Panic seizes me as my lungs constrict, the last of the air being pressed from my lungs.

This is the end. This is it. I'll drown in the one element I was never able to master.

My movements go still. Not with fear; with realization.

The elements.

I may be under water, but the other elements aren't lost to me.

My first need is air. I imagine a pocket of air, forming from the oxygen molecules that help make up water. I envision it growing into an enormous bubble, one large enough for me to swallow a lungful of breath. I can feel it. It's so close.

But why can't I see it?

Pain sears my chest. I won't make it much longer. I need to breathe.

I close my eyes, thinking of Minuette, the wind that constantly writhes around her. I imagine the feel of a breeze against my human skin, then rustling my fox fur as I run through the windblown forest. I focus on what the air element represents. Thought. Imagination. Innovation. I know air. I *know* it.

With calm certainty, I open my eyes.

Then I see it. A shimmering bubble of air unlike any ordinary bubble I've ever seen. It's enormous and round, maintaining its shape as if it were a solid thing, not one composed of air. It floats slowly through the black water, just feet from where I am. Jolting into motion, I kick out my legs, pull my arms, swimming toward the bubble. My vision fades with every inch I close between myself and the air I so desperately need, and I fear I'll lose consciousness before I reach it. Still, I keep going, focusing on my connection to the element of air, imagining it filling my lungs long before it truly does.

Then finally it's there. My lips press against the bubble, and I suck in an enormous breath. My chest still aches, but at least I've given myself more time.

Now how to reach the surface?

I immediately know the answer, and it surrounds me like a shroud.

Water. I must connect to the element of water. Work with it. Make friends with it.

Face it.

I already know what it will bring, but I have no other choice. Closing my eyes, I allow myself to feel the icy sea against my skin, taste the salt on my lips, feel its pressure squeezing me at all sides.

Then I open myself to it, using all my will to take it to the Twelfth Court.

There I fall into a chasm of grief.

31

A bullet. Blood. Death.

I'm back in the courtroom where Mother's death plays out before me. The violet haze of the Twelfth Court does nothing to take from the pain of this memory, and the emotions that accompany it swallow me whole. Pain and regret. Guilt and shame. Sorrow. Sorrow. Endless sorrow.

I want to open my mouth and wail, but a small part of me remembers where I truly am, knows what will happen if water rushes in through my lips.

My next instinct is to pull away, swallow the painful emotions or burn them with my fire. I can do neither of those things, for my fire is tempered by the water around me, and the only way out of this is through it. I don't know how I know that, but I do.

Mother's death plays again and again. I watch the life leave her eyes as a bullet strikes her forehead. Blood streams down her face, filling the tub she's kept in. She sinks lifeless into the crimson water, the color bright against the violet haze that falls over everything else.

Gone. She's gone.

Dead.

And it was all my fault.

I admitted as much to Amelie, and once again, I confess it to myself.

It was all my fault. All my fault. All my fault.

I'm so sorry, Mother.

The pain that drags me down is too much to bear. I can feel it sinking me deeper, deeper toward the ocean floor.

A bullet. Blood. Death.

A bullet. Blood. Death.

Again.

Again.

Mother's lifeless form sinks into a tub of her own blood—

"Stop!" The voice freezes the scene, crimson water suspended midair in the moment it was about to splash over Mother's head. Everything else in the image is frozen as well—the guards, the councilmen, the jurors, Mr. Duveau—but all is blurred aside from the tub. "Stop this, Evelyn," the voice says, and I know who it belongs to. It's a voice I never thought I'd hear again.

Mother.

I blink at the frozen scene just as movement begins to stir inside the tub. With equal parts joy and terror, I watch as Mother rises from the bloody water. "Why do you always return to this scene?" she asks, eyes pleading as rivulets of scarlet trail down her face.

"Because it haunts me," I whisper. "It's the moment I saw the consequences of my choice."

She shakes her head. "It wasn't just your choice." With a flick of her wrist, the image begins to reverse, the blurred shapes of the guards returning to their posts, Mr. Duveau's gun swinging away from Mother and instead to me. Mother's arms are outstretched, wrists locked in the iron cuffs. Her expression is defiant.

I recalled this moment in the cell with Amelie. The moment Mother sought her flames when she should have been at her weakest. The moment she wanted me to fight.

The rest of the image returns to stillness, but flames ignite over Mother's hands, turning her cuffs a molten orange. "I chose to fight here, Evelyn."

"I know." My voice comes out with a tremble. "But then...I tried to use the councilman's true name. Tried and...failed. That's why he shot you. To punish *me*."

"No, my love," she says. "I chose my death before he pulled that trigger. And I would choose it again and again if it saves your life. If it saves your sister's life. You cannot take that moment from me, Evelyn. It is mine, not yours."

Tears stream out of my eyes, but they float from my cheeks like twinkling violet stars floating through a stream. No, an ocean. Part of me remembers where I truly am, knows that I'm drowning, while the rest of me remains in the violet courtroom, eyes locked on Mother's face.

"I could stay here," I say, voice small. "With you. This could be the end of all my pain, all the fighting."

Mother's face falls, eyes turning down at the corners. "You cannot stay here with me. There's so much more for you to do. For you to live for. Love for. And yes, fight for."

Aspen's face flashes through my mind, then Amelie's, Foxglove's, Lorelei's, and Nyxia's. I see Franco's face and Breeda's. Dune's face and Marie Coleman's and Fehr's, and all the other people and creatures I'm sworn to protect. "But I'm running out of time. I don't know how to get out of this."

"You do." In a flash, Mother's chains are gone. She exits the tub and comes to me, her steps slow and swaying, trailing water with every move. Just like my tears, the water doesn't remain in place but lifts into the air in glittering droplets. When she reaches me, her hands come to frame my face. "You are a queen. This element is yours. Even if you weren't a royal, you would still have access to it. Do you know why?"

I shake my head, eyes glistening as I luxuriate in the feeling of her gentle, familiar touch.

"Because water is the element of emotion. And the most powerful emotion of all is love, which you are no stranger to. All you have to do is open to it. All of it."

"But it brings so much pain."

"I know. But you're stronger than the pain. You are stronger than you know. You'll never see just how strong you are, though, if you don't allow yourself to."

I continue to study her face, memorizing every crease at the corner of her lips and eyes. The violet haze lifts from her, revealing the emerald shade of her glittering irises, the bright copper of her hair, the peachy hue of her skin.

"It's time for you to go," she says.

I want to argue, but I know she's right. I can feel the compression of my lungs, my single breath of air already running out. With a sob, I nod.

My heart lurches as she takes one step away, then another, retreating from me. The water from the tub begins to rise, spilling over the edges. Mother smiles as she backs up another step, paying no heed to the water that floods the courtroom, darkening it. I watch as she continues to back away from me, watch her smile even as we both go under the rising tide, until we hang suspended in the cold, dark sea.

I love you, Evelyn, she says straight into my mind.

I love you too, Ma.

You can do this. It's the last thing she says before she disappears.

My heart feels like it will break in two, and I sink into that feeling, noticing how similar it feels to drowning. But it won't drown me. Not this time. For alongside that grief lies every memory that uplifts me—Mother brushing my hair from my head after a bad dream. Mother kissing my wounds and laying her hands over scrapes and bruises, telling me her love will mend them. Then I see Amelie and me laughing, playing, fighting, then making up over mugs of warm tea that Mother offers us.

The memories bring equal parts joy and sorrow, and I accept them, giving both emotions equal places in my heart. Allowing the memories to wrap around me, hold me, lift me, I open my awareness to the feeling of water. I know I'm nearly out of air, but I manage to keep my panic down, manage to fight the urge to control the water, and instead surrender to it. Grow one with it. Flow with it. Become it.

The pressure begins to ease around me, giving way to a sense of rising, floating. A shimmer of light in the dark sea draws my attention. Is that the surface? I kick out, my arms stroking through the water as I reach for hope. Air. Safety. Drawing near, the light begins to grow brighter. Brighter. And at the center of it is a figure with dark copper hair streaming around her like a halo.

My heart leaps. It's Amelie!

I swim faster now, and she swims toward me. Her movements are far more elegant than mine are; her limbs cut through the water with ease, propelling her forward to close the distance between us in seconds. Her hand grasps mine, and she pulls me toward her, circling an arm around my waist as she turns us back in the direction she came. Swimming with one arm, she guides us up, up, closer to that shimmer of light. Then finally, our heads breach the surface into the light of the morning sun. I gasp, coughing up water as I suck in the most delicious breath I've ever tasted in my life. A second later, a wave crashes over our heads, but another gulp of air is on the other side.

Amelie sputters, skin pale and cheeks ruddy. "Can you swim to the shore?" she asks, voice hoarse.

I look in one direction and then another, finally spotting the lighthouse. We're a good distance away from the shore, and I've never swum so far in my life. "I...I don't know. Can you?"

She nods. "Selkie experience." Steel flashes over her expression.

Another wave douses our faces, leaving me gasping in its wake. "I'll try." My words come out with a cough.

"Perhaps I can help." A shadow blocks out the light overhead, and I look up to find Franco, partially shifted between his two forms—mostly seelie but with an enormous set of raven wings spanning out on either side of him. His lips quirk in a crooked grin as his outstretched arms reach for me.

I cast a glance at Amelie, who eyes Franco with suspicion. She may have seen his diversion on the boat, but they aren't well acquainted yet. I attempt a smile, despite the seawater dripping over my face. "We can trust him," I tell her, lifting my arms for Franco to grasp beneath my armpits.

Amelie's gaze locks on mine as Franco hoists me into his arms. "I'll see you on the shore," she says with a nod, then dives beneath the waves.

32

I barely have time to secure my arms around Franco's neck before he takes off toward the shore. As it comes into view, all I see is smoke and sand, but the closer we draw near, the more obvious it is that the fighting is still underway. However, most of the commotion seems to be coming from near the lighthouse. I try to lift my chin to see over the wall, seeking any sign of Aspen, but just as the fighting becomes visible, the sight drops from view.

"No!" I cry, fighting against the arms that secure me. "Take me to the lighthouse."

He shakes his head. "You don't want to go there right now."

"Is Aspen there?"

He gives a short nod.

"Then that's where I want to be."

"He told me to get you to safety so you can get out of here." Ignoring my protests, Franco continues our descent toward the beach where the fighting has condensed to the far end. Several soldiers remain locked in physical combat with what is unmistakably Cobalt, still in his blue nix form, as well as a few other sea fae who look like the guards I've seen in his employ. Franco's momentum slows as we near the ground on the abandoned end of the beach, where only carnage remains. My stomach roils as I take in the blood that coats the sand, along with dismembered body parts of dead soldiers. I'm momentarily stunned with the realization that

Cobalt likely did all this. But as soon as we land, I remember where I need to be.

I'm barely out of Franco's arms before I round on him. "Bring me up to the lighthouse."

"Your mate can take care of himself," he says. "Nyxia and Estel are there too, as well as four of my sister's soldiers. We need to wait here."

I furrow my brow. "For what?"

He turns his eyes to the sky, squinting through the smoke that hangs in the air. Then a smile tugs his lips. "For that."

I follow his gaze, unsure of what he's looking at. There's nothing there. Nothing out of the ordinary, at least.

Then I see it.

A red light hovers in the sky, darting this way and that as if in search of something. Franco waves his arms wildly in the air until the light pauses. After only a moment's hesitation, it shoots down toward us. As it draws near, I see the unrestrained joy on Breeda's tiny face. "Your Most Beautiful Esteemed Majesty!" she squeals, flying around my head with dizzying speed. When she stops, she extends her arms, revealing a silver disc. "Look what I brought you."

A Chariot. *My* Chariot. The one I hid in the planter outside my bedroom window.

I open a palm and she sets the device upon it, then brushes her hands together. "That was heavy."

"We have what we need," Franco says. "Now it's time to leave."

I close my fingers around the disc and narrow my eyes. "I'm not leaving without Aspen or Amelie."

He grasps me by the shoulders, desperation in his eyes. "Aspen and the others have their own Chariot, Evelyn. As soon as we're away, Breeda will fly up and give the signal. The others will follow us."

My heart sinks at the thought of leaving without Aspen. But if he's only stalling for me to get away...

"We at least need to wait for my sister." I turn to where the waves lap upon the bloody shore, my eyes seeking any sign of life between here and the wreckage of the boat, where flames and smoke continue to rise into the sky. Behind that, the hulking warship remains. With the sea so wild, I can't make out much else at all. Then finally, I see movement halfway down the beach.

Amelie falls to her knees as she fights her way out of the waves to catch her breath. She made it.

I rush toward her, Franco close at my side. "Amelie!" I call out.

She turns to face me, her eyes lighting with relief. But it's short lived as her attention is drawn to the other end of the shore.

Every muscle in her body stiffens, and I watch as her fingers curl into fists.

The air leaves my lungs when I realize what has her so distracted. It's Cobalt and the sea fae, fighting more human soldiers. I see now that some of the humans have built a barricade to hide behind, revealing their faces only to take aim with their rifles. The rest of the soldiers engage the sea fae in close physical combat. Cobalt's blue scales are shredded in places, revealing bloody gashes. Some lesions go as far down to the bone. And yet he fights just as fiercely as if he were unwounded. There's almost a madness to the way he dodges the blasts of the guns, falters for only seconds when struck by an iron bullet. He presses on despite every wound.

Fueled by Amelie's command. *Kill these men.*

My gaze returns to my sister, but she continues to watch her mate. Without taking her eyes off him, she reaches into the sand, retrieving a discarded blade. Then, to my complete horror, she charges into the fight.

"Amelie, no!" I halt, my scream shattering the air, yet it doesn't reach her.

"Evelyn, watch out!" Franco yanks me roughly by the arm as a figure nearly barrels into me. We stumble back as Mr. Duveau rises clumsily to his feet, dripping seawater. He's lost his jacket and waistcoat, his shirt torn and stained crimson. He darts forward again, but a red flame sears his face, making him lurch back.

"Stay away!" Breeda shouts, brandishing a tiny fist. "I am charged with protecting Her Most Beautiful and Gracious Majesty."

Duveau blinks, eyes unfocused in the heat of the fire sprite. Then, with a shout, he swipes his hand through the air, right through Breeda's flames, and sends her spiraling through the air.

Franco pushes me behind him, and shadows begin to writhe around his shoulders. As he grows taller, the skin prickles on the back of my neck. I don't need to see his face to know what he looks like. I've seen how terrifying he can be, how he can transform his features into those of a nightmarish monster at will. The true origin of the haunting vampire tales of my youth.

I back up a step, catching a glimpse of the councilman.

Duveau, however, seems nonplussed. He grimaces but shows none of the terror the drivers of the ship revealed. "You forget, princeling. I've been dealing with the fae my whole life." In one swift move, he reaches for the waistband of his trousers to withdraw his revolver.

Fear floods me, but I know the gun is wet. Surely it won't work...

Mr. Duveau swipes out, and that's when I realize he hadn't pulled out his gun at all, but a blade. Franco doubles over and staggers back, grasping the left side of his torso. Blood flows through his fingers, and I can only hope the cut sliced over his ribs and not into his heart.

My preoccupation with Franco is all Duveau needs, and he lunges for me yet again. He tackles me to the ground and crawls on top of me, straddling my hips. I expect to feel the edge of his blade strike me next, or for his fingers to wrap around my throat. But all his efforts are thrown into grasping my right hand. He twists my wrist, making me cry out. Then his weight releases me, and I scramble to my feet.

Duveau retreats, flashing me a wild gaze before turning his attention to what he holds in his hand. My Chariot. With a grin, he opens the lid, the bright golden light wrapping around him in an instant. I dive forward, but in the blink of an eye, he's gone.

I stand staring at the empty air for a few moments, until more pressing concerns steal my focus. I whirl toward Franco and Breeda. The prince's face is pale as he grasps his wound, but he shakes his head.

"I'll be fine," he says. "It isn't deep and there's no iron embedded in me. I'll heal once we return to the other side of the wall."

I then study Breeda, who seems dazed but unharmed.

My next thought is Amelie, and I take off running. Franco tries to call me back, but I let his voice die out behind me, focusing on the fighting at the other side of the beach, seeking a glimpse of copper hair amidst the spray of sand and gunfire. The scene has become clouded by a smoky haze, making it impossible to see much of anything. Then a blue-scaled sea fae clears the haze, darting toward the ocean. Just before he reaches it, an explosion strikes right where he was about to step.

I stop in my tracks as what was once a sea fae is now a radius of flying debris. Bile rises in my throat as pieces of gore land just feet in front of me. I look wildly about, but there's no sign of my sister. "Amelie!" I call her name again and again, but my voice is drowned out by another explosive blast.

Then I see her.

Near the base of the cliff, she clears the wall of smoke and sand. Cobalt limps after her, no longer a blue nix. In his seelie form, his wounds look far worse, skin a sickly green, his shirt a darker shade of red than Mr. Duveau's was. What little is left of his collar is grasped in Amelie's fingers. She squeezes the cloth so hard, her knuckles are white. Once they're far enough away from the barricade, she releases him, pushing him to the ground. He falls to his knees as he struggles to right himself, hands clasped as if in prayer.

I run toward them, but neither seem to notice my approach.

Amelie looks down her nose at Cobalt, a cruel smile twisting her lips. Then she extends her hand, pointing her dagger at her mate. He hangs his head, but she shouts something at him. With trembling fingers, he accepts the weapon. Not bothering to lift his gaze, he raises his forearm, one already torn to shreds. Pressing the tip of the blade to a patch of ragged skin, he makes a cut.

Words she spoke just days ago ring through my head. *I don't care if I have to force him to peel every inch of skin from his own body. I will do whatever it takes to watch the life fade from his eyes.*

She's doing it. Despite the violence and danger around her, she's pursuing vengeance like it's the only thing that matters.

It makes my stomach turn with dread.

Then something else makes my gut drop even deeper. A cylindrical object flies from the haze and lands at Amelie's feet.

Cobalt's gruesome ministrations go still, his attention fixated on the grenade. Amelie's eyes find it next, going wide, draining all the deadly malice from her expression. She retreats a step away from it just as Cobalt lunges forward. Grasping it to his chest, he darts toward the haze.

It explodes.

Again, I stop in my tracks, the sound of the explosion ringing through my ears. This one, however, isn't the same that ended the life of the sea fae. For Cobalt's body isn't obliterated at once. Even so, he lays unmoving, face buried in the sand. I pump my legs to close the distance between me and Amelie, reaching her just as she grasps Cobalt and rolls him onto his back.

I come up behind my sister, recoiling at the sight of the male below her. The damage caused by the explosive may not have been immediate like the other grenade was, but this blast is just as lethal. Cobalt gasps for breath, chest gaping open, his skin coated black. Tiny shards of what I can only imagine is iron pierce everything from his face to his arms, as well as every open lesion.

I'm reminded of the grenades Ustrin had threatened to use against his fire fae when he confronted us in the cave. These must be the same. Cruel, human weapons technology crafted for the fae.

And Cobalt took the entire brunt of it himself to save Amelie.

Amelie's sobs come out short and heavy, her hands shaking as she attempts to touch him but can find no place uninjured. I want to reach out to comfort her, to pull her away, but I can't bring myself to move, nor can I bring myself to look away.

He's dying. Even without the iron puncturing his insides, I doubt even a fae could heal from this type of wound. Especially not on this side of the wall. While the thought of him dead should come as a relief, the sight before me only makes me feel empty.

Amelie's shoulders slump. "I was supposed to kill you," she whispers.

His face turns toward her, but I can't tell if even his good eye remains intact. "And I was supposed to love you," comes his raspy voice. "I was supposed to bring peace to the isle with a radical seelie reign. I failed at everything. Everything."

Amelie hangs her head. "Your blood was mine to spill. How dare you take that from me!"

He attempts to lift a hand but doesn't make it far. "Instead, you have my heart. Always."

Amelie convulses with the weight of her sobs. "I don't want it, Cobalt. Do you hear me? I don't want it."

"And yet..." He takes a few strangled breaths. "It's yours."

His body goes still.

Amelie throws her head back and wails, and a light begins to shimmer over her skin. Then it turns to a deep red flame that dances over every inch of her, rising higher and higher. Her skin begins to blister beneath the heat.

Driven by urgency, I allow myself to place a hand on her shoulder. I ignore the sharp bite of flames that are not my own, and when she whirls to face me, a snarl pulls her lips. Then recognition crosses her face, and she reaches for me. Her flames settle to a gentle roar as I wrap my arms around her, igniting my own flames alongside hers as I fall to my knees at her side. With my fire protecting me from hers, I brush the tangled, blood-soaked hair from her brow and let her rest her head in the crook of my neck.

33

I know we should get up. I know we should run. We've already seen one grenade reach this far. We're defenseless, should the army throw another. But I also know what Amelie is feeling, this debilitating pain that drags her down. Whether it's from the loss of Cobalt or her vengeance, I can't say. All I can do is hold her, be here for her.

And yet, we need to move. Retreat. Find Aspen and the others.

"Amelie," I say, my words coming out quiet, strangled. "We should get to safety."

She only wails harder, grips me tighter.

"I'm here, Ami," I whisper into her hair, although it dawns on me she might not be able to hear me. Our proximity to the blast has left my ears ringing, my own voice muted. But as my flames dance over my skin, fueling my healing, my ears begin to clear.

Yet it's still quieter than it was before.

Too quiet.

Gunfire still rings out in the distance, but the beach is almost silent. No... there *is* a sound. One that sets my heart racing, my flames retreating.

Marching footsteps approach, and I whirl around to face the human soldiers who close in on us, rifles raised. Amelie must realize the threat too, for she stills, clinging to me as she turns in my arms, her fire extinguished.

Six men spread out in a semi-circle around us. My eyes flash from them to the barricade, which now seems empty. Are these the only survivors? Two look vaguely familiar, dripping seawater. They must be guards from the boat I set aflame, those who were able to swim to shore like Duveau. I hazard a glance at the other side of the beach, seeking Franco and Breeda, but I see no sign of them.

"Stand up," orders a soldier, one of the guards from the boat.

Shakily, I rise to my feet, pulling Amelie up with me. Keeping my breathing steady, I reconnect to my flame, readying it. Until the end, I will fight.

The man who spoke steps closer. "Hands where I can see them."

As we raise our hands, I assess the distance between us and the soldiers, process scenario after scenario of possibilities to take them down. There are only six of them. Two of us. And we both wield fire.

"What are we doing with them, Averson?" asks another soldier, expression wary.

The man before us, Averson, narrows his eyes to study us. "Mr. Duveau wanted these two brought to the king."

"But they're creatures," says another. "They have no place in Bretton."

Averson's lips curl into a cold smile. "I agree. Besides, we don't take orders from Duveau."

"Then we—"

"Yes." Averson nods. "Execution."

I flinch as he raises the barrel of the rifle to my forehead, but my fire burns hot inside me. Locking eyes with him, I seek to draw in the imagery of the bird in the cage. At such a close distance, I could glamour him. But no matter how long his eyes remain on mine, the imagery doesn't come.

The soldiers must be wearing rowan.

"Turn around," Averson orders.

Keeping my voice steady, I say, "I'd rather look at you while you shoot me." But I'm not looking at him. Not anymore. My attention is now fixated on his gun, the metal that formed it, shaped it from elements of the earth. Elements I can control.

"Fine," Averson says, then nods to the soldier on his right. Another man steps forward and levels his gun between Amelie's eyes.

My inner fire falters. Damn. I can't focus on two guns at once. "Kill me first," I say, voice trembling. If I can keep his attention, keep his gun from firing just a few seconds longer...

"Very well." Too soon, Averson reaches for the trigger.

But it isn't a trigger he finds.

Averson bites back a yelp as the metal that was once a trigger melts onto his finger, burning red-orange. He pulls his finger away, but the barrel too begins to glow. Then it...bends. With a shout, he drops the rifle and takes a step back. The soldier with the gun on Amelie trembles, his own weapon glowing hot in his hands. Just like the first gun, the barrel melts and bends toward the sky. The man drops it just as it fires overhead.

The other soldiers watch their guns with terror in their eyes, retreating several steps. Theirs too begin to glow, and the two soldiers the farthest back are lost in a fiery blast, their guns exploding in their hands.

I'm stunned as I watch all this unfold.

This isn't me. I'm not the one doing this.

I glance at Amelie, but she seems just as dumbfounded as I am.

Then the four remaining soldiers all seem to see the same thing. Their eyes grow wide, mouths agape as they retreat farther. Farther.

Grasping Amelie's hand in mine, we whirl around.

There, coming down the steps from the cliff is the most terrifying yet beautiful sight I've ever seen.

My mate.

His arms are outstretched, his feet barely touching the stone steps as he glides down, drawing nearer. His blue-black hair swirls wildly around his face, pupils so dilated, his eyes look black. His golden skin is paler than I've ever seen, every vein visible beneath his flesh, lips peeled back from his teeth. He flicks his fingers this way then that. Behind me, I hear another gun explode, then another. Then the sound of waves rising to a roar. A gurgling scream. Despite my curiosity about what's happening to the soldiers, I can't take my eyes off Aspen.

Aspen in all his terrifying, haunting glory.

This is the creature I was raised to fear.

And I've never loved him more.

At the base of the cliff, his feet meet sand. I watch in awe as he stalks across the beach, past the bodies of the dead soldiers, to the edge of the shore. There he pauses, water lapping up his legs as if in praise of him. Not too far out I see two figures, frantically swimming out to sea, making a desperate bid to reach the warship which appears to be retreating as well.

Hands raised toward the water, palms facing the sea, he thrusts outward. In answer, the water recedes, gathering in a wave. It swallows the two swimming men, drowning them in its depths as the wave grows higher. Higher.

All reason tells me this wave can only crash back into us, but instead, the water shifts, rising, twisting, lurching in an impossible direction. Away from the shore. Toward the warship.

An eruption of sound startles me, and Amelie squeezes my forearm. What follows is a deafening crash into the face of the cliff, rocking my feet beneath me. Ducking from flying debris, Amelie and I scramble to the far end of the shore, to the abandoned barricade built from large bags of sand. We kneel behind it as another blast strikes the cliff.

My heart hammers in my chest, and I hazard a glance over the top of the barricade, seeking Aspen. Once the rubble clears, I find him, still at the edge of the shore. His wave continues to build, rushing toward the warship.

Another blast.

Biting back a scream, I duck, covering my head with my hands. Amelie's arms wrap around me. But as soon as the trembling begins to fade, I leap back up again, eyes darting immediately to Aspen.

Still unharmed, his arms tremble as if pushing an incredible weight.

He opens his mouth in a scream that doesn't reach my ears over the raging wave. Gathering speed, his wave finally reaches the warship, dousing it in a roaring crash. The ship goes under, disappearing beneath the sea. To my horror, it reappears seconds later, rocking erratically. It has ceased firing its enormous guns, but the ship remains whole.

Aspen staggers his legs and thrusts again, gathering another wave. The ocean grows wilder, darker. His arms, however, begin to tremble more, his shoulders starting to sag.

That's when I notice the blood dripping down his torn calves, the puncture marks in his side, his arms.

He looked so strong when I first saw him coming down the side of the cliff; I hadn't seen how wounded he'd been.

Without a second thought, I leave the safety of the barricade and run to his side.

"Evie, stay back," he shouts through his teeth. The veins in his face and neck are more visible than they were before, and even worse than that— black tendrils spiral up the skin on his arms, and dark threads mingle with the blood that seeps from a few of the lesions. He has iron embedded in him.

A painful lump sears my throat. "I'm not leaving you."

"Go!" he roars, sending his newest wave crashing over the warship. Again, the ship goes under, only to reappear.

I don't know why he's so adamant about destroying the ship, especially when it clearly taxes his strength. I want to argue him away, force him to abandon his mission so I can tend to his wounds.

But something stills my heart, fills me with a profound calm.

I do know why he's doing this. Safety. Protection. Love. Vengeance.

We can't let them get away.

Planting my feet firmly beneath me, I stand at his side and raise my arms. I open myself to love and grief, connecting to the element of water. With rage and fury, I connect to fire. My duty as queen to protect my people links me to earth. And my mind, piecing all of this together with precise thought, connects me to air.

Like Aspen, I thrust out my arms, giving strength to his wave, shaping it into something more. The water builds higher than ever before, then separates, reaching for the warship like two monstrous hands. Fire heats the metal hull of the ship, a crack forming at its center. Then, in tandem, Aspen and I curl our fingers into fists. The two waves mimic our motions, wrapping around opposite ends of the ship. With a final thrust downward, the waves snap the warship in two.

Lowering my hands, I watch as smoke barrels into the sky. Smaller waves continue to pummel the broken ship, forcing the two halves to drift apart. One begins to sink. Then the other.

Terror surges through me as I watch the shattered warship sink and become swallowed by the hungry waves. I shudder, shoulders trembling at the sight.

Aspen's fingers brush against mine, and my racing pulse begins to calm. Together we watch the sea, watch the roiling waves toss and rage, all signs of the warship gone.

I take his hand fully in mine and lift my chin. We may have done an ugly thing, but it needed to be done. There may be dozens more, but this enemy warship won't be coming back to take out the fae. My people. My home.

It's one thing. One small, infinitesimal feat in a much larger war.

But we did it.

And we did it together.

34

———————

We continue to watch the sea as the waves subside, satisfied in the wake of its meal, until footsteps sound behind us. I turn to find Amelie approaching. Behind her, Breeda flutters down from the cliffside.

Aspen shifts to face them as well, but his legs give out beneath him. Gasping, he falls to his knees, face contorted as he clenches his chest.

"Aspen!" I shout, lowering to his side.

"The iron," he bites out, teeth bared.

My throat goes dry as my gaze falls on the black tendrils spiraling up his neck, his arms. If he wasn't already weakened by the iron embedded in his wounds, he certainly is now. Any feat of magic is nearly impossible on this side of the wall. For him to do what he did...

To do what *we* did.

"What's wrong?" Amelie asks, eyes wide.

"He's taken several iron injuries." My hands fly frantically over him, assessing what little I can through the grime and blood.

"You can help him," she says, a flicker of hope weaving in between her furrowed brows.

"I need tools. I need..." My breath hitches as I recall the medical tent I spotted in the camp outside the lighthouse. I rise to my feet to intercept Breeda as she draws near. "Where are the others?" I ask her. I can no longer hear fighting anywhere, not just on the beach.

Her color is muted, her characteristic joy absent from her face. "Prince Franco and I went to warn the others that we lost the Chariot," she says, her voice so much slower and weaker than usual.

The blood leaves my face. "Was anyone hurt?"

"There was hardly anyone who wasn't hurt," she says. "So much blood. So much...death."

"Where are the others?" I ask again.

"Pursuing the retreating army. Franco joined the fight, and I came to you."

"What about the camp?"

She shrugs. "It's empty. Unless you count dead bodies." Her color goes a shade paler. "I don't suggest you count the bodies."

I spin toward Amelie. "Help me. Please."

She nods, then lowers to the other side of my mate. Aspen lets out a pained groan as we help him to his feet. We make our way across the beach and to the stone stairs. It's slow going as Amelie and I help Aspen climb, but we eventually make it to the top, sweat soaked and gasping for breath.

We assist Aspen, guiding him toward the wall of the fortification where he can lean his weight. Once he's settled, I race to the medical tent with hardly a glance at the blood and carnage Breeda had mentioned. I pull open the tent flap with force.

I startle as I enter, finding a human woman doing the same. She whirls to face me, her hand flying to her mouth. My eyes move from the cases of supplies she's gathering, then to the symbol of the winged staff on her tan uniform. She's a nurse. And not just any nurse. Considering how quickly Dahlia's injury was treated after I stabbed her, the nurses in this camp are trained to treat the fae. Sliding my gaze to her left wrist, I find a strand of red beads. I lurch forward and grab her forearm tightly in my fingers, nails digging into her flesh. With the other hand, I rip the strand of rowan beads from her wrist and toss them to the floor. She cries out with alarm, cowering away from me, but I grab her by the shoulders and shake her into silence. Bringing my face close to hers, I lock her gaze with mine. The imagery of the bird in the cage comes at once. Her face goes slack, pupils dilating.

Just like that, I have her under my control.

"You will tend to my mate at once."

IT ISN'T UNTIL HIS SURGERY IS OVER THAT I FEEL I CAN FINALLY BREATHE AGAIN. After tedious hours spent helping the human nurse remove every bit of iron embedded in his skin, all we can do is wait for the others to return. Luckily, laudanum proved effective on him, easing his pain and allowing him to slip into unconsciousness. I now watch him sleep, taking in the rise and fall of his breaths. The tendrils of black have ceased their spread, although I doubt they will begin to recede until we return to the Faerwyvae side of the wall.

But he *will* heal.

I place my hands over his chest, willing my inner fire to strengthen his, to speed his healing.

The nurse stands at his head and checks his pulse. "He's stable," she says. Still under my glamour, her moves are precise, her tone even.

I lock my eyes with hers. "You will continue to tend to him until I release you."

Her face slackens further than it already is. "I will."

I return my attention to Aspen. I don't know how long my glamour over the nurse will last. I've always known a mental glamour isn't nearly as strong as using one's true name. But in case my friends return wounded, I'll need all the assistance caring for them that I can get.

Sudden commotion comes from somewhere outside the medical tent— several sets of footsteps and what sounds like sobbing. Fear prickles the back of my neck as my thoughts immediately go to Amelie.

"Stay here," I order the nurse. Then, with a final glance at my dozing mate, I dart from the tent.

My eyes find Amelie at once, rushing from the door of the lighthouse tower, followed by Breeda. The two had gone to the top to keep watch for the return of our friends. But the commotion comes from the far end of the camp. Amelie joins my side as we eye the spaces between the tents. Flames erupt from my fingertips, shaping into an orb, but my sister stills me with a touch. "It's them," she says. "Estel and the Lunar Queen. I saw them from the lighthouse."

Relief washes over me, and a second later, I see Nyxia leading the party. Shadows writhe around her, but she remains in seelie form. Her black trousers and tunic are torn, and nearly every inch of her skin is coated in blood. But that's not the most shocking sight. Wailing and sobbing at the Lunar Queen's side is Dahlia, stumbling while Nyxia drags her forward. The normally composed Summer Queen is covered in dirt, blood, and grime, one of her yellow butterfly wings bent at an unnatural angle. "Phoebe," Dahlia cries out, shoulders heaving.

"Phoebe is dead," Nyxia says through her teeth.

Estel follows closely behind Nyxia, her shimmering particles a dull glow, although she seems otherwise unharmed. Franco limps next to her, but the fact that he's alive tells me the wound Mr. Duveau gave him wasn't too bad after all. The only other figure is a single fae soldier—one of Nyxia's wraiths. His robes flutter on an invisible wind, but I can't help noticing the trail of blood he leaves behind. Is it his? Or that of his enemies?

"There are less than we came with," Breeda says, fluttering by my ear. "I am most certain we traveled with four guards."

My heart sinks at that. When they finally stop before us, Nyxia shoves Queen Dahlia, who falls to her knees, her sobs never ceasing. "You know what to say," Nyxia says, her tone thick with venom.

Dahlia flashes a miserable look at me before sitting back on her heels, mumbling something unintelligible?

"What's that?" Nyxia prods. "It doesn't count if she can't hear you."

Dahlia takes several shaking breaths. This time, her words are clear. "I accept and acknowledge your rule. You are the rightful Queen of Fire."

Nyxia's lips peel back in a triumphant grin. "The Renounced are defeated. Phoebe is dead and Dahlia has surrendered on behalf of the rest."

My mouth falls open, but I'm not sure what to say. In light of the devastation of battle, I hadn't given a moment's thought to how we fared against the Renounced. With Cobalt's death and Dahlia's surrender, there's no other fae to stand against us. Unless the pretender kings and queens count, which I'm certain they don't. We've won. "And the human army?"

"Retreated," Estel says. "We pursued as many as we could, but we couldn't stray too far south. We're already far enough from the wall as it is."

"Wait, where's Aspen?" Nyxia asks, looking around the camp.

"He's stable. He went under surgery to remove the iron bullets embedded inside him, but we need to get him back to Faerwyvae. Do you still have a Chariot?"

Estel nods. "We'll depart at once."

"What are we doing with her?" Nyxia tilts her head toward Dahlia. Then her gaze falls on my sister, and she wrinkles her nose. "And her?"

I exchange a glance with Amelie and reach for her hand. She places her fingers in mine, and I give them a squeeze. "Amelie has proven herself trustworthy, and her loyalties will no longer be questioned."

My sister lets out a heavy sigh.

Releasing Amelie's fingers, I put my hands on my hips and watch Dahlia through narrowed eyes. "But I too want to know what we plan on doing with this one."

"We could present her to the rest of the Alpha Alliance," Estel says. "We can let her acknowledge the rest of us the same way she did with Evelyn just now. Then she can send out an official declaration urging her allies to acknowledge our rule and a return to the Old Ways."

"Or we can execute her here and now," Nyxia says. Her eyes find mine. "What do you think?"

I clench my jaw, recalling all that she's responsible for.

Dahlia's eyes are wide with terror as she looks up at me, hands pressed together in supplication. "Please," she says. "I've already lost everything."

I take a slow step toward her. "You tried to trade me and my sister to Mr. Duveau in exchange for a human army. You were going to let our enemies onto fae soil."

"It was my last chance to defeat you," she says, tears streaming over her cheeks. "My final opportunity to secure peace with the humans. We would have drafted a new treaty—"

"No, you wouldn't have." I let out a bitter laugh. "Do you still not get it? Mr. Duveau was using you. He needed me and my sister to save face with King Grigory, but the alliance you made with him was a farce. You were a pawn to get human armies into Faerwyvae without conflict. After they destroyed us, they would have destroyed you too."

She pales, shaking her head. "No. No, we made a bargain."

"Not a watertight one, obviously," Franco mutters under his breath.

"He's right," I say. "You made a joke of a bargain. When I met with you to arrange a ceasefire, I meant what I said. We had proof that the humans sought to obliterate the fae."

"You mentioned the warships," she argues. "I already knew they were coming. They were sent for my aid."

"You honestly believed that? They were invading whether you let them in or not."

She opens her mouth, but she can't seem to find the words. Instead, she purses her lips, regaining some of her haughty air. "How do you know? What is this proof you claimed to have that revealed the humans wanted to destroy all fae and not just the rebels?"

I crouch down, balancing on the balls of my feet. It takes everything in me to control the rage that comes from being this close to her. "Have you heard of the Parvanovae?"

She leans back, hand flying to her chest. Her voice comes out barely above a whisper. "It's a myth."

I study her expression, the way her eyes widen in fear. Up until now, I wasn't entirely convinced she hadn't known about it from the start. There was still a chance she'd been after it when she sent her pretender king to occupy my palace. After learning about her alliance with Mr. Duveau, the possibility remained that they were working together to find it. But the look on her face tells me, despite her claim that the star bomb is a myth, she's terrified of it.

No, she wouldn't have worked to bring the bomb to the humans. She may be a fool for believing Mr. Duveau's promise of an alliance, but she's not stupid enough to put the most dangerous weapon known to man and fae alike in human hands.

Reading the truth on my face, she shakes her head. "It can't be. It was supposed to be destroyed."

"It wasn't. But you will be if you make one more move against me and my allies. Say even one thing against us, and I will tear the wings from your body shred by shred. Then I'll burn you alive."

She swallows hard and gives me a short nod.

I rise to my feet and address the others. "I agree with Estel. She can come back with us alive, so long as she works with us and acknowledges our rule. I doubt the broken bargain will stop the warships from coming, but at least we can face the armies as a united front."

"Does even a united front stand a chance against a dozen warships?" Franco asks. "I'm not sure we would have survived a single army, if they hadn't retreated."

"I don't know," I say, "but we must try. Besides, Aspen and I were able to destroy the ship in the cove before it could get away."

Nyxia assesses me from head to toe, eyes alight with appreciation. "Nice work."

"Thanks. Now, we need to get back to Faerwyvae so everyone can heal and we can make a plan. Aspen is still unconscious. Can he travel by Chariot in such a state?"

"No," Estel says. "He must be awake."

I turn around and start back toward the medical tent. "I'll see if I can wake him, but he has laudanum in his system—"

"Wait." Estel's voice freezes me, and I whirl to face her. The particles shift rapidly over her face, her expression lost beneath the movement.

"What is it?" I ask.

The particles go still, revealing a look of deep concern. "Franco said you lost your Chariot."

I nod. "Mr. Duveau stole it from me."

"Where did he go?"

Dread fills my stomach, but I don't know why. "To safety, I assume. Once I destroyed the transport boat, he knew he couldn't get me to the warship. It was over for him."

"But you aren't certain where he went?"

"Of course not." My heart hammers in my chest as the particles begin to shift and swirl over her face again. "What are you getting at, Estel?"

With a quick stride, she closes the distance between us and thrusts out her palm, revealing a silver disc. "Take this and return to Irridae at once," she says, voice trembling as she presses the Chariot into my hand.

I accept it, although I don't understand the urgency. My eyes seek hers, then the others, who all look equally as perplexed as I feel. "Me? Alone? You already used this once to get here, haven't you? That means it only has one more use left tonight. Shouldn't we use this to return together?"

"Go to Irridae right now. Let the Chariot charge by starlight and return to us at dawn."

"But why?"

Estel releases a shuddering breath and lowers her voice. "Go to Irridae. Travel straight to the weapons room."

"The weapons room," I echo. Then the horrible truth dawns on me. My legs tremble as I grasp the source of her fear. "You think Mr. Duveau used the Chariot to take the Parvanovae."

She nods. "Your Chariot was not used to arrive here, which means it has two uses. Mr. Duveau has been to Irridae. He's very likely been inside the weapons room itself. Now that Fehr has opened the palace, the councilman won't need to attempt an invasion from the courtyard. If he wanted, he could travel straight to the bomb. In the next second, he could be safely back home."

My stomach churns. When I stalled him on the boat with my questions, I all but confirmed I had the Parvanovae at my palace. That's why he didn't kill me when he had the chance. That's why he grabbed the Chariot instead. "No, no, no."

"Go," Estel says, voice firm as she ushers me forward "None of us can come with, not as weak as we are right now. Your molten river would debilitate us."

"I'll go," Amelie says, coming up beside me and lacing her fingers through mine.

I nod. With the Chariot in my free hand, I flip open the cover with my thumb. Recalling everything I know about using the Chariot, I focus on the golden light as it grows around me, the energy that pulses and hums through my bones.

Estel steps out of the radius's light, just as it blocks my view of everything around me. Closing my eyes, I picture the weapons room at Irridae Palace, fueling my need to go there with every ounce of my will. I repeat the name of my destination to myself over and over. When I open my eyes, the light grows brighter, brighter. In a blink, the light goes out, plunging us into darkness.

I squeeze Amelie's hand to confirm she's still with me.

"I'm here," she whispers, returning the squeeze.

As my eyes adjust to our new surroundings, the glow of my molten river illuminates the weapons room. I stand at the center of the room with a few boxes of explosives to my left. Those were the only weapons, aside from the selection of daggers I claimed, that I hadn't melted. I turn in a slow circle, seeking any sign of a small wooden crate.

But there's nothing else there.

The Parvanovae is gone.

35

———————

I don't sleep a wink that night, opting instead to stare blindly out my bedroom window, waiting for the first light of dawn to creep over the horizon. Amelie sleeps in my bed while Lorelei dozes on my couch, her soft snores falling upon my ears.

After discovering the star bomb gone, I barely had the energy to carve a path through my molten river for Amelie and me to get through. Once we made it to the atrium, I collapsed, both from exhaustion and grief. That's where Lorelei found Amelie and me, covered in blood and sand and looking near-death. She's refused to leave us since.

She wasn't the only one worried. After Lorelei coaxed us into the bedroom to get cleaned up, Foxglove and Fehr peeked in on us, asking the same questions Lorelei had.

What happened?

Is everyone all right?

Are you all right?

They each got the same answer. *It's over. It's gone.*

Whether Amelie explained more, I hadn't had the energy to notice or care. All I could think about was Aspen. The bomb. Aspen. The bomb.

It's still all I can think about now as I wait for dawn to arrive.

No sooner than I catch the first blush of sunlight creeping behind the distant mountains, I'm on my feet. I cast a glance at Lorelei and Amelie. I don't bother waking either of them before I retrieve the Chariot from my planter box and flip open the lid. I fill my mind with thoughts of the light-house. Varney Cove.

The light of the Chariot wraps around me, energy buzzing, humming, and growing. Seconds later I'm at the army camp. A gentle breeze carrying the tang of salt washes over me, bringing memories of fighting. Blood. A broken warship.

The camp is quiet, and seemingly empty, aside from the raven who flies overhead. Franco must be on guard duty. He caws down at me, but I can't bring myself to offer so much as a halfhearted wave.

Lowering my head, I start toward the medical tent. As I draw near, move-ment rustles the tent flap, stealing my attention. A pale hand emerges first, then a heavily bandaged forearm. Finally, Aspen slowly limps out of the tent. His eyes find me at once. At the sight of my mate, my heart awakens for the first time since I found the bomb missing. There's still a heaviness upon it, but my love for him releases me from the overbearing numbness I've felt all night.

With a strangled sob, I rush to him, closing the distance between us. His arms wrap around me, and I press myself to his chest, careful not to squeeze him too tight. He brushes a hand down my hair, saying nothing as I cry onto his bandaged chest.

When I think I can manage to find my voice amidst my sobs, I pull away and meet his eyes. There's sorrow in them, something that tells me Estel has already warned him of her fears. "It's gone," I croak out.

He nods, shoulders drooped in resignation.

"It's gone," I repeat.

He lifts a hand to brush my cheek, lips pulling into a feeble smile. "Let's go home."

THE FOLLOWING DAYS PROCEED WITH TENSE SOBRIETY. AFTER RETURNING TO Irridae with the rest of the party from the lighthouse, the other royals leave for their own courts. Luckily, as soon as we settle in at home, Aspen's wounds immediately begin to heal at a much more rapid pace, the tendrils of black receding from his skin more and more each day.

It's the only thing that brings me comfort in all this. However, not even that can take away from the sense of doom that falls over me with every day that goes by, knowing any moment could bring the detonation of the Parvanovae. The end of everything I love.

On the sixth night since Mr. Duveau stole the bomb, Aspen convinces me to join him in the bath. I don't know if he thinks I need to relax or if he's noticed how badly I've been neglecting my bathing habits. Whatever the case, I follow him to our bathing chambers and into the enormous sunstone tub. The aromas that invade my senses bring me a comforting feeling of nostalgia—rosemary, marigold, cinnamon, and cloves. It smells like fall. Like Aspen. Like the baths he used to draw for me at Bircharbor Palace.

I bite back tears of gratitude as I recline at one end of the tub, the warm water reaching my shoulders. Aspen climbs in after me, watching me carefully as he lowers down at the opposite end.

I hate the way he eyes me like I'm made of glass. Somehow, he's managed to handle the news of our impending doom with far more grace than I have.

"Do you like it?" he asks.

"I do." I force a weak smile, although I can't meet his eyes. Instead, I watch as sprigs of rosemary float over the surface of the water. Then a thought tugs my heart. "We should have a bath like this drawn for Amelie. She loved the ones at Bircharbor."

"Already done," he says.

This surprises me enough to bring my eyes to his. "Really?"

"Lorelei's taking care of it."

I blink a few times, taking in the sincerity on his face. "Thank you."

Ever since our return, Aspen and I have had the royal bedroom all to ourselves, and Amelie has taken residence in the guest room next door. I must admit, part of me feels she's still too far away.

For the first time, it isn't distrust that makes me feel that way. After everything we've been through together, I feel closer to Amelie like never before. My heart is linked to hers. Not only that, but I worry about her. She's been almost as withdrawn as I've been this past week. How will she recover from everything she's done? From the loss of her vengeance? The loss of a mate she once loved and hated to equal degrees?

Then again, how much time will she even have to recover? How much time do any of us have?

Aspen's touch brings me back to the present as he leans forward and runs a hand over one of my arms. "Are you all right?" he asks.

I meet his eyes again. "I should be asking you," I say. "You're the one still healing from iron injuries."

He looks down to examine his naked torso. Puckered skin remains over his chest, abdomen, shoulders, forearm—plus many other places hidden by the water—where incisions were made to remove the bullets. But nearly every tendril of black has disappeared. "Almost good as new," he says.

"Any updates from Lunar?" I swallow hard, not sure I want to know the answer. I saw one of Nyxia's owls arrive at the palace hours ago. Could she have discovered when and where the bomb will be detonated?

He steels his expression, which shows he's equally as unsure about whether he wants to tell me.

"It's all right," I say. "I've already resigned myself to our fate."

He sighs. "It isn't over, Evie."

I lean back further, letting the water come up to my chin. "Mr. Duveau has a weapon that could end all life on the isle. If it isn't over one way, it will be over in another. Now tell me what Nyxia said in her message."

"Her owls reported seeing the warships turning course back toward the mainland."

It doesn't come as a surprise, nor is it particularly encouraging. "That makes sense, considering the entire isle is about to be obliterated. King Grigory might as well get his expensive warships safely out of harm's way."

Aspen leans forward again and reaches a hand to my cheek. "Evie," he says with some force. "It's *not* over."

Tears well in my eyes as I take in all the hope he holds in his. "He has the bomb," I say, voice strained. "What better gift to give the king he so disappointed?"

"They might not even use it here," he argues.

"They will."

"They might not."

"They. Will." A lump rises in my throat, but I make no effort to swallow it down. I'm done ignoring the truth. "And it's all my fault."

Aspen pulls me closer, cradling me against his warm, sodden chest. "It's not your fault, Evie."

"I'm killing everyone on this isle."

"Enough," he says, tone firm yet gentle. "I don't want to hear another word of that."

I lift my head to meet his eyes again. "But it's true."

He shakes his head. "We don't know that. Until I see a blinding blast coming to end my soul, I will assume my lengthy lifespan will continue on as ever before."

The way he speaks so casually, so free, lifts some of the burden from my heart. "This is a strange time to be stubborn," I say through my tears.

"I could say the same to you."

I lower my head back to his chest, sinking deeper into the warm water. "If I knew what was coming—*when* it was coming—I would fight. It's the not knowing that is killing me. Draining my will."

"Don't let it do that to you, my love," Aspen whispers against my hair. "Don't let an unknown evil take you away from me before it's even time."

"I'm still here," I say with a sigh.

"No. You're already slipping away from me. It crushes my heart to see you like this. To see the fire extinguished from you."

I shrug a shoulder. "What else would you have me do?"

He reaches a finger for my chin, tilts it back until I'm looking at him again. "Live. If these truly are our last days, why aren't we living them to the fullest?"

"Because it isn't realistic."

"Evie, I don't give a centaur's bare ass what's realistic right now."

A corner of my lips quirks up against my will. "Is that so?"

He nods. "Meeting you has made me enjoy my life for the first time. You've made me feel like I *deserve* to enjoy it. With you. I'm not going to give that up just to sulk in the doom and gloom of reality."

"I think Nyxia would say that's all very sunny and idealistic of you."

He grins. "And yet it doesn't lack execution."

My lips mirror his. "So, what do you propose?"

"Let's pretend it never comes."

"Pretend? I never thought you'd be one to play pretend."

"Then you must know very little about your own kind. The fae excel at playing pretend. Isn't that all a glamour is?"

His oddly light mood has mine lifting as well, even though I know it won't last. I suppose the least I can do is humor him. "What are we pretending, then?"

He sits up straighter, and I return to my place across from him in the tub. "Let's pretend this is a year from now," Aspen says.

"A year from now?"

"Yes. All that nonsense with the bomb—an entire year has passed since then. Agreed?"

I shrug. "Fine. I'll play. Where are we a year from now?"

"Well, first of all, remember when that idiot Mr. Duveau took the Parvanovae to the mainland and accidentally blew it up in the king's face? Remember how the blast destroyed Bretton, but we had our wall up in time to protect against it? Then Estel found some crazy solution that protected the isle better than our original plans? Remember that?"

My heart sinks. "If that were true, everyone on the mainland would be dead. That's only slightly less depressing."

"All right, let's not talk about the bomb at all," he says. "That was almost a year ago, besides. Let's talk about now."

"And what are we doing *now*?" I roll my eyes on the last word, my tone full of mockery.

"Right now, we are living in our new palace."

"Oh, we have a new palace?"

"We do," Aspen says. "We built it on the border between Fire and Autumn. There the weather is warm, but only perfectly so. The red leaves of Autumn mingle with the warm breeze of fire. And we have a lake for swimming. An ample bathtub even larger than this one. Oh, and an enormous table that rivals Nyxia's."

I bark a laugh. "What do we use this immense table for?"

"Certainly not meetings," Aspen says. "Only sex. Same goes for every viable surface in our palace. Our household staff knows exactly when to make themselves scarce and which rooms they should vacate at once."

"How do they know?"

His eyes unfocus as he thinks for a moment, a devious smirk tugging his lips. "We have a bell."

"A sex bell?"

"Yes. It warns all those within our vicinity that no surface is safe from us and all eyes must be averted at once."

"I'm guessing we pay our staff very well."

"They have a handsome salary indeed," he agrees.

"All right, so we spend our days fornicating all over the furniture. What else do we do?"

He waves a dismissive hand. "Tedious royal business of course. Signing papers. Holding court. Making appointments and ironing out conflicts. But no matter how taxing the day was—"

"From all the sex, of course."

"—I end my night laying at your side, thanking the gods that you came to the wall all those months ago and stole my heart."

My chest fills with warmth, tears glazing my eyes. I inch closer to him, and his hand finds my calf. He runs it idly over my skin, eyes drinking me in. When I speak, my voice comes out quiet. "What do we do after?"

His eyes sparkle with mischief as he reaches forward, grasping me beneath my hips and hoisting me into his lap. Water splashes over the side of the tub at the movement. "I think you know what we do after," he says, a teasing growl in his voice.

I lean closer to him, bracing my hands on the rim of the tub as I rock my hips over his. Once. Twice. I feel him stiffen against me. "Is tonight any different, then?"

He brings his lips to mine in a soft brush of a kiss. "Tonight is only a little different, for I must be gentle with you."

I quirk my brow. "Why is that?"

He gives me a shy smile. "Well, we've just begun to suspect you might be carrying my child."

I freeze, my body going still. "Your child? How do you know I even want children?"

Heat flushes his cheeks. His voice is hesitant as he asks, "Do you?"

I allow myself to ponder it before pulling my shoulders into a shrug. "Maybe someday. Not right now."

His expression regains its previous mischievous humor. "Well, we have hundreds and thousands of years to decide about children. If that isn't part of your one-year plan, then I suppose I don't need to be gentle with you after all." He grips my waist tight, then nips playfully at my neck. I squeal, but his bites dissolve into kisses, his lips trailing my collarbone.

Passion returns to my core. I tip my head to the side to allow him to nuzzle closer. My hips begin to rock again, and I bring one hand to his chest. I feel every hard muscle beneath my palm as I trail my hand down his torso, reaching his lower stomach.

"Are you sure you even want to?" he whispers against my neck, a hint of jest in his tone. "I mean, we've been doing it twice a night for a year now."

I pull back and look at him, my lips stretching into a grin. "Twice a night?"

"Ok, you're right. Most nights it's thrice. And that does not include what we do on the furniture." His face contorts with a pretend grimace. "But aren't your hips beginning to ache? Besides, at this rate, you're sure to be with child far sooner than you're ready."

I bring both hands to his shoulders. "Shut up and kiss me."

"Whatever you say, my dearest mate. My wife."

Again, I'm taken aback. "Wife?"

"Yes, my *wife*. Have you already forgotten our wedding? I seem to recall you being owed one when you were named my Chosen."

"That was a term of the treaty, *remember*? And we broke the treaty."

"Ah, but I am still a man of honor. I wasn't going to defile your human side too long without trapping you beneath the bonds of wedlock."

I roll my eyes. "How romantic."

"It was romantic. After all that business with the bomb, we settled down in our new palace, enjoyed a very human wedding, and even exchanged human wedding rings. You wore a hideous human dress which you glamoured from some poor, unsuspecting dressmaker. That was a night where we made love *four* times, if I remember right."

"Four? My, my, I think we have a record to break."

"Surely, we've broken it at least once this year."

I lean in close, planting a kiss at the corner of his jaw. "Nope."

"Well, the night grows late. We should get started trying to break it."

I place a kiss on the other side of his jaw, then pull back just enough to meet his eyes. "Aspen?"

"Yes?"

"Did you just propose to me?"

His lips curl into the most beautiful grin I've ever seen him wear. "I suppose I did. Do you accept?" He runs a hand up and down my spine, the touch eliciting a shudder of pleasure. Fire heats every part of me, my heart, my flesh, the apex of my thighs. It mingles with the joy that wells in my chest, the love that radiates to every corner of my being.

I don't care if it's pretend. I don't care if this year we're imagining never comes to pass.

In our minds and in our hearts, we're living it now.

"Yes, Aspen. I'll marry you."

His lips crush into mine, and a second later, I feel myself being lifted from the tub. Wrapping my arms around his neck, we kiss with every step he takes from the bathing room to our bed. He lays me down on our warm blankets and presses himself close. Before he can get too comfortable, I shift my legs, then roll my weight over his. He complies, allowing me to turn him onto his back. I climb upon him, arching my back as one of his hands caresses my hips, the other lighting over my breast. There he teases another wave of pleasure. A moan escapes my lips and I fall forward, catching myself on my hands.

"Always and forever, Evie." Aspen's voice comes low and rough. "No matter how many days that is."

I claim his lips with mine, then lower myself onto him. "Always and forever, Aspen."

36

The next morning, I wake in a tangle of sheets and limbs with Aspen's arm sprawled over my naked chest. Hazy morning sunlight peeks through the shutters in our bedroom, bringing with it the desert heat, already warming my skin. I shift beneath Aspen's arm to roll toward him, settling my hand on his side and bringing my face just below his. A smile comes to my lips as I study his slack expression, feel his soft breaths brush my cheeks. His antlers hang over the back of our mattress, his hair in tangled disarray, curled from last night's sweat and our time in the bath. Memories of our passion rise to my mind, as well as the playful words we exchanged. I can't say if we made love four times or not; it's hard to say for sure at this point. Even lying still, my body aches from our time spent together, engaged in our game of pretend. Pretend that also wasn't pretend.

Aspen begins to stir, and as he blinks his eyes open, he catches my gaze. A wide grin plays over his lips, and he immediately nuzzles closer, bringing our mouths to touch. "Good morning," he says, between kisses.

I wrap my arms around his neck, and he shifts his body slightly over my upper half. Pulling away, his eyes wander every inch of me, drinking me in with clear pleasure in his eyes. One hand is propped beneath my neck while the other explores my skin in a soft caress, roving lazily from my neck to my torso, then down my legs.

Just like that, fire ignites inside me. "If you aren't careful, we're never getting out of this bed," I say, voice husky.

He leans in for another kiss, his tongue dancing against mine. When we separate, he snags my lower lip gently between his teeth. "I can think of far worse fates."

The blood leaves my face at the mention of worse fates, and Aspen's expression turns apologetic.

"I could have phrased that better." His hand finds mine and laces our fingers together.

With him so close, with his body so warm against me, it's impossible for the flash of dread I felt a moment ago to linger. Our game last night taught me something valuable—that if we must face certain doom, I don't want to do it sulking and living in fear. I want to face it without regrets. I want to live my last days to the fullest because they matter.

I smile up at him, breathing in the scent of his skin. "How do you do it?"

"Do what?" His smile mirrors mine, and it's his sweetest one, the kind that crinkles his eyes, free from mischief and teasing.

"How do you know exactly what to do to get me out of a mood?"

He shrugs. "I think you would know how to do the exact same for me."

I ponder that for a moment. Is he right? If the tables were turned, would I know how to get him out of the darkest humor? "I'd probably just fight with you."

Now the mischief melts into his grin. "Exactly. We work well together, you and I." He brings our lips to meet once again, and this time, we let our kisses linger, deepen. I'm almost certain we're nearing an encore of last night when a knock sounds at the door.

We pull away, breathless and smiling. "We slept late," I whisper. "I suppose we should attend to our duties."

"Must we?"

I ignore him and shout toward the door, "Coming!"

"She's actually not," Aspen adds, "thanks to you."

I swat him playfully as I extricate myself from his arms. He steals several kisses in the process, and by the time I'm at the door, wrapped hastily in a crooked robe, my cheeks are flushed with heat and happiness. However, the face I see on the other side of my threshold has my brow furrowed. It's Marie Coleman.

"Your Majesty," she says with a clumsy curtsy. She's dressed in loose slacks and a cropped, sleeveless linen top, its drape flowing in several folds gathered from a wide, bronze ring around her neck, revealing a flash of skin over her stomach. Although it isn't a dress, I'd know an Amelie design anywhere now. And I'd say Marie seems comfortable in her new Fire Court attire if it weren't for the way she wrings her hands, shifting from foot to foot.

"What is it, Marie?"

Aspen's footsteps approach from behind, and I feel him place a comforting hand on my lower back.

She looks from me to my mate and back again. Finally, she withdraws an envelope from her pants pocket. "My uncle sent me a letter," she says, a guilty look passing over her face.

I take the envelope, unsure why she's handing it to me. "Your uncle knows you're here?"

She lifts her chin in defiance, although the guilt remains in her eyes. "I wrote to him so he can tell my parents I'm safe. I may not have wanted to go back to them, but I didn't want them to worry either."

I bite back my argument. I'd already warned Marie it isn't safe for humans in Faerwyvae when we're at war. Informing her relatives of her whereabouts could create major complications I don't have time for. Especially when her uncle is the Mayor of Sableton. Someone not entirely fond of me, at that.

I turn the envelope over in my hands. The seal has already been broken. "How did you even get a letter to or from him?"

She wrings her hands again. "I may have used an ambassador's seal. I was with Lorelei when she found the one belonging to the former Fire Court ambassador. Once I had my letter, I sent Dune with it. I didn't expect him to bring one back."

"Dune took a letter to Sableton?" My voice comes out sharper than I intend. How did this happen without me knowing? The answer comes to me at once. I've paid very little attention to much of anything this past week, focusing only on my dread. With a sigh, I soften my tone. "That was reckless, Marie. Dune could have been in danger going to Sableton like that. There's no telling if the humans will even honor an ambassador's seal right now, especially one borne by an unseelie."

"I know. I'm sorry."

"So, what did your uncle say? Is he demanding your return home?"

She shakes her head. "The letter he sent back isn't about me at all. He wants to meet with you."

"About what?" Aspen asks, stepping closer.

"He says he has information regarding the safety of the isle."

I exchange a glance with Aspen. His expression is equal parts suspicious and intrigued. I lower my voice to a whisper. "Do you think he knows about..."

Aspen shrugs. "Can you trust him?"

I recall my last interaction with Mayor Coleman at Mother's trial. While he may not have shown the same cruelty as Mr. Duveau, he did make it quite clear he was against me in every way. My pulse races as I pull the letter from the envelope. Aspen leans forward and we read the letter together.

It contains very little more than what Marie has already said. Mayor Coleman claims to have vital information pertinent to the safety of the Fair Isle and requests an urgent meeting with me to discuss it. The only other statement the letter contains is a promise that he offers this conversation in peace, even going so far to use fae verbiage of a *peaceful exchange of words.*

I return my gaze to Aspen, who runs a hand through his hair. "I don't know," he says. "This could be a trap."

He's right, but I don't think I can pass this opportunity up. If there's even the slightest possibility Mayor Coleman knows anything about the Parvanovae, I have to take the chance. "This could give us the ability to prepare. To fight."

He stares at the letter in my hand as if he could decipher the mayor's intents between the inked words. Finally, his expression softens, gaze meeting mine. "I already know you're going to go, so I'll go too."

"He might not speak with me if you're there."

"If he's desperate enough to reach out to you, he will. And if it's indeed a trap...I can protect you."

There's no use telling him I don't need protection. If Mayor Coleman hides some devious plan, I might need all the protection I can get.

I return to face Marie, who eyes us warily. She seems unsurprised by our whispered conversation, although she can't be fully aware of all that Aspen and I know, either. We've only made public to our people the news that we won the war against the Renounced but still face an even greater threat from the humans. One we might not be able to win. "What do you think, Marie? Can we trust your uncle?"

She shrugs. "I can't say for certain. I know he resented you becoming King Aspen's Chosen instead of my sister and me after the Holstrom girls died. And yet I think you might be right about his desperation. He seems worried about something." Her eyes unfocus as she goes silent for a moment. Then excitement crosses her face. "I know! Bring me. Use me as a hostage in case he tries anything."

"Marie, no—"

"He'll make no move against you if I'm there."

I cross my arms, giving her a pointed look. "Somehow I doubt he values you quite as much as you suggest. If he was eager to ship you off to Faer-wyvae, I can't imagine you'd make a great hostage."

"You don't understand," she says. "He's always been fond of me. He may not love the fae, but he considers the marriages forged from the Hundred Year Reaping to be a great honor for human families. Promoting and protecting his family is all my uncle cares about."

"That still doesn't make you a good hostage," I say. "Besides, I think that goes against a peaceful exchange of words."

She rolls her eyes. "We won't call me a hostage. I'll come under the pretense of wanting to see him. My presence will merely be a veiled threat." Her grin glows with mischief as she presses her palms together. "Please, Your Majesty. Let me be useful for something."

I look to Aspen, who shakes his head as if to say he's not the one to ask. I'm probably not the best to ask either, for as much as I want to protect the girl, I must admit her presence could provide just the right amount of collateral to ensure the mayor behaves.

"All right," I say, much to Marie's morbid delight. "You can act as my sort-of-hostage."

"Thank you, Your Majesty," she says, standing straight. I almost expect her to salute. "I'll be the best hostage you could ever hope for."

I shake my head in amusement. Never in all my days could I have expected to hear those words. "Go find Dune," I say. "Since he's so fond of delivering messages, let him take my response back to your uncle."

37

Three days later, after sundown, Aspen, Marie, Dune, and I make our way through the Spring axis toward the wall near Sableton. Dune lights the way, the blue flame hovering over his tail creating a soft glow as he pads quietly across the forest floor. Marie nearly skips with excitement, her enthusiasm unhampered by the exertion of our journey. Luckily, our travels haven't been too strenuous, for Queen Tris granted us permission to transport our party directly to her Spring axis from my Fire axis, something I previously hadn't known we could do.

Marie lifts her face to the night sky, arms spread out before her as she breathes in deeply. "I could get used to this. Everything smells like cherry blossoms in the Spring Court."

"Enjoy it now," I say. "Once we cross the wall, it will be very much fall." I tug my newly made cloak around my shoulders in anticipation of the cool weather that awaits. I can already see the telltale fog that lines the Faerwyvae side of the faewall, telling me we'll reach our destination in a matter of minutes. My heart races at the thought.

I feel Aspen's gaze on me, and I turn my head to meet his eyes. "Are you ready for this?" he asks.

I nod, although I know I can't hide the trepidation I feel. Despite the mild weather of the Spring axis, my nerves have me sweating. None of us know what to expect from this meeting with Mayor Coleman. His reply to my acceptance of his offer to meet was brusque at best. I pat my hip and the dagger strapped around my waist—my newest blade forged from the molten river. It may not be as elegant as my obsidian blade was, or the daggers I took from the weapons room, but it is far more carefully crafted than the one I made at Varney Cove.

We slow our pace as the wall of fog draws closer. Only when we are beneath its blanketing quiet does Marie's enthusiasm begin to wane. "What is the purpose of the fog?" she asks, wrapping her cloak around her.

"Privacy," Aspen says. "To keep humans from crossing the wall."

"Not that it kept them out completely," I add, remembering Mr. Osterman—the Butcher of Stone Ninety-Four—and his vile traps. Even Amelie and I once crossed it when we were younger, driven by a bold dare made by Maddie Coleman. That was a night that changed everything, solidifying my hate for the fae, and my distrust for my mother. My heart sinks with regret. I was wrong about so many things back then.

With the thought comes a chasm of grief, but I allow it to open beneath me, let my body sink into it. Tears prick my eyes and I breathe past the lump in my throat. Instead of swallowing me whole, the grief washes over me, moves with me and through me. Then its power diminishes, turning it into more of a companion than a threat.

Aspen's fingers find mine, and I catch his reassuring smile through the dense fog.

"Foxglove told me the fae are extending the wall around Faerwyvae to protect us from human attack," Marie says. "Is that true?"

I mutter a curse. I really need to have a chat with Foxglove about spreading gossip. Even when it's true. "Well, we were."

"We still are," Aspen says, and I flash him a surprised look. I hadn't realized the efforts were continuing now that the Parvanovae is gone. Then again, maybe I shouldn't be surprised, considering not everyone else reacted to the theft with the same level of apathy as I did. And to be honest, I haven't had much communication with the other royals since then. We've had only one meeting of the Alpha Alliance since our return from Varney Cove, and that was primarily to present Dahlia to the others so she could make her surrender known. When talk turned to the subject of the Parvanovae, and Flauvis began growling insults over my incompetence, I left the meeting. But not before tossing him a rude gesture.

Aspen continues. "The process is slow going, but now that the Renounced have been defeated, King Aelfon has been able to coordinate building efforts in all courts.

"To what end, though?" I ask, lowering my voice. "Without the ability to infuse the wall with an enchantment..."

He shrugs. "Who says it can't be infused with an enchantment? We may not be able to proceed with the one Estel's sister had designed long ago, but that doesn't mean we can't protect the wall."

Hope begs to rise in my chest, but it doesn't go far. Even if we could find a new enchantment to protect Faerwyvae, will we be able to finish the wall before the next attack? And if we are...what if the humans detonate the bomb in Eisleigh instead? Is there any enchantment strong enough to protect from the blast of an exploding star?

"I sense a human," Dune says from up ahead, shaking me from my thoughts. His blue flame is muted by the mist, and I can barely make out the kitsune as more than a white shape. He pauses for us to catch up. "Stone Eighty-Five, I believe."

"Do you sense only one human or multiple?" I pat my dagger again, wrapping my fingers around its hilt.

"One," he says to my relief. That lessens the chances that this is a trap.

I let my fingers leave the dagger. "Take us to him."

Dune leads us through the mist, the towering stones of the wall now in full view. Aspen's hand remains locked in mine as we make our way between two stones and onto human soil.

The chill is the first thing I notice, the bite in the air sharp against my skin, even through my clothing. My previously warm cloak now feels thread-bare, making me wish for a heavy winter coat instead. The next thing I notice is the smell of the forest on this side of the wall, the aroma of dirt and rotting leaves, of waste and pollution in the villages beyond. Finally, I spot the human figure stepping out from behind one of the trees. The sight of the heavy-set mayor sends my mind reeling back to the night of Mother's trial, igniting fire in my blood, but I do my best to keep my rage under control.

Marie nearly starts forth when she sees her uncle, but I place a warning hand on her shoulder to hold her back. If she's going to serve as a warning to keep the mayor in line, I can't have her skipping around without a care. "Somber, remember?" I whisper.

She nods in understanding, slowing her pace to remain close at my side.

We come to a stop several feet from the wall and wait for Mayor Coleman to close the remaining distance. He narrows his eyes at my companions, going a shade paler at the sight of Dune. It's rare for a human to come into contact with a fae who isn't an ambassador, and it's an even rarer thing for them to see an unseelie. When they do, it almost always ends in trouble from one side or the other.

"I thought you'd come alone," the mayor says as he halts before us.

I keep my posture erect, my chin lifted in a regal air. "You thought wrong, Mayor Coleman."

He turns his gaze to his niece, offering her a curt nod. "I certainly didn't expect to see you here, Marie."

She gives him a small smile. "I wanted to see you, Uncle. Her Majesty was so kind as to offer me the chance."

He shifts his jaw, making his bushy mustache twitch. "Are you being treated well?"

"Of course I am," she says. "That's why I've chosen to stay with Queen Evelyn and King Aspen."

I put my arms around her shoulders and pull her close to my side, doing my best to appear domineering despite the fact that Marie is nearly my same height. "We've been given no reason to treat her with anything but kindness." My words come out slow to emphasize the feigned threat beneath them.

"Right," the mayor says, and I can see in his eyes that he understands completely.

I withdraw my arm from Marie's shoulders and bring it to my hip. "So, why did you ask me here to talk?"

"I said in my letter. I have vital information regarding the safety of the isle."

I pin him beneath a glare. "You're going to need to be more specific than that."

With a deep breath, he takes a step closer, flashing a wary glance at my mate. "Eisleigh's council has been given a twofold warning, straight from King Grigory," he says. "First, that the isle will be under attack by the king's own army coming from the mainland. And second, that only the most prestigious families are to be given notice and urged to vacate."

Dread sinks my stomach, but I do my best to appear aloof. "This news isn't surprising. The fae already know we're at war with the humans. It was only a matter of time before the King of Bretton got involved with the matters on the isle."

"There's more." His expression darkens. "I looked into this matter, spoke to someone I thought would know more. Turns out he knew a great deal more."

From the way he speaks, I already know who he's referring to. "And what did this dear friend of yours say?"

The mayor opens and closes his fists, his cheeks turning crimson. "The king is in possession of a weapon that could destroy all life in a matter of seconds. Not just the fae. *All* life here on the isle."

Marie bites back a cry of alarm, pressing a hand to her mouth to stifle it. It's obvious this is the first she's heard of the Parvanovae and its threat.

I can't keep the steel from my gaze. Even though the news is of little surprise to me, it confirms Mr. Duveau gifted the bomb to King Grigory. Not just that, but he did so fully aware of the power the weapon possesses. Part of me has kept a flicker of doubt over whether he sought it without understanding how powerful the bomb could be, but now all doubts are erased. He knew all along that the bomb would destroy the isle, and he gave it to the human king.

The king who now seeks to kill his own people just to end the fae.

The mayor's eyes go wide. "You knew about this too."

I press my lips tight.

"Do you know when the king plans to unleash this weapon?" Aspen asks.

The mayor looks from me to my mate, shaking his head. "No, but I'm sure it's soon. The last of the covert ships transporting the elite to the safety of the mainland depart from Eisleigh tomorrow night." He opens and closes his fists again, forehead wrinkled. "Do you know what the weapon is?"

There's no use denying it now. "A bomb," I say. "One created by the fae at the end of the first war. I was tasked with protecting it from being used until it could be destroyed, but your dear friend stole it from me."

Mayor Coleman scowls. "Mr. Duveau is no friend of mine or the council's."

I raise a brow. "Is that so? It seemed at my mother's trial he had all of you wrapped around his finger."

"That was before the treaty broke," he says. "We may not know what happened, but we know he failed to keep the treaty intact. And now I know he's directly responsible for this newest threat."

I release a frustrated sigh. "Well, I appreciate the warning, Mayor Coleman, but if you have no more specific intel on the king's plans to attack, then I must bid you a goodnight."

"Wait." He takes another step closer, lowering his voice. "That's not the only reason I requested we meet."

"What else could we have to say to each other?"

He brings a hand to his face, rubbing his mustache as if it will help him find his words. Then his gaze falls on his niece, eyes turning down at the corners at the sight of her flushed cheeks, her unshed tears. He goes still. With a resigned grumble, he pins his arms stiffly at his side. "I need your help. *We* need your help."

I pull my head back in surprise. "Who's we?"

"The humans, Miss Fair—I mean, Your Majesty."

I'm so shocked to hear my honorific coming from his lips that my mouth momentarily falls open. I hurry to hide my astonishment behind a look of skepticism. "Why is that?"

He clenches his jaw as if it pains him to answer the question. "King Grigory has forsaken us, left his people to die just to be rid of a powerful nuisance."

I bristle at hearing the fae referred to as a *nuisance* but clench my jaw to keep from interrupting.

He continues. "He's willing to sacrifice an entire population to wrest total control from the fae once and for all."

"He won't have much to rule over when he blasts the entire isle to smithereens," Aspen mutters.

The mayor nods. "I think he'd rather lose the isle than face possible defeat."

"Why come to me?" I ask. "What is it you expect me to do about it?"

"You're one of them. One of the fae. You have the ear of the other royals. Not only that, but I trust that you care about the fate of the humans."

"The fae are already doing our best to prepare for it. We will defend Faerwyvae at all costs."

"I know," he says, "but we need you to defend Eisleigh too."

I'm dumbstruck, words stripped from my throat as I stare at the mayor in disbelief. "You've got to be kidding. You want the fae to protect the *humans*? The humans who we are at war with?"

"We will set our squabbles aside."

"So, what? You're offering a temporary ceasefire?" I scoff at that, remembering how poorly my last negotiations over a ceasefire ended. "That's not good enough. We need your total surrender."

The mayor throws his hands in the air. "We have no king anymore, Evelyn. Eisleigh is broken. If you want our surrender, you can have it. It's nothing more than the plea of dying men."

Aspen and I exchange a glance. *He's desperate*, he says through the Bond.

Suspicion has my gaze returning to the mayor. "Why are you so willing to bargain with me? In fact, why are you even on the isle still? You said the king sent word to the council with a warning for the elite families to vacate. Shouldn't that include you?"

His voice comes out small. "I have more than just my household here. Yes, I have my wife and children. But also brothers and sisters." He waves a hand toward Marie. "Nieces and nephews."

"All of whom are among the wealthy elite," I say, narrowing my eyes. "Marie's parents own the most prosperous trade ships on the isle. Their ships could take your entire extended family to safety."

"Every one of their ships is out on trade," he says through his teeth. "As soon as the treaty was broken, the king sent word to all the ports, forbidding ships from returning to Eisleigh. That's when he launched his warships."

I frown. "None of the other ships would take you?"

"I'm not leaving my family," he says. "My wife won't leave her sisters. My brother won't leave without his daughters." His gaze turns to Marie, and his face falls. "Maddie won't leave Bircharbor, awaiting the return of her husband."

I bite back my urge to break the news that Maddie Coleman will be waiting indefinitely. With Cobalt dead, she's no longer the wife of a fae king.

The mayor gestures at his niece. "I doubt this one will leave the fae, for whatever godforsaken reason has her enamored with your kind. Please, I'm begging you. Tell me there's something you can do for the humans."

I close my eyes and bring my fingertips to my temples, my mind whirling with thoughts, questions, solutions. It's already an impossible enough task to come up with a way to protect Faerwyvae. How can we possibly make a plan that could save Eisleigh too? And if I agree to defend the humans myself, is there anything I can do to get the other royals to join me? I can already imagine Flauvis trying to convince the others that we should take this opportunity to eradicate the humans.

Aspen's voice comes through the Bond like a smooth caress. *What are you thinking, my love?*

I think you know, Aspen.

You want to protect everyone on the isle. But is it possible?

I open my eyes to find his, my answer pulsing through the Bond. *I don't know, but we have to at least try.*

Then you know what needs to be done, he says. *We must craft a bargain. One tempting enough for the other royals to accept.*

He's right. Already, I know what I must offer.

Marie comes up to me and Aspen, tears streaming down her cheeks. "Please help them."

"I will," I whisper to her. It's more than a statement. It's a promise made from the bottom of my heart. Even if I fail, I know I must at least try.

I face the mayor. "We shall make a bargain. If we save the humans, the Fair Isle falls under fae rule from then on. Agreed?"

His expression darkens. "You have the surrender of Eisleigh's council. We will not fight you. We will set all grievances aside and forge a new treaty. But turning rule over to the fae is too much. It's asking me to give up my position as mayor. My livelihood."

I let out a bitter laugh. "Oh, so your job is worth dying for?"

He mutters a curse under his breath. "No. But why would you require such a sacrifice?"

"It's the only way the rest of Faerwyvae will agree. I can only do so much on my own. To save the isle, we need all fae—seelie and unseelie alike—fighting for the same cause."

He shakes his head rapidly. "They'll eat us alive. Literally."

"Not if it's part of the bargain," I say. "Humans surrender to a fae rule. The fae in turn work to save the isle from the bomb. No humans rise against us, no humans are harmed."

His chest heaves as he studies me, a sheen of sweat coating his face.

"Do you agree?" I ask.

He gasps a breath, and with it comes another string of muttered curses. "Fine," he bites out. "On behalf of Eisleigh's council and people, I agree to this bargain."

A sob of relief escapes Marie's lips, but my own comfort is short lived. This bargain brings even more challenges. More to lose.

"Will you spread the word?" I ask. "Assure us no one will rise against the fae or our efforts to do what must be done?"

"I will."

"Good. Then I promise I will do whatever it takes to save the isle. However, it would be a lot easier if we knew when or where the bomb will be detonated. If we can steal it back, we could destroy it the same way we'd previously planned. You're sure there's nothing else you can tell us?"

"No," the mayor says, a dark glint in his eye, "but I know someone who can."

My heart races. I already know exactly who he means. "Mr. Duveau?"

The mayor nods. "I can tell you where to find him."

38

―――――――

I've never run so fast in my life. Even with the increased swiftness my fox form allows, I know I'm pushing myself to the limit. Still, I run on and on, fueled by necessity. Need. Hope. With every panting breath, I keep my destination fixed firmly in my mind.

Port Denyson. Port Denyson.

That's where I'll find Mr. Duveau, catching the last ship from Eisleigh, leaving under the veil of night. Why he's taking a ship off the isle when I damn well know he has my Chariot, I cannot say. All I can do is pump my fox legs as fast as they can go, skirting around the most populated cities and towns in favor of forests. When towns can't be avoided, I rush through cobblestone streets, fully aware that my glowing fur won't allow me to pass as a regular fox.

Luckily, very few people catch sight of me, and those who do make no move against me. What could they do, anyway? To them, I am the unseelie beast they were taught to fear. Until Mayor Coleman's message about our bargain circulates the isle, that's all I and the rest of the fae will be.

There is one tangible threat to my progress, and that is exhaustion. At first, my flames are sufficient fuel to revitalize me just when I'm about to slow down. But the farther I get from the faewall, the weaker my fire becomes, and the more often I must stop for rest. With Port Denyson being at the southeastern end of Eisleigh, so distant from the wall and the magic of Faerwyvae, my travels grow more taxing as the hours drag on.

Hours. I've been running for hours and still have several more to go. My journey began soon after the meeting with the mayor, once I'd convinced Aspen to take Marie and Dune back to Fire so he can round up the other royals for an emergency meeting when I return. It took a bit of arguing to get him to agree to part ways, but he eventually conceded, knowing Duveau is our best shot at gaining an advantage over the coming threat.

But only if I make it in time.

Despite my aching paws, I continue to run.

ANXIETY RUSHES THROUGH ME AS THE SUN BEGINS TO LOWER IN THE SKY. MR. Duveau's ship is set to sail after nightfall—a coward's escape. I hate that the elite families of Eisleigh get to flee to the safety of the mainland while the unsuspecting villagers sleep, no clue what terrors await them. Not yet at least. If the mayor keeps his side of the bargain, the humans will know what's coming soon enough. They'll know they've been betrayed by their king with no one but the fae to save them.

My muscles are screaming as night fully falls over the forest, but still I press on. Just when I'm starting to lose hope that I'll ever find the port, the tang of salty air begins wafting in on the breeze, a sure sign my destination is near. Finally, the trees of the forest give way to a small seaside town. I slow my pace as I enter its sleeping streets, trying to orient myself. The sound of waves falls on my ears, but I'm not just looking for the sea. I need to find the port. The docks. The ships.

I attune myself to every sound, every smell, my fox instincts sharp as they take in every bit of data that filters through my senses. Then I hear it. The low hum of a boat's foghorn. I dart forth again, listening deeper, seeking the telltale sound of waves lapping against the hull of a boat.

I reach the beach, docks in sight. Racing forward, I search for signs of Mr. Duveau's ship. Yet all I see at the end of each pier are small fishing boats. I locate the larger docks where trade vessels and cruise ships would be. They're all empty. I run to the end of one, rich with recent scents of human bodies. One distinct, familiar aroma stands out above all the rest, turning my stomach. He was here. I can smell it.

I sit back on my haunches and stare out at the dark water. There, hundreds of meters out to sea, sails the last ship to the mainland. I'm too late.

Disappointment lashes through me, so strong it has me shifting out of my fox form and into my human body. I stumble back, catching myself on my forearms to keep from toppling over completely.

No, no, no, no. I can't have missed it. I ran as fast as I could.

My mind whirls with calculations, recalling every minute I wasted on rest. I now regret letting myself catch my breath, rest my paws. If only I'd pushed harder. If only I'd…no. There's still a chance.

I rise to my feet and undo my cloak, letting it fall to my feet as I assess the distance between here and the ship. I could swim to it, couldn't I? Or harness the element of water and get it to propel me to the ship? But even if I somehow could catch up, could I board it somehow? Pretend to have fallen off and call for a life raft? Then what? Do I question Mr. Duveau on the ship and then swim back here before it can take me too far?

No, no, none of this is logical.

My anxiety rises higher and higher with every inch of space that grows between myself and the ship. I know I must take action. Do *something*, logical or not. I must jump, swim.

I reach a hand out to the water, connecting to its element. Depth, emotion, sorrow—

Nothing.

I feel nothing.

I try to connect to my flame, my rage, my passion, but it's hardly more than a flicker inside me. This is the farthest south I've ever been from the wall—farther than Grenneith, and way farther than Sableton or Varney Cove. All I feel is aching muscles, blistered toes. My exhaustion is so heavy, I doubt I could shift back into my fox form if I tried.

Sinking to my knees at the edge of the dock, I stare down at the black water. It's over. Our last chance to get answers from Mr. Duveau. My last shot at vengeance. Gone. Gone.

"Please," I mutter, although I know not who I beseech. The Great Mother above? The All of All? "Please!" I call out again, louder now. "He doesn't deserve to get away."

The water has no answer for me. Nothing but the steady rise and fall of waves rippling from the motion of the departing ship. The ship bearing my enemy.

"He doesn't deserve safety," I say through my teeth. Then, closing my eyes, I throw my head back and shout into the night, "He doesn't deserve to live!"

"I say that about most humans."

I startle at the voice, drawing back from the water and the equine head that breaks above its surface, eyes red like rubies. Its fur is midnight black, dark mane floating around it, tossed by the waves. The rest of its body is hidden beneath the water, but I don't need to see it to know what creature this is.

Kelpie.

In a flash, I reach for the belt at my waist, retrieving my iron blade. "Stay back."

"I do not come to hurt you," he says, though his tone is far from comforting.

I assess the kelpie through slitted lids. "How are you even here?"

"I swim," he answers without humor.

"We're too far from the wall. There's no magic out here."

The kelpie rumbles with hissing laughter. "No wall can separate magic from the sea. It is everywhere."

I shake my head. "I can't feel it. No matter what I try, I don't feel connected to the elements here."

"That's because you are not of the sea."

"Perhaps," I say, "but fae are never seen this far from Faerwyvae, not even sea fae."

"Melusine forbade us," he says. "Although I prefer to think I have no master, no king or queen, I obeyed this order. It was for our protection. Sea fae do not like it on the human side of the sea. We can hardly stand to swim through the polluted waters, and when we do, the iron nets and barbed hooks are enough to keep us from coming back."

"Then why are you here now? I am not lost. I am in no need of your services."

"No, I suppose you are not." His tone holds a hint of regret. "Although, I hoped you would find yourself lost today, for you owe me a life. Yet every time I spied you running past my rivers and streams, you were a fox. And the fox knew the way."

A chill runs down my spine. The kelpie has been watching me? For how long? I saw no sign of him during my travels here. Then again, my focus wasn't on seeking out other creatures; it was on finding the port.

When I say nothing in reply, the kelpie releases an equine snort and begins to rise from the waves.

I take one step back, then another, keeping my blade between us as the kelpie pulls himself onto the dock with a sinuous agility a normal horse would never possess.

Righting himself on four enormous, ebony hooves, he pins me with his ruby stare, paying no heed to the threat I hold in my hand. "I saw what you and your mate did to the vile ship."

I furrow my brow; it takes me several moments to comprehend what he's referring to. "You were at Varney Cove?"

"The seelie rat who called himself king summoned my kind to his aid. Very few obeyed. The rest of us came only to watch."

"I'm sure it was great entertainment for you," I say, a bitter edge to my voice. Aspen and I could have used some assistance on the beach that day. If the sea fae weren't going to help Cobalt, they could have helped us instead. Especially considering Cobalt's death makes Aspen Regent of the Sea Court until another sea fae can gain the blessing of the All of All.

"We approve of your actions against the ship."

I put my free hand on my hip and toss him a sardonic glare. "Thanks for your approval."

A stretch of silence falls as the kelpie continues to watch me with his unsettling gaze. I'm considering the best way to extricate myself from the conversation when the kelpie speaks again. "You call yourself unseelie."

"I do."

"And yet you do not hate all humans."

"I do not."

The kelpie's eyes burn a shade brighter. "And yet you hate the one on the ship."

I shudder. "Yes."

"Would you like to speak with him? I could bring him to you."

The hair rises on the back of my neck. As much as I want to say yes, I can feel the threat of a bargain hanging in the air. I squeeze my dagger tighter. "What will it cost me?"

The kelpie's long, serpentine neck curves to the side, allowing him a glance behind him at the ship. When he returns to face me, his serrated teeth are bared. Whether the expression is supposed to be a threat or a smile, I know not. "A life."

I shake my head. "I will not give you my life."

"You need not," he says. "The life of the one you hate will do."

My pulse pounds rapidly, my eyes flashing to the ship. It's so far out now, it's nothing more than a dark shape amidst the equally dark night.

"Do we have a bargain?"

I swallow hard. "Yes."

39

____

The kelpie leaps off the dock and into the sea, disappearing from view. All I can hear are waves and the pounding of my own heart as I watch the ocean, the ship, unable to see anything taking place on it from here.

With bated breath, I stand vigil as several anxious minutes pass. With every inhale I take, doubts creep in, and I begin to wonder if the kelpie had been tricking me. He only insinuated that he'd bring Mr. Duveau to me at once, but a specific timeline wasn't part of the bargain. In fact, we never even agreed on who exactly I sought. Then again, the kelpie must have some strange ability to track travelers. He found me when I called for help in the coral cage, then located Aspen soon after on his rampage toward Sableton.

Sweat pools under my arms, behind my neck, despite the chill in the air. Several more agonizing minutes pass and there's still no sign of the kelpie. I begin to pace, ready to curse the kelpie and myself for making such a reckless bargain. Then motion stirs in front of the dock, sending my heart into my throat. I inch forward for a closer look, only to leap back as the kelpie suddenly breaches the surface. I stare open mouthed as he pulls himself onto the dock with a male figure locked on his back.

Terror and delight mingle in my gut as I watch Mr. Duveau gasp for breath from the kelpie's back, sputtering water from his blue lips. His elegant evening attire is dripping seawater, his hands and neck red where the kelpie's mane strangles his flesh.

"I brought you the one you hate," the kelpie says. His mane begins to shift, slithering from around Mr. Duveau like the coils of a snake. Once freed from the kelpie's bonds, the councilman falls to the dock at my feet.

Mr. Duveau coughs up water as he pushes himself to his hands and knees. Before he can do anything else, I'm upon him, my blade at his throat as I push him onto his back. His eyes are wide as he blinks the water from them, holding his palms out in surrender.

"Miss Fairfield?" His tone is laced with surprise, his voice rough from swallowing so much saltwater.

I press the blade closer until it knicks his flesh and heave myself over him. With my free hand, I reach beneath his jacket and retrieve his revolver. I chuck it over the other side of the dock and return to my search, bringing up two knives, which also make it into the sea. Further digging proves fruitless, as his pockets are empty of the one thing I'm looking for. "Where is the Chariot?"

"Please don't hurt me," he gasps.

"Wrong answer." I press the dagger closer, drawing a stream of crimson to trail down his throat. I avert my gaze, seeking something else of the same hue. Then I find it—a strand of red rowan beads circling his left wrist. Lifting my blade from his neck, I slice the bracelet off and toss it behind me.

Now the fear truly shows in his eyes as I lower my face toward his. He blinks rapidly, his chest heaving with his sharp, shallow breaths.

"Stop blinking or I'll cut your eyelids off."

"I'll tell you anything," he says, lids still fluttering. "Do anything."

"I know you will." I bring the dagger to the corner of his eye, letting the tip pierce his skin. "Now. Stop. Blinking."

Trembling, he obeys, face going a sickly shade paler.

I lock my eyes with his, drawing his attention to me. The imagery of the bird doesn't come, which makes me wonder if he's hiding rowan elsewhere on his body. Then I recall my difficulties connecting to the elements, the magic of Faerwyvae. Does that mean I can't glamour him?

No. I have him. He's not getting away.

I bring my face even closer until our noses nearly touch. His pupils grow so wide, they devour his irises. I focus on that black void, summoning my rage, my fury, my inner fire. The flame I touch is barely a flicker, but it's there. I call it forth, let it wrap around me, move through me, growing as large as it can despite this world without magic that threatens to tamp it back down.

Maintaining a steady awareness on my inner flame, I again seek the imagery of the bird in the cage, drawing his eyes to me, locking his attention in my grip...

There.

His consciousness becomes a bird, and my will is its cage, grasping him tight within my hands.

I have him.

His face goes slack, but his body remains rigid. My control over him feels tenuous at best, but at least it's something.

"Where is the Chariot you stole?" I ask.

His body trembles beneath me, but he answers without hesitation. "I gave it to King Grigory."

Fury courses through my veins as my lips peel back from my teeth.

"It won't work from Bretton anyway," he adds, as if that makes his treachery any better.

"And the Parvanovae?"

"I gave that to him too."

"And what is he going to do with it?" I already know the answer to this, but I want to hear it from his lips.

"He has ordered it to be detonated on the isle."

"When?"

"Five days from now."

"Five days?" My heart leaps into my throat. It takes all my effort to keep hold of the glamour. "Where will it be detonated?"

"Just beyond the wall in Faerwyvae."

I'm a little surprised at this. I'd assumed the army would try to detonate the bomb on the Eisleigh side of the wall, especially now that Mr. Duveau's broken alliance with Dahlia removes their opportunity to enter Faerwyvae unfettered. "How will the army get into Faerwyvae?"

"A warship."

"The warships were sent back to Bretton."

He gives a subtle shake of his head, but his eyes remain involuntarily locked on mine. "Not all will truly return. Tomorrow, one of the warships turns course and heads straight to its destination."

"Which is where?"

"Here. The warship will dock in Port Denyson."

My mouth goes dry. Of course the warship would come here, to one of the farthest points from Faerwyvae. That way, even if the fae were able to intercept the army, they'd be too far from their magic to do much harm. Still, it's a reckless plan. It will take the humans days to get from Port Denyson to the wall, especially with such precious cargo demanding a careful pace. There must be more to it than that. "How are they transporting the bomb?"

"I don't know."

Rage courses through me as I raise my voice to a shout. "How are they doing it! Tell me!" Just like that, I'm stripped from my concentration, severing the glamour. My body feels weak in its absence, but I force my limbs to remain steady as I bring the blade back to Mr. Duveau's throat.

Free from the glamour, he closes his eyes and whimpers like a broken animal. My lips curl in disgust; the sight of him so helpless makes me feel cold, sick, empty. Somehow, seeing my enemy brought to his knees is far less satisfying than I expected it to be. I can't help but think of Amelie sobbing over Cobalt's remains.

"Thank you," he says, snapping my attention back to the present. "Thank you for releasing me."

I purse my lips. If he wants to believe I released the glamour on purpose, I'll let him. But that doesn't mean this is over.

Reconnecting to my inner fire, I remind myself of everything he's done. All the pain he's caused. Rage courses through my veins. "I'll ask you one more time," I say through clenched teeth. "How are they transporting the bomb?"

"A...a tank. I think."

A tank? I curse under my breath. I've only seen the armored vehicles depicted in the broadsheets. From what little I know of them, they're strong and deadly.

"Let me go," Mr. Duveau says, voice trembling. "I must catch up with that ship."

"Perhaps you should have thought twice before condemning the isle to death."

He shakes his head. "I never wanted this to happen."

"Oh, is that why you stole the Parvanovae from me and gave it to King Grigory?"

"I didn't think he'd use it *here*. I thought he'd use it on a distant enemy, not the Fair Isle."

I clench my jaw. "If that's true, then you're a bigger idiot than I ever thought before."

"You left me with nothing," he says. "The treaty stripped me of my position, my pay. My wife was made a social pariah. My sons—"

"Sons?" The blood leaves my face. All this time, I never imagined Mr.

Duveau as anything other than a monster. Never could I have imagined him as a husband or father.

"Yes, my sons," he says, desperation straining his voice. "They're on that ship with my wife. Please, just let me return to them. They're only five and eight."

Darkness crawls into my heart, turning my voice cold and cruel. "Why should your sons' father live when my mother had to die?"

His eyes go wide, shoulders trembling. "I was following the letter of the law."

My lips peel back from my teeth. "No, you weren't. You were saving your pride."

"I was saving the treaty," he argues. "For my family. For peace. I never sought the isle's destruction. Giving the bomb to the king was wrong; I see that now. For all I know, the blast will reach Bretton and my family will die there too. Just let me be with them when it happens. That's all I ask now."

Despite my burning rage, watching him plead sends the darkness draining from my heart, leaving only emptiness in its wake.

He must see my resolve faltering, for the color rushes back into his cheeks. "Please, Evelyn. I'm so sorry."

With a heavy sigh, I toss my iron blade to the side, letting it skitter a few feet away. Then I pull myself to my feet.

Mr. Duveau scrambles back, eyes wide as if he can hardly believe I'm letting him go. "Thank you."

"Don't thank me," I say, turning my attention to the kelpie waiting silently at the edge of the dock. "It's all up to you now, Mr. Duveau."

He slowly turns his head to follow my gaze.

"Miss Fairfield," he whispers. "Please don't."

"I'm sorry." I take one step back, then another. At the same time, the kelpie inches toward its prey. "But I made a bargain."

Mr. Duveau's gaze flashes to my discarded blade. The kelpie takes another step forward.

"At least you can swim," I say, tone flat. Just as the kelpie lunges at him, I turn around, squaring my shoulders as I retreat down the dock.

The last thing I hear is Mr. Duveau's strangled scream cut off by a thunderous splash.

40

The journey back to Fire takes almost two days. I push myself nearly as hard as I did getting to Port Denyson, but as exhausted as I am, I force myself to rest far more often. As I cross the faewall, I find Aspen waiting for me in his stag form, and together we run the rest of the way to Fire, utilizing the axis line for the fastest travel. Once we make it back to Irridae Palace, I barely have time to clean myself up and change before I'm rushing back down the stairs to the atrium where my fellow royals await.

I slow my pace at the final staircase before the atrium, taking in slow, deep breaths to compose myself. With each breath comes an awareness of the magic flowing through my veins. After being nearly stripped from it at Port Denyson, I don't think I'll ever take this feeling for granted again. Nor will I curse the heat of the Fire Court. The heavy warmth that envelops me as I make my way across the atrium feels like a luxury after the bone-deep chill of a human autumn.

I approach the sunstone table, where all the other royals gather, some seated, others standing. Aspen turns to face me, a comforting smile on his lips, contrasting with his furrowed brow. On our journey from the wall to Irridae, I relayed to him all the details I'd learned from Mr. Duveau, but neither of us are looking forward to sharing the news with the others.

Squaring my shoulders, I take my place at Aspen's side. All of Faerwyvae's royals are here, not just the Alpha Alliance. However, with Cobalt's death leaving Aspen as Regent of the Sea Court, the only newcomers at my table are Dahlia and an ambassador from the Solar Court. Aspen told me earlier that Phoebe's heir has yet to be established, considering our victory over the Renounced brings an official return to the Old Ways. The radical seelie courts will have the hardest time adjusting to this, I'm sure.

The Solar ambassador bends in a bow of respect, while Dahlia gives me a tight-lipped nod. I offer her a saccharine grin, silently praying that someone gains the blessing of the All of All to dethrone her as soon as possible. My gaze moves around the table to far more welcome faces—Nyxia, Estel, Aelfon, Tris, Minuette, and...well, compared to Dahlia, I suppose Flauvis' wolfy sneer is a welcome sight too.

Aspen's hand brushes mine, and he gives my fingers a squeeze. The warmth of his skin makes my chest feel light, and my breaths come easier.

"Thank you for gathering for this urgent meeting," I say. "We have much to discuss, so I'll get into it at once. I know when the Parvanovae is set to strike."

Flauvis rumbles with a mocking growl. "You mean the weapon you let some pathetic human steal from you—"

"Flauvis!" Fire ignites over my body, rippling in tricolor flame from my head to my toes as I fix the Winter King with a furious scowl. "If I hear one more asinine comment from you—*one more*—I will leap over this table and tear out your throat with my teeth."

He opens his mouth, and I expect his high-pitched imitation to follow. Yet, to my surprise, he says nothing. His lips curl at the corner of his muzzle in a canine smirk...but he doesn't speak.

I return my attention to the others, waving my hand across the table. "The same goes for the rest of you."

Aspen snickers at my side and Nyxia struggles to hide her grin behind an air of boredom.

I extinguish my flames. "The Parvanovae comes in three days. It is set to strike just beyond the wall in Faerwyvae. One of the retreating warships will be turning course, if it hasn't already. It will then dock at Port Denyson, and the army will take the bomb north to the wall. If my intel is correct, the Parvanovae will be transported by an armored weaponized vehicle called a tank."

The table is silent as all eyes stare unblinkingly back at me. I expect gasps, shouts of alarm, arguments. But there's nothing. Nothing but quiet trepidation humming across the table.

"This means we still have one more chance to steal the Parvanovae back and use it to enchant the wall," I say, then face the Star Queen. "Estel, did you find your sister's blueprints for the enchantment?"

The particles shift and sway over Estel's face, obscuring it. She hesitates before finally saying, "I did."

I frown. "And?"

The particles continue to shift until they settle on a well-composed smile. "And it can be done. If we expand the wall around Faerwyvae, I can transmute the Parvanovae to fuel the enchantment. No one but the fae will be able to cross the wall, whether entering or leaving. To any human, it will be as if a solid barrier exists."

Hope flutters in my chest, making me want to bounce on the balls of my feet. Reeling in my excitement, I turn to the Earthen King with every ounce of grace I can muster. "Aelfon, how is the progress going with building the wall around the perimeter?"

"Now that the fae are no longer fighting amongst themselves," he says, "I've been able to send builders into every court that touches the sea. They've made progress, but it would be impossible to finish their work in three days."

My stomach sinks at that. "What about fae from other courts? Can we get all fae with an affinity for the earthen element to aid their efforts?"

Aelfon tilts his head one way, then the other, considering my suggestion. "That could help. I still doubt we could build an entire wall around Faerwyvae by then, but with more fae on the job, it's possible."

I bite back a grimace. "There's more. We don't just need a wall around Faerwyvae. We need it around the entire isle."

Nyxia's eyes go wide as she throws her hands in the air. "Why would we do that?"

"It wouldn't be possible," Aelfon says. "Our magic is too weak on the other side of the wall."

"Not if we first destroy the border wall," Aspen says. I'm grateful my mate already knows my plan, my ideas. Knows what a daunting task it will be to get everyone else on board. At least someone here is already on my side.

Flauvis leans forward, panting, eyes glinting with enthusiasm. "Yes! We will break down the wall, unleash our magic, and destroy the humans! Finally, an idea I can support."

"No," I snap. "We aren't breaking down the wall to destroy the humans. We will free our magic so we can face the soldiers at Port Denyson with our full strength. But also..." I resist the urge to wring my hands, clenching my fingers into fists instead. "I've made a bargain with the humans."

Gasps and growls rumble from around the table. Even Nyxia looks murderous as she stares daggers at me.

"They've surrendered to the fae," I say. "The isle belongs to us now. All of it. But only if we protect it from the bomb. That means we must protect the humans too."

Minuette lets out an angry whistle through her teeth. "You never should have bargained without coming to us first."

I put my hands on my hips. "Would you have chosen differently? Would you have given up the opportunity to regain control over the land that first belonged to the fae?"

"No," Nyxia says, arms crossed over her chest, "but I may have worded things differently."

"Yes, how exactly did you word it?" Tris asks.

"And who will rule the portion of land that is now Eisleigh?" Dahlia asks, her voice like razors down my spine. "Are you claiming it yourself?"

I narrow my eyes at the Summer Queen. "No."

"Can we make the humans our slaves?" Minuette asks.

Flauvis runs his tongue over his muzzle. "Can we kill them after we save them?"

"Excuse me," Tris adds. "Must I remind you *again* that I do not support the extinction of humans? However, I don't want them living too close to me, either. Not with their...smells." She wrinkles her nose. "What will we do with them after we save them?"

Aelfon clears his throat, a sheepish look crossing his face. "I agree we shouldn't kill them, but I do think we should take the land back from them."

Dahlia leans forward with hunger in her eyes. "But how will we divide it?"

"Pardon," the Solar ambassador says, "but I do not think a conversation regarding land ownership should happen until the Solar Court has an official ruler blessed by the All of All."

"—*blessed by the All of All*," mimics Flauvis. "I say only those who were part of the Alpha Alliance should have rights to the new lands. The rest of you can—"

"Enough!" Aspen shouts, his voice ringing through the atrium.

That silences the others, but fire heats my core. "This is not what I called this meeting to discuss," I say through my teeth. "I don't know what we will do with the isle after we face the human army, but first we need to survive this war. This isn't the time to fight over land and power. We need to come up with a plan."

Nyxia runs a hand over her silver tresses, smoothing them away from her face as she releases a grumbling breath. When she speaks, her words are strained with poorly hidden animosity. "A plan would be far easier to come up with if you hadn't bargained the isle in exchange for more work from *us*."

"It may be more work," I say, "but it's in our best interests."

Nyxia raises a skeptical brow. "How so?"

"Well, returning the isle to the fae, for one."

Aelfon nods his agreement and Dahlia runs her tongue over her lips, as if she can already taste the extra land she hopes to claim.

I continue. "For another, this gives us a chance to free Faerwyvae's magic all over the isle. We won't be trapped on this side or drained of power on the other. With the humans' surrender, we can enter Eisleigh free of reproach. We can go *anywhere*. We can face the troops who invade at Port Denyson as soon as they touch land. We can meet them on our terms."

Nyxia lets out a resigned sigh. "All right. You have a point."

"There's still the issue of the wall," Estel says. "If we are to extend it around the southern half of the isle, we must first break down the border wall to release our magic. Then we must gather enough builders to finish the job before the invasion. With only three days, I don't know if it can be done."

"She's right." Aelfon leans back in his chair, arms crossed over his wide torso. "These aren't just ordinary stones. Each one is crafted with earthen magic, forged from crystals, rock beds, and soil. Not only must we destroy the thousands that make up the border wall, but we'll have to craft hundreds of thousands more. I don't know if it can be done in three days."

"Not to mention," Tris says, "even those of us with powerful earthen fae in our courts will need to reserve a fighting force."

Minuette nods. "We'll need to defend our courts, send soldiers to fight the men from the warship..."

"Prepare to defend the area beyond the border wall in case the army gets through our fighters," I add, my stomach sinking.

Aspen faces me, lips pulling into a frown. "That's a lot to prepare for in three days."

I look from him to the others. "There must be a way. Even if we can't finish the wall, we can at least pour all our efforts into stealing back the bomb. Then we can finish the wall once we have the Parvanovae."

"The human king will only send more warships to harry our efforts," Nyxia says.

"Then we'll keep fighting," I say. "We'll keep fighting and building until the wall is complete and Estel can perform the enchantment."

The responses uttered from around the table are mostly halfhearted mumbles of agreement.

"There is another way." The voice that speaks doesn't come from the gathering. I look toward the source and find Fehr watching us from the other end of the atrium. With slow steps, he approaches. His face is unreadable, but I see apprehension in the tense set of his shoulders.

"What is it, Fehr?" I ask.

"The wall. It can be built in three days."

"How?"

"You can use a djinn."

41

───────

"A djinn?" Flauvis falls into a fit of howling laughter. "You mean, like you? You've got to be kidding."

I ignore the Winter King, keeping my eyes on Fehr. "You think you can move the wall?"

Fehr lifts his chin. "The djinn are the most powerful of the fae, and I am no exception. Fire may be my primary element, giving me the power to create, but the earthen element obeys my command nearly as well. My strong affinity for air lets me move swiftly through time and space. I could break down the border wall and build one around the perimeter of the isle before the earthen fae can so much as fortify a single court."

Excitement rises inside me, but an obstacle remains that keeps his plan from being sound. "But you can't leave the palace."

"No," he says, "I cannot."

"He wants you to free him," Flauvis says, still shaking with mirth. "The creature who rose against his people wants release from his Bond so he can do it again."

Fehr turns a slow scowl to the Winter King. "My kind are all but extinct, and not one lives outside the bonds of slavery. There will be no uprising from us again."

Minuette watches the djinn through slitted lids, her blue hair rippling wildly about her face. "You just admitted the djinn are the most powerful fae. If you can singlehandedly build a wall around the isle, you could turn on us."

"I could," Fehr admits, a haughty smirk tugging his lips before he returns his gaze to me. "But I won't. If you free me from my Bond to Irridae Palace, I will build the wall. I will fight against the human army. Then, when the battle is won, I will return to serve you of my own free will."

"Do I smell a bargain?" Nyxia lifts her brow, assessing the djinn.

Fehr's jaw shifts back and forth. "Yes," he says through his teeth. "I will make a bargain."

I study Fehr, seeking signs that he plans to betray me, manipulate me. Abandon us when we need him the most. I recall how cold he was with me when we first met. How reluctant he was to serve me. But things have changed between us. He may not laugh or smile or chat at ease with me the way I caught him doing with Foxglove, but...he doesn't hate me.

"All right," I say. "We'll craft a bargain."

The table goes still, silent, with my breathing as the only sound. Each set of eyes watches me with anticipation; those on the far end of the table lean forward with keen interest.

I toss a glare at the royals. "We shall craft our bargain *after* the meeting and do so in private."

Rumbles of disappointment circulate the table as I return to it. Fehr bows low and steps back.

"So, we have a plan," I say. "Fehr will aid Aelfon's earthen fae in building the wall. The rest of us will prepare our soldiers. As soon as the border wall is down, we'll march to Port Denyson. There we'll fight the human army with the primary target to steal back the bomb. We must fight them with care, however, so we don't accidentally detonate it."

"Then when we have it," Estel says, her shimmering particles once again swirling rapidly to obscure her face, "I'll transmute it."

I can't help but feel there's something she isn't telling me. Or perhaps it's just because her particles keep hiding her expression. Is she simply nervous? She has every right to be, I suppose.

My gaze leaves hers to fall on the others. "Are we in agreement?"

"Are you sure we can trust the djinn?" Flauvis asks, teeth bared.

"I'll deal with him myself," I say. "Now are we in agreement or not? I need a yes or no so we can get to work."

Nyxia huffs. "When I said I'd support your claim as queen, I never anticipated you'd be so bossy."

My eyes lock with hers, and I lift my shoulders in a casual shrug. "You aren't the only one who's had to learn not to underestimate me." My gaze slides to Dahlia for a moment, and I let my lips peel back from my teeth until the Summer Queen blanches.

Nyxia's mouth quirks into an approving grin. "Well then. I agree to your plan, little foxy." She turns her gaze to the others. "And you? I've got places to be, you know."

The rest of the table adds their agreement.

Just like that, we stand a fighting chance.

WE FINALIZE THE DETAILS OF WHAT TO DO OVER THE NEXT THREE DAYS, AND then the royals begin to funnel out of the atrium to return to their courts. Fehr follows them into the courtyard to see them off.

Aspen lingers behind, turning to face me. His arms wrap around my waist and I bring my hands to his shoulders. Tilting my head back, I look into his eyes, finding true joy in them. Even though he hadn't fallen into the pits of apathy like I had last week, he hadn't seemed convinced we'd actually come out on the other side. He seemed more...at peace with death than anything else. But the expression he wears now contains true conviction. Optimism. Hope.

He smiles down at me. "Have I told you lately what an incredible queen you are?"

My lips turn up at the corners. "Well, that's the first time I've heard it today."

He brings his lips to mine, our first kiss since I returned from Port Denyson. Every second since has been clouded with anticipation of today's meeting, but now that it's over...

I retreat a step until I feel the edge of the table come up against my back. "You know, we've still never tested out this table. To see if it rivals Nyxia's?"

His irises glitter and his lips curl with mischief. "Important research. I agree it must be done. Do you think the royals have all left yet?" Pressing his body close, he places his hands on the table, framing my hips. His lips return to mine, his kisses slow and teasing. I lean back, drawing him against me.

A throat clears, and I find Fehr has already returned from escorting the royals.

"We really need that bell we spoke of." Aspen's voice is a husky growl in my ear.

I giggle and reluctantly push him away. "You might be right. But I should speak with Fehr. I'll come find you later."

After claiming my lips in a final kiss, my mate leaves me alone with Fehr.

I straighten the skirts of my saffron gown—another Amelie creation—and approach the djinn.

"We should craft the bargain sooner rather than later," he says. "That way I can get to work on the wall at once. I'll begin tearing down the border wall tonight."

"Very well. So, how do I release you from your Bond to Irridae Palace?"

He frowns. "Shouldn't we craft the bargain first? That way you can ensure I return to your service like I said I would?"

"Fehr, we're not making a bargain."

His eyes widen, then narrow with suspicion. "You aren't releasing me." He shakes his head, lips pursed tight. "I understand your concern, Your Majesty, but this might be the only way to finish the wall in time."

"I'm releasing you, but not into a bargain."

He blinks at me a few times. "I don't understand."

"You've been trapped beneath the Bond since before humans knew fae existed. I can hardly comprehend how long that has been. You may have rebelled against the fae, but I think you've paid the price for that already."

He assesses me through slitted lids. "No one would dare free a djinn, much less release one without a bargain. Most fae consider us monsters. Traitors. Murderers."

"You aren't the only one in this room who could claim those same titles." Mr. Duveau's chilling scream before he was taken by the kelpie rings through my mind. "I've killed my share. I've fought those whom I once considered my people. Used my magic for harm."

"No one would deem your crimes equal with mine."

"You know what, Fehr? I don't care. I don't care what the other royals would choose if they were in my shoes. Nor do I care what you've done to deserve your punishment. I told you from the start. I'm not Ustrin. I won't force you to serve me."

His breathing grows rapid, dark eyes glittering with hope. "You're truly going to set me free?"

"Yes. However," I lift my chin and I burn him with a steely gaze, "if you betray me at any point, I will hunt you down and kill you with every bit of strength I have. Understood?"

Swallowing hard, he nods.

"Good. Now, how in the bloody name of iron do I free you?"

~

ONCE MY BUSINESS IS DONE WITH FEHR, I MAKE MY WAY THROUGH THE PALACE halls, searching for a head of copper hair. Finally, I spot Amelie where I should have thought to look first—in the seamstress' quarters. There I find her hunched over a swath of gauzy crimson fabric spread out before her. My newly appointed seamstress—a fae with tan, fuzzy skin and eight long, dexterous limbs—bends into a graceful bow, then returns to her work at a loom nearby, weaving yards of pale blue spider silk. I yearn for a closer look at the fae, for I'm almost positive she's making the silken strands from her own body, but I'll have to save that for another day. One where I'll have time to ask a lot of questions.

Instead, I approach Amelie, watching as her hands fly over the fabric, creating a row of neat stitches. It didn't take long for Amelie to find her way here after we returned from Varney Cove, and she's been here nearly every day since, working alongside her new mentor.

She looks up, grinning when she sees me. Her face is bright, making her look so much like she did when we were younger. But not quite the same. Dark circles hang under her eyes, and there's a density to her energy that not even the biggest smile can hide. At least she's found a way to channel that energy and whatever else lurks within her heart in the wake of Cobalt's death.

She rises to her feet, showing off the length of the gown-in-progress. "I'm making this for you."

I eye the ruby silk and the row of golden jacquard that lines the bottom hem. "It's beautiful, Ami."

She returns to her seat and immediately gets back to sewing. "How did the meeting go?"

I cast a glance at the seamstress, who'd paused her work to watch us. Averting her gaze, she seems to get the hint and scurries out of the room on all eight legs.

Once I'm sure the spider fae is out of earshot, I perch at the edge of the table Amelie works at. "It went well," I say, struggling to maintain a casual air. I'm still trying to sort out how to speak to Amelie without a figurative wall between us. It doesn't feel quite natural yet, but I know we'll get there. "We have a plan. There's a chance we can intercept the Parvanovae."

"Good," she says. "There would be a lot of nice dresses going to waste if we all end up obliterated." She says it with a sardonic laugh, but I can't bring myself to join. There's a very real chance this plan could fail, making it all too real to joke about.

Bringing my hands to my lap, I anxiously pick at a fingernail. "I also released Fehr from his Bond to the palace."

Amelie looks up from her work, eyes wide. "Why would you do that?"

"He's going to help build a wall around the isle."

She furrows her brow but returns to sewing. "That's helpful, I suppose."

"Yes, it was interesting how I was able to free him. There's something he never told me—something I probably could have guessed if I'd thought about it."

"What's that?"

I bite the inside of my cheek. "He told me I've had the power of his true name all along. Since he was Bonded to Irridae, he was essentially Bonded to its ruler as well. When I took his hand that first time he confronted us outside the palace steps, the power of his true name was given to me."

Her stitches begin to slow. "So, then you released him?"

I nod, feeling a lump rising in my throat. "He told me how."

She stops sewing altogether, her gaze slowly lifting to meet mine.

I can hardly see her through the sheen of tears that glazes my eyes. "Amelie Fairfield, by the power of your true name, I release you from our Bond."

Something snaps inside me, and a tangible weight is lifted from my heart, my shoulders. Amelie leans back with a sharp inhale, as if finding her lungs suddenly larger than they were before. We stare at each other for several seconds, both trembling as we orient ourselves in this moment. One where my sister is no longer my slave, my subordinate, and I no longer carry the burden of her name.

Then her face crumples. No sooner than she rises from her feet, I close the distance between us, wrapping her in my arms. Tears stream from our eyes as we sob into each other's hair, taking our first steps at returning to what we were always meant to be.

Sisters.

42

Later that night, I pace alongside one of the ponds in the palace courtyard, pulling my cloak tight against the chill in the air. I'm still getting used to how cold the desert can be at night, but the coolness helps counteract how badly I'm sweating.

Sweating and avoiding sleep.

A dark shadow swoops overhead, making me jump, but one glance tells me it's just Venitia the moon dragon. The shadow of his mate glides over the mountains in the distance. Earlier, I ordered the dragons and firebirds to establish sky patrols. Even though we still have three days before the risk of invasion, I want to be prepared. I want eyes on every stretch of land from here to the faewall, in case the humans manage to break through our forces at Port Denyson.

With a sigh, I return to my pacing. It's the only thing that seems to keep my heart rate from skyrocketing. Perhaps I should have joined Aspen in preparing our soldiers. They'll be working through the night to ready themselves to march to Port Denyson. And since my nerves won't let me find sleep...

"Are you going to do this all night?" comes a voice from the palace steps. It's Lorelei. I whirl toward her, finding Foxglove at her side. The two ambassadors slow as they draw near, and Lorelei raises a questioning brow at me.

"No," I say. "Just until I feel tired enough to sleep."

Foxglove lets out a low chuckle, shaking his head. "Sweetie, we all know that's not going to happen. Might as well enjoy your insomnia." He thrusts a cup toward me, then reveals two more.

Now I see Lorelei holds two bottles in her arms, cradled like twin infants. "You never did try Agave Ignitus wine. It's the Fire Court equivalent of Midnight Blush."

I make to return the cup to Foxglove, but he pointedly ignores me. "I don't want to drink anything," I say.

Lorelei sets one of the bottles down and wrestles the cork out of the other. "Sure you do. It will settle your nerves." Refusing to hear my protests, she fills my cup, then hers and Foxglove's.

"Drink up, Your Majesty," Foxglove says with a wink.

I shake my head. "You two enjoy it without me. I can't indulge tonight. We could set out to march at any moment."

Lorelei barks a laugh. "Evelyn, you've already been marching for an hour."

Foxglove's eyes turn down at the corners. "We saw you pacing from the window."

"And it isn't helping a thing," Lorelei adds. "The best thing you can do right now is relax."

I stare at the amber liquid in my cup. "I'm not in the mood to get drunk."

"Drink," Lorelei says, lifting her glass. "Don't get drunk. If I can manage a clear head and a couple glasses of wine, so can you. Let's enjoy what might be one of the last nights of our lives."

At those words, my heart leaps into my throat, and wine just might be the only thing to coax it back down. Besides, she's right. If everything goes wrong, this could be one of my last calm moments with my friends. One of my last calm moments *ever*. And what did Aspen teach me about living each day to the fullest? I doubt pacing counts as that.

"Fine," I say, "but I'm only having one cup."

I HAVE THREE CUPS. FOUR.

But the wine is unlike any other I've had. The flavor is sweet, warming my stomach in the most comforting way. My mind remains strangely clear while my body is completely and utterly relaxed.

Foxglove, Lorelei, and I lay on our backs in the sand next to the pond, staring up at the stars. I can't help but miss the view from the telescopes at Lunar, but the sky is still impressive from here.

Foxglove lets out a dreamy sigh. "What do you think Fehr's doing right now?"

"Breaking down the wall," I say. I expect a rush of anxiety to wash over me at the mention, but it doesn't.

Lorelei rolls onto her side, propping herself up on her elbow to face Foxglove. "Has he kissed you yet?"

"Stop, you're embarrassing me," he says with a giggle, although I can tell he's relishing the attention to his love life. "Powerful beings are delicate creatures to seduce, all right? Maybe after all the doom and gloom is over."

My heart clenches. Of all the things that could upset me right now, the thought of Foxglove and Fehr never seeing their budding relationship through is oddly painful. Yet another reason why we must win this war. "Do you really think we can do this? Steal the bomb back?"

Lorelei sits upright and points a forbidding finger at me. "No, Your Majesty. We are not talking about war right now. We are relaxing."

"I'm relaxed," I say, and it's true. Even though my worries remain in the back of my mind, they don't send me pacing like they did earlier. "Just humor me. Is our plan crazy?"

She purses her lips with a glare, then finally relents. "No," she says with a sigh. "It isn't crazy. We're going to meet a single warship with the full might of Faerwyvae and its magic. There's no way they'll make it past us."

"We'll have to hold back, though," I remind her. "We can't do anything too reckless in case we jeopardize the bomb."

A corner of her mouth quirks up. "Is that a warning to me? Will I have to reel in my roots?"

"I'm more worried about the winter fae. Flauvis is bad enough."

Foxglove sniffs. "I'm glad I'll be away from the fighting altogether. I'll be perfectly content keeping things running here at the palace while you bloodthirsty warriors go do your fighting." He waves a fluttering hand.

I laugh. I can't even imagine Foxglove in combat. Verbal combat, perhaps. But physically fighting another? No way. It does make me wonder, though...

"Foxglove, what's your unseelie form?" I ask. "You once told me you're a flower fae, but I've never seen you shift into anything else. Nor have I seen you manipulate the elements in any visual way."

His expression falters, and Lorelei bites her lip, a warning in her eyes. Blazing iron, did I say something wrong?

I'm about to apologize when he releases a sigh. "I'm not too fond of my unseelie form," he says, shoulders slumped.

"Why is that?"

"Let's just say, I was never a very pretty flower. My parents were quite unimpressed with me. That's why I'm so fond of human things and the ability to maintain a seelie form. This way, I can be anything I want, look however I want. I get to shape my own beauty."

I can't help but smile at that. While he may not be tall, and he's neither slim nor muscular like most other fae males I've met, he *is* beautiful. Inside and out. "What powers do flower fae have?"

"We create beauty," he says with a shrug. "Each flower fae expresses that in a different way. Some create the most exquisite glamours. Others build impressive gardens. I haven't explored my own abilities too much, but I think I may start to one day."

"You are really good with hair," I say, recalling how he'd styled Amelie and me when we first came to Bircharbor.

"I am," he admits. "But I'm thinking even bigger than that. Palaces, perhaps."

Warmth fills my chest at the mention of palaces, bringing to mind the game of pretend Aspen and I played. "When this is all over, Aspen and I may have something in mind."

He opens his mouth to reply, but a rushing sound, like a bellowing wind, enters the courtyard, drawing our attention to the tile walkway. There, a whirl of sand barrels toward the front doors. Foxglove is on his feet before anyone else, smoothing the front of his burgundy jacket, then adjusting his spectacles and hair. "Fehr," he says, a blush of color rising to his cheeks.

The cyclone pauses outside the palace doors, then dissipates to reveal the djinn. His dark hair is wind-tossed, bare chest rippling with more muscles than I can count. I'm not sure if it's the wine, or if freedom has made Fehr look more majestic than ever, but Foxglove isn't the only one blushing as the djinn approaches us.

Fehr spares a glance at Foxglove, lips pulling into a subtle smile, before his eyes lock on mine. "Your Majesty, I have broken down the border wall."

"Already?" Seeking my inner fire, I summon my flames to flood me, burning away all remnants of the wine. Euphoria slips away, leaving my pulse racing in its absence.

"That was the easy part," he says. "Now the building begins."

That's not all that begins, I think to myself. If the wall is down, that means it's time.

I curl my fingers into fists to keep my arms from shaking. "All right then. Go to the other royals. Tell them it's time to march."

43

Standing at the edge of a bluff just outside the docks at Port Denyson, I look out at the dark shape that crosses the Channel of Bretton. Dawn is barely a blush on the horizon as the warship makes its journey, still just a tiny speck in the distance. My eyes dart from the ship to what lies beyond—the mainland. From this high up on the bluff, I can just make out a sliver of land on the other side of the channel. It's strange to think that such a sight would have once inspired longing. Now it only fuels my rage. For there lies the seat of King Grigory, the man who would annihilate my people.

I rest my hand on the comforting hilt of a dagger—one of several obsidian blades gifted from Nyxia that now ring my waist. The weapons belt is cinched around the slim black tunic I wear beneath a bronze, lightweight breastplate, while thick leather trousers hug my legs. My hair is braided tight in a coronet around my scalp.

I steal a glance at Aspen, who stands at my side. His clothing is nearly identical to mine, aside from the belt of knives. He seems to think his antlers will suffice. His breastplate is also much larger and heavier than mine is, carved with maple leaves. Sensing my gaze, he turns and meets it. His eyes reflect everything I feel—rage, anticipation, trepidation. Fear. Neither of us can find smiles in this moment, but a look is all we need to express all that must be said—that we will fight to the death if we must, but first we shall fight to live.

A raven caws overhead, making its descent to the bluff. As it lands, Franco takes its place and makes his way to his sister, who stands in tense silence next to Lorelei. Aspen and I join them, as does Estel. The rest of the royals and fighting forces await down below, hidden just out of sight from view of the beach.

Lorelei gives me a tight-lipped smile as we approach, her usual swagger gone. She's outfitted in black trousers and bronze armor as well, which makes me realize I've never seen her in anything but a dress. It somehow makes her look even smaller than she is, and with that comes a wave of panic over her safety. But even though her presence puts her in mortal danger, there are few others I'd rather have fighting at my side. I've seen what she can do with her powers. Petite or not, I know how fierce she can be.

"I got a closer look at the warship," Franco says, shoulders rigid.

"Anything unusual?" Nyxia asks. Like always, her appearance is stunning, with shimmering black slacks that look unlike any fabric I've ever seen, and armor made from scales of moonstone and obsidian.

"What's unusual is the warship isn't alone. There are three smaller ships with it."

"Three!" Nyxia rounds on me. "You said a single warship. You mentioned nothing about three more."

"Neither did Mr. Duveau," I say. "I compelled him under a glamour. If he didn't mention the three ships, then he didn't know." Either that or my glamour wasn't strong enough, considering how weak my magic was. Of course, I don't say this out loud.

"The three smaller ships may be a naval guard for the warship," Estel says. "Were they armed?"

"Not like the warship," Franco says. "They seemed heavily armored and staffed, but they don't look like fighting vessels."

"Then we wait and see what they do," Aspen says. "They aren't expecting an ambush, so the warship won't attack until prompted."

"Won't they see the wall?" Franco asks. "I saw the stones on my return from spying. They'll know something has changed when they see it."

I look out at the beach and docks where Fehr has yet to complete the wall, then at the rows of stones that begin farther down. We know the warship will simply blast down any stones that interfere with its ability to dock, creating more work for Fehr, so we've decided to save this portion of the wall for last. As soon as we have the Parvanovae, we can destroy the warship without hesitation. Until then, we must treat our enemies like glass.

But Franco's right. With the rising sun illuminating the port, they'll see the stones once the ship draws near. They may not know an ambush is coming, but they'll be wary of attack.

A rush of wind swirls over the bluff, revealing Fehr when it comes to a stop. "The wall is finished," he says, chest heaving as he catches his breath. "I just erected the last stone, aside from the port. We're ready."

Relief has my shoulders dropping, chest open with an easy breath. "Thank you, Fehr."

"Finally, some good news," Nyxia says.

I turn to Estel. "Will you be ready to perform the enchantment once you have the Parvanovae?"

Like at our last meeting, the particles disperse over her face to hide her expression. This topic must truly make her nervous. "Yes. All I need is contact with one of the wall's stones."

I nod. "Good. Once we're in possession of the Parvanovae, you get to the wall. We'll destroy the warship—"

"I wish I could do it right now," Aspen says through his teeth, fingers clenched into fists as he casts a dark glance at the channel. "It will take all my restraint not to rip it to shreds as soon as it docks."

I suppress a chill, visions of the broken ship at Varney Cove flooding my mind. With his full strength and all the magic he needs at his beck and call, there's no doubt he'll be able to destroy it on his own.

"As soon as we get that bomb, it's all yours," I say. Then I turn to Fehr. "After the warship is destroyed, you will build the final stones."

The djinn nods. "I'll await the signal."

"And when the last stone is in place, I'll perform the enchantment," Estel says.

Nyxia lifts her chin with a smirk. "Then the isle will belong to us."

MORNING ILLUMINATES THE SHIPS AS THEY DRAW NEAR THE PORT. WE REMAIN on the bluff, crouched down to keep out of sight. Just when I think the warship will pull in toward the dock, it slows and turns starboard. My heart races when I consider it might be leaving and returning to the mainland. I can't tell if I'm angry or relieved, for we still need to regain possession of the Parvanovae. So long as it's in human hands, no one is safe.

But the warship doesn't change course; it remains in place with its port side facing us. The three smaller ships proceed forward, leaving the warship in the channel.

Panting breaths and the heavy padding of enormous paws tells me Flauvis has arrived. Not bothering to keep out of sight, he runs to the edge of the bluff. "Is the beast too scared to get close?" he says with a teasing laugh.

"Don't let your arrogance make you comfortable," Nyxia says. "The smaller beasts still come."

"Perhaps they're scout ships," Lorelei says. "Come to scope out the territory before they bring the troops in from the warship."

She might be right, but the sight of the smaller ships unsettles me. They may not be heavily armed like the warship, but there's still something terrifying in their design. What's even more unsettling is that the three ships don't head for the docks; they close in on a long stretch of beach beneath the bluff we're hiding on. Which means, if they hadn't noticed the new wall before, they must now, for Fehr left off his progress at the far end of the beach.

"Why are we hiding up here like fools?" Flauvis asks. "Why aren't we swarming these humans as soon as they touch land?"

"You know why," Aspen snaps. "We can't do anything reckless until we know who has the bomb. Trust me, it's making me crazy to do nothing too."

Flauvis grumbles in response, but he doesn't argue.

With bated breath, I watch as the three ships come in closer to the beach, expecting them to run aground at any moment. But instead, the bow of the three ships moves easily from water to sand, revealing a flat keel that keeps the ships upright as they ground.

"What kinds of ships are these?" Franco mutters.

I shake my head. "Nothing I've ever seen. They're amphibious. At least, partially so."

Flauvis' hackles rise and he begins to pace. "These ships bring death. We need to attack."

The same trepidation has the skin prickling on the back of my neck. Everything in me wants to keep whatever is on those ships at bay, wants to destroy them before a single soldier can emerge. But one of these ships could have the bomb. Destroying them could detonate it. "Just...wait."

Voices ring out from below, commands too distant to hear. Then, to my horror, the bow of one of the ships splits, swiveling outward like two doors. Once open, a ramp is lowered from inside. The other two ships follow suit, bows gaping wide. I can't help but imagine the ramps they spew as tongues lolling from the maws of great iron beasts. I expect fire, teeth, a guttural growl, but the inner belly of each ship remains dark, hiding what it contains.

"I don't like this," Aspen says next to me.

I don't either, but I can't find my words. I can hardly blink as I watch those platforms, sound roaring to life from inside each ship. Then movement.

From the first gaping mouth comes an ironclad vehicle, rolling down the platform on two rows of elongated tracks. Its front is mounted with an enormous gun.

My blood goes cold. It's a tank.

Another one follows as the first drives down the beach, crawling over sand and driftwood with ease. Then the other two ships deploy their cargo, and soon six tanks are driving toward the docks.

That's when the soldiers emerge from the ships, crawling over the beach like a swarm of ants.

I turn to the others, heart hammering against my ribs. "The Parvanovae is in one of those tanks."

"We need to get to them," Nyxia says.

"Without blowing them up," Lorelei adds.

Flauvis paces anxiously at the edge of the cliff. "Well, isn't that just great," he growls. "They're made of pure iron. I can smell it from here. No one is getting inside one of those *unless* we blow it up."

"No one except me," I say. "I'm the only one who can get close enough."

Aspen clenches his jaw, and I can see the worry in his eyes. But he knows what must be done. "I'll cover you."

"As will I," Lorelei says.

"Those tanks are armed with guns, and possibly other explosives," I say, voice trembling. "I can't use my fire on them."

Aspen exchanges a glance with Lorelei. "We'll use earthen elements," Aspen says.

"Good idea," I say. "Let's get to our forces. Tell them the plan. Engage the soldiers but focus our efforts on keeping those tanks from breaking past us. Estel—"

"I'll remain here," she says. "So long as I have this vantage, I can watch for the Parvanovae. If I discover which tank is carrying it, I'll come to you."

"And I'll await the signal to finish the wall," adds Fehr.

Aspen and I lock eyes, and I feel an invisible embrace reach down the Bond. Then I meet the gaze of Franco, Nyxia, Lorelei, and Flauvis. Terror, hunger, and rage swim in their eyes, echoed in the pounding of my blood.

With a steadying breath, I curl my fingers around the hilts of my daggers as flames heat my core. "Time to fight."

44

The fae stream down the abandoned streets of the port town, racing for the beach. Guttural cries fill the air, mingling with animal sounds and the roar of the approaching tanks. My blood throbs in my head as I run, Aspen and Lorelei on either side of me. Gunfire greets us as we arrive at the street outside the docks. My two companions extend their hands, reaching toward the earth. They draw out enormous roots that tear through cobblestones to block the bullets. The three of us huddle behind a wall of roots as we steal glances of what lies ahead, ducking behind the roots just in time to avoid another blast. Other fae rush past us, deftly dodging bullets. Human screams follow, then more gunfire.

I glance around the edge of the root wall, splotches of crimson catching my eye. I don't let my gaze linger long enough to see whether it belongs to human or fae. Instead, I seek the first tank, eyes locking on it as it draws closer. Soldiers march on foot ahead of it, keeping anyone from getting too close. Just as I retreat back behind the roots, I catch sight of a brown, shaggy wolf taking down one of the soldiers.

"It's coming," I say. The roar of the tank draws closer. Closer. Footsteps pounding ahead of it.

Aspen looks around our barricade, then back at me. "Now!" He leaps from behind the roots and runs toward the tank, Lorelei and I following just behind. We split formation to avoid the eye of the tank's enormous gun, Aspen running to one side, Lorelei and I to the other. Reaching for the ground, he sends several coils of roots springing up, lashing at the soldiers surrounding the vehicle. An enormous, gnarled limb sweeps their legs out from under them, sending gunshots wild. The tank's gun swivels toward Aspen, but he closes in and under its reach, its fiery blast soaring overhead. Another tangle of roots erupts from the ground to pummel the bodies of the men still standing.

Lorelei and I race to the other side. With a roar, she pulls up a network of roots to wrap around the tracks of the tank. The tracks grind against their bonds, while another set of roots—either hers or Aspen's—rise from the ground to wrap around the barrel of the gun, locking it in place.

More fae join the fight, tackling any soldier who moves in to defend the tank. The fae fighters carve a path straight to the side of the vehicle, which Lorelei and I rush to take advantage of.

"I need to get inside," I say once we reach it, gasping for breath as I press in close to the side of the tank.

"How?" Lorelei grimaces, her skin ashen as she struggles to maintain such a close proximity to the iron beast.

Craning my neck, I eye the top and spot the rungs of a ladder set at the back of the vehicle. "There. We need to move around back."

As if in answer, a wall of roots shoots up at the rear of the tank, and Aspen dives behind it. His tunic is already torn, bronze armor dented in places, forearms splattered with blood. At least the blood doesn't appear to belong to him. "Go!" he shouts.

I race to the back of the tank and hoist myself up the rungs. Keeping my flames burning hot within my core, I utilize their power to fuel my strength, moving me up the ladder which was clearly designed for a much bigger person. At the top of the tank, I find a circular hatch with a handle shaped like a wheel. Grasping it with both hands, I turn it with all my might. It doesn't budge. Does it lock from the inside? I pause my efforts to stare at the hatch, pondering how I can break through. I could try and melt it, but I'm hesitant to use fire around a vehicle that carries explosives. And possibly the Parvanovae itself. I'm about to shout down at Aspen for assistance from his powerful roots, when sound splits my right ear. A wall of roots shoots before me, just in time to block the bullet. Even so, I feel the sting of something sharp graze my shoulder. Ignoring the feel of hot blood raining down my arm, I ignite a layer of flames to heal my torn flesh and return my efforts on the handle. Then, to my surprise, I find it shifting easily in my grasp.

I leap back as the hatch pops open, and out from it emerges a soldier, rifle leveled at me. Fire leaping to my palms, I duck beneath the barrel of his gun and grasp the front of his uniform, fire lapping up his chest. I realize my mistake too late; if he falls back into the tank, the flames could ignite whatever is inside. My fear is short lived, however, as a sharp root climbs up the side of the tank and spears the man through the chest. Then it lifts him from the shaft, taking him and my flames from the tank and tossing the man through the air. From the ground, Lorelei meets my gaze with a nod.

I don't hesitate a second more, leaping through the hatch and down the shaft. As my feet meet the floor inside, I reach for the hilt of one of my blades and send it soaring toward the figure who stands at the tank's enormous scope. I connect to the element of air to control the trajectory of the blade. My dagger meets its mark, striking his gut, and the soldier collapses with a grunt. I see no one else in the main chamber, so I race toward the front. There I find the driver, trying desperately to move the vehicle past the tangle of roots. Before he can react, I unsheathe another dagger and bring it to his throat. His eyes meet mine, pupils dilating as his mind bends to my will.

So, not all the soldiers here are outfitted with rowan. Good to know.

"Where is the Parvanovae?" I ask.

"I don't know what that is." His voice is flat, toneless.

"Where is the weapon your king sent you to detonate?"

"I don't know. It's covert. Only the troop that carries it knows."

"Is it on this tank?"

"No."

"Are you sure?" My heart pounds so hard in my chest, I feel like it will explode.

"I'm certain. We're a diversion."

I curse under my breath. Even though I knew it was unlikely I'd find the star bomb so quickly, I can't fight the crushing disappointment. Keeping my eyes on his, I say, "Stop fighting. It's over. Abandon your tank and raise no more arms against the fae."

He gives a subtle nod, and I release him. I then return to the man I stabbed, finding him still alive, hunched over on the floor beneath the scope. With a groan, he pulls the blade from his gut. When I reach him, my fist moves into his hair, pulling his head back until his eyes lock on mine. Trapping him beneath my compulsion, I repeat the same orders I gave his companion. Then, retrieving my bloody blade, I return it to its sheath and scramble up the shaft.

Once on the ground outside the tank, I fight to catch my breath, seeking signs of Lorelei and Aspen amidst the chaos. The roar of another tank sends the ground rumbling as it skirts around this one. I clench my teeth and run after it. *Please let it be there.* My nerves are already frazzled after infiltrating just one tank. There are six in total. Six that could be carrying the bomb.

Roots reach for the tracks, lacing between them. A man emerges from the top hatch, shooting at the ground. I dance back to avoid the spray of gunfire. Lorelei pursues the tank with more roots. A second man joins the first at the top of the tank, blasting the roots with his keen aim. Each time one root gains hold, it's blasted in half. And it doesn't take the men long to realize an even faster way to deal with their woes—one of the men lifts the barrel of his gun and points it at Lorelei.

With a shout, I dive for her, pulling her back. Her body lurches, and she lets out a cry. Her roots uncoil, freeing the tank and it takes off down the street. Lorelei moans, grasping her bicep. I pull her toward me, ushering her into the shadow of the disabled tank, and inspect the wound.

"Were you shot?" I ask, voice trembling.

She throws her head back with a hiss, but says, "It doesn't feel like iron." Finally, she pulls her hand away, revealing a gash but nothing embedded in her flesh.

Relief washes over me. The bullet must have ricocheted off her breastplate.

"I'll heal," she says. "The iron in the air is making it worse, though. I'm not as strong as Aspen in that sense."

I look around, past fighting pairs, blasts of sand and gunfire. "Where is he?"

"He went to disable the tanks still on the beach," she says. "But you need to get after the one that got away."

"Can you stand?"

She pushes to her feet, and I can see the skin around the wound has already begun knitting back together. We're about to take off when another tank barrels toward us. Lorelei reaches for it, and again roots shoot from the earth to wrap around the tracks. She turns to lock eyes with me. "Go!"

With a nod, I turn in the direction the runaway tank was heading and find it's nearly reached the end of the street. To catch up, I'll need speed. With a shudder, I shift into my fox form, taking off on all fours. In a matter of seconds, I close the distance between myself and the tank, but without Aspen or Lorelei, how do I stop it?

The ground rumbles beneath my paws, then the cobblestones ahead seem to come to life, rising from the ground in front of the tank. Aelfon rounds the corner, flanked by dozens of earthen fae, some with horns and hooves, others with limbs like gnarled trees. The tank fires its gun, blasting a hole in the barricade, but in its place sprouts another stone. Another. As I race toward the tank, the hatch opens and out pour three men, storming from the tank to engage the surrounding fae on the ground. If each tank holds only three men like the first, that means the tank is empty.

This is my chance.

Skirting behind the fighting men, I leap onto the tank and scurry up the rungs, through the open hatch, and down the shaft. Inside, the belly of the tank is empty. I pad around it, seeking any sign of the Parvanovae. Tuning into my senses, I sniff for anything familiar, listen for the strange hum that always accompanies the presence of the bomb, feeling for its vibrations. But there's nothing. Unless it's well hidden, it isn't here.

Damn. Two down, four to go.

I race back to the shaft, paws on the lower rungs, when a shadow darkens the opening above me. The soldier freezes when he sees me, and I give him a warning growl. Then, tossing something down the shaft, he slams the hatch shut.

Shifting back into my human form, I climb the rest of the way up the shaft and grasp the handle. But as my hands close around it, I remember the object the soldier had thrown.

The skin prickles at the back of my neck as my eyes lock on the cylindrical object beneath my feet.

A grenade.

45

Biting back a scream, I wrap my hands around the handle of the hatch and turn with all my might. Just like it was outside the first hatch, this one is impossible to turn. There must be a locking mechanism I don't know about.

Sweat beads at my brow as I cast another glance at the grenade. My inner fire can sense the spark devouring the unseen fuse inside the device, and I know I only have seconds before it reaches the detonator.

My lungs collapse as fear locks me in an iron grip. How do I get out of this? How? I could melt the iron walls, but will that be fast enough? If I wrap myself in my flames, will they protect me from the blast? I may be strengthened by fire, but I can't see how that will help if my body is blasted to tiny pieces. The memory of Cobalt and the other sea fae I saw obliterated by a grenade has me trembling.

I need to be invisible. No, ethereal. If I could walk through walls like a wraith...

I sense the spark racing toward the detonator.

This is the end. It's here.

And all I feel is fear.

Take it to the Twelfth Court.

I don't know whose voice it is—is it Aspen's? Mine? —but I obey. Gathering all my fear around me, I close my eyes and wait for the blast.

When it doesn't come, I blink into a world of shimmering violet.

My first thought is that I'm dead.

The grenade exploded, and in my journey to the Twelfth Court, I avoided pain but not the physical blast. However, if I were dead, I'd like to think the afterlife wouldn't leave me in the same place I died. And that's exactly where I am now, inside the tank with a grenade below my feet. The only thing that has changed is that all matter is now composed of shimmering particles of violet light.

I study the grenade, surprised that I can see through its outer shell to the inner spark that has slowed to a snail's pace. Like the first time I visited the Twelfth Court, time neither moves nor stands still. Everything around me is in motion, alive, active, and yet seconds and minutes and hours don't seem to exist. Neither do walls. Although the tank surrounds me, its particles shift and sway, and the longer I look at them, the less substantial they become. Soon the walls appear paper thin, a mere layer I can peel back with my thoughts, providing a view of what's on the other side. Squinting through the particles, I see a soldier suspended in midair, as if he were leaping from the tank. Another is doubled over as an earthen fae's horned head rams him in the gut. Other fighters are nearly frozen in battle.

I pull my attention back to the inside of the tank and examine myself. I too am composed of violet light, still clinging to the top rung of the shaft. My body feels weightless, as if I could float away if I simply let go of the rungs. The rungs seem both firm and weightless at once, given shape only by my hands. As if...

My heart has grown calm since entering the Twelfth Court, my mind steady. With my intent fueling each move, I lift a hand from the rung and press it against the vibrating particles that form the wall nearby. It feels firm beneath my hands yet yielding at the same time. Shifting my attention to the layers of swirling light outside the tank, I extend my hand. As if the tank were made of air, my hand slips through it. Angling my body away from the rungs, I slip both hands through the walls, pushing out as if swimming through slow, murky water. With my body fully outside the tank, my feet seek the ground, touching down just as a bone-chilling vibration rattles the air behind me. Moving faster than the other figures in my proximity, I run, tackling the nearest earthen fae in the process, hoping I can push him as far from the tank as I can. Each step I take feels heavy and yet strangely buoyant. I'm halfway down the street by the time the tank explodes, sending slow, violet flames and debris unfurling incrementally outward.

I turn to watch, hypnotized by the deadly dance of flame and shards of iron, but more pressing concerns urge me on. Surging into the mass of languid fighters suspended in battle, I race back to the beach. There I see Lorelei, frozen in time, her roots wrapped around a tank like a cocoon. Willing my sight beyond the walls of the tank, I see three human figures, electrical wires, mechanical panels, crates of guns. But no orb of powerful, dangerous light that I'd expect from the Parvanovae. I continue on, to where Aspen stands before the last three tanks. The closest one is nearly buried in sand, while the farthest one back is tangled in ropes of seaweed.

I gaze through the violet particles that compose each tank, beyond every layer, but I see no sign of the Parvanovae.

It isn't here at all.

WITH THIS REALIZATION COMES A RETURN TO SOUND, TO COLOR, TO substance. The Twelfth Court vanishes, leaving me in the midst of chaos. Fighting rages all around me as I struggle to orient myself with this new location and the flow of time. I only have a moment to gape over the fact that I truly escaped the exploding grenade through the magic of the Twelfth Court. But now that I'm here, new dangers await. Igniting my flames over my skin, I race to Aspen.

"I don't think the Parvanovae is in any of these tanks," I shout over the din once I reach his side.

He looks at me, temples pulsing as he thrusts outward, pushing the nearest tank back, burying it deeper in the sand. "How do you know?"

"I just do." At least I hope I do.

The tank struggles to climb from the sand, but it gains just enough purchase for the barrel of its gun to swivel toward my mate. Before it can fire, Aspen flicks his hand, and the enormous gun twists and bends, like the rifles he manipulated at Varney Cove. With a blast, the gun backfires, imploding the tank with a modest burst of flame.

"Well, it wasn't in that one, that's for sure," Aspen says.

"They all must be diversions," I say. "There must be another tank. Perhaps they sent another landing ship farther down."

"One of the fliers would have seen it," he says.

I turn my eyes to the sky, but only a few members of the aerial team remain there. Most must have joined the fighting on the ground. But that gives me an idea. "I'll go back to the bluff," I say. "Ask if Estel has seen anything unusual."

"Be careful," he says. "I'll take care of the rest of the tanks."

With a nod, I shift into my fox form. Racing on all fours, I take off back to the cobblestone streets, dodging blasts and bullets as I head for the bluff.

WHEN I REACH THE BLUFF, I FIND ESTEL AT THE EDGE. SHE LOOKS OUT AT THE fighting below, perfectly still. All that moves are the particles on her face, crawling rapidly and blurring her features.

Shifting back into my human form, I stand at her side and look down on the chaos. Flames dance into the sky above two of the tanks, while another sinks into the sea, strands of seaweed pulling it deeper down until it disappears from view. The beach is coated in blood and debris, the air clouded with smoke. I look away, seeking signs of any other evasive force at work. But there's nothing.

"I don't feel it," Estel says.

I turn to look at her, watch as her expression settles into one of concern. "Feel what?"

"The Parvanovae," she says. "I thought I would be able to sense it, but I can't."

"Have you ever sensed it before?"

"The day you brought it to the meeting of the Alpha Alliance, I sensed something. Before you even presented it to us, I felt it shifting the weight of the air. However, I never noticed it before, in all those years it was kept at Irridae Palace. Perhaps it wasn't always in the weapons room. Perhaps when it was, the iron clouded my senses. That's what could be clouding them now."

"Estel, none of the tanks are carrying the bomb."

She sighs. "It could be on the warship. They might be holding back just to see if they can wear us out fighting the tanks first. For all we know, a greater force awaits."

"Maybe I can find out." From this vantage, the warship is in full view. If I can return to the Twelfth Court...

With a deep breath, I close my eyes, fueling my intent with a need to see beyond the limitations of physical form. Just like before, the world returns to shimmering violet when I open my eyes. Time slows down once again, while the particles composing everything both dead and alive move rapidly over my vision.

I immediately look to the warship. It's difficult to see anything except the ship itself at first, but then the layers begin to split, revealing what lies beyond. I see human bodies, pulsing and shifting. Their numbers are far less than I expect, perhaps only a fraction of the men one of the landing ships brought. The brightest, most vibrant lights represent motors and sources of massive energy, but there's nothing to suggest the Parvanovae.

Breathing out, I let the haze of the Twelfth Court fall away and come back to the present moment. "I don't see it on the warship, either."

Estel turns to me, shimmering brow furrowed as she studies my face. "You can see beyond time and space?"

I'm not sure how to answer that, so I shrug. "I journeyed through the Twelfth Court."

Her eyes go wide, a small smile curling her lips. "You truly have been blessed by the All of All, haven't you?"

I open my mouth but can't find my words. It's never occurred to me that my experiences in the Twelfth Court are anything but ordinary to the fae. It's through the magic of the mysterious realm that the fae learn to shift forms. But I remember what Foxglove said when I first prepared to journey there to fight for Aspen's throne. *Going there is a rare thing. A sacred and dangerous excursion.*

Estel lifts her chin. "The All of All wants us to win."

"Then we need to steal back the Parvanovae. But where the blazing iron is it?"

Estel only shakes her head, lips pulling into a frown. "I don't know, but I think something's wrong."

Her words chill me. I'm about to ask her what it could be, when something draws my attention from the corner of my eye—a dark shape hovering in the sky. At first, I think it's Franco, or a dragon perhaps, but it looks impossibly large for how far away it is.

I skirt around Estel, squinting into the sky. There, stark against the canvas of cloudless blue floats an enormous, wingless beast.

46

The object is hardly more than a speck at this distance, but there's no mistaking what it is.

An airship. A great and terrifying master of the skies.

Just like the tanks, this is something I've only seen depicted in the broadsheets, and everything I've read about them does little to comfort me. Filled with hydrogen gas, its shape is long and cylindrical, tapered at both ends with fins at the rear. It's able to soar at impossible heights, evading enemy reach to drop bombs from the sky.

Estel turns and follows my line of sight. Her words come out breathless. "What is that?"

I shake my head, my heart pounding against my ribs at an agonizing tempo. "This is all a diversion," I say. "All of this. They have our fighting forces concentrated far from where they intend to drop the bomb. It doesn't matter that we've released magic. It doesn't matter that we're overpowering all of their tanks. The Parvanovae isn't coming by sea. They're sneaking it in by air."

I can't help but wonder...did Mr. Duveau know all along? Did he fight my glamour and feed me the lie that played us right into King Grigory's hands? Or did he not know the truth?

Estel squints at the sky. "It's coming in from the south of Eisleigh. I...I think I can sense something."

"It's there, isn't it?"

"I can't be sure unless I get closer. But I swear I can feel it."

Her words give me an additional idea. "If we can get close enough, I can try and glimpse it through the Twelfth Court, see if there's any sign of the Parvanovae. That way, if it's there, we'll know exactly where it is onboard."

Estel walks forward, as if a few feet closer could provide a better vantage. The truth is, we're about as high as we can get in Port Denyson, and the airship is already heading away from us toward the center of Eisleigh. "We must get closer. If we can confirm the Parvanovae is on the flying beast, we can send word back to our fighters to destroy the warship at once."

"Then Fehr will finish the wall."

Estel nods. "And I'll cast the enchantment."

Sweat beads at my brow as I watch the airship slip farther and farther from view. "How do we get close enough to the airship for a better look?"

She opens her palm, revealing a Chariot. Where she stores items on her shimmering, ethereal person, I'm not sure I'll ever know. And this isn't the time for such questions. "We must get somewhere along the flight path that isn't in Faerwyvae. If they reach beyond the border, it will already be too late."

I pace a few steps, mind reeling. "I can take us to Grenneith," I say in a rush. "If the airship plans on dropping the Parvanovae, they'll target a central location after they cross the border into Faerwyvae. Based on the ship's trajectory, it's sure to pass over Grenneith."

Without question, she hands me the Chariot. "Let's go."

I TRANSPORT US TO THE STREET RIGHT OUTSIDE THE SPIRE, TO THE VERY PLACE I once stood with Aspen, Franco, and Foxglove while we plotted how to infiltrate the prison so I could visit my mother. One look at the building has me suppressing the shudder that writhes through me, but I know I must be strong. There is a proper time to sit with my grief, and this is not one of them. Not when the isle is at stake.

Pocketing the Chariot, I summon my inner fire to strengthen my will and lead Estel up the steps through the doors. Inside, the building is eerily quiet. Now that I think about it, even the streets outside were oddly empty for so early in the day. Word of the fighting must have traveled the isle, either from the people at Port Denyson who we evacuated, or from Mayor Coleman. Whatever the case, we don't encounter a single soul as we run through the building and enter the staircase that leads up the central column of the

Spire. It isn't until we reach the lower level of the cellblocks that we meet company.

Rounding a corner to the next flight of stairs, we come face to face with a pair of guards. They startle, hands flying to the hilts of their swords. I'm so used to seeing guns that I'm flooded with relief as one draws his blade and advances forward.

"Stop!" I shout, lifting my palms and letting blue flames dance over my fingers. "We are your new queens, and you will let us pass. Otherwise, I will have to hurt you." Or glamour them, I suppose. But right now, violence feels like the fastest solution.

"Queen," the guard echoes, eyes flashing from my face to my flames, then to the shimmering fae at my side.

"Yes, your new fae queens," I say. "Here to save the isle from complete annihilation. Now, let us pass or you will regret it."

The guard sneers, taking a step forward. "I'll bow to no fae." It seems violence will be the answer after all, until the second guard grasps his comrade by the shoulder, pulling him back. The two exchange a tense glance, and the second guard gives a subtle shake of his head. Chest heaving, the first guard considers his friend's silent warning before reluctantly returning his weapon to its sheath. Then, with another nudge from the second guard, they both step aside.

Estel and I brush past them and continue up the ring of stairs. We pass cellblock after cellblock until we finally reach the highest point in the tower. There I lead us to the end of the hall where one of the old, glassless windows welcomes a chill of autumn air. I lean forward, searching the sky for any sign of the airship. I know we beat it here. Only minutes have passed, and we crossed a great distance by Chariot. However, the airship was already far north of the port by the time we saw it. It must be nearly—

Then we see it.

It starts as a speck in the sky, then grows closer, crossing the east side of the city at a diagonal and heading straight our way. The nearer it comes, the more detail I can make out, from the gondolas suspended beneath the airship to its engine carts and motorized propellers.

"The Parvanovae is there," Estel says, eyes fixated on the approaching threat. The conviction in her voice is unwavering. "I can feel it with every speck of my being."

Even though I believe her, I want to see for myself. Turning inward, I close my eyes and seek the Twelfth Court. When I open them, the airship is beneath the violet haze, vibrating with shimmering particles. I don't even need to deepen my investigation, for there near the rear of the hull is an orb of blindingly bright light. I spare the rest of the ship a brief study, counting a dozen living figures, spread mostly between the rear and control gondolas, with a few figures lingering in the keel corridor.

I pull back from the Twelfth Court, blinking into the present. "I saw it. I know where it is."

"We must retrieve it. Now."

"Let's return to the port, gather an aerial force—"

"We can't attack the airship," Estel says. "If we destroy it, we destroy the Parvanovae. Even if it detonates from the air, it would be just as destructive as it would be on the ground."

"Winged fighters could invade the ship and take the Parvanovae back."

"No," she says. "I will not risk anyone but myself retrieving it. One wrong move could send it careening to the ground, resulting in our doom."

My eyes go wide. "How do you expect to get up there? You'll at least need someone to fly you up."

"No, I won't." Her palm flicks out, another Chariot appearing.

I check the pocket of my trousers, finding the one I used to bring us here still there.

"I brought a second," she says, eyes fixed on the sky. "It is my last. I will use it to transport myself directly to one of the gondolas."

I look from her to the airship, brow furrowed. "You're going to try and travel from here to a soaring object? One you've never been on? Can you even do such a thing?"

She nods, expression somber. "It's dangerous, and no one but a star fae should ever attempt such a risk with a Chariot. But if I can fixate on what those gondolas look like, and a specific space in the sky, I can transport myself there."

I want to argue, but time is running out. The airship is already at the center of Eisleigh. If we return to Port Denyson to gather an aerial team, we might not intercept the ship before it crosses into Faerwyvae. And even if we do, the crew could decide to drop the Parvanovae earlier if they sense our attack.

"Fine," I say, "but you're taking me up with you."

"No," she says with stern calm. "I already told you that using the Chariot without a clear mental picture of where you're going is dangerous, if not impossible. There's a chance I could miss my target."

"Then you better take me, because if I try it myself, you can be damn sure I'll miss my target, then you'll have my death on your hands."

She burns me with a scowl, an expression I've never seen her wear. "I could have your death on my hands if I *do* take you."

I ignore her. "If you're transporting yourself to one of the gondolas, you still have to make your way into the ship's hull. There are a dozen men on board. You'll need me to cover you."

"Aspen will have my head."

"He'll probably have mine too. Now, let's go. Oh, and aim for the center gondola. It's vacant."

Her expression disappears behind a buzz of particles, demonstrating her irritation, before they settle back down to reveal pursed lips. "Very well. But when I say it's time to leave, open that Chariot I gave you without question. Understand?"

I nod.

She takes a long look at the airship, now passing overhead, then flips open the lid of the Chariot. "Are you ready?"

I swallow hard, my pulse pounding in my ears. "No. But we should probably go."

47

―――

The light of the Chariot encircles us, buzzing around our bodies with its bright golden illumination.

In the next moment, the breath is stripped from my lungs as a rush of air has me reeling backward. Orienting myself to our new location, I find that we are not in the center gondola at all, but on the narrow gangplank that connects all three. My feet slip on the metal grate, sending me sprawling toward the side. I bite back a scream as I clasp my hands around the slim guardrail, scrambling to regain purchase on the gangplank.

Estel seems far more composed, arms outstretched to maintain balance. "Are you all right?"

Vertigo seizes me, my stomach churning. "If I don't look down," I shout over the rushing wind.

She looks over her shoulder toward the rear of the ship. "I can feel it. It's over there."

"That's where I saw it too." With my hands closed around the guardrail in an iron grip, I force myself to study the rear gondola. It's barely more than a boat-like metal box, partially enclosed at the far end where most of the crew are preoccupied with their tasks. Just above the middle of the gondola is a hatch that opens to the hull, a shaft of metal rungs leading to it from the gondola. "We need to get to the ladder—"

Just then, a figure rushes to the end of the gondola, shouting something I can't hear. I have only a second to react before he levels his gun and aims.

The sound of bullets striking metal rings out around me as I fight my terrified reluctance to move. With a deep breath, I let go of the guardrail and dart toward the center gondola, away from gunfire. Just before I dive behind the safety of the gondola's wall, something sharp slices into the back of my thigh. I've been shot. Collapsing to the metal floor, I press myself as close as I can into the side walls, safe from the blasts. I look for Estel and find her crouched on the opposite side.

Pain sears my leg, and I call forth my flames to combat it. The pain lessens, but I know it won't fully heal until I remove the bullet. And now might not be the best moment to try and do that.

"What now?" I call to Estel, but the wind and gunshots eat my words. There's a sudden break in gunfire. I pull myself onto all fours, prepared to dart across the gondola to Estel's side, but the appearance of a sudden figure has me retreating against the wall. The figure, however, joins me there. That's when I see it's Aspen, rippling with the violet aura of the Bond. His eyes are wide as he presses himself against the wall, arms splayed against it. "Where the bloody oak and ivy are you?"

"Aspen!" I shout, scrambling closer to him. "What's happening at the port?"

He stammers for words, looking wildly about, then finally manages to speak. "The warship has begun firing at the beach. We've destroyed all the tanks, and their soldiers are overpowered, but there's still a lot of fighting. The iron is growing thicker in the air and the fae are getting weaker."

I clasp his hands in mine. "We know where the Parvanovae is. We're about to steal it back."

"By flying in the air on a moving beast? This is madness."

I ignore him, giving his hands a tight squeeze. "Listen to me. Destroy the warship. Destroy everything. Then have Fehr finish the wall."

Finally, he nods, then his expression turns serious. "When this is all over," he says through his teeth, "I'm going to murder you for putting yourself in danger like this."

"Looking forward to it," I bite back. "And I love you too."

His lips pull into a subtle smirk, then he's gone. When I return my attention to the space between me and Estel, gunfire rains down from both sides. It seems we've drawn the attention of the forward control gondola too.

Estel crouches on all fours, looking both ways between blasts. Then, with a leap, she darts across to my side of the gondola. Bullets fly toward her, but I swear the particles of her body part to let them pass through the other side. She squeezes in tight next to me, appearing unscathed.

"Estel, can you die?" I've never seen her or any other ethereal being mortally wounded by a physical attack. I've often wondered if it were even possible.

"I can shift and reform my mass at will, which helps me avoid most injuries," she says. "However, if iron strikes me before I can avoid it, my form will become more solid and I'll be vulnerable to further injury."

"So...I'm not the only one in mortal peril right now."

"I told you this would be dangerous."

I clench my jaw, trying to put on my bravest face despite the pain lashing the back of my thigh. "What do we do now?"

She cranes her neck to peer over the side of the gondola, ducking to avoid another bullet. "I must get to that shaft and into the hull at once. They could decide at any moment that we're putting their mission at risk and drop the bomb early. I have an idea, but it's a risk. We might not make it out before getting caught." She releases a sigh. "This would be so much easier if the wall were complete."

"It should be any time now," I say. "Aspen is destroying the warship as we speak. After that, Fehr will finish the wall."

She eyes me with curiosity. "How do you know?"

"Aspen and I can communicate through our Bond."

"Ah," she says. "He told me about your mysterious connection before we came to rescue you at Varney Cove."

Just then, Aspen returns, eyes bulging as he struggles to keep his balance amidst the rushing wind. "It's done," he says, crouching down before me. "The warship is destroyed, and the wall is complete."

My pulse races at this news. "Thank the Great Mother," I say under my breath.

Aspen's expression turns hard again. "Now get out of here, Ev—" He doubles over, clutching his side while blood streams between his fingers. Then, with a lurch, he closes his eyes and begins to stumble back. In the blink of an eye, he's gone.

"Aspen!" I lunge for the place he was, but Estel pulls me back, just in time to save me from a flying bullet. My mind reels to comprehend what I just saw. One moment he was there, and the next he was...he was...

He couldn't have been injured by the bullets here, for he traveled through the Bond. That means...

I shake my head. No, I can't think of that. He must be all right. He must. Surely, I'd feel it through the Bond if he were...

I swallow hard.

Estel takes me by the shoulders, shaking me gently.

Trembling, I meet her gaze. "The wall is complete." My voice is hollow, my throat dry.

Her eyes widen. "You're sure?"

I nod.

She rises into a partial crouch, as if ready to spring back into the fray. "Then I need to transmute the bomb here. Now."

Her words clear my mind, and it takes all my will to force myself back to the present. Everything in me wants to travel to Aspen through the Bond to ensure he's all right, but I committed myself to this job. One that is the difference between life and death for everyone on the isle. Swiping errant tears from my cheeks, I take a deep breath and refocus on our task.

"We need to get to it first," I say. It takes me a second longer to comprehend what else she said. "Wait, when you say *now*, do you mean *now* now? As in from the airship?"

Her expression turns hard, determined, fixated on the rear shaft. "Yes."

"Don't you need to be at the wall to transmute the bomb?"

"No. This is actually better, and I know exactly what I must do."

Pulling myself upright, I glance at the rear gondola, still teeming with armed soldiers. Half the crew is there, guarding the gangplank, our only path to the shaft. "What will you do?"

She lifts her hand and the Chariot within. "I'm going to transport myself straight to the shaft and pull myself into the hull. I'll need you to distract the crew so they don't see me."

"Wait," I hold out my hands as a better idea comes to me. "I can enter the Twelfth Court and go myself. Time slows when I'm there. I can make it past the soldiers before they see me coming."

"No." I've never seen Estel look so stern; not even when I manipulated her into bringing me up here. "I must be the one to get it. As soon as I touch the Parvanovae, I'll begin the enchantment. You must distract them only long enough for me to climb up. Once I'm out of sight, use the Chariot and get back to the bluff. Don't wait a second longer. Understand?"

I open my mouth to say yes, but a chilling thought dawns on me. "If I use my Chariot to return to the bluff, how will you get back? You're going to utilize your Chariot to transport yourself to the shaft, which means you'll have used it twice."

Estel's eyes turn down at the corners. "I'm not coming back, Evelyn. Not from any of this. I never was."

Suddenly, it all makes sense—how ambiguous she's been at every mention of the enchantment, masking her expression behind her swirling particles. She was never planning on surviving this. "I don't understand."

She gives me a sad smile. "I discovered why my sister didn't destroy the Parvanovae like she said she would. I can't transmute the bomb unless I detonate it. To guide its transmutation, I must absorb the blast, become one with it. My final act of consciousness will be to fuel the energy with my intent, transmuting it into protection. It's the only way the enchantment will work."

"And that...will destroy you?

"It will, but I'm ready. I've *been* ready."

I shake my head, eyes wide. "You can't! You should have told us. We never would have agreed to let you do this."

"This is my choice, Evelyn. You can't take this from me. I'm sorry."

All further arguments are stripped from my throat as her words resonate deep inside me, echoing against ones said by my mother when I spoke to her in the Twelfth Court beneath the sea.

You cannot take that moment from me, Evelyn. It is mine, not yours.

Acknowledging them both, I nod.

Her eyes glaze with shimmering light as she places a hand on my shoulder. "I'm glad to have known you, Queen Evelyn of Fire."

I nearly choke on a sob. "I'm glad to have known you too."

"Promise me you'll leave as soon as I enter the hull."

With a deep breath, I force the words from my lips. "I promise."

Without another word, she opens the lid of the Chariot and disappears into golden light.

I turn around and face the rear gondola, glancing above the edge of my hiding spot. A flash of light ignites inside the shaft over the gondola. One of the men makes to turn toward it, but I rise to my feet with a roar. Filling my palms with fire, I draw their attention to me, connecting to the element of air to send orbs of flame down the gangplank. My diversion has them thoroughly preoccupied, and I only have a second to duck before they return my attack with gunfire.

When I peek back over the side wall, I catch only a glimpse of a shimmering foot. Then nothing; she's inside the hull. It takes everything in me not to charge the crew and follow her up that shaft. To respect the promise I made. Breaths harsh and shallow, I crouch back down behind the side wall and reach into my pocket. My fingers tremble as I flip open the lid of the Chariot and fill my mind's eye with the bluff.

The golden light swallows me whole, vibrating, humming, growing, then blinks out, leaving me surrounded by salty air at the edge of the bluff. Heart hammering against my ribs, I turn away from the sea to the northwest, where Grenneith should be. I find no sign of the airship from here, but still search the skies. What I'm looking for, I don't know...

Then a shudder vibrates through me, through everything, like a wave of sound washing over the land. A blindingly bright light appears in the sky, brighter than the sun.

My stomach drops.

No.

All I can think is that it didn't work; Estel detonated the bomb but wasn't able to transmute the energy. Or perhaps she was caught before she could.

I'm transfixed as I watch the light grow, awaiting with cold dread for the end.

But the end doesn't come.

Instead, the light retreats, pulling back to a single point in the sky. Its radiance shifts from a blinding golden hue to a collection of shimmering white particles. Then, with another wave of vibration, the particles blast outward, spanning in every direction until it curves up, out, and toward the ground. For a moment, the light of the sun is hazy, filtered through a dome of shimmering particles surrounding all that I see.

Then it's gone.

Invisible.

But not broken, for I can feel it humming all around.

Estel's enchantment is complete.

48

As a fox, I make my way down the bluff, following a violet tether in my mind's eye. Shifting into my fox form is the only way to make the journey bearable, with the bullet still lodged in my thigh. I summon my fire again and again, which helps keep me conscious, but at this point, I've lost a lot of blood. On three legs, I hobble down the hill, the violet tether pulsing like an artery, guiding my every step.

Only when I reach the first buildings of the port town, does the silence reach my awareness. There's no gunfire. No blasts. No shouts. And yet the evidence of battle lies all around, blood and bodies and discarded weapons. I refuse to look too closely, not wanting to recognize any faces amongst the dead and, instead, fixate my attention on that violet tether, padding after it on silent paws.

When I reach the main street near the docks, I finally see movement, hear sound. The first thing I hear are whimpers, cries, mingling with the hollow ringing in my ears. Then I begin to pick up strands of solemn conversation. The fae are here, gathering the dead, tending to their injured comrades.

What's strange, however, is the presence of humans. Humans that were not fighters. A dozen or so men and women, dressed in the clothing of regular townspeople, weave about the fae, kneeling next to the broken, conversing with the strong. Those who kneel have boxes at their sides. Boxes full of cloth, blades, bottles, and herbs. They're healers. Nurses, perhaps.

And yet, they wear no uniform, no insignia to represent a specific medical practice. I furrow my brow. These people are...helping us? Of their own accord?

Of course, not all fae receive them with warmth. Nearby, a white wolf lies on his side, the bottom half of his body coated in blood. It takes me a moment to realize the wolf is Flauvis. Despite his injuries, he snaps his teeth when a human woman tries to come near. She holds her hands out in a sign of peace, saying something I can't hear, but Flauvis only bares his teeth. Part of me wants to go to him, shift back into my seelie form and inspect his wounds. But there's someone else I need to see. More than anything in the world.

Following the tether, I continue padding down the street, skirting around bodies as I reach the site of the first disabled tank. I hazard a glance at the beach, which makes me pause. The shore is littered with debris and the remnants of the ruined tanks. The three landing ships, now crushed as if squeezed by an enormous hand, sink into the channel beyond the row of stones that make up the new wall. There are more dead here, but the living gather too. On one of the docks, I spot human soldiers, survivors of the battle. They cluster at the center of the dock, just before the pair of stones that flank it. More of the human healers move about there, tending to the injured.

Evie.

My heart hammers at the sound of my name. The feel of it. A lump rises in my throat, a sensation so human I'm thrust from my fox form. With a cry, I stumble to right myself on my good leg, then return my attention to the violet tether, feeling it pulsing stronger now.

I limp forward. One step. Another.

Evie.

Faster I move, summoning my flames to burn the pain from my leg, fueling my pace as I continue down the street, past melted guns, more broken bodies, shattered cobblestones, mangled roots.

"Evie."

My breath hitches in my chest, a sob building there alongside it, as my mate steps into view. His breastplate is gone and there isn't a part of him not covered in blood, but he's standing. Standing on two feet. Standing and alive.

I rush forward, but he's faster, closing the distance between us and shrinking the tether that links us with every step. Then finally, he's here, wrapping me in his arms. I press myself into him, cry into his chest, let my weight sag into his.

"I was so worried you were gone," I whisper.

He strokes my hair, lips pressed against my forehead. "I was. For just a second."

I lift my face to study his, assessing every scratch, cut, and bruise beneath the dirt and blood. "What happened?"

"I was shot in the side, and another soldier struck me in the back of the head."

My eyes go wide. "Struck you?" My fingers tremble, yearning to reach for the back of his head, but terrified of what I'll find.

"With the butt of his gun. His bullets were out."

"That's not all the story," says a voice nearby. It's Franco.

My heart lifts as I whirl to face him, although my arms don't leave my mate. He lowers to the ground with his enormous raven's wings, arms crossed over his chest. He too is coated in blood, his silver hair slick with it.

Aspen purses his lips and releases a warning grumble. "We're kind of busy here."

"Busy leaving out the best part of the story," Franco says. He turns his gaze to me, lips curled into a haughty grin. "I saved your dearest mate here."

Aspen shakes his head. "I would have crushed them with my bare hands."

"Not if you're unconscious."

"I was only out for a second."

"And it would have been forever, if the armed soldier came in for another shot. However, I took the human for a little flight."

With a roll of his eyes, Aspen says, "Fine. You might have saved my life. Do you want a medal?"

Franco winks. "I just wanted to hear you say it." With a shudder, he leaps into the air in his full raven form, then calls overhead, "We might become dear friends after all, Aspen." Then he's out of sight.

I return my gaze to Aspen's. "Where are the others?"

"Nyxia is tormenting the soldiers who wouldn't stand down after they'd clearly lost. Aelfon and Minuette are with their troops. Lorelei is helping one of the humans bind fractures with her roots. Flauvis is, well..."

"I saw. He doesn't look too good, and he's not accepting help from the humans." I furrow my brow. "Who are these healers, anyway?"

He pulls back just enough to lift the hem of his bloody tunic to reveal his bandaged side. "They came to our aid as soon as the fighting stopped. They called themselves *veterinarians*." He says the last word slowly.

I quirk a brow. "Veterinarians came to our aid?"

"The one who tended me said Mayor Coleman sent word to them days ago, urging them to come to the port."

"Mayor Coleman sent animal doctors to tend fae wounds? Of course he did." I shake my head. Whether he did it as an insult, or if they were the only healers he knew would aid my people, I suppose it matters not. With this many wounded and with so many of the injuries being from iron, these tasks would have fallen on my shoulders alone without their aid. "I should probably go tend to Flauvis. I doubt the veterinarians will have any luck with him."

I make to pull away, but my injured leg gives out beneath me. Aspen catches me in his arms, brow furrowed with concern. "You're hurt."

Pain sears the back of my thigh again. "It's fine," I say, voice hoarse, summoning my flames to ease the agony.

"It's not fine. You need to see one of the healers at once."

"No, I need to help—"

Aspen grasps me by the shoulders, voice firm. "Evie, take care of yourself first."

I want to argue, but he's right. No matter how much fire I summon to regenerate my blood and weave my flesh, the wound won't heal until the bullet has been removed. And I'm in no condition to try and remove it myself. "All right. I'll...go to the vet."

"Good," he says with a nod. Then his lips curl into a crooked grin. "Besides, Flauvis should probably suffer just a little longer."

As soon as the bullet is removed and my wound is tended and bound, I go to the wolf king. He still snaps his teeth at me like I saw him do to the veterinarian, but after a few stern words, he gives in and lets me approach. My stomach sinks when I take in the severity of the wound. His entire back leg is mangled, torn to shreds by what looks like numerous rifle shots.

He'll need amputation. And from what I know about fae healing, the leg won't grow back. He, of course, does not take the news well. Luckily, chloroform seems to suffice in shutting him up.

"If I can hobble on three legs, so can you," I whisper as he slips into unconsciousness. "Perhaps it will humble you a bit too."

The veterinarian who tended my wound assists me now, lending me her tools for the amputation. When it's over, I examine my work, running my hands over Flauvis' filthy fur in search of any other minor injuries. But now that the amputation is complete, taking with it all remnants of iron, the rest of his wounds begin to heal on their own.

"We should probably be out of sight when he wakes up," I tell the veterinarian. "He's not going to be happy about being a three-legged wolf."

She blanches and rises to her feet.

"Thank you," I say to her. "For helping him, me, and all my kind."

"You're one of them," she says. "Your ears are rounded, but...you're fae."

I lift my chin with pride. "I am."

"You're the one we've heard about, then. The human-fae queen. The one who bargained for our protection."

I'm taken aback as I contemplate her words. Is this what Mayor Coleman has told the people of Eisleigh? Or has rumor spread on its own?

When I don't reply, she speaks, voice trembling. "What happens now? You...your kind...rule us. What does that mean for humans on the isle? For our cities and towns? Our way of life?"

Her words echo questions of my own, questions I have no answers to. So I give her honesty. "I don't know what the future of the isle looks like. Yes, it belongs to the fae now, but it is still your home. We won't hurt you."

She studies me, shoulders rigid. "Do the others feel the same as you do?"

The truth will frighten her, but it's all that I have to offer. "No, but I promise that I will fight on your behalf." I can feel the promise ringing through my bones, and I know it's one I can keep. I will fight for the humans, and I will fight for the fae. I will fight for a fair way of life for all people. Seelie. Unseelie. Human. I may not know what that balance looks like yet, but I will work to build it. And I know Aspen will too.

I extend an open palm to the human. After a moment's hesitation, she takes it in hers and gives it a squeeze. "Fae promises are binding, right?" she asks.

I give her a solemn nod. "They are. I will not break this one."

With a small smile, she dips into a curtsy, then turns away in search of more work to be done.

I too scan the street, looking for who I can help tend to next, but the sight of someone at the corner of my periphery has my heart leaping in my chest —Lorelei. She grins wide when I meet her gaze, and we both run to each other. As soon as she's in reach, I fling my arms around her, squeezing her petite frame close. Tears stream down my cheeks, and from the way her shoulders heave, I can tell she's crying too. When our sobs turn to laughter, we pull away, although our arms remain linked.

"The wall works," she says, eyes bright as she bounces on the balls of her feet. "Nyxia tested it on the soldiers."

"What do you mean?" I ask.

Her words come out faster than I've ever heard her speak, as if she can hardly contain them. "Nyxia glamoured one of the soldiers to attempt to pass between the stones near the dock. He couldn't. No human can, neither on nor off the isle, not unless accompanied by a fae. It's like a tangible barrier exists, one only the fae can cross. No weapon can pierce it either. Now Nyxia is escorting the surrendered soldiers onto fishing boats so we can ship them back to the mainland. They're never coming back. Ever."

This sends a rush of excitement to my head. My relief is so overwhelming, I have to squeeze Lorelei's arms to keep from swaying where I stand. Even though I already knew the enchantment had been completed, hearing that it's been tested and proven successful is a much-needed comfort amidst the grim aftermath of battle.

Lorelei's eyes sparkle as she bounces on her feet again. "She did it, Evelyn. Estel's enchantment works."

My face falls at the mention of the Star Queen, fresh tears pricking my eyes. "Yes, it does."

Lorelei's smile melts off her lips. "Where is she, anyway?"

My chin quivers as I summon the words from my heart. "Estel has returned to the stars."

Lorelei's shoulders droop, her hold on me growing slack. Her eyes are keen, telling me she knows there's much more to this story.

But it isn't one I want to tell right now. Not when there is still much work to do. Hearts to soothe. Wounds to tend. Dead to burn or bury.

When we're done, I'll tell them. I'll tell everyone.

Not a single soul, neither human nor fae, will go without knowing that Estel, Queen of the Star Court, saved the Fair Isle.

The days that follow are solemn ones.

We remain at the port while our wounded are tended to by myself and my fellow healers. When we run out of supplies, we go to town and get more. When we grow tired, we rest, only to wake up a few short hours later and return to our duties.

It takes two days to heal what can be healed, mend what can be mended. In the physical sense, at least. Then some of our fighters begin to leave.

Traditions are followed for every court regarding the care of the dead. Some bodies are wrapped in cloth and taken away with their comrades to return to their families. Others are burned on the beach. Still others are feasted on. While the latter turns my stomach, I've already learned from my fire fae subjects that life and death are treated differently by each court, each culture, each species of fae. The seelie and unseelie will always handle things differently, as is their right. A right I'm determined to see is never stripped from either side.

On the third day after the battle, Aspen, Lorelei, and I guide our troops back to Irridae Palace.

On the fifth day, we're home.

The moon illuminates the courtyard as we enter the palace gates, cool night air brushing my skin. We hardly take two steps down the tile walkway before Foxglove and Amelie rush out the front steps to intercept us. As soon as Amelie is in my arms, we dissolve into tears, falling on our knees while we hold one another. I hear a similar reunion between Foxglove and Lorelei taking place nearby. When Amelie and I can finally bring ourselves to separate, I see Aspen has joined the two ambassadors, arms draped over their shoulders as he brings them to his chest.

Rising to my feet, I wipe the tears from my cheeks as more figures stream out of the palace—Marie Coleman, Dune, the spider seamstress, and then Breeda with a girlish squeal. Then other fae funnel into the courtyard—the mushroom crab and his family, blue wisps, firebirds, dragons. The courtyard erupts in cheers and yips and excited conversation. Amelie runs to Lorelei and Foxglove, Breeda flutters around my head, speaking too fast for me to hear, and Dune taps from paw to paw, asking if I brought any dead for him to feast on.

As the commotion grows wilder around me, my attention is drawn to a figure who stands silently amongst the crowd. It's...Fehr. No one has seen him since he finished the wall. I'd expected he'd take his freedom and make himself scarce for a while, but he's...here.

He steps forward and takes a knee before me. "I'm sorry I didn't come directly to you, Your Majesty. I sensed unrest growing near parts of the wall in Eisleigh. Humans were rioting, trying to take down the stones."

The news fills me with dread. It's not that I hadn't anticipated some rebellion from the humans. I doubt everyone is so willing to accept a fae rule, no matter what we accomplished for the greater good. Still, hearing unrest has already begun to stir makes my bones feel tired.

"Even though the enchantment prevents harm from coming to the stones, I've dealt with the rebels," Fehr says. "I ushered them to the other side of the wall where they can either rot or try and make it to the mainland."

"You did well," I tell him. "We will find...other ways to deal with rebels in the future."

He rises to both feet. "I have returned to your service, Your Majesty."

I lift a brow. "Of your own free will? You know we have no bargain."

The corners of his mouth quirk up, and I see his gaze flick to a certain bespectacled ambassador in the process of uncorking a bottle of Agave Ignitus. "Of my own free will. I shall go where you and your mate go." He bows low, then disappears into the crowd.

I sense Aspen long before I feel him. His arm circles my waist, and I turn to him, pressing my head against his chest, silent as I watch our people celebrate our return home. With the sparkling lights coming from the wisps, fire sprites, and kitsune flames, it feels like the start of a revel.

As tired as I am from our journey, I hesitate to give in and join. But after everything we've been through, after all we've lost and won, perhaps a revel is what we need. Perhaps it's what *I* need.

I lift my gaze to my mate's, arms circling his neck. Our Bond pulses between us, saying everything we don't have words to express. Joy, gratitude, exhaustion, sorrow. Beneath it all is that which links us whether near or far, regardless of tether or Bond, life or death. It's the same element that connects me to my people, my sister, my friends. My mother. Estel. Those I've lost and those I still have near. It's that which makes me fight. Protect. Risk my life.

It's love.

With it comes waves of grief, chasms of pain and longing. And with it comes passion and joy. It's what it means to be human. What it means to be fae. Seelie and unseelie alike, whether they admit it or not, feel love. Humans and fae, despite their differences, are bound by the same element of love.

I am bound by love. Its depths and shallows, streams and waves. Its darkness and light. I'm open to all of it now.

Pulling Aspen's lips to mine, I initiate the night's revelry with a kiss.

EPILOGUE

Foxglove leads the way through a stand of slim white birches surrounded by an elegant citrine wall. A canopy of crimson leaves dance in the mild breeze overhead, the sun shining through the boughs to create the ideal climate. The air that caresses my skin feels like the warmest day of the most perfect autumn, warm enough that a lightweight dress will suffice, but cool enough that I wouldn't be sweating if I chose to wear a cloak or jacket. Foxglove extends his arms. "Here you'll find the autumn garden. There's a pond, several benches, a brook. Then on the opposite side of the palace, there's a lovely desert courtyard with cacti and succulents. I selected each one myself. It's also a great place for sunbathing. Oh, and your pool is there too. Shall I take you to it?"

Aspen and I exchange a glance. "Perhaps show us inside the palace first," Aspen says.

Foxglove adjusts his spectacles. "Very well. How about your bedrooms?"

Hand in hand, my mate and I follow after the ambassador-turned-palace-designer into a set of double doors. There we enter an enormous hall with intricately carved marble walls and a blue tile floor. Heads of servants bow as we pass, while guards in bronze armor stand at attention.

"It seems the palace staff has already settled in," I say.

Foxglove grins. "Yes, most of your households have already arrived. The rest will be coming tonight. Well, except for Lorelei. She'll be staying at Lunar a few more days."

I purse my lips to hide my smile. Even though I only sent Lorelei to exchange a single message with Nyxia, it seems she and the Lunar Queen are getting along far better than they used to. Or perhaps they've grown fond of their fights and have been unable to extricate themselves from their most recent one.

I return my attention to the elegant halls, finding it impossible to take in all the splendor at once. When Aspen and I brought Foxglove the idea of building a new palace on the border between our courts, he immediately went to work. In every wall, tapestry, table, and vase, I see the beauty of Autumn and Fire combined. Leaves mingle with flames in fiery yellows, deep reds, and rich browns. It's even more stunning than I could have imagined.

We make our way up an immense staircase to the sleeping quarters. At the end of the hall, we find our bedroom, which is far larger than anything I've lived in yet. The ceiling is domed and painted like a clear autumn sky, while the walls are carved marble. The floors are deep-orange carnelian. The middle of the room hosts an enormous bed, its posts made from twining roots blooming with red leaves. The windows stand from floor to ceiling across the far wall, filling the room with warm sunlight. I scan the rest of the room, finding a sitting area, a table laden with fruit and wine, and then—

When my eyes land on the tall oak wardrobe, I find Amelie there, resplendent in a gown of lilac chiffon.

"Don't tell me you made me more dresses," I say, crossing the room to join her at my very full wardrobe.

She shrugs, suppressing a grin. "I won't tell you then. But I will tell you, you should see the bathing chamber."

Foxglove claps his hands together. "Yes, the bathing chamber! Your mate was quite specific on the size of the tub you would need."

I eye Aspen, finding the corner of his mouth quirking up. "It had to be big enough for two."

With a blush, I follow Foxglove into the adjoining room. Everything from the floor to the ceiling is pink and orange sunstone, with an enormous recessed rectangle at the center, filled with steaming water. Sprigs of rosemary and marigold heads float over the surface. Just looking at it makes me want to sink beneath its depths.

"Not yet," Foxglove says, as if my thoughts are written on my face. "We have much more to see."

WE CONTINUE THE TOUR, MOVING FROM ROOM TO ROOM, WING TO WING, FLOOR to floor. There's a ballroom, a library, several studies, a medical wing, and countless guest rooms. Of course, Foxglove is most excited to show me my parlor, one that is a near-replica of the one he made for me at Bircharbor, filled to the brim with human knickknacks, doilies, and other atrocities. His pride over the room is so palpable, it's infectious, and I find myself not having to fake my smile at all.

Finally, he leads us to the throne room on the main floor of the palace. "Aspen said he wanted me to show you this last," he says as he throws open the doors. The room is nearly as large as our bedroom, with towering ceilings, long windows, two ornate thrones, and...

I nearly bark a laugh at what rests in the center of the room. An obsidian table, twice as large as Nyxia's. I meet Aspen's smirk with a quirked brow.

"So," Foxglove says, wringing his hands. "What do you think? Is it suitable? The palace, I mean."

I go to him and take his hands in mine. "Yes, Foxglove. I love it more than I could ever say. You've done an amazing job."

His cheeks flush pink at my praise.

A knock sounds on one of the open doors, and we turn to find Marie Coleman. She curtsies, then crosses the room to hand me two envelopes. "Another trade proposal to bring to the Alpha Council, and the most recent correspondence from my uncle."

I take the letters from her. "What's the latest from Representative Coleman?" I mutter as I break the seal of the second envelope.

Before I can open it fully, Aspen's hand covers mine. "Work can wait until later," he says in a conspiratorial whisper.

I lift my eyes from the envelopes and find heat in his gaze. It's enough to send my heart flipping in my chest. "I suppose you're right," I say, tucking the letter into the pocket of my dress.

"Are you in need of anything else, Your Majesties?" Marie asks, cheeks flushed as she suddenly finds the floor at her feet very interesting.

"No, thank you, Marie," I say.

She hurries to the door, but Foxglove remains in my periphery, grinning wide at me and my mate.

Marie pauses and clears her throat. "Foxglove," she hisses in a too-loud whisper. "I, uh. I think Fehr wants you to show him your room."

"Oh!" Foxglove jumps, wringing his hands when he gets the hint. Then, "*Oh*," when he understands what Marie is suggesting.

As soon as the doors close behind them, Aspen's lips find mine. I retreat toward the obsidian table, and he hoists me on top of it. I spread my knees to pull him closer, wasting no time in getting him out of his jacket, his waistcoat. Then he shrugs out of his shirt with haste, losing a button in the process. I run my hands up and down his golden chest, leaning back as he returns his lips to me. One of his hands cradles the back of my neck, while the other moves up my knee, my thigh, climbing beneath the folds of my skirt to the roundness of my hips.

I pull away, my voice breathless when I say, "I have a surprise for you."

His eyes brighten with curiosity. "Do you?"

I put a hand on his chest to gently push him a step back. Then I reach for the ribbon tied behind my neck, one that holds up the bodice of my lace gown. Once the knot is free, I pull the bodice down to reveal thick black satin stiffened by bone stays.

Aspen pulls his head back at the sight of the undergarment. "What the bloody oak and ivy?"

"It's a corset, remember?"

His eyes lock on my breasts, the tops bulging above the painfully tight torture device. As his gaze moves down the length of it, his brow grows more furrowed. "I thought you hated corsets."

I lean back, propped on my forearms, lips pulling into a mock pout. "I do. I hate them so much I can hardly bear it. In fact, I think I might die if I'm not freed from it at once."

He eyes me with concern a moment more before his mouth quirks with devious delight. Stepping forward to return to the space between my legs, he frames my waist with his hands on the tabletop. "I should rescue you then. Although, I must warn you. The corset might not survive my valiant efforts."

I lift my chin, lips parting as my breaths grow heavier. "Do what you must."

Our kisses return with a fierce passion, his tongue caressing mine as his hands grasp the bodice of the undergarment. With one pull, he has me out of it, and his hands rove over my bare skin. I scoot back on the table until I'm at the center of it, and he follows, kissing up the length of my torso. His tongue stops to rest over each mound of my breast, sending heat burning at the apex of my thighs, then he trails his lips over my collarbone, then up my neck—

"Oh, hello, Your Most Beautiful Majesty. And His Most Handsome Majesty."

My head whips toward the fire sprite, and I find Breeda fluttering just a few feet away without a care in the world for what she might be interrupting.

"What are you doing?" Breeda asks with innocent curiosity. "Are you expecting the other royals to join soon? This is your meeting room, isn't it?"

Aspen laughs into the crook of my neck. "Where in the hell is that bell?"

Stifling my own laughter, I say, "Will you give us some privacy, please? In fact, will you stand guard outside this room and see that no one disturbs us until we leave?"

Breeda spins in a circle and salutes. "It will be done." Then, in a flash, she's gone.

I bring my left hand to Aspen's cheek, running my thumb along the crease outside his mouth, the one that forms only with his biggest smiles. The light from the windows catches the bright orange of my carnelian ring —one gifted to me from Aspen during the human wedding ceremony we had earlier this year. A sunstone band circles the ring finger on his left hand.

My chest feels warm as I'm reminded of the conversation we had just over a year ago, one I thought was pretend. One I hardly dared to hope would ever come true.

And yet here we are.

Of course, there is one thing missing.

"I can't believe after all the work Foxglove put into this palace, it never once occurred to him to make us a bell," I say.

Aspen snorts a laugh. "You're the metalworker. I thought you were going to make one."

"Perhaps I shall." I look into his glittering irises, breathe in the rosemary cinnamon scent of his skin.

He reaches for my free hand, weaves our fingers together. "Evie, have I ever told you how grateful I am that you almost killed me with an iron blade?"

"Excuse me?"

He lights a kiss on my cheek, then my jaw. "The day we met at the wall."

My grin stretches across my face at the memory. "Where would we be now if I hadn't?" The question takes me down several paths, one to a future where nothing changes, where lives are kept but a tense treaty remains. The other brings me to where we are now, past a history of grief, bloodshed, love, and joy. In between lie several other forks and paths leading to unknown fates. All I know is I'm glad I'm here.

Now.

With him.

"Always and forever, Aspen," I whisper to him.

His eyes lock on mine. "Always and forever, Evie."

Our kisses return slow and gentle, his bare skin warm against mine as our hearts hammer between us, beating a rhythm for our love. My favorite song. One I want to hear every day for the rest of my life, however long that will be. It could be endless. It could be an eternity, and I would never tire of its melody. Not when he's here.

As much as I want to linger in the luxury of our simmering fire, an inferno begs to be released. I smile against his lips. "Let's put all other tables to shame once and for all."

And we do.

NOT READY TO LEAVE FAERWYVAE?

WHAT ABOUT FRANCO? If you're wishing a certain snarky vampire fae would get his happily ever after, then you'll want to continue on with my next series, *Entangled with Fae.* It takes place twenty years after the events of *The Fair Isle Trilogy* and features familiar faces!

Entangled with Fae is a fantasy romance series of fairytale retellings with a fae twist. Each can be read as a standalone in any order. Happily ever after guaranteed.

In *Curse of the Wolf King: A Beauty and the Beast Retelling*, you'll fall in love with Flauvis (yes, I promise you will love him!) aka Elliot Rochester, after he loses his memories and is cursed to live in a human body.

In *Heart of the Raven Prince: A Cinderella Retelling*, Franco finally gets his love story when he convinces a servant girl to pose as his fake fiancé.

More Faerwyvae fairytales are still to come to help keep the magic alive. Thanks for reading!

-Tessonja Odette

ALSO BY TESSONJA ODETTE

ABOUT THE AUTHOR

Tessonja Odette is a fantasy author living in Seattle with her family, her pets, and ample amounts of chocolate. When she isn't writing, she's watching cat videos, petting dogs, having dance parties in the kitchen with her daughter, or pursuing her many creative hobbies. Read more about Tessonja at www. tessonjaodette.com

instagram.com/tessonja
facebook.com/tessonjaodette
tiktok.com/@tessonja
twitter.com/tessonjaodette